VAL McDERMID

Val McDermid grew up in a Scottish mining community then read English at Oxford. She was a journalist for sixteen years, spending the last three years as Northern Bureau Chief of a national Sunday tabloid. Now a full-time writer, she divides her time between Cheshire and Northumberland.

Her novels have won international acclaim and a number of prestigious awards, including the Gold Dagger for best crime novel of the year, the Anthony Award for best novel, and the *Los Angeles Times* Book of the Year Award. Her thriller series featuring criminal profiler, Tony Hill, has now been adapted for television under the generic title Wire in the Blood and stars Robson Green and Hermione Norris.

For the latest news, visit www.valmcdermid.co.uk

By the same author

The Grave Tattoo
The Distant Echo
Killing the Shadows
A Place of Execution

TONY HILL NOVELS
The Last Temptation
The Wire in the Blood
The Mermaids Singing

KATE BRANNIGAN NOVELS
Star Struck
Blue Genes
Clean Break
Crack Down
Kick Back
Dead Beat

LINDSAY GORDON NOVELS
Hostage to Murder
Booked for Murder
Union Jack
Final Edition
Common Murder
Report for Murder

NON-FICTION
A Suitable Job for a Woman

VAL McDERMID

The Torment of Others

The Mermaids Singing

HarperCollins*Publishers*
77–85 Fulham Palace Road, London, W6 8JB

The HarperCollins website address is:
www.harpercollins.co.uk

This omnibus edition published 2008
2

Typeset in Meridien by Palimpsest Book Production Limited,
Polmont, Stirlingshire

Printed and bound in Great Britain by
Clays Ltd, St Ives plc

Extract from *The Four Quartets* by TS Eliot
(published by Faber and Faber Ltd) reproduced by
kind permission of Faber and Faber Ltd.

The Torment of Others

Acknowledgements

As usual, I owe a debt of thanks to those who generously give of their time and expertise in a bid to keep me within the bounds of accuracy. I am grateful to the Greenfield Girls for letting loose the dogs of narrative; Angus Marshall for advice on the forensic aspects of computing; Dr Ray Murray for geological assistance; Dr Sue Black for matters pathological; Brigid Baillie for legal procedure; and the late Kathy Wilkes for first introducing me to the mind/body problem.

For their perennial support, Julia Wisdom and Anne O'Brien at HarperCollins; Jane, Broo, Anna, Claire and Terry at Gregory & Company; Trina Furre at Riverdale; and Sandra, Ken and Robson at Coastal.

For Leslie, Sandra, Julia, Jane, Maria, Mel, Margaret, Nicky, Jenni, Mary, Julie, Paula, Jai, Diana, Stella, Shelley, Daphne and Bunty Al – my personal monstrous regiment of women who brought back the wounded from the battlefield and tended me till I was better. With love and thanks.

But the torment of others remains an experience
Unqualified, unworn by subsequent attrition.
People change, and smile: but the agony abides.

TS Eliot
'The Dry Salvages', *Four Quartets*

All torment, trouble, wonder, and amazement
Inhabits here. Some heavenly power guide us
Out of this fearful country!

William Shakespeare
The Tempest

PART ONE

Just because you hear voices, it doesn't mean you're mad. You don't have to be well smart to know that. And even though you did all that stuff that made the jury look sick to their stomachs, at least you're clever enough to know that doesn't make you a nutter. All sorts of people have other voices in their heads, everybody knows that. Like on the telly. Even though you can believe it when you're watching it, everybody knows it's not real. And somebody's got to have dreamed it up in the first place without them ending up where you have. Stands to reason.

So you're not worried. Well, not very worried. OK, they said you were insane. The judge said your name, Derek Tyler, and he tagged you with the mad label. But even though he's supposed to be a smart bastard, that judge didn't know he was following the plan. The way to avoid the life sentence that they always hand down when somebody does what you did. If you make them believe you were off your head when you did it, then it isn't you that did the crime, it's the madness in you. And if you're mad, not bad, it stands to reason you can be cured. Which is why they lock you up in the nuthouse instead of the nick. That way the doctors can poke around in your head and have a crack at fixing what's broke.

Of course, if nothing's broke in the first place, the best thing you can do is keep your mouth zipped. Not let on you're as sane as them. Then, when the time is right, you can start talking. Make it look like they've somehow worked their magic and turned you into somebody they can let out on the street again.

It sounded really easy when the Voice explained it. You're pretty sure you got it right, because the Voice went over it so many times you can replay the whole spiel just by closing your eyes and mouthing the words: 'I am the Voice. I am your Voice. Whatever I tell you to do is for the best. I am your Voice. This is the plan. Listen very carefully.' That's the trigger. That's all it takes. The intro that makes the whole tape play in your head. The message is still there, implanted deep inside your brain. And it still makes sense. Or at least, you think it does.

Only, it's been a long time now. It's not easy, staying on the wrong side of silence day after day, week after week, month after month. But you're pretty proud of the way you've hung on to it. Because there's all the other stuff interfering with the Voice. Therapy sessions where you have to blank what the real nutters are going on about. Counselling sessions where the doctors try and trick you into words. Not to mention the screaming and shouting when somebody goes off on one. Then there's all the background noise of the day room, the TV and the music rumbling round your head like interference.

All you have to fight back with is the Voice and the promise that the word will come when the time is right. And then you'll be back out there, doing what you've discovered you do best.

Killing women.

Find them in the first six hours or you're looking for a corpse. Find them in the first six hours or you're looking for a corpse. The missing children mantra mocked Detective Inspector Don Merrick. He was looking at sixteen hours and counting. And counting was just what the parents of Tim Golding were doing. Counting every minute that took them further from their last glimpse of their son. He didn't have to think about what they were feeling; he was a father and he knew the visceral fear lying in wait to assail any parent whose child is suddenly, unaccountably not where they should be. Mostly, it was history in a matter of minutes when the child reappeared unscathed, usually grinning merrily at the panic of its parents. Nevertheless it was history that left its mark bone deep.

And sometimes there was no relief. No sudden access of anger masking the ravages of ill-defined terror when the child reappeared. Sometimes it just went on and on and on. And Merrick knew the dread would continue screaming inside Alastair and Shelley Golding until his team found their son. Alive or dead.

He knew because he'd witnessed the same agony in the lives of Gerry and Pam Lefevre, whose son Guy had been missing now for just over fifteen months. They'd dragged the canal, combed the parks and wasteland within a two-mile radius, but not a trace of Guy had ever surfaced.

Merrick had been the bagman on that inquiry, which was the main reason why he'd been assigned to Tim Golding. He had the knowledge to see whether there were obvious links between the cases. But beyond knowledge, his instincts already nagged that whoever had snatched Guy Lefevre had now claimed his second victim.

He leaned against the roof of his car and swept the long curve of the railway embankment with binoculars. Every available body was down there, combing the scrubby grass for any trace of the eight-year-old boy who had been missing since the previous evening. Tim had been playing with two friends, some complicated game of make-believe involving a superhero that Merrick vaguely remembered his own sons briefly idolizing. The friends had been called in by their mother and Tim had said he was going down the embankment to watch the freight trains that used this spur to bring roadstone from the quarry on the outskirts of the city to the railhead.

Two women heading for the bus stop and bingo thought they'd caught a glimpse of his canary yellow Bradfield Victoria shirt between the trees that lined the top of the steep slope leading down to the tracks. That had been around twenty to eight. Nobody else had come forward to say they'd seen the boy.

His face was already etched on Merrick's mind. The school photograph resembled a million others, but Merrick could have picked out Tim's sandy hair, his open grin and the blue eyes crinkled behind Harry Potter glasses from any line-up. Just as he could have done with Guy Lefevre. Wavy dark brown hair, brown eyes, a scatter of freckles across his nose and cheeks. Seven years old, tall for his age, he'd last been seen heading for an overgrown stand of trees on the edge of Downton Park, about three miles from where Merrick was standing now. It had been around seven on a damp spring evening. Guy had asked his mother if he could go out for another half-hour's play. He'd been looking for birds' nests, mapping them obsessively on a grid of the scrubby little copse. They'd found the grid two days later, on the far edge of the trees, crumpled into a ball twenty yards from the bank of the disused canal that had once run from the railhead to the long-silent wool mills. That had been the last anyone had seen of anything connected to Guy Lefevre.

And now another boy seemed also to have vanished into thin air. Merrick sighed and lowered the binoculars. They'd had to wait for daylight to complete their search of the area. They'd all clung to a faint hope that Tim had had an accident, that he was lying somewhere injured and unable to make himself heard. That hope was dead now. The frustration of having no leads bit deep. Time to round up the usual suspects. Merrick knew from past experience how unlikely it was to produce results, but he wasn't prepared to leave any avenue unexplored.

He pulled out his mobile and called his sergeant,

Kevin Matthews. 'Kev? Don here. Start bringing the nonces in.'

'No sign, then?'

'Not a trace. I've even had a team through the tunnel half a mile up the tracks. No joy. It's time to start rattling some cages.'

'How big a radius?'

Merrick sighed again. Bradfield Metropolitan Police area stretched over an area of forty-four square miles, protecting and serving somewhere in the region of 900,000 people. According to the latest official estimates he'd read, that meant there were probably somewhere in the region of 3,000 active paedophiles in the force area. Fewer than ten per cent of that number was on the register of sex offenders. Rather less than the tip of the iceberg. But that was all they had to go on. 'Let's start with a two-mile radius,' he said. 'They like to operate in the comfort zone, don't they?' As he spoke, Merrick was painfully aware that these days, with people commuting longer distances to work, with so many employed in jobs that kept them on the road, with local shopping increasingly a thing of the past, the comfort zone was, for most citizens, exponentially bigger than it had ever been even for their parents' generation. 'We've got to start somewhere,' he added, his pessimism darkening his voice.

He ended the call and stared down the bank, shielding his eyes against the sunshine that lent the grass and trees below a blameless glow. The brightness made the search easier, it was true. But it felt inappropriate, as if the weather was insulting the anguish of the Goldings. This was Merrick's first major case since his promotion, and already he suspected he wasn't going to deliver a result that would make anybody happy. Least of all him.

Dr Tony Hill balanced a bundle of files on the arm carrying his battered briefcase and pushed open the door of the faculty office. He had enough time before his seminar group to collect his mail and deal with whatever couldn't be ignored. The psychology department secretary emerged from the inner office at the sound of the door closing. 'Dr Hill,' she said, sounding unreasonably pleased with herself.

'Morning, Mrs Stirrat,' Tony mumbled, dropping files and briefcase to the floor while he reached for the contents of his pigeonhole. Never, he thought, was a woman more aptly named. He wondered if that was why she'd chosen the husband she had.

'The Dean's not very pleased with you,' Janine Stirrat said, folding her arms across her ample chest.

'Oh? And why might that be?' Tony asked.

'The cocktail party with SJP yesterday evening – you were supposed to be there.'

With his back to her, Tony rolled his eyes. 'I was engrossed in some work. The time just ran away from me.'

'They're a major donor to the behavioural psychology research programme,' Mrs Stirrat scolded. 'They wanted to meet you.'

Tony grabbed his mail in an unruly pile and stuffed it into the front pocket of his briefcase. 'I'm sure they had a wonderful time without me,' he said, scooping up his files and backing towards the door.

'The Dean expects all academic staff to support

fundraising, Dr Hill. It's not much to ask, that you give up a couple of hours of your time –'

'To satisfy the prurient curiosity of the executives of a pharmaceutical company?' Tony snapped. 'To be honest, Mrs Stirrat, I'd rather set my hair on fire and beat the flames out with a hammer.' Using his elbow to manipulate the handle, he escaped into the corridor without waiting to check the affronted look he knew would be plastered across her face.

Temporarily safe in the haven of his own office, Tony slumped in the chair behind his computer. What the hell was he doing here? He'd managed to bury his unease about the academic life for long enough to accept the Reader's job at St Andrews, but ever since his brief and traumatic excursion back into the field in Germany, he'd been unable to settle. The growing realization that the university had hired him principally because his was a sexy name on the prospectus hadn't helped. Students enrolled to be close to the man whose profiles had nailed some of the country's most notorious serial killers. And donors wanted the vicarious, voyeuristic thrill of the war stories they tried to cajole from him. If he'd learned nothing else from his sojourn in the university, he'd come to understand that he wasn't cut out to be a performing seal. Whatever talents he possessed, pointless diplomacy had never been among them.

This morning's encounter with Janine Stirrat felt like the last straw. Tony pulled his keyboard closer and began to compose a letter.

Three hours later, he was struggling to recover his breath. He'd set off far too fast and now he was paying the price. He crouched down and felt the rough grass

8

at his feet. Dry enough to sit on, he decided. He sank to the ground and lay spreadeagled till the thumping in his chest eased off. Then he wriggled into a sitting position and savoured the view. From the top of Largo Law, the Firth of Forth lay before him, glittering in the late spring sunshine. He could see right across to Berwick Law, its volcanic cone the prehistoric twin to his own vantage point, separated now by miles of petrol-blue sea. He checked off the landmarks: the blunt thumb of the Bass Rock, the May Island like a basking humpback whale, the distant blur of Edinburgh. They had a saying in this corner of Fife: 'If you can see the May Island, it's going to rain. If you can't see the May Island, it's already raining.' It didn't look like rain today. Only the odd smudge of cloud broke the blue, like soft streamers of aerated dough pulled from the middle of a morning roll. He was going to miss this when he moved on.

But spectacular views were no justification for turning his back on the true north of his talent. He wasn't an academic. He was a clinician first and fore-most, then a profiler. His resignation would take effect at the end of term, which gave him a couple of months to figure out what he was going to do next.

He wasn't short of offers. Although his past exploits hadn't always endeared him to the Home Office estab-lishment, the recent case he'd worked on in Germany and Holland had helped him leapfrog the British bureaucracy. Now the Germans, the Dutch and the Austrians wanted him to work for them as a consultant. Not just on serial murder, but on other criminal activity that treated international frontiers as if they didn't exist. It was a tempting offer, with a guaranteed minimum that would be just about enough to live on. And it would give him the chance to return to clinical practice, even if it was only part-time.

Then, there was Carol Jordan to consider. As always when she came into his thoughts, his mind veered away from direct confrontation. Somehow, he had to find a way to atone for what had happened to her, without her ever knowing that was what he was trying to do.

And so far, he had no idea how he could achieve that.

Day Two. And still no trace of Tim Golding. In his heavy heart, Merrick knew they were no longer searching for a living child. He'd visited Alastair and Shelley Golding that morning, cut to the bone by the momentary flash of optimism that lit their eyes when he walked into their neat Victorian terraced cottage. As soon as they'd comprehended that he had nothing to offer them, their eyes had glazed over. Fear had gnawed at them till there was nothing left inside but barren hope.

Merrick had left the house feeling bleak and empty. He glanced down the street, thinking ironically that Tim Golding had, in a way, been a victim of gentrification. Harriestown, where the Goldings lived, had been a working-class enclave until enterprising young couples in search of affordable housing had begun buying up decaying properties and restoring them, creating a trendy new suburb. What had been lost was a sense of community. The avid followers of *Changing Rooms* and *Home Front* were interested in their own lives, not those of their neighbours. Ten years before, Tim Golding would have known most of the people on his street and they would have known him. On a summer evening, people would have been out and about, walking to allotments or from the pub, standing in their doorways chatting as they soaked up the last rays of the sun. Their very presence would have protected the boy. And they would have noticed a stranger, would have clocked his passage and kept an eye on his destination. But these days, those residents of Harriestown not whipping up some exotic recipe from a TV chef in their exquisitely designed new kitchens would have been in their back yards, cut off from neighbours by high walls, designing their Mediterranean courtyard gardens or arranging the Greek urns that held their fresh herbs. Merrick had scowled at the blank doors and windows of the street and longed for a simpler time. He'd headed back to the incident room, feeling ill at ease and jaded.

His team had worked through the night, interviewing the known paedophiles on their patch. Not a single pointer had emerged to move the inquiry forward. A couple of punters had phoned in, reporting a white Transit van cruising slowly round the narrow streets at about the time Tim had disappeared. By chance, one of them had remembered enough of the index number to make it worth checking out on the Police National Computer. They'd identified half a dozen possibles in the local area, which had given the incident room a fresh surge of energy.

But that lead had died on its knees within a matter of hours. The third van on the list belonged to a company who made home deliveries of organic vegetables. The driver had been going slowly because he was new to the round and wasn't sure of the layout of the local streets. That alone wouldn't have been enough to get him off the hook. But the clincher was that he'd been accompanied by his fifteen-year-old daughter, augmenting her pocket money by helping him out.

Back to square one. Merrick shoved his hands in his trouser pockets and glared at the pinboard in the incident room. It was pitifully bare. Usually by this stage in a missing-child inquiry, information was pouring in. It certainly had in the Guy Lefevre case, although it had all proved fruitless in the long run. But for some reason all they were getting was a pathetic trickle. Of course there were the time-wasters, calling to say they'd seen Tim on the Eurostar train with an Asian woman; in a McDonald's in Taunton with a grey-haired man; or shopping for computer games in Inverness. Merrick knew these so-called sightings were worthless. Whoever had taken Tim certainly wouldn't be parading him round the streets for everyone to see.

Merrick sighed. The images in his head now were not of a small boy playing with his friends. What he saw when he closed his eyes was a shallow wood-land grave. A flash of yellow football shirt in the long grass of a field margin. A tangle of limbs in a drainage ditch. Christ, but he felt inadequate to the task.

He racked his brains for some other avenue of approach, summoning up the images of previous bosses, wondering how they would have handled things differently. Popeye Cross would have been convinced their abductor was someone they already had on the books. He'd be sweating the nonces, determined to get a confession out of someone. Merrick was confident he'd covered that already, even though his team knew better than to exert the kind of pressure Popeye had been famous for. These days, you leaned too heavily at your peril. Courts had no patience with police officers who bullied vulnerable suspects.

He thought of Carol Jordan and reached for his cigarettes. She'd have come up with some tangential line of attack, he had no doubt of that. Her mind worked in ways he'd never managed to fathom. His brain was wired differently from hers, and he'd never in a million years arrive at one of her inspired angles. But there was one thing Carol would have done that he could pursue.

Merrick inhaled and reached for the phone. 'Is the boss in?' he asked the woman who answered. 'I'd like to talk to him about Tony Hill.'

John Brandon climbed the steps up from the Barbican station. The dirty yellow bricks seemed to sweat and even the concrete underfoot felt hot and sticky. The air was stuffy with the thick, mingled smells of humanity. It wasn't the best preparation for what he suspected was going to be a difficult conversation.

No matter how much he'd tried to prepare himself for his meeting with Carol Jordan, he knew he didn't really have a clue what he'd find. He was certain of only two things: he had no idea how she felt about what had happened to her; and work would be her salvation.

He'd been appalled when he'd heard about the botched undercover mission that had ended with the violent assault on Carol. His informant had tried to stress the significance of what her operation had achieved, as if that were somehow a counterbalance to what had been done to her. But Brandon had cut impatiently across the rationale. He understood the demands of command. He'd given his adult life to the police service and he'd reached the top of the tree with most of his principles intact. One of those was that no officer should ever be exposed to unnecessary risk. Of course danger was part of the job, particularly these days, with guns as much a fashion accessory in some social groups as iPods were in others. But there was acceptable risk and unacceptable risk. And in Brandon's view, Carol Jordan had been placed in a position of intolerable, improper risk. He simply did not believe there was any end that could have justified such means.

But it was pointless to rage against what had happened. Those responsible were too well insulated for even a Chief Constable to make much of a dent in their lives. The only thing John Brandon could do now for Carol was to offer her a lifeline back into the profession she loved. She'd been probably the best detective he'd ever had under his command, and all his instincts told him she needed to be back in harness.

He'd discussed it with his wife Maggie, laying out his plans before her. 'What do you think?' he asked. 'You know Carol. Do you think she'll go for it?'

Maggie had frowned, stirring her coffee thoughtfully. 'It's not me you should be asking, it's Tony Hill. He's the psychologist.'

Brandon shook his head. 'Tony is the last person I'd ask about Caról. Besides, he's a man, he can't understand the implications of rape the way a woman can.'

Maggie's mouth twisted in acknowledgement. 'The old Carol Jordan would have bitten your hand off. But it's hard to imagine what being raped will have done to her. Some women fall to pieces. For some, it becomes the defining moment of their lives. Others lock it away and pretend it never happened. It sits there like a time bomb waiting to blow a hole in their lives. And some find a way to deal with it and move forward. If I had to guess, I'd say Carol would either bury it or else work through it. If she's burying it, she'll probably be gung ho to get back to serious work, to prove to herself and the rest of the world that she's sorted. But she'll be a loose cannon if that's what she's trying to do, and that's not what you need in this job. However . . .' she paused, 'if she's looking for a way through, you might be able to persuade her.'

'Do you think she'd be up to the job?' Brandon's bloodhound eyes looked troubled.

'It's like what they say about politicians, isn't it? The very people who volunteer for the job are the last ones who should be doing it. I don't know, John. You're going to have to make your mind up when you see her.'

It wasn't a comforting thought. But he'd since had support from a surprising quarter. The previous afternoon, DI Merrick had sat in his office asking Brandon's sanction to bring Tony Hill in to profile the disappearance of Tim Golding. As they'd discussed the case,

Merrick had said almost wistfully, 'I can't help feeling we'd be doing better if we still had DCI Jordan on the team.'

Brandon's eyebrows had shot up. 'I hope you're not having a crisis of confidence, Inspector,' he said.

Merrick shook his head. 'No, sir. I know we're doing everything we can. It's just that DCI Jordan looks at things differently from anybody else I've ever worked with. And with cases like this . . . well, sometimes it feels like it's not enough to cover all the bases.'

Brandon knew Merrick had been right. All the more reason why he should do everything in his power to bring Carol Jordan back into the world again. He squared his shoulders and headed for the concrete labyrinth where Carol Jordan waited at the epicentre.

John Brandon was shaken to see the change in Carol Jordan. The woman who waited in the doorway for him to emerge from the lift bore almost no resemblance to his memory of her. He might well have passed her in the street. Her hair was radically different, cut short at the sides, the heavy fringe swept to one side, changing the shape of her face. But she had altered in more fundamental ways. The flesh seemed to have melted from her face, giving it a new arrangement of planes and hollows. Where there had been an expression of intelligent interest in her eyes, now there was a blank wariness. She radiated tension rather than the familiar confidence. In spite of the warmth of the early summer day, she was dressed in a shapeless polo-neck sweater and baggy trousers instead of the sharply tailored suits Brandon was used to seeing her in.

He paused a couple of feet from her. 'Carol,' he said. 'It's good to see you.'

There was no smile of welcome, just a faint twitch of muscle at the corners of her mouth. 'Come in, sir,' she said, stepping back to allow him to enter.

'No need for formality,' Brandon said, taking care to keep as much physical distance as possible between them as he walked into the flat. 'I've not been your boss for quite a while now.'

Carol said nothing, leading the way to the pair of sofas that sat at right angles to each other with a view through the floor-to-ceiling windows of the old church at the heart of the Barbican complex. She waited till he sat down, then offered him a drink. 'Coffee, tea?'

'Something cold. It's warm out there today,' Brandon said, unfastening the jacket of his charcoal suit. Catching her sudden stillness, he stopped awkwardly at the third button and cleared his throat.

'Mineral water or orange juice?'

'Water's fine.'

When she returned with two glasses of water still hissing their effervescence into the air, Carol set Brandon's in front of him then retreated with her own to the furthest point from him. 'How are you?' Brandon asked.

Carol shrugged. 'Better than I was.'

'I was shocked when I heard what had happened. And upset too. Maggie and I . . . well, I know how I'd feel if her, or my daughters . . . Carol, I can't imagine how you begin to deal with something like that.'

'There isn't anything like that,' Carol said sharply, her eyes on his. 'I was raped, John. No other violation comes close except death, and nobody's reported back on that yet.'

Brandon took the rebuke on the chin. 'It should never have happened.'

Carol let out a deep breath. 'I made mistakes, it's true. But the real damage was caused by people who set up the operation and never levelled with me about what was really going on. Sadly, not everyone is as scrupulous as you.' She turned away and crossed her legs tightly. 'You said there was something you wanted to discuss with me?' she continued, changing the subject irrevocably.

'That's right. I don't know how current you are with recent changes in the service in the north?'

Carol shook her head. 'It's not what I've been paying attention to.'

'No reason why you should,' he said gently. 'But the Home Office in their wisdom have decided East Yorkshire is too small a force and it should be amalgamated. And since my force is the smaller of the two involved in the merger, I'm the one who's had to give up the top job.'

Carol showed the first sign of animation. 'I'm sorry to hear that, John. You were a good Chief Constable.'

'Thank you. And I hope I will be again. I'm back on my old stamping grounds.'

'Bradfield?'

Brandon noticed Carol's body relaxing slightly. He had, he thought, penetrated the hard outer shell.

'That's right. They've offered me Bradfield Metropolitan Police.' His lugubrious face creased in a smile. 'And I've said yes.'

'I'm very pleased for you, John.' Carol sipped her drink. 'You'll do a good job there.'

Brandon shook his head. 'I didn't come here for flattery, Carol. I came here because I need you.'

Carol looked away, her eyes fixed on the marled grey stone of the church. 'I don't think so, John.'

'Hear me out. I'm not asking you to come and fly a desk in CID. I want to do something different in Bradfield. I want to set up an operation like the Met has for dealing with serious crime. A couple of elite major incident squads on permanent standby to catch the tough ones. All they do is the big cases, the really bad lads. And if there's a lull in the action, the squad can pick up cold cases and work them.'

She turned her head towards him and gave him a shrewd, considering look. 'And you think I'm what you need?'

'I want you to be in charge of the unit and to have hands-on leadership of one squad. This is the sort of stuff you do best, Carol. The combination of intelligence and instinct and solid police work.'

She rubbed the back of her neck with a hand chill from her water glass. 'Maybe once,' she said. 'I don't think that's who I am any more.'

Brandon shook his head. 'These things don't go away. You're the best detective I ever had working for me, even if there were times when you came close to overstepping the mark. But you were always right when you pushed it that far. And I need that level of skill and guts on my team.'

Carol stared down at the brightly coloured gabbeh on the floor as if it held the answer. 'I don't think so, John. I come with rather too much baggage these days.'

'You'd be reporting directly to me. No petty bureaucrats between us. You'd be working with some of your old colleagues, Carol. People who know who you are and what you've achieved. Not people who are going to make snap judgements about you based on rumour and half-truth. The likes of Don Merrick and Kevin Matthews. Men who respect you.' The unspoken hung in the air. There was nowhere else she could expect that sort of reception and they both knew it.

'It's a very generous offer, John.' Carol met his gaze, a world of weariness in her eyes. 'But I think you deserve an easier ride than hiring me will get you.'

'Let me be the judge of that,' Brandon said, his natural air of authority suddenly emerging from the mildness he'd shown so far. 'Carol, your work was always a large part of who you were. I understand why you don't want to go back into intelligence and, in your shoes, I wouldn't touch those bastards with a ten-foot pole. But policing is in your blood. Forgive me if this sounds presumptuous, but I don't think you're going to get over this until you get back on the horse.'

Carol's eyes widened. Brandon wondered if he'd gone too far and waited for the whip of irony that he'd once have earned, regardless of rank.

'Have you been talking to Tony Hill?' she demanded.

Brandon couldn't hide his surprise. 'Tony? No, I

haven't spoken to him in . . . oh, it must be more than a year. Why do you say that?'

'He says the same thing,' she said flatly. 'I wondered if I was being ganged up on.'

'No, this was all my own idea. But you know, Tony's not a bad judge.'

'Maybe so. But neither of you can know much about what it's like to be me these days. I'm not sure the old rules apply any more. John, I can't make a decision about this now. I need time to think.'

Brandon drained his glass. 'Take all the time you need.' He got to his feet. 'Call me if you want to talk in more detail.' He took a business card from his pocket and placed it on the table. She looked at it as if it might suddenly burst into flames. 'Let me know what you decide.'

Carol nodded wearily. 'I will. But don't build your plans around me, John.'

It's never silent inside Bradfield Moor Secure Hospital. Well, not anywhere they've ever let you go. All the films and TV shows you've seen make you think there are probably padded cells somewhere no sound can reach, but you'd probably have to go completely tonto to end up there. Scream, foam at the mouth, deck one of the staff – that sort of thing. And while the idea of being somewhere quiet is appealing, you reckon it won't do your chances of release much good if you fake a full-on madhead attack just to get enough peace to hear the Voice properly.

When you first arrived at Bradfield Moor, you tried to get to sleep as soon as the lock's click signalled you were shut in for the night. But all you could hear were muffled conversations, occasional screams and sobs, feet slapping down corridors. You pulled the thin pillow over your head and tried to blank it. It didn't often work. The anonymous noises scared you, left you wondering if your door would suddenly burst open and front you up with who the fuck knew what. Instead of sleep, you'd get edgy and wired. Morning would come and you'd be exhausted, your eyes gritty and sore, your hands shaking like some fucked-up alkie. Worst of all, in that state, you couldn't tune in to the Voice. You were too wound up to find the technique to beat the background.

It took a few weeks, a few hellish, terrifying weeks, but eventually your slow brain worked out that it might be worth trying to go with the flow. Now, when the lights go out, you lie on your back, breathing deeply, telling yourself the noises outside are meaningless background chatter that you don't have to pay attention to. And sooner or later they fade like radio static, leaving you alone with the Voice. Your lips move silently as you relive the message, and you're gone somewhere else. Somewhere good.

It's a beautiful thing. You can replay the slow build-up to your greatest achievements. It's all there, spread before you. The choosing of a sacrifice. The negotiation. Following her to the place that you're going to transform with blood. The stupid trust they had that Dozy Derek wasn't going to hurt them. And the look in their eyes when you turned to face them with their worst nightmare in your hand.

The rerun never quite makes it to the finale. It's the eyes that do it, every time. You relive the moment when it dawns on them, the terror that turns them the colour of milk and your hand tightens on your cock. Your back arches, your hips thrust upwards, your lips stretch back over your teeth as you come. And then you hear the Voice, triumphant and rich, praising you for your role in the cleansing.

It's the best moment in your cramped little world. Other

people might think differently, but you know how lucky you are. All you want now is to get out of here, to get back to the Voice. Nothing else will do.

PART TWO

Ten weeks later

He can't remember the first time he heard the Voice. It makes him ashamed these days that he didn't recognize it instantly. Thinking about it now, he finds it hard to believe it took him so long to get it. Because it was different from all the other voices he heard every day. It didn't take the piss. It didn't get impatient with him for being slow. It didn't treat him like a stupid kid. The Voice gave him respect. He'd never had that before, which was probably why he didn't get the message for so long. It took a while before it dawned on him what was on offer.

Now, he can't imagine being without it. It's like chocolate or alcohol or spliff. The world would go on without them, but why would anybody want it to? There are times and places where he knows he'll hear it: the message service on his mobile, the minidisks that turn up without warning in the pocket of his parka, alone in bed late at night. But, sometimes, it comes out of the blue. A soft breath on his neck and there it is, the Voice. The first time that happened, he nearly crapped himself. Talk about blowing it! But he's learned since then. Now, in public places, he knows how to react so nobody thinks twice about what's going on.

The Voice gives him presents, too. OK, other people have given him things in the past, but mostly worthless crap they didn't want or second-hand stuff they were finished with. The Voice is different. The Voice gives him things that are just for him. Things that are still in their boxes and bags, bought and paid for, not nicked. The minidisk player. The Diesel jeans. The Zippo lighter with the brass skull and cross-bones that feels good when he rubs his thumb over it. The videos that fire him up with thoughts of what he'd like to do to the street girls he sees every day.

When he asked why, the Voice said it was because he was worthy. He didn't understand that. Still doesn't, not really. The Voice said he would earn the gifts, but it didn't say how, not for ages. That was probably his fault. He's not quick on the uptake. It takes him a while to get the hang of things.

But he likes to please. That's one of the first things he can remember learning. Make people smile, give them what they want and there's a better chance of avoiding a beating. So he paid attention when the Voice started to teach him his lessons because he knew that if he kept the Voice happy there was more chance it'd stay around. And he wants it to stay around, because it makes him feel good. Not many things have ever made him feel good.

So he listens and he tries to understand. He knows now about the poison the girls spread on the street. He knows that even the ones who have been kind to him are only after what they can get. This makes sense to him; he remembers how often they've tried to sweet-talk him into doing them a better deal, and how vicious they get when he sticks to what he's supposed to give them in exchange for their crumpled notes. He knows now those bitches have to be cleansed, and that he's going to be part of that cleansing.

It won't be long. Every night when he turns out the light, the Voice whispers through the silence, telling him how it will be. At first, it scared him. He wasn't sure he could handle the way the walls seemed to be talking to him. And he didn't think he could do what was being asked of him. But now when he listens in that half-world between wakefulness and sleep, he thinks maybe he can do this. One step at a time, that's how you get where you want to be. That's what the Voice says. And if he looks at it step by step, there's nothing so hard about it. Not till the very end.

He's never done anything like that before. But he's seen the videos, again and again. He knows how good it feels to watch. And the Voice tells him it'll be a million times better to do it for real. And that makes sense too, because everything the Voice has told him so far has been the truth. And now the time has come. Tonight's the night.

He can hardly wait.

Carol Jordan tossed her briefcase on to the passenger seat and got into the silver mid-range saloon she'd chosen specifically for its anonymity. She put the key in the ignition, but couldn't quite bring herself to start the engine. Christ, what was she doing? Her hands were clammy with sweat, her chest tight with anxiety. How the hell was she going to walk into a squad-room and energize her troops when her mouth was so dry her tongue stuck to her teeth?

She stared up at the small windows high on the walls of the underground car park. Feet hurried past, making their way to work. Polished loafers, scuffed shoes, kitten heels and pumps. Legs clad in suit trousers, jeans, opaque black tights and sheer nylon. City-centre hikers, taking the morning in their stride. Why couldn't she do the same thing?

'Get a grip, Jordan,' she muttered under her breath, turning the key and firing the engine. It wasn't as if she was going to have to confront a room full of strangers. Her squad was small, hand-picked by her and Brandon. Most of them she'd worked with before and she knew they respected her. Or at least they once had. She hoped their respect was still strong enough to withstand the temptation to pity.

Carol eased the car out of the garage into the street. It was all so familiar and yet so different. When she'd lived and worked in Bradfield before, the loft apartment in the converted warehouse that occupied a whole block had been her home, a high eyrie that allowed her to feel both part of and apart from the city she policed. When she'd moved to London, she'd sold it to her brother and his girlfriend. Now she was back living inside the same four walls, but this time as the reluctant cuckoo in a nest created by Michael and Lucy. They'd changed almost every aspect of the flat, making Carol feel even more out of place. Once, she'd have shrugged off that feeling, secure in the knowledge that she had a workplace where she was at home. What she feared today was that she'd feel as much of an outsider inside the police station as outside.

Even Bradfield itself felt like a too-familiar stranger. When she'd lived and worked here before, she'd made a point of learning the city. She'd visited the local museum in a bid to understand the forces that had shaped Bradfield over the centuries, turning it from a hamlet of shepherds and weavers into a vigorous commercial centre that had vied with Manchester to be the northern capital of the Victorian empire. She'd learned of its decline in the post-war era, then the reinvigoration that had been kick-started by successive waves of immigration at the tail end of the last century. She'd studied the architecture, learning to appreciate the Italianate influences on the older buildings, trying to see how the city had grown organically, attempting to imagine what the hideous 1960s concrete office blocks and shopping centre had vanquished. She'd mapped the city in her mind, using her days off to walk the streets, drive the neighbourhoods until she could grasp immediately the kind of environment she was about to enter just from the address of the crime scene.

But this morning, Carol's old knowledge seemed to have fled. New road markings and one-way systems had mushroomed in her absence, forcing her to concentrate on her bearings in a way she hadn't expected. Driving to the central police station should have been automatic. But it took her twice as long as she'd estimated and relief washed through her as she eventually turned into the car park. Carol nosed forward towards the dedicated parking spaces, pleased to see that at least one of John Brandon's promises had already been kept. One of the few empty slots bore the freshly painted designation, 'DCI JORDAN'.

Walking into the station itself provided a brief moment of déjà vu. Here at least nothing seemed to have altered. The back entrance hall still smelled faintly of cigarette smoke and stale fat from the canteen on the floor below. Whatever cosmetic changes might have been imposed on the public areas, no decorators had been charged with making this entrance more appealing. The walls were still the same industrial grey, the noticeboard covered with what were possibly the same yellowing memos she'd last seen years ago. Carol walked up to the counter and nodded a greeting at the PC behind the desk. 'DCI Jordan reporting to the Major Incident Team.'

The middle-aged man rubbed a hand across his grizzled crew cut and smiled. 'Welcome aboard,' he said. 'End of the corridor, take the lift up to the third floor. You're in Room 316.'

'Thanks.' Carol managed a thin smile and turned to push open the door as the lock buzzed. Unconsciously squaring her shoulders and tilting her chin up, she walked briskly down the corridor, ignoring the occasional curious glance from uniformed officers she passed on the way.

The third floor had undergone a facelift since she'd left. The walls were painted lavender to waist height, then off-white. The old wooden doors had been replaced with plate glass and steel, the central sections frosted so the casual passer-by could see little of what was going on inside the offices. It looked more like an advertising agency than a police station, she thought as she reached the door of 316.

Carol took a deep breath and pushed the door open. A handful of curious faces glanced up at her then broke into smiles of welcome. First on his feet was Don Merrick, newly promoted to inspector. He'd been her bagman on her first serial killer inquiry, the case that had proved to those who cared about that sort of thing that she had what it took to go all the way. Solid, reliable Don, she thought gratefully as he crossed the room and extended his hand.

'Great to see you back, ma'am,' he said, reaching out to cup her elbow with his free hand as they shook. Although he towered over her, Carol was pleasantly surprised to find nothing unsettling in his bulk. 'I'm really looking forward to working with you again.'

Detective Sergeant Kevin Matthews was right behind Merrick. Kevin, who had redeemed himself after an act of monumental stupidity had nearly cost him his career. Even though she'd been the person responsible for uncovering his treachery, Carol was nevertheless glad to see he'd apparently rehabilitated himself. He had been too good a detective to waste on the mindless routine of uniformed work. She hoped he wouldn't mind too much that they'd once been equals in rank. 'Kevin,' she acknowledged him. 'Good to see you.'

His pale, freckled skin flushed pink. 'Welcome back to Bradfield,' he said.

The others were crowding round now. 'Good to see you, chief,' a woman's voice said from behind her. Carol half-turned to see the slight figure of Detective Constable Paula McIntyre grinning up at her. Paula had worked on the periphery of the murder squad that had tracked down the psychopath who had butchered four young men in the city. She'd only been a CID aide on secondment then, but Carol had remembered her attention to detail and her empathetic way with witnesses. According to Brandon, she'd since established herself as one of the best interviewers in the city's CID. Carol knew exactly how important that could be in a murder inquiry, where everything happened against the clock. Someone skilled at persuading people to remember all they knew could save time at a stage when time could mean lives.

Paula pushed forward a mixed-race man standing

beside her. 'This is DC Evans,' she said. 'Sam, this is DCI Jordan.'

Carol extended a hand. Evans seemed almost reluctant to take it, not meeting her eye as they shook. Carol gave him a quick look of appraisal. He wasn't much taller than she was; he must barely have made the height requirement, she thought. His tightly curled hair was cut close to his head, his features more Caucasian than African. His skin was the colour of caramelized sugar and a fuzzy goatee gave him an air of maturity at odds with the unlined youthfulness of his face. She summoned up Brandon's notes on the young detective: 'A quiet lad. But he's not afraid to speak up when he's got something to say. He's smart and he's got that killer knack for pulling information together and making sense of it. He wants to go all the way, though he hides it well. But that means he'll pull out all the stops for you.' It looked like she'd have to take Brandon's word for it.

One person hung back on the fringes of the group. DC Stacey Chen had a small, fixed smile on her face. She was the unknown quantity. These days, any major inquiry needed an officer who understood how the systems worked and who could manage the volume of information generated. Carol had asked Brandon to recommend someone, and he'd come back within twenty-four hours with Stacey. 'She's got a Masters in computing, she knows the systems inside out and she's a grafter. She keeps herself to herself, but she understands the importance of being part of the team,' he'd said. 'And she's ambitious.'

33

Carol remembered what that felt like. Ambition had deserted her along with her dignity in Berlin, but she could still recall the sharp burn of desire to be on the next rung of the ladder. Carol sidestepped Evans and offered her hand to Stacey. 'Hi. You must be Stacey. I'm glad to have you on the team.'

Stacey's brown eyes never left Carol's. 'I appreciate the chance,' she said in a strong London accent.

Carol's eyes swept the room. 'We're one short,' she said.

'Oh yeah,' Merrick said. 'DS Chris Devine. We had a message yesterday: her mother's been diagnosed with terminal cancer. She's requested permission to stay with the Met for the time being. The Chief agreed.'

Carol shook her head, faintly exasperated. 'Great. We're under strength before we even get started.' She looked around, assessing the room for the first time. There were half a dozen desks, each with a computer terminal. Whiteboards and cork boards lined one wall, next to an overhead projector. A large-scale laminated map of Bradfield filled most of the space by the door. The windows that ran the length of the opposite wall were obscured by vertical blinds, cutting out the distractions of the cityscape. It was a decent size: not too cramped, not so big they'd feel marooned. It would do, she decided. 'Don, where's my office?'

Merrick pointed to the far end of the room where two doors closed off a pair of offices. 'Take your pick. They're both empty.'

And neither offered much in the way of privacy, she thought. She chose the one that had windows on the outside world and turned to Merrick, who had followed her down the room. 'Call whoever's responsible for housekeeping round here. I want some blinds for the internal window.'

Merrick grinned. 'Don't want us to know when you're playing Solitaire, eh?'

'I prefer FreeCell, actually. Give me half an hour to get settled in here, then we'll have a briefing.'

'Fine by me.' He ducked out of the room, leaving her alone. It was, she thought, a relief. She switched on the computer. Seconds later, she saw Evans approaching, his arms laden with a bundle of files. She jumped up to open the door.

'What's all this?' she asked.

'Open cases – the most recent ones. They were delivered yesterday teatime. What we're supposed to be working on while we wait for the next big thing.'

Carol felt her blood stirring. At last, something she could focus on. Something that might just lay her demons to rest. Or at least shut them up for a while.

Aidan Hart studied the man sitting opposite him with a degree of wariness. He knew many of his colleagues thought he was too young at thirty-seven to be clinical director of Bradfield Moor Secure Hospital, but he was confident enough of his skills to write off their disapproval as the product of disappointment and envy. He knew that none of them presented any professional challenge to him.

But his latest appointment was in a different league. Dr Tony Hill came with a reputation for both brilliance and awkwardness. The only rules he observed were the ones that mattered to him. He wasn't a team player, unless the team in question was one he'd chosen. He'd won loyal respect and engendered fury in equal measures among those he'd worked with. When Tony Hill had applied for a part-time post at his hospital, Aidan Hart's first reaction had been to refuse. There was room for only one star at Bradfield Moor, and that was him.

Then he'd had second thoughts. If Hill was only there as a part-timer, his work could be carefully channelled. His successes could be parlayed into more credit for Hart himself, the visionary clinical director who had tamed the maverick. It was a tempting prospect. He could portray himself as the man who persuaded high-flyer Tony Hill back into clinical practice. He had convinced himself that while the patients might benefit from Hill's famous empathetic skills, the ultimate beneficiary would be Aidan Hart himself. His second thoughts had been reinforced when he'd met Hill in the flesh. Aidan Hart knew all about dressing to impress, but within seconds he realized Hill had obviously missed that particular tutorial. The little guy in the chair opposite with the bad haircut, brown shoes with black trousers and greenish tweed jacket with frayed cuffs wasn't going to make ripples in the sort of pond Hart intended to swim in. Hill had seemed embarrassed by the high profile his work with the police had earned him and had stressed that he didn't want to find himself in the public eye ever again. Whatever profiling he did in future would be behind closed doors and beyond distant borders. Hill's eagerness to get back into harness at the sharp end of clinical practice was almost pathetic.

At the time, Hart had been smugly satisfied that taking a chance on Tony Hill would be the best possible decision. Somehow he'd missed the penetrating intelligence of the eyes, the unmistakable charisma the man wore like a well-cut suit. Hart wasn't quite sure how that had happened. Unless, of course, Hill had deliberately disguised it in order to make a quite different kind of impression. And that was a very unsettling thought. He liked to think of himself as the analyst. He was uncomfortable with the idea that this time, he might have been played by a higher master in the art of reading human behaviour. He couldn't help wondering whether he was the latest object of scrutiny for those startlingly blue eyes that seemed to absorb every nuance of his body language. He didn't like the thought that he'd have to monitor his every word and movement in his newest employee's presence. Aidan Hart had his secrets, and he didn't want Tony Hill probing too closely into them.

He didn't think he was being paranoid. Hill had only been in the building for an hour, but already he'd played a blinder. He'd found out about the latest admission and now he was sitting opposite Hart, one ankle casually propped on the opposite knee, making an irresistible rationale for first crack at the new patient. It was the sort of case that led to published papers in well-respected peer-reviewed publications, and already Hill was staking a claim to territory Hart wanted for himself. 'After all,' Hill said, 'since we've got a new admission, it makes sense for me to take the case on. That way I won't have to go over old ground. And nobody's nose gets put out of joint because I'm taking over their patient.'

'It's a pretty extreme place to start,' Hart said, affecting concern. 'And you have been out of the field for a while.'

Tony's mouth twitched in a half-smile. 'Extreme is my comfort zone, Aidan. And I do have very direct experience of dealing with people who kill for reasons that most people dismiss as madness.'

Hart shifted in his chair and spread his hands, as if discarding responsibility. 'So be it. I look forward to seeing your initial report.'

Carol leaned against the whiteboard and waited for her new team to settle down. Then she moved closer to them and perched on the edge of a desk. 'Before we get down to business, there's something I have to say to you,' she said, trying to sound more relaxed than she felt. 'I know how rumours spread in this job and I expect you've all heard some version of my recent history.' She could tell by the way the men all found something more interesting to study that she'd hit the target.

Don Merrick gazed at the floor. 'Nobody here's interested in gossip,' he muttered. 'Just results. And your record speaks for itself on that.'

The shadow of a smile crossed Carol's face. 'Thank you, Don. Nevertheless, if we're going to make this unit work, we need to have an open, honest atmosphere. What happened to me happened because of secrets and lies. I'm not prepared to work in an environment like that again.' She looked around, saw she had their attention and continued.

'I was selected for an undercover operation that left me in a very exposed position. Because I wasn't thoroughly briefed by my bosses, I couldn't cover my back properly. And as a result, I was raped.' She heard a sharp intake of breath but couldn't identify its source. 'I don't expect to be handled with kid gloves. What happened to me won't affect the way I do my job. Except that it has made me very sensitive to issues of loyalty. This squad can only function if we all put teamwork first. I don't want any glory hunters here. So if any of you has a problem with that, this is the time to ask for reassignment.' She looked around at her group. Stacey and Evans looked surprised, but the others were nodding their acquiescence.

Carol stood up straight and picked up the top file. 'Good. Now, until we land our first job, we're supposed to be looking at unsolved open cases. They've given us two murders, a rape, two armed robberies, a serial arson and a pair of child abductions. Over the next few days, I want you each to go through three separate files. Don, work out a rota so all the cases get looked at. Include me in it – since we're one light, I'll make up the numbers. On each file, I want you to list suggested actions for moving the case forward. Then, when you've all made your lists, we'll sit down together, look at what you've come up with and see which cases offer the most promising prospects for further investigation. Any questions?'

Kevin raised a hand. 'Is this a non-smoking office?'

Paula groaned. 'It's a non-smoking building, Kevin.'

'Yeah, but that doesn't mean we can't have smoking areas, does it? I mean, what is the point of air conditioning if you don't make it earn its keep?'

'It's bad for the computers,' Stacey pointed out.

'We could have one corner,' Evans said. 'Under the air-conditioning vent.'

As the discussion rolled over her, Carol felt the first twinges of homecoming. Never mind the adrenaline of working a case, this was the kind of argument that told her she was back where she belonged. Pointless wrangling about the small issues that made life bearable, that was the hallmark of the police service. 'Sort it out among yourselves,' she said with an air of finality. 'I don't care. I've got a door I can close. Oh, and I've got a job for you, Sam . . .'

He looked up, surprise on his face. 'Guv?' He shifted in his seat, turning slightly to one side. It was the movement of a man unconsciously reducing his target area, assessing the situation before committing himself to fight or flight.

'Pop out to the shops and buy us a kettle, a cafetière and a dozen mugs.' His eyes hardened as Carol's words sank in. 'Tea and some decent coffee, milk and sugar. Oh, and some biscuits. We're not going to win any popularity contests in the canteen, digging over what other officers will see as their failures. We might as well entrench ourselves here.'

'Can we get some Earl Grey tea?' Stacey Chen's contribution sounded more like an order than a request.

'Don't see why not,' Carol said, turning away and heading for her office. She'd learned something already. Evans didn't like what he saw as menial work.

Either he considered it to be women's work or he thought it was beneath his capabilities. Carol stored the information away for future reference. She had almost reached the door when Merrick's voice reached her in a protest.

'Ma'am, do you know why the files on Tim Golding and Guy Lefevre are in here?' he demanded indignantly.

Carol swung round. 'Who . . .?' She was aware of a sudden stillness in the room. Paula's stare was wary, while the others' expressions varied from surprised to incredulous.

Merrick's genial face had tightened. 'Tim Golding's the eight-year-old who went missing nearly three months ago. Guy Lefevre vanished into thin air fifteen months before. We turned the city upside down looking for them. We even got Tony Hill to draw up a profile, for all the good it did.'

It was Carol's turn to feel surprise. Tony had said nothing to her about profiling, never mind profiling in Bradfield. But then, he had been uncharacteristically quiet since they'd discussed whether she should take up John Brandon's offer. He'd encouraged her to accept the job, but since she'd told him of her decision to go ahead, his emails had been curiously bland and noncommittal, as if he was deliberately making her stand on her own two feet. 'What's your point, Don?' she asked.

'Tim Golding was my case,' he said angrily. 'And I was the bagman on Guy Lefevre. There's nothing we left undone.'

'Now you understand why we're going to be the station pariahs,' Carol said gently. 'There are another

41

half-dozen SIOs out there smarting because cases they couldn't close have been passed on to us. I wouldn't be surprised if Tim Golding's case had been put in deliberately to keep us on our toes. So even though I have every confidence that you did all you could, we're still going to treat this case just like the others.'

Merrick scowled. 'All the same, ma'am . . .'

'There are people in this organization who would probably be very happy to see us fail. If you let this wind you up, Don, you're playing into their hands.' Carol gave him her warmest smile. 'I trust you, otherwise you wouldn't be in this room. But we're all capable of missing something, no matter how much we think we've covered all the ground. So I don't want the officers reviewing this case to keep their thoughts to themselves for fear of offending you. Like I said earlier: no secrets or lies.'

Carol didn't wait for a reaction. She walked into her office, leaving the door open. Was this the first sign that someone was out to undermine her squad and, by extension, their new Chief Constable? She knew she fell too easily into mistrust these days, but she'd rather be too cautious than blithely oblivious to someone putting the shaft in. After all, it wasn't paranoia if they really were out to get you.

She'd barely settled behind her desk when Don Merrick appeared in the doorway carrying a file. 'A word, ma'am?'

Carol gestured towards the visitor's chair with her head. Don sat down, holding the file to his chest. 'Tim Golding,' he said.

'I hear you, Don. Hand it over.'

He pulled it even closer to him. 'It's just that . . .'

'I know. If anybody's going to poke their nose into your case, you'd rather it was me than one of the new faces.' Carol reached a hand out.

Reluctantly, Don shifted forward in his seat and extended the file towards her. 'We couldn't have done more,' he said. 'We just kept hitting brick walls. We couldn't even give Tony Hill enough to go on to make a profile worthwhile. He said himself it was a waste of resources. But I couldn't think of anything else to try. That's why it's ended up as a cold case this early on.'

'I wondered about that. It seems very soon to consign it to the back burner.'

Don sighed. 'There just wasn't anywhere else for us to go with it. We've still got a couple of DCs keeping an eye on it, feeding the press whenever they decide to take another crack at it. But nothing active's happened for at least a month.' Don's misery was written all over him, from the hangdog eyes to the slump of his shoulders.

It provoked a sympathetic echo in Carol. 'Leave it with me, Don. I don't expect I'll see anything you've missed.'

He got to his feet, a rueful look on his face. 'Thing is, ma'am, I remember when I was working the case that I wished you were around. Just so I could run it past you. You always had the knack of seeing things from a different angle.'

'What is it they say, Don? Don't wish too hard for what you want because you might get it.'

Tony Hill leaned forward and gazed intently through the observation window. A neat, balding man sat

43

folded in the chair bolted to the floor. He looked some-where in the region of fifty, though his placid expression went some way towards erasing the lines etched into his face. For a fleeting, incomprehensible moment, Tony thought of a child's lollipop, tightly wrapped in cellophane, Sellotape wrapped around the stick.

His stillness was preternatural. Most of the patients Tony encountered had difficulty with immobility, never mind tranquillity. They twitched, they fidgeted, they chain-smoked, they fiddled with their clothes. But this man – he checked the notes – this Tom Storey had an almost Zen-like quality. Tony glanced through the notes again, refreshing his memory from the previous evening's reading. He shook his head, fighting his anger at the stupidity of some of his medical colleagues. Then he closed the folder and headed for the interview room.

He felt the spring in his step, even in that short journey. Bradfield Moor Secure Hospital wasn't generally associated in people's minds with the notion of contentment, but that was precisely what it had given Tony for the first time in months. He was back in the field, back in the world of messy heads, back where he belonged. In spite of his constant efforts to assume a series of masks that would help him blend in, Tony knew he was an outsider in the world beyond the grim institutional walls of Bradfield Moor. It was a feeling he did not care to examine too closely; it said things about him that he wasn't entirely comfortable with. But it was impossible to deny that the exercise of empathy was what gave meaning to his days. There was nothing quite like that moment when the tumblers of someone else's brain clicked into place for him and allowed him to penetrate the knotted logic of another mind. Really, truly, nothing.

He pushed open the door to the interview room and sat down opposite his latest challenge. Tom Storey remained immobile, only his eyes shifting to connect with Tony. In his right hand, he cradled a heavily bandaged stump where his left hand had been until a few days previously. Tony leaned forward and arranged his face into an expression of sympathy. 'I'm Tony Hill. I'm sorry for your loss.'

Storey's eyes widened in surprise. Then he gave a small snort. 'My hand or my kids?' he said sourly.

'Your son and your daughter,' Tony said. 'I imagine the hand feels like a blessing.'

Storey said nothing.

'Alien Hand Syndrome,' Tony said. 'First recorded in 1908. A gift for horror-film scriptwriters: 1924, *The Hands of Orlac* – Conrad Veidt played a classical pianist who had the hands of a killer grafted on after his were destroyed in a train accident; 1946, *The Beast with Five Fingers,* another pianist; 1987, *Evil Dead II* – the hero takes a chainsaw to his possessed hand to stop it attacking him. Cheap thrills all round. But it's not so thrilling when you're the one with the hand, is it? Because when you try to explain what it feels like, nobody really takes you seriously. Nobody took you seriously, did they, Tom?'

Storey shifted in his seat but remained silent and apparently composed.

'The GP gave you some tranquillizers. Stress, that's what he said, right?'

Storey inclined his head slightly.

Tony smiled, encouraging. 'They didn't work, did they? Just made you feel sleepy and out of it. And with a hand like yours, you couldn't afford to relax your vigilance, could you? Because there was no telling what might happen then. How was it for you, Tom? Did you wake up in the night struggling for breath because the hand was round your throat? Did it smash plates over your head? Stop you from putting food in your mouth?' Tony's questioning was gentle, his voice sympathetic.

Storey cleared his throat. 'It threw things. We'd all be sitting eating breakfast, and I'd pick up the teapot and throw it at my wife. Or we'd be out in the garden and the next thing I'd know, I'd be picking up stones from the rockery and throwing them at the kids.' He leaned back in his chair, apparently exhausted from the effort of speech.

'I can imagine how frightening that must have been. How did your wife react?'

Storey closed his eyes. 'She was going to leave me. Take the kids with her and never come back.'

'And you love your kids. That's a hell of a dilemma for you. You've nothing to fight back with. Life without your kids, it's not worth living. But life with your kids places them in constant danger because you can't stop the hand doing what it wants. There's no easy answer.' Tony paused and Storey opened his eyes again. 'You must have been in complete turmoil.'

'Why are you making excuses for me? I'm a monster. I killed my children, that's the worst thing anybody can do. They should have let me bleed to death, not saved me. I deserve to be dead.' Storey's words tumbled over each other.

'You're not a monster,' Tony said. 'I don't think your kids are the only victims here. We're going to run some physical tests. Tom, I think you may be suffering from a brain tumour. You see, your brain comes in two halves. Messages from one part reach the other across a sort of bridge called the corpus callosum. When that's damaged, your right hand literally doesn't know what your left hand is doing. And that's a terrible thing to live with. I can't blame you for being driven to the point where you thought killing your children was the only way to keep them safe from whatever you might do to them.'

'You *should* blame me,' Storey insisted. 'I was their father. It was my job to protect them. Not kill them.'

'But you couldn't trust yourself. So you chose to end their lives in the most humane way you could. Smothering them while they slept.'

Storey's eyes filled with tears and he bowed his head. 'It was wrong,' he said, his voice choking. 'But nobody would listen to me. Nobody would help me.'

Tony reached across the table and laid his hand on the bandaged stump. 'We'll help you now, Tom. I promise you. We'll help you.'

Carol arched her back and rotated her shoulders, swivelling round in her chair to stare out of the window. Across the street stood a white Portland stone building with a fine neoclassical portico. When she'd last been in Bradfield, it had been a bingo hall. Now it was a nightclub, its cold neon tubes spelling out 'Afrodite' in fake Greek script. Buses rumbled past, advertising the latest movies and console games. A traffic warden stalked the metered parking, his computerized ticket machine held like a truncheon. A world going about its business, insulated from the unpleasantness that was her stock in trade. She'd read the material on Guy Lefevre and now she was close to the end of Tim Golding's file. The words were starting to blur. Apart from a half-hour break for lunch, she'd been reading solidly all day. She knew she wasn't the only one. Every time she'd raised her head, the rest of the squad had been equally engrossed. Interesting how their body language seemed to reveal so much more of their personalities than the slightly awkward and guarded conversation over the lunchtime sandwiches Stacey had fetched from the canteen.

Don sat hunched over his desk, one arm round the file like a kid who doesn't want anybody copying his work. He wasn't the quickest wit Carol had ever worked with, but he made up for it with his stolid persistence and total commitment to the team. And if there was one person whose loyalty she could depend on without question, it was Don. He'd proved himself in the past, but she hadn't realized until this morning how important that knowledge was to her.

Kevin's wiry body sat erect in his chair, papers neatly aligned. Every now and again he would pause and stare into the middle distance for as long as it took to smoke a cigarette. Then he would scribble something on the pad next to him and return to his reading. Carol remembered how he'd always seemed so buttoned up. It had made it all the harder to believe when he'd gone off the rails. But like most repressed individuals, when he had finally broken the rules he'd been more reckless than the wildest risk taker. And it had led him into betrayal. Carol told herself that he'd never make that mistake again, but she was still reluctant to trust. She hoped he couldn't see that in her eyes.

Sam Evans was hunched in the chair opposite Kevin, his jacket carefully arranged on a hanger hooked over a filing-cabinet drawer handle. His shirt was crisp and white, the careful creases of the iron still clean cut on his sleeves. He and Kevin had staked out smokers' corner on the opposite side of the room to Stacey and her computers. Evans' reading style seemed almost nonchalant, as if he were drifting through the Sunday papers. His expression gave nothing away. But occasionally his hand would snake into his trouser pocket and emerge with a minidisk recorder. He'd mumble a few words into it then slip it back out of sight. Carol didn't think much was getting past him.

Paula, conversely, was a spreader. Within half an hour of starting, the whole of her desktop was covered in stacks of papers as she sorted through the file in front of her. But in spite of the appearance of untidiness, it was clear she knew where everything was. Her hand moved, apparently independent of her eyes, confidently picking up the next piece of paper she needed. It was as if she had a mental map of her arrangement, a neat grid stamped firmly on her brain. Carol wondered if that was how she worked interviews; slotting every piece of information into its own socket till the connections linked together and lit up like a completed circuit.

Stacey couldn't have been more different. Even her dress style was at odds with Paula's casual T-shirt and

49

jeans. Stacey's suit fitted as if it had been made to measure, and the fine polo-neck sweater beneath it looked like cashmere to Carol's eye. A surprisingly expensive outfit for a detective constable, she thought. When it came to work, it was almost as if Stacey resented the presence of paper. She'd balanced the file she was studying on a pulled-out desk drawer to leave her work surface clear for interaction with the machine. The twin screens of her computer system held most of her attention. She would swiftly scrutinize the file material, then her fingers would fly over the keys before she cocked her head to one side, ran her left hand through her glossy black hair and clicked a mouse button. Manipulable virtuality was seemingly what she craved over reality.

It was, Carol thought, a group with enough variety in their skills and attributes to cover most of the bases. The key question was whether she could get them to bond into a unit. Until they felt part of a team, they would be less than the sum of their parts. She sighed. Somewhere in her near future, she could see a night out with her officers. On balance, she'd rather have spent a day in the dentist's chair without benefit of anaesthetic. She hadn't been out on the town since she'd come back from Germany. Even going to familiar restaurants with friends had been beyond her. The idea of raucous, crowded pubs and clubs curdled her stomach. 'Get over it,' she muttered angrily to herself as she turned back to the Tim Golding file.

She reread the statement given by the organic vegetable deliveryman. My, how Harriestown had changed in the few years she'd been gone. The previous occupants of the area would have been interested in organic vegetables only as potential missiles. So engrossed was she that the sharp rap of knuckles on her door jamb made her start. The pages she was holding fluttered to the desk unheeded as Carol pushed back in her chair, heart thudding, eyes wide. This was new, she thought. The old Carol Jordan was a lot harder to startle.

'Sorry, I didn't mean to creep up on you.' The woman in the doorway looked more amused than apologetic.

It was Carol's habit to form descriptions of new encounters as if she were registering their details for the National Criminal Intelligence database. Medium height; wiry as Carol herself. Straight shoulders, full breasts, narrow hips. Wavy brown hair cut in a tousle that had been fashionable a few years before, but which she'd probably hung on to because it suited her incongruously cherubic face. The cast of her features made her look as if she was perpetually on the verge of a smile. Only the eyes gave her away; she had the long flat stare of the cop who'd grown weary of the variety of human viciousness and misery. She wore black jeans, a black silk T-shirt and a leather jacket the colour of crème caramel. Whoever she was, Carol was certain she'd never met her before. 'I was miles away,' she said, getting to her feet.

'And who wouldn't be, given half a chance.' The woman's eyes crinkled in an easy smile as she moved forward, extending a hand. 'Detective Sergeant Jan Shields. I work Temple Fields.'

'DCI Jordan,' Carol said, accepting the warm, dry handshake. She gave a wry smile. 'You're the Vice, then?'

Jan groaned. 'Oh please. One bloody TV series and we're back with a label from the bad old, sad old days. Yeah, I'm the Vice. That'd be why we get the scuzzy office and you get the management suite. How are you settling in?'

Carol shrugged, slightly uncomfortable with the assumption of camaraderie from an officer junior in rank though probably roughly equal in years. 'We're feeling our way. So, Sergeant Shields, is this a social call? Or is there something I can help you with?'

'I think it might be me that can help you.' Jan waved a slim manila folder, this smile a tease.

Carol raised her eyebrows, moving back behind her desk. 'Really?'

'Your team's working cold cases till you hit a fresh jackpot, right?'

'We're taking a look, yes.'

'And one of those cases would be Tim Golding?'

'You're well informed, Sergeant.'

Jan shrugged. 'You know how it is. Gossip travels faster than a speeding bullet.'

'And we're today's hot news.' Carol sat down. She wanted to give the impression of confidence. 'So what is it you have for me?'

'It's a bit of a long story.' Jan gestured to the chair opposite Carol. 'May I?' She sat down and crossed her legs with easy confidence.

Carol leaned forward. 'Let's have it, then.'

'When you were here before, I was on secondment to a Home Office team working with the FBI on a long-term investigation into paedophiles using the internet. You've probably heard of Operation Ore?'

Carol nodded. The news media had leapt on

52

Operation Ore with the avidity of a starving coyote in a meat-processing factory. The investigation had netted thousands of potential arrestees on both sides of the Atlantic: men who surfed the net and used their credit cards to buy access to sites where they could download child pornography. But the sheer scale of the results had made Operation Ore a victim of its own success. Overstretched law enforcement agencies looked at the mountain of evidence and threw their hands up in despair. Carol had heard one colleague estimate that with the officers at his disposal it would take nine and a half years simply to interview all the names from his patch, never mind to seize and analyse their hard drives. 'You were involved in that?'

'In the early stages, yes. I've been back here two years now, and most of what I've been doing since then has been prioritizing our hit list, in between the usual shit on the streets. In the last six months, we've started pulling in our prime candidates. What we do is kick their doors down and seize their computer equipment. After a preliminary interview we usually release them on police bail till the analysis is done.'

'Which can take weeks, I imagine?'

Jan's mouth twisted in a half-smile. 'If we're lucky. Anyway, I got a stack of stuff through yesterday from the techies. They'd stripped out a pretty rich seam from a guy we pulled in a couple of months ago.' She shook her head. 'You'd think I'd be used to this by now. The guy's a senior NHS manager. You need a hip replacement or a new knee at Bradfield Cross? He's the one you blame for the length of the waiting list. Respectable house in the suburbs, wife's a teacher, two teenage kids. And his computer's like a fucking sewer. So, I'm wading through his shit and I find this –' She flipped open her file dramatically and pulled out a print of a digital photograph, blown up to cover most of an A4 sheet. She passed it across to Carol. 'I recognized the kid from the media blitz.'

Carol studied the photograph. The background showed a dramatic rock formation. Slender birch branches crisscrossed one corner. A skinny child stood naked and hunched in the middle of the frame. Sandy hair, Harry Potter glasses. Features she'd memorized in the course of her long day's reading. There was no room for doubt: this was Tim Golding. She felt the familiar rush that came with a fresh lead and hated herself for it. This wasn't something to rejoice over. Carol understood that now better than she ever had before. 'Are there any more?' she asked.

Jan shook her head. 'I've been right through the archive. Nothing.'

'What about the other missing kid – Guy Lefevre?'

'Sorry. That's the only one. And it doesn't mean my guy is the one you're looking for. These sick bastards swap shots all the time. The fact that there's only the one pic of the Golding boy would suggest to me that my target wasn't the photographer.'

'I'm inclined to agree with you. But I want to talk to him nevertheless.' Carol met Jan's eyes in a long, measured stare. 'I'd like his file now and I'd like him in an interview room first thing in the morning. Do you want me to clear that with your senior officer?'

'Sorted already. My guvnor agrees you get first crack. Full house beats a flush.'

'Thanks, Sergeant. I appreciate it.' Carol slid the

print back towards Jan. 'This background – any idea where it might be?' She pointed to the unusual rock formation.

Jan shook her head. 'Not a clue. I'm a city girl, me. I get the shakes if I'm more than five miles from Starbucks.'

'It looks pretty distinctive to me. But for all I know, there could be rocks like this from Land's End to John o'Groats.'

'Yeah. But there's only one Tim Golding.'

Carol sighed. 'Wrong tense, I think.'

'Sorry?'

'Looking at this, I think we should be saying there *was* only one Tim Golding.'

His hands are sweating. They slither and slip in spite of the thin layer of talc inside the latex gloves. It makes the prep-aration difficult. He's not really used to anything that requires finer control than rolling a joint. When his fingers fumble and a blade nicks him through the glove, he swears out loud at the beads of blood that ooze from the wound.

He's glad the Voice isn't here to see him fucking up. And that reminds him that he has instructions about what to do if his blood gets on the stuff. 'Put anything stained with even the smallest drop of blood to one side. Replace it and start again. Only one blood, that's what we want. Only one blood.' The words echo in his head and he does what he's told. He pulls a page out of that evening's paper and places the bloody blade on it. Then he strips off the gloves and adds them to the pile. He doesn't have an Elastoplast, so he tears off a corner of the newsprint and sticks it clumsily over the place where the blood is seeping. Then he takes another pair of gloves from the box. And starts again.

He really wants to get it right. He knows that if he gets it right, this will be the best thing he's ever done. He knows because that's what the Voice told him. And everything else the Voice has said has been right.

All day, he's been thinking about what's to come. All day, his mind's been in a spin. Though he tried to keep it hidden, people noticed. But they don't expect much of him at the best of times, so they didn't notice in a way that they'll remember afterwards. Mostly, they just made a joke of it, although one or two used his slowness or stupidity as an excuse for giving him a bad time. But he's used to that too. Until the Voice came along and said he deserved better, that was how it was for him. The tree every dog pissed up. The one who was so crap everybody else looked good next to him.

Tonight, he's going to prove them wrong. Tonight he's going to do something none of them would dare. And he's going to do it right.

Isn't he?

The car park was a place of shadows, hemmed in by high brick walls topped with razor wire. When it had been built, nobody could have anticipated the explosion in car ownership, so it was always over-full, double-parked and a source of irritation to those who had to use it.

It was also supposed to be secure. A sturdy metal barrier had to be raised to permit entry or egress, and the officer in charge of it was supposed to monitor each entrant carefully. But the man leaning on one of the cars understood how to circumvent systems. When he'd been here before, he'd made allies of the security team, aware that there would probably be a time when he'd want to come back without the necessary authority.

That time was tonight. He'd been waiting for the best part of an hour, resting against the bonnet of the silver saloon, reading steadily through the papers he'd stuffed into his briefcase, his peripheral vision alert to anyone leaving the tall building in front of the car park. But the light was fading fast and the air held the crisp promise of winter. Waiting was becoming less attractive. He glanced at his watch. Just after six. He'd give it half an hour, then he'd slip away into the night. He didn't want to lurk in the darkness, for a variety of reasons.

A few minutes later, he saw what he'd been waiting for. A gleam of blonde hair caught in the security lights by the back door, and he was on the move. He shoved the file back into his briefcase and stood upright, moving towards the back of the car to cut off his target before she could reach the driver's door.

She looked over her shoulder, calling out a farewell to a colleague. When she turned back, he was only a few feet from her. Shock and astonishment shot across her face and she stopped dead. Her mouth formed an exclamation, but no sound emerged.

'Hi, Carol,' Tony said. 'Fancy a curry?'

'Jesus,' she exhaled, her shoulders dropping. 'You nearly gave me a heart attack. What the hell are you doing here?'

He spread his arms wide, a parody of innocence. 'Like I said, inviting you out for a curry.'

'Freaking me out, more like. What are you doing in Bradfield? You're supposed to be in St Andrews.'

He raised one finger in admonishment. 'Later. Now, are you going to unlock the car? I'm freezing.'

With an air of bemusement, Carol obediently popped the locks and watched him walk round to the passenger seat. She couldn't help smiling. There was, she thought, nobody quite like Tony Hill.

Twenty minutes later, they'd found a relatively quiet corner table in a cheap and cheerful Bangladeshi café on the fringes of Temple Fields, the area of the city centre where the gay village sat uneasily alongside the red-light district. Their fellow customers were a mixture of students and individuals poised to go looking for love in all the wrong places. Carol and Tony had discovered the café when they'd first worked together on a case centred on Temple Fields, and it seemed the obvious place for this reunion.

'I can't believe you're here,' Carol said as the waiter departed to bring them a couple of bottles of Kingfisher.

He held out his arm. 'Go on, pinch me. I'm real.'

She leaned forward and gave his shoulder a gentle punch. 'OK, you're real. But why are you here?'

'I jacked the job in. I was a fish out of water there, Carol. I needed to get back to the work I know I'm good at. I'd already got an offer of consultancy work over in Europe. And when John Brandon told me you were coming back to Bradfield, I got on to Bradfield Moor and asked for part-time clinical work.' He grinned. 'So here I am.'

'You came back to Bradfield because of me?' Carol's expression was guarded. 'I don't want your pity, Tony.'

'It's nothing to do with pity. You're the best friend

58

I've got. I have some idea of how hard this is for you, Carol. And I want to be around if you need me.'

Carol waited for the waiter to deposit their beers, then said, 'I can manage, you know. I've been a cop for a long time. I'm capable of catching villains without your help.'

Tony took a long drink from the bottle of Indian lager while he considered how to deal with her wilful misunderstanding. 'I'm not here to help you do your job. I'm here because that's what friends do.' He gave a crooked smile. 'And besides, it suits me to be here. You should see the nutters they've got locked up in Bradfield Moor. It's a dream come true for a weirdo like me.'

Carol snorted, spraying the paper tablecloth with beer. 'Bastard! You waited till I had a mouthful of beer to make me laugh.'

'What do you expect? I'm trained to provoke reactions. So, where are you living?'

'I'm camping in Michael's spare room while I look for somewhere to rent.' Carol studied the menu.

Tony pretended to do the same, though he already knew he'd choose the fish pakora followed by the chicken biryani. The lack of commitment implied by Carol's decision to rent rather than to sell up in London and buy in Bradfield was understandable. She wanted to leave herself an escape route. But it troubled him nevertheless. 'That must feel strange,' he said. 'It having been your flat in the first place.'

'It's not ideal. I don't think Lucy's crazy about having me there. She's a barrister, remember? She does a lot of criminal defence work, so she has a tendency to regard me in the same light as a chicken

59

farmer regards a fox.' The waiter returned and they ordered their meals. As he departed, Carol met Tony's eyes. 'What about you? Where are you living?'

'I was lucky. I sold my cottage in Cellardyke practically overnight. I've just bought a place here. Near where I used to live. A Victorian semi. Three bedrooms, two receptions. Nice big rooms, very light.'

'Sounds good.'

The waiter plonked a plate of poppadums and a tray of relishes in front of them. Tony took the opportunity to busy himself with something other than Carol. 'Thing is, it's got a cellar. Pretty much self-contained. Two big rooms, natural light. Toilet and shower. And a little boxroom you could easily turn into a kitchen.' He looked up, the question in his eyes.

Carol stared at him, clearly unsure if he was saying what she thought. She gave an uncertain laugh. 'What would I do with a kitchen?'

'Good point. But it does give you somewhere to put the washing machine.'

'Are you seriously offering me your cellar?'

'Why not? It'd solve your accommodation problem. And having a copper on the premises would give me a sense of security.' He grinned. 'More importantly, Nelson would keep the mice away.'

Carol fiddled with the lime pickle. 'I don't know. Does it have a separate entrance?'

'Well, of course. I wouldn't want to compromise your reputation. There's a door that leads to a flight of steps up to the back garden. And an internal door down from the house, obviously. But it would be a simple enough thing to fit a lock to that.' He smiled. 'You could have bolts too, if you wanted.'

'You've been thinking about this, haven't you?'

Tony shrugged. 'When I viewed the house, it seemed like a good way of making it work for a living. I didn't know what your plans were. But the builders started work on it yesterday. And I'd rather have you living there than a stranger. Look, don't make a decision now. Think about it. Sleep on it. There's no hurry.' There was an uncomfortable silence while they both tried to figure out where to take the conversation next. 'So how was your first day back in harness? What are you working on?' Tony asked, moving the conversation away from treacherous shoals.

'Until we get a new major case, we're taking a look at a bunch of unsolveds.' Carol looked up as the waiter brought their starters.

'That must be pretty soul-destroying.'

'Normally it would be.' She reached for her aloo chat. 'But amazingly enough, we actually scored a break this afternoon. Purely by chance, a detective from another squad stumbled across a new lead. I can't help seeing it as a positive omen.'

'That's a great start.'

Carol's expression was rueful. 'Yes and no. You remember Don Merrick? He's the DI on my team. And the trouble is that the break came on one of his cold cases. Which makes him feel pretty sick.'

'Not Tim Golding?'

Carol tipped her head in acknowledgement. 'The one he called you in on. Thanks for telling me, Tony,' she added ironically.

He looked embarrassed. 'To tell you the truth, I was afraid of muddying the waters while you were considering coming back to Bradfield. I didn't want to influence your decision one way or the other.'

Carol smiled. 'Oh, you think your presence in Bradfield would have been such a draw?'

He put down the pakora that was halfway to his lips. 'The truth, Carol? I was afraid if you knew I was here, it would be the last place on earth you'd want to be.'

Don Merrick stared glumly into his pint of Newcastle Brown Ale, his Labrador eyes sad and brooding. 'Stop looking on the fucking bright side, Paula,' he grumbled. 'Because there isn't a fucking bright side, all right?'

Paula ran her finger down the condensation on her bottle of Smirnoff Ice. They were the last survivors of the bonding session the team had decided on after DCI Jordan had called it a day. There hadn't been much of a celebratory atmosphere, truth to tell. Stacey and Sam had excused themselves after the first round, and Kevin had been sucked into a drawn-out game of pool in the pub's ratty back room. Neither Paula nor Merrick minded. They'd worked together long enough to slip the bonds of rank once they were on their own time. 'Please yourself, Don.'

'That photo . . . I can't help thinking about what that lad went through before he died. And don't try to contradict me,' he continued, holding up a hand to fend Paula off. 'We both know that the kind of scum who'd do that to a kid wouldn't leave a witness. Tim Golding's dead. But he was alive long enough to be taken off somewhere in the middle of nowhere and subjected to Christ knows what. That picture was taken in daylight, which means he was still alive the next morning. And that's what I'm having trouble with. If I'd done my job, we'd have found him.'

Paula reached across the table and helped herself to one of Merrick's cigarettes. 'If you're getting maudlin, I need a smoke.'

'Thought you'd stopped.'

'I have.' She inhaled deeply. 'That's bullshit, what you were just saying. We worked that case into the ground. You've got to stop beating yourself up like this, Don. Apart from anything else, we need you not to be fucked up. We've already got a fucked-up DCI. The last thing we need is a fucked-up DI as well.'

Merrick looked at her in surprise. 'You think Carol Jordan's fucked up?'

'Of course she is. She was raped, Don. And it happened because a bunch of suits thought so little of her they staked her out like a Judas goat. However you cut it, she's not playing with a full deck right now. Her judgement's compromised.'

Merrick shook his head. 'I don't know, Paula. She seemed pretty much on her game to me.'

'It's easy to talk the talk when there's no pressure. But I'm not sure she'll be able to walk the walk any more.'

Merrick looked doubtful. 'It's far too soon to be talking like that. Carol Jordan's the best guvnor I ever worked for.'

'I thought so once too. But now . . .?' Paula swigged the rest of her drink. 'Let's see if you're saying that in six months' time. So what do you make of the newbies?'

'Early days.' Merrick shrugged. 'That Stacey knows her way round the machines, that's for sure.'

'I keep catching myself wondering if she is a machine,' Paula giggled. 'She's not one of the girls, that's for sure. I keep trying to get her talking, but she's definitely not one for idle chit-chat.'

Merrick grinned. 'Yeah, somehow I can't see her gossiping about men and make-up in the toilets. But she's quick enough to weigh in when somebody needs a bit of help with the computers.'

'What about Sam? What's your take on him?' Paula asked.

'Seems all right. He doesn't have much to say for himself.'

'I'm not sure about him. There's something a bit creepy there,' Paula confided. 'One of my mates used to work with him over at Downton, and she said he was slimy. Never said much, but never missed a chance to put one over on everybody else. And always incredibly well informed about what everybody else was up to. Apparently, he likes to look good to the bosses, does our Sam.'

'Well, we all like to make a good impression,' Merrick said.

'Yeah, but not necessarily at the expense of our colleagues. Oh, and she said he was never at ease with her or the other women on the squad. She thought he was a bit of a secret sexist.'

Merrick laughed. 'Paula, these days we're only allowed to be sexist in secret or else you and the sisters come down on us like a ton of bricks.'

She punched him affectionately on the arm. 'You know what I mean.' She contemplated her empty bottle. 'You ready for another?'

'I should be getting home,' Merrick said reluctantly.

Paula got to her feet, grinning. 'That'll be another brown ale, then?'

He knows these streets like the inside of his pocket. He's walked them, worked them since he was a kid. He knows the faces, he knows the places where certain people can be found at particular times of the day and night. He never thought anything of it before, it was just the way the world turned. But the Voice has made him understand that knowledge is power, that what he knows makes him king of the streets.

He shambles along in his usual fashion, trying his very best to look like he would on any other night. He does a bit of business, just to cover himself, just to make it look like any other night. The Voice said he should do that. So that when the questions come, people will place him in the usual haunts, doing the usual things.

But soon it's time. He knows where to find her. It's where she always is between punters. He clears his throat and walks up to her. He tells her what he wants. She looks amused, as if she can't quite believe it's him asking for it. 'No discounts for mates, mind,' she says. He blushes and squirms. It makes him uncomfortable that she calls him a mate. Because what he's about to do to her is nothing like the things that mates do to each other, no way. But she doesn't see what's in his mind. She sees what she expects to see: a punter who feels awkward because he's a fish out of water.

He tells her he wants to go back to her room. He knew

about the room even before the Voice. He knows much more about what goes on round here than anybody gives him credit for. He follows her round the corner into the ginnel where her room is, giving a quick glance over his shoulder. Nobody is paying any attention. Even if they wanted to, it's too dark round here; the dealers smash the streetlights so often the council's given up replacing them. And even if they had eyes like a cat, they'd assume it was him working, not getting her to work for him.

Up the stairs she goes, her arse tight in her short skirt. It's amazing, but he feels himself getting hard at the sight of it. He's seen these girls a million times before, they're just part of the landscape, they don't normally register any more. But tonight, watching Sandie's gyrating hips, he's turned on. He remembers dimly what he's supposed to do at this point and he pulls out the digital camera and snaps her as she goes. The flash makes her stop in her tracks and whirl round. 'What the fuck are you up to?' she demands.

He waves the camera at her. 'I just wanted something to remember you by,' he says, the rehearsed words tripping out with hardly a stumble.

She frowns for a second, then laughs. 'That'll cost you.'

He snaps another shot. 'I can afford it,' he says. She carries on upstairs and he follows. At the door, she stops. 'Let's see the colour of your money,' she says. 'You want to tie me up, you pay upfront.'

He takes out the money the Voice left with his instructions and peels off some notes. Sandie snatches at it and shoves it into her little handbag. 'Business must be better for you than it is for me,' she says, her voice bitter as the coffee in Stan's Café. She opens the door. 'Come on then, let's get it over with.'

He smiles. She wouldn't be saying that if she knew what

66

he's got for her. But then, if he does what he's told, she won't be saying anything again. Ever.

Temple Fields hadn't changed much in the past couple of years, Carol thought as they walked back to her car. The same litter tumbling along the gutters, the same mixture of self-conscious seekers after what passed for pleasure rubbing awkward shoulders with those who had already found it and lost all inhibitions along the way. Her police officer's mind clocked them as she passed: the frail-looking rent boys, the bored hookers, the shifty sellers of chemical promises, and the easy marks who moved among them, obvious in their fake confidence. But the woman behind the badge shivered at the traffic in human flesh and folly. She didn't want to think of the acts that would take place in this square mile before morning. Carol felt as though she'd lost a layer of skin somewhere, and wondered how long it would take to grow back.

'Same old same old,' she said wearily. 'Look at them – they think they've made a deal with the world that will keep them safe. They've no bloody idea how fragile they are.'

'They can't afford to think about it,' Tony said, his eyes taking in the parade on streets splashed with garish neon from the bars.

They walked on in silence. 'I'll give you a lift,' Carol said as they neared her car.

'No, you're all right. I feel like walking.'

Carol raised her eyebrows. 'Thinking time?'

Tony nodded. 'I saw someone today and I need to figure out how to keep the promise I made him.'

'Your latest crusade?' Carol smiled.

Tony looked surprised. 'Is that how you see what I do?'

'I think it's how you see what you do. A one-man crusade to mend the damage.'

He shrugged. 'I wish it was that easy. So, you'll come round tomorrow night to see the house?'

'I will. Then maybe I can decide if I want to be the mad woman in the cellar. Shall I bring pizza?'

He considered. 'Chinese,' he said finally.

'OK.' She reached for the driver's door. 'Tony – thanks for tonight. And for being here in Bradfield.'

He looked surprised. *Why would I be anywhere else? Everything I need is here.* Instead of speaking his thoughts aloud, he patted her awkwardly on the shoulder. 'See you tomorrow.'

She climbed into her car and drove off, conscious of him in her mirrors, standing on the pavement, watching her out of sight. She knew it was guilt that had brought him there. Once, that would have made her uncomfortable and angry. But she was a different woman now and that woman had learned to be grateful for good things, however complicated the package they arrived in.

Sam Evans edged the office door open cautiously. No lights inside. He slipped through the narrow gap and closed the door behind him, turning the lock. Then he flicked the light switches on. The fluorescent strips flickered then settled their hard glare over the Major Incident Team's squadroom. Sam surveyed the array of desks and made straight for Paula McIntyre's.

He sat in her chair and noted the position of the piled paper on the desktop. The case she was working on would come to him next. Carefully, he riffled through each stack, trying to figure out the reason for the alignment she'd chosen. He flicked open the notepad and read down the list of points Paula had made. Some of them were pretty perspicacious, he thought, storing them away in his mind for when he came to review that case.

He inched open Paula's desk drawers one by one, stirring the contents with a pencil, leaving no prints to indicate he'd been there. It was always useful to see what people kept out of sight but close at hand. Tucked right at the bottom of the drawer, he found a photograph of Don Merrick with his arm round a woman in what looked like a pub or a club. On closer inspection, he realized with a jolt of surprise that the woman was Carol Jordan. Her hair was longer, her face fuller, but it was undoubtedly her. They were both toasting the photographer with what looked like glasses of champagne. Very interesting, he thought. And almost certainly useful.

He closed Paula's drawer and moved on to Kevin Matthews' desk, where he repeated the same process. People said you should know your enemies. But Sam Evans also believed in making damn sure he knew the people who were supposed to be on the same side. He was, as John Brandon had spotted, ambitious. But he didn't just want to excel; he wanted to make sure nobody outshone him. Ever.

Knowledge was power. And Evans knew that nobody ever handed out power as a gift. You had to grab it whenever and wherever you could. If that meant stealing it from someone else, so be it. If they were too weak to hold on to it, they didn't deserve it.

He did.

He checks the image in front of him against the one planted there by the Voice and the videos. Sandie's spreadeagled on the bed, her wrists handcuffed to the cheap pine frame. Her feet are tied to the legs. He had to use rope for them because the ankle cuffs wouldn't stretch that far. It's not right, but it's the best he can do. He's grateful to the Voice again for reminding him to take rope as well as the cuffs in case the bed wasn't right.

He wishes the room was nicer, but there's nothing he can do about that. At least the lights are dim. It's easy to ignore the needle tracks on her arms and the fact that she's too skinny. She could almost be the dream girl from one of the videos, the trimmed triangle of hair hiding the secrets he's about to possess.

He turns away from her and snaps the latex gloves over his hands. 'Come on,' she says. 'What are you waiting for? I haven't got all night.'

Only he knows how true that is. He reaches into his back-pack and takes out the padded leather gag. He turns back to face her and now she's starting to look worried. He moves towards her and she starts to shout. 'Wait a fucking minute! You never said nothing about that . . .' But her words are lost as he rams the gag home, jerking her head forward to fasten it behind. Her eyes are bulging now as she struggles to scream. But all that can be heard is the faintest of grunts.

He remembers to wipe the handcuffs clear of any finger-prints, then he grabs the video camera and sets it up on its little tripod, checking that he can see the whole bed. Next,

70

the laptop and the webcam. Sandie pushes against her restraints, but there's no point.

He takes out a bundle wrapped in a thick wad of kitchen towel. He steps into shot and slowly unwraps it. When Sandie sees what he's holding, the veins in her neck stand out. The air fills with the smell of piss. He smiles sweetly. He's hard now, harder than the videos ever got him. But he mustn't lose control. He needs to make the Voice proud of him, and that means no evidence.

He takes a deep breath, trying to steady his pounding heart. He's sweating, he can feel it running down his neck and soaking his T-shirt. He grips his weapon tightly. The razor blades glint sharp and savage in the lamplight. 'I hope you're ready for me, Sandie,' he says softly, just like the Voice told him to.

Then he begins.

Carol stared through the two-way mirror at the man in the interview room. Ronald Edmund Alexander looked nothing like the popular image of a paedophile. He wasn't shifty or sweaty. He wasn't dirty or sleazy. He looked exactly like a middle manager who lived in the suburbs with a wife and two children. There was no dirty raincoat, just an off-the-peg suit, an unassuming charcoal grey. Pale blue shirt, burgundy tie with a thin grey stripe. Neat haircut, no vain attempt to hide the way he was thinning on top. He'd been complaining bitterly when the two uniformed officers had brought him in. They had no right, he insisted, no right at all to come marching into his office at Bradfield Cross as if he was some common criminal. He'd co-operated, hadn't he? All they had to do was pick up a phone and he'd have been straight over. There was no need, no need at all to embarrass him at his place of work.

Carol had watched from across the custody suite, trying to work out if she disliked him more because of what she knew he held on his computer or because he exemplified every petty bureaucrat who had ever driven her to thoughts of violence. She'd wanted to get straight into him, but had been frustrated by the tardiness of his solicitor.

So they'd stuck him in a cell while they waited for his brief to arrive. He'd been remarkably calm, she thought, wondering what Tony would have made of Alexander's demeanour. He'd taken a look round then calmly sat on the bunk, legs apart, arms folded across his chest, gazing into the middle distance. Zen and the art of façade maintenance, she thought wryly.

Finally, the door to the observation room opened. Paula stuck her head round the door. 'Showtime, chief. His brief's here.'

'Who is it?' Carol asked, dragging her eyes away from Alexander.

'Bronwen Scott.'

Carol remembered the defence lawyer from her previous spell in Bradfield. Unlike most legal aid lawyers, Scott seemed to have the wherewithal to dress in Dolce & Gabbana, with matching shoes and handbags from Prada. Her perfectly groomed shoulder-length black hair and flawlessly painted nails always made Carol feel like she'd been dragged straight out of bed into their interviews. It would have been almost bearable if the lawyer hadn't been as sharp and combative as she was expensively immaculate. The general view was that if you could afford

Bronwen Scott, you'd probably done it. 'Oh good,' Carol said, heading for the door.

She came face to face with Scott as she emerged into the corridor. 'Inspector Jordan. What a surprise. I thought you'd left us for pastures more glamorous,' Scott said, her voice cool and amused.

'It's Chief Inspector, actually. And you should know better than anyone that there's nothing glamorous about what we deal in. Shall we go?'

Scott shook her head. 'I don't know where you've been hiding, Chief Inspector, but up here in Bradfield we still allow lawyers to talk to their clients in private. And before I do that, I'd like some disclosure.'

Nothing unexpected there, Carol thought. 'When your client was arrested, his computer equipment was confiscated. It has subsequently been analysed. He will be interviewed fully about that at a later date, but there is one image on his machine that links directly to a major inquiry which I am leading. It is that single image I want to talk to him about.'

'That image being . . .?'

'I'll be happy to discuss that in the interview. And to show you and your client a copy.'

Scott shook her head. 'You really have forgotten your manners, haven't you, Chief Inspector? Before I can have a meaningful conversation with my client, I need to know what we're talking about here.'

There was a long silence. Carol could feel Paula's eyes on her back, measuring her. There really wasn't anything to be gained by holding back at this point. It wasn't as if Ron Alexander was a serious suspect in the disappearance of Tim Golding. If she refused to give Scott anything, then she'd end up with a 'no comment' interview, nothing surer. If she tried waiting until the interview to spring the photo on him, Scott would simply demand time out to talk to her client. Carol considered. She wanted co-operation. She didn't care what that might or might not do to any wider case against Ron Alexander. 'We might as well speed things up,' she said. 'Your client's computer held an image of Tim Golding. The eight-year-old –'

'Yes, I know who Tim Golding is,' Scott said impatiently. 'But since you people disseminated images of the child all over the country, it's hardly a big deal that my client has a photo of the boy on his computer.'

'It's a big deal when the picture in question shows a terrified, naked child.' Carol turned on her heel and walked off. 'Let me know when you're ready to talk,' she said over her shoulder as she rounded a corner, Paula hard on her heels. 'I see Bronwen Scott hasn't mellowed with age,' she commented.

'It's a pain you had to give away so much,' Paula said, falling into step beside her boss.

'You know the rules, Paula. They ask for disclosure, we have to give it.'

'Couldn't you have held back on the ID, chief? Then hit him with it in the interview?'

Carol stopped and gave Paula a speculative look. 'You think I was weak back there, don't you?'

Paula looked horrified. 'I never . . .'

'Giving in isn't always a sign of weakness, Paula. There was no point in holding out. I know how Scott works. Alexander would just have gone "no comment" from the off. This way, she might just see it as a bargaining chip.' Carol walked off, feeling the tension in her shoulders. Maybe they didn't trust her quite as much as she'd thought.

He sleeps late. It's nearly noon when he wakes, and even then he has to force his eyes open. He feels like somebody spiked his brain with Valium. His head's muzzy, it takes him a moment to realize where he is. At home, in his own bed, curled into himself like a baby. But it's a different person inside his body this morning.

He's not the fuck-up that everybody laughs at any more. He did it. He did exactly what he was supposed to. Just like the Voice told him to. And he's got his reward. He's got the money, even though he explained that wasn't why he'd done it. He'd done it because he understood. It's not the money that makes him feel like he finally made it. It's hearing the Voice say good things about him. It's knowing that he's done something hardly anybody else could do. Something special.

Thank God he managed to hide the way he really felt when he reached the moment itself. He'd been excited, aroused, on the point of coming inside his pants like a teenager. But when it came to it, when he had to stick that thing inside her again and again, he wilted. It wasn't sexy. It was bloody and terrible and frightening. He knows it was the right thing to do, but at the very end, it wasn't exciting at all. Just messy and sad.

But the Voice didn't see that. The Voice just saw that he'd done what he was supposed to do, and he'd got it right.

As he wakes up properly, he feels a buzz in his veins. It's pride, but it's fear too. They're going to be looking for him. The Voice promised he'd be all right. But maybe the Voice has got it wrong.

Maybe he wasn't as clever as he thought.

* * *

Tom Storey stared out of the window, watching the leaves detaching from the trees and swirling in the brisk breeze that had sprung up towards noon. He sat motionless, his bandaged stump gripped in his other hand. Tony watched him for a good ten minutes, but Storey never budged.

Eventually, he walked across the day room and pulled up a chair next to Storey. He noted the purple bruise along his cheekbone. According to the orderly who had shown Tony in, one of the other patients had punched Storey during a group therapy session. 'Even these mad bastards draw the line at child killers,' the man had said casually.

'We've all got two personalities, you know,' Tony said conversationally. 'One in each hemisphere of the brain. One's the boss, it shouts down the weaker one. But you sever the diplomatic links, and there's no telling what the subservient one will do once it gets the taste for power.'

Storey still didn't move. 'I can still feel it,' he said. 'It's like a malevolent ghost. It won't leave me alone. Supposing you find out I've got a brain tumour. And supposing that doesn't kill me. There's still going to be a war going on in my head, isn't there?'

'I won't lie to you, Tom,' Tony said. 'There's no quick fix here. See, you've got the dominant left side of the brain. That's in charge of the three R's – reading, writing and arithmetic. And you've got the right side. It's illiterate, but it comprehends form, solid geometry, music. I suspect it gets frustrated because it can't express itself readily in the ways that humans generally communicate. That's why it goes off the rails

76

when the left side loosens its grip. But that's not the end of the story.'

'Just the end of Tom Storey.' His voice was bitter.

'Not necessarily. The brain's an amazing structure. When it gets damaged, it retrains other areas to take over the jobs that used to be done by the bit that's redundant. And there are things we can do to retrain the rebellious part of your brain. I can help you, Tom.'

Storey took a breath so deep it raised his shoulders. 'Can't bring my kids back, though. Can you?'

Tony looked out of the window at the flurry of golden and scarlet leaves. 'No, I can't. But what I can do is help you live with that absence.'

Tears spilled out of Storey's eyes and trickled unheeded down his cheeks. 'Why would you want to do that?'

Because it's the only thing I'm good at, Tony thought. What he said was: 'Because you deserve it, Tom. Because you deserve it.'

Carol walked into the interview room with an assumption of confidence she didn't really feel. It had been many months since she'd interviewed anyone, witness or suspect, and she was afraid of her emotions bleeding into the professional sphere. It didn't help that she was conscious of Paula at her side, weighing her up. At least Ron Alexander's composure seemed to have slipped a little. He was refusing to meet her eyes, fiddling continuously with his wedding ring.

'Right,' Carol said, settling into her chair. 'I'm Detective Chief Inspector Jordan and this is Detective Constable McIntyre. As your solicitor will have explained, Mr Alexander, we're looking for your help in respect of another inquiry that's not related to the reasons you were originally arrested. We would appreciate your co-operation.'

'Why should I talk to you?' Alexander blurted out. 'You'll only twist anything I say to make a case against me.'

Bronwen Scott put a hand on his arm. 'You don't have to say anything, Ron.' She looked directly at Carol. 'My client is concerned that any co-operation he offers you will be reflected in any subsequent proceedings.'

Carol shook her head. 'You know it's not up to us, Ms Scott. It's the CPS who make the deals. But I'm perfectly willing to make representations to them at the appropriate time.'

'That's not good enough.'

Carol shrugged. 'It's the best I can do. Your client might like to consider the converse, however. If he fails to help us in such a sensitive case, nobody's going to cut him any slack anywhere down the line.'

'Is that a threat, Chief Inspector?'

'Just a statement of fact, Ms Scott. You know as well as I how emotions run high in the case of a missing child. Sex offenders have a hard enough time in prison without adding to their problems. It's up to you, Mr Alexander.' Carol eyed Alexander, who was shifting uncomfortably in his chair. She opened the folder in front of her and took out the photograph Jan Shields had supplied. She placed it in front of him. 'We found this on your computer. Do you recognize this child, Mr Alexander?'

He glanced at the image then looked away,

desperately scanning the wall as if it would give him the answer. 'Yes,' he said, his voice barely above a whisper.

'Can you tell me who it is?'

'His name's Tim Golding.' He picked up Scott's pen, gripping it in both hands as if trying to snap it in two. 'His picture was in the papers. And on the TV.'

'When did you acquire this photograph?' Carol leaned forward slightly, forcing warmth and intimacy into her voice.

He flashed a look at Scott, who nodded. 'I don't know exactly. A few weeks ago, I think. It came in an email attachment. I was shocked when I opened it.'

'Shocked because you recognized Tim Golding?'

He nodded. 'Yes. And because of . . . because of how he looked.'

'What? You're not used to receiving pictures of naked, frightened children?'

'Don't answer that, Ron,' Scott said quickly. 'Chief Inspector, if we're going to make any progress here, I must insist you stop asking questions whose answers might tend to incriminate my client.'

Yeah, right. Carol took a deep breath. She slid another photograph from her folder. 'Do you recognize this boy?'

Alexander frowned. 'Isn't he the one who went missing last year? Guy something or other?'

'Guy Lefevre,' Carol said. 'Have you ever been sent photographs of Guy Lefevre?'

'No.' Alexander's eyes flicked from side to side. Carol couldn't decide whether he was panicking or lying. But with Bronwen Scott patrolling her every question, there was nothing to be gained by pressing the point.

'What did you do when you recognized Tim Golding?' she asked.

'I erased the picture right away,' he said. 'I didn't want it on my machine.'

Carol stripped her voice of challenge and tried to sound sympathetic. 'You didn't think about contacting the police? You could have printed it out and sent it to us anonymously. You've got children of your own, haven't you, Ron? How do you think you'd feel if one of them went missing? Wouldn't you want to believe that anyone who had information that might help the inquiry would pass it on to the police?'

A sheen of sweat appeared on his forehead. 'I suppose,' he said.

'It's not too late to put that right,' Carol said. 'Who sent you the photograph, Ron?'

He breathed out noisily. 'I don't know. People don't use their real names on email, you know?'

Carol knew. They used nicknames and mixtures of letters and numbers even when they had nothing to hide. Her own personal email address was a combination of her surname and the last four digits of a previous phone number because, when she'd signed up, 'caroljordan' had already been taken. 'OK. You didn't know the identity of the sender. So what was his email address?'

He spread his hands. 'I don't know. I didn't pay attention. I just wiped the whole thing. The email and the attachment.'

'Presumably it was someone who had sent you things before?'

'I'd advise you not to answer that, Ron.' Scott laid a hand on his arm again.

Carol glared at the lawyer. 'You seem to be losing sight of what's at stake here, Ms Scott. A child is missing. We both know the chances are he's dead. I'm trying to find out what happened to him, and that's all I care about.'

'Very commendable, Chief Inspector. But my concern is my client's best interests. And I will not sit quietly by while you draw him into potentially incriminating statements.'

Carol gathered herself together and turned her attention back to Alexander. 'Ron, can you remember anything that might lead us to the person who sent you this picture?'

He shook his head. 'Honestly, if I knew anything useful, I'd tell you. I want to help, I really do.'

'OK. Let's try a different tack. Why do you think he sent it to you? Why would he have thought this was the kind of thing you might like to see?'

'I don't think . . .' Scott began.

'It's all right,' Alexander said. 'I don't know the answer to that either. Everybody gets unsolicited email. Spam blockers don't get rid of it all.' He sat back in his seat, clearly more relaxed now he'd figured out how to play the game.

Carol felt irritation rising. 'Fine. If that's how you want to play it, Mr Alexander, that's the way we'll go.' She pushed her chair back. 'This interview is over. But I should tell you that we're going to be trawling every byte on your hard disk. We're going to follow your footsteps round the web. You may think you've cleaned up your computer, but our technicians are going to demonstrate just how misguided you are. You've had your chance, Mr Alexander. And you just blew it.'

Carol marched out of the interview room and headed back to her office, not even bothering to check if Paula was following her. 'Stacey? My office, now,' she said as she crossed the squadroom. Paula and Stacey arrived together. 'What did we get from the techies on Ron Alexander's computer?' Carol asked Stacey, waving a hand to indicate they should sit down.

'Not as much as they'd hoped for,' Stacey said. 'People are so dim about this stuff. Alexander thought he'd erased everything from his hard disk. He probably panicked when he saw the earlier newspaper reports about Operation Ore. But like most people, he thought if he just deleted them then emptied the Recycle Bin, they were gone for good. And like most people, he never bothered to reformat or even defrag –'

'Defrag?' Paula asked faintly.

Stacey rolled her eyes. 'It's when you –'

'Never mind,' Carol said. 'So there was still stuff lurking there?'

'Well, yes, of course there was. File fragments, some complete files. Like the photo of Tim Golding.'

'And can we find out where that came from?'

Stacey shook her head. 'Not a trace. It's an orphan.'

Paula opened her mouth but before she could speak, Carol said hastily, 'Never mind, Paula, we get the idea. That's a blow, Stacey.' She rubbed the bridge of her nose between her fingers. The lead that had seemed so promising the day before was turning into another dead end. 'What about his email service provider? Any chance they could help?'

Stacey shrugged. 'Depends when he got the email. They're not really techies, ISPs, just bean counters,' she said disparagingly. 'They're only interested in billing, not in keeping records of traffic. Most only keep detailed records for a week. Some for a month. If he got that attachment more than a month ago, we've got no chance. And we'd need a court order before they'd hand over the information anyway.'

'So we're screwed.' Carol's flat statement hung in the air.

Stacey pushed her hair behind her ear. Her self-satisfied smile and her dark almond-shaped eyes made her resemble a cat. 'Not necessarily. Images like this, there's more to them than meets the eye. Literally. You sometimes get other information encoded in them.'

Carol perked up. 'Like the sender's details?'

Stacey's sigh fell just short of obvious exasperation. 'Nothing that straightforward. You might get the serial number of the camera that took the picture. Or the registration number of the software the photographer used to process the image electronically. Then it's a matter of contacting the manufacturer or the software licence holder and seeing what information they can provide.'

'That's scary,' Paula said.

'It's bloody good news,' Carol corrected her. 'So what are we waiting for?'

Stacey stood up. 'It's going to take time,' she warned.

'Doesn't everything?' Carol leaned back in her

chair. 'Anything you need, Stacey, just let me know. Paula, find out who Ron Alexander's ISP is and see what they can tell us. It's time we brought Tim Golding home.'

The doorbell came as a welcome relief. Tony pushed aside the philosophical text on the mind/body problem that had been stretching his brain and hurried down the hall. He opened the door to find Carol leaning against the porch, a bulging plastic carrier in one hand. 'You ordered a takeaway?' she said.

'You took your time. It's at least twenty-two hours since I placed my order,' he said, stepping back and following her down the hall. 'The kitchen's straight ahead.'

Carol looked around, taking in the pine units and the tiled breakfast bar. 'Very eighties,' she said.

'Is it? You think that's part of the reason I got it so cheap?'

She smiled. 'Could be. It looks in good nick, though.'

'All the drawers work, which is a definite improvement on anywhere I've ever lived before. Now, do you want to eat first or tour the cellar?'

'What I'd really like is a glass of wine. It's been a frustrating day.'

'OK. Wine we can do.' He reached for an opened bottle of Australian Shiraz Cabernet and poured them each a glass. 'Here's to . . . I don't know, what should we drink to?'

'An end to frustrations? For both of us?'

Tony raised his glass and chinked it against hers.

'That's as good as anything. An end to frustrations.' He watched her drink, noting the dark shadows under her eyes and the wariness in her body language. She was, he thought, a long way from herself. 'So, would you like to see the cellar – sorry, basement flat?'

Carol smiled. 'Why not?'

She followed him back into the hall. He opened a door that looked as if it should be the cupboard under the stairs. Instead, it gave on to a narrow, steep flight of steps illuminated by a bare lightbulb. Tony led the way into a surprisingly high-ceilinged space. 'This would be the living room,' he said, ushering her into a large room that had two shallow but wide windows set high in the walls. 'It gets a fair bit of natural light. And we could put glass panels in the outside door and build a little porch at the bottom of the steps for security,' he added eagerly. 'I already suggested that to the builder. I know it's hard to imagine now, with the walls still being bare brick, but all this will be plaster-boarded. Wood floors. It'll look really nice.'

It was a good size. Plenty of room for all she would need, Carol thought. The bedroom was almost as big as the living room, with a surprisingly large bay window. Carol looked around, a smile tugging at the corners of her mouth. 'It's not bad, you know. I can imagine waking up here.'

Tony looked at the floor, suddenly embarrassed. 'Good,' he said. 'Think about it.'

On the way back upstairs, he showed her the recently installed toilet and shower room. White tiled walls gleamed bright under their ceiling spotlights. *Clean, fresh, untainted. New,* she thought with a surge of excitement. *A place without ghosts.* 'I don't need to think about it,' Carol said. 'When's it going to be ready?'

Tony grinned like a small boy. 'The builder reckons three weeks. Can you stand it at Michael's till then?'

Carol leaned against his breakfast bar. 'I can stand anything if I know it's going to end. You think you can stand having me as your downstairs neighbour?'

'Only if you promise always to have milk.' He pulled a wry face. 'I'm very good at running out of it.'

Carol smiled. 'I'll stock up on UHT.'

Waiting is never easy. Especially when he knows exactly what he's waiting for. By the time he got out on the street today, he was expecting cops everywhere, police tape cordoning off the ginnel where Sandie worked. He was expecting huddles of people on street corners, muttering about murder and mutilation. He was expecting uniformed officers with clipboards asking people where they were and what they were doing last night.

He remembers what it was like last time. The whole of Temple Fields felt like it had overdosed on whiz. Everybody talking nineteen to the dozen like speed freaks, even the miserable gits who never normally had the time of day for him or anybody else. Until the bizzies walked in. Then silence fell like somebody dropped a blanket over everybody's head.

That's what he expected this time. But when he went into Stan's Café and ordered his usual bacon butty and mug of tea, it was just like any other day. A few of the working girls clustered round greasy tables, taking the weight off their feet for half an hour. A couple of kids from the rent rack cuddling cups of coffee. Various eyes clocking him, wondering if he was carrying any gear. Looking away in disappointment when he gave them a slight shake of the head. He'd get hassle off Big Jimmy when he showed up to collect today's stock. He'd bollock him for being late. He'd hoped the excitement on the street would give him an excuse, but there isn't any.

So he finished his breakfast and moseyed on round to Big Jimmy's flat for some stuff to sell. Luckily, the big man wasn't in and he only had to deal with that fuckwit scaghead Drum who's too far out of the world to care what anybody else is doing. Within the half-hour he was back on the pitch, doing the business, hoping nobody wondered where he'd been all morning. Hell, most of them had probably still been out cold themselves.

But now it's evening, and still nothing's stirring on the streets. It makes him uneasy. Part of him begins to wonder if he dreamed the whole thing. He almost wants to walk round to Sandie's pitch to see if she's standing on her usual corner, acting as if nothing out of the ordinary had happened.

He wishes the Voice was here right now to tell him what's going on. But since he delivered, he's heard nothing. He begins to wonder if he's been abandoned, if all the promises were a dream too.

It wouldn't be the first time.

Tony raised his glass and reached across the debris of the Chinese. 'Here's to one of our rare non-Catholic meals.' They chinked glasses.

'Non-Catholic meals?' Carol frowned.

'Mostly, when we eat together, it's in the middle of a case.' He picked up a piece of pancake. 'Here is my body which I sacrificed for you.' He ate the pancake, then raised his glass again in mock-ceremony. 'Here is my blood which I shed for you.'

Carol nodded, getting it. 'Only, in our case, the confession comes after the communion.'

'Only if we're right.'

She pulled a rueful face. 'Right, and lucky.' She took his glass from him and sipped from the opposite side. She felt a crackle of electricity in the curiously intense moment. Before she could hand back the glass, the intimacy was shattered by the insistent ring of her mobile. 'Damn,' she said, scrabbling for her bag.

'Speaking of lucky . . .' Tony muttered.

'DCI Jordan,' Carol said.

Don Merrick's familiar voice sounded in her ear. 'We've got a body. I think you'll want to see this one.'

Carol stifled a sigh. 'Fine. You'll have to send a car for me, I've had a couple of glasses of wine.' Tony stood up and started shovelling the tinfoil containers into their plastic bag.

'No problem, ma'am. You at your flat?'

'Actually, no, Don. I'm at Dr Hill's house.' She caught Tony's glance and raised her eyes heavenwards as she gave Merrick the address. She was aware of muffled conversation at the other end of the phone. Then Merrick came back on.

'I've asked a car to pick you up there.'

'I'll see you shortly, Don,' Carol said, ending the call. She drained her glass of wine and said, 'Seems we've got a body.' She got to her feet. 'I didn't exactly mean the evening to end like this.'

Tony picked up the dirty plates. 'Well, it's probably best to stick to what we know we're good at.'

*   *   *

Temple Fields' tawdry glitter was blurred by the slant of autumn rain. The car tyres hissed on the block paving of the pedestrianized zone at the heart of the area. The driver turned into a narrow side street. Redbrick and seedy, it harboured shop fronts with little allure and small entrepreneurial businesses with bedsits on the floors above. Halfway down, access was blocked by a pair of parked police cars. Vague figures hurried beyond the cars, heads down against the weather. As the car pulled up, Carol lowered her head, took a deep breath and climbed out.

Approaching the squad cars, Carol saw that the entrance to a smaller ginnel was closed off by crime-scene tape. Her stomach lurched in anticipation of what she was about to be confronted with. Please God, let it not be sexual. She ducked under the tape, giving her name and rank to the officer logging access to the scene, and spotted Paula standing at a grubby door leading to a stairwell. Seeing Carol, she broke off her conversation with a uniformed officer and turned to her.

'It's upstairs, chief. Not a pretty sight.'

'Thanks, Paula.' Carol paused on the threshold, snapping a pair of latex gloves over her hands. 'Who found the body?'

'One of the street girls. Dee. She and the dead girl used to share the room. Somewhere to take punters.'

'Was Dee with a punter, then?'

Paula gave a grim little smile. 'According to Dee, as soon as he realized there was something wrong, he was out of there like a rat off a sinking ship.'

'Where's Dee now?'

'On her way back to the nick to make a statement. With Sam.'

Carol nodded in satisfaction. 'Thanks, Paula.' She edged past a fingerprint technician lifting prints from the narrow banister and headed up. At the top of the steep, uncarpeted stairs, an open door cast an oblong of pale light on to the landing. The air was thick with the coppery smell of blood and the darker, deeper stink of human excrement. Though she'd been steeling herself against it, Carol felt herself slide into flashback and almost lost her footing. But the sight of the SOCOs coolly going about their business anchored her back in the present, banishing the kaleidoscope of images that threatened to overwhelm her. *Further up and further in.*

As she reached the doorway, Carol was conscious of Merrick and Kevin turning to look at her. At first, she concentrated on the external details, working up gradually to deal with what lay at the heart of the room. It was a spartan space, shoddy and cheaply decorated with old stained woodchip emulsioned in what had once been magnolia. A pine bedstead, a couple of armchairs that looked like they were rescued from the tip, a sink, a card table and not much else. Nothing to distract her from the body on the bed.

The woman was tied down, her legs and arms spread in a hideous parody of ecstasy. Her blue eyes stared blankly at the ceiling. It wasn't hard to read panic and pain there. Her short bleached blonde hair was plastered to her head; the sweat of fear had soaked it and time had dried it into a stiff helmet. She was still dressed, her skirt a blood-soaked ruck around her hips. A sea of gore engulfed her lower body and soaked the thin, sagging mattress. Carol cleared her throat and moved closer. 'That's a hell of a lot of blood,' she said.

'According to the police surgeon, she pretty much bled out,' Merrick said. 'He reckons it took her a while to die.'

Carol struggled with the emotions tormenting her and tried to remember how to do her job. 'He's been and gone already?'

'Yeah, so happened he was at a dinner at the Queensbury. We'd hardly got here ourselves.'

'So, what have we got?' she asked.

Merrick consulted his notebook. 'Sandie Foster, twenty-five, prostitute, convictions for soliciting and possession. But before we get into that . . . ma'am, this is the identical MO to a series of four murders that happened two years ago, not long after you left us.'

'Were all the victims clothed, like this?'

'Like I said, it's identical.'

'Well, maybe this time we can solve them.'

Merrick and Kevin exchanged a glance. Kevin looked faintly apologetic. 'That's the thing, guv. We already did.'

'What?' Carol said.

Merrick shoved his gloved hands into his pockets. 'Kevin and I worked the case. Derek Tyler – he pleaded guilty. He's in a secure hospital.'

'Could we have got the wrong man?'

Merrick shook his head, his lower lip jutting in stubborn denial. 'No room for doubt. The forensics nailed him. DNA, fingerprints, the lot. Derek Tyler. He pleaded guilty. He even made a confession of sorts, claiming the voices in his head told him to do it. And as soon as Tyler was arrested, the killings stopped. Even more proof, as if we needed it. They locked him up in Bradfield Moor and he refused to say another word about the murders.'

'Can we check if Tyler has been released?' Carol asked.

'I already have. I just came off the phone. Tyler is tucked up in bed, sleeping far better than he has any right to, so it's not him.'

'Perhaps we missed something last time.'

'The forensics nailed him,' Merrick insisted.

'Maybe we should talk to Dr Hill,' Kevin said. 'Making sense of things is his line, isn't it?'

'Good idea, Kevin,' Carol said. Tony was always complaining he was never called in early enough on complex murder inquiries. She stepped outside the room and dialled Brandon's mobile. When he answered, she briefly outlined the circumstances. 'On the face of it, it looks impossible,' she said. 'I'd like to bring Dr Hill in for a consultation.'

'Isn't it a little early for that?' Brandon asked.

'Normally I'd agree with you, sir, but if there's any possibility we're looking at a copycat, I think he could give us a quick answer. Like he did the first time we all worked together.' Carol held her breath while Brandon considered.

'All right, go ahead. We'll talk more fully in the morning.'

As the call ended, Carol stepped to one side to allow the mortuary staff access to the crime scene. 'Does Dr Vernon know about this?' she asked.

The one bringing up the rear nodded. 'Yeah, he

wants to cut and shut early tomorrow, he's got some conference or other to go to. He said to tell you he'll be ready to roll at seven.'

Merrick and Kevin joined her on the landing, to allow the technicians room to manoeuvre the dead woman into the body bag. 'Kevin, Sam's interviewing the woman who found the body. I want you to come back to the station with me and sit in with him. You worked the case before, there might be something you pick up on that Sam wouldn't know about. Don, you and Paula start organizing door-to-door inquiries. We need to talk to all the street girls and rent boys we can get our hands on, as well as bar staff, punters and the like. Find out where Sandie Foster worked. Somebody must have seen her with her killer.' She stripped off her gloves and shoved her hands in her pockets, unconsciously hunching her shoulders. 'And let's all keep an open mind for now.'

Kevin found Sam Evans slouched against the wall outside one of the interview rooms. 'How's it going?' he asked.

'Am I glad to see you,' Evans groaned. 'That woman in there most definitely does not like people of colour. How come we say one word out of place and we get hit with a complaint of racism, but she gets to call me a jungle bunny?'

Kevin winced. 'You want me to take a crack at her?'

'Be my guest.' Evans waved a hand at the door. 'I can't get a single word out of her. I'm going for a smoke.'

He handed Kevin a folder and walked off. Kevin

opened it and saw a single sheet of paper that told him nothing more than name, age and address. 'You weren't joking, were you, Sam?' he said softly.

Kevin looked through the spyhole in the door to see a bleached-blonde woman in a short, tight, black dress. The notes said she was twenty-nine but, from this distance, she looked closer to nineteen. She was pulling her skimpy jacket close to her as if the room was chill. She was smoking, and judging by the thickness of the air, it wasn't her first cigarette. So much for Brandon's non-smoking policy. Kevin remembered the first day he'd tried to enforce it. The suspect he'd been interviewing had threatened him with a complaint under the human rights legislation for cruel and unusual punishment. He wasn't going to be telling Dee Smart to put her fag out. She was the nearest they had to a useful witness so far, and this case was far too important to take chances with.

He walked in and treated her to his best sympathetic smile. 'Thank fuck,' she said. 'A human being.'

'You have a problem with my colleague?' Kevin said, a sympathetic smile on his face.

'He gives me the creeps,' she muttered. 'He's got that Ali G chip on his shoulder. "Is it because I is black?" No, mate, it's because you is an arsehole. Somebody should tell him even whores are higher up the food chain than the shit on his shoe. Where does he get off, looking down his nose at me?'

'He's a bit lacking in the social skills department.'

'You can say that again.' She blew out a stream of smoke and scowled. 'So are you going to treat me any better?'

Twenty minutes later, the two of them were almost

cosy. The mugs of tea he'd brought as an ice-breaker were empty, and they'd got through the hardest part, the actual discovery of the body. 'Just how long had this arrangement been going on?' Kevin asked conversationally.

Dee lifted one shoulder in a half-shrug. 'About three months, I suppose. Sandie used to share the room with another girl, Mo, but she moved back to Leeds so Sandie asked me to come in with her.'

'How did it work in practice?'

Dee flipped open her cigarette packet and looked in disgust at the three remaining cigarettes. 'You're going to need to find a fag machine if we're going to be at this much longer.'

'Don't worry about that. Tell me about the arrangement.' Kevin gave her his best sympathetic smile.

Dee scowled. It brought the fine lines on her skin into sharp relief, making her look her age. 'Sandie has the early shift. Most nights she likes to knock off about ten. She's got a kid. A little lad, Sean. Her mum looks after him. Sandie likes to get home in time to get a decent kip before she gets him up in the morning for school. Any time after half past ten, the room was mine.'

Kevin tried not to think how Sean would be feeling when he woke up tomorrow morning to discover his mother had been murdered. Instead, he concentrated on what Dee was saying. 'So how come you didn't find her there last night?' he asked.

'I wasn't working last night.' She clocked the look of surprise on his face. 'If you must know, I had the shits. I must have eaten something dodgy. There was no way I could turn tricks, the state I was in.'

It made sense. Even whores could throw a sickie, Kevin thought. 'So as far as you knew, everything was normal? When you went up with your punter you expected the room to be empty?'

Dee closed her eyes and shuddered at the memory. 'Yeah.'

'Had you seen Sandie at all earlier in the evening?'

Dee shook her head. 'I wouldn't have unless I was working, and I wasn't. I had a couple of drinks in the Nag's Head before I got started, but I never saw Sandie.'

'Where did she normally work?'

'Down the end of Campion Boulevard. Just past the mini-roundabout.'

Kevin pictured it in his mind's eye. Only fifty yards down the side street and Sandie would have been at the entrance to the alley where the shared room was. 'What about regulars?' he asked.

Dee suddenly lost her composure. Her eyes welled up with tears and her voice emerged as a strangled wail. 'I don't know. Look, we shared the room and the rent, we didn't live in each other's pockets, I don't know what she did or who she did it with.'

Kevin reached across the table and took her hand. Astonishment overcame her emotional outburst and her mouth fell open. 'I'm sorry. We just need to explore every possibility if we're going to have any chance of catching him.'

Dee snorted derisively, pulling away from him. 'Listen to you. Anybody would think it was a respectable mother of three who'd been killed, not some throwaway tart.'

Kevin shook his head sorrowfully. 'I don't know

who you've been listening to, Dee, but we don't treat anybody as a throwaway victim here. My guvnor wouldn't stand for it.'

Dee looked momentarily uncertain. 'You mean that?'

'I mean it. Nobody on this investigation is giving any less than a hundred per cent. Now, I want you to come upstairs with me and look at some photographs. Will you do that for me, Dee?'

'All right,' she said. It was hard to say who was the more surprised.

After midnight, the fluorescent lights in Carol's office seemed indecently bright, turning skin tones grey. Carol was reading the scant computer files on Derek Tyler's murders when the door opened and Tony walked in. 'It's rubbish, you know,' he said without preamble.

Carol, accustomed to the vagaries of his conversational style, humoured him. 'Thanks for coming in. What's rubbish?'

'Copycats. They don't happen. Don't exist – not in sexual homicide.' He dropped into the chair opposite her desk and sighed.

'What are you saying, Tony? That Derek Tyler managed to be in two places at once?'

'I don't know anything about Derek Tyler until I read the files. What I do know is that whatever we've got here, it's not a copycat.'

Carol struggled to make sense of what she was hearing. 'But if the MO is the same . . .?'

'Then you've got the same killer.' He gave her an apologetic smile and shrugged.

'That's not possible. From what Don says, and from what I've read here, there was no doubt on the forensics. And Derek Tyler is behind bars.'

Tony yanked the chair forward and leaned on the desk. His face was inches from hers. 'What is sexual homicide about?' he demanded.

Carol knew the answer to this one. 'The perverted gratification of desire.'

'Good, good,' he said, moving even closer. 'How many lovers have you had?'

Flustered, Carol looked away. 'What's that got to do with anything?'

'More than one, right?' he continued insistently.

Carol gave in. It was easier than the alternative. 'More than one,' she agreed.

'And have any of them ever behaved identically in bed?' Tony asked, as if the answer would settle an important argument.

Carol started to see a glimmer of where he was going with this. 'No.' Tony's intense blue eyes were irresistible. In spite of herself, she grew tense at his physical closeness. Whether he recognized that or not, he gave no clue.

His voice dropped, becoming intimate and gentle. 'My particular needs can only be met by one specific ritualistic process. I need you bound to the bed, I need you clothed, I need your voice stilled by a leather gag, I need you in my power and I need to destroy the manifestation of your sexuality.' He took a deep breath and pulled back. 'What are the chances that there are two of us out there who want exactly the same thing?'

Comprehension dawned on Carol. She relaxed now the immediacy of the intimacy had receded. 'Point taken. But we're still left with an identical MO. Which is a problem for me.'

Tony leaned back and his voice changed. Carol recognized the shift. Now he was thinking out loud, unformed conclusions bumping into each other. It had taken him a while to be comfortable enough with her to riff like this, but now it was almost as if he saw her as an extension of himself in these moments of verbal reverie. 'Unless of course someone wanted to get rid of Sandie specifically and thought it would be clever to do it in a way that made us run around like headless chickens looking for an impossible killer.'

'I suppose that's conceivable,' Carol said reluctantly.

'I mean, if it wasn't for the history, tying it into past cases, it wouldn't be that far out of the ordinary. Extreme, but not extraordinary.'

'Jesus, Tony,' Carol protested. 'You think what he did to her wasn't extraordinary?'

'Divorce your personal response from your professional one, Carol,' he said quietly. 'You've seen worse than that. A lot worse. Whoever did this still has a lot to learn about sexual sadism.'

'I'd forgotten how far from normal you are,' she said wearily.

'That's why you need me,' he said simply. 'Probably the only really interesting aspect of it is that she wasn't undressed. I mean, if you go to the trouble and expense of going back to a room with a hooker, I'd have thought you'd want her to take her clothes off. I know I would. Otherwise, you might as well just do it in the back of the car or up against a wall.'

'So what does that say to you?'

'Rape.' The word hung in the air between them. For months it had been unspoken and unspeakable. But now it was out in the open. Tony raised his shoulders in an apologetic shrug.

Carol struggled to stay in the professional zone. 'Why do you say that? There's no sign of a struggle back there. Presumably Sandie agreed to be tied up. Presumably he'd agreed to pay her.'

'Absolutely. But he wants it to feel like it's rape. So he doesn't want his victim undressed. That way he can fool himself that he's a rapist.'

It was Carol's turn to look puzzled. 'He wants to pretend he's a rapist? And then he kills them? Why can't he just pretend to be a murderer?'

Tony sighed. 'I don't know that yet, Carol.'

It's ironic, but he's calmer now the streets are full of cops. It's what he expected, and it's always comforting when what he expects happens, even if it's bad shit. Because at least then he knows it's not something worse.

He was doing a bit of business in the toilets at Stan's Café when he saw the blue strobe of their lights through the high frosted-glass window. One set of lights could have been anything, but three together had to be Sandie. And he didn't panic. He's proud of that. Before the Voice, he probably would have run, just as a matter of principle. But now he carried on selling rocks to the nervy black kid, acting surprised when he tried to hurry the action along because of the bizzies outside.

The kid had barely walked out the door when the conversation started. 'They've found her,' the Voice said, warm and caressing. 'They're going to be all over Temple Fields tonight. They're going to want to talk to everybody. They're going to want to talk to you. And that's fine. Just fine. You know what you're going to say, don't you?'

He gave the door a nervous glance. 'Yeah. I know.'

'Humour me. Let me hear it again,' the Voice coaxed.

'I was round and about, just like usual. Dropped in at Stan's, had a couple of beers in the Queen of Hearts. I never saw Sandie all night. I sometimes used to see her down the end of Campion Boulevard, but I never saw her last night.'

'And if they ask you for alibi names?'

'I just act thick. Like I can't tell one night from another. Everybody knows I'm a bit slow, so they won't think anything of it.'

'That's right. Vague is good. Vague is what they expect from you. You did a great job last night. Wonderful footage. When you get home tonight, there'll be a little reward waiting for you.'

'You don't have to do that,' he protested, meaning it. 'I'm sorted.'

'You deserve it. You're a very special young man.'

He felt a warm glow inside, a warm glow that's still there. Nobody but the Voice has ever thought anything about him was special, except his educational needs.

So now he's out there, mooching around like usual. He checks out the cops, a mixture of uniforms and obvious CID. They're working their way down both sides of the street. He could go back to Stan's and wait for them to come to him, or he could amble towards them like a fool with nothing to hide.

He recognizes one of the CID from before, when they were all over Temple Fields a couple of years ago. A big Geordie. Geordie didn't treat you like shit. He changes his angle of approach to come close to Geordie and the woman he's working with. They're talking to a punter, but he's got

101

nothing to say, he can't wait to be away. He's probably given them a moody name and address and he wants to skip before they catch him out.

They step back and the punter scuttles off sideways like a crab. The cop looks up and sees him. He's got that 'I know you but I can't put a name to you' look. He gives Geordie a stupid grin and says hi. Geordie says he's Detective Inspector Merrick.

He repeats the name a couple of times to fix it good and proper because he knows the Voice will want to know everything. He tells Geordie his name and address almost before he asks and the woman cop writes it down. She's not bad looking. A bit on the skinny side, but he's learning to like them like that. The cop asks if he'd heard about Sandie and he says yes, everybody's talking. And he comes out with the lines that the Voice has carved on his brain. Word perfect.

They ask if he saw anybody acting strangely. He laughs loudly, playing up to the image of the Gay Village idiot. 'Everybody acts strange round here,' he says.

'You're not kidding,' the woman cop mutters under her breath. 'Can anybody vouch for your movements last night?'

He looks puzzled. Mr Merrick says, 'Who saw you around? Who can confirm where you were last night?'

He opens his eyes wide. 'I dunno,' he says. 'Last night, it was just the same as every other night, you know? I don't remember stuff too good, Mr Merrick.'

'You remembered you didn't see Sandie,' the woman chipped in. Smart-arsed cow.

'Only because that's what everybody's talking about,' he says, feeling a tickle of sweat at the base of his spine. 'That's a big thing, not a little thing like who was in the café or the pub.'

Mr Merrick pats him on the shoulder. He takes a card

out of his pocket and tucks it into his hand. 'If you hear anything, you give me a call, right?' And they're off, ready for the next friendly little chat.

Not a flicker of doubt. Not a breath of suspicion. He fooled them. They were talking to an assassin and they had no idea. So who's the thickie now?

Carol eased the door shut, not wanting to disturb Michael and Lucy. She was aware how even slight noises carried in the high-ceilinged loft. She slipped out of her shoes and padded through to the kitchen at one end of the open-plan living space. The concealed fluorescent strips that cast light on the worktop were turned on, revealing her cat Nelson sprawled on his side, soaking up the warmth. He twitched one ear as she approached and let out a low rumble that the charitable might have interpreted as a welcome. Carol scratched his head, then noticed the sheet of paper he was half-obscuring. She slid it out from under him, ignoring his wriggle of protest. *'Hi, Sis. Lucy's doing an armed robbery in Leeds tomorrow and Thursday, we got last-minute tickets for the opera so I'm staying over there with her tonight. See you Thursday night. Love, M.'*

Carol crumpled the paper and tossed it in the bin, allowing herself to be momentarily wistful about the prospect of a night at the opera in good company. Anything was better than thinking about a night alone in the apartment. Opening the fridge to take out the half-eaten tin of cat food, she was drawn irresistibly to the bottle of Pinot Grigio sitting in the door. She took both out, fed the cat and contemplated the wine.

In her battle for restoration, Carol had resisted the

easy comfort of drink, nervous of its easy promise of oblivion. She'd told herself she didn't want to sleep-walk through the aftermath of the rape. She wanted to deal with it, to unpick its effects and put herself back together in something approximating the right order. But tonight she wanted erasure. She couldn't bear the thought of closing her eyes and seeing the images she'd brought home from the mortuary. Without anaesthetic, there was no way she was going to sleep. And without sleep, there was no way she could effectively lead the hunt for Sandie Foster's killer. Carol raked through the cutlery drawer for the corkscrew and hurriedly opened the bottle. Full glass in hand, she leaned against the worktop and buried her fingers in Nelson's fur, grateful for the beat of his heart against her skin.

Before last night, she'd had nothing in common with Sandie other than their gender. But what had happened to the prostitute had given her a sort of kinship with the woman charged with hunting down her killer. They both possessed a victimhood that had been conferred because they'd both been guilty of being female in a world where some men believed they deserved never to feel powerless. Sandie hadn't merited what had happened to her any more than Carol had.

Carol drank steadily, topping up her glass whenever it fell below the halfway mark. She understood the terror Sandie must have known as she realized there was no escape from her attacker. She knew that sense of utter helplessness, knew the absolute fear of the prey that has no defence against the predator. But in one crucial sense, perverse though it sounded,

Sandie had been luckier than Carol. She hadn't had to find a way to live with what had been done to her.

Tony stood by Carol's side, his eyes focused on Sandie Foster's lifeless face. He didn't mind being present at post mortems. If he was honest, it intrigued him to watch the pathologist uncovering the messages contained by the dead. Tony read corpses too, but his was a different text. What they had in common was that they both received communication from the killer via the conduit of his victim.

The body lay in a pool of halogen light, the surrounding room a collage of shadows. Dr Vernon, the pathologist, stooped over the body. It offered a gruesome illustration in contrast. Below the waist, Sandie's body was still caked in blood, a study in scarlet. Above the waist, she was apparently untouched. The plastic bags covering her hands partially obscured the bruising at her wrists, allowing the illusion of wholeness to persist. 'Poorly nourished,' Vernon said. 'Underweight for her height. Signs of intravenous drug use –' He pointed to the needletracks on her arms.

He leaned forward and gently probed her mouth open. 'Slight bruising on the inside of the mouth. Most likely as a result of the gag we removed earlier. Some indications of long-term amphetamine abuse.'

'I know you hate it when we jump the gun,' Carol said. 'But can you give me any indication on cause of death yet?'

Vernon turned and gave her a wintry smile. 'I see you haven't acquired patience in your time away from us, Carol. So far, I see nothing to contradict the obvious. She bled to death as a result of injuries inflicted vaginally. The tissue in the area is macerated almost beyond recognition. Not a pleasant way to go.'

'She didn't die quickly?' Carol asked. Tony could feel anxiety vibrating from her. He could also smell stale alcohol on her breath. He'd only managed four hours' sleep himself; God alone knew how little sleep Carol had managed to squeeze in between the bottle and the morgue. It certainly hadn't been enough, judging by the bruised smudges under her eyes.

Vernon shook his head. 'No. No arterial bleeding. This was slow exsanguination. She would have been alive probably for an hour or more, in terrible pain and shock.'

There was a long silence as they absorbed the information. Tony hoped Carol was not contemplating Sandie's suffering too closely. He gave himself a mental shake. He had to stop concentrating on Carol. He had a job to do, and while that job might be easier if he could help Carol on a personal level, he had to keep enough distance to allow himself to do what he was paid for. Mapping the mind of a murderer was never an easy task, and he couldn't afford to ignore an opportunity as good as this for finding a way in.

A long, slow, painful death. 'He watched her die,' he said softly.

Carol's head jerked round. 'What?'

'That's the whole point of a lingering death. The killer wants to savour what he's created. He'll have recorded it as well. Video, probably. But you might want to check the room for fibre-optic cameras. It's possible he wanted to watch the discovery of the body too.'

'He stayed around till she was dead?'

Tony nodded. 'High risk. He's confident, this one. He knew enough about Sandie's routines to feel safe that they weren't going to be disturbed. He's probably paid her to have sex before so he could check out the lie of the land. He won't have been able to manage intercourse, but he'll have wanted to talk, to find out her regular patterns. You should ask around, see if she mentioned anything to any of her mates.'

Carol filed the information away for future action. Vernon unpeeled the plastic bags from Sandie's hands and began taking scrapings from under her nails. 'Any thoughts on time of death?' Carol asked.

'An imprecise science at the best of times,' Vernon said drily. 'My best guess would be somewhere between midnight and eight yesterday morning.'

'No way to tell if she had sex before she was attacked, I suppose?' Carol asked.

'No chance. The damage to the surrounding tissues is so severe it will be impossible to tell whether there was any ante-mortem bruising. If it's any comfort to you, there's no apparent sign of any gross anal penetration.'

Before Carol could respond, the door behind them opened. Tony glanced over his shoulder. That single look told him the woman who had entered was a police officer. There was something unmistakable about her casual air of authority in this context. She wore a long black leather coat, the collar turned up against the blustery weather outside, making her look as if she was auditioning for a feminist version of *The Matrix*. She barely glanced at the body on the table before crossing to Carol.

'Morning, DCI Jordan,' she said. 'Mr Brandon said I'd find you here.'

Carol hid her surprise, though not from Tony. He knew her well enough to read the faint rise of the brows, the slight widening of the eyes. 'Sergeant Shields,' she said. 'What brings you here?'

'Mr Brandon didn't call you?' Jan's face showed consternation.

'No.'

'Ah. I expect he's left a message on your voice-mail. I tried to call you myself earlier and I couldn't raise you. Anyway, he's seconded me to your team for this investigation. He said you were a sergeant under strength and thought it might be useful to have someone on the team who knows the street scene.'

'That makes sense.' Carol's voice had ice at its heart. Already Brandon seemed to be reneging on his promise to give her a free hand, and she didn't like what that said about her.

'He seemed to think so,' Jan said, turning towards Tony. 'And this must be the man who reads our minds.'

Tony assumed the expression of a man who's heard it all before. 'Only if you're a sexually motivated serial offender.'

Jan laughed. 'My secrets are safe, then.' She held out a hand. 'I'm Jan Shields.'

Tony returned the handshake. Strong, warm hand. Exactly what he'd expect from someone who'd just demonstrated how sure of herself she was.

Jan turned back to Carol. 'Another one bites the dust, eh?'

'In a particularly unpleasant way,' Carol said repressively.

Jan shrugged, stepping forward to see better what Vernon was doing. 'It's a high-risk occupation.'

'So is being a cop,' Carol said. 'But when one of us dies, we get a little respect.'

Jan gave an apologetic smile. 'Sorry, I don't mean to sound callous. But when you've been in Vice as long as I have, they all start to look like meat while they're still on the hoof.'

Tony didn't find Jan's attitude surprising. He'd met too many cops – and clinical psychologists – on the edge of burnout not to have some sympathy with the defensive positions they adopted. He took a step away, moving closer to the table. 'Did you do the post mortems two years ago?' he asked.

Vernon nodded. 'I did.'

'What do you think?' Tony asked.

'If I didn't know better, I would say this woman had been the victim of the same killer. The pattern of the wounds is quite distinctive. Unique, really. The only time I've seen it before was in the murders Derek Tyler was found guilty of.'

'What did he use? A knife of some sort?'

'As I recall, Tyler never gave up the weapon. At the time, I surmised it was something home-made,' Vernon said. 'The wounds certainly don't match any implement I've ever come across. And I did ask one of my colleagues who's an expert in toolmarks for an opinion.'

'So, what kind of home-made?' Carol interjected.

Vernon studied the blade of his scalpel. 'It's hard to be certain. The wounds are consistent with a narrow, flexible blade. A razor blade rather than a craft knife. But there are dozens, hundreds of cuts. The best guess my colleague and I could come up with was something along the lines of a latex dildo with a series of razor blades inserted quite deeply into it.'

Carol's intake of breath was audible. 'Jesus,' she said.

'Danger, nutters at work,' Jan said bitterly. 'That right, Dr Hill?'

Tony frowned. It made no sense. Nothing added up. If the police had captured the wrong man, the real killer should have reacted by taking another victim then and there. Sexually motivated murderers didn't like other people being given credit for their handiwork. To wait two years to strike again was all wrong. He needed to talk this through. 'Carol?' he said softly.

But her attention was elsewhere. She indicated Tony with a movement of her head without looking at him directly. 'Jan, Dr Hill thinks our man had been with Sandie before. Can you find out who she hung around with, see if she mentioned a punter who wanted her to talk about herself? Chances are he couldn't maintain an erection.'

Jan snorted. 'That hardly narrows it down. You'd be amazed how many punters can't get it up when it comes to it. That's often why the girls get smacked around. But yeah, I'll see what I can come up with.' She pulled her coat collar closer. 'I'll hit the bricks, then. Catch you later.'

Tony watched her melt into the shadows, waiting till he heard the door close behind her before

110

returning to Carol's side. The room was quiet save for the clink of metal on metal as Vernon exchanged one instrument of deconstruction for another. 'Carol, I keep coming back to what I said earlier. This is an impossible scenario. If Derek Tyler really did commit the murders he was convicted of, it's beyond the bounds of credibility that somebody else would find satisfaction in such a precise replication of his crimes. It goes against every psychological truth I know. Somebody's setting the scene, creating what they want us to see.'

'But the forensics –'

'I know what you said,' Tony interrupted her. 'But your team needs to look at those files, to see if there was any possibility of a mistake. And if there was, you need to start looking at men who've been recently released from prison or from Bradfield Moor after a two-year stretch. That's the only explanation for the time lag. Because I'd stake my reputation on the fact that whoever killed those women two years ago also killed Sandie Foster.'

Carol stared at him, the glimmering of an idea at the edge of her consciousness. 'Tony? What if that's exactly what our killer is gambling on?'

'Sorry?' he looked puzzled.

Carol's words tumbled over each other in her excitement. 'What if the person who murdered Sandie Foster is gambling on the fact that we'll be forced to draw precisely that conclusion? What if killing Sandie was incidental? What if the killer's real intent is to have Derek Tyler's conviction set aside?'

Tony cocked his head to one side, considering. 'That would work? You could base an appeal on

111

that? In spite of the overwhelming evidence against Tyler?'

'You could have a damn good try. Especially with someone like you in the witness box staking your not inconsiderable reputation on it.'

'Ah,' he said. 'So I take it you don't want me shouting that from the rooftops?'

'Especially not when there are lawyers or journalists present,' Carol said. 'But what do you think? Is it motivation enough?'

'Hard to say. It would have to be somebody who cared passionately about Derek Tyler and who was smart enough to figure out how to pull our strings. It's not a likely scenario, but it's possible.' He smiled. 'This is why we work so well together. You think like a detective, I think like a nutter.'

After the morgue, it was almost a relief to be back inside Bradfield Moor. Front-desk security told him where to find Derek Tyler. Because he'd been classified as a non-violent inmate, he was allowed to eat his meals with others in the same category in the dining room. It was a low-ceilinged barn of a room that smelled of chip fat with undertones of overcooked brassicas. The walls had been painted indigo and yellow in line with what Tony privately considered to be the junk science of colour therapy. Any beneficial effects that the décor might have provoked were probably compromised by the scuffs and stains that marked the paintwork from floor to ceiling. Through the security-glass windows there was a view of a shrubbery that consisted mostly of spotted laurel and rhododendrons. If they weren't depressed when they came in here, Tony thought, they soon would be.

He asked one of the orderlies to point out Tyler, then he helped himself to a tray of macaroni cheese and peas, choosing a table off to one side, where he could observe the man who had been found guilty of the murders of four prostitutes over a period of six months, a man who had blamed his urge to kill on the voice in his head. A few of the other inmates glanced Tony's way, some openly staring. But nobody made any attempt to approach him.

Tyler was a lanky, scrawny individual in his mid-twenties. He hunched over his sausage, egg and chips like a miser with a hoard of gold, head down so Tony could see little of him apart from the top of his shaved head and the tattoos on his skinny forearms.

Tony absently munched his way through his lunch, washing the bland food down with strong tea. Tyler showed none of the physical tics of the obsessive compulsive. He ate with preternatural slowness, as if he were stretching the meal out as long as he could. It seemed a pretty good strategy for passing the time, Tony decided.

Tyler had progressed to his last few mouthfuls when Aidan Hart slipped into the chair next to him. 'I didn't expect to see you in today,' he said.

'It's all right, I won't be claiming overtime,' Tony said.

'There's better grub in the staff restaurant, you know.'

'I know. But I wanted to take a look at a patient.'

Hart nodded. 'Derek Tyler.' Noting Tony's look of

113

surprise, he said, 'Security told me when I came in. What's your interest?'

'Bradfield police found a murder victim last night. They've asked me to consult on the case.' At the mention of the police, Hart perked up, his eyes gleaming with interest. Tony reckoned he'd been right when his first instinct had placed Aidan Hart firmly in the box marked 'careerist'. Just what he needed. More of the professional politics he was so bad at. He'd have to be very careful how he handled this. 'On the surface, it looks like a copy of Derek Tyler's murders.'

Hart stroked his cleanly shaved chin. 'Interesting.'

'Oh yes, it's that, all right.' Tony finished his tea. 'He looks a bit young for this kind of offence.'

'I guess the profile has to be off the mark some-times,' Hart said smoothly. 'Given that we're working with the law of averages.'

'Which is why I always warn the cops it's not an exact science. So, what can you tell me about him?'

Hart looked across at Tyler, who had come to the end of his meal and was staring down at his empty plate. 'Very little. He's one of the most unco-operative patients I've ever come across. Don't get me wrong. It's not that he's disruptive – quite the opposite. He's totally passive. In one sense, he's no trouble at all. But in another, he's completely intractable. He won't participate in any aspect of the therapeutic regime. He won't speak. He's not catatonic. He just chooses not to.'

'Ever had any trouble with him?'

'Only once. They've got integral radios in their rooms. They can choose from half a dozen preset stations, and we can use the system to broadcast

114

announcements. Derek never uses his, but somehow something went wrong with it. The radio came on and it couldn't be turned off. And Derek lost it. Smashed the room up, went for the nurses. We had to sedate him, and he wouldn't go back in his room until we had the radio removed.'

Tony gave a small smile. 'Interesting,' he said. If Hart noticed the echo, he didn't react.

'But not very illuminating.'

Tony let the comment lie. He wasn't ready to share his thoughts with anyone, least of all someone he felt an instinctive mistrust towards. 'What do we know about him before the killings?'

Tony watched the eye movements that indicated Hart was accessing memory not lies. 'Not a lot,' Hart said after a short pause. 'Borderline special needs. According to the report from his GP, he was highly suggestible, eager to please, mild obsessive compulsive. But nothing to merit treatment. And nothing to indicate he was heading for a career as a serial killer. Then again, GPs – what do they know?' His smile was complicit, one expert to another, calculated to build an alliance. Tony read it for what it was and instinctively fought against it. Hart pushed his chair back. 'Do you want to meet Derek?'

'I'd appreciate it if you could arrange it. It'd be good if I could talk to him in his room.'

Hart looked surprised. 'That's not normal procedure. We usually talk to patients in one of the interview suites.'

'I know. But I'd like to see him on his turf. I'd like him to feel he has a measure of control. And you've said yourself, he's not violent.'

Tony could see Hart weighing up the arguments and deciding to keep his powder dry. 'All right. I'll page you when we're set up. But you'll be wasting your time, you know. He's not spoken to a member of the medical staff since the day he arrived here.'

Tony didn't take his eyes off Derek Tyler as Hart bustled off. He spoke under his breath: 'You like the voice, don't you, Derek? You like to listen to it. You don't want anything to interfere with it. So what do I have to do to make you want to listen to mine?'

When she'd woken up only three hours after falling into bed, Carol had blamed lack of sleep for the way she felt. But as the morning had worn on, it became clear to her that she was in fact hung over. She felt as if someone was cutting through her brain with cheesewire after cruelly turning the lights several hundred watts higher. Still, it was almost worth it for the dreamless stupor that had kept the nightmare images of Sandie Foster's death at bay. She swigged from a bottle of water and surveyed her team. They all looked fresher than she felt. She walked out of her office and took up station in front of the white-board that was already adorned with photos of Sandie, alive and dead.

'Good morning,' Carol said, trying to imitate an energy she didn't possess. 'Sandie Foster died at some time between midnight and eight a.m. on Tuesday morning. Which means she was probably attacked somewhere between ten on Monday night and four on Tuesday morning. Given that she normally knocked off at ten, we can assume she was in the company of her killer before then. According to Dr

Vernon, she bled to death and it would have taken her at least an hour to die. Dr Tony Hill, who will be working with us on this case, believes that the killer probably stayed with her while she bled out. So we're looking for someone who has two or three hours they can't account for in that time period.' She turned to the whiteboard and wrote up the crucial times.

'Preliminary forensics indicate we're not going to have much to go on here. Plenty of prints, but none on the handcuffs or the bedstead. They've been wiped clean. The top of the table was green baize, so nothing for us there either. Chances are the remaining prints are from punters who had nothing to do with this. Nevertheless, if and when we get any matches, we need to follow up on that. So far, we've not found any traces of sperm. The blood boys are checking to see if they can find any blood that isn't Sandie's, but that's a slim chance.' Carol perched on the edge of a desk, forcing her thoughts into order.

'I know you're all aware of the similarities between this case and a series of murders that took place two years ago. However, there is nothing to suggest that Derek Tyler's conviction was unsafe. I've read the files, and even without his admission of guilt, that case was as open and shut as we're ever likely to get. So while we treat this as an individual case, we should be aware that it's possible Derek Tyler had a fan a couple of years ago. A sick bastard who sees it as his role to replicate Derek's crimes. It might even be the case that someone is trying to get Derek Tyler out of Bradfield Moor and sees this as the way to do it. Make a case for linkage between the murders, and you make a case for a miscarriage of justice.'

'Don't you think that's a bit far-fetched, ma'am?' Don Merrick interjected.

'At this stage, Don, I'm not ruling out anything, however off the wall it might seem.' Carol noticed Paula catch Merrick's eye and give him a small shake of the head. Indicating that she thought her guvnor had lost it? Or was Carol just being paranoid? Was Paula acting out of team solidarity, signalling it wasn't appropriate for Don to question the boss's judgement when there were others present? Carol cleared her throat and continued. 'We all know this is not a straightforward murder because of the resemblances to the previous series. But I want that knowledge to stay in this room. Nobody talks to the press. Leave that to me and Mr Brandon. Now, what have we got?'

Not much, Carol thought miserably as she listened to the team run through the scant high points of their results so far. Nobody admitted to having seen Sandie with a punter after nine o'clock. Sandie's distraught mother knew nothing of the details of her daughter's other life; it had been tacit between them that what Sandie did to earn her keep was something not to be spoken of in the family home. The only lead they had was that Sandie had been seen getting into a black Freelander 4x4 around half past eight. An obliging prostitute had noted the last three digits of the number plate.

'OK,' Carol sighed. 'Kevin, get on to the number plate. Chances are it's not our man, but at least if we can find out when he dropped her off, we narrow down the time frame for our killer. Don, Paula – I want you to collate all the interviews from the street last night. Work with Stacey to draw up a plan of

118

who was where, when. Then we'll have an idea who might be worth reinterviewing. Stacey, I want you to carry on working on Ron Alexander's computer files as well. Let's not lose sight of our other priorities. Jan, you're with me. Sam, you can start backtracking on Derek Tyler's known associates. The rest of you I want out on the streets in Temple Fields – saturation coverage. I want everybody who was out and about on Monday night interviewed.'

The room filled with the hubbub of conversation as officers organized themselves. Jan Shields wove through the bodies and reached Carol as she was about to enter her office. 'What have you got in mind for us?' Jan said conversationally, following Carol inside.

'Kevin did a good job with Dee Smart, but I think she might have more to give us. It's always worth trying a different approach. And I thought you might know some of the levers to pull.'

Jan leaned against the door frame. 'Sure. We're probably wasting our time, but you never know.'

'It's better than spinning our wheels.' Carol was opening and closing her drawers, looking for the paracetamol she was sure she'd stashed there. No trace. She was going to have to manage without.

'You really think somebody's trying to get Derek Tyler off the hook?' Jan asked.

Carol looked up. 'I don't know. But, frankly, it's a more comfortable notion than any of the alternatives.'

Tony knocked on the open door and waited. Silence. Worth a try, he thought, unsurprised that the tactic hadn't worked. He stuck his head round the door.

Derek Tyler was sitting on his bed, knees bent, arms wrapped round his legs. 'Can I come in?' Tony asked.

Tyler didn't move. 'I'll take that as a yes, then.' Tony walked into the small room, keeping his eyes on Tyler. There would be plenty of time to take in the room without making the man feel his environment was under scrutiny. 'I'll sit down, shall I?' Tony continued, making for the single wooden chair that was tucked into a bare table.

He pulled the chair out and turned it so he was sitting at an angle to Tyler. He deliberately chose a relaxed posture, body open and unthreatening. Tyler moved his head so Tony was out of his line of vision. Tony glimpsed a raw-boned face with deep-set pale eyes. He had the sense that Tyler was perfectly capable of connection but that he chose to avoid it. 'My name is Tony Hill,' he said. 'I work here at the hospital. But I also work with the police. And that's why I wanted to talk to you.' He waited, taking in the bareness of the room. It was like a monastic cell. No books, no family photographs tacked to the walls, no Page Three girls. The only personal item in the room was a large framed black-and-white photograph of Temple Fields, looking down the pedestrianized street with the canal off to one side.

After a few long minutes, Tony decided it was time to get to work. His strategy was, he knew, basic. But it was the best he could come up with on short notice with a patient he'd no previous clinical engagement with. 'I understand why you might not want to talk about it. Who could possibly comprehend what it was like to do the things you did?'

Tyler shifted slightly, but his bony face remained

120

resolutely turned away. Tony lowered his voice, making it warm and sympathetic. 'But that's not the main problem, is it? The trouble is, when you start to talk, everybody just wants to talk back at you. And that way you can't hear the voice, can you, Derek?'

Tyler jerked his head round momentarily, a flash of surprise on his face. It was over so quickly that Tony could almost have believed he'd imagined the response. 'It's still there, isn't it?' he said. Then he waited a good two minutes before speaking again. 'You can hear it when I shut up, can't you?'

Nothing from Tyler. But that single glance had told Tony he was moving in the right direction. 'But the voice can only tell you stuff from before. It can't tell you what's happening now, outside here. You have to rely on me for that. You know why that is? You know why it's all gone quiet? It's because your voice is talking to somebody else now.'

Tyler's whole body swivelled round till he was facing Tony. He was all attention now, his grey-blue eyes shrouded under his heavy brows. Tony spread his hands in a conciliatory gesture. 'I'm sorry, Derek, but that's the way it is. You're shut up in here, you're no use any more. I told you I work with the police. The reason I'm here is that somebody else is doing exactly what you did, Derek. And that has to be because the voice isn't talking to you any more. It's talking to him.'

Anger flared in Tyler's eyes. His hands tightened their grip on each other, the veins on his thin arms standing out like cords. Tony wondered if anyone on Aidan Hart's team had ever provoked this tightly coiled violence in Tyler. He doubted it. If they'd seen what he was looking at now, he didn't think Tyler would be allowed into the general population. 'I'm not making this up, Derek,' Tony said reasonably. 'The voice has left you for somebody else. All you've got is memories.'

Abruptly, Tyler jumped up and walked past Tony to the doorway. He rang the call button on the wall and banged on the door with his fist for good measure.

Tony continued speaking as if nothing had happened. 'I'm right, aren't I? The voice isn't yours any more. So you might as well talk.'

A nurse in white scrubs appeared in the corridor. Tony could see Aidan Hart hovering behind him. Tyler stood meekly by the door.

'What's happened?' the nurse asked.

Tony smiled. 'I think Derek wants to go away and think about what I've been saying to him, don't you, Derek?'

'You're OK, are you, Doc?'

'I'm fine. In good fettle and in good voice.'

The nurse looked from Tony to Tyler and back again, unable to fathom what was going on. 'Come on then, Derek, we'll take you down to the day room.' The nurse reached out for Tyler's arm.

In the doorway, Tyler turned and growled in a voice rusty from disuse, 'You're not the voice. You could never be the voice.'

Aidan Hart's mouth fell open. He watched speechless as Tyler walked down the hall, head high, narrow shoulders thrown back. Tony stood up and replaced the chair. 'Well, that's a start,' he said cheerfully, walking past his new boss at a brisk pace.

*   *   *

Stan's Café featured in none of the tourist guides to Bradfield. Even the indie internet websites that prided themselves on offering their readers the *echt* experience normally only available to natives shuddered away from a greasy spoon frequented principally by hookers, rent boys, homeless people and drug dealers. Unlike some low-life dives that made it into alternative guides, nobody went to Stan's for the food. The clientele frequented Stan's because it was somewhere to go out of the cold and rain. When Temple Fields glamorized itself into the Gay Village in the nineties, the bar owners had started to become more picky about who they allowed across their thresholds, especially if they were the sort of customers who could make a half of bitter last hours. The only beneficiary of this more stringent approach was Stan's. Fat Bobby, who owned Stan's, didn't care who occupied the split and sticky vinyl seats as long as they bought food and drink and fags from him.

That morning, half a dozen tables were taken. Two young Asian men were hunched over eggs on toast, a velvet jeweller's roll of knock-off watches half-exposed between them. They were clearly brothers, sharing the same tight, sharp features, the same slack-lipped mouths stained with tomato sauce. In between mouthfuls, they argued prices and pitches. A gangling youth lounged against the fruit machine, frowning at the reels as they spun and settled in response to the coins a chunky lad with classic Black Irish looks was feeding into the machine. 'Why d'you keep doing it when you don't win?' the spectator asked.

'If I don't do it, I won't win, will I?' the player grunted. 'Fuck off, you're bringing me bad luck.'

Dee Smart sat at a corner table near the toilets, back to the door, huddled over a cigarette. Her eyelids were puffy and heavy, her mouth downturned and tight. She stared into a grey cup of coffee, looking miserable. A gawky, slack-jawed youth emerged from the toilets and caught sight of her. He slid into the seat opposite. 'You sad about Sandie, Dee?' he said. He had some sort of problem with his speech which turned everything he said into a long drawl.

Dee took a drag on her cigarette and sighed. Jason Duffy was not what she needed right then. 'Yeah, Jason, I'm sad about Sandie.'

He patted her hand awkwardly. 'You need something to take the edge off? I got some nice skunk.'

'Not a good idea just now, Jason. I'm waiting for the dibble,' Dee said wearily. 'Besides, you know I don't buy from you.'

Jason's face twitched with nervous anxiety and he edged quickly out of the seat, almost falling over his feet in his haste. 'Be seeing you, then.' He headed for the door without a backward glance.

The youth by the slot machine abandoned his post and moseyed over to the counter to order a tea. The door to the outside swung open and Jason Duffy nearly ran head first into Carol Jordan in his haste to be gone. Carol sidestepped him and walked in, her stomach rebelling at the steamy, smoke-filled atmosphere. Stale bacon fat and vinegar conspired in a foul miasma that made her regret her excesses of the previous night once more. Jan followed her, eyes dredging the room for Dee Smart. 'Over there,' she said, indicating Dee with her head. 'You want a coffee?'

Carol wrinkled her nose. 'You're kidding, right?'

'They don't do mineral water,' Jan said acidly. 'A Coke might settle your stomach.'

Carol tried to hide her surprise. 'Sorry?'

'You've been looking off colour all morning. The morgue will do that to you.' Jan weaved through the tables to the counter. Carol followed, checking out the room. She might as well have been invisible for the amount of eye contact she could garner. Every time she looked at someone, their eyes slid off her like water off wax. 'Who's who?' she asked.

Jan's eyes swept the room. 'The lad playing the fruit machine is Tyrone Donelan. He nicks cars.' As if he'd heard her, Tyrone Donelan took one glance over his shoulder and made straight for the door to the toilets.

'The two Asians, that's Tariq and Samir Iqbal. Snide watches, pirate DVDs – that kind of thing. Their old man's a serious player in the counterfeit game. I think he got a tug a year or so back, did three months.' The Iqbals suddenly lost interest in their eggs on toast, grabbed their stash of watches and hurriedly left.

'What about the kid who nearly knocked me over when we came in?'

'Jason Duffy. Low-level dealer. Smack and whiz mostly. He's not the full shilling, Jason. His claim to fame is that his mother was the first person in Bradfield to be arrested for dealing crack.' She indicated the gangling youth with a sideways jerk of the head. 'That's another one from the same mould: Carl Mackenzie. He mostly deals to the street girls. More of a range than Jason, but not much smarter. As far as what we're looking for goes, there's not one of them that would be as much use as a chocolate chip pan.'

Carol nodded. 'Thanks.' She moved at a leisurely pace towards Dee and sat down opposite her. Dee raised her head and gave her a calculated stare. Carol took in the lank hennaed hair and the weary, suspicious eyes.

'Who are you?' she demanded.

'Hi, Dee,' she said. 'I'm sorry I didn't get the chance to meet you yesterday. I'm Detective Chief Inspector Jordan. Carol Jordan.' Carol smiled and extended a hand.

Obviously taken aback, Dee shifted her cigarette from one hand to the other and accepted the shake. 'Right,' she said. 'So you obviously know who I am.'

'I'm sorry about Sandie,' Carol said.

'Not half as sorry as I am.'

'Naturally. She wasn't my friend. But I want you to know that I'll pursue whoever killed her just as hard as if she had been.'

The sincerity in Carol's voice seemed to penetrate Dee's carapace of toughness. 'That's what the other bloke said. That you'd take it seriously.' She sounded surprised.

Jan reached the table, a can of Coke in each hand. She dumped the drinks on the table and plonked herself down in a chair at right angles to the other two women. 'Dee, this is . . .' Carol began.

'I know who this is,' Dee said. Her manner had shifted back to her earlier truculence.

'Hi, Dee. How are you doing?' Jan asked.

'How do you think?' She angled herself away from Jan.

126

Carol popped the top of her Coke and took a mouthful. Sugar and caffeine and bubbles hit her, giving her an instant lift. 'I know this is a hard time for you, but we do need your help.'

Dee sighed. 'Look, like I said when you phoned. I told everything I know to that bloke last night.'

Jan shook her head. 'There's always more, Dee. We all know that. Stuff you think isn't important, stuff you think is too important. Who did she score from?'

Dee looked panicked. Her eyes swivelled towards the counter, where Carl Mackenzie was leaning, mug in hand, talking to the girl behind the counter. 'I dunno,' she mumbled.

'Course you do.' Jan followed Dee's glance in time to see Carl heading for the door, throwing a nervous glance in her direction.

'Was that Carl Mackenzie going out just now?' Jan asked.

'I don't have eyes in the back of my head. And if it was, what of it? It's still a free country, isn't it? People can have a cup of coffee wherever they want, can't they?' Dee was talking too much, Carol thought.

Jan clearly agreed. 'Sandie scored off Carl, didn't she?'

Dee snorted scornfully. 'Sandie wasn't a low-life. I don't know who she used, but it wasn't Carl, OK? You stay off his back, he's harmless.'

'That would be because he's dealing to you, would it?' Jan drawled wearily.

'Fuck off. Look, she might have got some stuff off Jason Duffy now and again, but that's all I know.'

'Did she have a pimp?' Carol asked.

Dee shook her head. 'There's less poncing round Temple Fields than you'd think. Her lot saw to that,' she said, gesturing towards Jan with her thumb.

'We cleared out a lot of the pimps a while back,' Jan said to Carol. 'We made it clear we were going to nail their earnings under the Proceeds of Crime legislation.' She turned to Dee. 'I'd have thought you lot would be grateful to us for getting them off your backs.'

'We'd have been a fuck of a sight more grateful if you hadn't tried to get the punters off the streets at the same time,' Dee said bitterly. 'You're the ones who pushed us off the main drags and into the side streets. And now it's all happening again.'

Carol felt the rapport she'd started to build with Dee slithering away out of her reach. 'We want to stop it happening,' she insisted.

'Yeah, well, I've told you all I can.' Dee pushed her chair back.

Carol tried a last desperate appeal. 'If you remember anything at all, however insignificant it seems, it could be important for our investigation, Dee. We're here to help.'

Dee snorted. 'Yeah, well, it's not helping me earning a living, sitting in Stan's being clocked talking to the dibble. I'm out of here.'

She grabbed her skimpy denim jacket from the back of her chair and stalked off. Carol looked after her, fed up and puzzled. 'She was a lot more co-operative with Kevin last night,' she said.

Jan shrugged. 'Maybe she prefers men.'

'She seemed edgy about Carl Mackenzie.'

Jan looked bored. 'She scores from him. She doesn't want us taking him off the streets. He's harmless. Mental age of about ten. The girls treat him like a pet.'

'You think Dee was telling the truth? About Sandie not using him?'

Jan considered, rolling her drink between her palms. 'Probably. If Sandie bought off Jason, she wouldn't have been using Carl as well. They're both street dealers for the same middleman. Plus, what's Dee got to gain by lying about it?'

'Like you said, it keeps her source on the street, where she needs it,' Carol pointed out.

Jan pulled a dubious face, making her look like a pouting cherub past its sell-by date. 'I can't see it. I'll check the overnights, see if he's been spoken to, if you like.'

'That'd be good. And if he hasn't, maybe you could have a word.' She'd skimmed the reports herself that morning, but she couldn't remember the detail. 'Same goes for Jason Duffy.'

Carol knew she was clutching at straws, always tempting when an investigation didn't throw up solid early leads. She was beginning to have a bad feeling about Sandie Foster's murder. It was showing all the hallmarks of a case that was going nowhere fast. If they didn't get a break soon, Carol's squad would be transformed from great white hopes to scapegoats. And that wasn't something she thought she could handle right now.

He's big news. Front page of the evening paper. He can't read well, but he can manage big headlines. He wasn't expecting it to be like that, not with Sandie being just a whore. The cops must be pissed off, he thinks. Big headlines about murder make them look bad.

He can tell by the way the streets are full of them, talking to anybody they can get their hands on, that they don't know where to look. They're desperate to find what he knows isn't there. He knows it's not there because he did it exactly as he was told.

He's proud of himself. He can't remember ever feeling like this before. There must have been a time when he did something right, something he could hold his head up about. But when he searches his fucked-up memories, nothing surfaces.

The Voice understands that. The Voice is proud of him too. He knows because when he got back to his place last night, there was a reward. A small parcel was sitting on top of his TV/video combo, wrapped in nice shiny holographic paper with a big gold ribbon round it. It was so beautiful that he almost didn't want to open it. He wanted to swagger round with it so people would realize he was the kind of person who got special presents. He didn't, though. He knew that would be stupid. And he's trying very hard not to be stupid these days.

Instead he sat on the bed for ages, turning it over in his hands. Eventually, he decided to unwrap it and see what was inside. He had a pretty good idea, but he wanted to be sure. First, he untied the ribbon, forcing his clumsy fingers to go slow over the knot rather than ripping it apart with his teeth or cutting it with his Swiss Army knife. Then he folded up the paper and ribbon carefully, before putting it away in a drawer.

Inside was the reward he expected. A video cassette. With sweating hands, he slid it into the slot in the video, reaching for the remote to turn on the TV. And there it was, in all its glory. His first mission, his first cleansing.

This time, he didn't lose his erection.

PART THREE

Three weeks later

He used to have nightmares when he was a kid. He hasn't thought about them in years; they stopped once he started spliffing. He can't recall the last time he went to bed without at least one joint humming in his veins, so likewise he can't recollect the last time a bad dream woke him screaming and quivering between the sheets. But he does remember how there was always someone towering over him, mouth opening and closing, spewing violent words. He seemed to shrink under the attack, while the shouting figure swelled like a monster in a manga comic. He could never make out the words, but they seemed to strip the very skin from him till he felt raw and bleeding.

What made it worse was that he had nothing to make it better when he woke. There was no comforting memory of gentleness or kindness to set against the sound and fury of his nightmare.

It's hard to believe how much things have changed. Now he falls asleep lulled by the rockabye rhythms of the Voice. He wouldn't mind betting that if he gave up the weed, he'd sleep like a baby these days. Not that he's about to give it a try. He likes life without nightmares too much to take a chance.

Tonight, he's making plans. The Voice is in his head, telling him it's time to move again. Time for the next chapter of the lesson, according to the Voice. Time for another cleansing.

Tomorrow night, he'll come home to find his supplies neatly laid out on his bed. Tomorrow night, he'll get set, just like the last time. He tries not to think of the target as a human being. That way, his head won't get tangled up like it did with Sandie right at the end, when he started to feel like he maybe shouldn't be taking her life away, when it all went muddled and only the memory of the Voice kept him going.

This time, he won't think of her as someone with a name. He'll just think of her as rubbish that has to be got rid of before it poisons the world he has to live in. Then he'll ride the dragon all the way to glory. He'll be a hero, just like in the movies. Blood and glory. Blood and glory and the Voice.

Once upon a time the only way respectable people could buy sex toys was to send off for what catalogues described with bizarre coyness as a 'cordless neck massager'. But by the first decade of the twenty-first century, almost every fair-sized town in the United Kingdom had at least one emporium dedicated to the fulfilment of most imaginable sexual desires. They'd started as seedy shopfronts with blacked-out windows regularly picketed by protesters ranging from evangelical Christians to women reclaiming the night. But they'd rapidly progressed to well-lit, inviting retail palaces, shelves stacked with everything from whimsical fake-fur handcuffs to implements whose functions mercifully eluded most of the customers who were intent only on having a good night in.

There was about most of these stores a relentless cheerfulness. The Pink Flaming-O was typical of the breed. It occupied a double-fronted shop that had once been, ironically, a toyshop, at the less fashionable end of the main shopping street in Firnham, one of the half-dozen satellite towns that circled Bradfield. The windows were painted opaque shocking pink to avoid offending those citizens of Firnham who steadfastly maintained their lack of interest in its contents. Given that most businesses at that end of Deansgate had a life expectancy of somewhere between six and eighteen months, and given that the Pink Flaming-O had been thriving for four years, the assumption had to be that the town boasted enough people with a lively interest in the wilder shores of sex to outweigh the censorious.

Certainly there was no lack of custom towards the end of a late autumnal Sunday afternoon. A pair of teenage girls were giggling incredulously at a display of outsize dildos, but the other half-dozen customers were giving far more serious attention to items as various as cock rings, anal-sex kits, bondage equipment, inflatable love dolls and penis pumps.

As the teenagers moved on to wonder at the range of clitoral stimulators, their place by the display of dildos was taken by a customer who had been browsing a rack of videos. A hand gloved in black leather reached out for one of the display models, a lurid scarlet latex imitation penis. Strong fingers tested its pliability and, satisfied, replaced it on the shelf. The hand picked up a boxed example of the dildo and carried it across to the counter, picking up a couple of pairs of handcuffs and ankle restraints along the way.

There was nothing sinister in the cash transaction, nothing to rouse a moment's suspicion in the mind of the shop assistant, who was frankly more interested in Bradfield Victoria's prospects in that evening's premiership match than in the putative sex life of his customers. It was probably as well for his peace of mind that he had no idea that within forty-eight hours, his merchandise would have been transformed into the accoutrements of murder.

The customer walked out of the shop and turned down a side street that led to a busy supermarket. Fifteen minutes later, a blank-eyed checkout assistant rang up a basket of purchases without thought. A loaf of sliced wholemeal bread. Half a dozen premier pork sausages. Four toilet rolls. A bottle of vodka. And three packets of razor blades.

The Voice was ready.

Carol surveyed the stack of cardboard cartons, her good spirits evaporating. It had seemed a good idea at the time to order the furniture for her new home online from a chain retailer. But now she was faced with a couple of dozen flatpacks, and she knew that what lay ahead of her was a long evening of splintered fingernails and muttered oaths. Still, she told herself, it would be worth the effort. The builder had made a good job of turning the basement into an attractive flat. The acrid pungency of fresh paint still hung in the air, but that was a small price to pay for having her own space again.

Carol pulled the cork on a bottle of Viognier, sloshed it into a glass and savoured the cold freshness of the wine as it slid down. It had become a familiar ritual at the end of the working day. After Michael and Lucy were in bed, she had taken to sitting by the window, Nelson wrapping himself round her legs. With her bottle and her glass for company, she would process the fruitless activities of the day and try to avoid thinking about what lurked in her personal shadows. She knew she was growing too reliant on the comfort that came from the wine, but the only alternative that suggested itself was the talking cure, and she had little confidence that she could find a therapist she would respect enough to trust. She could talk to Tony, of course. But she needed his friendship too much to want to turn him into a therapist.

She drained the glass and refreshed it, then set to work. Bed first. Then at least she'd have somewhere to collapse when the frustration of always having three screws and a piece of wood left over grew too much.

Carol was wrestling the slats of the bed base into place when the unfamiliar sound of her doorbell pealed out. She grinned. Nothing like setting the ground rules early on. She walked through to the living room and opened her door to the outside world. Tony stood at the foot of the flight of steps, a bottle of champagne dangling from his hand. 'I would have brought flowers,' he said, 'but I didn't know if you had a vase.'

She stepped back and waved him in. 'Two, actually. They're in the kitchen, stuffed with enough lilies to take the edge off the paint.'

He handed over the bottle. 'Welcome to your new home.'

Carol put a hand on his shoulder and kissed his cheek. It was the closest they'd come in months, and the familiar smell of his skin tripped a chain reaction of confused feelings. 'Thank you,' she said softly. 'You've no idea how much this means to me.'

Tony patted her back awkwardly. 'You're doing me

a favour. Having you on the doorstep might just save me from becoming an eccentric recluse.'

Carol laughed, stepping away from him as the closeness grew too much. 'I wouldn't bet on it.'

He looked around at the cartons leaning against the wall. 'Let's make a start, then,' he said, rolling up the sleeves of his sweatshirt. 'I warn you, I am to DIY what George Bush is to the philosophy of language.'

'That good, eh? Tony, I know it runs counter to your instincts, but all you have to do is follow the instructions.'

Two hours later, they'd assembled all the bedroom furniture, two bookcases and three of the dining chairs. They sat slumped in exhausted stupor, each clutching a glass of champagne in stiff and bruised fingers. 'God, I'm aching in muscles I'd forgotten about,' Carol moaned. 'I keep telling myself it'll be worth it to have a place of my own again. Michael's been very sweet, but it's so wearing, coming home from work and having to make small talk.'

Tony winced. 'You had to make small talk? That definitely comes under the heading of cruel and unusual.'

'It was that or listen to Lucy laying down the law about the incompetence, stupidity or bloody-mindedness of the police.'

'Not what you need,' Tony agreed.

'Especially not when it feels like she might be right. My supposed crack squad has two cases to work, and we're going nowhere fast with both of them. We've come to a full stop on Tim Golding.

Stacey managed to extract the serial number of the camera that took the photo, but whoever bought it paid cash in a superstore in Birmingham and never filled in the guarantee registration. There's nothing fresh on Guy Lefevre either. The Operation Ore techies are trawling all they've got to see if they can come up with any more images of either boy, but according to them, that's like looking for a needle in a field full of haystacks. I've got the three-week review of Sandie Foster's murder tomorrow morning, and it's going to be a nightmare. What have we got to show for all that slog and a huge spend? Bugger all. A handful of dead ends and not a single new idea to bless ourselves with. Canvassing Temple Fields took us nowhere. Chasing up Derek Tyler's known associates took us nowhere. Forensics took us nowhere.' Carol crossed her legs and wrapped her arms across her chest. 'We questioned Jason Duffy, the kid she bought her drugs from. He claims he hadn't seen her for a couple of days, and there's nothing to put him with her that night. So that's another dead end. We had a make on a four-wheel drive that Sandie got into earlier in the evening, but the punter is alibied solid from nine onwards.' Carol longed to tell him that the punter in question was his new boss, Aidan Hart, the squeaky clean poster boy for psychiatric care. Given that he was one of the handful of people with full access to the details of Derek Tyler's crimes, there had been a heartstopping moment when Carol had thought she had the killer in her sights. But his alibi had checked out. While Sandie Foster had been enduring the hellish attack that had killed her, Aidan

140

Hart had been sharing a late dinner in an expensive restaurant with a senior civil servant and an MP. According to Sam Evans, who had interviewed him, Bradfield Moor's clinical director had nearly crapped himself when he'd realized the woman he'd paid for a blow job was the victim whose killer Tony Hill was profiling. But that was one confidence she knew she couldn't share.

'I'm sorry I couldn't provide much of a profile,' Tony said, breaking eerily across her thoughts.

'Not your fault. It's the nature of what you do, I know that. You need data to work with, and one case doesn't provide enough.'

Tony got to his feet and paced the room. 'No, it doesn't. It's one of the worst things about this job. The more times an offender walks out on the high wire and struts his stuff, the easier it becomes to figure out what the important elements of the crimes are. With a single episode, you can't separate the background noise from the message. But the more he does it, the more I can draw out of his actions. Which leaves me in the outcast zone – I'm the only one who benefits when he strikes again. It's no wonder some of your colleagues treat me like a leper.'

'Maybe he won't strike again,' Carol said, her voice lacking all conviction.

'Carol, he already has. Even though I profiled it as a singleton, this is really number five.'

She shook her head. 'I've been through the original case, Tony. There's no question about Derek Tyler's guilt. And there's no indication that he was working with anyone. You've told me yourself: in all the cases where killers work as a pair, there's a high level of codependency and intimacy. They're inseparable. There was nobody like that in Derek Tyler's life. Sam Evans went through it with a fine-tooth comb. Tyler grew up in care. He lived alone. He didn't have a girlfriend. Or a boyfriend, come to that. He didn't even have close friends. Which also means there's nobody out there who cares enough to replicate his crimes in a bid to get him out on appeal.'

Tony leaned against the wall. 'I hear what you're saying, Carol. And I've no comfort to offer. I don't understand what's going on here. There isn't a workable theory that doesn't fly in the face of everything I know about the psychology of sexual homicide.'

'You've not had any fresh thoughts?'

He shook his head. 'My best shot is what I said to you right at the start. Your killer gets off on the idea of rape. But he wants to take rape way beyond the act itself. He's the ultimate rapist, the bench-mark everyone who comes after him will have to measure up to. That's how he sees himself. This is about power and anger, not straightforward sexual gratification.'

Carol snorted. 'Like sexual homicide is ever straightforward.'

Tony waved his arms expansively, tipping cham-pagne down his arm. Startled, he rubbed the dribble of liquid away impatiently. 'It is straightforward, Carol. It all comes down to the acting out of fantasy. Unravel the fantasy and you've got the mainspring of the crime. Ninety-nine times out of a hundred, the fantasy is primarily about getting your rocks off. But this is about more than that. This is about the assertion of absolute power. And part of that is about manipulating us. Controlling our reactions and masterminding the whole production.' He stopped, suddenly lost in thought. Carol knew better than to interrupt, sipping her champagne while she waited him out.

'There's something that's been bothering me about this profile,' he said eventually, pushing himself off the wall and returning to his pacing. 'The typology of rape was established way back in the seventies by Nicholas Groth and, although it's been refined, it's still basically the same. Now, if Sandie Foster's attacker hadn't killed her, he'd be a classic Power Assertive type. He's a planner. He uses bondage because it increases the foolproof quality of his attack. He wants his victim submissive from the start. Rather than take a victim off the street, our guy has used a prostitute that he's paying to tie up. With this kind of rapist, there's no fondling, no kissing, no foreplay – which I'm betting was the case here. He cut away enough of her clothing to let him do what he wanted; that's his idea of foreplay. There's no sign of him taking souvenirs, though I suspect he probably videoed his actions. So far, so classic. But then he kills her. And that's totally off the scale for Power Assertive rapists. All we know about this type tells us that they only use enough force to achieve their ends. They're not sadists, by and large. That's the first problem.

'The second problem is much more significant for us.' He paused in his restless movement to top up

143

his glass. 'The Power Assertive rapist has a high ego. He's assured in his masculinity. He operates in his comfort zone and he is confident that he can con his victim into a position where he can assert his power. That's beyond probability. That's a virtual certainty.' He fixed Carol with the full force of his magnetic blue stare. 'Does that sound like Derek Tyler to you?'

Carol pushed her short blonde hair back from her forehead. 'You know it doesn't. But that's not an argument that trumps the forensics. Do you think there's any point in you having another go at Derek Tyler?'

Tony dropped back into his chair. 'I've tried. But apart from what he said the first time, he hasn't uttered a word. It's like he's learned to tune me out. If you want me to try again, I will. But don't expect anything.'

'At this point, Tony, you're all I've got.'

DC Paula McIntyre drove slowly down the unfamiliar street, looking for the Penny Whistle pub. Rows of cramped sixties houses and maisonettes huddled together, showing the unmistakable signs that came with private ownership of former council housing – ugly jerry-built porches, nasty cheap doors, incongruous diamond-paned windows. A couple of years previously, the only reason Paula would have been in Kenton would have been in response to another drive-by shooting in the drugs war that had ravaged the inner city suburb. These days, Kenton had emerged from its no-go status thanks not to proactive policing but to its location, close to Bradfield Cross hospital and to the university, which had led to its being colonized apparently overnight by young health professionals and anxious parents who wanted to make sure their privileged offspring didn't have to do anything as tasking as search for decent rental property.

Even so, it wasn't a district that Paula had had non-professional reasons for visiting. She knew a couple of women who had bought round here, but not well enough to have been to their homes. It wasn't Don Merrick's usual stamping ground either, which was why she'd been even more surprised by his choice of venue than by his phone call asking her to meet him for a drink.

Although a friendship had grown between the two that transcended rank out of working hours, they seldom made special arrangements to meet, nor did they tend towards the sharing of intimacy about their personal lives. They'd often go for a drink after work, but they both had other concerns that ate up most of their off-duty time. When he'd called to invite her for a drink, her first instinct had been to refuse. She'd been planning to join some friends in a country pub. But there had been something in Merrick's voice that had snagged her attention, so she'd agreed. Now, as she pulled up outside an ugly 1960s barn of a pub, she was regretting it.

When she opened the door, a blast of smoky air, stale beer and male sweat hit her. The only other women in the place occupied a booth on their own. They looked ground down by poverty and children in spite of their best efforts at denial. Several of the men at the bar turned to look at her, nudged in the ribs by their friends. 'Over here, darling,' one of them shouted.

'In your dreams, saddo,' Paula muttered. She spotted Merrick in a corner booth, staring gloomily into a half-drunk pint. His shoulders were slumped, his head drooped. The country music playing in the background and the electronic cacophony of the fruit machine might as well not have existed. Paula walked over to the bar, ignoring the pathetic attempts of the drinkers to catch her attention, and bought a couple of drinks.

Merrick didn't even look up when her shadow fell across the table. She placed a fresh bottle of Newcastle Brown Ale beside his glass. 'There you go,' Paula said, sliding into the booth beside him.

'Thanks,' he sighed.

Paula sipped her Smirnoff Ice, wondering what the hell was going on. 'So, here we are. What's up, Don?'

Merrick folded his arms across his chest. He looked like a man who didn't know how to begin. 'Why should something be up? Can't we just meet up for a drink on our night off?'

'Course we can. But this is far from our usual watering hole in every sense. And you're sitting there with a face like a wet weekend in Widnes. And because I'm a detective, those two facts tell me some-thing's up. You can either tell me what it is, or we can sit here in this charming hostelry like a pair of bookends. Your call.' She leaned forward, reaching for his cigarettes. The light caught her bleached blonde hair, making it luminous against the dark wood of the booth.

'Lindy's thrown me out,' he said without preamble.

Paula froze, the cigarette halfway to her mouth. *Oh shit,* she thought. *Here comes trouble.* 'What?'

'I took the kids swimming this afternoon, and when I came back, she'd packed two suitcases. Said she wanted me out.'

'Jesus, Don,' Paula protested. 'That's cold.'

'You're not kidding. I couldn't even argue, not with the kids there. She stood in the hall, telling them Daddy has to go away for a few days because of work. And that look on her face, like she was daring me to contradict her.'

Paula shook her head, trying to imagine what that must have felt like and failing. 'So what did you do?'

'I picked up my bags and walked. Got in the car and drove around for a bit. I just couldn't get my head round it, you know? I tried phoning Lindy, but she wasn't picking up. I parked up and I just wandered round the city centre. Then I called you.' He picked up his glass and drained the remaining half-pint in one.

'I'm so sorry, Don.'

'Me too, Paula.' He picked up the fresh bottle and poured it carefully into his glass, watching intently as the beer cleared and formed a head.

'Do you know what brought it on?'

He made a wordless noise in the back of his throat. 'What always brings it on for cops?'

'The job,' Paula said heavily.

'The job,' Merrick agreed. 'You know what it's been like the past few weeks. We've been working all hours, then having a pint to unwind, because you need a space. You can't go home till you've put a bit of distance between you and the day, otherwise you just trail the shit in behind you. And when you do go home, it's the cold shoulder. Either that or it's, "You're never here, you never see the kids, you've no idea what it's like trying to cope with everything, I might as well be a single parent." Ever since I got the promotion, it's been relentless.'

'Did you try talking about it?'

Merrick's mouth twisted miserably. 'I'm not good at talking about feelings, Paula. I'm a bloke. I tried to explain about how it is, how what I do matters, but she just twists it round so it sounds like I think the job's more important than her and the kids. It's been brewing a while, but this case has just been the last straw. She accuses me of preferring to spend my time talking to hookers than to her.'

Paula put a hand on his arm. 'From what you're saying, I wouldn't blame you if you did. What about relationship counselling? Have you thought about that?'

Merrick tipped his head back and stared up at the ceiling. 'Thing is, Paula, I'm not even sure I want to go back. I'm not the same man who married Lindy. I've gone in one direction and she's gone in another. We've nothing in common any more. Did you know she's gone back to college part-time? She wants to be an educational psychologist. Can you believe it? Feels like the only psychology she's learned is how to put me down.'

'So you've maybe been staying in the pub a bit longer than you would otherwise?' Paula wasn't quite sure where this was going, nor how she wanted to play it.

'Maybe. But whatever's going on between me and Lindy, I don't want to lose my kids. I love my lads, you know that.'

'I know that, Don. But leaving Lindy doesn't mean losing your kids. You can still be their dad even if you don't live with their mum. You can still take them to the footie, go swimming with them, take them on holiday even.'

Merrick snorted. 'And how easy is that in this job? How often do we knock off when we're supposed to?'

'You're an inspector now. You don't work shifts, you don't have to do the overtime like you used to. You can make a space for your boys in your life. If you want it badly enough, you'll do it.'

He gave her a pleading look. 'You think so?'

'I think so.' Paula glanced over to the bar where a bunch of men in their twenties were arguing loudly about the football. She made an instant decision she hoped she wouldn't come to regret. 'This is a dump, Don. Have you got somewhere to stay?'

He looked away. 'I thought I'd check into a hotel.'

'Don't be daft. If you and Lindy are going to split up, you're going to need all your pennies. You can have my spare room,' Paula said gruffly.

'You mean it?' He seemed genuinely surprised.

'If you don't mind sharing it with the world's biggest pile of ironing.'

The ghost of a smile spread across Merrick's face. 'Didn't you know I'm shit hot with the iron?'

'Perfect. Just don't use my razor, OK?'

*   *   *

Sam Evans cracked open the window of his car to let a trickle of smoke out. One thing about doing stake-outs in red-light districts was that nobody paid much attention to a lone man sitting in a car. Nobody except the working girls, but they'd steered clear after he flashed his warrant card at the first to approach him. He'd stressed he wasn't interested in them, and they'd left him alone.

Aidan Hart's alibi might have been enough for Carol Jordan, but when he had interviewed the psychologist, Sam Evans had sensed a man with some-thing to hide. He wondered what that something was and whether it might be turned to his advantage. If there was a way to put Aidan Hart in the frame for murder, it would be to Evans' advantage in every possible way.

So he'd taken to watching Hart whenever he got the chance. One thing soon became clear: Hart and his wife led virtually separate lives. He didn't know if that was from mutual preference, or if it had evolved because Hart only seemed to go home to sleep. His evenings were usually spent in bars and restaurants, drinking and dining with men who looked like him – prosperous, well-groomed and self-satisfied.

But there was another side to Aidan Hart's life that Evans wouldn't mind betting was unknown to his drinking buddies. On the nights when he wasn't engaged in career-building and male bonding, he picked up women for sex. The shock he'd had when Evans had confronted him obviously hadn't been enough to still his appetite. All it had done was to relocate it.

Instead of trawling in Temple Fields, Hart had gone further afield. Manningham Lane in Bradford, Whalley Range in Manchester and now Chapeltown in Leeds. From what Sam could glean, he went for women who had a place to go rather than settling for a blow job in his gleaming black 4x4. On two occasions, he'd gone back for seconds after adjourning to an Indian restaurant for a meal.

Hart's apparent addiction to hookers didn't trouble Evans on a moral level. He'd shagged a few of them himself over the years. But it did make him wonder about what was going on inside Hart's head. Certainly, it was providing Evans with ammunition that he might be able to make something of. Everybody knew that sexual murderers often used prostitutes, everybody knew that exposure to extreme behaviour desensitized people. Hart was starting to shape up nicely as a suspect, even if Carol Jordan had taken him out of the picture.

Evans was determined that his assignment to the Major Incident Team would be the next step on his upward climb. And if he had to make Carol Jordan look derelict in her duty to achieve it, well, so be it.

He was the one with the knowledge, after all. And knowledge was power.

The knock on his office door was the usual perfunctory rap of the hospital staff. 'Come in,' Tony called.

One of the nurses stuck his head round the door. 'You wanted to see a patient in here, that right? Not in an interview room?'

'That's right.'

The nurse raised his eyebrows in a sceptical expression as if to absolve himself of any responsibility for what might happen. 'I'll go and get him, then.'

While he waited, Tony wondered about the strategy he was about to pursue. Thinking outside the box was his speciality, but he didn't normally impose his wilder ideas on vulnerable people. He barely had to rehearse the arguments against it, so strong were they: it was unprofessional, it potentially put a patient in danger and it was against all the principles of treatment to ask something of a patient that had no direct relevance to his therapeutic regime. On the other side of the balance, he had constructed his own argument. The possibility of saving lives should override all other considerations. The patient wouldn't be in physical danger because this was a controlled environment. The best thing he could do for this particular patient was to raise his self-esteem, and setting him an achievable task was a good way of doing that. Of course, it was arguable whether this was an achievable task, so Tony would have to take care to make it apparent he thought it was close to impossible, that it was a last throw of the dice.

Which it was, of course.

There was no time for further speculation. The nurse pushed the door open and moved back to allow Tom Storey to enter. He took a couple of uncertain steps across the threshold, then paused. His stoop had become more pronounced, Tony noted. Storey looked around, an expression of faint puzzlement on his placid features. His grey eyes swept round shelves already crammed to bursting with books, box files and padded envelopes with torn corners. They came to rest on Tony, who had swivelled round on his chair so he had his back to the paper-strewn desk and faced out into the room. 'Come in, Tom,' Tony said, getting to his feet. 'Take a seat.' He gestured towards one of a pair of low chairs arranged in a corner.

Storey frowned. 'We don't normally meet in here,' he said uncertainly.

'No, we don't,' Tony said.

'Does that mean you've got bad news for me?'

Tony wondered fleetingly whether an operable brain tumour was good or bad news for a man in Tom Storey's position. 'I have got some news for you, it's true. But also we're here because today I need your help. Come on, sit down.' He took the older man's elbow and steered him to one of the chairs then sat opposite.

'How are you doing, Tom?' he asked.

Storey averted his eyes and stared down at the place where his hand used to be. The club of bandages had given way to a lighter dressing, making it look as if he had a particularly uninteresting sock-puppet on the end of his arm. 'You were right. They say I've got a tumour in my brain.' He rotated his head, as if trying to relieve a stiff neck. 'Funny, not so long ago that would have seemed like the worst thing in the world.'

'It's never a good thing. How would you feel if I told you that the tumour is operable?'

A faint sheen of sweat appeared on Storey's bald head. He gazed mournfully at Tony. 'This is a terrible thing to say, but I'd want them to operate. I'd want to live. I know that a lot of the time I feel like I've got nothing left to live for, but if you ask me whether I'd rather take a chance on living, I'd say yes.'

Tony couldn't help the swelling of pity for Tom Storey's ruined life. So unnecessary, so final. So much the worse because Storey was clearly an intelligent man who now had devastating insight into his condition. 'You feel guilty about that, don't you, Tom? On top of all the other stuff you have to feel guilty about, you feel guilty because you want to live.'

Eyes sparkling with tears, Storey nodded. 'I'm a coward,' he stammered. 'I . . . I can't face myself for what I sent them to.'

'You're not a coward, Tom. Dying, that would be the coward's way out. Living with yourself is what takes courage. You can't give back what you took away, but you can live what remains of your life with good intention.'

'So is it operable, then? This tumour, can they get rid of it?'

Tony nodded. 'So they tell me. Like I said before, it won't cure what's wrong inside your mind, but we can help make that easier for you. You'll have noticed a difference already with the meds we've put you on?'

Storey nodded. 'I feel a lot calmer. A lot more in control.'

That was, Tony thought, good news for his plan. 'And that should continue to improve,' he said. 'What the operation will do is to give you a future. And I think you can make use of a future, Tom. I really do.'

Storey rubbed his eyes with the back of his

remaining hand. 'They won't ever let me out of here, will they?'

'It's not impossible, Tom. A lot depends on you, and a lot depends on us.'

'So I suppose you want to write about me? Make yourself a name by treating me? Is that how you want me to help you?' There was a faint but unmistakable note of resentment in his voice.

Genuinely taken aback, Tony cursed himself for assuming he'd won a more secure place in Tom Storey's confidence than he clearly had. 'I'm sorry you think we're here to exploit your pain, Tom,' he said, trying to recover ground he hadn't even known he'd lost.

'It's how you people get on, isn't it? You put the likes of me under the microscope, then you turn us into articles and books.'

Tony shook his head. 'That's not how I operate, Tom. Yes, I do write up cases sometimes, but not out of ambition.' He spread his hands, encompassing the room. 'Does this look like the habitat of an ambitious man to you?'

Storey looked around him again, this time making his assessment more obvious. There were no degrees or diplomas on the walls, no books with his name on the cover prominently displayed, nothing that indicated Tony wanted to impress anyone with his position or achievements. 'I suppose not,' he said. 'So why do you do it if it's not to make yourself look good?'

'I do it because what I've learned from someone like you could mean my colleagues giving better treatment to the people who come to them for help.

That's certainly the only reason I can be bothered reading what other doctors have to say. If I was ever going to write about you – and at this point, that's not on my list of things to do because I don't know what the outcome's going to be for you – I'd be writing to try and raise the awareness of your condition so that the next Tom Storey gets the support he needs sooner than you did.' Tony spoke with passion and sincerity, and Storey visibly relaxed as the words sank in.

'When you say you want my help, what are you getting at?'

'I've been watching the way you interact with the other people who live here. You're very good with them. You seem to have the knack of connecting with people who don't always respond very well with the staff.'

Storey shrugged. 'I was always good with people before . . .'

'Before you got ill?'

'Before I went mad, you mean. Why don't you just say it? Nobody ever says the word in here. Nobody calls us nutters, or loonies or even patients. You all pussyfoot around, as if we don't know why we're here.'

Tony smiled, trying to defuse Storey's irritation. 'Would you prefer it if we did?'

'It would be more honest. You expect us to be honest all the time in therapy, but you dress our world up in euphemism.'

Tony sized up the moment. If he was going to rewrite the rule book, this was his opening. 'OK, I'll try to be more direct. You're good with the nutters. They trust you. They like you. They see you as one of them, so they don't feel threatened by you.'

'That's because I am one of them,' Storey said.

'But most of the time you're still the person you were before your body betrayed you. And I'm gambling that that's how you can help me.' Tony took a deep breath and leaned back in his chair. 'I have another job. When I'm not here, I help the police. I analyse the behaviour of offenders and try to give them pointers that can help them catch criminals before they commit more crimes.'

'You're a profiler, you mean? Like Cracker?'

Tony winced. 'Not much like Cracker. And even less like Jodie Foster. There's nothing very glamorous about what I do. But yes, I am a profiler. Right now, I'm working with Bradfield police. There's a killer they need to catch before he takes any more lives.'

Storey looked confused. 'What's that got to do with me?'

'A patient in here was convicted two years ago of killing four women. There was no doubt about his guilt. The forensic evidence was compelling, and he admitted what he'd done. But now another woman has died in exactly the same way. Whoever is doing it knows everything about the original crimes, including details that were never made public.'

'And you think the man in here is innocent? And you want me to help you prove it?' Storey sounded eager, his face animated.

'I don't know if he's innocent, Tom. All I know is

that he has information locked away in his head that might help us stop any more women dying. And he won't talk to me. He won't talk to anyone. He's scarcely said a word since he arrived here. What I want you to do is to persuade him to talk to me.'

Storey looked uncertain again. 'Me? You think he'll talk to me?'

'I don't know that either. But I've tried everything else I know to get him to open up, and I've failed. So I'm willing to try anything, however crazy it might seem.'

'Crazy's the word.' Storey gave a little snort of amusement. 'The lunatics have taken over the asylum.'

Tony shrugged. 'Only part of it. So, what do you think? Will you give it a try?'

Carol ran her wrists under the cold tap, trying literally to cool down after her case-review meeting with Brandon. She'd always found Brandon a reasonable boss, someone who hadn't forgotten what the job was like at the sharp end. But today she'd felt demoralized and uninspired, and she knew he'd been disappointed in her performance. She couldn't blame him: she was disappointed herself.

At least she'd managed to persuade Brandon not to pull her budget from under her feet and reduce the level of the Sandie Foster inquiry to her own small team. She could still call on other officers as and when she had something for them to do. But it was galling to feel his frustration mirroring her own and to be unable to suggest a course of action that would remedy it. She knew one of the reasons for her success as a detective was her ability to think laterally, to come up with the tangent that nobody else had considered. But on these two cases, she felt trapped in deep ruts of conventional thinking, unable to see over the rims.

And part of that reason was that another of her gifts had turned into a curse. Carol had perfect recall of speech. It made her masterly in the interview room, enabling her to trap her victims in the toils of their own words. But these days, the tape that kept looping through her brain more often than not had nothing to do with what she was working on. She was working so hard not to hear the fragments of dialogue that crept under her guard that she had no space in her mind for those promptings of her subconscious that might just take her further forward.

Carol leaned her forehead against the cool mirror and closed her eyes. What she wouldn't give for a glass of wine right now.

The door to the ladies' toilets banged open and Paula rushed in. Carol jerked erect, taking in the startled reflection of her junior in the mirror. 'Hi, Paula,' she said wearily. Paula had been even more distant than usual at that morning's briefing. Carol tried not to take it personally, working on convincing herself that Paula had been scratchy with everyone. But she hadn't managed it.

'Chief,' Paula said, hesitating on her way to the cubicle. 'How did the review go?'

Carol pulled herself together, assuming the appearance of calm authority she knew she needed with a detective she feared was already on the road to writing her off. 'As you'd expect. Nobody's very happy with such conspicuous lack of progress in two very expensive inquiries. But at least they're not scaling us back just yet.' Carol made to pass Paula and head for the door. But Paula wasn't finished with her.

'I've been looking at the Tim Golding file again,' she said, her body language already on the defensive.

'Something strike you?' Carol tried to keep her voice as neutral as possible.

'That photo, chief. I don't know much about rocks and stuff, but the background looks pretty distinctive to me. I was wondering if there was any mileage in blacking out the image of the boy and asking climbing and rambling magazines to print it, see if anybody recognizes where it was taken?'

Carol nodded. Once that would have occurred to her. Now her thought processes were blurred with too many bad memories. *And too much wine*, a small voice in the back of her head muttered. 'Good idea, Paula. Ask Stacey to work something up and we'll get the press office to send it out asap.' Carol had taken a couple of steps towards the door when something in Paula's words triggered a faint memory. She half-turned just as Paula pushed open the cubicle door. 'Paula? What do you know about forensic geology?'

Paula looked puzzled. 'Forensic geology? Never heard of it, chief.'

'I heard something on the radio a few months ago. I wasn't really paying attention, but they were definitely talking about forensic geology. I wonder if someone like that might be able to help us narrow the location down?' Carol was thinking out loud rather than talking to Paula, but she was suddenly taken aback to see the DC's face light up in appreciation. It was as if this was the moment she'd been anticipating for weeks. It should have pleased Carol that she seemed finally to be dispelling the doubt she'd felt emanating from Paula. Instead, it saddened her to think that she'd been so far removed from her former self.

'That's a brilliant idea, chief,' Paula said, giving the thumbs-up sign.

'Maybe,' Carol said. 'For all I know, these guys just do the Sherlock Holmes thing of looking at the mud on your trousers and revealing which field you got splashed in. But it's worth a try.'

She walked back to the squadroom, telling the small condemnatory voice inside her that the white wine hadn't completely done for her brain cells. 'Sam,' she called as she crossed the floor. 'Get on to the BBC website and see what you can find under forensic geology.'

Sam looked up from his desk, startled by the unfamiliar vigour in Carol's voice. 'Sorry?'

'BBC website, forensic geology. Print out what you can find then get me somebody local to talk to,' Carol said over her shoulder. 'There's probably someone at the university earth sciences department who can point you in the right direction.' She closed her door behind her, shutting out the main room behind the recently installed blinds. She dropped into her chair and put her head in her hands, feeling a slither of sweat under her fingers. Christ, but it had been a long time coming, this small and blessed inspiration. It wasn't enough to solve anything. But at least it was a start. And she had some breathing space to explore it.

He looks at the tools of what has become his trade laid out before him. The handcuffs, the ankle restraints. The leather gag. The pliable rubber dildo. The razor blades. The latex gloves. The cameras. The laptop. The mobile. All he has to do now is slip the blades into the dildo then swaddle it in kitchen roll so it doesn't take his fingers off.

He presses <play> on his minidisk player and the Voice floods over him, taking him through it one more time. He doesn't need this reminder of what has to be done; he knows it by heart. But he likes to listen. Nobody ever made him feel this good, and what he does in return seems like a very small price to pay for something so right.

The Voice tells him who to pick, makes it easy for him. There's nothing left to chance. Tonight he'll find her round the corner from the shitty hotel just off Bellwether Street where they rent rooms by the hour to women like her. She'll be leaning against the big cast-iron litter bin, like as not. She'll be amused when he tells her what he wants from her, like as not. The women don't expect anything from him except always having good gear. He's just there. Part of the landscape. Not worth paying attention to.

But she'll pay attention tonight. It'll be the last bit of attention she pays to anybody. But it will be paid to him, and that means something.

The streetlights hung like luminous boiled sweets in the thin fog of the early evening. Bradfield's rush hour had spread like a middle-aged stomach even in the few years Tony had been away. But that evening, he was oblivious to his surroundings, working his way across town from Bradfield Moor to his new home on automatic pilot. Music spilled out of the tape player; he'd no idea what it was. Something soothing, minimalist and repetitive. One of his students back at St Andrews had given him the tape. He couldn't remember why now – something about brainwave function. He liked it because it covered up the background interference, shutting out road noise, other people's engines, the low subdued roar of the city's life.

He wondered about the task he'd set Tom Storey. Was he asking too much of a profoundly damaged man? Would Storey feel so pressurized that he'd blow up again? Tony didn't think so, but he couldn't know for sure. He'd gone way outside the limits this time, and he knew how bad he'd feel if it had any adverse effect on Storey.

It dawned on him that feeling bad might be the least of his worries. Aidan Hart would go ballistic if he found out what Tony had done. It flew in the face of every therapeutic regime in the book, but in Tony's view, the book had been written by people with at least as many problems as those they professed to treat. He knew this because he was one of them. His own difficulties with personal relationships of any kind, the impotence that had dogged him for most of his adult life, his failure to turn his feelings for Carol into any functional shape; these were all measures of his closeness to the ruined personalities he tended in his clinical role.

At least he knew he could do that with some semblance of competence. His empathy with their dysfunctionality made it possible for him to tease out useful treatment programmes. If it sometimes left him feeling uncomfortably complicit, that was a bearable trade-off.

What he couldn't reconcile himself to was the guilt he felt towards Carol. Right now, the best way to help her heal seemed to be helping her to do her job. And the key to that was Derek Tyler. Which went some way to providing him with self-justification for the process he'd set in motion.

'Oh, Derek, Derek, Derek. You crave the silence because that way you can still hear the voice,' he said out loud, continuing a conversation he'd been having with himself since he'd left the hospital. 'The voice does what?' He paused, thinking and feeling, before he answered himself. 'It reassures you. It tells you that what you did was good. If you couldn't hear the voice, you might have to consider that what you did was bad. So you need to hear the voice. So you don't talk, because that way nobody talks to you. So who's the voice?'

He turned off the main drag into a side street. It was only when he couldn't find a parking space that he realized he had come home to the wrong house. He was in the street where he'd lived the last time he'd worked in Bradfield. His automatic pilot had taken him to quite the wrong part of town.

Jackie Mayall walked into the hotel lobby. It wasn't much of a reception area; it wasn't much more than a large room with an alcove cut off by a chest-high counter. It had the kind of carpet visitors knew their feet would stick to. She leaned behind the counter, stretching to reach for a key. 'It's Jackie,' she shouted over the muffled hectic sound of Sky Sport coming from a room to the left of the grimy Formica counter. 'I've taken twenty-four.'

'Right. That's ten past six,' a voice called back. 'I'm writing it down, so don't you take the piss.'

'As if,' she muttered, heading for the threadbare narrow stairs that led up to the room on the second floor that she knew too miserably well. She let herself in and tried not to notice her surroundings. It was about as unappetizing a place for sex as it was possible to imagine. It could have served as a dictionary definition of scruffy, grimy or down-at-heel. A worn blue candlewick spread covered the sagging bed. The dressing table's cheap veneer was chipped and peeling. One upright chair sat by a dirty sink.

Jackie looked at herself in the mottled mirror. About time she dyed her hair again. She didn't care about the half-inch of black showing at the roots, but she understood the virtue of window dressing. Her skimpy skirt, halter-neck top, knee-length boots were all smarter than most of the girls on the street. She reckoned that was why she could afford to charge enough to bring most of her punters here, instead of shagging in shop doorways and bobbing over blow jobs in the backs of cars. Impatiently, she turned away, tossing her bag on the bed. She sat down on the edge of the bed, wondering if she should take off her boots or whether he'd want to see that for himself. He was paying her good money, after all. He deserved the best she could do for him.

A tentative knock at the door brought her to her

feet again. She yanked the door hard, to overcome the way it always stuck. She eyed him up and down, sardonic amusement in her eyes. 'Come on then, the meter's running,' she said, turning her back on him and heading straight for the bed. 'I've got no time for men who take all night.'

As soon as Tony walked through the door, he dialled Carol's number. 'Who's the voice, Derek?' he said, absently listening to the ring tone.

'Carol Jordan,' she said abruptly.

'Who's the voice, Carol,' he demanded without preamble. 'It doesn't make sense. None of the usual voices make sense.'

'Nice to talk to you too, Tony,' she said, weary humour in her tone.

'The thing about voices, they're a bit like past-life regression.'

'I'm sorry?'

'When people do those past-life regressions, they've never been a stable boy or a mill hand. They've always been Cleopatra or Henry the Eighth or Emma Hamilton. It's the same with people who hear voices. They don't hear the milkman or the woman who sits behind them on the bus every morning. They hear the Virgin Mary or John Lennon or Jack the Ripper.'

'Well, it's hard to imagine your average milkman giving out detailed instructions about carrying out sexual homicide,' Carol said drily.

Tony paused for a moment. He grinned. 'So you think it's more likely the Virgin Mary would be behind that?' Carol giggled. Tony felt a quick flash

166

of pride. He'd done something very human. He'd made her laugh. He'd almost forgotten how much he liked the sound of her laughter, it had been so long since he'd heard it. 'But anyway,' he continued, covering up his momentary lapse from the professional, 'what I'm trying to get at is that these are grandiose voices. They live inside the head of the person hearing them and they are dynamic. What they say changes according to circumstance. You don't have to worry about silence. You don't need silence because the voice doesn't mind noise. It just makes itself heard when it wants to be, whenever it's convenient. Well, convenient for the person hearing the voice, not usually convenient for the rest of us,' he added hastily.

'And you're saying Derek Tyler's voice isn't like that?'

'That's exactly what I'm saying. It's as if he's scared of losing it. Scared that it might get swallowed up in the background noise. I've never come across anything quite like it, not in life, not in the literature. It's as if . . .' He shook his head. 'I need to go and do some more research. There must be something in the literature . . . Unless we're breaking completely new ground.' His voice tailed off.

'Tony?'

'I'll call you. I need to think about this. Thanks for listening to me.' Whatever she said in reply was lost as he hung up the phone. He'd never encountered anything like Derek Tyler's voice. If it broke all the rules, maybe it was time for him to do the same thing. Instead of working with probabilities, maybe he should start considering improbabilities. He headed upstairs to his study, muttering, 'Six impossible things before breakfast.'

DS Kevin Matthews stood behind the Woolpack Hotel reception desk, notebook in hand. There wasn't much room behind the counter, which meant he was uncomfortably close to the seedy individual who had introduced himself as Jimmy de Souza, night manager. In spite of the stench of sweat, cigarettes and stale pizza that ballooned around de Souza, Kevin preferred this view to what was upstairs in room 24. One quick look had been enough to tell him that interviewing the man who had found the body was definitely not the short straw. Much better to be down here where there was nothing more disturbing to see than a cheesy night manager and a stream of SOCOs and cops going in and out.

De Souza was stocky, with a round belly that strained his grubby white T-shirt and the waistband of his shell-suit trousers. His black hair was greased back from a sharp widow's peak, and a rosebud mouth over a plump, rounded chin gave him a look of petulance. 'Look, I told you,' he said, a faint trace of distant parts underpinning his Bradfield accent, 'I only come out if somebody rings the bell. People like their privacy. That's what they're paying for.'

'By the hour,' Kevin said, his voice acidic.

'So? It's not against the law, is it, renting rooms by the hour? People have needs.' De Souza started to pick his nose then thought better of it as he noticed Kevin's lip curl in distaste.

'So you rented out room twenty-four when exactly?'

De Souza pointed to a thick desk diary lying open on the ledge beneath the counter. 'There. Ten past six.'

Kevin glanced at it. The time and a name scrawled next to it in a clumsy hand. 'And who did you rent it out to? I'm assuming – correct me if I'm wrong – it wasn't Margaret Thatcher.'

'Slag calls herself Jackie. Skinny bit of stuff with bleach-blonde hair. She used to come in most nights a few times.'

'You don't know her surname?'

De Souza leered. 'You kidding? Who's interested?'

'Who was she with?'

'I dunno. I was in the back, watching the football. She shouted through that she was taking the key and I just wrote down the time. She'd settle up on her way out. I like to give the regulars a bit of leeway.'

'So you didn't see who was with her?' Kevin asked again.

'I don't even know if he was with her. Often the blokes hang back a few minutes, so nobody sees them. The girls just tell them what room to come to.'

'Very handy,' Kevin said bitterly. 'So what made you go up there?'

'Her time was well up, wasn't it? Normally, she's out of there in half an hour or so. Like I said, she'd settle up and I'd go and change the sheets. When the match finished at the back of eight, the key was sitting there on the hook. I was pissed off, I thought she'd done a runner on me. So I went up to see if she'd left the money in there. I went to twenty-four and let myself in . . .' For the first time, de Souza looked uncomfortable. 'Christ, I'm not going to be able to let that room out again in a hurry.'

Kevin looked at de Souza as if he'd like to hit him. 'My heart bleeds for you.' He reached over with his pen and snagged the key of room 24 off its hook. He slipped it into a paper evidence bag and tucked it away in his pocket. 'We'll need to hang on to that for the time being,' he said. 'But, like you said, you're not going to be needing it any time soon.'

His words roused de Souza's self-interest. 'How long are you lot going to be keeping us out of business?'

Kevin smiled sweetly. 'As long as it takes. This is a crime scene now, pal.'

As he spoke, the street door opened again and Carol Jordan strode in. 'Where am I going, Kevin?' she said.

'Second floor, guv. Room twenty-four. Don's up there with Jan and Paula. And the SOCOs.'

'I'm on my way.'

Tom Storey hadn't been lying when he'd said he had people skills. His work as a housing benefits officer had been fraught with the underlying threat of violence, both verbal and physical. Until his recent erratic behaviour had seen him sent home on sick leave, he'd always been known as the one the bosses could rely on to prevent an awkward client losing it in the worst way. That was why the task Tony Hill had given him seemed less a burden than a genuine challenge he thought he might be able to rise to.

Incarcerated in Bradfield Moor, burdened both with crushing guilt and the fear of the unknown invader eating away his brain, he'd tried to distract himself by watching his fellow inmates. It helped him stay in control of his mind if he had something outside himself to focus on. Of course, the ones who were allowed a certain freedom of movement were the ones who were regarded as safe in the sense that they weren't about to run amok with a sharpened fork: the obsessive compulsives who were mostly a danger to themselves; the schizophrenics meekly medicated; the manic depressives kept on a level by lithium. In a way, they were more interesting to him than the violent. Tom found it easier to understand how they'd slipped the cogs of normalcy. He didn't like to think of the personality-disordered ones; he'd seen enough sociopaths in the course of his previous professional life to last him the rest of his days.

When Tony had described Derek Tyler, Storey had known at once who he meant. He'd been aware of his silent stillness, mostly because there was so little of it around the place. Even those drugged up to their eyeballs tended towards the twitchy. But Tyler seemed to exist in a little oasis of quiet. Not that there was anything tranquil about him. He gave off an air of tension that made others wary.

He didn't join in, either. That was something else that marked him out. He displayed no interest in social activities, and his passive resistance to anything approaching communal treatment was impressive, all the more so because Storey reckoned he wasn't that bright.

All of this made him easily identifiable. But very hard to reach. This was no straightforward undertaking that Tony Hill had laid on his shoulders. Storey had spent most of the day covertly watching Tyler whenever he got the chance, trying to figure out a way to crack the carapace. Nothing suggested itself.

In the early evening, when most of those conscious and out of their rooms were watching the TV soaps, he saw Tyler sitting alone at a table in the corner of the day room. On the spur of the moment, Storey helped himself to one of the jigsaws stacked on the bookshelves and walked across to Tyler's table. He sat down without asking, struggled to open the box with one hand but managed it at last. He tipped out the pieces, finding a moment to wonder how many of the 550 would be present and correct.

No reaction. Tyler seemed to withdraw further into himself. But Storey could see his eyes drawn to the muddle of die-cut cardboard in spite of himself. Storey started sorting through the pieces awkwardly, looking for edges and sky. 'The easiest bit and then the hardest bit,' he said. 'After you get the sky done, the rest feels possible.'

Tyler said nothing. The silence endured while Storey constructed the border of the picture. It was an Alpine view, a funicular railway ascending a mountain that turned from meadow to icecap. He made a couple of deliberate mistakes, but Tyler didn't react. So he corrected himself and carried on.

'I'm feeling quite cheerful tonight,' he said, carefully not looking at anything other than the jigsaw. 'I've got to have an operation, but after that, I think

I'm going to be out of here.' He glanced up at Tyler. 'You know what I did, right?' It was a fair bet. In spite of the best efforts of the clinical staff to prevent patients gossiping about the past transgressions of others, news travelled Bradfield Moor like rats mapping their nocturnal territory. 'I killed my kids.' He couldn't help it; tears welled up in Storey's eyes and he brushed them away impatiently. 'I thought that was it. I'd never see the outside world again. To be honest, I wasn't about to argue with that. I mean, how could I be trusted? How could I trust myself? If I could take the lives of the people I loved most in the whole world, how could anybody be safe?'

Tyler showed no sign that he had heard a word. Storey persevered. It wasn't as if he had anything else to do. 'And the way the staff treat me, I can see that, behind all their professionalism, they think I'm beyond redemption. They're used to dealing with sick people. But they make me feel like I'm special, like what I've done sets me even further apart than everybody else. That's the one thing nobody ever forgives, killing your children. Or so I thought, until I met this new doctor they've got.' He smiled. 'Dr Hill. He's not like the rest of them. He's big on getting people out of here. He made me see that it's not impossible to be made better. To start again on the outside. I tell you, you want to get out of this dump, he's the one you need to see.'

Tyler reached out a tentative finger and pushed a piece towards Storey. It was the next in a sequence of jagged grey that would eventually reveal itself as a glacier, hard up against the left-hand edge. Storey

173

tried not to show his delight. 'Thanks, mate,' he said nonchalantly. He carried on in silence for a few minutes.

'I wish to Christ I'd met Dr Hill months ago,' Storey eventually said, this time speaking from the heart with genuine resentment. 'He knew right away what was wrong with me. If my GP hadn't just fobbed me off with a bottle of pills, if he'd sent me to see somebody who knew what they were doing, I wouldn't even be here now. My kids would still be alive and I wouldn't be here.'

Tyler shifted in his seat, turning away from the table. Storey sensed he had somehow lost momentum with the silent man. 'But the thing about Dr Hill . . . he's making me see that that's not the end of my life. That I can go back into the world and start again. And next time, I can do better. I can get it right, maybe. With help, I can get it right.'

Storey wasn't sure what it was that he'd said, but something had worked. Tyler moved back towards the table. He studied the pieces, then picked one up and slotted it in. His eyes met Storey's and there was a flicker of some unidentifiable emotion. Tyler nodded slowly, then got to his feet. He walked past Storey, pausing to pat his shoulder. Then he was gone, a silent shadow slipping out of the room and into the hallway.

Storey leaned back in his chair, a faintly perplexed smile on his face. He wasn't sure if his tactics had worked, but he had a feeling he might have earned himself some brownie points with the man who could set him free, both from Bradfield Moor and from the prison of his thoughts.

*   *   *

Carol had taken one look at the crime scene and called Tony. Now he stood by the bed, his head bowed, reverential. Carol could almost believe that he was blind to the tide of scarlet that had swept the dead woman's life away, so focused did he appear to be on her gagged face. She didn't have that luxury. The corpse on the bed felt like a personal affront, a calculated reminder that she and her team had failed the challenge of this killer's last outing. Intellectually, she knew it was nothing of the sort; men who did this sort of thing were far less interested in their audience than in the contents of their own sick heads. But emotionally, it felt like a slap in the face.

'There's no doubt about it, is there?' she said softly to Tony.

He looked up at her, his eyes unreadable in the weak light from the sixty-watt bulb inside its dusty paper shade. 'None whatsoever. Whoever killed Sandie killed this one too.'

Carol turned to Jan and Paula, standing on the threshold waiting for their orders. 'Do we know who she is?'

Jan nodded. 'Jackie Mayall. She's relatively new on the scene. A smackhead, but one of the more or less functioning ones.'

'Did she have a pimp?'

'Not any more. When she started, she was working for Lee Myerson. But he's doing five for dealing smack. When we lifted him, we put the word out that his team was to leave the girls alone unless they wanted a taste of the same medicine. Since we started waving the Proceeds of Crime legislation around, a lot of shitty little ponces have had to trade in their fancy motors.'

'OK. So Jackie worked solo. But she must have had mates. Jan, I want you and Paula to hit the bricks. Get out there and talk to the women. Find out who else uses this flophouse. Who was here tonight. Who saw Jackie earlier on. Whether she had any regulars. You know the drill.'

The two women were already on the move. 'Paula, where's Don?' Carol called after them.

Paula turned, her face startled. Her voice said, 'I don't know, chief,' but her expression was a wary version of *Why are you asking me?*

'He was here earlier,' Jan said. 'He told Kevin to interview the manager. He got me and Paula to check out the other rooms. Of course, nobody heard anything or saw anything, not even when we threatened to tell their wives. Then after the police surgeon did the preliminaries, I think Don went off with Sam to see what they could pick up on the street.'

Carol hid her irritation. If Don Merrick wanted to be taken seriously as a DI, he had to start behaving like one. Canvassing the streets was a job for junior officers. He should have been here co-ordinating the rest of the team, at least until she arrived, not rushing off into the night. 'I want him at the post mortem,' she said. 'Tell him to liaise with Dr Vernon's team.'

Tony had moved away from the bedside to allow the scenes of crime technicians room to practise their arcane mysteries. Carol crossed to his side, close but not quite touching. 'It looks like she's bled every drop of blood from her body,' she said. 'He's out of control.'

'It's not a lack of control. It's overkill, true, but it's

overkill in a very specific way. It's about power. The abuse of power taken to the nth degree.'

'And he's going to do it again,' she said heavily.

'No doubt about it. He enjoys it far too much to stop now. And I think he's getting more confident.'

Carol's face wrinkled in distaste. 'What do you mean?'

'Remember Vernon said Sandie must have taken at least an hour to die? And yet he set this one up in a room that rents by the hour. He was taking the chance that he would run over time. He must have felt assured enough to deal with that if he had to.'

Carol shook her head. 'That would be a hell of a risk. He'd multiply his chances of being seen, surely?'

'There's that,' Tony agreed. 'But he doesn't seem to be prone to risk-taking. Power Assertive, remember? Keep the dangers to a minimum. Maybe it's got more to do with his confidence levels. Maybe he feels assertive enough now to know that he could kill his way out of the problem.'

Carol drew her breath in sharply. 'I don't like the sound of that.'

'No. But it's something you have to consider.'

'Who am I looking for, Tony? What can you give me?'

He frowned. 'He's white, male, mid-twenties to mid-thirties. He's not good with authority – he thinks he's underestimated by the world. If he has a job, his employment record will be spotty. But I think he's more likely to be self-employed, semi-skilled. Hires himself out casually to whoever has a job for him, but he never lasts long with the same employer because he thinks he knows best. Only he doesn't. Socially he gets by. He doesn't have close male friends, but he's got a circle of acquaintances. He's very unlikely to be in a relationship with a woman.' Tony pulled a wry face. 'And he'll be impotent except when he's doing this.' He shrugged. 'Not much to go on, I'm afraid.'

'It's a start,' Carol said, knowing how often unpromising beginnings led somewhere productive with Tony. 'And God knows, right now any kind of start is something I'm not going to sniff at.'

He feels good tonight. He's kept his promise to himself. This time it worked. He was strong and he was a man. Now, sitting in the bar sipping lager, acting like it was any other night and he was having a well-deserved pint, he hugs his secret to himself, knowing the activity on the street is all down to him.

They found this one quicker, just as the Voice planned. OK, the delay in finding Sandie worked to his advantage. Time had passed and any witnesses had scattered to the four winds, leaving only the regulars who wouldn't even notice him. But it had been nerve-racking, waiting and wondering. None of that this time, though. He knew Jimmy de Souza would be up those stairs like a rat up a drain as soon as he realized the key was back on its hook and he hadn't been paid. Greedy little shit. Served him right, coming face to face with something that would put him right off his food for days. He remembers de Souza taking the piss once, years ago. It feels good to get payback. Two birds with one stone.

But it was scary, being in the hotel room with her bleeding to death. It seemed to take forever, and although that really

178

got him excited, he felt exposed there in that room in a way he wasn't with Sandie. There were other people in the building. There was greedy Jimmy to consider. But the Voice had told him what to do if he was spotted. He hadn't relished the thought of unsheathing his knife and plunging it into someone's belly. It felt out of control, not part of their carefully staged cleansing. But the Voice had explained how it might one day be necessary, and he'd told himself he was ready for it, capable of it.

He looks out of the big picture window of the bar into the street. There they are, the plod, notebooks out, taking names and addresses that'd be bullshit half the time. Asking people what they'd seen, where they'd been. Looking for alibis, looking for witnesses, looking for a killer who was under their noses. But they can't smell him. He's out of their reach, safe and sound in the pub with his pint. He smiles and remembers a tag from childhood. 'Run, run as fast as you can, you can't catch me, I'm the gingerbread man.' That's him, all right. The gingerbread man.

Jan and Paula decided to start close to the hotel. There were a couple of bars in Bellwether Street close to the narrow entry that led to the Woolpack Hotel. As they walked down the street, Jan shivered in the foggy night air and pulled on her gloves. 'It's bitter tonight,' she said. 'The girls who work out of doors won't be doing so well.'

'Bloody awful life,' Paula said with feeling, turning up her coat collar against the chill clinging hand of the mist.

'So what's it like, living with Don Merrick?' Jan said conversationally.

179

Paula flashed her a look of surprise. 'News travels fast,' she said.

'No secrets in a nick,' Jan said.

'Then you'll know I'm not living with him in the biblical sense,' Paula said sharply. 'He's sleeping in my spare room. Just till he gets himself sorted out.'

Jan laughed. 'He'll be there for a while, then. It's all right, Paula, I know you're not shacked up with Don.'

There was something in her tone that made Paula uneasy. 'Good. So you won't mind keeping everybody else straight on that one.'

'Is that what you want? You really want me to tell everybody how I can be so sure you're not sharing your bed as well as your microwave with Don?' There was a playful, teasing edge in her voice now.

Paula stopped in mid-stride. 'And what's that supposed to mean?' she asked, a hollow feeling in her stomach.

Jan wheeled round to face her, a smile turning her cherub's face into a picture of innocence. 'Rainbow Flesh, Leeds. On the dance floor. I think it was the dance mix of Beth Orton's "Central Reservation". Your partner was very cute. Mixed race. Tat of a snake on her shoulder.'

Paula tried not to show the shock that seemed physically to ripple through her muscles. 'Not me,' she said automatically, not even pausing to figure out that even by asking this, Jan was making her own confession. She started walking again. 'You obviously have more time off than I do if you're out clubbing,' she added, trying to make light of this moment when her worst fear had assumed the shape of reality. She felt sick.

'It's all right, Paula, I'm not going to tell,' Jan said, falling into step beside her. 'Think about it. I've got as much to lose as you do. We both know that, no matter what the brass say, the street cops aren't going to be our friends if we're out.'

'There's nothing to tell,' Paula said sharply. She wanted time to think about this, not fall into false comradeship with someone she didn't know well enough to trust. She headed across the street, not bothering to see if Jan was following her. 'There's a woman over there, looks like she's working. Let's go and check her out.'

Jan followed, the cherub smile still on her face.

Next morning, the fog had thickened to a dismal shroud, a pale grey tinged with sulphurous yellow. Traffic crawled through the city streets and the morning DJ on Bradfield Sound was beginning to betray his exasperation at the length of the traffic reports. Normally, it wouldn't have impinged on Tony, who would have used the time to escape inside his head. But this morning he was impatient to get to work.

He'd come home from the ugliness in room 24 of the Woolpack to a message on his answering machine from Aidan Hart. When he'd returned the call, his boss had sounded both bemused and faintly annoyed. 'Derek Tyler wants to see you,' he'd said.

'He asked?' Tony wondered what on earth Tom Storey had done to break the logjam of Tyler's silence.

'He didn't use his voice, if that's what you mean. He wrote a note, gave it to one of the nurses. "I want to see Dr Hill." That's all it said. But the nurse thought it was enough of a breakthrough to call me on my mobile,' he added petulantly.

'I'm sorry your evening's been disturbed,' Tony said, not bothering to thread regret into his voice. 'That's great news. Thanks for letting me know.'

'I've booked you an appointment with him at nine tomorrow morning,' Hart continued.

Sorry, Carol, he thought. 'That's fine. I'll be there.'

'In the interview room with the observation window,' Hart added. 'I want to see this for myself.'

Tony cursed the weather and the traffic and wished he knew the back streets of Bradfield well enough to get off the main drag and cut through the back doubles to his destination. At this rate, he was going to be late, and he had a feeling that would bring altogether too much pleasure to Aidan Hart.

Suddenly, for no apparent reason, the cars in front of him started to move at something approximating the speed limit. Tony surged forward, saying a prayer of thanks to whatever god governed Bradfield's erratic traffic flow. *Must be a malicious bastard*, he thought irreverently.

He arrived at the hospital with seven minutes to spare. Tony didn't bother going to his office; he made straight for the observation booth behind the interview room. As he turned into the corridor, he bumped into one of the orderlies. 'Sorry,' he said, stumbling slightly.

The orderly put a hand on his elbow to steady him. 'It's OK, Doc. You're here to see Tyler, right?'

'That's right. He's not changed his mind, has he?' he asked, seized by a sudden apprehension.

The orderly shrugged. 'Who knows? Tyler's not saying. Your boss had a crack at him last night and got nowhere.'

'Dr Hart spoke to him last night?'

The orderly nodded. 'Soon as he got the message, he was out here, telling Tyler that he might as well save everybody's time by talking to him instead of you.'

Politics, Tony thought bitterly. *He wants the glory of getting Tyler to talk.* He spread his hands in a gesture of innocence and opened the door of the observation room. Hart was already there, lounging in a chair, one ankle balanced on the other knee. 'Glad you could make it,' he said.

'Traffic,' Tony said. 'Fog.'

'Yes, I was glad I set off quarter of an hour earlier than usual,' Hart said smugly. 'Well, this is a bit of a turn-up for the books. I thought Tyler had put you in your place the last time you spoke. But it seems he wants to say more. How did you do it?' He straightened up and leaned forward. He really wanted to know. But now Tony knew about Hart's attempt to muscle in the night before, he was determined not to tell.

'Natural charm, Aidan. Natural charm.' Tony smiled and walked out. He was waiting in the interview room when the door opened and Derek Tyler entered. He walked with a kind of cramped stoop that made him look older than his years. The knobbly skull gleamed in the lights as he sat down opposite Tony, who gave him an encouraging look. 'Hello, Derek,' he said. 'Nice to see you again.'

Nothing. But at least this time Tyler was staring at

him, not acting as if there was nobody in the room other than himself. Tony stuck out his legs, crossed them at the ankle and put his hands behind his head. It was as open and relaxed a position as it was possible to adopt on a hard plastic chair. 'So, what did you want to talk about?'

Nothing. 'OK,' Tony said. 'I'll start. I think you're just about ready to give up. You've kept the faith. You've stayed true to the voice in your head. But now you're wondering if there was any point in that. Like I told you when we spoke before, somebody else has taken over your job. He's out there, doing what you were doing. And he's cleverer than you, because he's not been caught yet.'

Tyler blinked several times, like a matinee idol fluttering his eyelashes. His lips parted and the tip of his tongue flickered from one side to the other. But he said nothing.

'I think the voice has given up on you.'

Tyler's eyes narrowed and his thumbs rubbed against the tips of his index fingers.

'Because you can't give satisfaction any longer, can you, Derek? You can't take these bitches off the street any more.'

Tyler shook his head. He seemed frustrated. Then his mouth opened and the words spilled out, dry and cracked. 'I know what you're trying to do. You don't want to help me, you want me to help you. But you can't take the Voice away from me. It's mine. I only do what it tells me to. And until the Voice tells me I can talk to you, I can't.' He pushed his chair back and abruptly stood up. He walked to the door and knocked, a demand for release.

He didn't look back. If he had, he would have seen a slow grin spreading across Tony's face.

Carol leaned against the wall of the mortuary, watching Dr Vernon make his initial assessments of the remains of Jackie Mayall. The acrid traces of chemicals combined with the ripe aromas coming from the body to make her sinuses ache. At least, that was how she explained her headache to herself. Vernon was taking the scrapings from under the victim's fingernails when Don Merrick burst through the door, looking anxious and faintly dishevelled. 'Sorry, ma'am,' he said, his eyes hangdog. 'The traffic was a nightmare. The fog . . .'

'Same fog for all of us, Don,' Carol said.

'I know, but . . .' His voice tailed off. He couldn't explain that he'd miscalculated because he was unfamiliar with the traffic patterns where Paula lived. Not without explaining everything else.

'And last night,' Carol said, keeping her voice low so the mortuary staff wouldn't hear her giving Merrick a bollocking. 'What was that about? You were the senior officer on the scene and you left it to go and do a job that should be left to DCs and uniforms. When I arrived, Paula and Jan were standing around like a pair of spare parts, not knowing whether they were supposed to be working the streets or waiting for me.'

'I told them to interview everybody else in the hotel,' Merrick said defensively.

'Which didn't take them very long since only two other rooms were occupied, and by people who were more interested in their own activities than in anything else that was going on. Don, you're not a sergeant any more. I need to know you're on top of things when I'm not there. You can't just walk away from the scene of a murder and expect everybody else to do the right thing.'

Merrick hung his head. 'I'm sorry, ma'am. It won't happen again.'

'It better not. I've got enough on my plate without having to worry about covering your back from above and below.'

Merrick flinched at the sharpness in Carol's tone. He hoped the information he could provide might go some small way to redeeming himself in her eyes. 'At least we got an address for the victim,' he said. 'It took a while, but we tracked her down to a bedsit in Comb Moss. We got the landlord out of bed at three this morning and turned the place over.'

Carol's severe expression relaxed a little. 'So what do we know?'

'Jackie Mayall moved to Bradfield about eighteen months ago. Originally she came from Hayfield. I spoke to one of the local lads on my way in. Usual sort of story. One of four kids, parents long-term unemployed. Left school at sixteen, not much work around. She did casual shifts in one of the factories, but never managed to land a full-time job. Time-keeping wasn't her strong point, apparently. She drifted into heroin and then into prostitution to pay for the stuff. Little place like Hayfield, it was hard to avoid getting nicked, so she moved up to the big city. The landlord says he knew she was on heroin, but he wasn't bothered because she was no trouble as a tenant. I tell you, her bedsit was the cleanest, tidiest place I've ever seen a smackhead living in.' Merrick could see it now: a neatly made double bed, a couple of cheap armchairs with brightly printed throws covering their threadbare upholstery; a spotless cooking area with a combi oven scrubbed to a gleam; clothes hanging neatly on a rail; TV and video free from dust, and half a dozen chick-lit paperbacks on the mantelpiece. It had been pitiful, really. A sad simulacrum of normal life lurking behind the chipped door in one of the poorest parts of town. 'Not much of a life,' he said.

Carol sighed. 'Even so, it was still hers. And then some bastard comes along and takes it from her.' She cleared her throat and stepped forward. 'What do you think, Doc? Same killer?'

Vernon glanced up at her. 'She was killed in the same way. If anything, her injuries were more severe. I'd guess that her killer used a longer implement this time. The internal damage goes deeper. Chances are she didn't live as long as Sandie Foster. The pain must have been excruciating. She would have gone into shock fairly soon after the initial attack.'

Carol shuddered. 'What kind of person does this?'

'That's a question for Dr Hill, not for me. All I can tell you is what he does, not why he does it. Except that he's definitely getting some sort of sexual thrill from it.'

'That's hardly news,' Merrick muttered.

Vernon gave him a sharp look. 'I deal in the realms of fact, Inspector, not theory. I know he's getting some sort of sexual thrill because there are traces of semen on Jackie Mayall's stomach.'

*　　*　　*

The steam on the inside of the windows of Stan's Café always made it look as if mist was hanging along the canal in Temple Fields. DS Kevin Matthews pushed the door open and went from cold fog to warm fug. He wasn't sure it was an improvement. He took a folded A4 sheet of paper from his pocket and sat down at the first table by the door. The vacant-looking young man in a hooded top who was already seated there looked surprised, as if Kevin had broken some unwritten rule. Kevin unfolded the paper, revealing a computer printout taken from a snapshot of Jackie Mayall that Merrick had found in her flat. It showed Jackie raising a glass to the camera, her blonde hair bleached white by the flash. Merrick had tinkered with the photograph to get rid of the red-eye. Now it just looked as if her pupils were unnaturally dilated. 'Probably not so far off normal,' Sam had grunted as he'd picked up his copy and set off with Kevin to do the rounds. They'd split up, Sam taking the convenience store and the burger bar round the corner.

'All right, mate?' Kevin asked.

The young man nodded eagerly. 'Yeah. I'm all right. I'm Jason.'

And you're a few bricks short of a wall, Kevin thought, adjusting his attitude without condescending. 'Hi, Jason, I'm Kevin. I'm a policeman.'

He held out the picture of Jackie. Jason looked at it, then raised his eyes to Kevin. 'Why have you got a picture of Jackie? Is she your girlfriend? Have you lost her?'

'You knew Jackie?'

'Jackie. I know Jackie. Jackie comes in here for cups of hot chocolate.'

'I'm sorry to have to tell you that Jackie's dead. She was murdered last night.'

Jason's mouth fell open. 'No. Not Jackie, that can't be right. Jackie's a nice woman. You must have made a mistake.'

Kevin shook his head. 'No mistake, I'm afraid. I'm sorry.'

'That doesn't make sense. Jackie was nice,' Jason repeated.

'Did you ever talk to her?'

Jason looked embarrassed. 'Not really. Not talk talk. Just "Hello, how're you doing?"'

Before Kevin could ask more, a couple of youths unpeeled themselves from the fruit machine and dropped into the other two chairs at the table. 'You a cop?' one asked.

Kevin nodded. 'And you are?'

The stockier of the two youths squared his shoulders in a pathetic parody of manliness. 'I'm Tyrone Donelan.'

'And what do you do, Tyrone?' Kevin asked, trying to keep the sarcasm from his voice.

'About thirty-five to the gallon.' He guffawed at his own joke. 'I'm a mechanic,' he said. 'Anything to do with cars, I'm your man.'

Anything to do with nicking cars, Kevin thought cynically. 'And who's your mate?'

Donelan jerked his head towards the other lad. 'This is Carl. Carl Mackenzie. Say hello to the nice policeman, Carl.'

Mackenzie grunted something and looked away, tracing lines in a scatter of spilled sugar on the tabletop. 'And what do you do, Carl?' Kevin asked.

Mackenzie's mouth twitched as if he wasn't sure what was expected of him. 'Nothing much,' he said.

Kevin pushed the photograph of Jackie towards them. 'Either of you know Jackie Mayall?' Before they could answer, the door opened and Dee Smart walked in. She looked around and, seeing Kevin, crossed straight to the table and stood glaring down at him. The lads all seemed to brighten at the sight of her. 'This is Dee. This is Kevin,' Jason recited like a child who's proud of recently acquired social skills.

'I know Kevin,' Dee said sourly, fixing him with a hard stare. 'I thought you said you lot cared about us? That we weren't just throwaways?' Her voice was loud enough to attract attention from the surrounding tables.

Kevin flushed an ugly red, his freckles seeming to darken. 'You're not,' he said quietly.

'So how come there's another one of us lying in the morgue? And how come you've got nothing better to do than harass an innocent kid? Why don't you get off your arse and find out who's killing my mates?' Dee turned on her heel and teetered off to the counter.

Jason gave a pained smile while Carl tittered. 'I don't think Dee likes you, Kevin,' Tyrone jeered.

Kevin looked around at the hostile stares pointed in his direction. 'I don't think she's the only one, Tyrone.' He stood up wearily, knowing there was nothing more to be gained in the café while Dee was in this mood.

It was impossible to miss the police presence in Temple Fields that morning. Tony saw several officers he recognized as he walked through the streets and lanes.

190

The fog was slowly dissipating, leaving the odd swirling pocket that seemed to swallow people whole as they walked into it. It was hard not to feel the weather was responding to the atmosphere of foreboding in the city's dark heart.

Tony stopped outside his destination. The window was brightly lit, its contents mostly innocuous; sex, it implied, was always and only fun. He pushed open the door and walked in. He'd been in sex shops before, but not for a while. What surprised him was how matter-of-fact it all seemed. Upbeat techno music played in the background. There was nothing hidden or coy about the items on display; everything was laid out for the customers to choose from. The implied message was that whatever consenting adults wanted to do in private was fine and dandy.

He wandered round, taking it all in. There were things here whose purpose he could only guess at, which he found slightly disturbing, given his area of expertise. Tony stopped by a section of shelves dedicated to bondage restraints. Chains, cuffs, gags, nipple clamps and various arcane objects clustered together like varieties of baked beans in a supermarket. Tony picked up a set of leather ankle restraints that looked similar to those they'd found on Jackie. He looked at the price and raised his eyebrows. 'Whatever you are, you're not cheap. Power has its price and you're willing to pay.' He spoke softly, but not so softly that it didn't catch the attention of the man behind the counter. He emerged from his station and walked over to Tony.

'Can I help you, sir?' he asked.

Tony looked up, seeing a tall, lean figure wearing

a leather waistcoat over tanned and tattooed skin. The salesman had a line of twinkling diamond studs down the ridge of each ear. 'Sell a lot of these, do you?' he said.

'More than you might think. People like to spice up their love lives.' The look he gave Tony seemed to suggest he could well imagine his love life needed spicing up.

Tony fondled the cuffs absentmindedly. 'Maybe that's where I've been going wrong. What sort of people buy them?'

'All sorts.' The assistant looked wary.

Tony tried for the harmless look. 'My interest is purely professional. I'm a clinical psychologist,' he said apologetically.

The assistant rolled his eyes as if he'd heard it all before. 'Like I said, all sorts. You get your obvious S&M types, all piercings and black leather, but you get your suburban housewives too.'

'Sex. The great melting pot. Thanks. I'll take these.' He handed over the ankle cuffs and added a pair of metal handcuffs. 'All in the interests of research.' He headed towards the till, glancing back at the assistant, who was eyeing him as if he wasn't fit to be out on his own. It wasn't the first time Tony had caught such a look directed at himself. He didn't find it insulting; rather, he was impressed by their perspicacity. *Passing for human*, he thought. *Except I don't always succeed.*

He emerged a few minutes later, wondering idly if he could claim the cost back as a legitimate expense from Bradfield Police. On balance, he thought he'd prefer not to try. Carol might understand why he needed them, but he suspected some clerk in accounts would take a dimmer view. Especially once they found out, as they surely would, where Carol was living now.

He headed back towards his car. As he rounded a corner, he spotted DS Jan Shields talking to a woman in the skimpy uniform of a prostitute. The woman's body language said this wasn't a conversation she relished. Seeing him approach, Jan cut the interview short and watched the woman hurry away. As he grew closer, Jan pointed to his bag. 'Who's the lucky lady, then?'

Tony looked bemused. He looked down at the bag and saw the logo of the sex shop plastered along the side. He shrugged. 'Head games. I need to understand the killer's rules. It sometimes helps to play with the same toys.'

'You think this is a game? Women are being slaughtered like stuck pigs and you think it's a game?' Her tone was amused rather than outraged.

'He does. You have to remember that some people take their games very seriously. Life and death stuff, like Bill Shankly said.'

Jan nodded, getting it. 'And your job is to beat him at his own game?'

Tony considered her words. 'No. It's my job to figure out the rules. You're the ones who get to play out the endgame. How's it going?'

She shook her head. 'Slowly. Truth is, we need a lucky break. Someone has to have seen something. It's just a question of finding them before he does.'

Tony looked at her with surprise. It was an insight he hadn't expected. 'I think you're right,' he said slowly. 'I think he's ready for more.'

*   *   *

Oscar's, Paula thought, was one of those bars that had never been anything other than a dump. She could read the signs. Even on the day it had opened after its last makeover, it still would have looked exactly what it was – a cut-price version of anything approximating style. Everything reeked of cheapness. The lightbulbs were too low a wattage, but it was still possible to see where poorly applied varnish streaked the pine in a vain attempt to make it look like expensive hardwood. The signboards scattered round the walls screamed special offers on beer, shots and happy-hour doubles.

Paula looked around for her target. Her canvass of the streets had turned up a single nugget so far. One of the girls who worked in a sauna on the fringes of Temple Fields had told her that Jackie Mayall sometimes turned double tricks with a young hooker who worked under the street name of Honey. 'This time of day, you'll likely catch her in Oscar's. You can't miss her. She'll be the one in the red rubber dress with the Bacardi Breezer,' the girl had said, looking apprehensively over her shoulder to make sure nobody overheard her passing information to a copper.

It was a description that fitted perfectly the kid sitting at the corner table, swigging her drink straight from the bottle. Her dark hair was streaked with magenta; a shade one of Paula's friends had once characterized as 'prostitute purple', when her home dye job had gone wrong. Paula's heart contracted at Honey's obvious youth. She didn't look old enough to be served legally with what she was drinking, that was for sure. Paula went up to the bar where half a dozen early lunchtime drinkers nursed their pints morosely. She bought a mineral water and another Bacardi Breezer and walked across to the table. She placed the drinks on the table and sat down. Honey's look of surprise shifted to one of hostile suspicion. 'Cop,' she said derisively.

'Cop with a drink for you,' Paula said.

'You think I'm that fucking cheap?' Honey sneered.

Paula sighed. 'I didn't come here to pick a fight, Honey. I came here because one of your friends is dead.'

Honey gave her a look of pure hatred. 'You lot don't give a fuck about us. We're just shit on legs to you. Jackie wouldn't be dead if you useless fuckers did what you're paid for and protected us like you protect the nice people in their nice houses.'

'That's what we're trying to do. But it's not easy when all we get is silence and lies. I'm not after you, Honey. I'm trying to protect you and your colleagues. That's why I need your help.'

Honey snorted. 'Colleagues? Fuck, that's a new word for whores.'

Paula leaned forward, her face passionate, her eyes boring into Honey's. 'Can't have it both ways, Honey. Can't slag us off for dissing you then slag us off some more when we try to show a bit of respect. I don't think you're shit on legs, actually. I save that for the scumbags who use you and abuse you. And I don't think you deserve what you mostly get. The bastard who killed Jackie? I want to put him away for the rest of his natural life. So talk to me.'

Paula's intensity struck something inside Honey. She looked away and muttered, 'What do you want to know, copper?'

'The name's Paula. When did you start working with Jackie?'

'Who said I did?' It was the last defiance. Paula could see her heart wasn't in it.

'It's not exactly a state secret.'

Honey picked at the label on her drink. 'When I first went on the streets, about six months ago. She sort of took me under her wing, know what I mean? Like, I knew nothing. I just put myself out there, I was easy meat. And she kept me away from the bad shit.'

'So you hung out together on the street? What about after hours, Honey? Did she take care of you then too?'

'What are you getting at? She wasn't a fucking lezzie.'

Paula shook her head. 'That's not what I meant.'

Honey eyed her up. 'And neither am I.'

'I couldn't care less,' Paula sighed. 'Did Jackie help you get yourself sorted out?'

Honey wrapped her arms round her narrow frame, hugging herself. 'She got me a bedsit in the same house as her. She was like a big sister, that's all. We used to have a laugh, you know?'

'And when you worked together? How did that go?'

Honey gave her a sideways look, as if calculating how much she could hold back. 'You remind me of her, you know?'

As a diversionary tactic, it worked. Startled, Paula nearly knocked her drink over. 'What? I look like her?'

'A bit. But it's more – I don't know, it's like you listen, don't just treat me like a fucking kid.'

Paula wasn't quite sure if Honey was being truthful, but if she were, it might prove useful in getting the young hooker to open up. 'So tell me about working together.'

Honey pulled her packet of cigarettes towards her and lit up. 'Now and again, like, if some punter wanted to pay for a threesome, we'd take him to the hotel. You know – the Woolpack, where she . . . died.'

Paula tried to hide the excitement she felt at finally getting somewhere. 'Were any of them regulars?'

Honey grinned. It stripped her of her streetwise cynicism and made her look like the teenager she must once have been before the streets put years on her. 'Some of them came back for more, yeah. We were fucking excellent, you know?'

'Any rough stuff?'

'You can't avoid it,' said Honey, her face clouding over. 'Goes with the territory.'

'Anyone in particular?'

Honey shrugged. 'Jackie wouldn't have them back if they'd cut up rough.'

'We think the man who killed Jackie had been with her before.'

'You reckon that narrows it down?' Honey snorted. 'She was good, you know. The men who went with her, they often came back for more.'

'And one of them might have killed her. We need to try to identify them. See if any of them have a record of violence against women. Will you come back to the station and look at some photographs for me?'

'Me? Come to the nick? Are you kidding? You want me to walk out of here with you and come to the nick? You trying to fuck my life up completely? It's bad enough I'm talking to you. I walk down the street with you and I'm screwed.'

Drugs, Paula thought. *She's worried her dealer will see her with a cop and shut her off.* Thinking on her feet, she said, 'OK. You know the car park at the Campion Centre?'

Honey nodded suspiciously.

'Meet me on the top floor there in half an hour. I'll drive you to the station and take you back afterwards. Nobody will see you arrive or leave. How does that sound?'

Honey considered. 'OK,' she said reluctantly. 'But you better keep your word, Paula.' She used the name like an insult.

Paula smiled sweetly. 'I always keep my word, Honey. I'm famous for it.'

Honey gave her a look that stripped her bare. 'I bet that's not all you're famous for. Like I said, you remind me of Jackie.'

Paula blinked. It was an innuendo too far. She got to her feet and said gruffly, 'Top floor of the Campion Centre car park. Half an hour.'

She could feel Honey's eyes on her all the way to the door. It wasn't a comfortable sensation.

The only person in the squadroom when Carol got back was Stacey Chen. She glanced up from her computer screens. 'The Chief was in a while back looking for you. He said if you came in to call his office.'

'Thanks. Let him know I'm in,' Carol said. Just what she needed to take away the taste of Jackie Mayall's post mortem. 'Has Dr Hill shown up today?'

'I haven't seen him. And I've been here all morning.'

'See if you can track him down when you get a minute,' Carol said.

'I'll get right on to it. Oh, and Sam left you a note about the forensic geologist,' Stacey added.

As if she didn't have enough to do, Carol thought wearily. She closed the door behind her and settled behind her desk, raking through her top drawer till she found a bottle of Paco Rabane. She sprayed her throat and wrists, trying to rid herself of the smell she felt clinging to her. If Brandon was about to walk in, she didn't want to reek of the mortuary slab and the wine bar.

Carol reached for the note lying on her desk. In Sam's tight compact handwriting, it read:

I spoke to the Earth Sciences department at the university. They've got a guy who's done some work with the police before, but he specializes in soil samples, so he's not much good to us. But he gave me the number of Dr Jonathan France who apparently is The Man when it comes to limestone. Which is what we've got here. He's based in Sheffield, but he's going to be in Bradfield this afternoon, so I asked him to swing by around three. Do you want me to see him, or will you?

Carol thought about it for a moment. It never hurt to flatter experts with a sense of their own importance. Besides, she could use the sense of forward movement with at least one of her cases. She logged on to her computer and sent Stacey a message. 'Tell Sam I'll deal with Dr France when he comes in.'

She had barely sent the message when the door

opened and Brandon strode in without waiting for an invitation. Carol looked up in astonishment. In all the years she had worked with John Brandon, she had never seen him lose contact with good manners. His entrance told her more clearly than any words that he was under pressure from places she could only guess at. He tossed an early copy of the evening paper on her desk. SECOND CITY PROSTITUTE SLAUGHTERED, the headline blared. In smaller type it read, 'Did Police Catch Real Killer Two Years Ago?'

'He's laughing at us, Carol. Two killings in three weeks, and we're getting nowhere.'

'I wouldn't say that, exactly, sir.'

'No? You have a suspect? You have any notion of where to start looking for a suspect?' His long face was taut with frustration.

'Dr Vernon found sperm on the body of the second victim. It's heavily contaminated with her blood, but he's reasonably confident the lab can extract some DNA from it.' Carol tried to stay calm, but her heart was racing and she could feel a prickle of sweat at her neck.

Brandon made an impatient noise. 'Unless he's already in the database, that's little use until we have a serious suspect. What progress are you making on that front?'

Carol got to her feet, trying to minimize the distance between them. 'We're trying to trace as many contacts of the murdered women as we can, but it's not easy. Men don't like admitting they go to prostitutes.'

Brandon picked up the paper and waved it at her. 'We're taking a caning in the press. They're asking openly if we fitted up Derek Tyler two years ago. I've already had the TV on wanting a statement from me on the evening news. We need to make solid progress, Carol.'

'I've got Dr Hill working on a profile,' she said, desperately trying to find something to say that would give Brandon a life raft.

He shook his head. 'Not enough. We need to be proactive. I think we should smoke him out. I think we should set up a sting.'

Carol couldn't believe what she was hearing. After what John Brandon knew she'd been through, she couldn't believe he was suggesting that she would seriously consider exposing one of her officers to a risky undercover operation. She wanted to scream at him, to tell him he was no better than the men he'd claimed he wanted to rescue her from. She wanted to slap sense into him, to remind him how close she'd come to losing everything because of just such an operation. Somehow, she controlled herself and simply said, 'Surely it's too early to think along those lines?'

'Too early? He's already claimed two victims, Carol. And that's if we don't accept any connection to the four murders that Derek Tyler is inside for. We can't sit idly by and wait for him to strike again in the hope that he'll get careless and give us some hard evidence to work with.'

'We can increase security in Temple Fields, sir. More foot patrols. More CCTV.'

Brandon shook his head, exasperated. 'Carol, you know as well as I do that all that sort of policing achieves is to move the problem elsewhere. If we make Temple Fields too hot for him, he'll take his next victim from another part of town. That's why the Yorkshire Ripper started preying on so-called "innocent" victims – the police made it too hard for him to operate in the red-light districts. I'm not having that on my conscience.' He flipped open a folder he was carrying and spread out the contents. Six women looked up at Carol from enlarged snapshots that showed them looking far happier than their lifestyles had ever merited.

'There they are,' Brandon said. 'Look at the photographs. There's a definite type he goes for. The same type as Derek Tyler took.'

Carol dragged her eyes from the photographs, disturbed at the thought of lives cut short, lives she and her colleagues had failed to save. And, for a moment, transported back to a point where she wasn't sure how long she would hold on to her own life. 'I'm not disputing that. But –'

Brandon cut straight across her. 'And we have an officer who matches his type.'

Paula, Carol thought instantly. *Slim, short bleached-blonde hair, blue eyes.* 'DC McIntyre.'

'That's right. She'd be perfect.'

Carol felt her stomach turn over. The sense of déjà vu was overwhelming. 'I've experience of this sort of thing, sir,' she said as formally and as forcefully as she could manage. 'We'd be putting her at tremendous risk.'

Brandon seemed to collect himself, as if suddenly remembering who he was talking to. 'It's your very experience that makes me feel all the more confident that this will be handled properly. I think you're capable of containing that risk. And I think if we put this to DC McIntyre, she'd jump at the chance to help put this bastard behind bars.'

Just like I did. 'I'm sure she would. She's committed to the job. But I'm not sure we should be putting her on the spot like that. It's precisely because she's committed to the job that her judgement would be clouded.'

Brandon gathered the photographs together impatiently. 'What else do you suggest?'

She had nothing to suggest, and they both knew it. She stalled as best she knew how. 'We need to be sure it's a strategy that will work. I think we need to involve Dr Hill.'

'In the planning stage. Of course,' Brandon conceded.

'I think we need to talk to him before we get that far, sir. I think before we put an officer's life at risk, we need to be damn sure we're going to get the result we want.'

Empathy was always the answer, Tony believed. Every killer operated to his own interior logic. Find the logic and you could find the killer. The only problem was untangling the external symbols and translating their meanings. Everything connected back to the fantasies of the murderer, and every fantasy had its roots in a contorted vision of reality. Sometimes Tony could find his way through the maze with words; sometimes it needed something more concrete.

He had taken his purchases home, and he was working through his own version of the killer's game. He had fastened his ankles to a kitchen chair with the leather restraints, and now he had the handcuffs in his lap. He fastened one manacle round his wrist and tested its strength. 'Tie me up, tie me down. This way, you have to do what I want. Control without consent. That's what I need from you.'

He fiddled with the other manacle, putting it round his wrist without actually snapping it shut. But the ringing phone made him jump, and before he could stop himself, his fingers spasmed on the cuff, the ratchet gripping tight and locking in place. 'Shit,' he shouted as his answering machine cut in.

He heard his own voice say, 'I can't talk to you right now, leave a message after the tone.'

A long beep, then Carol's voice. 'Tony, call me as soon as you get this. I really need to speak to you. If I'm tied up, get them to interrupt me.'

He looked at the machine in wonder, then burst out laughing. 'If *you're* tied up?' He stared bleakly at the key, sitting on the table a few feet away from him. His toes barely touched the floor. He rocked the chair back and forth, trying to get some purchase on the tiled floor. After a few minutes, sweating and furious, he managed to get close enough to the table to pick up the handcuff key in his right hand. It took half a dozen attempts, but he eventually slid it into the lock. He twisted the key and felt the mechanism shift. He pulled against the cuff and miraculously, his left hand came free.

Unfortunately, so did the key. It shot across the room and clattered into the sink. A series of metallic clinks, then a hollow clank. 'Oh no,' he groaned. 'Let it not be the waste-disposal unit.'

He hastily undid the leather straps on the ankle

restraints and rushed to the sink. The key was not in sight. But the open maw of the waste-disposal unit mocked him with its greed. 'I couldn't have done that if I tried,' he muttered.

He glared at the phone. 'Women,' he said. He picked up the handset and dialled Carol's number. 'You wanted to talk?' he said when they were connected.

'Yeah. But not here.'

'Suits me. What about the gardens in Temple Fields?'

'Why there?'

'I need to go to the sex shop,' he said. 'I'll explain when I see you. Half an hour?'

After he left Carol's office, Brandon decided to pay a visit to the incident room. It never hurt to show the troops he was aware of their work. As he walked round from desk to desk, he had a word of encouragement for everyone, showing an interest in what they were pursuing. He was entirely unaware of Sam Evans' eyes on him.

When he turned to Evans' desk, the DC was making notes on his computer screen. 'How's it going, Sam?' he asked.

'Slowly, sir,' Evans said.

'What are you working on?'

Evans shifted in his seat, his expression embarrassed. 'I . . . uh . . .'

Brandon moved so he could see the screen. 'You've been mounting surveillance on Dr Aidan Hart?' He sounded startled.

Evans cleared his throat. 'Not officially, sir.'

'Explain yourself,' Brandon said, a note of severity in his tone.

'Well, we placed Dr Hart with Sandie Foster on the night she died. But he's alibied after nine o'clock, and Dr Vernon estimated the time of the attack later than that. So DCI Jordan decided he was off the hook.'

'And you disagreed?'

'It's all been on my own time, sir,' Evans said defensively. 'I just got a feel off him, like he wasn't totally kosher.'

Brandon frowned. 'And?'

'He visits prostitutes, sir. At least a couple of times a week. But not in Bradfield any more. He's hitting the other big cities.'

Part of Brandon wanted to congratulate Evans on his persistence. But he was too concerned about the implications of him having done the surveillance in contradiction of Carol's orders. What was she thinking, to let a potential suspect off the hook so easily? 'Report this to DCI Jordan at the first opportunity,' he said grimly. 'Well done, Evans. It never hurts to follow your gut instincts.' Even if it did leave Brandon with a problem.

By the time Carol arrived in the scrubby green space that passed for a city park, Tony was feeding chocolate to the pigeons and rubbing his wrist. She watched him for a moment, then walked up behind him and touched his shoulder. He jumped and swung round, startled.

'I know I'm not going to like the answer, but why did you have to go to the sex shop?' she asked, moving round to sit next to him on the bench.

He had honed his experience into an anecdote for her, and by the time he got to his return to the sex shop, she was giggling helplessly.

'So I walked in, and the bloke behind the counter gave me a funny look. Like, *I hoped I was never going to see you again*. And I could tell he really didn't believe my story. Anyway, he finally agreed to open another pack of handcuffs and set me free.' He pulled out the offending cuffs and dangled them in front of her.

'I think that's taking method profiling a little far.'

'You're not kidding. So, you wanted to talk to me.'

Suddenly sober, Carol got to her feet. 'Let's walk.'

Tony followed her down the path that led back to the street. When Carol said nothing, he filled the silence. 'Radio waves all around us. The air's full of voices we don't hear. Why does the killer hear one and not the others? What wiring in the brain makes him hear the world differently from you and me? It's like sexual predators – we see this as a place to walk, they see it as a place to steal sex. What makes the choices?'

Carol shivered. 'Right this minute, I make the choices. I choose a café – I'm freezing out here. But not in Temple Fields. The place is crawling with my officers. Come on, let's go to Starbucks in the Woolmarket.'

Ten minutes later, they were ensconced in a quiet corner of the café, exotic coffees in front of them. 'Remember when a coffee was just a coffee?' Tony said wistfully. 'I tell you, if I brought some of my patients in here, it would give them a breakdown just trying to decide what to drink.'

'Brandon wants us to smoke him out with a decoy,' Carol said abruptly.

Tony's mouth hung open. He'd known John Brandon a long time but would never have thought him capable of such insensitivity. 'He wants you to send someone undercover?' he said incredulously.

Carol took a deep breath and exhaled. 'Yes. He thinks Paula's the killer's type.'

'God spare us from the brainwaves of the bosses.'

'So you don't think it's a good idea either.' Carol's eyes held a plea for help.

'Psychologically, it might work. But we both know what a high-risk strategy it is. And we know the price of failure – you remember the fiasco of the Wimbledon Common case? That set the cause of profiling in Britain back ten years. Rachel Nickell's killer's still walking the streets. Leaving aside any personal considerations, that makes me very wary about anything that smells of entrapment.'

Carol shook her head. 'A judge wouldn't throw this out. We're not talking a systematic campaign targeted at a particular suspect.'

'So this sort of operation wouldn't count as entrapment?'

'You've been watching too many American courtroom dramas. Legally, there's no problem. It's the morality of it that bothers me. Knowing what I know, do I have the right to expose Paula like that?'

Tony's heart went out to her. He couldn't argue against her position. But he also understood the realities. 'Carol, if Brandon really wants this, he's not going to be swayed by your experience or your views. It's going to happen.'

'What if you tell him it wouldn't work?' She toyed with her mug, not meeting his eyes.

'He won't believe me,' Tony said starkly. 'You know as well as I do how dispensable the views of profilers are when it comes to disagreement on operational matters.'

Carol ran a hand through her hair. 'Shit!' she exploded. 'You'd think they'd have learned from what happened to me that you can't control the war once you take it to the enemy's territory.'

'They always think it won't happen to their operation,' Tony said. 'I don't suppose there's any chance that Paula will say no?'

'What do you think?' Carol's expression was sad, her voice resigned.

Tony reached out and took Carol's hands in his. 'Then we better make sure we don't screw up.'

Before she could respond, Carol's phone interrupted her. 'Carol Jordan,' she said impatiently.

'It's DC Chen,' Stacey said. 'Dr France is here. The geologist?'

Carol rolled her eyes. 'I'll be there in ten minutes, Stacey. Apologize for me, would you?' She jumped to her feet, coffee almost untouched. 'I've got to get back. There's a geologist from Sheffield waiting to see me.'

Tony looked bemused. 'I'll take that as part of your female mystique,' he said, following her. 'Can you take me back with you? I want to talk to Brandon about this undercover idea.'

She flashed a quick look of gratitude over her shoulder. 'Thanks. But no pity, remember?'

'No pity,' he agreed.

Whatever Carol had been expecting, it wasn't Dr Jonathan France. Tall, lean and thirty-something, he was dressed in dark blue bike leathers, the top unzipped to reveal a white T-shirt that showed off an admirable set of pecs. He lounged in the visitor's chair in Carol's office as relaxed as if he was in his own living room. He had thick, straight dark hair cut short enough to stand erect as a shoe-brush on top of his head, and his dark blue eyes were nested with laughter lines. For the first time in months, Carol reacted to an attractive man with interest rather than wariness. She was so shocked at her response she immediately retreated behind formality. 'I'm Detective Chief Inspector Jordan,' she said, extending a hand in greeting.

The hand that engulfed hers was warm and large, long blunt fingers ending in square-cut nails. 'Pleased to meet you. I'm Jonathan France,' he said. *Nice voice too*, she thought, hearing what sounded like a faint trace of West Country in his accent. He glanced around, letting her see him taking in his surroundings. 'Not quite what I expected,' he said.

'Me or the room?' Carol said. *God help me, I'm flirting*, she thought, appalled.

'Both,' he said. 'I didn't realize you would be . . .'

'A woman?' she interrupted, forcing herself to sound cold.

He smiled. 'I was going to say, so young. Isn't that a terrible cliché?'

Outflanked and disarmed, Carol took refuge behind her desk. 'I don't know how much you've been told?' she said.

'Almost nothing,' he said. 'Only that you had a photograph you wanted me to look at to see whether

I could help identify where it might have been taken.'

Carol opened the Tim Golding file and pulled out the blown-up photograph. Before she handed it over, she said, 'Have you ever worked with the police before?'

He shook his head. 'Never.'

'No problem. But I have to stress that everything we discuss is confidential. Even the fact that you are working with us. This investigation is live and we don't want to give the slightest hint to the perpetrator regarding our lines of inquiry. Whatever insight you can offer stays with us. Are you comfortable with that?'

He frowned. 'It's possible I might have to consult one of my colleagues. But I can do that without going into any detail as to why I'm asking.'

'That would be helpful. Of course, if we make an arrest and we get to court, you might well have to appear as a witness, with the attendant publicity that might bring. Are you comfortable with that?'

'Sure.' He gestured at his leathers. 'I clean up well. And I'm happy to have the chance to show the world that geology isn't boring.'

Fat chance of them thinking you're boring. 'Just for the record, can you run through your qualifications?'

'I took a first in Earth Sciences at Manchester, then spent a year doing postgrad work in the Carlsbad Caverns. I did my doctorate in Munich, then came back to teach at Sheffield, where I am a lecturer in geology. My area of specialization is calcite formations in limestone. That do you?'

Carol looked up from the notes she was taking.

211

'Sounds impressive.' She picked up the photo again. 'The boy in this picture is called Tim Golding. He was kidnapped nearly four months ago. Every possible lead we had is exhausted with the exception of this. If you can help narrow down where it might have been taken, it's possible we could make some progress in finding out what happened to him.'

He held out a hand and took the sheet of paper. He held it up at an angle to the light and studied it. 'This is a digital image, right?'

'It was sent as an email attachment.'

'And you've got the original electronic version?' He spoke absently, moving the photograph closer to his face then drawing it away.

'Yes, we do.'

He looked up and smiled. 'Good. Can you have someone send it to my mailbox? I've got some great software specially designed to enhance geological specimen photos. It should be able to give me something better to work with.'

'You think you can help us?' Carol had almost forgotten what hope felt like.

He cocked his head to one side, considering. 'It's possible,' he said at last. He straightened up in his chair. 'Yes, it's possible. Can I meet you for dinner this evening?'

Carol was surprised. 'You'll have something for us that soon?'

He laughed, a deep, warm laugh. 'Afraid not. But even Detective Chief Inspectors have to eat sometime. What do you say? Pizza, curry, Chinese? You choose.'

'Are you asking me out to dinner?' Carol couldn't keep the disbelief from her voice.

He spread his hands. 'Why not? I'm young, free and single, and if you're not, just say no.'

She couldn't have explained why, but there was something utterly unthreatening about Jonathan France. The idea of sitting opposite him in a restaurant didn't freak her out. For the first time since the rape, she could almost believe it might be possible to have something approaching a normal life. 'I don't know what time I'll be through here,' she hedged, still not quite trusting herself enough.

He fished a card from an inside pocket of his leathers. 'No problem. I've got a couple of meetings later this afternoon, then I'll just plug in my laptop and do some work till you're ready.' He placed the card on her desk. 'Text me when you're free.' He stood up, loose-limbed and unperturbed.

Carol followed him out into the squadroom. 'Thanks for your help,' she said.

'It's a pleasure.'

Stacey looked up from her computer screen. 'The Chief wants to see you in his office. Dr Hill's with him.'

Carol crashed back to earth. Paula. They had to figure out what to do about Paula. And how the hell was she going to explain Jonathan France to Tony?

Tony had marched straight into John Brandon's office, ignoring his secretary's attempts to stop him. The Chief Constable was sitting at his desk, dictating a memo into a hand-held digital recorder. He stopped, astonished, in mid-sentence. 'Tony,' he exclaimed. 'I wasn't expecting . . .'

'I know you weren't,' Tony snapped. He'd grown increasingly angry as Carol had driven him back to headquarters, though he'd made sure she didn't notice. In his professional life, he'd worked hard to keep his own responses battened down. But the more he thought about John Brandon's suggestion, the more outraged he felt. He stalked across the room and leaned on the edge of Brandon's desk, his hands fisted tightly. 'John, what the hell were you thinking, asking Carol to commit one of her officers to an undercover operation?'

Brandon stood up. 'You're well outside your remit, Tony. My operational decisions are nothing to do with you.'

'Don't hide behind protocol, John. You pay me to give you the benefit of my psychological insight. And that's what I'm doing right now. Carol Jordan was thrown to the wolves by people who have the same masters as you do. I understand you're under political pressure to solve these cases, but it was political pressure to get results that motivated the bastards who hung Carol out to dry in Berlin. Can't you see that, in her eyes, that makes you just like them? You held this job out to her as a lifeline, yet here you are, asking her to put a junior officer in the very same position that nearly destroyed her.' The words poured out of Tony in an angry torrent.

A dark blush spread up from the pristine white collar of Brandon's shirt, creeping up his neck and face. 'You're out of line, Tony.'

'I'm not. I'm telling you that you are going to do serious psychological damage to one of your best officers if you force her to run this operation.'

Brandon pounced. 'So it's not the operation you object to? Simply that I'm asking Carol to oversee it?'

Tony flung up his hands in exasperation. 'The operation's questionable. It'll only work if you sow the proper seeds in the media. But yes, my primary objection is the potential danger for DCI Jordan.'

'You think I haven't considered that?' Brandon said, his voice rising. 'Frankly, I'm already having some doubts about her self-confidence. I think it's affecting her judgement.'

Tony was shocked. 'What do you mean?'

Brandon shrugged off his question. 'Nothing I'm prepared to discuss with you. But just how good do you think it would be for her self-esteem if I put another officer in charge of it? This is her case, Tony, and she's desperate to prove she can still cut the mustard. She's the SIO on these murders. If I give the undercover to someone else, she'll think I don't trust her to do her job. And what's worse, her team will think the same. If we try this avenue of approach, Carol has to be in the driving seat. I'm not happy with that, but I don't see any alternative.'

Tony slammed his palms down on the desk. 'So hold off on it. Give them the chance to see if they can get anywhere with conventional methods. Let me try and get some more out of Derek Tyler. He's close to giving me something, I know he is.'

Brandon shook his head. 'Tyler's been silent for two years. Why should he suddenly start to talk now?'

'He spoke to me this morning,' Tony said.

Brandon's head jerked back. 'He what?'

'He spoke to me.'

'What did he say?'

Tony felt cornered. He knew Brandon would dismiss the prospect of getting information out of Tyler if he told the truth. But a lie would only cause more problems in the long run. 'He said he couldn't talk to me until the voice said he could,' he sighed.

'Well then,' Brandon said triumphantly. 'It's hardly progress, is it?'

'Of course it's progress,' Tony said, knowing from Brandon's expression and body language that he'd already lost. 'It'll take time, though.'

'We don't have that luxury. Time means more women dying. You more than anyone should know that,' Brandon said. 'So, what bait do I have to lay in the media?'

Tony rubbed his hands over his face, as if trying to erase his anger and fear and replace it with professional competence. He stared down at the floor. When he spoke, his voice was cold and distant. 'He's a Power Assertive rapist. He prides himself on his control of the scenario. He thinks he's covered all the bases. So you have to tell the press that this second murder has provided some valuable lines of inquiry. That the killer is not as careful as he thinks he is. That you believe you will be able to apprehend him before he can claim another victim. That way you prick his vanity, challenge him to prove you wrong. And then your decoy scenario might just work in the short term.' He straightened up and looked Brandon in the eye. 'And that's what you want, isn't it, John? A nice, quick, clean result.'

Brandon turned away and reached for his intercom button. 'Have DCI Jordan come up, would you?' With his back to Tony, he said, 'Yes, Tony. That's what I want. A nice, quick, clean result. And I think Carol can deliver that with an undercover operation.'

'For her sake, I hope you're right.'

Merrick walked into the squadroom, balancing a sandwich on top of his polystyrene cup of tea. Late afternoon and nothing much doing. Apart from Stacey, the room was empty. He called out a greeting, earned a grunt in reply and crossed to his desk. He was glad of the peace; he'd stuck his head round the door of the murder incident room, seen it was crowded and decided to write up his interview notes at his own desk. He sipped his tea, rubbed his eyes. He wasn't sleeping well. Nothing to do with Paula's spare bed and everything to do with the core of misery eating away at his heart. He missed his sons like a physical ache. Even though he'd often gone a few days without seeing much of them, knowing he wasn't allowed to be with them was a completely different experience.

He missed nothing about Lindy, and that was almost as disturbing. How could he not have noticed how the love between them had shrivelled and shrunk? It wasn't as if there was anyone else. He hadn't even been tempted to read between the lines of Paula's offer of somewhere to stay. Besides, there had been nothing in her behaviour to indicate that she was interested in him as anything other than a friend, even if he had been ready to consider the possibilities of solace. For now, recognizing the death of love between him and his wife had left him feeling curiously desolate.

Merrick sighed and roused his computer from its snooze mode. He'd just started typing in the mostly fruitless results of his interviews when Paula walked in. 'Hi, Stacey. Hi, Don,' she said brightly, walking over to his desk and perching on the corner of it. 'How's it going?' she asked.

He pulled a face. 'Pretty crap, really. I spent a bit of time out on the streets this morning after I'd sent the teams out. But I might as well have stayed here and read the paper for all the progress I've made. I'm just writing up what I've got, then I'm going to plough through the rest of the reports in the incident room.' He flipped through his notebook. 'Oh, I did get one laugh, though. I was talking to this young lad. Rent, you know? And he goes, "I hear the girls are refusing to play bondage games with their customers. You think maybe I should do the same?" I could hardly keep my face straight. "I don't think you're his type, son," I said.'

'At least you got a laugh,' Paula said. 'I've just spent the last hour going through the mug shots with a kid who calls herself Honey. She used to turn twosomes with Jackie sometimes. I thought she might be able to pick out some of their punters, but no joy. It's such a hidden world, Don, that's the trouble. These are lives that feed on secrecy. Jan says they're so used to turning a blind eye that in the end they just stop noticing.'

'She should know, the queen of the Vice,' Don said slightly sourly.

'You don't like her, do you?' Paula said.

'She's a smart-arse,' he said. 'And you know what they say?'

'Nobody loves a smart-arse,' they chorused.

Paula stood up. 'Better crack on,' she said. But

before she could make a move towards her own desk, the door opened and Carol walked in with Tony. When she saw Paula, she turned to share a quick look with Tony.

'Paula,' Carol said. 'Can you come through to the office? I'd like a word.'

Paula raised her eyebrows at Merrick behind Carol's retreating back then followed her and Tony into the office. Tony leaned against the wall, arms folded. Carol sat down and indicated that Paula should do the same. Paula could feel the tension in the room and wondered what was coming. She wasn't nervous; she'd done nothing to be worried about, after all. The only secret thing in her life wasn't something Carol Jordan would summon her to the office to discuss. Especially not in front of Tony Hill.

Carol fiddled with a pen, avoiding Paula's eyes. 'Paula, the Chief Constable has had an idea he wants me to put to you.'

Suddenly the tumblers clicked into place. Honey's words. Carol's unease. Tony's presence. 'You want me to go undercover on the streets. Be a decoy,' Paula blurted out.

Carol's head came up, her expression stunned. Out of the corner of her eye, Paula registered a look of faint amusement on Tony's face.

'How did you know that? Who told you?' Carol demanded.

Paula shrugged. 'Nobody told me. I worked it out for myself. One of the girls I was interviewing said I reminded her of Jackie, and I suddenly realized that, if I was on the game, I'd be his exact type. And we're not getting anywhere with the usual routines, so when you said Mr Brandon had had an idea . . . it just seemed to make sense, that's all.'

'And how do you feel about the idea?' Carol said. 'It's up to you, Paula. It's a dangerous, risky operation. You don't have to agree if you're not comfortable with it.'

Paula couldn't help herself. She was grinning broadly. 'I think it's brilliant, chief.' Her chance to shine, to show what she could do. Not even the look of concern she caught on Tony Hill's face was enough to dent her enthusiasm. 'So when do we start?'

He's watching the streets tonight. He's had a hard day; it's not easy to do what he does for a living when the place is crawling with coppers. But his customers need what he has to offer, so somehow it happens. He shifts the gear, relying on a sixth sense for avoiding trouble that's always kept him clear so far.

There's something soothing about prowling his familiar pitch, now transformed by his own actions. He'd never have believed he could change the world around him, but he has. People are moving differently. He catches the nervous glances every pedestrian throws at those they pass. They don't know if there's a killer among them, and they're scared.

He almost wishes he could stand in the middle of the street and shout, 'It's me. I'm the one you're all scared of.' Just to see the looks of disbelief. Because he knows he's not what they expect. He's not a monster. He's not even scary. He just looks ordinary.

It's what's inside that counts. And they've got no idea what's inside him. They've never heard the Voice. They're the ones that are ordinary. But him, he's become extraordinary. And this is only the beginning.

*   *   *

The low rumble of the motorbike engine cut through the quiet of the suburban street. Jonathan kept the big machine steady even at low speed. As they drew level with Tony's house, Carol unpeeled one arm from round his ribs and tapped him on the shoulder. The bike slowed to a halt and the engine died, leaving a shivering echo of itself inside her head. Carol dismounted, heart still racing, and took off the spare helmet Jonathan had given her outside the Italian restaurant where they'd eaten dinner.

Jonathan was next to her, placing his own helmet on the padded leather saddle. 'Not too terrifying, I hope,' he said.

'It's years since I've been on a bike,' she said, handing over her helmet. 'I'd forgotten how exhilarating it feels.'

Jonathan opened the topbox on the rear of the bike and stowed the spare. 'There's nothing like it,' he said. He moved closer to her. Instinctively, she put a hand against his chest, feeling the rough tweed of his jacket under her fingers. It was as if all her senses were heightened, on full alert. She could smell the tang of winter in the air, the warm masculine scent that rose from Jonathan's skin. He put his hands on her hips and she could feel a burn on her skin even through her clothes.

'Thanks for a lovely evening,' she said briskly. 'I enjoyed it.'

'Me too,' he said, leaning down for the kiss.

Carol shifted her head to one side so his lips brushed her cheek. Her pulse was hammering in her throat, her tongue dry against the roof of her mouth. The images flashing in her head were not of Jonathan

221

France, and no matter how hard she tried to tell herself this was not a threatening situation, she couldn't free herself from her history. She knew she wasn't being fair; their conversation had been flirtatious and fun, but that had been in the safe environment of a well-lit, busy restaurant. Here, now, she couldn't maintain the charade that she was like any other woman.

He sensed her tension and drew away, a puzzled look in his eyes. 'Was it something I said?' he asked, his tone light and teasing.

Carol released the breath she hadn't been conscious of holding. 'It's not you,' she mumbled, fixing her eyes on the sleeve of his jacket. She'd been surprised that he hadn't turned up in his leathers, but he'd explained that he always travelled with a change of clothes when he was working. The boy biker look had been replaced by a faintly fogeyish tweed jacket, faded jeans and a crew-neck cotton sweater.

'What's wrong, Carol?' he asked, his voice mild, entirely lacking in accusation.

'I'm sorry, I . . .' She didn't know what to say except the truth and she didn't know how to say that. His hands were still on her body and it was taking all her strength not to wriggle away from what felt like an invasion.

As if sensing her discomfort, he let her go. Her hand was still on his chest, and he gently covered her fingers with his own. 'It's all right,' he said. 'I'll go.' He stepped back, still holding her hand.

Carol closed her eyes. 'I was raped,' she said. The words hung in the air between them. His grip didn't alter. She opened her eyes, expecting to see shock, anger, pity, avidity.

But all she could read on his face was concern. Their eyes met in the silence. Then, tentatively, he said, 'Then it was pretty brave of you to come out with me tonight. Thank you for trusting me.'

She was taken aback. His reaction was unlike anything else she'd experienced. 'I don't know about brave,' she said. 'But I don't think it was very fair.'

He shook his head, the streetlights catching his hair and making it seem to sparkle. 'Don't be hard on yourself. Is this the first time you've been out with someone since it happened?'

Carol nodded. 'With someone I didn't know before? Yes.' She took a deep, shuddering breath. 'Seven months ago, and it still feels more vivid than anything I did today.'

'Then you should be proud of yourself. I'd never have guessed that there was anything preying on your mind other than work.' He smiled down at her. 'So. Probably best we call it a night.' He let her hand go and took a step back. 'Can I call you?'

'Please,' she said. On a sudden impulse, she darted forward and stretched up to kiss him. His lips were dry and cool, and he made no attempt to pull her into an embrace. They stood, slightly awkward, smiling at each other. 'Goodnight,' she said softly. She'd been lucky tonight. Lucky to have found herself with a man who didn't dismiss her as damaged goods, leap to the desire to avenge her, or recoil with ill-disguised disgust. He hadn't drowned her in pity or outrage, hadn't asked how such a thing could happen to a woman like her. A clutch of negatives that added

223

up to the first positive she'd encountered since the rape. It was, she imagined, how Tony would have reacted if he hadn't been so riven with guilt.

'Goodnight, Carol.' Jonathan reached for his helmet. 'I'll wait till you're inside,' he said, straddling the powerful machine.

She opened the gate and walked down the path, noticing for the first time that the light was on in the upstairs room that anyone else would have used as the master bedroom but which Tony had turned into a study. Her heart lurched and she hoped he hadn't seen the small drama they'd just played out.

Tony sat at his desk, eyes unfocused, turning over what he'd just witnessed. Ninety-nine times out of a hundred, he'd have missed it. Although his observational skills were the lynch-pin of what he did for a living, he didn't sit at his window spying on other people's worlds. And when he was working, engrossed in his reading, writing or analysis, it would take more than the unfamiliar note of a motorbike engine to rouse him from the focus of his concentration.

But when Jonathan France turned into his street, Tony was standing near the bay window, scanning rows of books for something he knew had to be there somewhere. That was the trouble with moving house; no matter how carefully you packed the books, they never ended up on the new shelves in quite the right place.

So when the motorbike stopped at his front gate, he was not in his customary state of oblivion towards the outside world. Curious, he glanced out of the window in time to see Carol shake her blonde hair free of the constraints of the helmet. His first instinct was to step away, to allow her privacy. But when she reached out her hand towards the tall man who had dismounted, he found he couldn't move. He told himself he was only watching to make sure she was safe. He knew that was a lie, but he didn't want to acknowledge the confused emotions tumbling beneath the surface. He watched as she avoided the first kiss, watched as the man stepped away, watched as they spoke and as Carol suddenly took the initiative.

Shamed, he made a harsh, dismissive noise and stepped back into the shadows as Carol turned towards the house. He dropped into his chair and slumped there, his face in his hands. Eventually he raised his head, blinking back tears.

Jealous. He was so jealous he could taste it like bile in his throat. He loved her; he'd known that for a long time now. But it looked as if the rift between them had grown too wide to cross. In spite of all his efforts, it appeared that Carol had chosen her own route to salvation. And it didn't include him.

The atmosphere in the incident room was heady with anticipation. A low buzz of speculation filled the air as the detectives wondered why DCI Jordan had called them together. 'I don't care what it is as long as it gets us out of talking to hookers in the rain,' Sam Evans confided in Kevin Matthews. 'It's like monkey city out there – see no evil, hear no evil, speak no evil.'

'You never know with Jordan,' Kevin said. 'If anybody's got off-the-wall tendencies, it's her.'

'But do they work?' Evans demanded. 'Her off-the-wall ideas?'

Kevin picked at a bit of dried food he'd just spotted on his trousers. 'She's got a spooky tendency to get it right,' he said. 'I've seen her float ideas that even Tony Hill thought were out of the box. And then she's turned out to be on the money.'

'Yeah, but after what happened to her . . . maybe she's lost her nerve for going out on a limb,' Evans pointed out. His late-night trawls through the desks of his fellow officers had yielded nothing from Carol Jordan. She seemed to commit very little to paper and even less to her computer. He needed to know what she was thinking if he was to achieve his goal, but it was taking a long time to get a handle on her. So far, he'd managed to avoid an opportunity to tell her about his surveillance on Hart. He was hoping Brandon would get to her first, make her feel vulnerable and put her on the back foot. But it didn't look as if that had happened yet.

'I wouldn't bank on it,' Kevin muttered as a hush fell over the room. He turned to see Carol making her way to the front through the serried ranks of officers. Don Merrick followed close on her heels. Kevin thought she was looking better than she had for weeks. Her skin had a glow to it and her eyes were bright.

Carol stopped by the murder board with its photographs of Sandie Foster and Jackie Mayall. She looked at their faces, made a silent promise to herself then turned to face the detectives. She'd been in the office since seven working on the undercover strategy, stifling her personal anxieties about the operation, and she still felt fresh and sharp. After leaving Jonathan, she'd gone straight to bed without even a nightcap. And she'd slept straight through till the alarm woke her at six. No nightmares, no restless tossing and turning. And almost no alcohol. Three glasses of wine with dinner scarcely counted, given her recent levels of consumption. She didn't think she'd climbed a mountain, but she thought she might have turned a corner, offering a new choice of direction.

'Good morning, everyone,' she said, her voice clear and brisk. 'First, I want to thank you for your hard work over the past few weeks. It's not the fault of anyone in this room that we have made so little progress. We're up against an organized and intelligent killer here, and we've had none of the breaks that open a case up. So it's time for an alternative strategy.'

There was a murmur of assent round the room. She saw nods of approval from her own team. She bit back her doubts and fears and carried on. 'It's a high-risk operation. It's going to mean a hundred per cent effort from every one of you. But I believe it can bring us results we're not going to get any other way.'

Carol opened the folder she carried and took out photographs of Derek Tyler's four victims. She pinned them up on the board behind her then swung back round to face the room. 'I know there's been a lot of speculation in the media about a connection between these two recent murders and the series of killings two years ago. At this point, there is no substantive doubt about Derek Tyler's guilt. However, one thing is clear: whoever is responsible for these murders is using Derek Tyler's crimes as a template. There's no point in wondering why. At this point, it's not going to take us any further forward. We simply have to accept that it's the case.

'What it does give us is a very clear idea of the physical type that our killer goes for. These women all have short blonde hair. They're all slim. They're all around the same height and build. These are his chosen victims.' Carol straightened her shoulders. 'With that in mind, we have decided to mount an undercover operation in an attempt to draw our killer to us.' A sudden hubbub of reaction threatened to drown out Carol's words and she raised her voice accordingly. 'The first part of that strategy came last night in the Chief Constable's press briefing. His comments were guided by advice from Dr Hill, and they were designed to goad our killer into action.'

She glanced across to Paula and nodded. Paula stood up. 'For those of you who don't know her, this is DC Paula McIntyre. She's going to act as our decoy on the streets.'

Paula grinned at the room. Carol's heart lurched. She remembered that gung-ho feeling, and where it had taken her. It was unbearable to think of someone else embarking on the same journey. But at least she could make sure Paula had blanket back-up, something she'd been forced to do without.

Sensing the excitement in the room, she immediately acted to subdue the natural thrill of anticipation provoked by the idea of something that would break the investigative logjam. 'I repeat, this is a high-risk strategy. We are going to saturate the area with undercover officers to make sure we keep Paula safe. That is our paramount consideration. If Paula is in any danger, then we abort. I want you all to be crystal clear about that.' She glanced at Paula. 'The first thing is to get Paula to look the part.'

'Hey, Paula, don't get too carried away now,' Kevin called.

'All right, Sergeant Matthews, save the adolescent humour for the little boys' room,' Carol said wearily. 'DS Shields, I want you to go with Paula over to one of the sex shops in Manchester, get her kitted out in the right sort of gear. We're not going to use anywhere local, on the off chance you might be spotted. Then we'll put Paula on the street tonight with full back-up. Don, can you run us through the technical stuff?'

Merrick stepped forward. 'Paula will be wearing a wire, naturally. We're also going to mount extra CCTV cameras at either end of the main drag in Temple Fields and at the bottom of Campion Boulevard, where they can't be easily seen. We'll have a team in the surveillance van, and there will be plainclothes units on the street. We'll stay in close radio contact. And we're trying to arrange it so that the wire feed will also be available in the cars so you will know what's going down.'

Carol spoke again. 'Like I said, the priority here is Paula's safety. I want you all to bear that in mind. She's taking all the risks. She deserves to know we're looking out for her. She deserves our best efforts. There'll be a full briefing here at six. Some of you – mostly the statement readers and the HOLMES team – will continue with what you've been doing. Others of you can take the rest of the day off. DI Merrick has your assignments.' Carol swept the room with a cool gaze. 'This could be our best chance to take this bastard off the streets before he kills again. I'm counting on you.'

She didn't wait for questions or comments. Anything she needed to hear would be relayed to her by Merrick, her eyes and ears among the thirty-odd detectives on the team. She concentrated on getting out of the room before her confident façade cracked wide open.

She'd barely made it back to the security of her own office, blinds drawn against the world, when there was a knock at her door. *If it's bloody Brandon, I'll scream.* 'Come in,' she said resignedly.

The door opened a few inches and Jonathan France's head appeared. 'Have you a minute?'

Flustered and surprised, Carol stammered, 'Yes, come in.' He slid round the door and closed it behind him. 'I didn't expect to see you so soon,' Carol gabbled. 'Have you got something for us already?'

'Not professionally,' he said. 'That'll take a little longer.' He pulled a plastic bag from his jacket pocket. Carol recognized the logo of a local independent book-shop. He held the bag out to her. 'I thought this might interest you,' he said.

Curious, Carol took it. She slipped the book from the bag. *Lucky* by Alice Sebold. She looked up, puzzled.

'It's a memoir of her own experience of rape,' Jonathan said. 'I don't mean to be presumptuous, but it struck me you might find it helpful.' He looked awkward, as if unsure of his ground. 'It's not schlocky or sensationalist or sentimental. And it's very well written.'

'You've read it?' Carol asked. It wasn't really the question she wanted to ask, but it filled the silence.

He looked faintly sheepish. 'Don't tell my rocky colleagues.' He stuck his hands in the pockets of his jeans. 'My sister is an arts bureaucrat. She's always punting stuff my way. I like things that make me think.'

Carol turned the book over and read the jacket blurb. She looked up. 'Thank you. I appreciate it.'

'You're welcome.' He backed towards the door. 'Look, I'll get off. We've both got work to do. Give me a call, yeah?'

More touched than she could express, Carol nodded. 'I'll do that.'

'I'll be in touch about the other thing – the photograph.' He gave her one last smile, then he was gone.

Carol stared at the door for a long time, trying to work out how she felt. His kindness was remarkable, not least because he delivered it with a grace that removed any sense of patronage. She'd enjoyed his company, found him attractive. But somehow, her heart remained untouched. Maybe she wasn't ready. Maybe it was still too soon.

Or maybe it was simply that he wasn't the one she wanted.

Before she could consider the matter further, another knock disturbed her. 'Come in,' she sighed.

Sam Evans stood in the doorway, his face giving nothing away. 'Can I have a word?' he said.

She gestured to the chair. 'Take a seat.'

He arranged himself in an attitude of confident relaxation. 'I thought I'd better come clean before Mr Brandon spoke to you,' he said without preamble.

Carol frowned. 'What are you talking about, Sam?'

'Aidan Hart.'

231

'Have I missed something? Only you're not making much sense.'

'I know you concluded that Aidan Hart was off the suspect list because of his alibi, but I wasn't convinced. So I've been following him.' Evans met her eyes, his mouth twisting in what might have been an apology. 'On my own time.'

'What?' Carol sounded incredulous.

'When I interviewed him, I got the feeling that there was something not quite on the square about Hart. And I was right,' he added. 'He's addicted to whores. Two or three times a week, he's buying sex from street girls.'

Carol stared at him in astonishment. She didn't know where to begin. She was furious that he'd taken matters into his own hands. But the gnawing bite of doubt had taken hold too. Had she been rash in discounting Hart? Was she losing her touch? Impatiently, she put such considerations to one side. 'And where does Mr Brandon come into this?'

Evans shrugged. 'He caught me entering the details on my computer. He wondered why I was following Dr Hart. So I had to explain.'

Carol felt a cold pit open inside her. 'You told the Chief Constable that you were pursuing a line of inquiry I had dismissed?' she said, her words clipped and tense.

He raised his eyebrows. 'I didn't put it like that. Not exactly.'

You bastard. She could barely trust herself to speak. The echo of betrayal rang in her head. 'I want a full report on your activities,' she said. 'I want it on my desk within the hour. And I don't ever want to hear

232

anything like this from you again. This is not the OK Corral. We're a team or we're nothing. You expressed no hint of your doubts about Hart to me. If you had, I might have been more reluctant to let him off the hook. I won't have this sort of underhand behaviour on my team. It undermines all of us. Consider this a warning, DC Evans. Now get out of my sight.'

He stood up and walked out, back straight, head erect. Carol saw nothing of the smile that lifted the corners of his mouth.

A watery sun had broken through the grey haze, giving a pale gleam to the streets of Temple Fields. The rest of the city was bustling, but at ten on a weekday morning, there was an air of deserted sleepiness about the district. Those who lived there had already left for work; those who worked there were mostly still trying to recover from the night before. A man in a business suit, his raincoat flapping with the speed of his passage, briskly walked a bull terrier along the canal towpath. A couple of women in jeans and leather jackets swung along the street arm in arm, cocooned in a bubble of smug self-satisfaction. And Tony Hill stood on a street corner, fumbling with the index of a Bradfield A–Z and a sheet of paper.

Should have done this before I came out, he thought as he tried to work out a logical order in which to visit the six addresses he'd jotted down when the spectre of a copycat killer had first reared its head. He flicked through the pages of the gazetteer, trying to find the locations of the crime scenes and fix them on his own mental map of the area. That way, he could start to get a feel for the killer's own view of his world. He hadn't chosen his victims at random so the chances were good that the area he'd culled from was one he knew well, one he held in his mind as a shape. Everyone had their own topography of the patch they called their own, traced by their personal routes, limited by their own needs. They could be blissfully unaware of whole chunks of territory entirely bounded by their own activities. The killer's Temple Fields would be uniquely his, and discovering what that consisted of might help Tony to understand more of who he was. Or at least who he wasn't.

He'd needed activity that morning. Although he knew Carol would be briefing her officers about the proposed undercover operation, he wasn't ready to see her yet. All night, he'd kept drifting up from sleep, the images of her and the motorbike man morphing in his mind's eye into new shapes and patterns. He despised himself for the violence of his reaction, and he didn't want that to taint his next encounter with Carol.

Eventually, he had his route clear in his mind. He set off, heading into the warren of ginnels and lanes that threaded through the hinterland of Temple Fields. He turned into an alleyway and stopped outside a doorway. He looked up at the grimy redbrick building, wondering which window had opened on to the bed where Derek Tyler's first victim had bled to death. According to the notes, Lauren McCafferty had often taken punters back to the bedsit where she lived. She'd thought it was safer than their cars; she'd thought it meant she was in control, surrounded as she was by other bedsits whose occupants might hear if things got out of hand and she had to call for help.

She hadn't bargained on an encounter with a killer who had forgotten more about control than she had ever known.

Tony stood for a few moments, letting his mind freewheel, then set off for the next place on his list. Half an hour and another four locations later, he was outside the Woolpack Hotel. 'What do they have in common, these places of yours?' he said softly. 'They're part of a network that's invisible to most of the people who visit Temple Fields to drink or find a sexual partner. But you're comfortable with them. So maybe you live or work there? Maybe you make deliveries? A courier? A postman? All the sites are near the busy streets but not on them. You like to be private, but you want your victims to be discovered before too much time has gone by. You stay with them till they're dead and then you leave, knowing they won't be alone for long. Can you not bear them to be lonely?'

He walked slowly down the alley towards Bellwether Street, thronged at this time of day with shoppers and those members of the underclass for whom the prospect of covered shopping areas was an improvement on the alternative. 'No, that's not it,' he mumbled. 'You don't care enough about them. They're not women to you, they're disposables. You want us to see your kills when they're fresh so we can admire your art. It was just bad luck that Dee had a night off and it took us so long to find Sandie.' He looked up, a radiant smile on his face. 'You're showing off, that's what it is. You can't bear to hide your light under a bushel. You're rubbing our noses in your power. You want the credit, the gratification, and you don't want to wait for it.'

Tony made his way down Bellwether Street to the Woolmarket, where he sat down on one of the benches that looked across the busy square. Unpacking the underlying message of the killer's actions was only the first step, but it was a necessary one. He had to move backwards into the unravelling before he could extrapolate how those deep motivations might shape the public behaviour of the man who was perpetrating these vicious actions. Until he could do that, he wouldn't be much use to Carol. Or to the killer's future victims. 'You've always looked for praise.' He spoke quietly, his lips hardly moving. 'But they never gave you enough of it, did they? They never valued you for what you wanted to be valued for. You wanted the power that people's admiration would bring you, and it never happened. So what do you do for a living? You'll have chosen something that offered you the prospect of lording it over the rest of us. You'd have liked the armed forces or the police or the prison service, but I'd guess you're not disciplined enough to handle that. So maybe a security guard? A nightclub bouncer? Temple Fields has plenty of those. Something where you can throw your weight around anyway.' He raised his eyes and let his gaze drift over the assortment of humanity going about its business. On the far side of the square, a woman in a dark blue uniform was tapping a stylus against a handheld computer. 'Or a traffic warden,' Tony muttered. 'They know the streets.'

He got to his feet impatiently. He didn't feel as if he was getting anywhere. For some reason, this killer's mind felt as slippery as saturated autumn leaves that would fall apart in his hands before he could examine them. He couldn't grasp those central threads that would lead him through the labyrinth. He'd never had this experience before, and he couldn't understand why it was happening now, with this case. Was it that he was too focused on his own guilt and his need to keep Carol safe? Or was there something about this killer that set him apart from the other twisted minds Tony had encountered?

He'd spent too many years working with serial offenders – rapists, killers, arsonists and paedophiles – to see them as one homogeneous group. Some were highly intelligent. Others, like Derek Tyler, seemed scarcely bright enough to have pulled off their crimes. Some had superficial social skills. Others would trip any normal person's weirdo detector at a hundred paces. Some were almost grateful to be caught, to be relieved of the burden of their compulsion. Others gloried in the celebrity a perverse media culture persisted in granting them. One thing was certain: their actions carried the unique stamp of their particular mindset, and that had always been the route Tony had been able to travel with them.

But this time, it was different. This time, it felt impossible.

Peccadilloes was tucked away on a side street in Manchester's Northern Quarter, a revamped part of the city centre where the rag trade had slowly been squeezed out by the economics of labour and replaced by craft workshops, inner city housing and boutique shopping for the hip. An uneasy mixture of redbrick streets, remodelled Victorian monoliths and modern vernacular architecture struggling to look as if it fitted in hugged the narrow pavements. Jan Shields navigated the one-way system like a native, pointing out their destination as they drove past.

'You know your way around,' Paula commented as she negotiated a tricky junction in line with Jan's instructions.

'I've been doing my Christmas shopping in the Craft Village for years,' Jan said. 'It's nice to get people something a bit individual, something they won't have seen in Bradfield. And there are a couple of decent restaurants where you can relax afterwards.' She directed Paula into a small pay-and-display car park where they found a slot.

It had been a quiet drive over the Pennines. Jan had spent most of the journey engaged in a text message conversation that seemed to afford her considerable amusement. She hadn't shared the joke with Paula. Almost the only conversation they'd had centred round whether or not Carol Jordan was up to the job. Paula had defended her boss, in spite of her own doubts. It was one thing to question Carol's judgement with Don, but Jan Shields wasn't really one of their team, so loyalty demanded that Paula support Carol to the hilt. Seeing she was getting nowhere, Jan had given up and turned to her mobile.

As they approached Peccadilloes, Jan became more animated. 'This is going to be fun,' she announced. 'Nothing like a bit of game-playing to put a spring in the step.'

'That's easy for you to say,' Paula muttered. 'You're not the one who's going to have to stand on a street corner freezing her arse off and dealing with grubby little fucked-up punters.'

Jan chuckled. 'No, I get to appreciate the view.' She pushed open the door. The interior of Peccadilloes was less glossy than its counterpart in Bradfield. The lighting was dimmer, the wares less exuberantly displayed. Behind the counter, a woman glanced up at them. She looked to be in her late thirties, multi-coloured hair gelled and twisted into curlicues and spikes. Bizarrely, she was wearing a fawn cardigan that would have looked more at home on the propri-etress of a wool shop. Paula suspected the outré hairdo was an attempt to draw attention from the strawberry birthmark that slid down one side of her face, looking as if someone had drawn a paintbrush loaded with blackberry sorbet down her cheek.

Jan glanced around, then led Paula to a rack of clothes at the rear of the shop. Jan flicked through the garments hanging on a rail and pulled out a skimpy black latex dress. 'Hey, girl, you'd knock them dead at Rainbow Flesh in this.'

'I wouldn't know,' Paula lied, trying to cling to her privacy in the teeth of Jan Shields' certainty. 'Anyway, it's not practical for tonight. I couldn't wear a wire under that.'

Jan grinned, her cherub's face looking incongru-ously wicked. 'Constable, you couldn't wear anything under that.'

She replaced the dress and raked along the rack. Her next pick was a scarlet PVC miniskirt. 'Now that is the business. Perfect for Temple Fields. You'll have Don Merrick slobbering into his tea in this.'

Paula giggled. 'That's meant to be a selling point?' But nevertheless, she took the skirt, setting it against her hips to gauge the fit.

Jan pointed to the skirt. 'You'll need to try it on,' she said. 'And you'll need a second opinion.'

Paula turned a frigid stare on the sergeant. 'I don't think that will be necessary,' she said, reacting to what felt like knee-jerk innuendo. She reached past Jan and pulled out a tight silver lurex top cut low in the neck. 'This should fit the bill.'

Jan raised her eyebrows. 'I swear you're starting to enjoy this altogether too much, DC McIntyre.'

This time, Jan's flirtatious tone made Paula feel flustered. There seemed to be a note of genuine appreciation in her voice that made Paula wonder fleetingly what it would be like to spend time with Jan outside work. 'I like to do my job properly,' she said, smacking down the idea. Relationships with colleagues were always a seriously bad idea. And besides, Jan Shields wasn't her type. Now, if Carol Jordan were to make a pass at her . . . Paula turned away, mentally rebuking herself for losing sight of why they were here.

'Of course you do. But maybe when all of this is over, you could give me a little fashion show all for myself?' Jan's voice was soft, her breath warm against Paula's neck.

'I swear, Jan, you're as bad as the guys,' she said wearily.

'Trust me, Paula, I'm better than any of them.' Jan put a hand on her shoulder, smiling when Paula flinched. 'The changing rooms are over there,' she said, pointing to a curtained-off cubicle behind the clothes rails. She stepped back, allowing Paula to pass without crowding her.

Five minutes later, Paula surveyed herself in the

changing cubicle mirror. Even without make-up and the right shoes, she knew her best friends would be hard pressed to recognize her. She barely knew herself. It was disconcerting how so superficial an alteration rendered her undeniably other. A shiver of apprehension gave her gooseflesh and she hastily stripped off and gratefully assumed her own personality along with her black jeans and white shirt. She yanked back the curtain, holding the clothes at arms' length. 'These'll do,' she said.

Jan held out a PVC bomber jacket that almost matched the skirt. 'What about this to finish it off?' she said. 'It'll be fucking freezing out there tonight.'

Paula shook her head. 'Jackie and Sandie weren't wearing jackets. I'm supposed to look as much like them as possible. But I do need some fuck-me shoes.'

'You need the jacket,' Jan insisted. 'You've got to have something to hide the wire going down your back and the bulge of the transmitter.'

'I hadn't thought of that. You're right.' Paula took her purchases to the counter and handed over her credit card. Thank goodness nobody she cared about would see the monthly statement.

'God, there's some weird stuff here,' Jan said, peering curiously into a cabinet containing bondage equipment.

'Takes all sorts,' the woman behind the counter said huffily.

Jan gave her a cool look. 'So it would seem.' She turned away. 'See you outside, Paula.'

When Paula joined her, Jan was leaning against the wall, rolling a cigarette. 'I didn't know you smoked,' Paula said.

'Only when I need to take the taste out of my mouth,' Jan said.

'I thought you were having a laugh in there.'

Jan licked the paper and efficiently finished the job. 'Did you? Whistling in the dark, Paula. That's what that was.' Her expression was unreadable, but her voice was softer than Paula had ever heard it. 'You're putting yourself on the line tonight. That's probably the scariest thing a cop can ever do.'

Paula sighed. 'Thanks, skip. And there was me trying to convince myself you lot would take care of me.'

Jan's smile looked forced. 'We will. Don't doubt it. But there are times, Paula, when it's sensible to be scared. And tonight is one of them.'

The day ticked relentlessly on. There was a ziggurat of paperwork in the incident room that Carol could have skimmed, but there were other officers to do that. Teams reading statements and reports, filling in slips for actions that needed to be pursued, detectives working their way through the actions in their in-trays, officers producing more paperwork for the statement readers to plough through. And Don Merrick to pull out the crucial stuff she needed to know about. The overwhelming volume of material in a case like this was terrifying, all the more so because it seemed to be taking them nowhere.

The undercover operation preyed on her like a fox on chickens. Every tiny intimation of what might go wrong multiplied in her mind, stirring up the silted memories of her own botched operation. Then there was Sam Evans. She couldn't figure out whether he was simply a glory-hunter or whether he was deliberately trying to undermine her. Either way, he must have planted doubts in Brandon's head at a time when she could least afford that. She didn't want him wondering if her own experience was going to affect Paula's undercover. Carol tried to force the poisonous thoughts away, but they wouldn't be ignored. Eventually, she gave in. If she couldn't evade the past, perhaps she should try confronting it. She took the book Jonathan had given her from the desk and gingerly opened it. She'd never been much of a reader outside her own very specific areas of interest, and since the rape she'd deliberately shied away from anything that smacked of self-help. But this seemed to be different. In spite of her reservations, Carol found herself drawn into a narrative that, while it had few parallels with her own experience, nevertheless seemed to speak to her at a level nothing and no one had touched before.

After forty pages, she had to put the book down. Her hands were trembling and she felt on the verge of tears. Her body craved a drink, but she was determined not to give in. For the first time in months, she understood that she had travelled so far down the route of survival that there was no longer any question but that she was going to make it. The Carol Jordan who emerged on the far side of what had happened to her would be very different, but she would be herself again. Damaged but not destroyed. Cracked but not broken. She wished Tony was there, not because she wanted to talk about it, but because she knew he would see the change in her and perhaps feel the beginnings of release.

As if in response to her wish, a knock sounded at her door. 'Come in,' she said, hastily shoving the book out of sight under some papers. But it wasn't Tony who appeared. Jonathan France was back again, clutching a folder under one arm. 'Twice in one day,' Carol said. 'People will talk.' She was idiotically pleased to see him, far more so than she expected to be.

He sat down, leaning back in the chair and stretching his long legs out. 'Much as I enjoy your company, this is a purely professional visit,' he said. 'I have some news for you.' He looked pleased with himself, a retriever carrying the soggy newspaper he knows will make somebody's day.

Carol's interest quickened. However much she might want to see Jonathan for personal reasons, that desire was always going to be trumped by her professional objectives. 'You've identified the location?'

He nodded. 'As soon as I saw the photograph, I thought I knew where it was. Not specifically, not down to pinpoint. But when I blew up the details on my computer, I realized I recognized it.' He opened the folder and drew out a couple of printed enlargements of sections of rock, passing them over to Carol.

She stared blankly at the photographs. To her, they looked like a couple of slabs of rock, grey with a faint reddish tinge, traced with what looked like dribbles and blobs of pale grey. 'What am I looking at?' she asked, almost immediately regretting the question. She knew only too well the perils of inviting experts to hold forth on their areas of specialism.

'It's called stromatactis,' Jonathan said eagerly. 'One of the persistent enigmas of the Devonian period. In lay terms, what you've got there is a flat-bottomed cavity with an irregular top filled with fibrous calcite. In geological terms, it's an autochthonous formation caused by the partial winnowing of unlithified sediment. Opinions differ as to how it was formed and what it represents. You see how it mimics the fabric of a coral reef? Some geologists say what you're looking at is the result of reef organisms, stromatoporoids, being piled up. Water filled the interstices and, under pressure, stromatactis was formed. Others believe they're essentially the fossils of soft-bodied organisms such as sponges. Yet others think they're the product of marine algae or cyanobacteria.' He grinned. 'And the creationists think they were thrown up from the deep ocean during Noah's flood.'

'All of which is fascinating, but . . .' Carol tried for an amused but quizzical expression.

'I know, I know – cut to the chase, that's what you want, right?' Jonathan said ruefully. 'OK. You get these formations in limestone. The Peak District has some remarkable examples. They tend to show up in clusters. And there are a few places in the White Peak that sad rockies like me positively salivate over. When I saw the blow-ups, I thought I could narrow it down to one place in particular. But I wanted to check it out first. So after I left here this morning, I went out there. And I was right. This is a piece of limestone reef in a spur off Chee Dale.'

Carol couldn't hide her excitement. 'You've identified it? Positively?'

Jonathan nodded. 'It's quite distinctive . . .'

Whatever he'd intended to say next was cut off by the opening of the door. Tony started speaking as he

245

walked in, initially oblivious to the fact that Carol had company. 'Carol, I think he works in Temple Fields. Maybe a security guard or a bouncer in one of the bars or clubs.'

'Tony,' Carol said, her voice a warning, her head indicating Jonathan, half-hidden behind the open door.

Tony craned his head round. His voice was friendly enough but his face seemed to lose all animation. 'Oh, sorry. I didn't realize . . . I'll come back later.'

She knew from his reaction that he'd seen something the night before. And she knew him well enough to understand he wasn't going to make allusion to it. Not here, not now. Probably not ever, knowing Tony's capacity for avoidance of the life emotional. 'It's all right,' she said. 'Come on in. This is Dr Jonathan France. He's a geologist. Jonathan, this is Dr Tony Hill.' Jonathan eased out of his chair and shook hands, towering over Tony. 'Tony's a clinical psychologist. We do a lot of work together.'

'A geologist,' Tony said, moving quickly away from Jonathan. He perched on the corner of Carol's desk. She suspected his move was completely deliberate, putting himself alongside her, demonstrating their allegiance, making Jonathan the outsider. 'It must be relaxing to work with something that moves as slowly as a tectonic plate.'

Jonathan lowered himself back into his chair. 'It gets me out of the house.'

Tony smiled. 'That's what some of my patients say about their psychiatric conditions.'

Jonathan looked faintly puzzled, as if unsure whether he was being disparaged. 'Not the agoraphobics, though,' he said.

Tony conceded the point. Before he could throw down the next verbal challenge, Carol intervened. 'Jonathan has identified the site where Tim Golding was photographed.'

Tony's professional instincts leapt to life. 'Really?' he said. 'Tell me more.'

'As I was just explaining when you came in, the geological features in the background of the picture are quite distinctive. I've visited the site on field trips more than once. It's a particularly striking example of stromatactis.'

'What kind of a place is it?' Tony asked. 'Isolated? Somewhere walkers go?'

Jonathan pulled another sheet from his folder. 'I photocopied the relevant section of the map.' He laid it on the desk and leaned forward to illustrate his comments. 'This is Chee Dale. Carved out of the limestone by the River Wye.' He traced the winding ribbon on the map. 'As you can see, there's a public footpath goes down the dale. It's a popular walk. So much so that the National Park has built stepping stones where the river breaks its banks and covers the path.' He stabbed the map with a long finger. 'And this little spur up here is called Swindale. The entrance is very narrow – it's easy to miss it. But the dale opens out once you're through that narrow neck and climbs up for about quarter of a mile. There's no footpath as such, and I'd bet that ninety-nine people out of a hundred wouldn't even notice the way in.'

'And that's where this stroma-whatsit is?' Tony asked, gazing intently at the map.

'Yes. About halfway up on the left,' Jonathan said.

'So it's pretty secluded? Not somewhere people would go for a picnic?'

Jonathan shook his head. 'Not unless you like mud and brambles and no view. That's the thing about the Peak District, there's a lot of hidden space. You get a quarter of a million people there on a Bank Holiday and still you can lose yourself.'

'So who would go there?' Carol asked.

'Geologists, professional and amateur. I did once see three guys climbing there, but it's not a great pitch, and there are a lot better rock routes nearby. But that's about it. Like I said, it's not got much to commend it in terms of scenery.'

'So whoever took Tim Golding there could be pretty sure they weren't going to be disturbed,' Tony mused. 'Which means they knew the terrain.' He glanced up. 'How near can you get a car to here?'

'There's a car park about a mile away at the old Miller's Dale station.'

'That's a tall order with an unwilling victim,' Tony said softly. 'I don't suppose there's any way of telling what time of day this picture was taken?'

Jonathan took the original print from his folder. 'That depends on the time of year. When did the boy go missing?'

'The second week of August,' Carol said without having to check.

Jonathan studied the photograph. 'That part of the dale is east-facing. It takes a while for the sun to climb high enough to clear the opposite cliff. I'd guess around nine or ten in the morning.'

Tony stood up abruptly and turned away, pressing his hands to the sides of his head as if suffering a

248

headache. 'Take a full team of SOCOs with you when you go, Carol. You're looking for a grave. Maybe even two.'

'You think Guy might be there too?'

Tony dropped his hands. 'Balance of probabilities? Yes. The overwhelming odds are that both Tim and Guy were taken by the same man. We both know that. If he's confident enough to put that picture out there, I'd say it's because he's already used that as his killing ground at least once.'

Carol caught Jonathan's dismayed expression. It was all too easy to forget how the horrors cops took in their stride could rip into the hearts of outsiders. Confronted with the uninflected reality that she and Tony had dealt with more times than they could count, the non-combatants in the war against chaos had no defences. 'It's too early to say,' she said, knowing in her heart Tony was right.

Tony whirled round, his face pale and drawn. Oblivious to Jonathan, he leaned his fists on Carol's desk and gazed into her eyes. 'He'll have got to the car park soon after first light. Tim was almost certainly lightly sedated. Enough to make him spaced out, docile, so he wouldn't put up a struggle. In that state, it will have taken a while to get him to Swindale. Then he'll have done his thing. Taken his time over it too. And taken his trophy pictures. So what does he do then? He's not going to risk walking back on a popular footpath with a messed-up kid on his hands. He's killed him, Carol. He's killed him there and disposed of the body in situ. A shallow grave under Jonathan's brambles.' He closed his eyes and muttered something she didn't catch.

'What?'

'I said, at least you can bring him home now.'

A long silence. Jonathan's face had sunk in on itself, his eyes slitted as if he was trying to block out the image Tony's words had conjured up. *Too much information for him,* Carol thought. She cleared her throat. 'We don't know that till we get there.' She pushed her chair back and stood up.

'Jonathan, there's nothing we can do today. The light is already going. But we need to get moving on your information as soon as we can. I know we're imposing a great deal on your time, but is there any possibility that you can take some of my officers to Swindale tomorrow and show them where this photograph was taken?'

His eyes widened, the implications of what he'd heard still reverberating in his head. 'I . . . I don't know,' he said.

'You wouldn't have to stick around,' Carol said gently. She moved to his side and put a hand on his shoulder. 'It would simply be a matter of leading us there, showing us the geological formation that corresponds to the picture. Then you'd be free to go. I promise you.'

'Will you be there?' His voice was neutral, but she sensed his need. It wasn't such a big thing to ask, not after what he had already done for her.

'I can't promise,' she said. 'I'm in the middle of another major inquiry. It depends on what happens tonight. If we make an arrest, I'll be needed here. But otherwise . . . yes, I'll be there. If you can be back here at eight tomorrow morning, we'll sort it out then.'

He nodded, reading the dismissal in her voice. 'Thanks, Carol.' He stood up.

'It's us who should be grateful, Jonathan. This is the first real break we've had since Tim went missing. If we do bring him home to his family, it'll be you they have to thank.' She patted his arm. 'See you tomorrow.'

Jonathan paused in the doorway and found a faint smile. 'Nice to meet you, Dr Hill.'

Tony nodded acknowledgement. As the door closed behind Jonathan, he said, 'I've lost count of the number of times I've heard that lie.'

Carol shook her head in affectionate exasperation. 'You really have to learn not to frighten the horses,' she said.

'I've always enjoyed a good stampede,' he said.

'If we find what you think we will, can you come out and take a look at the scene?' Carol asked.

'If you feel it will help.'

'Thanks.' She hesitated for a moment, wondering if and how she could raise the subject of Aidan Hart with him.

'So how are you doing?' he asked, returning to his perch on the end of Carol's desk. As he settled, he knocked into the pile of papers on her desk, revealing the Alice Sebold memoir. He frowned, picking it up. 'You reading this?' he said.

'No, I'm using it as a paperweight,' she snapped. 'What do you think?'

He raised his eyebrows. 'I think you might find it helpful.'

'You've read it?'

'Carol, I think I've read almost every serious work written about rape.' As she opened her mouth to speak he lifted a finger to stop her. 'And no, not because of you. Because of what I do.'

'So if you thought *Lucky* might be helpful, why didn't you suggest I read it?' Carol knew she sounded aggressive, but she didn't care.

'You would have listened?' Tony said mildly. 'You wouldn't have told me to butt out and let you deal with it in your own way?'

'Jonathan gave it to me,' she said baldly. 'He wasn't scared of being told to keep out.'

Tony's head moved back, as if avoiding a blow in slow motion. 'You told Jonathan.'

Straight to the wrong point, Carol thought bitterly. 'Yes, I told Jonathan.'

Tony nodded. 'Probably easier. Him being a stranger. No baggage. I'm sorry, Carol. If I'd thought you would have welcomed it, I would have suggested it. I read it wrong.' Suddenly he stood up. 'Right. Well, I'll be off.'

'You're not coming to the briefing?' He shook his head. 'And you're not going to run through the operation with Paula?'

'What would be the point?' he said. 'This isn't what I do. It's what you do.'

'You can give us insight,' Carol said.

'You've had my insight for the day. I think the killer works in Temple Fields. I think he's a security guard or a bouncer or maybe even a traffic warden. Other than that, I've got nothing to offer you right now.' He reached out and put the palm of his hand against the front of her shoulder.

She felt panic in her chest, a tight fist squeezing the air out of her lungs. 'You could help Paula.'

252

'I don't think so, Carol. You don't need me for this. This is cop business, not head business. There's nothing more convincing than experience. And nobody has more rigorous experience of undercover than you. You really don't need me.'

Paula found Don Merrick in the station canteen nursing a mug of tea. She slid into the seat opposite him, checking out his glum expression. 'You look like you could give Eeyore a run for his money,' she said.

'I got a letter delivered here from Lindy's solicitor. She wants a divorce.'

'Christ, she's not wasting any time, is she?'

Merrick sighed. 'She's right though, isn't she? We both know in our hearts that it's over. It's supposed to be blokes that are the tough ones, but when it comes to severing the ties and moving on, you women are bloody ruthless.'

'Not all of us,' Paula said, thinking back over her own calamitous past. Two relationships in the past six years, both of which she'd hung on to long past the sell-by date. They reminded her of a poem she'd once read about love being a kite you couldn't let go of till somebody gave you something better to do. Although she didn't like to see the effect Lindy's hard-headedness had on Merrick, she envied his wife her ability to cut herself free so readily.

But Merrick was too wrapped up in his own miseries to register Paula's regretful tone. 'At least if we get things formalized, I'll know where I am when it comes to seeing the lads,' he said. 'If I ever get any time off in this lifetime.'

'If we get lucky tonight, we'll be able to ease up a

253

bit,' Paula said, trying not to think what getting lucky would mean for her.

That got through. Merrick looked up, his mournful eyes showing a spark of interest. 'You all right about tonight?' he asked.

Paula twirled a short strand of hair round her finger. 'I'm a bit nervous,' she admitted.

'Nothing bad's going to happen to you,' Merrick reassured her.

'What? Like nothing bad happened to you when you were chasing the Queer Killer?' Paula said sarcastically. She'd only been a CID aide on the fringes of the investigation, but she vividly remembered the turban of bandages that had swathed Merrick's head after his own undercover operation had gone out of control.

Merrick looked embarrassed. 'That was my own fault,' he said. 'I put myself in harm's way. I thought I could handle the situation and I was wrong. So learn from my mistakes: don't take risks, don't leave anything to chance. If in doubt, abort. It's better we lose a chance at the killer than anything happens to you.'

Slightly uncomfortable in the face of his earnest concern, Paula said, 'I'm not really worried about something happening to me. I feel confident in the back-up. Face it, after what Jordan went through, she's not going to leave my back uncovered. If anything, she's going to go for overkill and scare him off.'

'So what is it that's eating you? Because I can see something's bothering you.'

'This is going to sound daft,' Paula said. 'But I don't

254

know if I can carry it off. I don't know if I can play the part. I don't think I've got the right kind of imagination.'

Merrick frowned. 'I'm not sure I understand you.'

'I'm a cop through and through, Don. I see the world in black and white. I don't get that empathy shit that Tony Hill's always banging on about. I don't catch villains by thinking the way they do. I catch them because they're stupid and I'm smart. Because I'm on the right side of the law and they're not. So how does somebody like me stand on a street corner and make some fucking psychopath believe I'm a hooker?' Paula said savagely.

Merrick struggled for an answer. 'Well, you've got the gear, right?'

'Yes, I've got the gear,' she said wearily. 'Shields knows all about picking the right trashy clothes. But I feel like a kid playing make-believe. You know how sometimes you dress up to go out, and you put something on that's a bit out of the usual run of what you wear and you think, "Yeah, wow, that's who I can be tonight"?'

Merrick looked at her as if she was talking Greek. 'I can't say I do.'

'Trust me, it goes that way. But when I put that stuff on, all I think is, "I so don't want to be this person." I'm not scared you guys are going to let me down. I'm scared I'm going to let you down.'

Carol tracked down John Brandon to the press briefing room, deep in discussion with one of the liaison staff. He looked up when she entered, and gave her a nod of acknowledgement. 'Carol, we're just talking about Tim Golding and Guy Lefevre. Shaheed's had one of the Sunday broadsheets on. They're apparently planning to revisit the cases this weekend.' He sighed. 'The way they go on, you'd think we'd been sitting on our hands for the past four months.'

Carol forced a smile. 'I might just have some news for you on that score, sir.' Briefly, she outlined the information Jonathan had given them.

Brandon's lugubrious face lit up. 'But that's excellent news, Carol. Whose idea was it to bring this geologist on board?'

'Mine, sir.' She was damned if she was going to refuse credit for the one good thing she'd achieved in a while.

'Good. Well done. Make sure you keep me posted on developments. And Shaheed too.' He stood up.

'If I might have a word, sir?' Carol said, drawing him to one side.

Brandon raised an eyebrow. 'Fire away.'

'I understand DC Evans told you he was following an unauthorized line of inquiry relating to Dr Aidan Hart?'

Brandon squared his shoulders. 'He did. And I'm bound to say I was most surprised that you had closed down that particular avenue. It's not as if you're awash with suspects on these prostitute murders. I know that Hart works with Tony, but . . .'

'That had nothing to do with my decision, sir,' Carol interrupted. 'I eliminated Dr Hart on the basis that he has an alibi for the time when the medical evidence says Sandie Foster was killed.'

Brandon shook his head. 'Not good enough, Carol.

We all know time of death is far from an accurate measurement.'

'Nevertheless, the timings don't stack up. He picked her up at half past eight. It would have taken a few minutes to get to her room. Then he's got to tie her up and brutalize her repeatedly. Then somehow he's got to drive across town, find a parking space and get to the restaurant by nine without a trace of blood on him. It's just not possible, sir, whatever bee Sam Evans has in his bonnet.'

Brandon scowled. 'In that case, DCI Jordan, you need to keep a tighter rein on your officers. Now, I'm sure you have work to do in preparation for this evening.' He walked past her and out the door, leaving Carol smarting at the injustice of his final remarks. Had she been wrong about Brandon? When the pressure for results was at its height, was he so very different from the others who had let her down before? One thing was certain: when all of this was over, there would be some adjustments in the Major Incident Team. But for now, she had to swallow her pride and get back to work.

Carol understood the disappointment she could read all over the faces of Kevin Matthews and Sam Evans. Tonight would be the first sniff of real frontline action they'd had since their supposedly elite squad had been inaugurated and she was pulling them off it for the sake of a good night's sleep. But if Tony was right about what lurked in Swindale, she wanted officers in charge who were alert to every possibility. She didn't want vital evidence slipping through their fingers either because the lead officers were dizzy and disorientated with tiredness or, conversely, high as kites because they'd got a result in another case.

She knew that when she'd called them in they'd been expecting some special assignment on the under-cover duty. They'd both demonstrated all the eager-ness and anticipation of lads let off the leash for a Saturday night on the town. She'd tried to let them down easy, but there was no way to sugar the pill. They wanted to be out there, standing shoulder to shoulder with their team mates, not tucked up in bed in preparation for the morrow's work, no matter how crucial that might turn out to be. No matter that they were all desperate to find out what had happened to Tim Golding and Guy Lefevre; when push came to shove, cops always wanted to be where the action was. And tonight, the action would be in Temple Fields.

'I thought we needed every body we could muster on the ground for this op,' Evans had protested even before she'd had the chance to brief them thoroughly.

'I'm not doubting your willingness, Sam,' she said, trying not to let her personal animus colour her response to what was close to insubordination. 'But I make the decisions about priorities round here. And as far as I'm concerned, finding out what happened to Tim Golding is every bit as high a priority as catching the person who killed Sandie Foster and Jackie Mayall before he can claim any more victims.'

'Even if it means putting an officer at greater risk?' Evans' betrayal of her to Brandon seemed to have given him a taste for undermining her. She had to end it here and now before it caused problems with the others.

'Believe me, Detective Constable, your absence will not be increasing the risk to DC McIntyre one jot. You are not so special that you can't be replaced. Tonight's team is at full strength. What I need is to have confidence that tomorrow morning's operation will be as thoroughly covered.' Carol's voice was sharp and cold as an icicle. Evans studied his shoes and mumbled something she was prepared to consider an apology.

'What's the drill tomorrow, guv?' Kevin asked, feeling sorry for his colleague and keen to divert Carol's annoyance.

'Dr France, the forensic geologist, thinks he's narrowed down where the photograph of Tim was taken. It's an isolated though not especially remote dale in Derbyshire. Dr Hill believes that there's a strong possibility Tim may have been murdered there and his body disposed of on site. So this isn't just a stroll in the country I'm sending you on. This could be the most significant development in these cases so far. You'll be going out with a full complement of SOCOs and you're going to treat the area as a crime scene. I need officers of your calibre because it's crucial that we don't miss anything that's down there that can take us nearer to what happened to Tim and who made it happen.'

'Do the local boys know we're going to be on their patch?' Kevin asked.

'I've spoken to them, yes. Stacey has the details of who you should liaise with if you come up with anything.' She stood up. 'I know you're both disappointed about tonight, but I've chosen you two because I have confidence in your ability to find whatever there is to be found out there in Swindale. So get a good night's sleep then go out tomorrow and prove me right.'

They filed out and Carol watched them glumly. *You're losing them,* she thought, trying not to panic. *You're losing them and they know why.*

The rules have changed. This time it's going to be different because the Voice says so. He doesn't make the rules, he just follows them. And if they change, there must be a reason. It doesn't worry him that he doesn't know what that reason is. He knows he probably wouldn't understand it even if he did. But the Voice understands. So even though things are going to be different this time, he'll still be OK.

Because it's going to be different, because there are new things for him to learn, the Voice is giving him longer to prepare. He has a new script to learn, a new set of instructions to be sure of. He's even got a new coat to make him look different.

He has a dim feeling that these changes mean danger. He's going to be taking more chances, which would be scary if it wasn't for the Voice giving him confidence. So tonight, he's staying home, making sure he knows without having to think about it what he'll have to do. He's sitting in his room, listening to the seductive voice on the minidisk running through the routine one more time. He's got a joint burning, good stuff he's been holding back for a special occasion.

As the words sink into his brain, spreading their warmth and comfort, he knows he was right to roll it. Occasions don't really come any more special than this.

Tony sat in the pool of light cast by the desk lamp in his office at Bradfield Moor. Like so many objects in the secure hospital, it had never been up to much in the first place, and now it was well past its best. The only two positions it would sustain for any length of time were either too high or too low for effective use. But at that particular moment, Tony was oblivious to his surroundings.

The killer was still eluding him. A disembodied voice he couldn't hear but which still seemed capable of pulling his strings. He had no more real sense of who this killer was now than he'd had on the morning after Sandie Foster's murder when he'd spoken to Carol about rape and murder and power.

He'd tried to speak to Derek Tyler again, but Tyler had refused to come out of his room. When Tony had attempted to see him there, Tyler had curled up in a ball on his bed and turned his face to the wall. There had been nothing equivocal in the gesture. So he'd gone back to his office and read through the case file that Carol had finally sent over. She'd been right. There was no wriggle room around Derek Tyler's conviction. Not unless he'd had a twin brother who shared his DNA. And there was no record of Tyler having any siblings, never mind a twin.

'What's in it for you?' he said, leaning back and staring at the ceiling. 'Where's the punchline in taking over someone else's crime?' He was at the point of beginning to doubt something he had always regarded as one of the few given truths in what he did: that no two people were subject to precisely the same reactions to stimulus in the area of sexual homicide. What if this case were to provide the exception that proved the rule?

He'd once been present at a forensic science conference where a prominent crime writer had been giving the after-dinner speech. He remembered the man leaning nonchalantly on the lectern, his soft Welsh accent making his words soothing and innocuous. Tony didn't have Carol's gift of total recall of speech, but he remembered the gist of it because it had chimed so perfectly with his own understanding. The writer was talking about a question that was frequently put to him by readers: did he worry about somebody stealing his imagined crimes and turning them into real ones? The writer said he didn't lose sleep over this for two reasons. Firstly, the chances of any individual having the identical motive springs for his action as the characters in the books was negligible. And even in the unlikely event of that happening, it still wasn't the writer's responsibility. The person committing the crime had to be predisposed in that direction; to blame the writer for the murderer's crime would be like blaming the breadknife for stabbing a spouse in the middle of a domestic.

But what if they'd both been wrong, the writer and Tony? What if a congruence of murderous fantasies wasn't as unlikely as he and his colleagues had always believed? What if someone out there had been so moved by Derek Tyler's crimes that he'd come to understand that the only way he could achieve his own dream of perfection was to act out what he'd realized was his fantasy too?

It was far-fetched. It would earn him ridicule from his colleagues. He could see the smirk on Aidan Hart's face at the conviction that Tony Hill had finally lost it completely.

More than that, it just didn't make sense. Because Tyler had confessed, because the forensic evidence had been believed to be impregnable, because he'd been deemed to be mad and not bad, the full story of Tyler's crimes had never been heard in open court. There were elements of the crimes that were not in the public domain, known only to Tyler himself, the police and the lawyers on both sides of the divide and those, like Tony himself, charged with his psychiatric care. And while it wasn't impossible that someone among that group could have gone to the bad, it wasn't a suggestion that was likely to inspire confidence from Carol or from Brandon.

Come to that, he didn't believe it himself. Trying it on for size only demonstrated what a bad fit it was.

He walked his chair back till he was out of the light and his head was touching the bookshelves behind him. Had he really lost his touch? Had he been out of the game for too long? Was he no better than those self-serving idiots who gave profiling a bad name?

It was a frightening thought. If he had lost the one thing he knew he was good at, what was left? He certainly couldn't console himself that he'd been able to use his professional acuity to help Carol. It had taken a man who spent his days looking at rocks to see at least something of what she needed and to act on it.

He wallowed for a few minutes longer, then abruptly sat upright. 'Mawkish self-pity,' he said loudly. 'Not a pretty sight.' Nor did it lead to behaviour he could be proud of. He'd walked away from tonight's undercover operation not because he genuinely believed there was nothing useful he could offer, but out of a combination of pique and a sense of acute failure. He'd let himself down. More importantly, he might have let Paula McIntyre down. And that was something Carol would find harder to forgive than his role in her own ruin.

'Oh, bugger,' Tony said, pushing himself out of the chair and grabbing his coat. It was time to stop the self-indulgence. It might not be too late to stop something very bad indeed happening to Paula McIntyre.

Carol watched the officers file out of the briefing room, their voices a low mutter of background noise. She'd pulled together just over thirty men and women to cover Paula's foray into the killer's world. Most would be on the streets in plain clothes, trying to blend in with the usual patrons of Temple Fields. Some would be parked up in cars just off the main drag, out of sight of Paula but in radio contact with the surveillance van. Others would be strategically placed in the warren of back alleys, ready to cut off any escape attempt. Carol herself would be in the surveillance van with Don Merrick, Stacey Chen, Jan Shields and a couple of technicians, sweating it out, staring into the CCTV screens, straining to hear what came in over the wire Paula would be wearing.

Carol tried to convince herself she was confident of a good outcome. She thought they'd achieved saturation coverage; any more officers and they'd have started to have a significant impact on the ambience. She knew that murderers like this were often finely tuned to their killing ground, and it was important not to alter the environment so much that their target would sense a disturbance in the atmosphere. That much she'd learned from Tony over the years. She could have used his input this afternoon. It wasn't that she didn't believe in her own ability to organize a major operation; it was more that she wanted another angle on what she had planned. She wanted Tony because he could look at it with the eyes of the hunted rather than the hunter. Paula would be offered up as prey; Carol didn't want her to end up as a sacrificial lamb, but equally she didn't want the wolf to sniff the air and take fright.

Tony was, she thought, behaving oddly. Given the level of concern he'd been showing for her since she'd come back to Bradfield, she'd expected him to be glued to her side tonight. It was hard not to see his absence as a reproach.

The last of the team left the room and Carol took a final look at the whiteboards where the strategy was outlined. Time to go and reassure Paula.

She found the young DC sitting in her office with Jan Shields. Paula was kitted up and ready to roll. She looked curiously pathetic in her trashy outfit, her bare legs already goosepimpled above the strappy stilettos Jan had found on a cheap market stall. Paula's face was masked with the exaggerated make-up of a street girl, eyes outlined in kohl and lips a scarlet slash. She looked as comfortable as a white mouse in a pit of vipers.

Carol looked her up and down. 'I know it feels horrible, but you look the business. Well, from a distance anyway. Up close, you look far too sussed and healthy.'

'Thanks, chief,' Paula said ironically.

Carol put a hand on her shoulder, feeling the stiff PVC cold against her fingers. 'We'll be close, all the time. We'll be watching you. We've got officers on the street as well as in vehicles. Have they wired you up yet?'

Paula nodded, swivelling in her chair and lifting the back of her jacket. Although the sparkly silver top revealed her midriff, the jacket reached the top of her hips, hiding the wire that ran from the mike between her breasts, round the line of her bra and down her back into the transmitter that was fixed just below the waistline of her skirt. The wire wasn't taped to her skin; there was enough slack to make sure it wouldn't be ripped out by accident if she had to bend over or crouch to speak to the driver of a car.

'You can't see anything when she's standing or walking,' Jan said. 'We've checked.'

'Good,' Carol said. 'What about an earpiece?'

Paula shook her head. 'The techies said it was too visible with my hair being so short.'

'And you're OK about that? About us not being able to talk to you?'

Paula shrugged. 'I'll be fine.'

'If we need to abort, one of us will do a walk-past. You're clear on the rest of the drill?' Carol asked.

She nodded unhappily. 'If I get a punter, I walk round the corner with him and find out what he wants. If he's just a regular punter, I flash my warrant card and tell him to disappear before he gets arrested.'

'That's right. We're not interested in saddo sales reps tonight. Save them for Jan's colleagues another time.'

'Thanks,' Jan said sarcastically.

'And when I get someone who wants a bit of bondage, I go along with him?'

Carol could see Paula was trying hard to maintain

bravado. But she knew the worm of anxious fear that was eating her. She knew because she'd lived with it for longer than she ever wanted to again. 'That's right,' she said. 'Then you ask him exactly what he's got in mind. If he's got somewhere to go or if he wants to use your place. Whether we think he's the killer or not, that's when we move in. Either to warn him off in no uncertain terms or to lift him. We'll be right behind you. We need to give him a bit of rope, but we'll be keeping close tabs to make sure nothing goes wrong.'

Paula braced herself visibly. 'But nothing's going to go wrong. Right?'

'Right.' The male voice came from behind them. The three women turned to see the Chief Constable in the doorway. 'I have every confidence in you and your team, DCI Jordan. You're in the best possible hands, DC McIntyre. I'm sure we're going to get a result. If not tonight, then very soon.'

Carol felt Paula stiffen under her hand. She realized that the DC hadn't understood that this might not simply be a one-off. 'Thank you, sir,' she said.

'I'd like a word, DCI Jordan?' Brandon said.

Jan and Paula left them to it. 'We'll wait in the briefing room,' Jan said, closing the door behind her.

'How are you doing, Carol?' Brandon asked, his brow furrowed in concern.

'I'm fine, sir,' she said, her voice clipped, inviting neither sympathy nor indulgence. After their earlier encounter, she found it hard to accept his concern was sincere. 'It's not me who's taking the risks tonight.'

'No, but it can't be easy for you, sending an officer out on an operation like this. After what you –'

'I do my job, sir,' Carol interrupted. 'If I thought my own feelings were compromising the operation, I would have asked you to relieve me of command.'

Brandon looked embarrassed. 'I wasn't suggesting that for a moment, Carol. And it wasn't what I was implying when we spoke before. All I meant was that I do understand that this must bring back uncomfortable memories.'

Carol fought to stay in command of herself against the rising tide of frustration and anger. 'With respect, sir, that's my business.'

Rebuked, Brandon turned away. 'As you say. Is Tony in the building?'

'No, sir. Dr Hill felt he had contributed all he could to this evening's undercover. He indicated that he thought the arrangements I had put in place were sufficient.' *Unlike you*, she thought with some bitterness. Suddenly, it dawned on her that Tony's absence might not be an admonishment. It could be his way of showing her that he thought she was back in command of herself again, back on top of her game.

If that's what it is, he couldn't be more wrong. She was more anxious than she'd been for a long time. But she was damned if she was going to let Brandon see that. She nailed a smile to her face and said, 'If you'll excuse me, sir, I need to show my support for DC McIntyre. It's time we got to work.'

Brandon stood aside to let her pass. 'Good luck, Carol,' he said.

She swung round. 'If we catch him, it won't be about luck, sir. It'll be about good police work.'

*   *   *

Temple Fields on a weekday evening. Sharp night air with an acrid edge of city pollution that caught the throat. Two generations back, the base note would have been the smoke from thousands of coal fires. Now it was the greenhouse gases from car exhausts and the stale exhalations of the city's hundreds of food outlets, from burger bars to Bollinger bistros. The garish neon lighting looked blurred through the lenses of the CCTV system. The four cameras that fed into the surveillance van were all targeted on Paula from a variety of angles and distances, showing her against the backdrop of a bustling street where all appetites could be met. People shopped in the mini-market on the corner, moved in and out of pubs, cafés and restaurants. Sex workers of all genders and sexes dawdled, their impatience for custom mostly numbed by alcohol or drugs. Cars cruised and drifted, some looking for parking spaces, others looking for sex. What their drivers didn't know was that every number plate was being logged by another set of cameras strategically placed at the main access routes into the area. If the killer didn't show his hand, each of those registered owners would have to be visited in a tedious, time-consuming ritual where everyone was assumed to have something to hide until they demonstrated otherwise. Marriages might founder in the wake of tonight's operation.

Carol Jordan didn't care. She knew the price that taking chances sometimes demanded and she had little sympathy for those who took their risks for such venal rewards. She stared into the screens, watching Paula intently. The young DC had staked out a corner by a mini-roundabout. She'd learned quickly, clocking the attitude and style of the other women on the street and now she was strutting her stuff like the rest of them. A few steps in one direction; a cocking of the hip, an insolent stare at the traffic. Then back to where she started.

When she'd taken up position, she'd been challenged by another woman whose pitch she'd inadvertently invaded. A quick flash of her warrant card would have seen off the opposition but might have threatened the whole strategy. So Paula had done a deal. The other woman backed off in exchange for a twenty-pound note. It wasn't much of a bribe, but Paula had invested her words with enough of a threat for the other woman to move a few yards down a side street without further complaint. Carol had been impressed. Given how nervous Paula had been earlier, it was a bravura performance.

'She did good,' Jan had said. 'That's one of the advantages of us clearing out the pimps. Not that long ago, if she'd have tried that stunt, she'd have had a knife at her throat in five minutes. But the women don't go in for that kind of response.'

'Don't they look out for each other?' Stacey asked, looking up from the computer screen where she was running the car numbers from the other cameras against the Police National Computer.

'Up to a point. But they're not exactly what you'd call a trade union,' Jan said sardonically.

It wasn't a busy night on the street as far as the hookers were concerned. But it was early yet. According to Jan, there would be more action after ten o'clock, reaching a peak between midnight and one. Carol, however, had already decided to close down the operation at midnight. All of the killer's victims, whether you counted it as two or six, had been taken off the streets between six and ten. This killer clearly didn't like working the night shift.

By half past eight, Paula hadn't had a serious nibble. The team in the van had been aware of a dozen or so transactions on the street, but none of the women involved had looked remotely like the killer's type, so they'd let them run their course without interference.

Suddenly, Jan pointed to one of the screens. 'Well, well, well,' she said. 'Look who it is.'

Walking down the street towards Paula, head down and jacket collar turned up, was the unmistakable figure of Tony Hill. Carol leaned into the screen, watching intently as he walked past Paula without a second glance. Then he turned into the first pub he came to. What the hell was he up to? Part of Carol wanted to jump out of the van and chase after him. But the better part of her knew she must sit tight. If anything went down, her place was here, right on top of the game, not running round the streets demanding to know what Tony was playing at. Besides, it went against all the rules of surveillance to have foot traffic in and out of the vehicle, drawing attention to its presence.

Her decision was made for her when a car glided to a halt next to Paula. 'Punter alert,' Merrick shouted. The tension in the van ratcheted up palpably.

Paula bent down to speak into the lowered window. The car obscured her face, but the camera behind her showed she was free and clear, and the wire gave a crackly but comprehensible rendering of the conversation.

'You working?' the driver asked.

'What are you after?' Paula said, the harshness in her tone evident even through the attrition of transmission.

'You take it up the arse?' the man said.

'You want me to take it up the arse, it'll cost you more than you could ever afford. Fuck off, pervert,' Paula snarled.

'Fucking cunt,' the driver spat back, shifting the car into gear and moving further down the street.

Paula stepped back from the kerb. 'I guess the price wasn't right.'

'Attagirl, Paula. Keep whistling in the dark,' Carol said softly. They all sat back in their seats and allowed themselves a degree of relaxation.

'He's sitting in the window,' Jan said.

'What?' Carol was still replaying Paula's encounter in her head.

'Dr Hill.' Jan pointed at one of the screens. It was just possible to make out a face that might possibly belong to Tony. 'He's just sat down. He's got a drink – look. He's found a seat where he can watch the street.'

'Just so long as he stays put,' Carol muttered.

Another fifteen minutes passed without incident. Then Merrick said, 'That bloke. He's walked past three times.' He pointed with his pen at a middle-aged, balding man, stocky but with a slight stoop. 'He's eyeing up Paula. Look.'

He was right. The man slowed as he approached Paula, his head moving up and down as he scrutinized her from the side and from behind. He passed her, then crossed the street. At the corner, he turned back. He sauntered in Paula's direction, then, when he was almost level with her, he crossed the street, quickening his pace.

'Uh, oh,' Jan said as he hit the pavement, crowding Paula so she had to take a backward step.

'Let's do some business, you and me.' The man's voice was a loud growl in their earpieces.

'What are you after?' Paula said, trying to stand her ground but having to back up as he moved in on her.

'I want you to suck me off,' he demanded, keeping up the pressure, angling Paula towards a break in the buildings where a narrow alley led to back yards.

'Team A, move into position,' Carol yelled. At once, four of the apparently aimless strollers on the street began to converge on Paula's position.

Now they were in the alley. It was hard to see what was going on, but they heard a thud then a cry of protest from Paula. 'Hey, shithead, cut the rough stuff,' she shouted.

'Shut your fucking hole,' the man grunted.

'Team A, stand by,' Carol said. The four bodies flanked the alley mouth. Carol heard sounds of movement in her ear. Then a yelp of pain. Then Paula's voice. 'This is a warrant card, asshole.'

'What the fu—'

'Yeah, I'm a cop.' Carol could hear Paula's breath coming fast and hard. 'Now fuck off fast before I'm tempted to do you for assault, shithead.'

Carol laughed out loud. 'Team A, stand down.'

The man shot out of the alley, breaking into a shambling trot, nearly stumbling as he looked over his shoulder, panic written all over his face. Behind him, Paula emerged from the alley, brushing down her skirt.

'She's good,' Jan said.

Carol wiped the sheen of sweat from her upper lip. 'She's very good. Let's just hope the killer thinks so too.'

Tony had his glass halfway to his lips when the hand descended on his shoulder. He started, slopping lager down his shirt. 'Shit!' he said, jerking backwards and batting pointlessly at the spreading stain. He looked up. 'Where did you come from?' he demanded.

Carol jerked her head towards the rear of the bar. 'Through the back door.' She put two bottles of Stella on the table.

'You scared the hell out of me,' Tony complained, reaching for one of the bottles and topping up his almost-empty glass.

'I'm supposed to scare the hell out of people. I'm a cop.' Carol sat down and took a swig of her beer. 'As you will have noticed, we just wound up for the night. I got the van to drop me off round the corner.'

'I noticed. I was just finishing up my drink then I was off to get the night bus.'

Carol grinned. 'Your sophistication never ceases to amaze me. What's wrong with a taxi?'

'You get a better class of nutter on the night bus. I blend in perfectly.'

She couldn't argue with that. 'So why are you here? I thought you were washing your hands of the undercover.'

He shook his head. 'I never said that. Just that I didn't think I had anything useful to offer.' He gave her a shrewd look. 'But I do now.'

She raised her eyebrows in a question.

274

'It's not going to work, Carol,' Tony said flatly.

From anyone else, it would have been grounds for offence. But she knew him better than that. 'What's the problem? You don't think Brandon's line will force his hand?'

Tony pulled a face. 'The challenge was fine. It's the bait that's the problem.'

'You don't think Paula looks like a hooker? I thought Jan had done a good job getting her kitted out. Or is it that you think she's not close enough to his type?'

He shook his head. 'She looks like a hooker. And she's his type. That's not it. Paula's right on the money. It's what you're doing with her that's the issue. Carol, this man knows Temple Fields. It's his stamping ground. Like I said earlier, I think the chances are high that he works here. Which means he knows these streets, he knows the women who work them. So if he saw Paula out there tonight, he knows she's new meat. And what did she do tonight?'

Carol thought for a moment. 'She acted like a street hooker.'

Tony put his glass down heavily. 'No. She didn't. Carol, she didn't go with a single punter. As a whore, she was a total failure. Now, if our man was watching her, he'll have thought one of two things. Either that she's a decoy, in which case you're blown. Or that she's so new to the game she's being too picky. In which case he's not going to chance an approach.'

Carol closed her eyes momentarily. With all she'd learned from Tony about putting herself in the shoes of the enemy, why hadn't she thought of that?

Because she'd been too wrapped up in her own reactions. Her priority had been taking care of Paula, not making sure the honeytrap was tempting enough. 'So what do I do now?' she asked wearily.

'You go back out on the street with Paula tomorrow night. And you set up some fake punters. A couple of guys in cars, a couple on foot. Make it look like she's learned not to be so fussy. Make it look like she's working and not standing around like cheese in a mousetrap.' He smiled. 'That's all I wanted to say. Now, are you going to give me a lift home or should I go and get the night bus?'

Rain drizzled depressingly from a battleship-grey sky, leaching all colour from the Derbyshire landscape. Their small cavalcade had swept out of Bradfield against the incoming tide of the morning rush hour, arriving at the car park by the remains of the old railway station in Miller's Dale just after nine. The brown gritstone of the walls seemed to weep moisture. Carol turned to Jonathan France, white-faced beside her in the back seat. 'Are you OK?' she asked.

They had spoken little in the car on the way over from Bradfield. Carol was lost in her plans for the next stage of the undercover. But even if she hadn't been, the presence of Sam Evans driving the unmarked CID car would have kept the conversation within narrow limits. As it was, Jonathan hadn't shown much inclination for talk. He'd mostly stared straight ahead, as if mesmerized by the sweep of the windscreen wipers.

'I'm ready, if that's what you mean,' he said, a deep breath lifting his shoulders. He grabbed the waxed

276

jacket that he'd placed on the seat between them, opened the door and got out.

Carol joined him. 'I do appreciate you helping us with this,' she said. 'As soon as you've identified the site, I'll have someone take you back to Bradfield.'

He nodded. 'I don't know how you deal with this stuff day in, day out,' he confessed. 'Just thinking about it makes me shiver.'

'Keeping faith with the dead. That's what Tony calls it.' Carol looked around her. The team was gathering, scenes of crime officers in their familiar white suits, designed to avoid any contamination of evidence. Kevin and Sam were struggling into their suits, both muttering complaints about the general level of discomfort. 'We should suit up too,' Carol said. She retrieved a couple of suits from the SOCO van and took the opportunity to have a word with Kevin and Sam. 'I didn't plan on being here,' she said. 'But Dr France had cold feet. It's your operation, I'm only here to observe. I won't stay long.'

Kevin gave her a tight smile. 'Thanks, guv.'

When everyone was ready, they set off along what had been the railway track. Now it was a public footpath, the rough stone chippings making for awkward going. It must have been a breathtaking journey back when the steam trains plied this route, Carol thought. Even on a miserable winter's morning, the light poor and the visibility worse, the drama of the landscape was obvious. Striated limestone cliffs and reefs loomed above them, occasional hardy patches of vegetation sprouting from the cracks. Mottled with more shades of grey than she could count, the huge bluffs stretched skywards, seeming to move towards closure above her head. She tried not to think how threatening it must have seemed to Tim Golding.

After a short distance, they left the track and cut down a steep slope towards a meadow. A handful of sodden sheep munched miserably at the pale grass while others huddled beneath the bare branches of a clump of trees. The ground was heavy underfoot and Carol could feel her walking boots add weight as the mud began to stick to them. It was a long and tiring forty minutes to the mouth of Swindale. They gathered at what looked like a cleft in the rock, no more than four feet across. Carol was sweating inside her protective suit, but her feet were freezing. Not even good quality boots could keep the water out when you had to walk through the river overflow. She turned to Jonathan. 'The scenes of crime officers will go in first. They'll tape off a narrow route as they go. That will be the route that we use in and out from now on. So if you go just behind them and direct them to the place you think we're looking for . . .?'

He nodded. He unzipped his suit and took out the blown-up photo of the rock formation. He'd laminated it, a sensible precaution against the weather. Carol stayed close on his heels as he followed the SOCOs through the narrow neck of the dale. To her astonishment, a few yards in, the walls of rock spread open dramatically, becoming a valley about fifty feet across. The rough vegetation on the valley floor thinned out in places, offering a faint path forwards. They carried on in, Jonathan occasionally steering them with a few words. 'Just there on the right,' he said eventually. Carol looked at her watch. Eight minutes from the mouth of the dale. She stepped up beside Jonathan and compared the picture in his hand to the rock in front of her. Even to her untutored eye, there seemed little room for doubt. But Jonathan took her through the common features, indicating the points of identity. 'I can't imagine there are two sets of stromatactis formations with those identical configurations,' he concluded.

Carol asked the photographer to start on a set of pictures, then she collared one of the uniformed officers she'd requisitioned for the search. 'Bryant? I want you to drive Dr France back to Bradfield. And then I want you to come back for me. I'll meet you in the station car park at one.' She turned to Jonathan. 'I'll keep you informed,' she said, putting a hand on his arm. 'Don't brood on it.'

He gave a rueful smile. 'I'll try not to.'

She turned back and watched Kevin go to his task. 'Right,' he said to the waiting team. 'Let's fan out from here. Three metres apart. Any sign of disturbed ground, uprooted plants . . . You know what we're looking for. Let's do it.'

Carol hung back, trying to find some shelter in the lee of the bluff a few yards from the site of the photograph. The officers were making slow progress, hampered by the brambles that twined through the dense undergrowth. While she waited, she took out her phone and started making the calls to reshape the undercover operation for that night. She'd just finished talking to Paula when a shout went up from one of the officers towards the right-hand end of the line. 'Over here,' he called.

At once, everyone froze. Two of the SOCOs who had remained behind headed for the man who had called out, spooling crime-scene tape behind them to make another narrow corridor of access. It took them a few minutes to reach the man, then another couple of nail-biting minutes while they looked at what had stopped him in his tracks. Then one of them turned back towards Carol and gave her the thumbs-up sign.

She reached the spot at almost the same moment as Kevin. They crouched down, the better to see what was being pointed out. Below the brambles, dead bracken had been piled in a vain bid to disguise the unmistakable hump of a shallow grave. To one side, the earth had been disturbed, presumably by a fox or badger. At first glance, it looked as if someone had strewn a handful of short grey-white sticks on the soil. But Carol knew different, knew what a scatter of finger bones looked like.

She stood up, head bowed, rain streaking her face. It looked as if they'd finally found Tim Golding. Or Guy Lefevre.

Or both.

Midnight. Carol rubbed eyes made tired by hours of peering at CCTV screens and sighed. They'd done everything Tony had suggested. But they were no further forward than they had been when Brandon had first insisted that they try the undercover. Carol wondered how long he would continue to sanction this level of expenditure and staff on such a labour-intensive operation. Following the discovery in the dale, they had two major murder inquiries on their hands. If the press got a whiff of how many officers were involved in the prostitute killings, there would be an outcry. Hysterical demands that more officers be allocated to the paedophile murders, that saving children was more important than saving hookers. It was logical to devote more attention to the Temple Fields murders at this point, because the killer was clearly active now, whereas the paedophile murderer seemed to be dormant for the time being. But logic was always the first victim when the press got their teeth into a campaign. They needed a quick result, both for morale and so that they could be seen to be throwing every resource at finding Tim Golding's killer. If they couldn't manage that, it would be Carol who would carry the stigma of failure in the eyes of her colleagues and junior officers. It wasn't the sort of start a supposedly elite unit needed, though she suspected there would be plenty who would savour her lack of success.

She pressed the transmission button on her radio and said, 'All units, stand down. Tango Charlie two three, pick up DC McIntyre. Full briefing tomorrow afternoon at four.' A man emerged from the café bar behind the van and climbed in, driving them back to base. Nobody spoke. They were all too tired and disheartened. When they arrived at the police station, the others filed out, leaving Carol and Merrick slumped in their seats.

Merrick glanced across at her. 'We're not going anywhere with this, are we?'

Carol shrugged. 'At least it stopped raining. What else is there to try?'

'We should be concentrating on finding Tim's killer. We both know he's going to kill again if we don't find him. And I don't want another kid's blood on my hands.'

'The man who killed Sandie Foster and Jackie Mayall is also going to kill again, Don. And he's got a much shorter killing cycle. The women on the streets deserve our protection as much as the kids do. We don't have the right to create a hierarchy of deserving victims. We leave that to the press. We treat them all the same, and we devote our resources where they're most likely to get a result.'

From the look on his face, Carol could tell Merrick didn't agree with her assessment. 'We can't keep this up indefinitely,' he said.

'And if Tony's right, we won't have to. Once our man accepts Paula as a fixture, he'll bite.' Carol sounded more confident than she felt.

Merrick pursed his lips. 'And until then, we keep putting Paula on the line?'

Carol reached for her jacket and stood up. 'It's her call. If she wants out, she only has to say.'

'But she's not going to say, is she?' Merrick challenged her. 'She's ambitious, she wants to do well. She wants you to think well of her. She sees backing down as bottling it.'

'You seem to be very clued up on Paula's thoughts,' Carol said. 'Has she told you she wants out?'

Merrick seemed embarrassed. 'Not in so many words, no. But I can see it for myself.'

Carol sighed. Sometimes she couldn't resist the feeling that Merrick had been shoved one rung up the ladder too far. He'd been a terrific sergeant, but he wasn't cutting it as a DI. 'Don, you're probably not wrong. But we haven't got the right to pull this rug out from under Paula. She's been asked to do something – asked, not ordered – and until she says she's reached her limit, she deserves not to have her courage undermined by us second-guessing her. So unless you think she's either a danger to herself or to anyone else, she keeps on keeping on.'

Merrick's dark eyes took on a sulky look. 'If you say so, ma'am.'

'I do, Don. And now I'm going home to bed. It's been a bitch of a day, and I've got to brief the Tim Golding team first thing in the morning.' As soon as the words were out of her mouth, Carol cursed herself.

'I was going to ask you about that,' Merrick said. 'I want you to put me on that inquiry.'

Carol shook her head. 'No, Don. I need you working this case. There has to be an inspector in charge of the statement readers and the action assignments. Somebody has to have an overview.'

'So get someone else,' he said impatiently. 'Tim Golding was my case. I worked on Guy Lefevre's disappearance too. Nobody's put more into finding those lads than me. I lost sleep over them, I worked my arse off for them. I know those cases inside out. I know the families. And they know me. Anybody else would be starting from scratch. And it would be just another case to them.'

Carol considered diplomacy and rejected it. She was too tired to go round the houses. And besides, it would probably be wasted on Merrick. 'That's a large part of the reason why I'm not transferring you. We've got a fresh scenario and I want someone running the shop who isn't bringing any preconceptions to it.' Merrick recoiled as if she'd slapped him. But Carol ploughed on. 'The other reason is that the Foster and Mayall cases are live and ongoing. Bringing someone else in to replace you would mean they'd have the impossible task of reviewing all that's already been done while still trying to keep on top of fresh statements and actions.' Belatedly, she tried to soften her response. 'Don, I know you took these disappearances very personally. And that's not a bad thing. It means you went the extra mile for Tim and Guy. But now it's time to step back. Sandie and Jackie had families too. They deserve answers as much as the Goldings and the Lefevres. And I need you by my side on this one.'

Merrick looked momentarily as if he wanted to argue. Instead his shoulders slumped and he stood up, bending over so he wouldn't crack his head on the roof of the van. 'I'll see you in the morning, ma'am,' he said bitterly. Then he was gone, leaving her to contemplate another piece of botched staff management.

'What a fucking day,' she said under her breath as she climbed out of the van and made for her car. She'd stood over a child's grave, then driven to the Goldings' home to tell them that in all probability it belonged to their son. Next she'd had to break the news to Jonathan before he heard it on the radio or the TV. Then four hours stuck in a van in an atmosphere pregnant with expectation. And now she'd pissed off her number two. Her nerves were shot. She needed a large drink, and she needed it soon.

The last thing she expected when she pulled up outside the house was to see Jonathan huddled over his motorbike. She glanced up at Tony's windows and was reassured to see they were all dark. She stifled a groan and got out. As she approached, he dismounted stiffly, stretching his long limbs and straightening his spine. She couldn't help admiring the sight. 'This is a surprise,' she said.

'I'm sorry,' he said. 'I didn't realize you'd be working this late. But once I'd waited an hour . . .' He shrugged and spread his hands.

'There's nothing more I can tell you, Jonathan. We don't have a positive ID yet, never mind a cause of death . . .'

'I didn't come because I wanted more information,' he said. 'I came because . . . well, I just couldn't settle. The whole thing kept going round in my head, and I thought how much worse it must be for you, and I thought it might help both of us . . .' He saw the look on her face and began to turn away. 'Obviously I was wrong.'

'No, no,' she said hastily. 'I was just taken aback, that's all. I'm not used to . . .' Her voice tailed off.

'People regarding you as human?'

She sighed. 'Something like that. Now you're here, would you like to come in for a drink?'

He looked uncertain. 'It's late, you probably want to get some sleep.'

'Both of those statements are true, but the first thing I was planning to do was to pour myself a very large glass of wine. You're welcome to join me.'

'If you're sure?'

Carol shook her head in mock exasperation. 'Can we not waste good drinking time standing here talking about it?'

She'd thought the ceilings in her flat were relatively

285

high, but Jonathan had barely a few inches of clearance. He sat down hastily, looked around her living room and smiled. 'You've not been here long, have you?'

Carol pulled a face. 'Does it feel so unlived in?'

'It's not that, it's just that there's no clutter. Me, I can make a place look like the wreck of the *Hesperus* in three days.'

'I'm not greatly given to clutter,' Carol said. 'But what there is of it is in my London flat.' She spoke over her shoulder as she headed for the fridge. 'White wine or beer?'

'Wine, please. So are you planning on selling your London flat?' he called after her.

Carol came back with the bottle and two glasses. 'Not sure yet. Right now it feels like too much of a commitment.' She handed Jonathan a glass and poured the wine. She turned on the CD player and slotted in Arvo Pärt's *Alina*, then sat down next to him. There was enough distance between them for the decision not to seem weighty. The lambent notes of the piano and violin eased the way into conversation.

'How do you get through this stuff?' he asked.

'I just open my mouth and swallow,' Carol joked. 'It's not that bad, is it?'

'You know that's not what I meant. OK, we'll talk about something else.'

'I'm sorry. I get so used to flippancy and graveyard humour I sometimes find it hard to shake off. You waited for hours in the cold, you deserve an answer. Except that I don't really have one. Some cops drink too much. Some focus so hard on catching the person who did it that they deliberately lose sight of the victim. Some go home and hug their kids. Some go home and beat their wives. And some crack up.'

'And you? What do you do?'

Carol stared into her glass. 'I try to turn the anger into positive energy. I try to feed off it, use it to drive myself to the edge of exhaustion and beyond.'

'Does that work?'

Carol could feel tears pricking at the back of her eyes. 'I don't know any more. I don't know a lot of things any more. Things I thought were bred in the bone. Now they sometimes feel like fairy tales I used to tell myself to stop me being afraid of the dark.'

He reached out and curled his arm round her shoulders. Without hesitation, she moved against his side. 'You haven't lost it, you know. You're still a good person. And a good cop.'

'How would you know?'

'I saw you out there today. I saw how you managed the scene without anybody realizing you were doing it. And with all that going on, you still found the time to be kind to me. And here you are, being kind to me again.'

Carol sighed, an exhalation that seemed to come from the very core of herself. 'Doesn't it occur to you that the person I'm being kind to is myself? Jonathan, I don't want to be alone tonight.'

She felt his muscles tense. 'You mean . . .?'

Another deep, heartfelt sigh. 'Yes, that's what I mean. But, Jonathan . . .' She pulled away so that she could see his face. 'Only if you're absolutely sure you're not in love with me.'

*   *   *

Just after five, Tony abandoned the unequal fight against wakefulness. He'd been drifting in and out of sleep for a while, troubled by thoughts of Tim Golding. And Guy Lefevre, the child almost forgotten in all the excitement. The message Carol had left telling him about the discovery in Swindale hadn't specifically asked him for help, but he had promised her he would look at the scene and he felt Bradfield police were still in credit on that case. He'd been asked for a profile in the early stages by Don Merrick, and he was painfully aware that he'd only been able to provide a very limited outline. That hadn't been his fault; he'd said right from the start that he needed more data before he could be of much use. But now he had more information, and a visit to Derbyshire would offer even more. It should be possible to come up with something a little more detailed.

He lay on his back, arms folded behind his head. The room was dark, but that was fine. He didn't have to see to think. He ran through what he thought he knew about the man who had taken Tim Golding and killed him. And probably done the same previously to Guy Lefevre. It would have been a man. There was an infinitesimal degree of doubt on that point. It was always about probabilities. But you had to keep an open mind at the same time, because the nature of sexual homicide was also very particular; it was about appetites that didn't occur often enough to form a proper statistical base.

So, a man. In age, anywhere between his late twenties and his early forties. It took time to mature into this kind of killer. Teenagers and men in their early twenties were often sexual predators but seldom took it to the point of no return. Sometimes they became murderers almost by accident, when restraining their victims went too far and ended in death. If they liked the way it made them feel, then the next time it wouldn't be an accident and another serial killer would be walking the streets. But mostly that first time was deliberate. And it took time for a man's fantasies to develop the commanding power that would drive him to take a life. So it was mostly safe to assume a higher starting age than for rape or sexual assault. The upper limit wasn't arbitrary either. By their mid-forties, the urgent rage of youth had faded or been dulled by alcohol. If they hadn't started killing by then, the chances were they were never going to take that step.

The fucked-up childhood was more or less a given too. Of course, it was possible to have all the markers without growing up to embrace the darkness. Tony knew that only too well; anyone examining his own past would have found a series of indicators that, in another man, would have been the first steps on the tortuous route to psychopathy. For him, they had provided the foundation of his empathy with those who had ended up on a different path. He was never entirely sure where the crucial fork in the road had been, but he had ended up a different kind of hunter. And just as the serial killer had a sure instinct for his victims, so Tony had an apparent sixth sense for tracking his prey. In spite of his public insistence that his was a scientific approach, he was well aware that his most crucial insights were drawn directly from the well of intuition. He was practised in hiding this aspect of his work; Carol was probably the only person who understood and forgave it.

So what could he safely say now about the abductor of Guy Lefevre and Tim Golding? Gender, age. Probably a loner, probably with superficial social skills but an inability to make deeper personal connections. He was at home in the countryside; he'd known a location isolated enough for a killing ground, and he'd known the area well enough to feel safe about parking in a public car park and transporting the boy a mile through the landscape to the final destination. He must have known there would be few people around at that time of the morning. But he was also comfortable in the environs of the city, since it was assumed he'd lifted Tim from a street in broad daylight.

At that point, Tony's thoughts stumbled. Assumption wasn't fact. There had been no witnesses. The cops had struggled to believe it could have happened without someone seeing something, even though there were precedents in this sort of case. The notorious child abductor and murderer Robert Black had snatched at least two of his victims from the street without anyone noticing. But what if it hadn't happened like that?

Tony reviewed the evidence. Guy had gone off into woodland to search for birds' nests. He'd never been seen again, though his map of the nests had been found near the canal. Tim had told his friends he was going down to the railway embankment to watch the freight trains. The women at the bus stop said they thought they'd glimpsed his yellow football shirt between the trees. What if their killer hadn't been in a vehicle on the streets? What if he'd been on the embankment or in the woods, waiting, ready with some tale that would enrapture a young boy and make him come willingly? Maybe a particularly exotic nest, or some piece of railway machinery? Interestingly, both locations were connected by transport links to the Derbyshire peaks, only a dozen or so miles from Swindale, though not links that the killer could have used. The canal led to a railhead with a direct line down into the dales. And that particular spur of the railway line led to a quarry on the fringes of the Peak District.

Galvanized by the thought, Tony jumped out of bed, grabbed his dressing gown and hurried through to his study. He wanted to get something down on screen, to make his ideas concrete so he could present them to Carol before the morning briefing he knew she'd be leading. They could discuss them over a coffee before she left for work.

While he waited for the computer to boot up, he ran downstairs and brewed some coffee. Mug in hand, he went back upstairs and crossed to the window to stare out at the sky while he marshalled the words he wanted to express his insight.

But it wasn't the sky that drew his eyes like a magnet. It was Jonathan France's motorbike, the one incongruity in a streetscape Tony had already grown familiar with. The bike squatted between Carol's car and the next-door neighbour's people carrier, imposing its presence with all the malevolence of a tank on the streets of Baghdad. Tony felt as if the breath had been sucked out of him, leaving him hollow.

Then emotion surged in, raw and relentless. It was more than jealousy; it was ragged pain, tearing at him like lacerating claws. *It's your own fault. Because you couldn't give her what she needed. Because you're a pathetic excuse for a man. Because you led her into the lion's den but you couldn't rescue her. Because love is only worth something if the actions match the words.*

Tony hurled his mug at the door, splattering the fresh paintwork and the nearby books with coffee. 'Fuck it,' he shouted. Then he threw himself into his chair and pulled his keyboard towards him.

Don Merrick was on his second cigarette of the morning when Paula pushed open the kitchen door. Her hair stuck up in an angled wedge on one side of her head, her eyes were puffy with sleep and her navy dressing gown had a streak of toothpaste on the lapel. 'How the fuck do you get to look so sorted first thing?' she grumbled on her way to the kettle.

'It's something to do with shaving,' he said. 'Even when you feel like shit, when you've had a shave you look better.'

'I'll have to give it a try some time,' Paula muttered.

'You not sleeping?' Merrick asked.

Paula coughed and poured boiling water on instant coffee. 'I'm OK once I get off. But that seems to be taking a while.' She sniffed, added milk to her drink and plonked herself down at the table opposite him. She reached for his cigarettes but he adroitly swiped them out of her reach.

'Slippery slope, Paula. You start cadging fags this early in the day, you'll be back on two packs before you know it.' He wagged a finger at her.

'Grrr.' She snarled, showing her teeth. 'I didn't realize I was inviting my mother to stay.'

'Your mother wouldn't have fags for you to nick. So, what are you planning to do today?'

She shrugged. 'Dunno. Might go down to the Spa, have a swim, see if I can get a massage. I need to do something to make me feel good about my body after two nights on the meat rack.'

'You don't have to do this, you know.'

Paula gave him a sidelong look. 'What do you mean?'

'I mean you could say you've had enough. That it's freaking you out.'

Paula snorted. 'Yeah, right. What a good career move that would be.'

Merrick's expression mingled concern and sympathy. 'Jordan would understand. She knows what it's like, she was on the sharp end when it all went pear-shaped. She's not going to hold it against you.'

'Even if you're right – which I'm not convinced of, by the way – that'd barely be fine if Jordan was the only senior cop in the world. I walk away from this, I'll always be the girl whose bottle went.'

'Better that than you end up as fucked up as Jordan.' Merrick studied the table. 'I'd never live with myself if anything happened to you on this one, Paula.'

Paula squared her shoulders. 'Get over it, Don. This is about you, not me. I'm holding together. I can do this.' She pushed the chair back, its legs grating on the tiled floor. 'You've got to stop trying to be the knight in shining armour. You can't save the world, Don. Concentrate on saving yourself.' She looked at the clock as she stood up. 'Isn't it about time you were getting a move on? Isn't there a briefing on Tim Golding at nine?'

Merrick grunted. 'I'm not invited to the party.

Jordan wants me to stick with the hooker murders. She wants a fresh pair of eyes on Tim Golding.'

Paula felt for him. She knew how much of himself he'd poured into the hunt for the boy. 'I'm sorry, Don. But maybe it's for the best. That case really ripped into you.'

He looked up at her, eyes wounded. 'So you think I blew it too?'

'Of course not. If they do crack it now, it'll be on the shoulders of your groundwork. Maybe Jordan's right, maybe she's wrong. But I'm your friend, and I'm glad you're not going there again.' She leaned over and hugged him, her breasts swinging against his chest. Hastily, she pulled back, embarrassed by the sudden flare of surprised interest in his face. 'I'll see you in the afternoon briefing, then.'

Merrick watched her go, conscious of her backside moving under her robe. He'd been disciplining himself, not allowing himself to appreciate her body, her air of contained sexuality. But now, finally, he was beginning to wonder whether he was in with a chance after all, whether her offer of the spare bed was really the disinterested kindness of a friend or something more. It was a cheering thought to take with him to the grimness of the murder room.

Carol waltzed into the station, conscious that her mood was not appropriate to what her day held. For the moment, she didn't care. She'd moved mountains in the night, shifted her world on its axis and she was going to savour the feeling for as long as she could. It wasn't that Jonathan had been the greatest lover she'd ever had; he'd been too cautious, too solicitous, too damn anxious about his steps in the ritual dance. The cynical cop's reaction occurred to her: perhaps he had culled his textbook responses from the very book he'd given her. Even if that were true, it didn't really matter. What was important was that she'd crossed the invisible, intangible line that had separated her from a crucial part of herself. She hadn't exorcized the rape. But she'd moved beyond it. Her body was hers again.

Jonathan had left shortly after six, and she hadn't been sorry to see him go. He'd tried to pin her down to another date, but she'd sidestepped neatly, calling on work to shelter her from an encounter she didn't want. She liked him well enough, but she didn't want to slip heedlessly into some sort of relationship with him. He wasn't the one she wanted to be with; but she'd always known that she couldn't expect Tony to be the one to bring her back to sex. That was a journey she would have to make without him. But having made it opened possibilities for them that had been closed down since Berlin.

She took the stairs two at a time and walked into the squadroom radiating confidence and good humour. Stacey glanced up casually from her computer at her entrance then did so obvious a double-take that it was almost comic. 'Good morning, Stacey,' Carol said cheerfully.

'Morning, ma'am,' Stacey said automatically.

'I've got a good feeling about today,' Carol said. 'You know how sometimes it feels like this is going to be the day when something breaks, when finally we get what we need to move forward?' Stacey nodded. 'Well, that's exactly how I feel this morning.'

'Dr Hill sent a document file for you,' Stacey said, not sure how else to respond to what seemed like unfounded optimism. Machines she could do; but people left her bemused, constantly searching for a way to exert the same mastery she applied so effortlessly to the cyber world.

Carol's mood sobered suddenly. 'What is it?' she asked.

'He's done a profile on the Tim Golding case. I printed it out. It's on your desk.'

'Thanks.' Carol was already moving, making for her office. She snatched up the printout as she shrugged out of her coat and started reading. At once, she recognized the familiar opening disclaimer:

Re: Tim Golding

The following offender profile is for guidance only and should not be regarded as an identikit portrait. The offender is unlikely to match the profile in every detail, though I would expect there to be a high degree of congruence between the characteristics outlined below and the reality. All of the statements in the profile express probabilities and possibilities, not hard facts.

A perpetrator of sexual homicide produces signals and indicators in the commission of his crimes. Everything he does is intended, consciously or not, as part of a pattern. Uncovering the underlying pattern reveals the killer's logic. It may not appear logical to us, but to him it is crucial. Because his logic is so idiosyncratic, straightforward traps will not capture him. As he is unique, so must be the means of catching him, interviewing him and reconstructing his acts.

This is a supplement to the draft profile I prepared earlier at the request of DI Merrick. As I stated previously, the perpetrator is likely to be male, between the ages of 27 and 42. He will probably live alone. It is likely that he has superficial social skills but he is unlikely to be capable of forming close friendships with either sex. In this case, given the age of the victim, I believe it to be unlikely that he has ever had a sexually functional relationship with any adult. He will have obsessive personal traits and may have an interest in the sort of hobby that provides an outlet for obsessional list-making such as trainspotting, birdwatching or philately. He is probably intelligent and functional enough to hold down a job, but it will not involve teamwork. He will prefer a role that allows at least the illusion of autonomy and will ideally spend much of his working day alone.

I believe that the same perpetrator is responsible for the abduction and probable murder of Guy Lefevre. However, given that only the body of Tim Golding has been discovered to date, I will confine myself initially to the specifics of his case.

It is clear that the killer is very familiar with the crime scene. He knew that the car park would be deserted at the time of day he chose to arrive. He knew he would be able to transport Tim Golding to Swindale without interference. He knew he would be able to use Swindale for his purposes without interruption. Therefore he must have a high degree of familiarity with the area. By taking Tim Golding to this particular spot, the killer is signalling that this is his place, somewhere special to him. When looking at suspects, a search of their home/workplace/computer will almost certainly uncover photographs or even paintings of the dale. I would suggest canvassing universities to see whether their field trips include Swindale; local amateur geological societies; climbing organizations; old railway enthusiasts; and of course, the Peak National Park ranger service, who, as well as being familiar with the area, are likely to know which other groups frequent Chee Dale and Swindale. I would also recommend a trawl of the literature; guide books, rambling publications. If this trawl proves negative, it strengthens the case against any putative suspect who can be shown to be familiar with the terrain.

It is likely that the killer may previously have attempted to lure other victims to Swindale. I would recommend checking with local police for any reports of stranger approaches to children in this area. The killer may have used the children's natural curiosity about their environment to draw them in (see below).

I have been giving further consideration to the means of Tim Golding s abduction. Given the absence of witnesses to support the theory that he was snatched from the street, and given we now know we have a perpetrator who is comfortable in a more rural environment, I would suggest that the killer made his contact with the victim AFTER he had left the street and made his way down the railway embankment. Given his familiarity with the country-side, the perpetrator could have found a credible approach to the boy along the lines of having some-thing to show him: a fox's earth, a badger's sett, a bird's nest. (This is even more probable in the case of Guy Lefevre, who was looking for birds' nests at the time of his disappearance.) Alternatively, playing on the boy's interest in trains, he could have posed as a railway enthusiast or employee promising him access to some special treat. There are several points further down the line where it would have been easy to take a child from the trackside to a parked vehicle with a low risk of being seen. In support of this contention, I offer the fact that this freight line runs away from Bradfield in the direction of the Peak District. Its terminus is a mere dozen miles as the crow flies from Swindale. The line moves from what we know now is our perpetrator's territory into Tim Golding's home territory. This is a connection that should not be ignored. We should also therefore consider the possibility that the perpetrator may be a railway worker or a railway enthusiast, particularly since part of the route he must have walked Tim Golding down is a former railway track.

He is more likely to live near the body dump than to the place where he originally picked up Tim Golding. He is more comfortable in the country than in an urban environment.

The perpetrator will also have private access to a computer. Given that the image of Tim Golding ended up on the computer of a known paedophile, it would be worth liaising with colleagues involved in the investigations into internet child pornography. It may well be that they have cases pending against others who have seen images of Tim Golding. These offenders may be willing to reveal their sources in exchange for some sort of deal. It may also be that in the vast volume of information held by Operation Ore but not yet acted upon is the name of our perpetrator. It may be worth running any names that crop up in the Tim Golding investigation against those in Operation Ore's databanks.

Finally, I would like to return to the disappearance of Guy Lefevre. As previously outlined, I believe there is a strong likelihood that whoever was responsible for the abduction of Tim Golding was the same person who took Guy Lefevre. That being the case, I think it is extremely likely that Guy's body will also be found in Swindale. The killer is clearly comfortable with his choice of body dump and his ability to get his victims there. It's likely he had already tested it out on Guy. When Tim's remains are clear of the grave, I suggest exploring the area immediately beneath him. If that produces no result, I would recommend widening the search to the rest of the dale.

Carol reread the profile. 'Thank you, Tony,' she said softly. As always, his concision and his insight had moved her inquiry further forward. She could go into the briefing this morning with a series of positive suggestions. Hitting the team with definite lines of inquiry always provoked their best work.

The only thing niggling at the back of her mind was why he had chosen to email the profile to her rather than bringing it in himself and going through it with her. They had always found it productive to test his hypotheses in argument and discussion. And there was no mention of a proposed visit to the crime scene. It cut into her good mood and made her feel uneasy.

Carol shrugged the thought aside and picked up

her phone. 'Stacey, can you find out who's in charge of the SOCOs we've been working with in Derbyshire? I need them to go back to Swindale and look for another body.'

Evans was looking pleased with himself. 'It's a start, at least,' he said. They were sitting in a tearoom in Tideswell, a pile of hot buttered teacakes on a plate in front of them next to a couple of slices of lemon meringue pie. Kevin had arrived first after supervising the further excavation of Tim Golding's grave. A mere fifteen inches below the first set of bones, more human remains had been unearthed. Carol Jordan had been right on the money, Kevin thought, pleased that his boss was so evidently back on form.

Now a full fingertip search of Swindale was under way. Two dozen cops were still on their hands and knees in protective white suits inching through the vegetation. Kevin felt he deserved self-indulgence after two hours standing in the rain feeling the waves of hatred from the officers Derbyshire had loaned them for the search, but Evans seemed oblivious to the treats on the table.

'Run it past me,' Kevin said.

'OK. I tracked down one of the three rangers who covers this patch. Nick Sanders, his name is. He told me that he had a report from some hikers earlier this summer of a flasher down that end of Chee Dale, near the entrance to Swindale. They'd spotted him exposing himself to a bunch of kids, and they chased him. But they lost him. Said he just seemed to disappear into thin air. Which of course fits with the entrance to Swindale. Later that afternoon, Sanders ran into them when he was doing a routine patrol and they gave him a description.' Evans flipped open his notebook and read it out. 'Early thirties. About five foot eight or nine, slim build, dark hair, bald on top. Wearing a Leeds Rhinos shirt, blue jeans and trainers.'

'It is a start, I suppose,' Kevin said, reaching for a teacake. 'But it's not like we're going to pull him based on that description.'

'We could release it, though. Somebody might recognize it.'

Kevin looked sceptical. 'Did Sanders report it to the local lads?'

Evans' lip curled in contempt. 'No. He says he meant to but it slipped his mind.'

'Great. Fucking woodentops out here.'

'But he logged it in his daily report. He's going to email me a copy of it when he gets back to base. He's also going to email me a set of photos the rangers took of Swindale and Chee Dale back in July.'

'What were they doing taking pictures down there?'

'It wasn't just there specifically. They did a photographic record of the whole of that part of the Wye Valley. Him and the other two guys who cover this patch were proposing a series of footpath improvements and they wanted to back it up with photographic evidence of the effectiveness of work that had been done in the past. Plus where it needed to be done now. He also told me that there was a team of conservation volunteers working in that part of the dale back in May. He didn't have names, but he says the Peak Park HQ should be able to provide those.'

'Helpful bloke, your Nick Sanders,' Kevin said. 'I wish the turnips Derbyshire sent us were as keen to do the business. Talk about "send in the clowns . . ."'

'He seemed genuinely upset about Tim and Guy,' Evans said. 'Nearly as upset as he was about the idea of somebody fucking with his precious park.'

'Nice work, Sam. So, have you got the other two rangers lined up for a chat?'

Evans glanced at his watch. 'Sorted. Gotta meet one in half an hour. Some place called Wormhill. Sounds tasty. The other one's on his day off today; I'll catch him first thing in the morning.'

'Better tuck in, then. Can't be expected to work on an empty stomach.'

Evans reached for a teacake. 'It'd be nice to nail this one. Make up for missing out on the action in Temple Fields.'

Kevin snorted. 'What action? That's turning into the biggest waste of time and money this side of the Yorkshire Ripper inquiry. A career graveyard, that's what that one's going to be, mark my words. A career graveyard.'

'It's brass monkeys out here.' Paula's words crackled in Carol's ears. She felt for the young DC. It was hard to imagine a worse night to be out on the streets. Freezing fog hung over the canal, sending tendrils of chill mist into the streets of Temple Fields. Moisture almost too fine to merit the name rain soaked through clothes, plastering Paula's hair to her head. There were few pedestrians, and those there were hustled down the street, heads down, umbrellas up. In all conscience, Carol knew she couldn't keep Paula out there for four hours. She made a mental promise to herself to knock it on the head at ten.

'Rather her than me,' Jan Shields muttered.

'She looks better in a miniskirt than you would,' Merrick commented.

'And light years better than you would, Don,' Carol pointed out. She chuckled suddenly. 'Hey, remember when you guys had to stake out the gay club on the Thorpe case? You made such a sweet leather queen, Don.'

'All right, all right, point taken,' he grumbled.

'Hang about, looks like we've got some action,' Jan said urgently.

The man had been walking down the street, snorkel parka hood pulled over his head, hiding his face. There was nothing suspicious about that in itself on such a night. But as he approached Paula, he slowed down. He came up to her from the side, obviously moving so quietly she hadn't heard his approach. He stretched out a gloved hand and touched her, one finger on her arm.

'Jesus Christ, are you trying to give me a fucking heart attack?' Paula's voice, loud and clear. She turned to face him.

'You working?' The man's voice was barely audible. It sounded muffled, as if he was speaking through a scarf.

'What does it look like?'

'I'm looking for something a bit unusual. You up for that?'

'Depends what you have in mind.'

'I'm willing to pay. Up front.' His hand emerged from his pocket. It was impossible to tell from the cameras what he was holding.

'That'll buy you a lot of unusual. But you still haven't said what you want. You gotta use a condom, you know that?'

'That's not a problem. Listen, I've got a place. You let me tie you up, I'll pay you two hundred. Straight up.'

Carol's mouth dried up. She pressed the button on her mike and croaked, 'All units, stand by. The eagle is hovering. Repeat, all units, stand by.'

Paula was still talking. 'Two hundred? Up front? Now?'

Even through the intermediary of the camera, the action was unmistakable. He peeled off notes and offered them to her.

Carol's nose was practically up against the screen but she still couldn't distinguish any of the man's details. 'Shit. We can't see his face.'

'Sounds like the real thing,' Jan said excitedly.

'All units, move to takedown positions. Move to takedown positions. Close off the area. Repeat, close off the area.' Carol's pulse was racing, the beat of her blood loud in her ears. On the screen, Paula was rounding the corner, the man's hand on her elbow. On the street, other bodies were closing in on them. It was going to work. Thank Christ, it was going to work.

Adrenaline had Paula in its electric grasp. Her breathing was shallow, her heart pumping like a drum. As they rounded the corner, she felt herself being shunted into a narrow ginnel between buildings. 'Where are we going?' she said.

In reply, he pulled her into an embrace, one hand

305

roughly groping her breast, the other circling her back. Paula was so focused on the pain in her tweaked nipple that she never felt the sharpened electrician's snips slicing cleanly through the wire that ran from her mike to the power pack.

She pushed him away, saying, 'Oy! I thought you said you had a place to go to?'

He swung her round by the arm. 'It's just here.' He leaned past her and opened a gate in the wall, so grubby it was almost invisible against the blackened brick. He steered her inside then slipped the snib on the lock, closing it fast behind them. He ushered Paula towards the back door of a building.

Nervous, but secure in the mistaken belief that she was still transmitting, Paula said sarcastically, 'Mmm, very glamorous back yard. Who'd have thought such a nondescript gate in the wall would hide so lovely a place? We going into this building here then? This your place?'

'Yeah,' the man said. 'Come on, get a move on. We haven't got all night.'

Carol was on her feet. 'Paula's gone dead. There's nothing coming through.' She turned to the two technical support staff. 'Is it our end or hers?'

Thirty seconds of unbearable suspense. Breath held. Prayers offered. Fingers crossed. Then one of the technicians shook his head. 'It's not our end. She's not transmitting.'

At once, chaos broke out. Carol shouted, 'Take down. Repeat, take down. The eagle has landed. All units, pursuit, pursuit.'

'Fuck, shit, fuck, shit,' Merrick kept repeating like

a mantra as he wrenched open the side door of the van. He leapt out into the street as Carol ripped off her headset and tore after him, Jan in their wake. Stacey stared after them, open-mouthed, uncertain whether to stay put and hold the fort or follow. She settled for closing the van door and picking up Carol's discarded comms equipment. Somebody had to keep track of what was happening. She didn't mind. She who controls the technology controls the world, she told herself. It was a far more interesting option than running around on the street. Nothing would happen without her knowledge here.

Carol pounded down the pavement, nightmare visions flooding her head. 'No, no, no,' she gasped on her out breaths as she covered the twenty yards to the corner where she'd last seen Paula. As she rounded the corner, she ran into the back of another officer, winding both of them. Carol staggered, then found her footing. She pushed past and found more officers milling around in the narrow ginnel where Paula had disappeared with the man. She shoved her way through, following the ginnel to its end. It led into another street intersected with lanes, alleys and back entries. It was a labyrinth.

'Fan out,' Carol shouted. 'Cover the area. They can't have gone far. Shit!'

'It's a rabbit warren round here, they could be anywhere,' Merrick said, his face haggard, his voice cracking.

'So don't stand here talking, start looking. And somebody get this gate open,' she added, pounding her fist against the door in the wall of the ginnel. 'See where it takes us and go through it with a fine-tooth comb.' Carol ran her hand through her hair. A sharp pain was rising from the base of her skull. How could this be happening?

Merrick was talking urgently into his radio. 'All units. Begin search of immediate area. Officer missing. Repeat, officer missing.' He glanced across at Carol. 'You want us to start door-to-door?'

She nodded. 'Jan, you take charge of that. And start with whatever's behind this gate.' Carol turned away, choking on her anger. As the officers around her dispersed, Carol wondered what she could have done differently. The worst of it was, she couldn't think of a single thing.

This one's a keeper. He doesn't know why, he just knows that's the way it has to be. The Voice makes the decisions, the Voice knows best, the Voice doesn't ever let him down.

She looks like all the others, like a whore, but this one's a cop. Knowing that makes him scared, but he still manages to do what he's supposed to. He can't get over how simple it's been to capture her. Just like the Voice said it would be. The Voice said she would come along with him, meek as a lamb, good as gold, and she has.

He plucks her off the street, easy as could be. Easier than the others, in a way, because he doesn't know this one from before. It isn't hard to think of her as a dirty piece of meat because she's never done anything to make him think otherwise. He gets her into the ginnel, then he cuts her wire just like he'd been practising all afternoon. Snip, snap, just like that. She doesn't notice a thing.

Into the yard, through the door, up the stairs. She never pauses for a moment, just keeps wittering on, thinking there's somebody listening to her giving directions to the room that's

308

been prepared for her. She doesn't even hesitate at the double door that looks just like a cupboard when you open the outer door on the landing. She comments on it, though, thinking she's passing the message on. When he tells her to lie down on the bed and spread her legs and arms, she does as she's told. He can smell the anxiety coming off her, but she isn't scared, not really scared, not nearly scared enough. The cuffs go on and still he can tell she's waiting for the cavalry to burst through the door and save her. She doesn't even kick when he fastens the ankle restraints.

But when the gag goes on, that's a different story. He can tell she doesn't like that, not one bit. Her eyes widen and a tide of colour sweeps up from her juicy round tits to her hairline. All at once it's dawning on her that maybe it isn't going to play out the way it's supposed to. That he is in control, not her and the pathetic plods on her side. He smiles at her then, the relaxed, triumphant smile of the winner.

'They're not coming,' he says. 'You're on your own.' He leans over and reaches under her body. He pulls the transmitter out from under her skirt. Then he reaches into her cleavage and yanks out the mike and its cable. He waves the cut ends in front of her eyes. 'You've been talking to yourself,' he taunts her. 'They don't have a fucking clue where you are. You could be anywhere in Temple Fields by now. You thought you could beat us, but you were wrong. You're fucked, plod.'

He turns away, ignoring the mewling noises coming through the gag. He takes out the dildo he prepared earlier. The bright light gleams on the sharp edges of the razor blades. It's fucking wicked, this death machine. He swivels on the balls of his feet, spinning round to face her. When she sees the dildo, the colour drains from her face, leaving her chest blotchy and ugly. He steps forward, pushes up her

309

skirt and rips her pants away. He waves the dildo in her face and grins.

That's when she pisses herself. Which annoys him, because it's going to make the room smell, and that's not very nice. Because this one's a keeper.

PART FOUR

It's a well-known fact that there exist books that change people's lives. If anyone were to ask me if such a book had ever swept through my life, I imagine they'd be profoundly surprised by the answer. But I can still remember the impact I felt when I first read John Buchan's The Three Hostages.

We were on a family holiday on the Norfolk Broads. It was as if my parents were aware of the concept of holidays but didn't really understand how they should be done. Other people got to spend the week messing about on boats, exploring the waterways and experiencing a way of life utterly different from their normal routines – locks, fens, waterfowl, the strange sensation of unreality when their feet hit solid ground after days on the water. But not us. My parents had rented a static caravan on a site where hundreds of the metal boxes sat in serried rows along a low bluff that looked out over the blue-grey waters of the North Sea. The van we'd ended up in didn't even have that view to commend it. All we could see from the windows was other caravans. It wasn't an improvement on home; even in a two-bedroomed council house, there was more space and privacy than in this thirty-two-foot tin can. I hated it, resented the other kids whose parents had taken them on a proper holiday, counted the hours till we'd be on the road home.

The weather didn't help either. A typically English summer week, grey drizzle alternating with days of watery sunlight when everybody from the caravan site trooped off to the shingle beach, stripped down to their bathing suits, hopping from one foot to the other over the painful stones to the water's edge. Then they screamed at the temperature, turned round and hopped shivering back up the beach again to flasks of hot weak coffee and egg sandwiches.

One afternoon when the rain was particularly undeniable my parents decided to go and play bingo in the community-hall-cum-snack-bar that squatted in a low concrete block in the middle of the vans. I had to go too, because at twelve I wasn't legally old enough to be left on my own. And my parents were always nauseatingly law-abiding. Smarting at the indignity, I trailed behind them, grudging and resentful. I wanted to hang out with Amanda, the beautiful blonde girl from the van two rows down, not watch a bunch of old fogeys playing bingo.

Dad bought me a Coke and a bag of crisps, pointed me in the direction of the ping-pong table and told me to amuse myself for a couple of hours and not to wander off. Like I was a little kid. Fuming, I stomped off. The ping-pong room was noisy with kids who looked at me like I'd dropped in from another planet. I slouched off towards the furthest corner and that's when I spotted the shelf of tattered hardbacks. I took a couple down from the shelves, but they didn't grab me. Then I picked The Three Hostages and from the first page, with its images of a

312

social milieu whose lives were utterly alien to mine, I was hooked.

Until that moment I'd never imagined it was possible to achieve total domination over another's conscious will. The Three Hostages *spoke to me of two things I wanted above everything else: absolute superiority, and access to a world of power and success. I'd been deprived of the latter by birth, but if I seized the former for myself, I could grasp at something almost as fine.*

The Three Hostages *was the first step on a long journey to the heart of other people's minds. That control was possible, I never doubted. That I could achieve it, I never doubted. That I could use it to change the world around me remained to be seen. But on balance, I thought I could probably manage it.*

At first, my path was less than clear. I chose information as my highway, tracking down everything I could about hypnosis, altered states, brainwashing and mind control. And the more I learned, the more I tried to demonstrate my abilities to myself. I practised on school friends, I sneaked under the guard of lovers, I even tried it at work. I soon learned that my skills weren't all I had hoped for. Sometimes I achieved remarkable results. But, more often, I failed. Most minds remained resolutely beyond my grasp. And no matter how hard I tried, I just couldn't break through.

Then I discovered that there was a category of weaker minds that had few defences against my techniques. People the rest of the world dismissed as slow and stupid could be bent to my will. Not perhaps the world-shattering effect I had dreamed of, but something that offered distinct possibilities.

The question then became what I would do with the

power I had prepared myself to wield. How could I magnify what was in my grasp?

The answer came out of nowhere. The power of two.

If knowledge was power, then the choice of how to disseminate it was power in action. So Sam Evans was always willing to trade a little to get a lot. It was surprising how much people would spill if they thought you were being candid with them. So it was with Kevin. In exchange for a couple of snippets he'd picked up about Stacey Chen's background, Evans had garnered a wealth of information about Don, Paula and Kevin himself. Just the sort of things that could come in useful as subtle little pressure points if he ever needed to push them off balance.

They were sitting in a country pub a few miles from Swindale, recharging their batteries with a well-earned pint after a long and frustrating day fighting petty turf wars and conducting painstaking interviews. They were supposed to be formulating a plan of action for the morning, but they'd tacitly acknowledged that they'd had enough of the grinding depression of dealing with the deaths of children. Station gossip was far more appealing.

Kevin broke off from the story he was telling when his mobile beeped, indicating the arrival of a text message. He looked incredulously at the screen. 'Is she at the wind-up, or what?' he exclaimed, turning the phone so Evans could read the screen.

Under the heading STACEY MOBY, it read 'Killr hs capturd Paula. She's missng.'

Evans shook his head. 'Not Stacey. Not her style.'

Kevin was already dialling. As soon as the line opened, he said, 'What do you mean, the killer has captured Paula? Is this some kind of sick joke?'

'I wouldn't joke about something like that,' Stacey said, clearly offended at the suggestion. 'I meant just what I said. He's got Paula. He took her into an alley and she went off the air. By the time we got there, they'd vanished. That was about half an hour ago and we've not seen hide nor hair of either of them since.'

'Shit,' Kevin swore. 'We're coming over. We'll be there inside the hour.' He ended the call and turned to Evans. 'She meant it. While we were sitting here enjoying a pint, our fucking colleagues sat on their hands and let the killer snatch Paula from under their noses.' He jumped to his feet. 'Come on, we're going back to Bradfield.'

Evans abandoned his half-drunk pint and led the way to the door. 'How the hell did that happen?' he said.

'I don't know,' Kevin said. 'Carol Jordan was so sure she had all the bases covered.'

Evans raised his eyebrows as he followed Kevin to the car. If anything happened to Paula, it would be goodnight, Vienna for Carol Jordan. He was glad he was well clear of the night's debacle, working a case that had a better prospect of resolution. It was every man for himself out there. Anyone who thought otherwise was prey. And prey got eaten.

He had no intention of being anyone's next meal.

It was just after three in the morning when Carol made it home. Paula McIntyre had been missing for a little over six hours. Every door in Temple Fields that would respond to a thunderous tattoo of knocking had opened, every respondent had been questioned. They'd shaken down massage parlours and brothels, accosted whores and rent boys, disrupted bars and clubs. Short of taking a battering ram to all the remaining doors of Temple Fields – shops, offices, flats, bedsits and who knew what else – they had done everything they could to find Paula. But it was as if she and her assailant had vanished into thin air. The maze of alleys, back yards and lanes had yielded nothing in the way of clues. Jan Shields had led a team through the gate in the wall and into the building behind it, which seemed mostly to serve as storage for a local printshop. Their search had turned up nothing to indicate that anyone had passed that way for days.

Finally, Carol had called it a night. Several officers had protested, expressing their willingness to continue searching, but Carol had vetoed their requests. Nothing of use could be done before daybreak, she said firmly. The best service they could offer Paula now was to get some sleep. What none of them was prepared to voice was their conviction that they were already too late.

Carol had walked back to the surveillance van with Jan Shields and Don Merrick in a despondent silence.

When they got there, Jan had shaken her head. 'I'm not coming back yet. I've still got contacts out there. There are people I need to talk to. You'll be amazed who ends up on our side once they realize it's a cop on the missing list. They'll want this sorted nearly as badly as we do.'

'Bad for business, is it?' Merrick said sourly.

'Yeah, you could say that.' Jan pulled her soft leather jacket closer to her face. 'I'll see you at the briefing.'

Carol made no attempt to stop her. They watched till she was swallowed up by the mist. 'I told her this morning she didn't need to go through with this,' Merrick said.

Carol could feel the heat of his hostility but was too weary to get into it with him. 'She knew that already, Don. It was her choice,' she said heavily. She yanked open the door of the van and climbed inside. 'I'm going home to get some sleep. I suggest you do the same rather than chase your tail round Temple Fields for the rest of the night.' She didn't wait for his response. When he hadn't followed her after twenty seconds, she slammed the door shut and ordered the driver to take them back to the station.

She thanked Stacey for holding the fort, then asked one of the technicians to run the CCTV footage of Paula's last encounter again. They watched it half a dozen times on the journey, but none of them saw anything new. When they arrived back at base, she ordered the technicians to do everything they could to enhance both sound and vision. Then she walked to her car, feeling so old and tired she could hardly put one foot in front of the other.

By the time she got to her door, she was trembling with a mixture of despair and exhaustion. She was pathetically grateful to see a light burning in Tony's study. She leaned on his doorbell. He opened the door dressed in jogging pants and a T-shirt, a puzzled look on his face.

'He's got Paula,' Carol said. Each word felt as if it had been dragged out of her. She closed her eyes tightly, tilting her head back. Tony stepped on to the freezing doorstep and put his arms round her. For a few seconds, her body remained rigid. Then her head was on his shoulder, tears coursing down her face. Tony said nothing. He supported her weight, letting her lean into him, feeling her body shudder as she let go her grief.

Eventually, the storm abated. Carol withdrew slightly, meeting his concerned look. 'I'm OK,' she said shakily.

'No, you're not.' Tony led her indoors and helped her sit. 'You want a drink?'

Carol nodded, wiping the tracks of her tears from her cheeks. 'Please.'

He nodded, heading for the kitchen. He reappeared a minute later with two glasses of white wine, handing one to Carol before sitting down next to her. 'You want to talk about it?'

Carol took a mouthful of wine. It tasted alien, as if something had chemically altered her tastebuds. 'Call it displacement activity if you want, but I can't talk about Paula until I know where we stand with each other.'

'Then you need to tell me what I need to know.'

Carol drank more wine. This time, it tasted closer

to what she expected. 'Since the rape, I've felt like I didn't own my body any more. It took me a while to realize that I needed a sexual experience that would show me I was still in control of my responses. I needed it to be about me and I needed it to be uncomplicated.' She put the palm of her hand on his back, feeling the warmth of his skin through his shirt.

He snorted. 'Which ruled me out on both counts.'

Her half-smile signalled agreement. 'And suddenly there was Jonathan. Understanding, generous, attractive and absolutely not somebody I could fall in love with. So I used him. I'm not particularly proud of that, but there's no reason for you to feel jealous. You get more of me every day than I let him have.'

'But I am jealous. I'm jealous that it's so easy for him and so hard for me.'

'I was trying to make it easier for both of us.'

'I know. But that's not going to happen any time soon, is it? For you and me to be at ease with each other?'

His voice was sadder than she'd ever heard it. 'I don't know,' she said bleakly. 'I just know that I . . .'

'Don't say it.' He cut across her harshly. 'I feel the same. But the timing's never right, is it? There's always something with a greater claim on us, something that pushes us apart. And right now, it's Paula. So tell me what happened tonight.'

Carol outlined the evening's events. 'She's dead. And I let it happen. Knowing what I know about how these things can go wrong, I still let it happen.'

Tony jumped to his feet and started pacing. 'I don't think she is dead. This killer wants his victims found,

320

and found while they're still fresh. He sets it up so they will be found. Paula hasn't been found, so logic dictates she's probably still alive.'

Carol shook her head. 'But why would he change his MO?'

'That's a good question. Maybe because he realized Paula's a cop. If you remember, I said to you after the first night that he might have spotted that she was a decoy.'

'Even so, why would that make a difference?'

'He likes power. It may be that he's keeping her alive because it gives him even more power to savour, having a cop under control. It gives him power over us as well as over her. He's the stage manager, the conductor of the orchestra. We have to dance to his tune if we want Paula back alive.'

Carol frowned. 'What do you mean, "dance to his tune"?'

Tony waved a hand impatiently. 'I don't know yet. Either he'll make that clear to us or we'll have to figure it out for ourselves.' He paced again then stopped abruptly and whirled round to face her. 'Carol, how did he know she was wearing a wire?'

'You answered that yourself. He must have figured out she was a decoy and realized she would be wired. That's probably why he started pawing her as soon as he got her in the alley.'

'This is way too sophisticated for Derek Tyler,' he muttered.

'But it wasn't Derek Tyler last night. Derek Tyler's banged up in Bradfield Moor.'

'I know, I know. But these are the same crimes, the same brain behind them. And it's not Derek Tyler's brain. He's not smart enough, not controlled enough.' He fixed Carol with a freshly energized stare. 'The person behind this isn't just pulling our strings. He's pulling the killer's strings too.'

Carol shook her head stubbornly. 'I don't buy it. People don't kill because somebody asks them to. Only contract killers do that. And if this is a contract killer, then he's doing it at the behest of someone who wants to send Derek Tyler a "Get out of jail free" card. We need to go back through his life again, find out who might want him out and why.'

'You're wrong, Carol,' Tony sighed. 'But if you're determined to go down that path, then maybe you should be looking into the lives of his victims, not Tyler himself.'

Carol drained her glass and stood up. 'His victims?'

'If I loved someone who was murdered, and their killer didn't even get life, if he just got sent to a mental hospital that theoretically he could be released from at any time, I probably wouldn't feel that justice had been done. I'd want that killer in my grasp. Given the kind of circles his victims moved in, it's not beyond the bounds of possibility that there's someone who loved one of his victims and who is now in a position to hire a contract killer to replicate those crimes, in the expectation that you'll have to let Tyler go as a result.' He shrugged. 'It has a kind of logic to it.'

Carol stared at him, her mouth open. 'Logic?' she stammered.

'No, Carol. It's bollocks. If there was anything in what I've just suggested, the person hiring the contract killer would also have sent a lawyer in to

Tyler, pushing him towards an appeal. And that hasn't happened.'

'There's time,' she said. 'Maybe he'll try to use Paula as a bargaining chip.'

'Carol, if you get a demand from the killer offering you Paula in exchange for an admission that Derek Tyler was wrongly convicted, I will buy you dinner every night for a year.'

'Deal,' she said.

He swallowed the last of his wine. 'And now I think it's time for sleep. We've both got important work to do . . .' He glanced at his watch and groaned. 'Starting in a few hours.'

'I didn't thank you for the profile in the Tim Golding case,' Carol said, following him to the front door 'It was very helpful.'

'You're welcome. I didn't think you got your money's worth before.'

'Will you go out and take a look at the scene?'

He spread his hands in a gesture of helplessness. 'I was thinking about going out there tomorrow. But with Paula missing . . .'

'It can probably wait.'

'Who have you got on it?' he asked.

'Kevin and Sam. And Stacey will do the liaison with the paedophile unit. Don wanted it back, but frankly I'm not convinced he's up to it. When all this shit is over, I think I'm going to ask Brandon to move him back to mainstream CID. Maybe by then Chris Devine will be able to move north. She'd make a good DI.' Her face clouded over. 'God, when I think how much I was looking forward to this assignment. I thought it was going to be my salvation. But right now, it feels like the last nail in the coffin.'

Stacey Chen loved her job. Her parents had embraced computer technology with eagerness when it first became generally available in the late eighties. They owned a chain of Chinese supermarkets and the capacity of the machines to keep track of stock and transactions enchanted them. Stacey could hardly remember a time when there hadn't been computers in her life. An only child, she'd taken to silicon the way other children took to Barbie dolls or books. Frustrated by the limitations of those early home computers, she'd learned programming code so she could write her own games for machines that had only ever been meant to do word processing and simple accounts. By the time she started studying computer science at UMIST, she'd already earned enough to buy a city-centre loft, thanks to a neat little piece of code she'd sold to a US software giant which secured their operating system against potential software conflicts. Her lecturers predicted a meteoric career for her in the dotcom world. None of them could quite believe it when she'd announced that she planned to join the police.

It made absolute sense to Stacey, however. She loved the unpicking of problems. Rooting around in other people's systems was meat and drink to her, and here was a way she could satisfy her urges without breaking any laws. And she had enough time off to pursue her own commercial interests without any of the potential clashes that might have arisen if she'd been working for a software company. So what if her police salary was peanuts compared to what she made in her own time? Her job gave her legitimate sanction to invade other people's secrets, and that was satisfaction enough.

She didn't even need to be in the office to creep through everyone else's data. She'd set up her own home computing systems to allow her network access to all the machines used by the Major Incident Team. And because she'd designated herself as a systems operator she didn't even have to go through the tiresome process of capturing their passwords. She could simply wander at will through their machines. And so she knew Kevin's taste for soft-porn sites where he could browse for free without handing over any personal details. She knew Don Merrick's penchant for American baseball, Paula's addiction to news websites and Jan's habit of ordering books from an online women's bookstore in York. She'd been intrigued by Carol Jordan's wariness to commit to the machine until she'd uncovered the information that her brother worked in software development. Carol was clearly only too aware of the footprints that any activity left on a computer.

She also knew about Sam Evans' late-night trawls. She'd sat in her flat noting his keystrokes, watching him trying to break into his colleagues' files and failing every time at the password hurdle. She should have felt that Sam was a kindred spirit, but instead she despised him for his incompetence. He should stick to hanging out on those gross post-mortem sites he liked so much. That was about his speed. God, but cops were weird.

Tonight she was alone on the system, however.

Wherever Sam was, he wasn't skulking round the office, trying to steal a march on the rest of them. And there was nothing new on the hard drive to interest her. She wondered what was happening over in Temple Fields. A few keyboard commands and a couple of mouse clicks and she could see what the cameras were feeding back to the computer.

Stacey poured herself another cup of coffee from the Thermos on her desk and settled down for a long hard look.

Paula had no idea how long she had been lying in the stark, oppressive room with its bare bulb making everything brutally vivid. At first, all she'd felt was overwhelming relief and gratitude that she was still alive. She had no idea why that should be; she knew his previous victims must have been attacked almost as soon as he'd snatched them from the street. And when he had produced that vile, horrifying implement, she'd been sure she was going the same way. But no. He'd simply exposed her genitals to the camera, brandished the lethal dildo in front of her and giggled. Then he'd checked her bindings and stepped back, fingering his cock through the faded denim of his baggy trousers. She'd thought then he was going to rape her, but that fear wasn't realized either. He'd gazed hungrily at her for a few minutes, stroking his erection as if it were a pet rat. Then he'd checked the video camera and the webcam and left.

Since then, she'd been alone. She'd struggled to free herself, but soon gave up, understanding that the only thing she was achieving was the fruitless expenditure of energy she might need later. She'd tried shouting for help, but the gag pressing against her mouth was far too effective to allow anything other than a moan to escape. There was nothing to do but lie there, shivering with cold and fear. The puddle of piss beneath her had soaked into the thin mattress and spread out, making her even colder.

Paula tried to convince herself they'd be coming to get her soon. Carol Jordan would never abandon her. That he'd left her alive made her think he believed they were close on his heels. He'd gone because he didn't expect to have the time to sit and watch her die once he'd cut her. But as the time trickled by, she began to lose faith. At one point she'd thought she heard faint footfalls and muffled conversation. But even as she strained to hear, the sounds faded and she was left wondering if it had all been her imagination.

This was all her own fault. How could she have missed him cutting the wire? If she'd been paying attention to her mission instead of freaking out because he'd pinched her nipple so painfully, she'd have known she was on her own. Then, as soon as they reached the room and she'd seen confirmation in the tools of his trade arranged on the table, she could have taken him by surprise and nailed him. But she'd dropped the ball. She'd focused on her reactions rather than on the job and now she was paying the price.

But she was still alive. As long as she was still alive, she could believe in rescue. Carol Jordan would break down every door in Temple Fields if she had to. She knew what it was like to be hung out to dry by her bosses, and there was no way she would allow that to happen to Paula. Whatever it took, Carol would find her.

The minutes ground by inexorably. Exhausted, Paula was drifting in and out of an altered state that bordered sleep but never quite crossed over. When the door opened, she couldn't be sure initially whether she was dreaming it. Her heart leapt in her chest. They'd found her!

Hope perished in seconds when the cruelly familiar shape of her kidnapper came into view. He'd swapped the parka for a hooded top, presumably to avoid being recognized. But she knew who he was only too well. 'Only me,' he said. 'Come to change the tape. The webcam's not very good, that's why we need the video too. So we can enjoy watching you suffer.'

If she strained her neck, she could see him move behind the video camera and remove the tape. He put it in his pocket, then leaned over and did something to the webcam. He leered at her. 'I'm not supposed to touch you. The Voice says I've to wait till the time is right. But the Voice doesn't see everything.'

He came towards her, one hand rubbing himself. He climbed awkwardly on to the bed. Paula smelled stale cannabis smoke and the acid tang of half-digested beer as he moved on top of her. He was heavy and clumsy, the zip on his jacket scratching the soft skin of her belly. Suddenly, she felt the smoothness of latex between her labia, fumbling towards her vagina. She tensed herself against him and he grunted. 'Don't make it harder on yourself, you silly cunt,' he growled in her ear. She tried to twist away, but her bonds were too tight and he was too heavy.

Then he was inside her, fingers pounding and thrusting while he rode her thigh. She could feel his cock rigid through his clothes. Paula bit down on the gag, fighting tears. She didn't want him to see how much he'd got to her. She tried to dissociate herself from what was happening to her body, but it didn't work.

Mercifully, it was over quickly. He hammered his hand into her, his hips forcing her thigh deep into the mattress as he speeded up. His head arched back and he yelped like a kicked puppy. Then he collapsed on top of her, his fingers slithering out of her bruised vagina. He rolled over and grinned. 'Tight bitch. I like that. It'll be more fun when I do you.'

He clambered off the bed, adjusting his jacket to cover the damp patch on his trousers. He slotted a new tape into the video camera, set the webcam running again and headed for the door. 'See you later, alligator,' he said, waving as he went.

The door slammed shut. Only then did Paula begin to weep.

Carol was in her office making notes for the briefing when Kevin and Sam arrived. 'Guv, can we have a word?' Kevin asked.

She waved them to take a seat with a resigned nod. She'd been half-expecting this. Just another messy conversation that would end up making her feel about as much use as a blind man in an archery contest. 'Let me guess. You want to help find Paula?'

'She's one of us, guv. You said at the start we had to be a team. It doesn't feel right that you've pulled me and DC Evans off on something else when one of the team is on the line,' Kevin said.

'I do understand how you feel,' Carol said. 'But I need to know I have the best possible officers running the Golding and Lefevre inquiry. You must have seen the papers this morning – they know two bodies have been found. They're speculating. The anti-paedophile hysterics are building up a head of steam, and we're directly in their paths. We have to be seen to be devoting our resources to finding their killer.'

'But they're dead, and Paula might still be alive,' Evans protested.

'They may be dead, but they're still important. And whoever killed them is still out there, possibly planning his next crime.'

'We're not saying they're not important, guv,' Kevin argued. 'What Sam means is that there's less urgency.'

'Yeah, it wouldn't hurt if we put it on hold for a day or two, just while the hunt for Paula's going on,' Evans interjected.

'We can't put it on hold, however much you might like to.' Carol tapped her finger on a file on her desk. 'Two positive IDs: Tim Golding and Guy Lefevre. Cause of death in both cases is most probably manual strangulation. We can't keep that from the press. You've already started stirring the pot with the park service and with other groups who may have visited Swindale. Unless our man is deaf and blind, he's going to know we're looking for him. I don't want to give him space to wriggle out from under. We need to keep up the pressure. I'm sorry, guys. You stay with Tim and Guy.'

Both men still looked mutinous. 'But, guv . . .' Kevin began.

'Kevin, the best thing you can do for Paula is to get an early result on this case. You know that'll boost morale, help everyone believe we can bring Paula home safe and catch whoever has taken her. There's no great skill in knocking on doors and chasing up official records, which is more or less all we have to go at this morning. Please, use your talents to give us something positive.' Carol felt faintly surprised at herself. It was the kind of persuasion she would have used without a thought in previous times. That it came so easily to her now restored some of the confidence she'd lost overnight.

Kevin at least fell for the bait. He visibly puffed up, basking in the glow of Carol's flattery. 'We'll do our best,' he said, getting to his feet.

Evans looked at him, then back at Carol. He shook his head in disbelief then followed Kevin out of the door. As they went, she heard him say, 'I can't believe you fell for that bollocks . . .'

Carol was on her feet and at the door. 'Evans,' she shouted. 'Back here. Now.' Startled, he turned back. 'Kevin, I'm taking Evans off you. Don't let me down.' She glared at Evans. 'My office. Now.'

Carol shut the door behind them. 'We're all under strain here, but that's no excuse for insubordination. I do not want my officers working with anything less than a whole heart, and it's clear to me that you are not prepared to give a hundred per cent to easing the pain of two sets of parents whose sons have been murdered.'

'That's not fair.' Evans' expression was mutinous.

'Don't talk back to me, Constable,' Carol said, each word enunciated with chill clarity. 'If you want to stay on this squad, you had better understand that I do not care about your personal preferences when it comes to assignments. I thought I'd already made that clear to you? I choose people for particular tasks because I think they are fitted to them. You're a talented detective, Evans, but that doesn't mean you have the right to question my decisions, especially not in my hearing. I'm reassigning you to the Temple Fields inquiry. But don't think you've won. As of now, you are number one on my shit list and it's going to take something very special indeed to get you out of that slot.'

A flicker of arrogance crossed Evans' face. 'You won't be waiting long,' he said. 'Ma'am.'

Carol shook her head in exasperation. 'It's time to grow up, Evans. Now get out of my sight before I have you reassigned to Traffic.' She watched him leave and sighed. One step forward and two steps back. Time to change the dance, she thought bitterly. Time to pick up momentum and crack the case.

On the giant TV screen, Paula once more stood on a misty street corner. The man in the parka approached and touched her arm. The dialogue boomed out, still crackly but more clear than it had been in Carol's earpiece the night before. Paula and the man rounded the corner and the screen faded to static. The sound-track continued to the point where it ended as abruptly as a slap to the face. There was absolute silence in the room as the lights went back on. Most of the team looked about as shit as Carol felt. *Showtime,* she thought, squaring her shoulders and stretching her fingers like a pianist. 'OK,' she said. 'That's the last we saw of Paula. She is still missing. Our job is to find her. Dr Hill believes the chances are good that Paula is alive. This killer wants his victims found while they're fresh. The fact that we haven't found Paula suggests she's not a victim yet. So let's get to her before that changes. Does anyone recognize that voice? Does that man look familiar? These are the questions we need to be asking.

'We have photographs of Paula at the back of the room. There are also stills from the video available to you. And we've got a limited number of microcassette recorders with tapes of the man's voice that you can play to people in Temple Fields, see if we can get an ID that way. There should be more tape machines available later in the day.

'I'm splitting you into three teams. DI Merrick will remain here, collating information as it comes in via statement readers and HOLMES operators. Sergeant MacLeod from uniform will be in charge of the team extracting details from the council tax registers of every property in Temple Fields. DS Shields will be in charge of the team who will interview every tenant and resident in the area, assisted by information from Sergeant MacLeod's team. No stone unturned, people. We've got an officer out there depending on us. And we're not going to let her down.' Carol's voice rang out with a confidence she didn't entirely feel. But it was her job to make them feel gung-ho, and she was determined to succeed. As they filed out, she called, 'DI Merrick, DS Shields and DC Chen, a word, please.'

The remnants of her squad gathered around her.

'You've all worked closely with Paula. Is there anyone we should inform about what's happened? Parents? Partner?'

'Her mum and dad live in Manchester,' Merrick volunteered. 'I can get an address. Do you want me to go and talk to them?'

'No, it's fine, Don. Get me the address and I'll deal with it myself.' *If anyone's going to get a kicking, it should be me.* 'So, that's it? Parents, no partner?'

'She hasn't got a girlfriend at the moment,' Jan said absently.

Merrick rounded on her angrily. 'What do you mean, a girlfriend?'

Jan gave Merrick a pitying look. 'A lover, a significant other, whatever. Who happens to be female, in Paula's case.'

'Bullshit,' Merrick exploded. 'Paula's not a dyke.'

Jan snorted with laughter. 'You're living under her roof and you hadn't noticed she's gay? Call yourself a detective?'

Carol did a double-take. Her DI was living with one of her DCs? Who happened to be gay? And she'd known nothing of it? There was something seriously amiss with the bush telegraph on this squad, which she'd have to rectify once they had recovered Paula and things had returned to something approaching normal. It wasn't that Carol wanted prurient gossip; simply that, if the squad was to work properly, she had to understand the personal dynamics.

'In your dreams, Shields. You're talking shite,' Merrick said contemptuously.

Jan shook her head, her cherub's face registering

amusement. 'If you say so, Inspector.' Merrick glared at her, frustrated.

Stacey, who had been watching the exchange like a Wimbledon spectator, suddenly spoke up. 'What does it matter who she likes to sleep with? She's not been abducted because she's gay or straight, she's been abducted because she's a cop and we put her out there to do our dirty work. And I'm going back to my computer to do what I can to put things right. Ma'am?' She looked to Carol.

'I couldn't have put it better myself, Stacey. For Christ's sake, you two, get with the programme. We've got a job to do. Shall we get on with it?'

Tony stared at the man curled up on the bed with his back to the room. Again, Tyler had refused to come either to Tony's office or to an interview room. But this time, Tony was not to be denied. He was going to prise something from the man. If Paula McIntyre didn't come out of this alive, he knew Carol would never work as a police officer again, and much as he found that idea personally attractive, he knew he couldn't sit idly by while she lost the one thing that had shaped her sense of herself as an adult.

He pulled up a chair close to the bed and leaned forward, elbows on knees. He gathered his thoughts, focused his energies and spoke conversationally. 'It's not nice, is it? Knowing you've been dumped in favour of somebody else?' Tyler didn't move a muscle.

'I mean, when you hear voices, the least you expect is that they'll be faithful to you. Not abandon you like a pair of worn-out shoes just because you can't deliver the goods any more.' Tyler's leg twitched.

'I can see that's a notion that upsets you. And no wonder. I'd be upset in your shoes. You've been cast adrift, Derek. I bet you thought your voice was going to get you out of here, didn't you? I bet that's why you played the "mad not bad" game, because the voice told you to keep your mouth shut. So one day you could start talking again and we'd think you were cured.' A definite movement, Tony thought. The shoulders tightened, the legs drew further up.

'It's a funny thing, but I've noticed over the years that with most people who hear voices, at some level they're using the voice as their excuse. Now me, if I thought the Virgin Mary was telling me to kill prostitutes, I wouldn't do it, because I've got no deep-seated desire to kill prostitutes. But a man who secretly believed prostitutes were evil would use the voice as an excuse to do what he thought was the right thing. Like Peter Sutcliffe claimed when he was trying to play the "mad not bad" game.'

Tony deepened his voice, aiming for warmth and sympathy. 'But I don't think that's how it was with you, Derek. I don't think you used the voice. I think the voice used you. And now it's using somebody else. Face it, Derek, you're not as special as you thought you were.'

Suddenly Tyler uncoiled and rolled over. He jerked into a sitting position on the edge of the bed, his face inches from Tony. Tony maintained his expression of compassion and concern. Time to play his ace. 'You've been loyal to the voice, but it's let you down. It's left you here to rot. It's found somebody else to do its bidding. It's betrayed you, Derek. So you might as well return the favour.'

The silence dragged out between them for a long minute. Then Tyler leaned even closer. Tony could feel the heat of the other man's breath against his skin. 'I've been waiting for you,' he croaked.

Tony nodded gently. 'I know, Derek.'

His eyes opened so wide Tony could see the iris as a perfect circle against the white. 'I'm supposed to be slow. All these doctors, they're supposed to be clever. But they never got it.'

'I know.'

'They all thought it was the voice of God or something. But I'm not daft, you know. I might be slow, but I'm not daft.'

'I know that too. So whose voice was it?'

Tyler's lips curled back in a triumphant sneer. 'The Creeper.'

'The Creeper?' Tony tried not to show disappointment. 'Who's the Creeper?'

Tyler withdrew a few inches and tapped the side of his nose. 'You're so bloody smart, you figure it out.' Then, in one single fluid movement, he rolled back into his foetal crouch, facing the wall.

If they'd only sussed it out soon enough, it could have been a field day for Bradfield's opportunist criminals. Every available officer was out on the streets in a kaleidoscope of encounters.

On a corner near the sex shop, putting potential customers off, PC Danny Wells: 'Have you seen this woman in the past twenty-four hours?' The photograph of Paula, grinning at the camera on a girls' night out with her colleagues. 'Do you recognize this man?' The video still. *It could be anybody, really,* Danny

thought. 'Listen to this voice. Do you recognize it?'
Play, stop, rewind.

In the newsagent's down the street from Paula's
pitch, DS Jan Shields. The Asian behind the counter
had the air of a man puffed up with righteous indignation. 'Have you seen this woman?' Paula's photo
placed on a pile of morning papers. A shake of the
head. 'Do you know this man?' The video still placed
next to Paula. A shrug.

'How do I know? It could be anybody. It could be
you,' he said insolently.

'Do you own this property?'

'No, I just rent the shop.'

'Only the shop? What about the upper floors?'

'Flats. Nothing to do with me.'

'OK. I'm going to need the name and contact details
of your landlord.'

The shopkeeper scowled. 'Why is this your business? Is there a problem?'

'Yeah, there's a problem, but it's probably not yours.
Can I see your back room?'

Suddenly his bluster was replaced with apprehension. 'Why do you want to do that? It's just a store-
room.'

Jan, not in any mood to argue, leaned on the
counter. 'Listen, I don't give a toss if you've got wall-
to-wall smuggled fags back there; that's not what I'm
looking for. Just let me take a look, OK? Then I'll be
out of here. Otherwise, I'll be on the phone to
Customs and Excise right now, pal.'

He glared at her, then lifted the counter flap to let
her through. 'I can explain . . .'

And in the offices of Bradfield Metropolitan

Council, Sergeant Phil MacLeod. He stood at the head of a group of five officers at the reception desk of the local taxation office. The woman behind the desk looked dubious. 'We shut at twelve today. It's Saturday,' she said.

'Not today you don't. This is a murder inquiry.'

She looked perplexed and frightened. 'I don't know what the procedure is,' she said.

'It's a matter of public record. All you need to do is show me the council tax register for these streets.' Sergeant MacLeod produced a list of the streets of Temple Fields.

'I'm going to have to get my boss.'

'Whatever. Just do it,' MacLeod snapped.

And in a house converted from former Victorian glory to an aggregate of bedsits, DC Laura Blythe. She knocked on a door. No reply. She walked down a hallway smelling of curry and cabbage and knocked on the next door. A bleary-eyed young man in boxers and a T-shirt opened up. Blythe produced her warrant card. 'DC Blythe, Bradfield Police. We're looking for a woman who has been abducted. I wonder if I might take a look inside your flat?'

'Do what?' He looked flabbergasted.

'I just need to satisfy myself that she's not here.'

'You think I've kidnapped somebody?' Incredulity and confusion.

'No, but she went missing very near here and it's my job to eliminate people from our inquiry. So, can I take a quick look?'

'You got a warrant?'

Blythe lowered her voice and went for menacing. 'Don't make me get one. I'm having a very bad day.'

She produced Paula's photo. 'I'm not interested in anything else. Just her.'

He gave a bemused shake of the head and pushed the door open to reveal the scuzzy chaos within. 'She's not my type, love,' he said ironically.

Carol stood in the doorway of Tony's office at Bradfield Moor. It looked like everywhere he'd ever worked – so crowded with books and paper it was impossible to discern any fundamental architecture. He was like a squirrel, building the same nest around himself year after year. 'You left a message on my phone? Sounded urgent.'

He looked up from his computer and smiled. 'Thanks for coming. I thought you'd just phone.'

'I was already heading out of town. I'm on my way to see Paula's parents.' She came in and sat down.

'Ah.'

'Quite. So, what have you got for me?'

'Tyler talked,' Tony said.

'You're kidding,' she exclaimed.

'Don't get too excited.' He ran through the conversation then looked expectantly at Carol.

She ran her hands through her hair. 'The Creeper? That's it?'

He nodded eagerly. 'I told you Derek Tyler hadn't got the wit to commit organized offences like this off his own bat. These murders weren't Tyler's idea. It was never his set-up.'

'So we're back to your theory of some puppet-master pulling Derek Tyler's strings? And now he's back at his old tricks?'

'That's one possibility. It would mean he's found

someone as suggestible as Tyler, which can't have been that easy. But maybe he's spent the last two years plucking up the courage to do it himself.'

'Oh God,' she groaned. 'You know how crazy this sounds?'

'I know. But it's the one thing that makes sense of all the information we have. Either the ringmaster has someone new to control or he's doing it himself.'

An anxious thought crept into Carol's mind. 'What sort of person would be able to control another person to this degree?' she asked, almost reluctant.

Tony frowned. 'You'd be looking at a strong personality. Someone with the ability to charm people, to get under their skin. They'd know a lot about brainwashing techniques. They would probably have developed skills in hypnosis.'

'Someone like you, in fact?' Carol tried to make it sound like a tease but failed.

Tony gave her an odd look. 'They'd have to have better social skills than me,' he said ironically. 'But yes, a practising clinical psychologist could probably do it.' He tilted his head to one side. 'Carol, what are you not telling me?'

'Nothing,' she said with a nervous laugh. This wasn't the time to mention Evans' obsession with Aidan Hart. First she wanted to figure out what she thought herself. 'I need to find the connection to Tyler. Whoever the Creeper is, he was in Tyler's life back then. And I need to get the teams on the streets asking if anyone's heard of the Creeper.'

Tony studied her for a long moment, puzzling over her words. Then he stood up and reached for his coat. 'And I need to think. I'm going back to where Paula

341

went missing.' He paused on his way out the door. 'She's still alive, Carol. I'm sure of it.'

And the kaleidoscope shifted. Inside a chichi pub with bed-and-breakfast rooms on the upper floors, DC Sam Evans. The publican was thirty-something, shaved head, leather waistcoat over a bare torso and leather trousers, polishing glasses with a bar towel. The questions, the photos and the tape. The publican shrugged. 'Doesn't ring any bells, mate.'

'So how many rooms do you have?'

'Eight doubles and two singles.'

'I'd like to take a look at them.'

'Four of them are occupied.' The publican put down his towel.

'I'd especially like to take a look at those ones.'

The publican leered at Evans. 'Into voyeurism, are you, pet?'

Evans leaned on the bar. He fixed the publican with a menacing stare. 'When does your licence come up for renewal? Sir?'

And in a room not fifty yards from the pub, Paula lay glassy-eyed on the bed, the fly captured by the spider. Her mouth was so dry her lips were gummed to the gag. Her captor had been back again to change the tape, but this time he'd left her alone, contenting himself with brandishing the dildo in her face. She had never been so afraid in her life. Her mind was beginning to slip its cogs, strange ideas tumbling over each other in her head. What if this was her punishment for doubting Carol Jordan? What if this was her punishment for being gay? Nothing made sense any more. All she lived for was the opening of the door and for it not to be him on the other side of it.

And on the streets that formed the web around the spider's prey, life went on in patterns too deep-set to be altered by the heavy weight of the police presence. People were more cautious than usual, but still the regular transactions continued. Dee had already found another fuckpad to entertain her customers in; that afternoon, she was bouncing mechanically on top of an office furniture sales rep whose wife was walking their two children home from school while he grunted under Dee. Honey was scoring a wrap of heroin from Carl Mackenzie, both of them well aware that the cops swarming the streets wouldn't have cared if it had been a kilo of pure Chinese white.

And a killer was swaggering on the streets of Temple Fields, wrapped in a sense of contemptuous invulnerability.

Alone in the elite squad's room, Stacey Chen noted the arrival of new email. Seeing there was an attachment, she ran it through her personal virus checker, then, satisfied it was safe to do so, she opened it. It came from Nick Sanders, a ranger in the Peak National Park, and included his log from July as well as a couple of dozen photographs of Chee Dale and Swindale. As she flicked through them, another program activated itself. Stacey had set up a capture program to analyse every JPEG file that her machine encountered, classifying them according to camera serial number when it could be found. She planned to offer the software to the paedophile investigation unit to help them sort files from a variety of sources into associated batches so they could see possible connections between different individuals, but she needed to be sure she'd ironed out any bugs first.

As she turned back to the files she'd been working on previously, one of the SOCOs came in. 'DCI Jordan around?' he asked.

'She's gone to Manchester. Can I help?'

He dropped a file on her desk. 'We managed to extract DNA from the contaminated sample on Jackie Mayall. It's a bit degraded – not good enough to run against the national database for a positive match, but certainly enough for elimination purposes. It won't nail your guy absolutely, but it'll give you a decent pointer if you get the right man.'

'Cheers. I'll make sure she sees it as soon as she gets back,' Stacey said absently, her mind already turning back to the task in hand.

She was surprised when she looked back at the screen to see a flashing window in the centre. <Camera match> it said. She sighed. Probably the same old glitch she'd been trying to solve for a week or two now. Instead of reading a group of images from the same source as a single batch, it was picking each of them up individually and telling her they were in fact matches against something already on the system. She'd thought she'd finally ironed it out, but clearly she'd been mistaken. All it would be telling her was that some of the photos in Sanders' attachment had been taken by the same camera as each other. Hardly earth-shattering stuff, and something she was going to have to work harder to sort out before she could let anybody else loose with the program. With no great hopes, she clicked on the window. And sat there staring, hardly able to believe the evidence of her eyes.

'Holy shit,' she muttered, reaching for the phone.

It had taken Tony longer than he would have liked to make it to Temple Fields. As he'd been leaving Bradfield Moor, he'd been collared by Aidan Hart demanding a case conference on one of Tony's patients. 'Not now, Aidan,' he'd said impatiently.

'Yes, Tony, now. This is one of the mornings you're contracted to work here, after all,' Hart had said implacably.

'You know that's just a formality. I put my hours in – hell, I put more than my hours in – at times that suit me and my patients.'

Hart had tried a conciliatory smile. 'What's so important that it can't wait a couple of hours?'

Tony ran a hand through his hair. 'It's the prostitute killer. He's kidnapped a police officer. I think she's still alive.'

'Surely that's a matter for the police? They don't expect you to search for her, do they?' Hart said, aiming for impish irony.

'No. But I've got something from Tyler and I need to figure out how it moves us forward.'

Hart looked startled. 'Tyler talked to you?'

'A bit. We've got a nickname for the killer. Or at least, the person behind the killer.'

Hart's eyes widened. 'A nickname?'

'I can't tell you, Aidan. It's still confidential.'

Hart's tongue flicked at the corners of his mouth. 'I think I understand confidentiality, Tony.'

'Even so . . .'

'OK, OK. But what do you mean by "the person behind the killer"?'

Tony frowned. 'I haven't got time for this now, Aidan. I need to get into town.'

Hart clamped a hand on his shoulder. 'I'm sorry, Tony. I need you at this case conference.' He steered him back down the corridor. 'So, what's this about a person behind the killer?'

'It's just an idea. I'm not really ready to talk about it,' Tony hedged, uncomfortable at what was starting to feel like an intrusion into the other part of his professional life. He'd clammed up then and sat through the case conference, his spirit chafing but his sense of duty requiring him to support his patient as best he could.

Eventually, however, he'd escaped. Now he was back on the streets of Temple Fields, retracing the steps of Paula's abductor, trying to figure out where he might have come from. As he walked, his lips moved, but he didn't notice the stares he earned from other pedestrians. Twice, he was stopped by police officers, brandishing photos of Paula, officers who were mildly embarrassed when he explained who he was and what he was doing.

'So where is she? Why haven't you given her back to us? You gave us all the others. Why not Paula? We know you've got the power. What are you trying to prove?' he said under his breath as he walked, the questions taking him round in circles that were far smaller than the ones his feet were tracing on the pavements and alleys.

He rounded another corner and walked straight into Jan Shields and Sam Evans, deep in conversation in the lee of a betting-shop awning. Not bothering with preliminaries, he said, 'The Creeper – what does that mean to you?'

Evans shrugged. 'Virginia creeper? Brothel creepers?'

Jan shook her head. 'Not a clue. Sounds like a nickname, but it's not one I've ever heard.'

Tony nodded. 'Pimps have nicknames, don't they?'

'Some of them, yeah. But, like I keep saying, we don't have many pimps left around here,' Jan said.

'Can you ask around, see if anyone's ever heard it?' Tony asked.

'Sure. But what's the relevance?' Evans asked.

Tony looked about him as if the answer might be lurking in one of the adjacent buildings.

'Tony?' Jan prompted.

'I think it's someone Derek Tyler knew,' Tony said, collecting himself. 'Someone who might be able to shed some light on these killings.'

'I don't remember seeing that in his file,' Evans said.

'It's not in his file. He told me himself.' Tony was still looking around, his mind already somewhere else.

'You got Tyler to talk?' Evans asked, incredulous.

Distracted, Tony took half a step beyond them. 'Not nearly enough,' he mumbled. 'And I don't think he's going to give me any more till I can prove I deserve it.'

He walked away, unaware of their looks of astonishment. He carried on to the end of the street, then traced a path through the lanes and alleys till he was in the place where Paula was last heard. 'I thought so,' he said. 'There had to be a circle.'

He leaned against the gate, entirely oblivious of its significance. 'You like to send us messages. So why have you gone off the air? You're the Creeper. You love the sound of your own voice. So why aren't you talking to us any more? Is it something we've done? Something we've said? Or is it the opposite?' He groaned and put his head in his hands. 'I wish I could work out what the hell is going on here.'

Kevin was already waiting for Carol when she returned to the office. She'd driven back from Manchester in the grip of conflicting emotions. Her encounter with Paula's parents had been harrowing. Paula's father, a self-employed electrician, had already been in a state of panic at her request that they both meet her. He was convinced she was coming with news of his daughter's death. Mrs McIntyre had seemed frozen, as if trying to hold back time so she wouldn't have to absorb what Carol told her.

Once Carol had explained the situation, her father's fear had turned predictably to anger. He wanted answers that Carol couldn't provide and he wanted to blame someone. Carol weathered the storm of his anger, did what she could to reassure them and eased out of the drab three-bedroomed semi with promises to keep them informed of any developments.

But the encounter had left her drained and guilty. The excitement she'd felt at Stacey's news had made her feel even more guilty; how could she take pleasure in anything when Paula was in the hands of a ruthless killer who savoured death too much to allow her to live indefinitely?

As if that wasn't enough, she had the troubling

problem of what to do about Aidan Hart. If Tony's bizarre hypothesis was right and a master manipulator had induced someone else to commit his crimes for him, she couldn't ignore what Sam Evans had uncovered about the clinical director of Bradfield Moor. No one was better placed to know every detail of Derek Tyler's crimes. He'd indisputably been in Temple Fields just before Sandie Foster's murder. And he had precisely the sort of skills Tony had outlined as necessary for that sort of mind control over another.

She knew she should discuss it with Brandon, but until she had something stronger to lay before him, she was reluctant to put herself so firmly in the wrong. She wanted to talk it over with Tony, but she was concerned about the possible conflict of interest. She'd never met Hart herself and knew little about Tony's relationship with his boss. She knew they weren't close, if only because nobody was close to Tony. Except possibly her. But she didn't want to put him in a difficult position if Hart was someone he liked and respected.

So she was glad of Kevin's presence because it meant she had something concrete to do, something that left no brooding space. 'Good news, isn't it?' she said, throwing her coat on top of the filing cabinet.

'That Stacey's bloody amazing,' Kevin agreed. 'It would never have occurred to me to do what she did.'

'Me neither. Where is she, by the way?'

'Gone to get a vase. Apparently we don't have one.'

Carol did a double-take. 'A vase?'

'You know, tall thing, you put flowers in it.' The grin was cheeky.

'Thank you, Kevin. And why do we need a tall thing for putting flowers in?'

'Because you got a bouquet,' he said, clearly delighted to be scoring a point off the boss.

'I got a bouquet?' she echoed, feeling stupid. 'Where?'

He gestured with his thumb in the direction of the main office. 'Stacey sat them in her wastepaper basket while she went to get a vase.'

Carol was already on her way back into the squad-room. She rounded Stacey's desk and stopped short at the huge bunch of roses and lilies propped up against the desk. 'Oh, fuck,' she muttered, reaching for the card pinned to the cellophane.

She ripped it open and her heart sank as she read: *Welcome back to the world. You're a very special woman. Love, J.* 'Fuck, fuck, fuck,' she said, screwing it into a ball and remembering at the last minute to stuff it in her pocket rather than toss it in the bin. She strode back into her office and gave Kevin a tight smile. 'So, what have we got?'

'Well, you've got flowers,' he said, not noticing her mood had slipped to the wrong side of geniality.

'Enough about the flowers. Show me what you've got,' Carol snapped.

Kevin covered the desk with the printouts Stacey had given him, arranging them in four groups. 'These are the photos Nick Sanders emailed to us. They've been taken by four separate cameras. The ones that we're interested in are these three –' He pointed to a trio of shots that Carol immediately recognized as being of Swindale. 'According to Stacey's program, they were shot on the same camera that took the picture of Tim Golding that turned up on Ron Alexander's computer.'

A slow, satisfied smile crept across Carol's face. 'So it's fair to assume that one of these three Park Rangers took that photo of Tim?' she said.

'Looks that way.'

'How do you want to proceed?' Carol asked.

'Well, given that we know the camera in question was bought for cash in Birmingham, it's not likely to be one of the ones that belongs to the National Park. So I thought I'd ask Derbyshire to do a simultaneous search of their homes and offices, bring in any cameras they find and see if we get a match.'

Carol considered the idea. 'Too much wriggle room,' she said. 'We start searching, we alert the killer that we're on to him. It gives him time to concoct an alibi, or even to disappear. No. Get their home addresses from the National Park. Take three teams down to Derbyshire, get on their tails and, when you're all in place, bring them in simultaneously. Arrest them on suspicion of murder. Then we'll ask Derbyshire to do the searches while we're questioning them back here. I want this guy scared, I want him off his patch, I want him sweating.'

'Where am I going to get three teams from?' Kevin asked.

'Go and see DI Merrick. Tell him I said you could have five bodies.' She raised a warning finger. 'But not Sam Evans.'

Kevin frowned. 'But it was him that got Sanders to send us the pix in the first place.'

'Exactly,' Carol said. 'But he didn't care enough to want to follow it through. Keep him away from the

351

endgame, Kevin. Maybe it'll teach him something.' She knew she was being harsh, but she wanted to rein in Sam Evans' maverick instincts, to make them work for him and not against him. It was a lesson Carol understood; it was the one she'd had most difficulty with herself in the early stages of her career. Going out on a limb was all very well, but you had to learn how to tell the solid wood from the rotten. And she suspected Evans was still a long way from that knowledge.

I'm savouring every minute of this, I admit it: the cops running around in circles because I've spirited away one of their own; front-page headline in the evening paper and an editorial slagging off the force hierarchy for putting an officer in harm's way without adequate back-up. Of course, it wasn't incompetence that cost them Paula McIntyre, it was my superiority. But I forgive the media that lack of insight, because it serves to make the police even more powerless. And power is like energy: finite. If one group loses it, somebody else benefits. And in this instance, it's me. I have the power to manipulate them, to frustrate them and to make fools of them.

My power is evident all around me. Even when I'm alone in my home, the wonders of modern technology allow me instant access to Paula's terror and pain. And my trained monkey brings me the digital videos at regular intervals. I can watch her, debased and helpless, on my TV screen or computer monitor while I lie on the sofa, naked and glorious. Whatever I want done to her, I can make it happen. I stroke my body, imagining her mouth on me, doing my bidding, her eyes fixed on mine, anxious to please. Imagination can be so much better than the reality, which so often disap-

points. *Not that I'm averse to taking my pleasure when it presents itself. I've always had a taste and a talent for making women do what I want. But compared to this exercise of total domination, that's just an appetizer. Soon the blades will slice into her cunt, the blood will start to flow and pool between her legs, and her body will arch and twist in a frenzy of pain . . .*

Sometimes I play one of the other videos, one of the ones that takes it all the way. But those make me come too quickly, and then I have to start all over again enjoying Paula.

The only thing that worries me is how I'm going to improve on this one.

After Kevin left, Carol had found it impossible to settle. She'd tried to call Tony, but only reached voice-mail and answering machine. She'd had a cup of coffee with Stacey, congratulating her on her inspired work and insisting she accept Jonathan's flowers. She'd spent half an hour in the murder room with Don Merrick, growing depressed at the dozens of names their street trawl had attached to the uniden-tified man who had snatched Paula. Finally, she'd decided to do what she'd previously criticized Merrick for; she needed to get out on the streets, to feel she was doing something more constructive than reviewing everyone else's work.

At first, she'd just walked around Temple Fields, speaking to the officers who were still knocking on doors and canvassing passers-by. It never hurt to offer the troops a word of encouragement, to let them see you were putting in the hours, just like them. As she chatted to one of the young uniformed officers, she noticed Dee Smart slipping into a well-lit doorway opposite. Carol ended the conversation with a metaphorical pat on the back and headed across the street and into Stan's Café.

Dee was already seated alone at a table with a mug of tea and a cigarette. Carol took the chair opposite and smiled. 'Hi, Dee.'

Dee rolled her eyes. 'Look, I've told you lot everything – you know more about me than my ex-husband. You're very bad for business, you know that?'

'And I appreciate your help, Dee. But something new's come up that I wanted to run past you. Did Sandie ever mention someone called the Creeper?'

Dee stared at her, open mouth revealing an unappetizing array of ugly fillings and stained teeth. 'The Creeper?'

Carol gave an apologetic shrug. 'I know, it sounds ridiculous. But did Sandie ever talk about anyone by that name?'

Dee shook her head, incredulity in her expression. '*You're* asking *me* about the Creeper?'

Carol's attention quickened. This wasn't the reaction she'd expected. Dee's incredulity was not sparked by the nickname but by the very fact that Carol was asking the question. 'You know who I'm talking about,' Carol said, knowing she was right.

Dee snorted. 'You think I'm going to tell you, of all people?'

This wasn't making any sense. 'What do you mean, me of all people?'

Dee said nothing. She shifted in her chair, as if she wanted to put visible distance between herself and Carol.

Carol persisted. It would have been impossible for her to do otherwise. 'Dee, if you know anything, anything at all, you'd better tell me. There's a woman's life at stake, and I'm not playing games. If I have to arrest you for police obstruction, I will.'

Dee crushed out her cigarette and stood up. 'You think you frighten me with your threats? Listen, cop, there are people out there I'm a lot more scared of than I am of anything you can do to me. I don't know what the fuck you're on about, OK?'

Carol jumped to her feet, trying to get between Dee and the door. But Dee pushed her to one side and picked up speed. 'Dee!' Carol shouted. A hush fell on the café as every pair of eyes turned towards them.

'Fuck off! I got nothing to say to you,' Dee shouted desperately over her shoulder as she barged out of the door.

Carol flushed scarlet, aware she was the remaining centre of attention. She felt a touch on her arm and swung round, ready to rip into anyone who was willing to have a go. 'Tony?' she said, taken aback. 'I didn't see you. Are you stalking me?' She wondered for one mad moment if he was on some mission to protect her.

'No, Carol. I've been walking and thinking.' He steered her towards the corner table in the rear where he'd been nursing a coffee and absorbing the atmosphere when Carol had arrived. 'You only had eyes for the woman you were talking to,' he said.

'That was Dee Smart.'

'The one who shared the room with Sandie?'

Carol folded her arms across her chest. 'I fucked

that up so badly.' She pursed her lips, furious with herself. 'She knows something about the Creeper. As soon as I mentioned him, she freaked out. She knows something and she sure as hell isn't going to tell me now.'

'What exactly did she say?'

Carol closed her eyes and summoned to her service her gift of perfect recall. 'She said, "You think I'm going to tell you, of all people?" And then she said, "You think you frighten me with your threats? Listen, cop, there are people out there I'm a lot more scared of than I am of anything you can do to me."'

'Interesting,' Tony said.

'Meaning what?'

'Not sure yet. There's something I'm close to, but I'm not quite there,' he said slowly. Carol knew there was no point in pushing him. Even though his hypotheses sometimes sounded like the product of a mind deranged, he never put them forward till he was sure they had assumed the shape of validity. She'd just have to wait till he was ready, frustrating though that might be when a life was at stake.

'It'd be nice if you could make it soon,' she grumbled.

'Do you want me to have a chat with Dee?'

Carol considered. It probably wasn't such a bad idea. 'You think you might get somewhere?'

He spread his hands in a self-deprecating gesture. 'Well, I'm not a cop. And I'm not a woman.'

She couldn't resist. 'I had noticed.'

He pulled a face. 'Maybe Dee will too.' He pushed his chair back.

'Tony . . .' Carol began.

He gave her a quizzical look. 'Yes?'

She sighed. 'Nothing. It'll keep. This isn't the place.'

He glanced around. 'I see what you mean. Later, then.'

She watched him leave, wondering when exactly would be the right moment to tell Tony she thought his boss might be a serial killer.

Sam Evans didn't believe in luck. Suckers believed in luck. He believed in hard work, preparing the ground and seizing the moment. That was the difference between making it big and never getting off the slow track to nowhere. So you had to go looking for whatever it was that would give you the edge. And that was what Evans had been doing all day. He was desperate to get off Carol Jordan's shit list. He didn't mind undermining her, but he didn't want her trying that on him. Besides, although he craved the attention of his bosses, this was definitely the wrong kind of attention and he needed to make it history, and fast. So in spite of the repetitiveness of his task, he'd had his antennae tuned for that little something a bit out of the ordinary. Tony Hill's account of Tyler and the Creeper seemed to offer the breakthrough he'd been looking for. It would be good to find someone who fitted the bill.

It had grown dark and chill on the streets of Temple Fields yet still he hadn't found a crack he could pry open. But just when he had almost given up hope, he felt that prickle along his hairline that told him he was on to something. He'd stopped a bleary-eyed young hooker and thrust Paula's picture under her nose. She'd looked away too hastily and shivered.

Evans was prepared to bet that it wasn't because of the cold night air.

'Let's go for a drink, you and me,' he said, taking her elbow and steering her into the nearest pub. Luckily for him it was low-life enough not to be bothered by his choice of company. He found a table near the back of the room and asked her what she wanted to drink.

When he came back with the Bacardi Breezer and his own pint of Guinness, she was still there. 'So, how come you know Paula?' he asked.

She swigged from the bottle and wiped her mouth with the back of her hand. It made her look about twelve. 'She was nice to me after Jackie died. She reminded me of Jackie, you know? Like, kind. But still a no-shit.'

'That's Paula all right. So, what's your name?' He placed a hand flat on his chest. 'I'm Sam.'

'Hi, Sammy. I'm Honey. So, has he got Paula, then? The geezer that did Jackie?' She dug a pack of cigarettes out and offered him one.

'Looks that way.'

'So you're really out to get him now, then?'

'We were always out to get him. I expect Paula told you that.'

Honey shrugged one shoulder. 'So she said. But, like, I knew you wasn't going to get your knickers in too much of a twist about a pair of dead prossies.'

'You knew Jackie?'

Honey sighed out a thin stream of smoke. 'That's why Paula wanted to talk to me. To see if I knew anything about who'd topped her. She even got me to look at some photos of geezers. But there wasn't anybody I knew.'

Evans wasn't about to let it go. 'You've had time to think since then, though. Have you remembered Jackie being scared of anybody?'

Honey gave him a derisive look. 'In this game, you'd be daft if you weren't scared out your mind half the time.'

'But was there anyone in particular that bothered Jackie?' Evans swirled his glass nonchalantly, making the creamy head stick to the inside.

'After I spoke to Paula, I remembered Jackie once warned me off a punter. I was going to get in his car and she practically dragged me out. Said he'd smacked her about one time and dumped her without paying.'

The door to the bar opened and Jan Shields walked in. Evans caught her out of the corner of his peripheral vision and gently shook his head. Either she didn't see the gesture or she had something that wouldn't wait. She headed towards them. 'What kind of car?' Evans asked quickly.

'One of them big four-wheel-drive jeep things. A black one.'

The connection sparked in Evans' mind: *Aidan fucking Hart.* He'd been right and Jordan had been wrong. If he fitted the frame as this Creeper that Tony Hill reckoned was involved in the murders, that alibi didn't necessarily clear him. 'You don't know what make?' he asked urgently. 'What model?'

Honey cast her eyes upwards. 'Do I look like somebody who knows about cars, Sammy?'

Jan arrived at the table and sat down. Honey jumped as if she'd been stroked with a cattle prod. She grabbed for her fags and began to slide off the banquette. Jan put up a hand to stop her. 'It's all right,

Honey, I'm not wearing my Vice hat. Nothing so trivial.'

Honey ducked under the hand. 'Yeah, well, I've got my rent to earn. See ya, Sammy.'

'Shit,' he said as Honey disappeared back to the streets. 'I thought I was getting somewhere with that one.'

Jan looked apologetic. 'Sorry, mate. My past working Vice has its downsides as well as its advantages. How're you doing?'

Evans pushed the remains of his drink away from him. He wasn't about to share his ideas with anybody else. 'Getting nowhere slowly. You?'

'Likewise. Nobody's ever heard of Tony Hill's Creeper. Not a hooker, not a pimp, not a punter. Waste of time, if you ask me.'

Evans got to his feet. 'So, nothing new there, then. Let's go make some more people miserable.'

Jan fell into step beside him. 'I keep seeing Paula's face. It's as if she's haunting me. Like I've failed her.'

'What do you think the chances are of us getting her back alive?'

Jan closed her eyes momentarily, as if a stab of pain had hit her. 'My honest opinion?'

'Yeah.'

'I think Tony Hill's full of shit. I think she's dead already.'

Kevin closed the door of the interview room behind him. He'd just spent forty minutes with the last of the three Park Rangers they'd arrested on suspicion of murder. He'd been determined to interview all three himself, in spite of the complaints of the duty

360

solicitors about being kept waiting. But he hadn't found a single discrepancy in their stories to offer any leverage. Nick Sanders, Callum Donaldson and Pete Siveright all denied having taken the photographs of Swindale.

They'd been happy enough to identify the other shots they had taken, but they were all adamant that they hadn't photographed the secret dale. They'd all denied ever having seen Tim Golding or Guy Lefevre other than via the media. They all claimed their work-sheets would show they'd been nowhere near Bradfield on the day of his abduction. That in itself was pretty worthless, however, since they all finished work at six and neither boy had been taken till after seven. Plenty of time to get from the Peak Park to Bradfield.

Bronwen Scott followed him out of the room. The solicitor looked depressingly fresh and alert. 'You've got nothing on my client,' she said. 'I'm going to make representations to the custody sergeant that Callum Donaldson should be released.'

Kevin leaned against the wall. As always when he was tired, his skin had paled to the colour of milk, his freckles standing out like miniature stigmata. 'Nobody's going anywhere till we get the results of the searches that Derbyshire Police are carrying out on our behalf.'

'That could take hours,' she protested.

'So go home. We'll call you when we're ready with the outcome of those searches and to reinterview,' he said, not bothering to hide his hostility. 'One of those three men abducted and killed two young boys. So your convenience isn't very high on my list of prior-ities, Ms Scott.'

She raised her eyebrows. 'I had hoped that DCI Jordan might introduce the concept of civility round here. Clearly I was wrong.' She swept past him towards the custody suite. As she reached the door, the custody sergeant yanked it open.

'Kevin,' he shouted, 'I've got some DC from Buxton on the line for you.'

Bronwen Scott turned as he hurried down the corridor. Her mouth looked as if she'd just bitten a pickle. Kevin enjoyed beaming broadly at her as he brushed past. 'Looks like you might not have so long to wait after all.' He snatched up the phone and introduced himself. For a couple of minutes he listened, saying nothing more than, 'Yeah . . . yeah . . .' Finally, he said, 'Give me that make and model and serial number again.' He reached for a pen and paper and scribbled down the details. Then: 'Thanks, mate. I owe you one. Let me have the paperwork soon as.'

He replaced the receiver and turned to give Bronwen Scott the full benefit of his smile. 'Derbyshire Police have just informed me that they have found a camera whose serial number corresponds to the camera that took the photographs of Swindale and the photograph of Tim Golding. Guess where they found it?'

Scott's lip curled in disdain. 'Get on with it, Sergeant.'

'They found it in the bedroom of your client.' He leaned against the custody counter and folded his arms. 'I guess you won't be going anywhere in a hurry, will you, Ms Scott?'

*　　*　　*

Driving round Temple Fields at night was a different experience from being a pedestrian, Tony thought. The perspective on the terrain was quite different. Walking around, the prostitution impinged, but it wasn't hard to ignore. Behind the wheel, the sex for sale was totally in his face; the vendors set out their stalls for the carriage trade, not the foot traffic.

On his first pass through, Tony was so absorbed in the distinctive feel of the night streets that he missed Dee. Second time round, he saw her on a corner, kerbside, legs apart, leaning towards the road. He slowed and pulled up beside her. As his window went down, she stepped forward and dipped, offering a view of her cleavage. 'What's it to be, then?'

'You're Dee?'

'That's right. Somebody recommend me, did they, sweetheart? Well, you came to the right place. What are you after?'

Tony felt faintly flustered. It was all so much more complicated in reality. 'I'm not a punter, Dee. I just want to talk to you.'

She backed up a step, but kept the cleavage on show. 'You a cop?' she said suspiciously.

He gestured at the car then at himself. 'Does this look like "cop" to you? No, I'm not a cop.'

'In that case, you want to talk, it'll cost.'

Tony nodded. It seemed reasonable. People paid to talk to him, after all. 'Fine. I'll pay. Do you want to get in?'

Ten minutes later, he pulled up outside a smart café bar on the edge of the financial district. Dee had tried to talk in the car, but he had asked her to wait.

'I'm not good at navigating and talking,' he said. 'We'll only end up in the middle of nowhere.'

They walked together to the entrance, where, to Dee's obvious astonishment, Tony held the door open for her. As they walked in, the unmistakable cube of a bouncer approached them. 'Hang on a minute, where do you think you're going?' he demanded, all belligerence and brashness.

'What's it to you, meathead?' Dee snapped.

'We don't want your type in here,' the bouncer said.

Tony intervened with a suaveness he could only achieve when it was nothing personal. 'And what type would that be?'

'Keep out of it, pal,' the bouncer advised him.

'This lady is with me. We came here for a quiet drink,' Tony said politely.

'Not in here, you don't.'

Dee put a hand on his arm. 'Leave it, Tony. We'll go somewhere else.'

He patted her hand. 'No, Dee. We won't.' He turned to the bouncer, ice and steel on full display. 'You have no basis for refusing my friend entry. She is dressed no less discreetly than at least three other women in here. She's not touting for trade, unlike the financial services jerks at the bar, and also unlike many of your other customers, she's not going to be using your toilet to take drugs. So unless you can come up with a compelling reason why we shouldn't, we are going to sit at one of your tables while we have a drink and a chat.' He nodded politely to the bouncer and steered Dee past him.

The bouncer, baffled, stared after them like a bull

who'd just missed the matador. Tony chose a table, pulled out a chair for Dee then sat down opposite her. She grinned at him. 'How did you get away with that?'

Tony looked pained. 'Natural charisma?'

Dee laughed, a deep, throaty sound that spoke of Embassy Regal and too many late nights. 'Balls of steel, more like.'

'Ah, that's what the problem's been all these years . . .' Tony looked up as the cocktail waitress approached and dumped a bowl of Japanese rice crackers on the table. He suspected the swiftness of her arrival came from curiosity to see the man who had bested the bouncer. Tony smiled sunnily at her. 'Good evening. My friend would like . . . ?' He gave Dee a questioning look.

'Rum and black,' Dee said.

'And I'll have a glass of your Shiraz Cabernet. Thanks.' The waitress departed, giving them a final curious glance.

Dee scrunched down in the leather armchair, savouring its comfort. 'So, what is it you want to talk to me about?'

'I think you know.'

Dee tipped her head back and sighed, as if to say she'd known it was too good to be true. 'Is this to do with what that woman cop was asking me about?'

Tony said nothing, simply fixing her with an expectant look.

Dee jackknifed forward, leaning across the table towards him. 'What's she to you, then? Why are you doing her dirty work for her if you're not a cop?' she asked savagely.

'I'm a psychologist.'

'A shrink? You going to make me lie down on a couch and tell you about my childhood?' she said scornfully.

'I don't have a couch.'

Dee gave a louche smile. 'Pity. I wouldn't mind lying on a couch for you.'

'Life is full of disappointments, Dee. Why are you so scared of the Creeper?'

'Who said I was scared?' The defiance was so fake it was almost laughable.

'Why else would you refuse to tell us what you know when there's a woman's life at stake? I don't think you're keeping schtum out of loyalty.'

Dee looked away. 'Why should I stick my neck out for some copper?' She shifted impatiently in her seat. 'You've no idea what you're dealing with here, do you?'

'Whatever it is, we can protect you. Who's the Creeper, Dee?'

Now she was angry, covering up her fear with spitting rage. 'You don't get it, do you? You might not be a cop, but you're still on the team. The only ones you look after are your own. Yeah, I'm scared. And I'm right to be scared. Nothing you can promise me can make any difference.' Suddenly she was on her feet, grabbing her bag.

'Wait, Dee!' Tony said urgently. But she walked away without a backward glance. 'You haven't even had your . . .' The waitress approached with her tray balanced at shoulder level. '. . . rum and black,' he sighed.

He sat alone for a long time, staring into his red

wine and occasionally over at the glass of rum and blackcurrant opposite him. Thoughts flashed in and out of his mind as he struggled to make a logical sequence from what he knew and what he surmised. The early-evening crowd dispersed, and the bar entered a hiatus before it would come alive again after nine. When he was almost the only person left in the place, he took out his phone and dialled the familiar number.

'Carol Jordan,' he heard.

'It's me. Can we talk?'

'I'm in the office. Do you want to come round?'

The last place he wanted to have this particular conversation. 'I don't think so,' he said. 'Can you come to mine?'

'I'm in the middle of something,' she said. 'It looks like we're close to cracking Tim Golding and Guy Lefevre.'

'That's great news. But I do need to talk to you, and not in the office.'

He heard her sigh. 'Give me an hour. I'll meet you at your place. And, Tony . . .?'

'Yes?'

'This better be good.'

Under pressure from the solicitors representing Nick Sanders and Pete Siveright, Kevin had released both men. He'd had no real choice once he'd given them the disclosure that was their right: namely, that the results of the searches had produced no evidence against their clients. Once Bronwen Scott had indicated she'd had enough time to consult with Callum Donaldson, he gave himself a few more minutes to prepare. He anticipated that Scott would advise Donaldson to go 'no comment', but he didn't want to take any chances.

Kevin felt the low thrum of excitement in his veins that always came when he was so close to a result he could touch it. These days, every good arrest, every conviction felt like another step towards rehabilitation. It was as if his previous disastrous mistake was a stain, like a street vandal's spraypainted tag. And everything that went well was another brushful of paint towards covering up the blemish. One day, there would only be a freshly painted wall, and he'd finally be back on track again.

Callum Donaldson felt right. He fitted the profile. He lived alone in a remote cottage between Chapel-en-le-Frith and Castleton. He was an avid birdwatcher who often led school trips into the Peak Park to show them the bird life. He was technologically adept – he had a state-of-the-art computer and a pager that automatically alerted him to the arrival of any rare species in the UK. Kevin had found him awkward and uncomfortable in their preliminary interview, and if he'd had to pick a killer from the three, Donaldson would have been his chosen one.

He gathered his papers together and walked into the interview room. He'd barely started the twin tape-decks and made the formal introduction when Bronwen Scott said, 'My client wishes to make a statement.'

Kevin couldn't hide his surprise. He smiled, wondering if it was really going to be that easy after all. 'Fine. Let's hear it.'

Scott perched a pair of rimless glasses on the end

of her nose and cleared her throat. 'My name is Callum Donaldson and I am employed as a ranger with the Peak National Park Service. I wish to make a statement regarding a Canon Elph digital camera which is presently in my possession. I purchased this camera on approximately 15th September of this year from my colleague Nick Sanders.'

Scott paused and looked up. Kevin understood she was enjoying the sight of the rug being pulled out from under his feet and he struggled to remain impassive. She allowed herself a tight little smile and continued. 'I paid him one hundred and fifty pounds for the camera. I paid this sum by cheque. The transaction took place in the Red Lion pub in Litton. Among those present were David Adams of Litton Mill and Maria Tomlinson, also of Litton Mill. I am willing to allow access to my bank records to verify this transaction and I am confident that David Adams and Maria Tomlinson will remember the occasion since we all took photographs with the camera in the pub that night.'

Scott handed him the statement, written out in her neat italic hand. 'Duly signed and witnessed,' she said. 'How soon will you be releasing my client?'

Kevin stared dully at the piece of paper, seeing his good night crumble before his eyes. He knew he should still ask his prepared questions, but suddenly time was of the essence. 'I'll need to speak to DCI Jordan,' he stalled. 'Interview terminated at seven forty-three p.m.,' he added, getting to his feet and hurrying out.

He ran down to the custody suite. 'When did you let Sanders go?' he asked the sergeant.

'When you said. About forty minutes ago,' the sergeant said.

'Who's driving him back?'

'They both declined the offer of transport. Said they'd seen enough of us for one day, they'd rather get back under their own steam.'

'Fuck,' Kevin exploded.

'We got a problem?'

'Too fucking right. We've let the wrong one go,' Kevin growled. He reached across and grabbed the phone. 'I need to speak to Buxton CID,' he told the switchboard. When the phone was finally answered, he identified himself then said, 'I need to speak to DC Thom . . . What do you mean, he's gone home?' After a prolonged conversation that led Kevin through three different officers, he finally secured a reluctant promise to go to Nick Sanders' cottage in Chelmorton and rearrest him when he arrived back home. Provided Kevin could have the request ratified by a senior officer.

He took the stairs two at a time and found Carol in her office, signing off on a stack of paperwork. She looked up expectantly, knowing how confident Kevin had been of a result. Quickly, he outlined what had happened. 'Oh, Christ,' Carol said, making no attempt to hide her dismay. 'Not your fault, Kevin, but . . . oh, Christ. Leave it with me, I'll speak to Derbyshire. And you'd better release Donaldson on police bail before Bronwen Scott starts waving the bloody Human Rights Act at us.'

As she watched Kevin go, she thought, *Actually, it was my fault*. They should have waited until they had the search results in from Derbyshire before interviewing the three men. But Kevin had been eager to get going and he was concerned that Derbyshire would drag their heels over the searches out of sheer bloody-mindedness. And because of the terms of the Police and Criminal Evidence Act, they could only hold the men for thirty-six hours before they'd have to go before the magistrates who would probably not understand the complex evidence relating to the camera and so would throw out the request for extended custody. Kevin had told her Derbyshire were becoming increasingly restive at what they perceived to be the big city boys expecting them to do the shit work. So, against her better judgement, she had sanctioned a series of preliminary interviews.

Carol squeezed the bridge of her nose between her fingers. She was making too many mistakes. It wasn't like her. It frightened her, with Paula's life at stake. Screwing up was bad enough on its own, but concern over screwing up could make her hesitate fatally; failure to reach a decision could be as damaging as making the wrong one in a case of this sensitivity. She sighed and made the call to Derbyshire. Then she reached for her coat. Time to go and see what Tony was being so mysterious about. And maybe she could get at least one of her worries off her chest at the same time.

She stopped in at the murder room, where Merrick was still ploughing through statements, his eyes heavy, his shoulders bowed. He looked up as she entered and slowly shook his head. Carol moved round the room, a supportive word for everyone. She ended up at his side, a hand on his shoulder. 'We'll find her, Don,' she said. 'Why don't you go home and get some rest?'

His face twisted in pain. 'Home? Ma'am, I'm living in her house. Going home just makes it worse. It feels like a reproach.'

Carol cursed herself for her insensitivity. 'Can't you go back to Lindy and the kids? Just for a few nights?'

'Too late for that. She's not even speaking to me.'

Carol squeezed his shoulder. 'Check yourself into a hotel, Don. Charge it to the inquiry. But get some rest, please.'

He gave her a crooked smile. 'I will if you will, ma'am.'

'Touché. But I am at least leaving the building now, Don. You should do the same.'

She was halfway down the corridor, lost in thought, when the familiar sight of Jonathan France swaggering towards her in his bike leathers jolted her back to earth. He grinned and quickened his step, not taking in the frozen expression on Carol's face.

'What are you doing here? How did you get in?' she demanded.

His step and his smile faltered. 'I wanted to see you. The guy on the front counter remembered me being here before, so he let me come up.' He looked hurt. 'I thought you'd be pleased to see me,' he added plaintively.

In reply, Carol threw open the nearest door, which led into an empty meeting room. 'In here,' she indicated with a jerk of the head. He followed her, perking up at the prospect of privacy, in spite of the contra-indications. Carol shut the door behind them and glared at him. 'What did you think you were doing, sending those flowers here?'

Shock flattened his features. 'I thought you'd like them.'

'So why not send them to my house?'

He shrugged. 'You're never there.'

'The florist would have left them with a neighbour. But no, you sent them here. Didn't it occur to you that a police station is a gossip factory? That my private life is now the subject of speculation from the canteen to the Chief Constable's office?'

'I didn't think . . .'

'No, you didn't. I'm running two major murder inquiries here, and the last thing I want is this kind of distraction.'

Stung, he rounded on her. 'Distraction? That's how you see me? A distraction?' Carol shrugged. Two patches of colour burned on his cheekbones. 'You used me,' he said, light dawning. 'You used me to prove to yourself you could get past the rape.'

She raised her eyebrows. 'You got what you wanted too – an image of yourself as the strong, sensitive saviour. But that wasn't enough for you, was it? You wanted it to matter to me, you wanted to be the man who would heal my heart. Well, Jonathan, I've got news for you. You never came near my heart, because somebody else has first claim to that.'

As so often happens in the throes of emotional argument, he seized on the least relevant point. 'You told me you weren't seeing anybody else. That night we had dinner, you told me.'

Carol clenched her fists. 'I'm not seeing anybody

else. Not in the sense you mean. But you can't reduce relationships to the simplicity of playground games.'

'You were dishonest,' he said bitterly. 'You were never emotionally available.'

She shook her head vehemently. 'I never said I was. You presumed. You saw what you wanted to see and you presumed the rest.'

'I don't deserve this,' he said, his voice shaky.

Carol's anger suddenly fizzled out, leaving her hollow and weary. 'No,' she said. 'You probably don't.' She opened the door. 'I'm not ungrateful, Jonathan. And I would have liked it if we could have been friends. But that's not going to happen now.'

He stepped through the open door. 'I don't envy him, this man you love,' he said bitterly.

'That's the first sensible thing you've said tonight,' Carol said sadly. 'Goodbye, Jonathan.'

She watched him go, feeling the last traces of adrenaline leave her. Christ, how much worse could it get tonight?

Tony sat at his desk, staring out at the cityscape that flowed down the hill towards the centre of Bradfield. In the distance, the office towers in the financial district showed irregular squares of light like half-completed seaside bingo games. 'You're out there somewhere,' he said softly. 'Making your plans, figuring out how to get us to play your game, deciding what to do with Paula.' A picture was starting to form in his mind of the person behind these crimes. It had been a struggle to grasp the shadowy mind of the puppetmaster, but at last he was piecing it together, gradually making sense out of the jumble of information in his head. Convincing Carol was going to be a lot harder, he thought.

He saw her car draw up and ran downstairs to let her in. He was shocked by how drained she looked. Her eyes were hollow, her skin slack and pale. 'You look shattered,' he said, stepping aside to let her in.

'I fucked up on the Tim Golding interviews. It looks like we ended up cutting the right man loose and holding on to the wrong one. Kevin seems to think the suspect is confident enough to go home so we can rearrest him. I'm not so sure. We're getting nowhere on the search for Paula. Don and Jan are at each other's throats because Jan says Paula's gay and Don says she's not. And Sam Evans thinks somebody died and made him God. The only one who's not doing my head in is Stacey, and that's because she only talks to machines.' She took off her coat and threw it over the newel post at the foot of the stairs. 'Where are we?'

'You want a drink? Or are you still working?'

'Yes, and yes. I'm waiting to hear from Kevin, but I'm out of the office now for the night unless something breaks on Paula.'

'Kitchen, then. I'll open a bottle.'

While Tony got the drinks, Carol settled herself at the kitchen table. 'I just gave Jonathan his marching orders,' she said.

Tony had his back to her, which he was grateful for. It meant she missed the leap of joy in his eyes, the smile that lit up his face. 'And how do you feel about that?'

Carol snorted with laughter. 'Oh, Tony, you're such a fucking shrink.'

He glanced over his shoulder at her. 'Sorry. But it wasn't a shrink question. It was a friendly enquiry.'

'I feel pissed off with him for pushing me into a corner. He sent the most ridiculous bouquet of flowers to the office, then he turned up there this evening. If he'd have just let it lie, we could have been friends. But it was that presumption, you know?'

Tony brought the glasses to the table. 'I know. "You slept with me, so how can you resist loving me?"'

'Exactly. And you know how I get when I'm cornered.'

He winced. 'Not a pretty sight.'

'I was horrible to him,' she admitted. 'But I didn't want there to be any room for doubt. I haven't got the time or the energy for that right now.' She sipped her drink gratefully. 'I just hope I haven't blown him as an expert witness.'

'I shouldn't think so. Given his behaviour so far, I suspect he'll want to impress you with his magnanimity. And of course, he'll want to believe that once a bit of time has passed, you'll realize what a good thing you let go by you. Don't worry, Carol, he'll be back.' Tony raised his glass to her.

She groaned. 'I hate you sometimes,' she said.

'You're going to hate me even more when you hear what I have to say.'

'Oh yes,' she said. 'There was a reason why I'm here, wasn't there? OK, spill.'

He'd never been good at the politics of information. Direct, uncomfortable, unvarnished, that was how his delivery always went. Even for Carol, he couldn't do diplomacy. 'Somewhere at the heart of this case, you're going to find either a cop or someone who's tight with the cops. A SOCO, that sort of thing.'

Carol's hand stopped halfway to her mouth. Carefully, she replaced her glass on the table. 'That's a hell of an allegation.'

'It's what makes sense. I believe Derek Tyler could not have constructed these crimes. Tyler's of low intelligence. He's stubborn, but he's also suggestible. If he was going to kill a prostitute off his own bat, he wouldn't have planned it like this. It would have happened on the street, with a knife or a half-brick. There would have been forensics all over the place. You'd have had him in custody the same night. He's not a sophisticated game player like our killer. But nobody fitted up Derek Tyler. So we come to the Creeper. Because there's one irresistible psychological fact here: Derek Tyler could not have imagined those crimes. This is somebody else's fantasy. Somebody else pulled the strings.'

'What if it's Tyler who's pulling the strings now? Getting someone else to do the crimes so he won't have to do the time?' She knew she should tell him about Hart. But she wanted to see where he was going with this, untainted by her suspicions.

Tony shook his head. 'Believe me, Carol. I've spent time with him. He just isn't smart enough.'

'So if it's the Creeper who's behind it all, why wait two years to start again?'

Tony closed his eyes and laid his hands, palms down, on the table. 'Because I'm careful. Because I want the dust to settle. Because it takes time to find another Derek Tyler. Because I don't have the desire to get my own hands dirty. Because the joy comes from exercising power twice over. Not just the power over the victim but also the power over the killer. And this time around, the power over the police.' He opened his eyes. 'But mostly because I don't want to be caught, and it takes time to arrange things in such a way that I can protect myself.'

'OK. That all makes some sort of sense,' Carol said grudgingly. 'What I don't see is how it points to a cop.'

'I spoke to Dee tonight.'

'And?'

'She won't tell us what we want to know about the Creeper. And she won't tell us because she doesn't trust us to protect her. That suggests either a cop or someone who is owed a duty of care by the cops. Someone on the team. Or even an informant . . .?'

Carol shook her head. 'No, I'm sorry, I don't buy it. It's just as likely that the Creeper is somebody out there who she sees as powerful enough to breach whatever protection we put round her. That doesn't spell cop to me. It could just as well be a pimp, a dealer.'

'She doesn't have a pimp. Jan says they've cleared out most of the hard nuts. And why would she imagine a dealer could breach witness protection?'

Carol gave him a cynical, knowing look. 'Because there is a perpetual assumption that drugs squad cops are bent, that you don't get to be a high-level dealer without having some cop in your pocket.'

Tony slumped in his chair. He'd given it his best shot, but he hadn't really expected her to go for it. 'Do me a favour: keep it in mind.'

She drained her glass and reached for the bottle.

'I appreciate your input on this, I really do. But I think you're way off beam.'

'Fair enough,' he said.

'Not the theory, Tony. I think that's nothing short of brilliant. But where you're pointing the finger, that's where you're off the mark,' she said.

Puzzled, he paused with his glass halfway to his mouth. 'What have I missed?'

'Someone with the skills to brainwash another person. Someone who has access to Derek Tyler, who can make sure he never tells what he knows. Someone who was in Temple Fields the night Sandie Foster was killed.'

Tony's eyes widened. 'What are you saying, Carol?'

'I'm saying that Aidan Hart fits your profile better than any cop.'

Tony snorted with laughter. 'Aidan Hart? You're kidding me.'

'Aidan Hart had sex with Sandie Foster the night she died. We traced his car and he admitted it. He had an alibi for the time of the murder so I didn't pursue it. But Sam Evans did. And he discovered that Hart uses prostitutes two or three times a week. I didn't think that was grounds for suspicion either. But if you're right, and the same person has orchestrated both series of murders, the alibi is worthless and everything else becomes more significant.'

Tony shook his head, struggling to take in what Carol was saying. 'No, that can't be right. The man's a buffoon. A careerist buffoon.'

'Or maybe he's just very good at presenting a fake front?' Carol said.

Tony swallowed a mouthful of wine, his brow

furrowed in thought. 'It doesn't work, Carol. It doesn't fit with what Dee said. There's no reason why she should know who Hart is, never mind be shit scared of him.'

'No? What do we know about her mental-health history? A man with Hart's power could write her up as delusional, have her sectioned, surely? Locked away forever?'

Tony looked doubtful. 'I don't know . . .' He jumped to his feet and paced. 'Wait a minute,' he said triumphantly. 'Two years ago. When Derek Tyler was active. Hart wasn't here then. He was still at Rampton. He's been in post here less than a year. He can't have been the man behind Derek Tyler's crimes. And if you concede that Derek couldn't have conceived those murders on his own, you have to concede that the same person is behind both series. Which rules out Aidan Hart.'

Carol stared at him. 'You're sure about that? He couldn't have been seconded here?'

'I'm sure as I can be. But it won't be hard for you to check out.' Tony pulled a rueful face. 'I'm sorry to rob you of a suspect. But, leaving aside the practicalities, I just don't figure Hart for this. I just don't think he's got what it takes.'

She sighed, not entirely convinced but unable to find a counter-argument. 'Fuck. Oh well, at least I don't have to make a fool of myself with Brandon.' She finished her drink. 'I need to get some sleep. It's been a shit of a day.'

'Keep me posted, yeah?' He walked her to the front door.

On the threshold, she turned and put a hand on

his shoulder, leaning into him and kissing his cheek. 'Thank you,' she said.

'What for?' He was surprised.

She grinned. 'You're the psychologist, you work it out.'

Then she was gone, leaving him alone to continue his journey into the dark spaces of someone else's mind.

Morning dawns sunny for a change, and I imagine those dull-witted coppers seeing it as a good omen. That's the thing about superstitions. The morons who believe in them never seem to consider that, by their very nature, omens must be indiscriminate. They look out their bedroom window and see the perfect rainbow arcing across the landscape and decide it means good fortune for them without realizing that it means precisely the same for their next-door neighbour who is their sworn enemy. So if the sunny morning is a good omen for my enemies, it must be one for me too.

I check out the webcam again. The refresh rate isn't brilliant, even with broadband, but at least it lets me keep an eye on Paula in real time. Except when that fuckwit leaned on the pause button by mistake the first time he changed the videotape. At least he noticed what he'd done and put it right before he left. He won't do that again in a hurry; I made my displeasure known and it reduced him to a pathetic jelly, desperate to win back my good graces.

So there she is, spread out the way I like her. I start to feel aroused by the sight, but I haven't got time to enjoy it, so I force myself to think of more practical things. I've never kept one this long before, and it does present certain problems. I know she can go without food for a long time, but I'm not sure how long she can manage without water. I

don't mind her getting delirious, but I don't want her to
die. Not until I decide the time is right. And when it is,
she'll die the way I dictate, not according to her physiology.
I decide to check it out on the net when I get a minute.

Letting her drink will be a problem. If he takes the gag
off, she'll try to scream. It should be possible to drip water
into her mouth through her teeth, but I'm not convinced the
trained monkey can manage something so delicate. I might
have to do it myself. Far from ideal. Not because there's any
danger she'll live to tell the tale, but because if she saw me
it would destroy the mystique.

The tip of my tongue slides between my teeth as I watch
her. She's good enough to eat.

Another fantasy to keep for later. But for now, there's
work to be done.

Paula was oblivious to the dawn. Inside her brightly
lit prison there was no day or night, just endless mute
brilliance. When she closed her eyes, the light burned
red through her eyelids, reminding her of the sea of
blood that had made islands of Sandie Foster and
Jackie Mayall. Her head hurt, a dull ache that had
started at the base of her skull and crept forward like
the vanguard of an enemy army till her brain felt as
if it would burst.

She could no longer keep her thoughts under
control. Something would pop into her mind, but
before she could examine it, it would slither away
or morph into something different. Memories segued
and elided into each other, people turned up in
places she knew they'd never been, their mouths
uttering things she knew they'd never said. Lovers
shape-shifted into colleagues, old school friends

shimmered and reformed as relative strangers. It was unnerving.

Sometimes she could barely remember who she was and how she'd got here. Her limbs felt heavy, as if they belonged to someone much bigger and softer. But that was more bearable than the agonizing cramps that shot through her arms and legs at unpredictable intervals.

The only clear knowledge Paula still managed to hold on to was that someone would come for her. She no longer knew who it would be; but she knew that, sooner or later, one way or another, it would end.

Tony closed the front door behind him and stood for a moment, savouring the sun on his face. He'd slept better than he'd expected but didn't want to think about why that might be. The sudden image of Paula McIntyre's face flashed into his mind and all at once, his pleasure in the morning evaporated. He hoped desperately that he was right, that she was still alive.

He got into the car and turned the key in the ignition. It coughed, wheezed like an emphysemic octogenarian and died. He frowned and tried again. A click, then nothing. He looked around as if there might be an answer inside the car. There was, of course. After Carol had returned to the office, he'd gone out for a Chinese takeaway. And he'd left the lights on. 'Bugger,' he sighed. Even if he could have laid hands on his roadside assistance membership card, he didn't have time to wait for the patrolman to turn up and jump-start him. And Carol had already left. He'd have bet serious money on her having a set of jump leads tucked away in her boot.

Grumpy now, he got out of the car and set off for the bus stop. He knew there was a bus that went near Bradfield Moor, but knew too from the complaints of visitors that the bus stop was a mile from the hospital gates.

Forty minutes later, a bus pulled up in the middle of nowhere and Tony got out. He stood for a moment, trying to figure out exactly where he was, then set off up a nearby lane. Freed from the clammy fug of the bus and its uneasy assortment of passengers, he let his mind run free over its problem.

'Two kinds of people are drawn to power: those who have it and those who don't,' he mused as he trudged on. 'That's where we have to start from.

'Those who don't have it usually don't have it for a good reason. Maybe they're not very bright or not very motivated or not very organized. Doesn't sound like you, does it?'

He was silent for a while, mulling it over. 'So we should probably assume that you have access to some degree of power. Which would work, if you're a cop – only Carol thinks I'm completely off the page on that one. The thing about having power is that those who have it always want more. Absolute power corrupts absolutely. And you like corruption, don't you? You like the taste and the smell of it. If you're a cop, you're a bent cop.' He stopped for a moment, digesting the implications of that thought.

'And that's why Dee's so scared of you. Because she already knows you don't play by the rules.' He was startled out of his reverie by a vast black all-terrain vehicle pulling up alongside him. The tinted window on the passenger side slid down and Tony found himself looking into the smug face of Aidan Hart. Given what he had learned from Carol about Hart's sexual proclivities, it was hard to resist the knowing remark that would wipe the smile from his mouth forever.

'Are you walking for pleasure or would you like a lift?' his boss asked.

Tony grinned. 'All things considered,' he said, 'I think I'd rather walk.'

'This is getting to be a bit of a habit,' Carol said, walking into her office with Kevin at her heels. 'People will talk.'

Kevin gave a tired smile. 'I don't think so. They all know I'm too cheap to send expensive bunches of flowers.'

'Kevin,' she said, her voice a dark warning.

'Sorry, guv,' he said ruefully.

'So, where are we up to?'

'Sanders never went home last night. After he left here, he disappeared into thin air. Siveright says Sanders told him he was going to visit friends in Bradfield and then he set off on foot. We've got Sanders withdrawing cash from the ATM in the Woolmarket about ten minutes after he left here. We've spoken to his colleagues at the park and I've alerted ports and airports but nothing's come up.'

'Shit,' Carol said. 'We need to put out an urgent press release with a photo. I want him caught, Kevin. I don't want him disappearing into some underground paedophile support network. He'll have contacts. People who will hide him. People who will give him transport, money, shelter.'

Before Kevin could speak, there was a knock at the door. 'Come in,' Carol said impatiently.

Stacey hovered on the threshold. 'Sorry to interrupt, but I just came up with something on Nick Sanders I thought you might both want to hear.'

Carol waved her in. 'Please tell me you know where he is,' she said with a half-smile.

Stacey frowned, as if uncertain whether Carol was serious. 'No. But I do have something that strengthens our case against him. You know he sent us his log from July with that report of the alleged flasher?'

'When he was being so "helpful",' Kevin said, his hands making speech marks in the air.

'Well, I dug a bit deeper. Guess what? That log was altered within an hour of the first news reports of a body being found in Swindale. He made up that log entry to divert attention away from himself.' Stacey looked pleased with herself.

'Thanks, Stacey, that's really useful. Well done,' Carol said. As she spoke, Don Merrick stuck his head round the door.

'Can I come in?' he asked. Carol nodded. 'I was looking for Kevin, actually,' he said. He consulted a sheet of paper. 'We've had an anonymous call from a punter claiming to be a former friend of Nick Sanders. The friendship ended because he caught Sanders taking pictures of his young son in the bath. He kept quiet at the time because he didn't want his kid being put through the ordeal of an investigation, but when a mate who works for the Peak Park told him Sanders was a suspect and that he'd legged it, he decided to come forward. Anyway, he reckoned Sanders would head for open country. He's got the skills to live off the land. Apparently there's a place in Sutherland, in the north-west of Scotland – Achmelvich Bay,' he said, stumbling over the unfamiliar name. 'Sanders was the warden at the Youth Hostel there years ago. We checked that out, by the way. It's on the CV he submitted to the Ranger Service. Anyway, according to our caller, Sanders spoke about something called the Hermit's Castle. He couldn't remember much about it except that some guy from London built it right out on the headland. Like a concrete pillbox, only smaller. Lived in it for a year, wouldn't speak to a soul. The caller said Sanders might head for there. I think we should check it out,' Merrick concluded eagerly.

'It's a pretty long shot,' Carol said.

Kevin made a noncommittal gesture. 'We could ask the local boys to keep an eye out.'

'If he worked up there, he probably knows the local boys,' Merrick pointed out. 'I think Kevin should go. There's a flight to Inverness at noon.'

Carol considered for a moment, then shook her head. 'It's too insubstantial. Kevin, speak to the local lads, ask them to check it out. But discreetly, yes? If there's any trace of Sanders, we'll follow it up. In the meantime, we concentrate on getting an appeal out nationally. Now, if you'll excuse me, I've got a briefing to prepare.'

There was pitifully little to impart at the morning briefing. And they all knew it. The determination of the morning before was tinged with desperation. They all knew that with every passing hour the chances of finding Paula alive diminished dramatically.

'We'll continue to follow up on the council-tax

data,' Carol said, trying to keep the energy in her voice high. 'I want us to speak to every landlord and tenant within the search area on the map here. I know it's a scattergun approach, but until we have something to narrow it down, we will do whatever it takes to find Paula. Inspector Merrick has the full list of assignments for today. In addition, I want you to ask in every interview whether the subject has ever heard anyone referred to as the Creeper.' She was conscious of a dubious stirring in the room.

'I'm aware it sounds bizarre. But this is good information. Derek Tyler has said nothing for two years. While it's possible he may have mischief in mind, Dr Hill is inclined to think he hasn't the wit to mislead us on this. So bear it in mind.

'The good news from forensics is that we do have DNA. Unfortunately, the sample is not of sufficiently high quality to run it for comparison against the national database.' Groans all round. 'However,' she said, raising her voice, 'it's good enough for elimination purposes. And I'm told that if we do get the right person, there will be enough common ground for it to have evidential value.'

She turned and pointed to the large-scale map of Temple Fields. 'She's there somewhere. So let's find Paula.'

As the briefing ended, officers moved in clusters towards Don Merrick, who looked as if he hadn't slept in this lifetime. 'Sam,' Carol called over the hubbub. He turned and gave her an enquiring look. 'A moment, please.'

He wove his way against the tide to her side. 'Yes, ma'am?' he said smartly.

'I want you to pull the files on the cases from two years back.'

'The Derek Tyler murders?'

'That's right. Once we'd arrested Tyler, everything else came to a halt. You and I are going to have a very boring morning going over those files and identifying any actions that were slated but never followed up.'

Evans tried to look enthusiastic. It wasn't convincing. Before Carol could say anything, she saw John Brandon's familiar figure moving through the press of bodies. He was plotting a course straight for her. 'Off you go, Sam,' she said firmly.

Brandon reached her and steered her to one side. 'Carol, is Tony fully abreast of the investigation?'

'Yes, sir.'

'I think we need a formal profile from him. I've got a press conference at noon and I'd like to give them something that makes it look as if we're making a degree of forward movement. Especially since we've lost Nick Sanders,' he added acerbically.

She tried not to smart under the implied criticism. 'Can we give them some of the video footage? To see if anyone recognizes the man?'

'I don't see why not. Whether they'll use it is another matter. The media care a lot less about a police officer at risk than we do. They're more excited about having a serial killer in their midst than they are about saving DC McIntyre.' Brandon moved away, taking the time to dole out some words of encouragement as he headed back to the relative peace of his office.

Carol looked around to see which of her officers was nearest. 'Jan?' she called.

Jan looked up from the sheaf of papers she was reading, caught Carol's eye and came over. 'Something for me?'

'Can you track down Dr Hill and get him to come over?'

'Sure. Have you got his mobile number?'

Carol reached for a piece of paper and scribbled it down. As she wrote, she said, 'He'll either have it turned off or he'll ignore it, though. I'm giving you his home address as well. I think he said he'd be there this morning.'

'And if he's not there?'

Carol shrugged. 'Try Bradfield Moor.'

Jan smiled. 'Like calling to like, eh?'

Carol bridled. It was precisely the sort of thing she would have said to Tony herself. But that was the prerogative of a friend, not the kind of sly remark she wanted to hear from her junior officers. 'We need him more than he needs us, Sergeant. Let's not forget that, eh?'

Jan shrugged an apology and left. Merrick approached Carol and ran a hand over hair greasy from lack of washing. Hollow-eyed, he stared at her bleakly over the rim of his mug, one leg jittering with nervous energy. 'I keep feeling there must be something else we should be doing,' he said, his voice gravelly with exhaustion.

'I know. But it's hard to imagine what that could be. And it's not going to help anyone if you drive yourself into the ground over this, Don,' she said gently.

She saw anger spurt into his eyes. 'Paula's not just one of my officers,' he said tightly. 'She's my friend. I know that might seem odd. I know most people can't get their heads round the idea of a woman and a man being mates. But that's how it is with us.'

And yet you didn't know she was gay, Carol thought. That probably said as much about Paula's instinctive caution as it did about Merrick's lack of insight. 'I believe you, Don,' she said. 'And I do understand how that makes it harder on you.'

'Do you?' He shook his head. 'She was like a dog with two tails when she got the posting to the squad, you know? She was excited about working with you. Ever since the Thorpe case, you've been her hero. That's why she agreed to the undercover even though it freaked her out. She wanted you to think well of her. She was determined that anything you could do, she could do too.'

His words cut Carol to the quick, even though she understood he was lashing out to ease his own guilty sense of failure. 'I think she was doing it for herself, Don. Not to impress me, but to keep faith with her own idea of what a cop should be,' she said. 'But whatever Paula's motives, there's no point in chucking blame around. We've got to concentrate on finding her.'

'You think I don't know that? But what's to concentrate on? There's hundreds of bits of paper there, and they all say the same shit. It's like she vanished into thin air.'

'We're getting there. We're narrowing down the possibilities all the time. We've covered a huge amount of ground in Temple Fields. According to your own figures, we've physically been inside more than seventy-five per cent of all the properties in the area. It comes down to time and method.'

He sighed. 'I know. I'm not thinking straight. Look, ma'am, if you don't mind, I'm going to take off and get some sleep. I'll check into a motel, get my head down for a few hours.'

'Good idea, Don. It won't look so bleak once you've slept.'

He turned away without a word and shambled off. It was only half past nine, but Carol felt she'd already done a day's work. When she'd taken on the challenge of a specialist squad, she hadn't considered quite how tiring it would be to spend her days trying to corral a bunch of cops whose natural abilities made them as difficult and bolshie as she'd been herself in her younger days. Sometimes, she found herself almost longing for Traffic.

The grounds at Bradfield Moor had not been designed for anything other than easy maintenance. But on a wintry morning, with the leaves off the trees, they offered a long vista across the moors to the north through the tall chainlink fence. It was possible to lose sight of the city below, to cut one's connections to the life of the streets. To walk there with a patient wasn't generally an option that staff were encouraged to take, but Tony had decided Tom Storey would only benefit from a short respite away from the oppressive surroundings of the hospital. They'd been out in the open for the best part of an hour, taking stock of Tom's most pressing current concerns.

They had come to a halt among a stand of birch trees, close to the fence, looking across the valley at the sparkle of a reservoir on the moors. Tony checked his watch. 'We should probably head back. I've got another appointment in a quarter of an hour.'

With one last look at the landscape, they turned back towards the ugly Victorian Gothic pile. 'I'm glad you came today,' Storey said.

'We had an appointment. Where else would I be?'

'I thought your police business might keep you away.'

'My patients come first with me. I work with the police, but that doesn't give them the power to dictate my movements.'

Storey gave him an odd look. 'That's a funny way to put it.'

'It is, isn't it? I suppose it's because I've been thinking a lot about power this morning.'

They walked in silence for a couple of minutes, then Tony said, 'What's your line on power, Tom?'

Twin lines formed between Storey's eyebrows as he tried to find a way to express what he felt. He was finding it less easy to communicate his thoughts now. 'You take it where you find it,' he said. 'It's always circumstantial. One man's power means another man's pathos.'

Tony stopped in his tracks. He wasn't quite sure how, but something in Tom Storey's words had triggered an idea in his head. He spoke so softly his patient had to strain to hear him. 'You look at the over-powered, there's a direct line back to the oppressor . . .' Tony raised his face to the sky. 'Find the thread, you find the killer.' He turned to Storey and smiled beatifically. 'Thank you, Tom. Thank you for that beautiful thought. I do believe I'm starting to see the light.'

But the light had to wait. As he'd said, Tony had another patient to see, a patient whose psychosis required the full focus of his attention. An hour later, he finally emerged from his office, head down, paying no attention to his surroundings. He was vaguely aware of shapes passing him, but he was almost at the end of the corridor when something penetrated his consciousness. He stopped and frowned, looking round impatiently as a voice repeated its Bugs Bunny impersonation.

Jan Shields was leaning against the wall outside his office, grinning. 'I said, "Nya . . . What's up, Doc?"'

He felt a quick surge of apprehension then dismissed it. If something bad had happened, she wouldn't be clowning with him. 'Don't give up the day job,' he said, walking back towards her.

'I wouldn't dream of it. I like it far too much.'

He drew abreast. 'Something happened?'

She pushed off from the wall. 'No. That's the trouble. Mr Brandon wants a profile. That way he'll have something to feed the reptiles. I'm here to drive you back. Shall we?' She gestured towards the main corridor and fell into step beside him.

'How did you know where I was? And that I didn't have my own car?'

She winked at him. 'I'm a detective.'

'What I do with my life isn't exactly a secret. You asked Carol.'

Jan smiled. 'When your car was at the house and you weren't, I called Carol. She said you'd probably have left the lights on. Or run out of petrol. So I called here.'

When they emerged in the car park, Tony was

surprised to see they were heading not for a nondescript saloon car but a low-slung Japanese sports two-
seater. 'Nice to see Bradfield CID taking care of their
officers,' he said, bending to fold himself into the
passenger seat.

'You really do have a weird sense of humour, Dr
Hill,' Jan said.

'Tony, please.' He gasped as she floored the accelerator and sped out into the narrow lane.

'So, what's in it for you?' Jan asked as she rattled
through the gears.

'In what?' he said, confused.

'The nutters in Bradfield Moor. Why bother? You
could spend your life profiling and teaching. Why earn
a pittance dealing with the dregs?'

He thought for a moment. 'Hope,' he said finally.

'That's it? Hope?'

'Don't underestimate the power of hope. And
besides,' he added, 'I'm good at it. There's a satisfaction in doing something you know you do better than
most people in the field. Don't you find?'

She drove fast into a tight bend, throwing him
against the door. 'Thanks for the implied compliment,'
she said. 'And do they help you with your current
profiling cases, your nutters?'

He grinned. 'Oddly enough, I place more trust in
my own judgement. Which is not to say they don't
occasionally offer an accidental insight.'

'Any insights today, then?'

Tony shook his head. 'Just a timely reminder that
I really should have been looking more closely at
victims. And what links them.'

'That's easy. They were all whores.'

395

'Apart from Paula.'

Jan pulled up at the junction with the main road and took the opportunity to give him a puzzled stare. 'But she looked like a whore.'

'If looks could kill, they probably will.' He smiled at her bafflement. 'There's something else they have in common.'

'What's that?'

'If your mission as a killer was cleaning up the streets, you might think getting rid of cops was as socially useful as getting rid of prostitutes. But of course that would only make sense if Paula was a bent cop . . .'

'There's more than one way of being bent.'

'Ah, yes, I'd heard you produced that revelation. Don Merrick seemed a bit put out at the notion.'

This time, there was no warmth in Jan's smile. 'It's so predictable, isn't it? Pretty girl like that, how could she be a dyke?'

'Still, you picked up on it,' Tony said. 'But then, I suppose you would.'

'Meaning what?' she said.

'Takes one to know one. Isn't that what they say?'

She flashed a quick glance at him. 'What makes you think I'm gay?'

'Is it supposed to be a secret?'

Jan blew a raspberry. 'Shrink's trick. Answer the question: what makes you think I'm gay?'

Because of the way you are with Carol, he thought, but was not prepared to say it because of what it would reveal about himself. He paused for a moment, finding another way of saying the same thing. 'Because of the way you are with men.'

'You think I hate men? What a cliché.'

'That's not what I said. You treat all of us with exactly the same mixture of amusement and charm and disdain. It doesn't matter if we're attractive or ugly, bright or dim, you don't differentiate. You're not interested in us beyond our professional interactions. It could be that you're one of those people who's just not interested in sex with either gender, but I don't think so. I sense a certain sexual charisma there. Does that answer your question?'

She slowed down and looked across at him. 'Thank you for taking it seriously. You're right, as it happens. And I'm right about Paula.'

'And you thought it was fair to out her?' Tony asked, curious rather than combative.

'Hey, you're the one saying we should be looking at every aspect of the victims. You think it matters? That she's gay?'

'I never gave it a moment's thought. It never seemed relevant,' he said indifferently.

'It can make you vulnerable on the street. Unless you take steps to turn it to your advantage. You can't rely on anybody else to do it for you. Of course, it's not the only thing that makes you vulnerable. Any sort of difference can have the same effect: race, being disabled . . . They're all things people have to compensate for.'

In every exploration he had made into the criminal mind, Tony had arrived at a moment where something crucial fell into place and made sense of everything. It wouldn't have registered if he hadn't been thinking so hard about power and vulnerability that morning, but because his mind was already running on those lines, it assumed the correct significance. At last he thought he understood. And he also knew he hadn't a hope in hell of convincing Carol or anyone else. Not wanting Jan to see his reaction, he looked out of the passenger window. 'I suppose. Must be just as hard for Evans and Chen,' he said nonchalantly.

'I wouldn't know, I've never asked them.'

'What? No solidarity among minorities?' Tony asked.

'I've got nothing against them. But I've got nothing in common with them either. Why should I expect them to fight my battles?'

'Fair enough. So I suppose Brandon wants this profile yesterday? That would be why they took the trouble to send someone to fetch me?'

'I guess so. Nothing else is going anywhere. Carol's even going over the old Derek Tyler cases with Sam to see if there were any loose ends they can chase up now.' She reached out and turned on the CD player. Bonnie Raitt sang that love had no pride.

'You think you're going to bring Paula home alive?' Tony asked.

'Honest answer?'

'Honest answer.'

'I think she's already dead. I think he's playing with us.'

More than anything else he'd heard that day, the words thrust a chill spear of fear into Tony's heart.

Evans marked his place with a finger and looked up. 'DCI Jordan? I can't seem to find any mention of Paula on the original inquiry list.'

Carol thought for a moment. 'She probably wasn't on it, Sam. She was a CID aide on the Thorpe case, but that was only a six-month posting. She'd probably have gone back to uniform by then. You think there's any significance in that?'

'If there is, I don't know what it could be,' he said. 'Just clutching at straws.' They went back to work, heads bent, minds on full alert, mining the mountain of paper.

Half an hour of silence later, they were disturbed by a SOCO. 'Are you DCI Jordan?' he said.

'Yes.' Carol tried to squash the quickening of interest. She couldn't bear any more false hope.

'We've been going through the bins in the search area and we've found the radio mike and transmitter that DC McIntyre was wearing,' he said, sounding pleased with himself.

Carol snapped to full attention. 'And?' She was half-aware of the arrival of Jan and Tony, but all her focus was on the SOCO.

'The wire from the mike to the transmitter had been snipped. There are two partial prints on the transmitter. We're working on them right now. We should know soon if they match anything on AFIS.'

Tony stayed discreetly in the background, but Jan dumped her coat and bag by her desk and moved closer to the action.

'Why has it taken this long to find?' Carol demanded. 'What have you people been doing for the past two days?'

He looked wounded. 'It turned up a couple of hundred yards away from where she was last seen. That's a lot of rubbish to get through.'

'It is when you work nine to five. Jan, see who you can rustle up to get back on the streets with you. Then widen the search area out from where they found the mike. Sam, you go too.'

Jan didn't pause to discuss the order, heading straight out the door towards the murder room. Evans capped his Cross fountain pen, slipped it into his inside pocket and followed her. Meanwhile, Tony casually sat down at Jan's desk, apparently waiting for Carol's attention.

'How long will it be before you get a result from AFIS?' she asked.

Unnoticed by anyone, Tony leaned down and flipped open Jan's handbag. He slid his fingers inside, probing till her found her bunch of keys. He closed his hand round them then silently lifted them clear and slipped them in his pocket.

'Hard to say,' the SOCO replied. 'It depends how much traffic there is on the system.'

Tony stood up. 'I'm just going for a coffee.'

Carol barely registered his words. 'Can't we put a priority status on it?'

'I already did,' Tony heard the SOCO say as he walked out of the office. He hurried downstairs and out into the front reception of the police station. He paused at the counter.

'Do you know where the nearest heel bar is?' he asked.

The civilian behind the counter thought for a moment. 'If you go into the mini-mall round the corner, there's one up the back in the basement.'

Tony left at a trot. He was breathing hard by the time he reached the heel bar. The smell of solvents and glue caught his throat and made his eyes water. Luckily there was no one waiting to be served ahead of him. He deposited the bunch of keys on the counter. As well as the car keys, there was a Chubb mortice, a couple of Yales and two small keys. 'I need copies of all of these, except for the car keys,' he said. 'And I'm in a hurry, I'm afraid.'

The youth behind the counter gave the keys a swift appraisal. 'No problem. Ten minutes do you?'

'Brilliant. I'll be right back.' He hurried out of the shop and ran through the arcade of stalls to the coffee shop by the escalators. Again, he was spared the tension of waiting in a queue. 'Large macchiato to go, please.' He drummed his fingers on the counter while he waited for the pitifully slow barista to get to grips with his technology and assemble the drink. He grabbed the carton then walked briskly back to the heel bar.

Five minutes later, he walked nonchalantly up to Jan's sports car. He put his coffee on the ground, unlocked the car and put the keys in the ignition. Then, trying to look like a man with nothing more demanding on his mind than coffee and a serial killer profile, he made his way back up to the squadroom.

He walked in just as Jan was upending the contents of her bag on to her desk. She looked up, frustration on her face. 'You didn't see what I did with my keys, did you?'

Tony scratched his head, frowning in recollection. 'You know, I don't remember you actually locking the car,' he said.

'Fuck.' Jan shovelled everything back into her bag, grabbed her jacket and ran from the room. Evans raised his eyebrows at Tony as he followed her at a more leisurely pace.

Tony shrugged. 'What can I say? I have that effect on women.'

Honey – whose real name was Emma Thwaite – had started to think of herself as streetwise. It had only been a matter of months since she'd left the shitty council flat in Blackburn to escape the responsibilities of raising three younger brothers while her mother spent her time in the pub, cadging drinks from men she would bring back and fuck on the living-room settee. But it felt like a lifetime. She could hardly remember who she'd been back then.

She knew she'd been lucky to end up under Jackie's wing, and she'd been naïve enough to believe she'd learned enough from that position of relative safety to manage on her own. But the past few days had thrust upon her the realization that she was a lot less capable of dealing with the world than she had thought. She wanted someone to take Jackie's place, someone to help take the edge off the fear and the loneliness.

So when she walked into Stan's Café that afternoon, she gravitated straight to the table where Dee Smart sat alone, smoking and staring out of the window. 'Hiya, Dee,' she said. 'Fancy another cuppa?'

Dee looked her up and down, as if calculating what the price might be. 'Yeah, go on,' she said with a shallow sigh.

Honey clattered off on her high heels, returning with two mugs and two chocolate biscuits. 'There you go,' she said, settling in opposite Dee and stripping the wrapper off her biscuit.

Dee carried on staring into the street. 'Bastard cops everywhere. They're scaring the punters away.'

'Sooner they catch whoever's doing this, the better for us,' Honey said.

Dee gave her a contemptuous look. 'That's not going to happen any time soon.'

'You think?' Honey tried not to let her apprehension show.

'I know. You think the Creeper isn't pulling the strings?'

The name took Honey by surprise. It had never occurred to her to connect it with the crimes that had turned her world difficult and sour. 'This has got something to do with the Creeper?' she asked.

'Of course it has,' Dee said impatiently. 'I've had them all over me, asking their questions. Do I know the Creeper? Do I know anybody who had it in for Sandie? Blah blah blah.'

'And you haven't told them?' Honey couldn't figure out why Dee would have kept silent about something so important.

Dee's eyes narrowed. 'You crazy? You think I want to be next on the hit list?'

Honey frowned. She knew she wasn't exactly Brain of Britain, but she didn't think what Dee was saying made sense. 'There won't be no hit list if the Creeper's locked up,' she pointed out.

Dee flicked the ash from her cigarette in a gesture of exasperation. 'Grow up, Honey. They're never going to lay a finger on the Creeper.'

'All the same . . .'

Dee shook her head vigorously. 'Don't even think about it. It'd be your funeral, girl.' She pushed her tea away from her, as if deciding that drinking it would place her under too much of an obligation. 'I'd have thought you'd have learned your lesson from what happened to Jackie. If you don't want to end up like her, keep your nose out of the Creeper's business.'

Honey watched Dee walk out. It hurt that her overture had been rejected, but she was more disconcerted by the reason than the fact itself. Maybe Dee was right, the best thing was to keep her head down and make sure she didn't rock the boat. But what if Dee was wrong?

Don Merrick decided he didn't like the Scottish Highlands. He'd never been anywhere so empty in his whole life. He remembered a trip he and Lindy had taken before the kids came along, a four-wheel-drive safari into the Sahara. Compared to this louring emptiness, the desert had felt positively thronged. It hadn't been so bad for a few miles after he'd left Inverness airport in the hire car, but when he'd turned off the main arterial road to strike out west, he had rapidly found himself in the middle of absolutely bloody nowhere. According to the map, this was supposed to be an A-road, but it was more like one of the narrow back roads of the Peak District.

You could go mad out here, he thought. Nothing but grey rock and greeny-brown vegetation. Correction. Nothing but grey rock and greeny-brown vegetation and the occasional grey-brown pond. Sometimes the grey rock manifested itself as the crumbling gable end of what might once have been a house or a barn. But signs of human life were few and far between. The only living things he could see were sheep. In an hour's driving he'd passed two vehicles, both travelling in the opposite direction: a Land Rover and a red minibus with PostBus emblazoned along the side. Don supposed some people might like the grandeur and the isolation, but he found himself longing for the bustle and scrum of the city.

When he'd looked at the map, he'd thought he could check out Nick Sanders' putative foxhole in a matter of hours. Before anyone would even notice he'd been gone. He'd capture the fugitive and restore his self-respect in one. Then the glory of success would bring forgiveness for his insubordination. Carol would be forced to respect his abilities if he brought Nick Sanders in before nightfall.

But the light faded faster up here too. It was only mid-afternoon, and already he felt twilight closing in. He'd be lucky if he made it to Achmelvich by night-fall, never mind back to Bradfield. He wished he'd brought a torch with him. He had a feeling that Achmelvich wasn't going to be well endowed with streetlights. If he ever found anything approximating civilization again, he'd stop and stock up on some essentials.

He wondered if they had chocolate up here.

Tony had chosen to sit at the desk Kevin Matthews normally occupied for the good reason that, from her office, Carol couldn't see what he was doing. She was still busy on the phone, which gave him the freedom to flick through the pages of the phone book. With one ear cocked, he ran his finger down a column of names. God, it was getting harder to read the small print, he thought. Time to have his eyes tested.

It sounded as if Carol was winding up her call. 'Yes, I do know that everybody thinks their request is a priority. But I've got an officer who's been abducted by a killer . . .' A pause. 'OK. I appreciate it.'

Just in time, he found what he was looking for. He jotted it on a piece of scrap paper and shoved it into his pocket as Carol emerged from her office and headed towards him. 'Did Jan fill you in?' she asked.

'Jan? Fill me in?' he echoed.

'Brandon wants a profile. He already told the noon press conference he was calling on the services of a psychological profiler. Which of course the local media will assume is you.'

'Oh, that. Right. Yes, she did say something,' he said, aware he was sounding flustered and hoping Carol would put it down to his customary vagueness. 'I take it you don't want me to refer to what we discussed last night?' he asked, hoping that might divert her from noticing anything unusual in his behaviour.

Carol raised her eyebrows. 'Not if you want Brandon to take anything else you say seriously.'

'And you? Have you thought about it?'

Carol pushed a hand through her hair. She looked frazzled and unhappy. 'Yeah, but it doesn't seem to take me any further forward. I'm sorry, Tony, but unless you've got something concrete, I haven't got time for this now.'

He stood up. 'That's OK. I understand. I'm going home. I'll work better there.'

'Fine, we'll talk later,' she said absently. Her mind was already on the next thing, the phone to her ear, her fingers on the buttons.

Out on the street, Tony hailed a taxi. He pulled the paper from his pocket and gave the driver the address. He sagged back into the seat and stared into the middle distance. So deep in his thoughts was he that he wasn't even aware of it when he started to speak out loud. Nor was he conscious of the apprehensive eyes of the driver in the rear-view mirror. All that interested him was the process of a killer's mind.

'You didn't get what you wanted,' he muttered. 'The bad fairy at the christening gave you a shit deal, and the brains to see how shit it was. So you learn how to take the power, hide the vulnerability. Get your retaliation in first. Hide your weakness behind a show of force. But sooner or later, the cracks start to show. You stop believing in your own publicity. You have to find a way to reassure yourself. A way to take more power to yourself. You become the voice.' He nodded in satisfaction. It made sense. It had the structure of a logical argument. Pretzel logic, but logic all the same.

'At first, you take your power from the weak. You find your listener in Derek. You make him do your bidding. You make him take your prey and you control every move of the puppet show. But Derek fucks up and you're back where you started. And it takes time to carve another will into the shape of your own.

'But, eventually, you get there. You find another mind you can dominate, another head you can perch inside. And it begins again. And then you get the chance to take on someone your own size. And you can't resist, can you?'

407

His reverie was broken by the anxious voice of the taxi driver. 'You all right, mate?' he asked.

Tony leaned forward. 'Not really,' he said. 'But I will be soon, I hope.'

One of the reasons for my success is my ability to think on my feet, to adapt my plans to accommodate changing circumstances. After the time it took to train him, I'd hoped to get more use out of this monkey, but it's become clear that sooner rather than later he's going to be fingered – and that presents a risk I'm not prepared to take. I was sure of Tyler, sure he would keep the faith because he had such a personal stake in the work I set him. But this one is weaker. He'll give me up without even knowing he's doing it.

I pull up round the corner from the shithole where he lives. It's getting dark now, and everyone's in too much of a hurry to get somewhere warm to pay attention to anybody else. I check the mirrors, just in case anybody's watching, then remove the gun from the glove compartment, enjoying the heft of it in my hand.

When the coast is clear, I get out, head down, and walk briskly to my destination. I have a key to the street door and I run up the stairs to the first landing. Two grubby green doors open off it. I reach up with a gloved hand and knock on the door with the number four painted on it.

I can feel my heart rate speeding up. I've never done this face to face before, and I'm curious to see how it will feel. Seconds pass, then the door inches open. Carl is peering out through the gap, dressed only in grey sagging jockey shorts and a crumpled T-shirt. He looks as if he's just woken up. His expression is suspicious, but when he sees it's me, his face clears.

'Hiya,' he says, a goofy grin on his greasy face. 'I wasn't expecting you.'

He steps back to allow me to enter. It's a dank, untidy room. Unmade bed, clothes in piles, Britney poster on the wall. It smells of masturbation and sweat. Every time I've been here, it's depressed me to think this was the best I could do.

Carl is gibbering something, but this afternoon I've no time for small talk. I'm supposed to be somewhere else. I pull out the gun and take pleasure in the panic that spreads across his face. He's not very bright, but even he knows what a gun means when it's at his head. I back him towards the bed.

'I did what you said. I never told anybody,' he whimpers. His legs hit the edge of the bed and he tumbles backwards. He scrambles towards the head of the bed. He's crying now. 'I promise, I won't give you up.'

I find the voice within myself. The one I know he is conditioned to obey. 'Lie down, Carl. Lie down and everything will be all right. I am the Voice. I am your Voice. Whatever I tell you to do is for the best. I am the Voice, Carl. Lie down.' And it works. His subconscious mind overrides his panic enough for him to do as he is told. He's shivering and sweating, but he's doing what he's told.

I reach for the pillow and put it to the side of his head. I press the gun barrel into the pillow. His eyes are wide with trust. 'I am the Voice,' I remind him. 'I am your Voice.' And I pull the trigger.

Carol looked up from the file she was reading and recognized the man who'd just entered the squad-room as one of the fingerprint technicians. 'We've got a result from AFIS,' he said.

'Who is it?' she demanded, getting to her feet and reaching for the sheet of paper in the technician's hand.

'Carl Mackenzie. Twenty-six. Possession of cannabis, possession of ecstasy, indecent exposure . . .'

'I know him, he's a small-time street dealer,' Kevin said. 'He hangs out in Stan's Café.'

'Last known address, Flat 4, 7 Grove Terrace, Bradfield,' Carol said. 'Come on, Kevin, let's hit it.' She pushed past the fingerprint officer, shouting for Merrick.

'He went off to get some sleep,' Kevin reminded her. 'I could call his mobile.'

Carol shook her head. 'Never mind. Stacey, get your coat,' she called across the room.

The technician stood in the doorway of Carol's office watching them go. 'Thanks for all your hard work, lads,' he mimicked sarcastically.

Carol, Kevin and Stacey pounded pell-mell down the corridor. 'We'll take my car,' Kevin shouted. 'I've got a noddy light.'

Carol nodded agreement as they hurtled down the stairs and into the car park. They piled into Kevin's car, Carol yanking open the glove box and pulling out the blue flashing light. Fumbling with the connector, she finally managed to plug it into the cigarette lighter slot, then opened the window and slammed it on the roof.

They were already out in the traffic, the rush hour jamming the streets with cars. Kevin leaned on the horn, the light flashed and it gradually dawned on other drivers that they needed to pull over. But it still felt like painfully slow progress.

Carol chewed on the skin by her thumbnail. *Please, God, let us find Carl Mackenzie. And please, God, let him lead us to Paula.*

* * *

410

Tony paid off the taxi and stood for a long moment, taking in the house in front of him. It was a modern detached brick building, part of a depressingly uninspired development on the outskirts of the city centre. It occupied the central plot at the head of a cul-de-sac with an unimpeded view of any car coming up the street. He wasn't in the least surprised. The Creeper would need to be in control of every possible aspect of her environment.

Jan Shields' house was even more lacking in personality than its neighbours, if that were possible. White paintwork, white front door, white garage door. Boring block paving on the drive and pathway. A tidy lawn with evenly spaced shrubs and conifers round the edge, all trimmed with obsessive neatness. Nothing that surprised Tony one whit.

He walked up the path and tried the mortice key in the lock. It was reluctant to turn at first, but Tony jiggled it a little and the tongue slipped back into its bed. The first Yale wouldn't fit, but the second slipped home easily. As the door opened, he heard the insistent beep of a burglar alarm's warning tone. He looked around for the control box, eventually spotting it behind him. His luck was still running; it was a key-operated system rather than one controlled by an electronic combination. He fumbled with the two small keys, his hands sweating as he jammed the first of them into the lock and turned.

Silence fell. Tony wiped the sweat from his face with both hands and turned to examine the house he believed to be the Creeper's lair. His evidence for that conviction was not the sort that would cut any ice with a cop. He could imagine Carol's face. 'It was

411

the way she spoke about power and vulnerability. Her contempt for the weak,' he'd say. And then he'd see the struggle on Carol's face between her desire to believe him and her copper's dependence on tangible evidence. Actually, there was something else too, but that was equally intangible. From the very beginning the cutting of the wire had troubled him. If Paula had noticed it happening, she'd have kicked off there and then. For her not to have noticed, it must have been done without fumbling. And for it to have been done without fumbling, whoever abducted her couldn't have relied on a lucky guess. He had to have known. And that narrowed it down to Carol and her team.

At first, he'd been more interested in Chen and Evans. They were the most obvious outsiders because of their racial backgrounds. It wasn't hard to imagine the resentments building up over the years as they perceived themselves powerless in the face of an organization that was implacably geared towards handing control to others. Chen had seemed particularly appealing because of her obsession with machines. Interacting with people was something that didn't come easily to her, which, if she was the killer, might tempt her to use the agency of another. There was a coldness in Evans too, a distance that suggested he might enjoy exploiting others for his own ends.

And then he'd realized Jan was not only another outsider but one with a unique connection to Paula. So he'd driven that morning's conversation in a direction that he hoped would tell him more about her. Which it had done. And then he'd remembered Carol mentioning that Jan had been with Paula when she'd chosen her outfit. Nobody was better placed to make sure the wire was where it was supposed to be. And so he was here, staking everything on his gut instinct.

He flicked on the light switches in the hall. It was a risk, but there wasn't any point in being here in the dark. The floor was covered in thick cream carpet as far as the eye could see. It extended into the living room and up the stairs and it was spotless. No children or animals here. He looked down at his feet and saw a pair of slippers by the front door. Nothing from the outside world was going to be allowed to soil this place.

He moved through to the living room, standing on the threshold and drinking it all in, moving from first impression to a fuller scrutiny. The room was big, an archway leading from the seating area to a dining space. Two big cream sofas dominated the first part of the room, each replete with four precisely placed burgundy velvet cushions. In front of one there was a glass-and-wood coffee table. On it sat a *Radio Times* and that morning's paper, each perfectly aligned. The walls were painted a deeper shade of cream than the carpet. Above the fake coal fire hung a reproduction of a geometric Mondrian painting. A flat-screen TV dominated one corner of the room, DVD and video players underneath it.

On the other side of the chimney breast bookshelves had been built into the wall. Tony crossed to look at them, but he was distracted by the sight of a laptop on the dining table. He ducked through the arch, opened it and pressed the button to turn it on. While he waited for it to boot up, he went back to the bookshelves. 'There's got to be a record,' he murmured.

413

The lower shelves contained videos, the upper ones books. Most of the books were lesbian fiction, from pulp romance to more serious literature by writers such as Sarah Waters, Ali Smith and Jeanette Winterson. Incongruously, half a dozen tattered hardbacks of John Buchan thrillers. On the top shelf, legal textbooks, police manuals. He bent over to study the videos. American cop shows like *CSI, NYPD Blue, Law & Order* dominated, though there were also a few lesbian classics such as *Bound* and *Show Me Love*. He took out a couple of cases at random, but the contents matched the covers.

'Gotta be a record,' he repeated. He went back to the computer and gazed at it. The trouble was, he wasn't much of a techie. He knew enough to run the programs he wanted to run and that was about it. He needed Stacey Chen. But that was about as likely as a moonwalk right now. 'It's not going to be here. You're too clever for that. You know what people like Stacey can do. No, you're going to want something tangible, something you can access without leaving footprints.' He looked around the room. There was nowhere to hide anything down here. Wherever the puppetmaster kept the records of her exercises in power, they weren't here.

Purposefully, Tony headed for the stairs. He wasn't worried about being disturbed; all Carol's officers were working flat out round the clock. Jan wouldn't be back for hours yet. Plenty of time to have a good look round.

The three cops thundered up the dimly lit stairs of 7 Grove Terrace, ignoring the open-mouthed student

414

who had let them in and who was now shouting, 'Hey, what the fuck . . .'

They stumbled into one another on the landing outside the door of flat 4. Carol banged the door with the side of her fist. 'Police, open up,' she shouted, venting all the anger, fear and frustration of the past few days.

No reply. Kevin pushed his way to the door and hammered so hard the wooden panel cracked. 'Open up, Carl. The party's over.'

'Kick it in,' Carol said.

Kevin stepped back and threw himself at the door. It vibrated, but didn't break open. As he backed up for another attempt, Stacey intervened. 'Gimme a chance,' she said.

Kevin almost burst out laughing. 'You what?'

But Stacey was already somewhere else. She stood side-on to the door, breathing deeply. She seemed to coil into herself then she erupted in a blur of movement, one leg shooting out and hitting the door right next to the lock. There was a splintering of wood and the door sagged open.

'Fucking hell,' Kevin said.

Carol gave Stacey a perplexed glance. 'You're full of surprises,' she said, pushing the door open. What faced them stripped away any sense of wonder or levity. Carl Mackenzie lay sprawled on the bed, blood and brains on the covers and the wall behind him. The air was thick with the salt metallic taste of blood. In his right hand, a gun lay, his fingers curled loosely around the grip.

'Gunshot wound to the right temple. Gun in his hand,' Carol said automatically.

'Oh Jesus, no,' Kevin shouted. 'Fucking bastard, why couldn't you give us Paula first? Fucking selfish bastard.'

'Looks like suicide to me,' Stacey said.

Carol bent forward to peer closely at the body on the bed. 'Except I can't see any powder burns round the wound.' She reached out and laid the back of her hand against his arm. 'Still warm. Very fucking convenient.'

Stacey frowned. 'Convenient for who?'

'For whoever wants us to believe that Carl Mackenzie was smart enough to plan a series of murders and to kidnap a cop.'

'I don't understand. His prints were on Paula's powerpack. Do you mean he was working with someone?'

Carol sighed. 'Not with someone, Stacey. For someone.'

It wasn't so bad after all. Nothing like as exciting as making the others do the work, but still a thrill. Having the power to take a life and having the nerve to exercise it; how could that not be close to as good as it gets?

I wonder how long the suicide scenario will hold water. It depends on whether they find him because they know they're looking for him for the murders or whether they just find him. If it's the ice blonde and her team of nodding dogs, it won't take them long to realize Carl wasn't alone when he died. It's a pity I had to use the pillow, but I didn't have a silencer and it was more important that I got away than that I made the scene watertight and some nosy neighbour clocked me leaving after the gunshot.

Maybe I should have tried the line that I was interviewing him when suddenly he reached for the gun and shot himself. I could have been the hero of the hour. But that would have been a high-risk strategy, and I haven't got this far by taking unnecessary risks. I've always stacked the odds in my favour. Like with the trained monkeys: I always made sure they were well in my debt before I started pushing the buttons to make them perform. With Derek, there was the evidence of the rape that I conveniently made disappear. With Carl, there were the drugs.

Now it's time to finish clearing up. I'm keeping an eye open for what I need, doubling down the side streets a couple of miles from Carl's place. And there it is, tucked down an alley. A builder's skip, full of wood and broken furniture and rubble. I pull up at the mouth of the alley and grab the ruined pillow. I stuff it under a broken sheet of chipboard and I'm back in the car inside a minute.

I need to get back on to the visible plane, but I want to see her first. I'm aching for her; it's been a long time since this morning, and Carl won't be bringing any more videos. I'm going to have to go there myself later to change the video cassette and to check on her. Shoving a dildo garnished with razor blades into a woman's vagina myself will be less satisfying. Making someone else do it, now that's worth the candle. But getting my own hands dirty was never part of the game plan.

But there's no other way out. Left to her own devices, she'll take too long to die. They'll have found where I'm keeping her long before that happens. And even though there's nothing there to point the finger at me, I'd prefer her to be dead when they get to her.

Of course, there might be more pleasure to be had in her staying alive . . . Watching her struggle with the damage my power has inflicted might just offer something rather *special to savour. It's possible that would amuse me while I look for another monkey to train.*

Yes. Perhaps for once the exercise of mercy might be a more entertaining route to take.

But first I want to see her suffer some more.

The immaculate cream carpet continued throughout the upper floor of the house. The room straight ahead was clearly the main bedroom. Although it was as perfectly ordered as the living room – no clothes thrown over chairs, bed neatly made, dressing table as organized as Dr Vernon's instrument tray in the pathology lab – it wasn't what he'd expected. Somehow, though the overall effect managed to be sterile, this was undoubtedly intended to be a boudoir. Decorated in peaches and cream, the curtains matching the bed linen, the room contained more flounces and frills than Tony had ever seen outside the bedding department of John Lewis.

'Who are you trying to be here?' he asked out loud. 'Who do you bring here? Are you trying to lull them into a false sense of security? Are you trying to kid them that you're not really a shark?' He walked over to the chest of drawers and, feeling uncomfortably like the sort of sexual pervert that ended up as his patient, he slid open the top drawer. It was crammed with excessively feminine lingerie of the kind Tony had only ever seen in expensive shops and then only in occasional glimpses. But even here, order prevailed. Bras on one side of the drawer, briefs that deserved their name on the other. He gingerly moved his hand among the lace and silk. Nothing untoward met his fingers.

418

The next drawer contained carefully folded T-shirts, many of them silk, and an assortment of hosiery. The bottom drawer was packed with sweaters. He closed it, having found nothing except clothes.

He looked over at the bed. Kingsize, traditional iron bedstead painted cream. It was, Tony thought, a measure of his intellectual investment in perversion that he could never contemplate such a bed without automatically thinking of bondage. On either side there was a bedside table complete with lamp. It was impossible to tell which side Jan slept on.

He checked the drawer of the bedside table nearest the door. Empty. The other offered a couple of books of lesbian erotica, one with an S&M theme, a dildo and a small anal probe. Nothing very remarkable, he thought. 'Of course, I could be wrong about you. It does run counter to the probabilities,' he muttered. 'And if I am, that could be very embarrassing.' He shut the drawer and looked around purposefully.

One wall of the room appeared to consist solely of doors. Tony tried the first and found himself inside a small en suite shower room. Not a hiding place in sight. The next door opened into a walk-in wardrobe stretching the rest of the length of the room. He moved slowly along, flicking through the clothes. Suits, trousers, jackets, blouses, a couple of formal evening dresses. Everything clean and ironed, some items still in their dry-cleaning bags. He got down on his knees to look behind the shoes. She had what he thought Carol would find a depressing penchant for cowboy boots.

Probing among the boots, his fingers brushed against the coolness of metal. Scrabbling under the footwear, he discovered a metal file case pushed back into a recess in the wall. 'Bingo,' he breathed. He pulled it out into the light and tried the remaining key he'd had cut.

The lock turned with the smoothness of frequent use. Hoping for more than a stash of porn, Tony opened the lid.

Carol stood on the landing in Grove Terrace, watching the SOCOs work their tedious magic. She could hear Stacey's voice floating down from the floor above.

'How well did you know Carl Mackenzie?'

Then a woman replying, 'I wouldn't say I knew him. We'd speak on the stairs, that sort of thing. But that's as far as it went. He wasn't the full shilling, poor lad.'

'Did you ever see other people coming and going from his flat?'

'Can't say I noticed anybody. A proper Billy No-Mates, that was Carl. Eager to please, but not the sort you'd want following you round.'

'And did you hear anything this afternoon?'

'Not me, love. I was watching the telly.'

Kevin walked up from the floor below. He shook his head. 'Nobody heard a thing.'

Carol sighed. 'They really didn't, or they conveniently didn't?'

'I think they were telling the truth,' he said despairingly. 'There's a little old lady downstairs, she'd love to have heard or seen something. She hasn't had this much excitement since the Boer War.'

'You know, Kevin, if Carl Mackenzie killed himself,

I'll apply for a transfer to Traffic. Get the uniforms to search the bins.'

'The bins? What are we looking for?'

'Look at the bed. What's wrong with this picture?'

Kevin looked but he couldn't see past the body steadily cooling on the soiled sheets. He shrugged.

'There's no pillow. Can you sleep without a pillow, Kevin?'

The penny dropped. 'A pillow with a hole in the middle.'

Sam Evans was fed up. He wasn't even sure what he was supposed to be doing. Jan Shields had marshalled half a dozen of them back down to Temple Fields to go over what was, as far as he was concerned, old ground. They were ordered to carry out another canvass of the area immediately surrounding the bin where the transmitter pack had been found. They'd dispersed on their rounds and he hadn't seen Shields since. He'd knocked on the doors assigned to him, asked the same questions, logged the same negative responses.

He decided to have a quick pit stop in Stan's Café. The coffee was terrible, but the atmosphere was marginally less depressing than that inside the police station. As he walked down the street towards the greasy spoon, he saw Honey on the kerb, touting for trade. 'Hey, girl, how're you doing?' he said easily.

'Hi, Sammy,' she said. 'Crap, actually. You lot are killing the trade.'

'Fancy a coffee?' He'd thought she had something for him in the pub, but Jan Shields' arrival had closed her down tight as a drum. Maybe he could loosen her up again.

'You buying?'

'I'm buying.'

'In that case, you can treat me to an all-day breakfast.'

He grinned. He'd always admired bottle. 'Come on, then.'

A few minutes later, Honey was attacking a monstrous fry-up with all the gusto of a starving dog. Mouth full of sausage and egg, she mumbled, 'Brilliant, Sammy.'

'It'll kill you, that shit,' he said censoriously. 'Clog up your arteries, make you fat.'

She shook her head. 'I never put a pound on, me.'

Evans gave her a cynical look. 'Can't imagine why that would be.'

She winked. 'All that exercise.'

'Not to mention the recreational drugs . . .'

She looked disappointed. 'Aw, Sammy, don't spoil it.'

'I'm a cop, Honey, I can't help it.' She acknowledged his reply with a sad little twist of her mouth. 'You know the other day when we were having a chat?' he continued. She nodded. 'I had the feeling you were going to tell me something. And then DS Shields turned up and you did one.'

Honey swallowed, buying herself some time, considering. Then she said, 'She disgusts me, that one.'

He shrugged. 'She's only doing her job. Just like me.'

Honey gave him a disbelieving look. 'Is that what it's called?'

This wasn't going quite where he'd expected but Evans was nothing if not a good listener, especially when it meant adding to his store of knowledge. 'Meaning what?' he prompted.

Honey cast her eyes upwards. 'Come on, Sammy. Don't tell me you don't know about the Vice and their freebies?'

At first, he didn't get it. 'Are you saying Jan Shields is on the take?'

She picked a piece of bacon rind from between her small, feral teeth. 'Not like you mean it. Not in money.' She understood his stillness. She knew he wanted her to spell it out, as if that would somehow make it easier to believe. 'She takes it in sex. She makes some of the girls have sex with her.'

Evans didn't much like Jan, but he thought she was a good cop. She'd been the one who'd spotted the Tim Golding photo. And she'd worked her arse off trying to find Paula. He didn't want to think of her in the light Holly was shining. 'Come off it, Honey,' he protested. 'That's just people taking a pop at a cop because she's an easy target.'

Honey put down her fork and knife. She looked both serious and miserable. 'She's had me. Face down on a table, rough and ready. She fisted me. I couldn't walk straight for days. Another time, she fucked me in the arse with a Coke bottle. Do you have any idea how fucking scary that is, someone ramming a glass bottle into you? That's what your precious detective sergeant likes.'

He recognized truth when he heard it, but he still didn't want to accept it. 'I'm finding this hard to believe, Honey.'

Her mouth twisted in a bitter line. 'Which is why she's been getting away with it for so long. You lot

423

don't want to hear this kind of shit about one of your own.'

'You should have made a complaint.'

'Yeah, right. Like anyone would believe that a nice lady cop would hit on a slag like me.' She picked up her cutlery and attacked a slice of fried bread, dipping it in her egg yolk and crunching angrily.

'Has this happened with other women?'

'Only a few, as far as I can make out. She's choosy. And we know to keep our mouths shut unless we want to be banged up on a charge. We all hate her. She drools all over us, makes us kiss her. And, like, that's the thing we don't do with punters, you know? It's sick. And you never know when she's going to be back for more. Out of the blue, suddenly she's there.' She gave him a side-long glance, knowing she was about to deliver the killer punch. 'That's why we call her the Creeper.'

He stared at her, open-mouthed and horrified.

'See, I knew you wouldn't believe me,' she said with a kind of sad triumph.

'What did you call her?' Evans strained to get the words out.

'The Creeper. It's what the girls she screws call her.'

He gave her the standard-issue policeman's hard stare. 'This better be the truth, Honey,' he said, pushing his chair back.

'I got no reason to lie about it, Sammy,' she said huffily.

Evans jumped to his feet and threw some money on the table. 'Right, Honey. On your feet. You're coming with me.' He marched her protesting to the door, pulling out his mobile as he went.

*　　*　　*

The first thing out of the file case was a thin stack of photographs. Tony recognized the top one immediately. Jackie Mayall lay spreadeagled on the bed where she'd died. But there wasn't as much blood as he remembered. In the following two pictures, more blood appeared. The final two shots showed crime-scene tape at the edges; in one a SOCO stood by the bed with a ruler in his hand. Tony's stomach turned over as he realized what he was looking at. 'Official crime-scene photos . . . and very unofficial ones.'

With a gesture of disgust, he put them aside and carried on looking. There were more photos, this time of Sandie Foster. They fell into the same two categories: official and unofficial. Under the photos he found a handful of DVD-ROMs. He leaned back on his heels and stared at them. 'Memories,' he said softly.

He'd been right. It had taken him far too long to get there, but he'd been right. He thought about phoning Carol, but the need to know, to be certain, was stronger. He gathered everything together and retraced his steps down to the dining-room table.

He sat down in front of the laptop and pressed the button to open the CD/DVD drive. Empty. He was about to insert one of the disks when it occurred to him that it might be worth checking out which websites Jan had bookmarked. He clicked on her comms program, then on the icon for favourite places. Her bank. The BBC website. Amazon. Something called lesbiout.co.uk. And one called simply 'webcam'. 'Oh shit,' he said.

Hurriedly, he checked there was a cable connecting the laptop to a phone line, then he clicked the icon to get online. Against the background sound of modems warbling to each other, he spread out the photographs on the table around him. A bright voice said, 'Welcome. You have mail.'

Ignoring the prompt to access the incoming mail box, Tony clicked on the webcam link. The screen went black. Then it filled with a blurred image. Seconds later, the pixels shunted into place and with pinprick clarity Paula McIntyre appeared on the screen. 'Holy fuck,' Tony said.

At first, he couldn't tell if she was dead or alive. There was no blood, which was a mercy. He frowned at the screen, trying to work out how to control the image, whether he could zoom in or not, whether there was any way to find where the image was coming from. He was so intent on what he was doing, he completely missed the drift of headlights up the cul-de-sac and the sound of a car engine cutting out only yards from the house.

She knew as soon as she turned into her street that something was seriously wrong. Her house was a blaze of light, upstairs and down. But there were no cars in sight, other than the ones she knew belonged to her neighbours. For a moment, she considered making a run for it. She'd have a head start and she had plans in place for precisely this contingency. However, she reasoned, if it was her colleagues who were on to her, she would have picked up something unusual in the radio traffic. But all afternoon, the police radio in her car had spat out the usual crap. Nothing out of the ordinary at all. She'd heard the call for support when Carl's body had been found and was glad she'd had the foresight to get rid of him before the fingerprint evidence came back. Besides, if it was her lot, Jordan the ice maiden would have made damn sure that she was well out of the way during the search, performing some pointless task on the other side of town.

So if it wasn't the cops inside the house, it had to be Tony Hill. She'd sensed something this morning in the car with him, but she'd thought she was being paranoid. Now, it seemed her instinctual nervousness might have been justified. Sudden realization dawned. He must have lifted her keys and had them copied. She swore under her breath. That's what had happened earlier. She hadn't been losing it at all. He'd tricked her. Outrage swelled inside her and she knew she wasn't about to run. Nobody got one over on her. Nobody.

If it was Hill and he was there alone, she could finesse the whole problem out of existence. Get rid of him, move her souvenirs where they couldn't be found, show terrible remorse at killing the psychologist she'd mistaken in the dark for a burglar. At the most, she'd do a couple of years.

If that was going to play, however, she'd need to make it look like she'd come home as normal. About thirty yards from her house, she cut the lights and switched off the engine, coasting into her drive on momentum and habit. She got out of the car, closing the door with the gentlest of clicks. From the darkness of the drive, she could see the length of her living room.

There he was, the cheeky bastard. Sitting at her dining table, using her laptop like he was Goldilocks and she was the three bears. Well, there was no doubt about it now. She was going all the way.

She crept round to the back of the house, ducking beneath the dining-room window as she passed. She leaned against the wall by the back door, raking through her bag to find the back door key, which she always kept loose, just in case she lost the rest of her keys. A cautious planner, that's what she was. And why she should have realized earlier that Carl wasn't her only problem.

She slipped the key into the lock and turned it with infinitesimal care. The click as the tumblers released was barely audible. She kicked off her shoes, pushed down on the handle and inched the door open. Gingerly she stepped through the gap and stood listening. She felt wonderfully alive, buzzing with the knowledge that she was in control, and he had no fucking idea. Through the half-open door between kitchen and dining area, she could hear the tap of keys and the click of the track-pad buttons.

So taut was she that she physically jerked when the sound of his voice cut through the silence. 'Where are you? Come on, tell me. Where are you, Paula?' Her heart rate dropped back as soon as she realized he was talking to the image on the screen, not to her.

She took a deep, silent breath. In the dim city glow bleeding in through the kitchen window, she could see the outline of her neat, sterile, modern kitchen. One of the few women she'd brought back to the house to fuck had commented that it looked like somewhere serious microwaving went on. She hadn't been invited back a second time. By the cooker, the knife block sat, its contents seldom used and still factory sharp. She reached out and gently removed a long-bladed boning knife, then walked soundlessly towards the dining-room door.

Carol reached out her free hand to the wall, unconsciously supporting herself against the weight of the information coming down the phone at her. 'Are you sure, Sam?' she said, knowing in her gut that he was right, that Tony had been right, that this was the worst of all possible scenarios for Paula McIntyre. The knowledge wormed its way into her brain, making sense of the loose connections that had been troubling her for days.

'I'm as sure as I can be,' Evans said solemnly.

'Where is she right now?' Carol asked. Kevin stopped on his way down the stairs, alarmed by the stricken look on her face, the dull inevitability in her voice.

'I don't know. I haven't seen her for hours.'

'We need to find her. Get out on the streets and see if you can track her down. Ask who's seen her. But keep it off the radio, you understand?'

'I understand.'

'Good work, Sam,' Carol said, knowing nobody else would ever thank him for what he'd achieved. She ended the call. She wanted to curl up in a ball and weep, but that would have to wait for later.

'Guv?' Kevin said, his tone concerned. Carol knew his anxiety wasn't really for her, but she forgave him anyway.

'The Creeper,' she said. 'Sam's got an ID from one of the street girls.'

Kevin's face lit up. 'But that's great news.'

'No, it's not,' Carol said flatly. It was as if she

couldn't bring herself to tell him. She turned away and began to run down the stairs. 'Stacey,' she shouted. 'And you too, Kevin. With me, now.'

Kevin caught up with her at the car, Stacey at his heels. 'Who is it?' he demanded. 'Who is it?'

Carol's face clenched momentarily in pain. 'Jan Shields,' she said.

Kevin recoiled as if he'd been struck in the face. He gave an incredulous little laugh. 'It's a wind-up,' he said. 'Somebody with a score to settle.'

'Sam says not,' she said heavily. 'I should have listened to Tony,' she added, running a hand through her hair. 'Can we get a move on, please, Kevin?'

Dazed, he unlocked the car and they piled in. 'Stacey, call the station and get a home address for Jan Shields,' Carol said over her shoulder. 'Fuck, I should have listened to Tony.'

'What? He said it was Jan Shields?' Kevin sounded incredulous.

'He said there was a cop behind this. I wouldn't believe him.'

'Where am I going?' Kevin said as Carol slammed the noddy light back on the roof.

From the back seat, Stacey shouted the address. 'It's on the Micklefield estate,' she said.

'We've still only got one hooker's word for it,' Kevin said as he carved a line through the traffic. 'And it makes no sense.'

Carol sighed as if she had the weight of the world on her shoulders. 'Oh, it makes sense all right. It's the first thing that's made sense since this whole fucking business began.'

*   *   *

Tony clicked another button, hoping it might provide some indication of where the webcam feed was coming from. He'd left the screen itself, unable to bear the sight of Paula's vulnerability. At least she was still alive. It was, he knew, time to call Carol. Stacey Chen was far better equipped for this task than he was.

He reached for his mobile. He'd barely got his hand out of his pocket when he heard a low voice behind him that chilled him to the bone.

'You're a burglar. I'm quite within my rights.'

He froze and slowly turned. Jan Shields was inches from him, her weight balanced perfectly, a glittering blade held almost carelessly in her hand. Her eyes were cold and steady, her whole attitude one of carefully contained violence. 'Drop the phone on the floor,' she added.

He did as he was told. He didn't doubt for a moment that she would have had no hesitation in cutting him if he hadn't complied. 'Might be a bit hard to argue reasonable force. I mean, everybody knows I'm a weed.'

Her lip curled in contempt. 'I don't think I'll ever have to make the argument. Because nobody knows you're here, do they?'

'Carol knows.' He said it casually, trying to make it convincing.

She shook her head. 'I don't think so. She does things by the book, does the lovely Carol. She would never let you come out to play by yourself. I rather think you're all mine, Dr Hill.'

She was so accustomed to dominating, he thought. The only way under her guard was to take the power

431

from her. Which was fine in theory. His problem was that he was woefully short on leverage. 'This isn't your style, Jan,' he tried for starters.

For some reason, his words had amused her. 'You think not?'

'It's way too hands-on. You like somebody else to do the dirty work.'

She raised one eyebrow. 'Are you suggesting I've got something to do with these murders?' she said, her cherub's face assuming a look of injured innocence.

'They're your murders, Jan. You should be proud of them. They're interesting pieces of work.'

'That's as maybe. But they're nothing to do with me, Dr Hill. Derek Tyler killed four women. And a retard called Carl Mackenzie did three more copycat murders before he topped himself in remorse only this afternoon. That's what the evidence shows.'

Oh Christ, she's killed with her own hands. The knowledge hit Tony with the force of a lightning strike. He felt his own chances shrivel to ash. But still, he had to try. 'Come on, Jan. There's no point in lying now. Carl Mackenzie hasn't done three murders. Paula McIntyre is still very much alive.'

'You obviously know more about it than I do. Maybe you're the person behind it all. Maybe you've set me up. Maybe you're the person who's been sending me all this sick stuff.'

He shook his head, aiming for an air of disappointment. 'That dog won't hunt. Carol Jordan knows me too well to fall for that.'

'I can make it look that way. With you dead and the ends all tied up, who's going to listen to your favourite blonde? Everybody knows she's lost it. Face it, Dr Hill, you're a busted flush.'

Kevin turned into the Micklefield estate and slowed to a halt at the end of the street where Jan Shields lived. 'What now?' he said. 'It's a cul-de-sac. If she's looking out for us, she's going to see us the minute we turn into it.'

'Your car's pretty nondescript. We could drive up and just turn into somebody's drive near her house. There's not much light, and it's not like we'd be doing anything suspicious.'

Kevin drove slowly up the cul-de-sac. Almost at once, he spotted Jan's distinctive car. 'Looks like she's at home,' he said.

'Stick to the plan,' Carol replied. 'There, that one on the right a couple of doors down from hers. The house will shield us from her line of sight if we pull right up the drive.'

'What now?' Kevin asked. 'We could just front her up. Arrest her on suspicion and do a search.'

Something was niggling at the corner of Carol's mind. 'Does anyone know where Tony is?'

'He said he was going home to write his profile,' Stacey reminded her.

Carol took out her phone and speed-dialled Tony's home number. It rang a few times then the machine kicked in. She waited for the beep, then said, 'Tony, it's Carol. If you're there, pick up. It's urgent.' She waited for half a minute, then cut off the call. She tried his mobile, but it rang out interminably without an answer. 'Oh shit,' she said, a terrible apprehension hitting her.

'There's no reason to suppose he's in there,' Kevin said anxiously.

'Apart from that little pantomime with Jan's lost keys earlier.' Carol felt the pieces sliding into place, the picture forming in her mind's eye.

'What little pantomime?'

'Jan mislaid her keys. And Tony stepped out of absent-minded professor role long enough to remind her she hadn't locked her car. How likely is that, on both counts? But I just didn't see it at the time.' She swallowed hard. 'He's in there, Kevin. In there with her.'

'We don't know that,' he said.

'We need to find out. Stay there,' Carol ordered, opening the car door, ignoring the looks of dismay on her colleagues' faces. She walked to the corner of the building and sneaked a look round it. She was at a tangent to Jan's house. She could see part of the living room, which was empty. The front window upstairs was also brightly lit. Anyone watching from in there would be visible from where Carol was standing. Time to take a chance.

She sprinted along the front of the house, jumping a low hedge and crossing the garden of the house next door. That brought her to the edge of Jan's drive, alongside her car. A big window towards the rear of the gable end spilled light on to the paved blocks of the drive and splashed it up the side of the garage. She calculated that if she could make it to the far end of the window undetected, she could use the shelter of the garage to look into the window from far enough away not to be obvious to anyone inside.

She crouched down and circled behind the car, making it to the gable end and flattening herself against the wall. She edged up until she was almost level with the window, then crouched down and crept along below the sill for a few feet before straightening up. She was just outside the oblong of light. Taking a deep breath, she covered the distance to the rear of the garage in seconds.

Relying on the pool of shadow to obscure her, Carol turned and stood up. She had a clear line of angled vision into the dining room. She could see Jan from the waist up. And, slightly to one side of her, she could see the back of Tony's head. Her chest tightened. *Why the fuck didn't you call me?* As she watched, Jan's right hand came up into view in what looked from that distance to be a casual gesture.

But there was nothing casual about the knife that refracted light in a gleaming line that seemed to cut to Carol's very heart.

The insistent chirrup of Tony's mobile stopped as suddenly as it had begun. Jan nodded. 'Good boy. You didn't even try to answer it.'

'This is what you like, isn't it? The moment of power. Control. The world bent to your will.'

She cocked her head. 'If you say so.'

'I know so. It was a beautiful idea. Working on mentally susceptible men, making them your tools. A double dose of power. You control them and they control the victim according to your script. I take my hat off to you. It can't have been easy, getting them word perfect.'

She smiled. 'I know what you're trying to do. And

it isn't going to work. There's no point in playing for time when the cavalry don't know where you are.'

He stood up. 'I'm not playing for time.'

'Sit down,' she ordered him.

'I don't think so,' he said. 'You know there's no way out for you.'

Her eyes narrowed. 'I told you. I can make it look like you tried to set me up. I caught you in the act, we struggled, you died.'

'Underestimating the opposition. It's the one mistake that brings people down more than any other.'

She gave a derisory snort. 'What's to underestimate? We both know where the power resides. I'm a cop. You? You're just a very strange little man who weirds people out.'

'No, no, you misunderstand me. I'm not your problem. I don't actually mind dying, you see. No, your problem is Carol Jordan. I told her what I suspected. OK, she laughed at me. But if anything happens to me, she'll come after you.'

She looked scornful. 'Carol Jordan doesn't scare me.'

'That's what I mean about underestimating the opposition. She should scare you. Because, contrary to what you think about her, she's not afraid of getting her hands dirty. She won't be hiding behind some poor inadequate sod like Derek Tyler or Carl Mackenzie. She'll take you down, and she'll do it in the worst way.'

'I'll take my chances.'

He turned away. 'I don't think so. You're too accustomed to making other people take them for you.'

'Where do you think you're going?' she yelled, her control suddenly slipping.

He glanced back at her. 'I'm tired of talking. You're history and I'm going home.'

Galvanized into action, she lunged forward and grabbed his arm, spinning him towards her. Then the knife was in the air, gleaming between them, searching for flesh.

As soon as she saw the knife, Carol knew there was no time for anything other than action. She raced to the back door of the house, making a lunge for the door handle. To her surprise, it gave under her hand and she half-tumbled, half-ran into the kitchen. She saw a freeze-frame of Jan bearing down on Tony, the weapon hidden from her by their bodies. His mouth opened in a scream of pain. 'Drop the knife,' Carol yelled desperately at the top of her voice as she crossed the kitchen in a handful of strides.

At the sound of her cry, Jan hesitated long enough for Tony to stagger out of the arc of her knife. She glanced back at Carol, turned to flash a look of hatred at him before Carol launched herself across the last few feet between them.

Carol's momentum drove them both crashing to the floor in a struggling tangle of limbs. At first, Carol had no idea where the knife was and she scrabbled for purchase so she could pin down Jan's wrist.

'Let me go,' Jan shouted. 'You're hurting me.'

'Drop the knife,' Carol yelled back, her face inches from the other woman's.

'I dropped it already.' The words came out almost as a scream. 'Get off me.' Her body bucked under

Carol. Then suddenly Tony was on the floor beside them, pinning Jan's shoulders to the floor with his knees. Blood was streaming from one of his hands, and he clutched it to his chest.

'The knife's on the floor, Carol,' he said.

Carol eased back, panting, her weight keeping Jan's lower body immobilized. 'You're making a big mistake,' Jan gasped.

'I don't think so,' Carol said. 'Jan Shields, I am arresting you on suspicion of conspiracy to commit murder . . .'

'You don't get it, do you?' Jan howled.

'Save it for the interview room. You do not have to say anything . . .'

'Carol, listen to me,' Jan said, dragging all her resources together to give her voice the note of assured command. 'I'm the victim here. You need to listen to me.'

Don Merrick couldn't remember ever having been so cold in his life. He'd gone beyond shivering and into a kind of physical trance, his body numb and heavy. And still no sign of Nick Sanders.

He'd reached Achmelvich in the early evening, at the end of a single-track road that cut high above the slender finger of a sea loch. The occasional tree he'd passed had been bent double, a marker to indicate the force and direction of the prevailing wind.

It was hardly worth giving a name to, he thought. There was the youth hostel, closed for the winter, and a handful of low cottages hunched along a spine of rock that stretched out into the sea. Only one of the cottages was showing a light. He wondered if he should ask for directions, but figured it couldn't be that hard to find this Hermit's Castle.

He'd been wrong, of course. He'd spent the best part of an hour clambering over rocks in the wrong shoes, stumbling on loose stones, nearly tumbling headlong into the sea at one point. When he'd finally found it, he'd almost walked straight past it.

Exhausted, cold and bruised, he shone his torch over the tiny concrete structure. It was nestled in a gap in the rocks, a grey box scarcely seven feet high with a small chimney curved over the roof like a tail. There was a doorway but no door. It led to a narrow passage that curved round, apparently designed to keep out the wind and the rain. It gave on to a tiny cell, barely six feet across. Along one side was a concrete shelf the size and shape of a single bed. Opposite was an open hearth. And that was it. Nowhere to hide, nowhere to do anything much. He couldn't imagine spending a day there, never mind a year.

Merrick went back outside and shone his torch around. Nothing to do but wait. He'd give it till ten, he decided, then leave. If Nick Sanders arrived after that, he wouldn't be going anywhere before morning. If, of course, he was coming there at all.

A short distance beyond the hideaway, Merrick found a sheltered space in the rocks and hunkered down. He'd come across a petrol station earlier where he'd managed to buy a heavy rubber torch, some cans of Coke, a couple of packets of biscuits and some crisps. He'd also bought a hideous handknitted jumper which he'd hoped might protect him against the cold. It didn't seem to be helping much.

The sound of the sea crashing against the rocks was hypnotic. There were moments when he felt himself drifting into a doze, starting awake only because his body shifted and some part of him hit a different bit of rock. Thoughts of Lindy and his sons drifted in confusion around his head. They were why he was here. Somewhere in the deep recesses of his mind, he knew that a large part of the reason he was so determined to bring Tim and Guy's murderer to justice personally was that he felt it would be a kind of talisman, an act that would protect him from the prospect of losing his own boys. It almost assuaged the guilt he felt at abandoning Paula. But there were dozens of people out there working to bring Paula back, and nobody but him who cared enough about Tim and Guy to take a chance on this most slender of leads.

It was just after seven when he realized that there was another sound in the distance, a different note from the surge and crash of the sea. There was no doubt about it. It was a car. He shifted his position, trying to rub some life back into his frozen limbs. Either it was one of the cottage residents returning after a day doing who knew what in the back of this godforsaken beyond. Or it was Nick Sanders, going to ground where he thought he'd be safe.

The minutes passed, slow as hours. Then a glimmer of light rose behind the rocks. It grew brighter and clearer then, as it rounded an outcropping, became clearly identifiable as the steady beam of a big torch. Merrick ducked lower, though he knew there was little chance of anyone seeing him against the mass of black rock.

The beam swung round and illuminated the Hermit's Castle. Merrick could see nothing of the person behind the torch at first. But as the light disappeared inside the narrow passage, he could make out the shape of someone with a tall rucksack on his back. The height and bulk of the figure was, as far as he could make out, much the same as the description he'd read of Nick Sanders.

Merrick counted to sixty, then he stood up. It took a couple of minutes for his legs to feel capable of carrying him. He used the time to make sure his handcuffs were open and ready, his grip firm on his torch. Then he picked his way across the rocks in the darkness and stepped into the mouth of the passage. He walked as lightly as he could, picking up the sounds of someone moving around. The clank of tins. The rustle of plastic bags. Then he was in the chamber, looking down at the man crouched by the concrete shelf, illuminated by the light of a lantern-style torch. There was no doubt about it. This was the man whose photograph was pinned to the whiteboard in the squadroom.

A slow smile of satisfaction spread across Merrick's face. 'Nick Sanders, I am arresting you on suspicion of murder,' he said, enjoying every word.

He relaxed too soon. Sanders sprang up from his crouch, his momentum carrying him into Merrick and knocking him off his feet. Sanders tried to scramble over him and into the tunnel, but the space was too confined. Merrick lunged at his leg and caught him off balance. Sanders crashed into the wall and tripped up, falling backwards and cracking his head on the bed shelf.

He grunted once, then went slack. Merrick dragged himself upright and staggered across to Sanders. He was, to Merrick's regret, still breathing. He rolled Sanders over on to his side, not caring about the first rule of head injuries, seeing with satisfaction a swelling welt across the man's forehead. He glanced away as he went for his handcuffs. Suddenly Sanders uncoiled and sprang upwards, grabbing the heavy torch and swinging it savagely at Merrick's head. It caught him on the temple and at once, everything went red then black.

Carol stared at Jan Shields, incredulity on her face. 'You're the victim here? Bullshit. Where's Paula?'

Jan's voice dropped into a warm, lower register. 'I have no idea, Carol. Why don't you ask Dr Hill? Like I said, I'm the victim here. I came home to find he'd made an illegal entry into my home. I found him typing something into my laptop. I grabbed a kitchen knife to defend myself against an intruder. I have no idea how long he has been here or what he might have planted.'

'Nice try, Jan,' Tony said, his voice strained. 'Carol, there's a webcam feed. She's got it saved in her favourites. It's Paula. She's still alive.'

'Does it say where she is?'

He shook his head. 'Maybe Stacey can find something?'

Jan continued as if neither of them had spoken. 'Like I said, Carol, I found him in my home. I have no idea what he's talking about.'

'Shut up,' Carol said savagely. She shifted her position so she could reach her phone. She dialled Kevin's number. 'Kevin, get up here now. Back door. Bring

Stacey with you. Call for an ambulance, a SOCO team and uniformed back-up, please.'

'You're going to look very foolish, Carol,' Jan said, a pitying smile on her lips. 'A well-respected police officer with commendations for bravery and experience of working with the FBI defends herself against an intruder in her home, an intruder intent on framing her for murder purely to protect the failing reputation of the woman he loves . . . That'll play beautifully in court, don't you think?'

Carol wished she could cover her ears and shut out the insidious poison coming from Jan Shields' mouth. 'Like I said, save it for the interview room. I hope you've got something put aside for a rainy day. Bronwen Scott doesn't come cheap.'

Jan chuckled. 'Oh, I think I can afford a few hours of her time. That's all it'll take before Mr Brandon realizes what a trumped-up mess of lies there is against me. And who's behind it.'

Carol was spared listening to any more by the hasty arrival of Kevin and Stacey. She summoned them with a jerk of her head. 'Cuff her and caution her, Kevin. I only got as far as "suspicion of conspiracy to commit murder". You might want to throw assault in for good measure. Tony, you can move away now,' she said. She waited till he was clear and Jan was flanked by the other two before she rolled off Jan's legs and got to her feet.

'I'm sorry you're being forced to take part in this charade, guys,' Jan said apologetically. 'I keep telling Carol I'm the victim here, but she's got her own reasons for preferring to believe Tony, hasn't she?' She smirked at Carol as she spoke.

'Get her out of my sight,' Carol said, crossing to Tony. 'As soon as we get some uniforms here, I want her taken back to HQ and banged up till I'm ready to talk to her.' She took in his pallor and pulled a dining chair across for him. He slumped on the chair, holding his hand against his blood-soaked sweater. 'How bad is it?' she asked.

'It hurts like hell. Won't stop bleeding.' Beads of sweat formed on his forehead. Carol hurried through to the kitchen and grabbed a couple of dishtowels from their hooks. She folded them into pads and made him press them against the long slash that transversed his hand.

After a couple of minutes that felt much longer, flashing blue lights washed across the front window. 'That's the ambulance,' Carol said. 'Come on, let's get you on your feet.'

By the time the paramedics had loaded Tony into the ambulance, Kevin was escorting Jan into the back seat of a police car. Stacey was about to climb in with them when Carol called her name. 'I need you back here,' she said. Stacey followed her into the house. 'There's a laptop picking up a webcam feed with live pictures of Paula. I need you to find out whatever you can, Stacey.'

The younger woman nodded. 'I'd be better off taking it back to the station,' she said. 'That way I have access to all my diagnostics.'

'Fine. Just do it as fast as you can. Paula's still alive. It's obvious Jan's not going to give her up, so we need to do whatever it takes to find her before that changes,' Carol said bleakly. She watched Stacey packing up the laptop, thoughts tumbling over each other in her head. She couldn't remember the last time she'd ever faced so complicated an endgame. It should have scared her, but instead it exhilarated her. She was definitely herself again. 'Oh, and Stacey – when you get back, can you call Don Merrick on his mobile and tell him I need him here. I'm going to the hospital to take a statement from Tony. I want Don to run the search here.'

Fifteen minutes later, she was addressing a mixed team of SOCOs and detectives. 'We need to find where Paula is. There must be something – a rent book, a utility bill, something. You have to be fast, but you also have to be unimpeachable. I don't have to tell you how vital this search is. Do what you need to do. Take up the carpets, shred the cushions if you have to. I don't care if you leave the place looking like a war zone, find Paula for me.'

She turned away and spoke to the senior officer at the scene. 'I'm going to the hospital to take a statement from Dr Hill before I interview Shields. As soon as you get anything, call me. I'll have my phone switched on. To hell with their bloody heart monitors.' She stopped on the threshold and gave the team a last level stare. 'I know I can rely on all of you. And so does Paula.'

Tony sat on the edge of the examination couch, a polystyrene cup of some indeterminate brownish liquid in his left hand. He'd waited less than ten minutes to be seen by the medical staff at Bradfield Cross A&E. Something to do with the amount of blood on his sweater, he suspected. Since then he'd been given a local anaesthetic, eight stitches and a cautious opinion that he probably hadn't done any permanent damage to his hand.

The curtains surrounding his cubicle moved and Carol's familiar face appeared in the gap. 'Hi,' she said. She slipped inside, closing the curtains behind her. 'How are you doing?'

'I'll live,' he said.

Carol hitched herself up on the bed beside him. 'I need to take a statement from you.'

He gave a tired, sad smile. 'What do you need to know?'

'I need to know what happened between you and Jan. The earlier stuff – how you got there, what the hell you thought you were playing at – that can wait for later. But I want to know how it went down.'

'I couldn't think of a way to make you believe me other than hard evidence,' he said. 'My failure.' He sipped from the cup. Tea, he thought, though he wouldn't have been willing to wager anything he cared about on it. 'Inside a file case that was hidden in her wardrobe, I found a bunch of photos and some DVD-ROMs. Photos of the victims before they were discovered. Photos presumably taken by Carl Mackenzie.'

'You know about Carl?'

He nodded. 'Jan told me the bare bones.' He continued with the story, up to the point where he had turned to walk away.

'She came after me,' he said. 'I thought she would. I wanted to make her feel powerless, to lose control. That was my only chance of finding a chink in her armour that might have got me out of there alive.' He smiled. 'And that's when you arrived.'

'She didn't actually confess?'

He shook his head. 'No. Sorry. She was already practising the line she used on you.'

'Never mind,' Carol said. 'We'll nail her.'

'Paula?' Tony asked.

'We're looking. We'll find her.' He could see the restored confidence in her face and hear it in her voice.

In spite of his concerns for Paula, part of Tony rejoiced.

Nick Sanders kicked the lifeless body at his feet. Bastard plod had screwed everything. He'd got it all planned. He was going to lie low for a week or two, until the hue and cry had died down and he'd had time to grow a beard. Then he was going to take the ferry across to Larne, drive down into Eire and disappear. It had all gone up in smoke now, thanks to this interfering copper. He'd have to hole up in some mountain bothy near the snow line, unable to risk venturing into populated areas. A child murderer would be off the front pages in a week by Sanders's reckoning, but a cop killer would be Public Enemy No.1 until he was caught. Sanders had no intention of allowing that to happen.

He repacked his rucksack, wiped the blood from the torch on Don Merrick's sweater, then set off back across the rocky outcropping to the place where he'd left the car. It was near the end of the narrow tarmacked track that led down into the hamlet of Achmelvich, tucked away between the last cottage and the rocky headland. The low cloud robbed the landscape of light, and Sanders had to use his torch to prevent himself breaking a leg on the jagged rocks that lay between him and safety.

Eventually he emerged on the narrow path between the boulders, his breath white in the chill air, a thin film of sweat on his back. He broke into a shambling trot. He was only feet away from his car when a set of headlights on full beam snapped on and blinded him, silhouetting his tall frame against the uneven skyline.

A strong Highland voice rang out across the short distance between them. 'Police. We'd like a word, sir.'

Sanders didn't pause. He took to his heels, running back down the path towards the sea. He heard the sound of heavy feet behind him and panicked. He veered from the path and started scrambling over the boulders. He'd barely gone a dozen yards when a pair of powerful torch beams started playing over the rocks around him, pinning him down after a few seconds. He carried on gamely, but his pursuers had the advantage of being fresh and being able to see where they were going.

It was over in minutes. Two burly officers hauled Sanders to his feet, handcuffed him and half-dragged, half-carried him back to the path and to their waiting car. 'What's this all about?' Sanders blustered as they went.

'You tell us, sir. Innocent people don't normally run away from the police,' the older of the two officers said.

'I was scared,' he said. 'I couldn't see if you really were the police. For all I knew you could have been going to rob me.'

'Aye, right.' At the car, they shoved him in the

back seat and turned on the interior light. 'Nasty bump you've got there,' the officer observed. 'It's not much of a disguise, though, Mr Sanders. We were expecting you. But we thought you'd be heading towards the Hermit's Castle, not running away from it.'

Sanders said nothing, mostly because he couldn't think of anything to say. A single tear slithered from the corner of his eye and trickled slowly down his cheek.

The older officer nodded. 'Fine. Constable Mackie is going to stay here with you while I go and take a wee look down by the sea. I'll not be long.'

The hospital had discharged Tony under the mistaken belief that he was going straight home to bed. Instead, he asked the taxi driver to take him to the police station. He was tired and in pain, but there was still work to be done. He knew the only practical thing he could do to help Paula was to advise Carol on the interview techniques that might penetrate Jan Shields' defences. So going home wasn't an option.

He arrived to find Carol deep in frustrated discussion with John Brandon. Jan Shields was refusing legal representation. She was also refusing to say anything whatsoever in a formal interview. Brandon looked surprisingly relieved to see Tony. 'How are you?' he asked, his expression one of concern and bonhomie.

'Sir,' Carol said, her voice a warning.

'I know, Carol, I know. But let me at least run it past him.'

'Sir, Dr Hill has suffered a traumatic experience tonight. He's been attacked and injured, he's exhausted and probably stuffed full of painkillers,' she said plaintively.

'Only local anaesthetic,' Tony said. 'I refused the painkillers. I thought I might need to have my wits about me if I was going to be questioned about planting evidence and illegal entry.'

Carol rolled her eyes at the ceiling. 'This is not the time or the place,' she muttered.

'Tony, we have a very unusual situation,' Brandon said. 'As you know, we have Jan Shields in custody. She is refusing to speak to anyone other than you. She says she will consent to a taped interview, but only if it's conducted by you. Anybody else and she will go no comment.'

'Would it be admissible evidence in court?' Tony asked.

Brandon shrugged. 'I don't know. I'll let the lawyers worry about that. What I'm concerned about is recovering Paula McIntyre alive. If Carol's right, then Shields knows where she is. I'm willing to take a chance on losing the product of your interview with her if it means getting to Paula. What do you say?'

'I think she just wants to play games with you, Tony,' Carol interjected.

'You're probably right,' he acknowledged. 'But so's John. If there's any chance of saving Paula, I have to take it.'

Tony took a last look over the notes Sam Evans had given him from his interview with Honey then took a deep breath and walked into the interview room. Jan Shields sat at the table, looking as relaxed as if she were conducting the interview. As he crossed the room, her eyes never left him. 'Nice of you to come by, Dr Hill,' she said. 'I imagine our positions will soon be reversed, just as soon as we can persuade a detective who isn't DCI Jordan to look at the evidence. Not that I'm saying you two are in cahoots. No, I think you acted entirely off your own bat. But you did it for her, and I'm sure she feels obliged to stand by you now.'

'You might as well save it for the tape,' he said genially, pressing the twin buttons as he'd been instructed. He intoned the date, time and names of those present. 'Just for the benefit of the tape,' he said, 'can you make clear the circumstances of this interview?'

'Certainly. I have waived the right to legal representation at this point. I have refused to communicate with any police officer and I have asked to speak to you, Dr Hill. The reason for this is that I wanted to confront personally the man who broke into my home and planted evidence there that would tend to incriminate me.'

'I don't think I've ever encountered anyone with a stronger taste for power,' Tony said conversationally. 'When did it start? What was the point where you understood that life had dealt you a crap hand? How did you come to realize that nobody gives power, that it has to be taken? What made you realize you could strip other people to the core and steal their power from them? How did you learn the hypnotic techniques you used on Carl and Derek? I tell you, it's going to be tough for you from now on, Jan. Because it's like a drug to you, isn't it? You can't give it up, can you? Even now, when you must know in

451

your heart that it's over, you still need to play the power games.'

'You're the one whose career is over, Dr Hill. You broke into my house.'

Tony shook his head. 'I had the set of keys you lent me.'

'Why would I lend you my keys?'

'I wanted to borrow your set of *NYPD Blue* videos and you didn't know what time you were going to get off work.' He pushed back in his chair. 'Any fiction you produce, I can counter it. But the weapon I've got that you can't trump is truth.'

'I don't think so.' She smiled.

'We'll see, shall we? Let's start with your sexual abuse of prostitutes.'

He thought he spotted a momentary flash of unease, but it was gone before he could be sure. 'You must be confusing me with someone else. I don't pay for sex.'

'I didn't say you paid for it. We've got a statement from a young woman saying you coerced her into violent sex by threatening her with arrest if she wouldn't co-operate.'

Jan laughed, a delighted gurgling chuckle. 'They're coming out of the woodwork tonight, aren't they? Dr Hill, one of the perennial risks of working Vice is malicious accusation. I can produce plenty of women with whom I have had consensual, non-violent sex. I don't need to threaten street hookers to get laid. I think, on balance, any court will take the word of a career cop with commendations over that of some junkie whore.'

'It's not a chance I'd be willing to take,' Tony said,

his manner mild and relaxed. 'Let's move on to the hard physical evidence I found in your house. Not just the computer, Jan. I found your stash. The photographs, the CD-ROMs. They'll have your prints on them.'

She sighed and looked down at the table. 'You've caught me out there, Dr Hill. Maybe I'll make it easier on myself if I just come clean now. Yes, I do possess the material you're talking about. But all I'm guilty of is withholding evidence. That material arrived anonymously in the post at my home. Maybe you have some idea where it came from? I know I should have turned the evidence in, but . . .' She spread her hands in a disarming gesture. 'What can I say? I'm not proud of this. I wanted to make a name for myself. I wanted to solve these crimes myself. Yes, I should have handed it over to DCI Jordan. But I wanted the glory for myself.' She lifted her gaze and met his eye. She gave him the twinkling cherub smile. 'I can only say how sorry I am.'

Tony couldn't help a sneaking admiration for her. He'd never seen anyone hold it together so well on the surface. He'd interviewed more than his share of stone-cold psychopaths, but he'd never encountered such supreme control. 'I've got to say, I don't know how you did it. It must have been a hell of a challenge, to get Derek and Carl to carry out your bidding so precisely. I've seen some skilled hypnotherapists in my time, but I doubt any of them could have exerted this level of mind and impulse control.'

She shook her head pityingly. 'I have no idea what you're talking about,' she said.

'No? I'd have thought you'd have wanted to share

the secrets of your success. You could make a lot of money teaching people like me how to achieve complete control over another human. Even if they are only pretty pathetic specimens like Carl and Derek.' Nothing. Not a twitch. He tried another tack. 'It's a shame Carl Mackenzie's dead. I'm sure he had an interesting tale to tell.'

'I think so too. And I suspect I'm more sorry than you that he's dead, because he could certainly have exonerated me. If someone was directing these murders – which I'm not convinced is true, by the way – Carl would have been able to reassure you that person was not me.'

'An interesting thought, Jan. But there is one person who can still set our minds to rest on this point. Once he realizes his voice isn't the omnipotent creature it pretends to be, once he knows we've got you in custody, Derek Tyler's going to talk. Derek is alive and well, and he will talk, I promise you.'

This time, her smile was cruel, her eyes dark with a savage humour. 'I wouldn't be too sure about that. About any of it, in fact.'

A sudden chill crept into Tony's heart. His mind flashed up the image of Jan leaning against the wall inside Bradfield Moor. How long had she been there waiting for him? Had she been anywhere near Derek Tyler? Had she had the chance to activate some long-buried suggestion?

'What's up, Doc?' Jan asked, clearly enjoying the confusion she could read on his face. 'Remembered something?'

Tony leapt to his feet and ran for the door. Carol emerged from the observation room at the same moment. They met in the corridor. 'She came to Bradfield Moor to fetch me,' he said urgently. He went for his phone, keying in the number of the hospital one-handed. 'This is Dr Hill, I need to speak to the duty charge nurse.' He looked at Carol as he waited to be connected. 'You need to get over there. Bring Derek Tyler here, keep someone with him twenty-four seven until I can persuade him to make a statement. He mustn't be left alone. She'll have programmed him to self-destruct.' He turned his attention to the phone. 'Vincent? It's Tony Hill. This is really important. How was Derek Tyler today?'

'Funny you should ask, Doc. He seemed quite bright, almost cheerful. Silent as usual, but a bit more animated somehow.'

'When did you last check on him?'

'Lights out, I suppose. There's no reason why he would have been checked again.'

Fuck. 'Vincent, can you do me a favour? Can you go and check on him yourself? Right now?'

The nurse sounded bemused. 'Sure, but . . .'

'And Vincent? Call me back as soon as you've done that.' He ended the call. 'Why are you still here, Carol? We need to get Tyler before it's too late. I need to talk to him.'

'Wouldn't it be better if you went and interviewed him there?'

He shook his head. 'Suicide watch there means observations every fifteen minutes. But you can put somebody in with him round the clock. That's what we need if we're going to keep him alive. Carol, you have to trust me on this.'

She hesitated for a second, then said, 'OK, you've

got it.' She took off down the corridor at a fast clip and Tony walked into the observation room. He stared through the one-way mirror at an apparently un-troubled Jan Shields. Her arrogance was monumental. Even when she knew her nickname was being bandied around in the investigation, she hadn't cut and run. She'd just carried on blithely, clearing up every potential problem before it caused her any diffi-culty. The scary thing was that she'd almost got him believing in her invincibility. She seemed to have an almost plausible answer for everything. She could, he feared, make a jury love her just enough to believe her. Or at least forgive her.

The minutes ticked by and Tony grew more and more restless. The longer the wait, the more he feared the worst. Four, five minutes at most from the nurses' station to Tyler's room. A minute to check, then the walk back. Ten minutes, no more. That's how long it should take Vincent to get back to him if all was well.

Ten minutes stretched to fifteen, fifteen to twenty. When his phone finally rang, Tony almost dropped it in his haste to answer it left-handed. 'Hello? Vincent?'

'It's me,' Carol said. Those two words told Tony all he needed to know.

'Shit,' he said.

'I got here five minutes ago,' she said. 'The place is in an uproar. They just found Derek Tyler dead in his room. Apparently he swallowed his tongue.'

'I don't believe it,' Tony groaned.

'Believe it,' Carol said grimly. 'This case is going belly-up and we're no nearer to finding Paula. I could weep.'

'You and me both.'

'I'll see you back at the station. Tony – don't go back in to Jan until I get back, OK?'

'Yeah. We need to figure out where we're going with this.' If indeed there was anywhere left to go.

The police station Stacey had returned to a few hours earlier bore little resemblance to the one she had left. Nothing travels faster than bad news within an organization as driven by information as the police. For days, Paula McIntyre's abduction had fuelled conversation and ambience alike with a mixture of outrage, hindsight and criticism. Everybody had an opinion. But the news of Jan Shields' apparent betrayal had delivered a shockwave to Bradfield police that had created something like the moment after an explosion when air and sound have been sucked from the epicentre. Corridors were hushed, movements subdued, faces angry and baffled. When she'd walked into the murder room, Stacey had felt hostile eyes on her, as if by having been present at the event she was somehow responsible for so brutal a blow to the force's self-esteem. Already, she knew, people would be rewriting history; some searching for ways to exculpate Shields; others who had been close colleagues distancing themselves from her; still others claiming always to have known she was dodgy. The fallout was going to be grim and painful.

Back at her own desk, Stacey dry-swallowed two paracetamol caplets and scrunched her face into an expression of concentration. It didn't take her long to determine that there was no easy route to the location of the webcam from the image on the screen. It made her stomach churn to see her colleague staked out like that, and she made a mental promise to Paula that she would make sure the images disappeared for good from every computer they'd ever contaminated once Paula was rescued. There was no way the sleaze-bags were going to get their hands on this. Paula wasn't going to end up as late-night entertainment for scummy vice cops. Or anybody else.

One of the officers from the HOLMES computer team had taken on the task of wading through all the easily accessible files on the laptop's hard disk. So far, he'd found nothing except a depressing amount of hardcore porn.

Stacey wasn't interested in what was visible. She knew that a criminal as organized as Jan Shields was not going to have left crucial information in plain view. She would have deleted anything incriminating and, because of her involvement with the paedophile investigations, she'd probably have learned to take basic steps to clean up her hard disk regularly.

That didn't mean there wasn't anything to find, and Stacey was determined to find it. After an hour's intensive investigation, she'd managed to isolate only three stray file fragments. At first glance, they'd looked like gibberish. But Stacey had tools at her disposal and it didn't take her long to translate the jumbled symbols into splintered words and phrases.

The first fragment yielded nothing of interest. It looked like the remains of an email attachment, prob-ably one of the thousands of jokes that circled the globe, given text such as 'wim in the pool' and 'so god sai' and 'out of the fish'.

The second fragment hit Stacey like a shot of vodka. '. . . rent in advan. . .osit in cash. . .edsit at !%. . .tron

Lane, Temp . . .rl Macke. . .' While the printer wheezed into life, she ran down the hall to the murder room, where a large-scale map of Temple Fields hung on the wall. She traced the street names with her finger. There it was. Citron Lane. The alley behind the street where Paula had disappeared.

Excitement welling up, she hurried back to her desk. The symbols ! and % were the shifted versions of 1 and 5. She'd got it.

Carol leaned her head on the steering wheel and felt the pain from her stressed muscles spread across her shoulders in a tight series of cramps. She couldn't get her head round Jan Shields. How much evidence could the woman wriggle out from? She'd clearly used all her experience in the job to figure out the perfect set of excuses and explanations for every aspect of her criminal activity. Carol was used to bluster from captured criminals, but she knew this went far beyond bluster into the realms of a kind of perverted credibility.

All of which she could possibly learn to live with if only she could bring Paula home. But that prospect looked no more likely now than at any point since her abduction.

Wearily she straightened up and started the engine just as her phone rang. 'Carol Jordan,' she said dully.

'It's Stacey,' the voice said. 'I've got it, I think.'

'Got what?' Carol couldn't let herself believe.

'Where Paula is – a bedsit at 15 Citron Lane, Temple Fields. Rented in Carl Mackenzie's name. We searched it on the night, but it was Sergeant Shields who led the search team and gave it the all clear.'

Carol felt her throat suddenly closing with emotion. 'Thank you, Stacey,' she managed to say before she choked up completely. 'I'll take it from here.' She ended the call and dialled Merrick's number. No reply. Where the hell was he? She didn't have time to chase him now, but she'd kick his arse when he finally reappeared. Cursing Merrick under her breath, she tried Kevin's number. He answered on the second ring. 'Kevin – 15 Citron Lane, Temple Fields. Meet me there. Bring a team. Do not, I repeat, do not go in till I get there. Is that clear?' She ended the call, shoved the car in gear and reached for her radio mike with one hand.

'DCI Jordan to control. Paramedic unit required at 15 Citron Lane, Temple Fields. Repeat, paramedic unit required at 15 Citron Lane, Temple Fields. Over.'

The radio crackled acknowledgement of her message. 'And I need someone to get over there with a set of boltcutters,' she added as an afterthought.

'Did you say boltcutters?' the radio operator asked.

'Yeah. The kind that cut through handcuffs.'

The room was on the third floor. As Stacey had said, Jan Shields had been responsible for giving the all clear to the building beyond the gate in the wall. Even if she hadn't managed to annex that search for herself, it would have been easy for officers in a hurry to miss its existence. At some time in the past, someone had created a double door. When the landing door was opened, it revealed a shallow cupboard with dusty shelves. But on closer examination, hidden under one of the shelves was a keyhole and a countersunk handle. The building was on the list of properties whose tenants were still to be queried with landlords. Another day and they'd have tied Carl Mackenzie's name to it.

Kevin Matthews and Sam Evans threw themselves at the inner door. It collapsed in a shatter of splinters and dust. Carol pushed her way through and entered ahead of them, heart in her mouth. At first sight, she thought they were too late. Paula lay motionless on the bed, eyes closed, unmoving. The room stank of sweat and piss. 'Get those cuffs off her,' Carol ordered, grabbing the corner of the sheet and yanking it free so she could cover Paula's nakedness. Evans rushed past her, boltcutters in his hand.

'Oh Jesus, Paula,' he moaned as he worked the boltcutters on the handcuff chain.

The paramedics crowded in, demanding room to do their job. Carol leaned over Paula and stroked her head. Her skin was warm and feverish, and Carol's heart sang. She stepped back to let the paramedics work, just as the metal on the second set of cuffs snapped under Evans' strength.

'How is she?' she asked anxiously as the paramedics started their tests.

'She's alive. But she's very weak,' one said without taking his eyes off her.

'Don't you dare lose her,' Carol said, backing towards the landing. She reached for her phone and called Tony. He answered on the first ring. 'Tony, we found her. We found Paula.'

'Alive?'

'Yes. Alive.'

'Thank God,' he sighed.

When she came off the phone, Carol was surrounded

by delighted detectives congratulating themselves and each other. The jubilation was so overwhelming that nobody, not even Carol, noticed the face that was missing. They were making so much noise she almost didn't hear her mobile ringing. She moved back into the room where Paula was being moved on to a stretcher so she could hear the call more clearly.

The voice at the other end was unfamiliar. 'Is that DCI Jordan?'

'Yes, speaking. Who is this?'

'This is Inspector Macgregor. I'm up here in Achmelvich,' he said, his voice gruff and solemn.

'Have you got Nick Sanders?' Carol hardly dared hope. But she could think of no other reason why someone of Macgregor's rank would be in a hamlet at this time of night unless a major arrest had happened. It was almost too good to be true. They'd found Paula, they had Jan Shields under arrest, and now they'd captured the man who had abused and murdered Tim Golding and Guy Lefevre.

There was a pause. Then Macgregor spoke, his voice packed with reservations. 'Aye. We do have Sanders in custody.'

'Is there a problem?' she asked, sidestepping to let the paramedics past with their burden. She reached out to brush her fingers along Paula's arm as she passed.

'DCI Jordan,' he said, 'do you have an Inspector Merrick on your team?'

A horrible suspicion formed in Carol's mind. 'What's happened?' she demanded.

'Look, I'm awful sorry. There's no easy way to say this: Inspector Merrick is dead, ma'am.'

Carol felt her legs collapse under her as she slid down the wall in a heap. It was too much to take in, on top of everything else that had happened in the past few hours. 'No,' she whispered. 'That can't be right. He's supposed to be here. Sleeping. In a motel. That can't be right.'

'I don't think there's any room for doubt, ma'am. He matches up with the photo ID he was carrying. It looks like he was staking the place out, waiting for Sanders. They had a fight and he took a bad blow to the head. We should have more information in the morning. I'm really, really sorry, ma'am.'

Carol ended the call and let the phone fall back into her pocket. She buried her face in her hands. Then she forced herself to her feet. There would be time for her grief later. For now, she had responsibilities.

She walked slowly to the door, planting one foot carefully in front of the other like a drunk. She took a long, shuddering breath and spoke as clearly and loudly as she could. 'I've got some bad news,' she began.

Tony was still standing by the one-way mirror. He knew he should be elated at the news of Paula's release, but all he could taste was the bitterness of failure. He'd finally met his match: a criminal who could withstand his probing, apparently effortlessly. The techniques she had developed to control the minds of others had given her the gift of control over her own responses to a remarkable degree. Perhaps with time he could break down her barriers. But he suspected he wasn't going to be granted time with her. If this ever went to trial, she would be charming, plausible – and would probably be declared not guilty.

If she did lose, she might well end up in a secure mental hospital, but he could guarantee it would be a long way away from anywhere he was practising.

Paula's survival was a huge consolation, of course. On a human level, it was the best possible outcome. But it didn't balance the despair he felt as he stared down at Jan Shields' complacency.

He had no idea how much time had passed when he heard a knock. Tony crossed the room and opened the door. A uniformed constable stood uncertainly on the threshold. 'I'm sorry to disturb you, Dr Hill. But this just came for you.' He thrust a small brown envelope at Tony. 'One of the nurses from Bradfield Moor brought it in.'

'Thanks,' Tony said. He closed the door and studied the envelope. His name was written in straggling capitals across the front. He didn't recognize the handwriting. He ripped open the flap and pulled out a single flimsy sheet of cheap writing paper. The same straggling capitals filled half the page. Beneath them was an awkward signature which read, DEREK TYLER.

Tony could hardly believe the evidence of his eyes.

DEAR DOCTOR HILL. DETECTIVE SARGENT JAN SHIELDS IS THE CREEPER. JAN SHIELDS MADE ME DO IT. SHE MADE TAPES FOR ME. THEY ARE BEHIND THE WATER TANK IN THE ROOFSPACE IN 7 ROMNEY WALK WERE I USED TO HAVE A BEDSIT. I AM NOT SORRY FOR WHAT WE DID BUT I DON'T WANT TO TAKE ALL THE BLAME.

There are few things more moving than the full pomp of a police funeral. Dozens of officers in dress uniforms, family and friends stunned with grief and carried along on the formal wave of an organizational farewell, the full solemnity that the Church of England can muster. Carol stood surrounded by her team, eyes front, chin tucked in, cap under her arm. John Brandon read the encomium she'd written to honour Don Merrick's memory while his boys clung to their mother, the only familiar element in this extraordinary scene.

Tony stood off to one side, his eyes never straying far from Carol and, next to her, a hollow-eyed and twitchy Paula. When he'd shown Tyler's note to Carol, she'd descended on the building where he'd had a ground-floor bedsit like one of the Furies. All her grief and rage at Merrick's death had manifested itself in the absolute determination to nail Jan Shields.

The tapes had still been there, three floors up, rammed down between the water cistern and the angle of the roof. And their chilling message was irrefutable and inescapable. The only person who didn't recognize the fact was Jan herself. But that didn't matter. No jury would free her now. Tony felt a shudder of pity for whichever establishment was unlucky enough to acquire her as an inmate.

The past few weeks had been a baptism of fire for Carol, he thought. There had been several points where he'd feared she wasn't going to make it. But she'd proved him wrong, and for once he was glad to be wrong.

Brandon reached the end of his eulogy and bowed his head. The twenty-one-gun salute crackled out across the graveyard. Carol turned her head to meet Tony's eyes. A small, almost imperceptible nod passed between them. It was, he thought, amazing how little we needed to survive.

The Mermaids Singing

Acknowledgements

It's always disturbing when life seems to imitate art. I started planning this book in the spring of 1992, long before the killings that shook the gay community in London. I sincerely hope that there is nothing in these pages that will cause grief or offence to anyone.

As ever, I have picked brains galore and thoroughly exploited my friends while researching and writing *The Mermaids Singing*. I'd particularly like to thank senior clinical psychologist and offender profiler Mike Berry of Ashworth Top Security Psychiatric Hospital in Liverpool for giving so generously of his time and expertise in the preparation of this book. The insights and information I gleaned from him have been invaluable, as well as stopping the conversation at dinner parties dead in its tracks.

Thanks too to Peter Byram of the Responsive College Unit in Blackburn, who gave me advice on the finer points of computer technology. Alison Scott and Frankie Hegarty provided helpful information on matters medical. Detective Superintendent Mike Benison of the Sussex Police generously made time in his busy schedule to fill me in on the handling of major murder enquiries. Jai Penna, Diana Cooper and Paula Tyler demonstrated yet again that some lawyers are generous with their time and knowledge.

For their support, patience and advice throughout, I'd particularly like to thank Brigid Baillie and Lisanne Radice. It can't be easy putting up with someone who spends her days inside the head of a serial killer . . .

The northern city of Bradfield is entirely a creature of my imagination. In particular, the attitudes and behaviour attributed to assorted professionals, including police officers, were chosen for reasons of fictional necessity rather than verisimilitude. In Britain, we are fortunate to have few serial killers; that's because most of them are caught after their first murder. Let's hope the profilers and the police can keep it that way.

For Tookie Flystock, my beloved serial insect killer.

I have heard the mermaids singing, each to each.
I do not think that they will sing to me.
'The Love Song of J. Alfred Prufrock'
T. S. Eliot

The soul of torture is male
Comment on exhibit card
The Museum of Criminology and Torture,
San Gimignano, Italy.

All chapter epigraphs are taken from
'On Murder considered as one of the fine arts'
by Thomas De Quincey (1827)

You always remember the first time. Isn't that what they say about sex? How much more true it is of murder. I will never forget a single delicious moment of that strange and exotic drama. Even though now, with the benefit of experience and hindsight, I can see it was an amateurish performance, it still has the power to thrill, though not any longer to satisfy.

Although I didn't realize it before the decision to act was forced upon me, I had been paving the way for murder well in advance. Picture an August day in Tuscany. An air-conditioned coach whisking us from city to city. A bus-load of Northern culture vultures, desperate to fill every moment of our precious fortnight's package with something memorable to set against Castle Howard and Chatsworth.

I'd enjoyed Florence, the churches and art galleries filled with strangely contradictory images of martyrdom and Madonnas. I had scaled the dizzy heights of Brunelleschi's dome surmounting the immense cathedral, entranced by the winding stairway that leads up from the gallery to the tiny cupola, the worn stone steps tightly sandwiched between the ceiling of the dome and the roof itself. It was like being inside my computer, a real role-playing adventure, working my way

1

through the maze to daylight. All it lacked were monsters to slay on the way. And then, to emerge into bright day and amazement that up here, at the end of this cramped ascent, there was a postcard and souvenir seller, a small, dark, smiling man stooped from years of lugging his wares aloft. If it had really been a game, I would have been able to purchase some magic from him. As it was, I bought more postcards than I had people to send them to.

After Florence, San Gimignano. The town rose up from the green Tuscan plain, its ruined towers thrusting into the sky like fingers clawing upwards from a grave. The guide burbled on about 'a medieval Manhattan', another crass comparison to add to the list we'd been force-fed since Calais.

As we neared the town, my excitement grew. All over Florence, I'd seen the advertisements for the one tourist attraction I really wanted to see. Hanging splendidly from lampposts, gorgeous in rich red and gold, the banners insisted that I visit the Museo Criminologico di San Gimignano. Consulting my phrasebook, I'd confirmed what I'd thought the small print said. A museum of criminology and torture. Needless to say, it wasn't on our cultural itinerary.

I didn't have to search for my target; a leaflet about the museum, complete with street plan, was thrust upon me less than a dozen yards inside the massive stone gateway set in the medieval walls. Savouring the pleasure of anticipation, I wandered around for a while, marvelling at the monuments to civic disharmony that the towers represented. Each powerful family had had its own fortified tower which they defended against their neighbours with everything from boiling lead to cannons. At the peak of the city's prosperity, there were supposedly a couple of hundred towers. Compared to medieval San Gimignano, Saturday night down the docks *after closing time seems like kindergarten, the seamen mere amateurs in mayhem.*

When I could no longer resist the pull of the museum, I crossed the central piazza, tossing a bicoloured 200-lire coin in the well for luck, and walked a few yards down a side street, where the now familiar red and gold hangings adorned ancient stone walls. Excitement buzzing in me like a blood-crazed mosquito, I walked into the cool foyer and calmly bought my entrance ticket and a copy of the glossy, illustrated museum guide.

How can I begin to describe the experience? The physical reality was so much more overwhelming than photographs or videos or books had ever prepared me for. The first exhibit was a ladder rack, the accompanying card describing its function in loving detail in Italian and English. Shoulders would pop out of their sockets, hips and knees separate to the sound of rending cartilage and ligament, spines stretch out of alignment till vertebrae fell apart like beads from a broken string. 'Victims,' the card said laconically, 'often measured between six and nine inches taller after the rack.' Extraordinary minds the inquisitors had. Not satisfied with interrogating their heretics while they were alive and suffering, they had to seek further answers from their violated bodies.

The exhibition was a monument to the ingenuity of man. How could anyone not admire the minds that examined the human body so intimately that they could engineer such exquisite and finely calibrated suffering? With their relatively unsophisticated technology, those medieval brains devised systems of torture so refined that they are still in use today. It seems that the only improvement our modern post-industrial society has been able to come up with is the additional frisson provided by the application of electricity.

3

I moved through the rooms, savouring each and every toy, from the gross spikes of the Iron Maiden to the more subtle and elegant machinery of pears, those slender, segmented ovoids which were inserted into vagina or anus. Then, when the ratchet was turned, the segments separated and extended till the pear had metamorphosed into a strange flower, petals fringed with razor-sharp metal teeth. Then it was removed. Sometimes the victims survived, which was probably a crueller fate.

I noticed unease and horror on the faces and in the voices of some of my fellow visitors, but recognized it for the hypocrisy it was. Secretly, they were loving every minute of their pilgrimage, but respectability forbade any public display of their excitement. Only the children were honest in their ardent fascination. I would have happily bet that I was far from the only person in those cool, pastel rooms who felt the surge of sexual desire between their legs as we drank in the exhibits. I have often wondered how many holiday sexual encounters have been spiced and salted by the secret recollection of the torture museum.

Outside, in a sun-drenched courtyard, a skeleton crouched in a cage, bones clean as if stripped by vultures. Back in the days when the towers stood tall, these cages would have hung on the outer walls of San Gimignano, a message to inhabitants and strangers alike that this was a city where the law exacted a harsh penalty if it was not respected. I felt a strange kinship with those burghers. I too respect the need for punishment after betrayal.

Near the skeleton, an enormous metal-shod spoked wheel leaned against the wall. It would have looked perfectly at home in an agricultural museum. But the card fixed to the wall behind it explained a more imaginative function. Criminals were bound to the wheel. First, they were flayed

4

with scourges that ripped the flesh from their bones, exposing their entrails to the eager crowd. Then, with iron bars, their bones were broken on the wheel. I found myself thinking of the tarot card, the wheel of fortune.

When I realized I was going to have to become a killer, the memory of the torture museum rose before me like a muse. I've always been good with my hands.

After that first time, part of me hoped I wouldn't be forced to do it again. But I knew that if I had to, the next time it would be better. We learn from our mistakes the imperfections of our actions. And luckily, practice makes perfect.

1

> Gentlemen, I have had the honour to be appointed
> by your committee to the trying task of reading the
> Williams' Lecture on Murder, considered as one of the
> Fine Arts; a task which might be easy enough three or
> four centuries ago, when the art was little understood,
> and few great models had been exhibited; but in
> this age, when masterpieces of excellence have been
> executed by professional men, it must be evident, that
> in the style of criticism applied to them, the public will
> look for something of a corresponding improvement.

Tony Hill tucked his hands behind his head and stared
up at the ceiling. There was a fine web of cracks around
the elaborate plaster rose which surrounded the light
fitting, but he was oblivious to it. The faint light of
dawn tinged with the orange of sodium streetlamps
filtered in through a triangular gap at the top of his
curtains, but he had no interest in that either. Subconsciously, he registered the central-heating boiler
kicking in, readying itself to take the edge off the
damp winter chill that seeped in round door and
window frames. His nose was cold, his eyes gritty. He

couldn't remember the last time he'd had a straight night's sleep. His concern about what he had to get through that day was part of the reason for the night's interrupted dreams, but there was more than that. Much more.

As if today wasn't more than enough to worry about. He knew what was expected of him, but delivering it was another story. Other people managed these things with nothing more than a short-lived flutter in the stomach, but not Tony. It required all his resources to maintain the façade he'd need to get through the day. In circumstances like these, he understood how much it took out of method actors to produce the fraught, driven performances that captivated their audiences. By tonight, he'd be good for nothing except another vain attempt at eight hours' sleep.

He shifted in bed, pulling one hand out and running it through his short dark hair. He scratched the stubble on his chin and sighed. He knew what he wanted to do today, but equally, he was well aware it would be professional suicide if he did. It didn't matter that he knew there was a serial killer loose in Bradfield. He couldn't afford to be the one to say it first. His stomach clenched on emptiness and he winced. With a sigh, he pushed the duvet back and got out of bed, shaking his legs to unfurl the concertina folds of his baggy pyjamas.

Tony trudged off to the bathroom and snapped on the light. As he emptied his bladder, he reached out with his free hand and switched on the radio. Bradfield Sound's traffic announcer was revealing the morning's projected bottlenecks with a cheerfulness that no motorist could have equalled without large doses of Prozac. Thankful that he wouldn't be driving that morning, Tony turned to the sink.

He gazed into his deep-set blue eyes, still bleary with sleep. Whoever said the eyes were mirrors of the soul was a true bullshit merchant, he thought ironically. Probably just as well, or he wouldn't have an intact mirror in the house. He undid the top button of his pyjama jacket and opened the bathroom cabinet, reaching out for the shaving foam. The tremor he spotted in his hand stopped him short. Angrily, he slid the door shut with a loud crack and reached up for his electric razor. He hated the shave it produced, never leaving him with the fresh, clean feeling that came from a wet shave. But better to feel vaguely scruffy than to turn up looking like a walking illustration of the death of a thousand cuts.

The other disadvantage of the electric razor was that he didn't have to concentrate so hard on what he was doing, leaving his mind free to range over the day ahead. Sometimes it was tempting to imagine that everybody was like him, getting up each morning and selecting a persona for the day. But he had learned over years of exploring other people's minds that it wasn't so. For most people, the available selection was severely limited. Some people would doubtless be grateful for the choices that knowledge, skill and necessity had brought Tony. He wasn't one of them.

As he switched off the razor, he heard the frantic chords that preceded every news summary on Bradfield Sound. With a sense of foreboding, he turned to face the radio, tense and alert as a middle-distance runner waiting for the starting pistol. At the end of the five-minute bulletin, he sighed with relief and pushed open the shower curtain. He'd expected a revelation that would have been impossible for him to ignore. But so far, the body count was still three.

On the other side of the city, John Brandon, Bradfield Metropolitan Police's Assistant Chief Constable (Crime) stooped over the washbasin and stared glumly into the bathroom mirror. Not even the shaving soap covering his face like a Santa Claus beard could give him an air of benevolence. If he hadn't chosen the police, he'd have been an ideal candidate for a career as a funeral director. He was two inches over six feet, slim to the point of skinny, with deep-set dark eyes and prematurely steel-grey hair. Even when he smiled, his long face managed to sustain an air of melancholy. Today, he thought, he looked like a bloodhound with a head cold. At least there was good reason for his misery. He was about to pursue a course of action that would be as popular with his Chief Constable as a priest in an Orange Lodge.

Brandon sighed deeply, spattering the mirror with foam. Derek Armthwaite, his Chief, had the burning blue eyes of a visionary, but there was nothing revolutionary in what they saw. He was a man who thought the Old Testament a more appropriate handbook for police officers than the Police and Criminal Evidence Act. He believed most modern police methods were not only ineffective but also heretical. In Derek Armthwaite's frequently aired opinion, bringing back the birch and the cat-o'-nine-tails would be far more effective in reducing crime figures than any number of social workers, sociologists and psychologists. If he'd had any idea of what Brandon had planned for that morning, he'd have had him transferred to Traffic, the present-day equivalent of Jonah being swallowed by a whale.

Before his depression could overwhelm his resolve, Brandon was startled by a banging on the bathroom door. 'Dad?' his elder daughter shouted. 'You going to be much longer?'

Brandon snatched up his razor, dunked it in the basin and scraped it down one cheek before replying. 'Five minutes, Karen,' he called. 'Sorry, love.' In a house with three teenagers and only one bathroom, there was seldom much opportunity for brooding.

Carol Jordan dumped her half-drunk coffee on the side of the washbasin and stumbled into the shower, nearly tripping headlong over the black cat that wound himself round her ankles. 'In a minute, Nelson,' she muttered as she closed the door on his interrogative miaow. 'And don't waken Michael.'

Carol had imagined that promotion to detective inspector and the concomitant departure from the shift rota would have granted her the regular eight hours' sleep a night that had been her constant craving since the first week she joined the force. Just her luck that the promotion had coincided with what her team were privately calling the Queer Killings. However much Superintendent Tom Cross might bluster to the press and in the squad room that there were no forensic connections between the killings, and nothing to suggest the presence of a serial killer in Bradfield, the murder teams thought differently.

As the hot water cascaded over Carol, turning her blonde hair mouse, she thought, not for the first time, that Cross's attitude, like that of the Chief Constable, served his prejudices rather than the community. The longer he denied that there was a serial killer attacking men whose respectable façade hid a secret gay life, the more gay men would die. If you couldn't get them off the streets any longer by arresting them, let a killer remove them. It didn't much matter whether he did it by murder or by fear.

It was a policy that made a nonsense of all the hours she and her colleagues were putting in on the investigation. Not to mention the hundreds of thousands of pounds of taxpayers' money that these enquiries were costing, particularly since Cross insisted each killing be treated as an entirely separate entity. Every time one of the three teams came up with some detail that seemed to link the killings, Tom Cross dismissed it with five points of dissimilarity. It didn't matter that each time the links were different and the dissimilarities the same tired quintet. Cross was the boss. And the DCI had opted out of the strife completely, taking sick leave with his opportunistic bad back.

Carol rubbed the shampoo to a rich lather and felt herself gradually wake under the warm spray. Well, her corner of the investigation wasn't going to run aground on the rock of Popeye Cross's bigoted prejudice. Even if some of her junior officers were inclined to grasp at the boss's tunnel vision as an excuse for their own uninspired investigations, she wasn't going to stand for anything less than one hundred per cent committed action, and in the right direction. She'd worked her socks off for the best part of nine years, first to get a good degree and then to justify her place on the promotion fast track. She didn't intend her career to hit the buffers just because she'd made the mistake of opting for a force run by Neanderthals.

Her mind made up, Carol stepped out of the shower, shoulders straight, a defiant glint in her green eyes. 'Come on, Nelson,' she said, shrugging into her dressing gown and scooping up the muscular bundle of black fur. 'Let's hit the red meat, boy.'

Tony studied the overhead projection on the screen behind him for a final five seconds. Since the majority of his audience had expressed their lack of commitment to his lecture by pointedly not taking notes, he wanted at least to give their subconscious minds the maximum opportunity to absorb his flow chart of the criminal profile generating process.

He turned back to his audience. 'I don't have to tell you what you already know. Profilers don't catch criminals. It's bobbies that do that.' He smiled at his audience of senior police officers and Home Office officials, inviting them to share his self-deprecation. A few did, though most remained stony faced, heads on one side.

However he dressed it up, Tony knew he couldn't convince the bulk of the senior police officers that he wasn't some out-of-touch university boffin there to tell them how to do their jobs. Stifling a sigh, he glanced at his notes and continued, aiming for as much eye contact as he could achieve, copying the casual body language of the successful stand-up comics he'd studied working the northern clubs. 'But sometimes we profilers see things differently,' he said. 'And that fresh perspective can make all the difference. Dead men do tell tales, and the ones they tell profilers are not the same as the ones they tell police officers.

'An example. A body is found in bushes ten feet away from the road. A police officer will note that fact. He'll check the ground all around for clues. Are there footprints? Has anything been discarded by the killer? Have any fibres been snagged on the bushes? But for me, that single fact is only the starting point for speculations that, taken in conjunction with all the other information at my disposal, may well lead me to useful conclusions about the killer. I'll ask myself, was the body deliberately placed there? Or was the killer too knackered to carry it further? Was he hiding it or dumping it? Did he want it to be found? How long did he expect or want it to stay hidden? What is the significance of this site for him?' Tony lifted his shoulders and held out his hands in an open, questioning gesture. The audience looked on, unmoved. God, how many tricks of the trade was he going to have to pull out of the hat before he got a response? The prickle of sweat along the back of his neck was becoming a trickle, sliding down between his skin and his shirt collar. It was an uncomfortable sensation that reminded him of who he really was behind the mask he'd assumed for his public appearance.

Tony cleared his throat, focused on what he was projecting rather than what he was feeling, and continued. 'Profiling is just another tool that can help investigating officers to narrow the focus of their investigation. Our job is to make sense of the bizarre. We can't give you an offender's name, address and phone number. But what we *can* do is point you in the direction of the kind of person who has committed a crime with particular characteristics. Sometimes we can indicate the area where he might live, the kind of work we'd expect him to do.

'I know that some of you have questioned the necessity for setting up a National Criminal Profiling Task Force. You're not alone. The civil libertarians are screaming about it too.' At last, Tony thought with profound relief. Smiles and nods from the audience. It had taken him forty minutes to get there, but he'd finally cracked their composure. It didn't mean he could relax, but it eased his discomfort. 'After all,' he went on, 'we're not like the Americans. We don't have serial killers lurking round every corner. We still have a society where more than ninety per cent of murders are committed by family members or people known to the victims.' He was really taking them with him now. Several pairs of legs and arms uncrossed, neat as a practised drill-hall routine.

'But profiling isn't just about nailing the next Hannibal the Cannibal. It can be used in a wide variety of crimes. We've already had notable success in airport anti-hijacking measures, in catching drug couriers, poison-pen writers, blackmailers, serial rapists and arson-ists. And just as importantly, profiling has been used very effectively to advise police officers on interview techniques for dealing with suspects in major crime enquiries. It's not that your officers lack interviewing skills; it's just that our clinical background means we have developed different approaches that can often be more productive than familiar techniques.'

Tony took a deep breath and leaned forward, grip-ping the edge of the lectern. His final paragraph had sounded good in front of the bathroom mirror. He prayed it would hit the right spot rather than stamp on people's corns. 'My team and I are now one year into a two-year feasibility study on setting up the National Criminal Profiling Task Force. I've already delivered an interim report to the Home Office, who confirmed to me yesterday that they are committed to forming this task force as soon as my final report is delivered. Ladies and gentlemen, this revolution in crime fighting is going to happen. You've got a year to make sure it happens in a form that you feel comfortable with. My team and I have all got open minds. We're all on the same side. We want to know what you think, because we want it to work. We want violent, serial offenders behind bars, just like you do. I believe you could use our help. I know we can use yours.'

Tony took a step backwards and savoured the applause, not because it was particularly enthusiastic, but because it signalled the end of the forty-five minutes he'd been dreading for weeks. Public speaking had always been firmly outside the boundaries of his comfort zone, so much so that he'd turned his back on an academic career after achieving his doctorate because he couldn't face the constant spectre of the lecture theatre. The ability to perform was not a reason in itself for doing so. Somehow, spending his days poking around in the distorted recesses of the minds of the criminally insane was far less threatening.

As the short-lived clapping died away, Tony's Home Office minder bounced to his feet from his front-row chair. While Tony provoked a wary distrust in the police section of his audience, George Rasmussen generated more universal irritation than a flea bite. His eager smile revealed too many teeth and a disturbing resemblance to George Formby that was at odds with the seniority of his Civil Service post, the elegant cut of his grey pinstripe suit and the yammering bray of a public-school accent so exaggerated that Tony was convinced Rasmussen had really been educated in some inner-city comprehensive. Tony half listened as he shuffled his notes together and replaced his acetates in their folder. Grateful for fascinating insight, blah, blah . . . coffee and those absolutely delicious biscuits, blah, blah . . . opportunity for informal questions, blah, blah . . . remind you all submissions to Dr Hill due by . . .

The sound of shuffling feet drowned out the rest of Rasmussen's spiel. When it came to a choice between a civil servant's vote of thanks and a cup of coffee, it was no contest. Not even for the civil servants. Tony took a deep breath. Time to abandon the lecturer. Now he had to be the charming, well-informed colleague, eager to listen, to assimilate and to make his new contacts feel he was really on their side.

John Brandon stood up and stepped aside to allow the other people in his row to move out of their seats. Watching Tony Hill's performance hadn't been as informative as he'd hoped. It had told him a lot about psychological profiling, but almost nothing about the man, except that he seemed self-assured without being arrogant. The last three quarters of an hour hadn't made him any more certain that what he was planning was the right course of action. But he couldn't see any alternative. Staying close to the wall, Brandon moved forward against the flow until he was level with Rasmussen. Seeing his audience vote with its

16

feet, the civil servant had sharply wound up his speech and switched off his smile. As Rasmussen gathered up the papers he'd dumped on his seat, Brandon slipped past him and crossed the floor towards Tony, who was fastening the clasps on his battered Gladstone bag.

Brandon cleared his throat and said, 'Dr Hill?' Tony looked up, polite enquiry on his face. Brandon swallowed his qualms and continued. 'We haven't met before, but you've been working on my patch. I'm John Brandon . . .'

'The ACC Crime?' Tony interrupted, a smile reaching his eyes. He'd heard enough about John Brandon to know he was a man he wanted on his side. 'I'm delighted to meet you, Mr Brandon,' he said, injecting warmth into his voice.

'John. It's John,' Brandon said, more abruptly than he'd intended. He realized with a spurt of surprise that he was nervous. There was something about Tony Hill's calm assurance that unsettled him. 'I wonder if we can have a word?'

Before Tony could reply, Rasmussen was between them. 'If you'd excuse me,' he interjected without any note of humility, the smile back in place. 'Tony, if you'd just come through now to the coffee lounge, I know our friends in the police will be eager to chat to you on a more intimate basis. Mr Brandon, if you'd like to follow us.'

Brandon could feel his hackles rising. He felt awkward enough about the situation without having to fight to keep their conversation confidential in a room full of coffee-swilling coppers and nosy Home Office mandarins. 'If I could just have a word with Dr Hill in private?'

Tony glanced at Rasmussen, noting the slight deepening of the parallel lines between his eyebrows. Normally, it would have tickled him to wind up Rasmussen by continuing his conversation with Brandon. He always enjoyed pricking pomposity, reducing the self-important to impotent. But too much hung on the success of his encounters with other police officers today, so he decided to forego the pleasure. Instead, he turned pointedly away from Rasmussen and said, 'John, are you driving back to Bradfield after lunch?'

Brandon nodded.

'Perhaps you could give me a lift, then? I came on the train, but if you don't mind, I'd rather not wrestle with British Rail on the way back. You can always drop me at the city limits if you don't want to be seen fraternizing with the Trendy Wendies.'

Brandon smiled, his long face creasing into simian wrinkles. 'I don't think that'll be necessary. I'll be just as happy to drop you at force headquarters.' He stood back and watched Rasmussen steer Tony to the doors, fussing all the way. He couldn't shake off the slightly disconcerted feeling that the psychologist had given him. Maybe it was simply that he'd grown so accustomed to being in control of everything in his world that asking for help had become an alien experience that automatically made him feel uncomfortable. There was no other obvious explanation. Shrugging, Brandon followed the crowd through to the coffee lounge.

Tony snapped the seat belt closed and savoured the comfort of the unmarked Range Rover. He said nothing as Brandon manoeuvred out of the Manchester force headquarters' car park and headed for the motorway network, unwilling to interfere with the concentration necessary to avoid missing the way in an unfamiliar city. As they cruised down the slip road and joined the fast-flowing traffic, Tony broke the silence. 'If it helps, I think I already know what it is you wanted to talk to me about.'

Brandon's hands tensed on the wheel. 'I thought you were a psychologist, not a psychic,' he joked. He surprised himself. Humour wasn't his natural mode; he normally resorted to it only under pressure. Brandon couldn't get used to how nervous he felt asking this favour.

'Some of your colleagues would take more notice of me if I was,' Tony said wryly. 'So, do you want me to have a guess and run the risk of making a complete fool of myself?'

Brandon snatched a quick look at Tony. The psychologist looked relaxed, hands palm down on his thighs, feet crossed at the ankles. He looked as though he'd be more at home in jeans and a sweater than in the suit which even Brandon recognized as well past its fashionable sell-by date. He could relate to that, remembering the scathing comments his daughters routinely passed on his own plain clothes. Brandon said abruptly, 'I think we've got a serial killer operating in Bradfield.'

Tony released a small, satisfied sigh. 'I was beginning to wonder if you'd noticed,' he said ironically.

'It's by no means a unanimous opinion,' Brandon said, feeling the need to warn Tony before he'd even asked for his help.

'I'd gathered as much from the press coverage,' Tony

said. 'If it's any comfort to you, I'm as certain as I can be from what I've read that your analysis is right.'

'That's not entirely the impression you gave in those quotes of yours I saw in the *Sentinel Times* after the last one,' Brandon said.

'It's my job to cooperate with the police, not to undermine them. I assumed you had your own operational reasons for not going public with the serial-killer angle. I did stress to them that what I was saying was no more than an informed guess based on the information that was in the public domain,' Tony added, his genial tone contradicting the sudden tensing of his fingers that ruched the material of his trousers into loose pleats.

Brandon smiled, aware only of the voice. 'Touché. So, are you interested in giving us a hand?'

Tony felt a warm rush of satisfaction. This was what he had craved for weeks now. 'There's a service area a few miles down the road. D'you fancy a cup of tea?'

Detective Inspector Carol Jordan stared at the broken chaos of flesh that had once been a man, determinedly forcing her eyes to remain out of focus. She wished she hadn't bothered to snatch that stale cheese sandwich from the canteen. Somehow, it was acceptable for young male officers to throw up when they were confronted with victims of violent death. They even got sympathy. But in spite of the fact that women were supposed to lack bottle anyway, when female officers chucked up on the margins of crime scenes they instantly lost any respect they'd ever won and became objects of contempt, the butts of locker-room jokes from the canteen cowboys. Pick the logic out of that, Carol thought bitterly as she clamped her jaws tighter together. She thrust her hands deep into the pockets of her trench coat and clenched her fists, the nails pressing into her palms.

Carol felt a hand on her arm, just above the elbow. Grateful for the chance to look away, she turned to find her sergeant looming above her. Don Merrick towered a good eight inches over his boss, and had developed a strange hunchbacked stoop when he spoke to her. At first, she'd found it amusing enough to regale friends with over drinks or the occasional dinner party when she managed to squeeze a night off. Now, she didn't even notice. 'Area's all cordoned off now, ma'am,' he said in his soft Geordie accent. 'Pathologist's on his way. What d'you think? Are we looking at number four?'

'Don't let the Super hear you say that, Don,' she said, only half joking. 'I'd say so, though.' Carol looked around. They were in the Temple Fields district, in the rear yard of a pub which catered primarily to the gay trade, with an upstairs bar that was lesbian three nights a week. Contrary to the jibes of the macho men she'd overtaken in the promotion stakes, it wasn't a bar Carol had ever had reason to enter. 'What about the gate?'

'Crowbar,' Merrick said laconically. 'It's not wired into the alarm system.'

Carol surveyed the tall rubbish dumpsters and the stacked crates of empties. 'No reason why it should be,' she said. 'What's the landlord got to say?'

'Whalley's talking to him now, ma'am. Seems he locked up last night about half past eleven. They've got bins on wheels behind the bars for the empties, and at closing time they just wheel them into the yard

21

back there.' Merrick waved over towards the back door of the pub, where three blue plastic bins stood, each the size of a supermarket trolley. 'They don't sort them out till the afternoon.'

'And that's when they found this?' Carol asked, gesturing over her shoulder with her thumb.

'Just lying there. Open to the elements, you might say.'

Carol nodded. A shudder ran through her that was nothing to do with the sharp north-eastern wind. She took a step towards the gate. 'OK. Let's leave this to the SOCOs for now. We're only in the way here.' Merrick followed her into the narrow alley behind the pub. It was barely wide enough for a single vehicle to squeeze down. Carol looked up and down the alley, now closed off by police tapes and guarded at either end by a pair of uniformed constables. 'He knows his turf,' she mused softly. She walked backwards along the alley, keeping the gate of the pub in constant view. Merrick followed her, waiting for the next set of orders.

At the end of the alley, Carol stopped and swung round to check out the street. Opposite the alley was a tall building, a former warehouse that had been converted into craft workshops. At night, it would be deserted, but in midafternoon, almost every window framed eager faces, staring out from the warmth within at the drama below. 'Not much chance of anyone looking out of a window at the crucial time, I suppose,' she remarked.

'Even if they had, they wouldn't have taken any notice,' Merrick said cynically. 'After closing time, the streets round here are jumping. Every doorway, every alley, half the parked cars have got a pair of poofs in them, shagging the arse off each other. It's no wonder the Chief calls Temple Fields Sodom and Gomorrah.'

'You know, I've often wondered. It's pretty clear what they were up to in Sodom, but what do you suppose the sin of Gomorrah was?' Carol asked.

Merrick looked bewildered. It increased his resemblance to a sad-eyed Labrador to a disturbing degree. 'I'm not with you, ma'am,' he said.

'Never mind. I'm surprised Mr Armthwaite hasn't got Vice pulling them all in on indecency charges,' Carol said.

'He did try it a few years back,' Merrick confided. 'But the police committee had his bollocks barbecued for it. He fought them, but they threatened him with the Home Office. And after the Holmwood Three business, he knew he was already on thin ice with the politicians, so he backed down. Doesn't stop him slagging them off every chance he gets, though.'

'Yeah, well, I hope this time our friendly neighbourhood killer has left us a bit more to go on, or our beloved leader might just pick another target for his next slagging off.' Carol straightened her shoulders. 'Right, Don. I want a door-to-door of the businesses, now. And tonight, we're all going to be out on the streets, talking to the trade.'

Before Carol could complete her instructions, a voice from beyond the tapes interrupted. 'Inspector Jordan? Penny Burgess, *Sentinel Times*. Inspector? What have you got?'

Carol closed her eyes for a brief moment. Dealing with the recalcitrant bigots in the chain of command was one thing. Dealing with the press was infinitely worse. Wishing she'd stayed in the yard with the grisly corpse, Carol took a deep breath and walked towards the cordon.

'Let me get this straight. You want me to come on board for the duration of this murder enquiry, but you don't want me to tell anyone?' The look of amusement in Tony's eyes masked his anger at the reluctance of influential policemen to accept the value of what he could do.

Brandon sighed. Tony wasn't making it easy for him, but then, why should he? 'I want to avoid any suggestions in the press that you are helping us. The only chance I have of getting you formally involved with the investigation is to persuade the Chief Constable that you're not going to be stealing the limelight from him and his coppers.'

'And that it won't become public knowledge that Derek Armthwaite, the Hand Of God, is turning to the mumbo-jumbo men for help,' Tony said, an edge in his voice betraying more than he wanted to.

Brandon's face twisted in a cynical smile. It was good to see that it was possible to ruffle that smooth surface. 'If you say so, Tony. Technically, it's an operational matter, and he's not really supposed to interfere unless I'm doing something that's counter to force and Home Office policy. And it is the policy of BMP to use expert assistance whenever it is appropriate.'

Tony snorted with laughter. 'And you think he'll accept me as "appropriate"?'

'I think he doesn't want another confrontation with the Home Office or the police committee. He's due to retire in eighteen months, and he's desperate for the knighthood.' Brandon couldn't believe what he was saying. He didn't even voice this kind of disloyalty to his wife, never mind to a virtual stranger. What was it about Tony Hill that had made him open up so swiftly? There must be something in this psychology lark after all. Brandon comforted himself that at least he had harnessed that something in the service of justice. 'So what do you say?'

'When do I start?'

Even that first time, I planned the event more carefully than a theatre director plans the first production of a new play. In my mind, I crafted the experience, till it was like a bright and shining dream, there every time I closed my eyes. I checked and rechecked every choreographed move, making sure I hadn't missed some vital detail that would endanger my freedom. Looking back on it now, the mental movie I created was almost as pleasurable as the act itself.

The first step was to find a place where I could safely take him, a place we could be private together. I immediately dismissed my home. I can hear my neighbours' squalid arguments, the barking of their hysterical German shepherd and the irritating thud of their stereo's bass; I had no desire to share my apotheosis with them. Besides, in my terraced street, there are too many curtain twitchers. I wanted no witnesses to Adam's arrival or his departure.

I considered renting a lock up garage, but rejected that for the same reasons. Besides, it seemed too seedy, too much of a cliché from the world of television and film. I wanted something in keeping with what was going to happen. Then I remembered my mother's Auntie Doris. Doris and her husband Henry used to farm sheep on the moors high above Bradfield. Then, about four years ago, Henry died. Doris tried to keep things going for a while, but when her son Ken invited her out last year for an extended holiday with his family in New Zealand, she sold the sheep and packed her bags. Ken had written to me at Christmas, saying his mother had suffered a mild heart attack and wouldn't be coming back for the foreseeable future.

That night, I took advantage of a lull in work to call Ken. At first, he sounded surprised to hear from me, then muttered, 'I suppose you're using the phones at work.'

'I've been meaning to ring for ages,' I said. 'I wanted to know how Auntie Doris was doing.' It's much easier to appear solicitous via satellite. I made the appropriate noises while Ken bored on about his mother's health, his wife, their three kids and their sheep.

After ten minutes, I decided I'd had enough. 'The other thing is, Ken, I was worried about the house,' I lied. 'It's so isolated up there, someone should keep an eye on the place.'

'You're not wrong,' he said. 'Her solicitor's supposed to be doing that, but I don't reckon he's been near it.'

'Do you want me to pop out and check it over? Now I'm back living in Bradfield, it would be no bother.'

'Would you? That'd be a hell of a load off, I don't mind telling you. Between ourselves, I'm not sure Mum's ever going to be well enough to go back home again, but I'd hate to think of anything happening to the family home,' Ken said eagerly.

Hate to think of anything happening to his inheritance, more like. I knew Ken. Ten days later, I had the keys. On my next day off, I drove out there to check the accuracy of my recollection. The rutted track leading to Start Hill Farm was *much more overgrown than the last time I'd been there, and my four-wheel-drive jeep struggled to climb the three miles from the nearest single-track lane. I cut the engine a dozen yards from the grim little cottage and sat listening for five minutes. The biting wind from the high moors rustled the overgrown hedges, occasional birds sang. But there were no human sounds. Not even the distant thrum of traffic.*

I got out of the jeep and had a look round. One end of the sheep shed had collapsed into a random pile of millstone grit, but what pleased me was that there was no sign of casual human visitations; no picnic remains, no corroding beer cans, no crumpled newspapers, no cigarette butts, no used condoms. I walked back to the house and let myself in.

It was little more than a two-up, two-down. Inside, it was very different from the cosy farmhouse I remembered. All the personal touches – photographs, ornaments, horse brasses, antiques – were gone, packed up in crates in storage, a very Yorkshire precaution. In a way, I was relieved; there was nothing here that could trigger off memories that would interfere with what I had to do. It was a blank tablet, with all humiliations, embarrassments and pain erased. Nothing of my past lurked to surprise me. The person I had been was absent.

I walked through the kitchen towards the pantry. The shelves were empty. God knows what Doris had done with her serried ranks of jams, pickles and home-made wines. Maybe she'd shipped them to New Zealand as a hedge against being fed alien food. I stood in the doorway, and stared at the floor. I could feel a foolish grin of relief spread across my face. My memory hadn't let me down. There was a trapdoor in the floor. I squatted down and pulled the rusty iron ring. After a few seconds, the door swung back on creaking hinges. As I sniffed the air from the cellar, I grew

28

more convinced that the gods were with me. I had feared it would be damp, fetid and stale. But instead, it was cool and fresh, slightly sweet.

I lit my camping gas lamp and carefully descended the flight of stone stairs. The lamp revealed a sizeable room, about twenty feet by thirty. The floor was flagged with stone slabs, and a broad stone bench ran the length of one wall. I held the lamp high and saw the solid beams of the roof. The lath and plaster ceiling was the only part of the cellar that showed any signs of disrepair. I could easily fix that with plasterboard, which would serve the double purpose of preventing any light escaping through the bare floorboards above. At right angles to the stone bench was a slop sink. I remembered the farm was served by its own spring. The tap was stiff, but when I finally managed to turn it, the water ran out pure and clear.

Near the stairs stood a scarred wooden workbench, complete with vices and G-clamps, Henry's tools hanging in neat rows above. I sat on the stone bench and hugged myself. A few hours' work was all that was needed to turn this into a dungeon far superior to anything the games programmers had ever come up with. For a start, I didn't have to think about creating an in-built weakness so my adventurers could escape.

By the end of the week, coming out to the farm in my time off, I had completed the job. Nothing sophisticated; I'd fixed padlock and internal bolts to the trapdoor, I'd repaired the ceiling, and covered the walls in a couple of coats of whitewash. I wanted the place as light as possible to improve the quality of the video. I'd even run a spur off the ring main to provide me with electricity.

I'd thought long and hard before I'd decided how to punish Adam. Finally, I'd fixed on what the French call the

29

chevalet, *the Spanish* escalero, *the Germans the* ladder, *the Italians* veglia *and the poetic English 'The Duke of Exeter's Daughter'. The rack got its euphemistic name from the resourceful John Holland, Duke of Exeter and Earl of Huntingdon. After a successful career as a soldier, the duke became Constable of the Tower of London and somewhere around 1420 he introduced that splendid instrument of persuasion to these shores.*

The earliest version consisted of an open rectangular frame raised on legs. The prisoner was laid underneath it, fastened by ropes round his wrists and ankles. At each corner, the ropes were attached to a windlass operated by a warder pulling on levers. This inelegant and labour-intensive device became more sophisticated over the years, ending up more like a table or a horizontal ladder, often incorporating a spiked roller in the middle so that, as the prisoner's body moved, his back was shredded on the spikes. Pulley systems had also been designed which linked all four ropes together, making it possible for the machine to be used by one person alone.

Fortunately, those who have applied punishment through the ages have been thorough in their descriptions and drawing. I also had the photographs in the museum handbook to refer to, and with the assistance of a CAD program, I'd designed my very own rack. For the mechanism, I'd cannibalized an old-fashioned clothes wringer that I picked up in an antique shop. I'd also bought an old mahogany dining table in an auction. I took it straight up to the farm and dismembered it in the kitchen, admiring the craftsmanship that had gone into the solid timber. It took a couple of days to build the rack. All that remained was to test it.

2

Let the reader then figure to himself the pure frenzy
of horror when in this hush of expectation, looking,
and indeed, waiting for the unknown arm to strike
once more, but not believing that any audacity could
be equal to such an attempt as yet, whilst all eyes were
watching . . . a second case of the same mysterious
nature, a murder on the same exterminating plan,
was perpetrated in the very same neighbourhood.

As soon as Brandon started the engine, the mobile
phone mounted on the dashboard trilled. He grabbed
the handset and barked, 'Brandon.' Tony could hear
the computerized voice say, 'You have messages. Please
call 121. You have messages . . .'

Brandon took the phone from his ear, hit the keys
and jammed it back again. This time, Tony couldn't
hear what was said. After a moment, Brandon dialled
another number. 'My secretary,' he explained briefly.
'Sorry about this . . . Hello, Martina? John. You were
looking for me?'

A few seconds into the answer, Brandon squeezed
his eyes shut, as if in pain. 'Where?' he asked, his voice

dull. 'OK, got it. I'll be there within the half-hour. Who's dealing? . . . Fine, thanks, Martina.' Brandon opened his eyes and ended the call. He carefully replaced the handset and twisted in his seat to face Tony. 'You wanted to know when you could start? How about now?'

'Another body?' Tony asked.

'Another body,' Brandon agreed grimly, turning back and slamming the car into gear. 'How do you feel about scenes of crime?'

Tony shrugged. 'I'll probably lose my lunch, but it's a bonus for me if I get to see them in a fairly pristine state.'

'There's nothing pristine about the way this sick bastard leaves them,' Brandon growled as he shot on to the motorway and made straight for the outside lane. The speedo read ninety-five before he eased back on the accelerator.

'Has he gone back to Temple Fields?' Tony asked.

Taken aback, Brandon shot him a quick look. Tony was staring straight ahead, his dark eyebrows corrugated in a frown. 'How did you know?'

That was a question Tony wasn't prepared to answer. 'Call it a hunch,' he stalled. 'I think last time out he was scared that Temple Fields might be getting a bit too hot. Dumping the third body in Carlton Park shifted the focus, maybe stopped the police concentrating on one area, probably relaxed people's vigilance a bit. But he likes Temple Fields. Either because he knows the patch really well, or else it's important to his fantasy. Or maybe it makes some kind of statement for him,' Tony mused aloud.

'Do you always come up with half a dozen different

hypotheses every time someone tosses you a fact?' Brandon asked, flashing his lights at a BMW that was reluctant to give up possession of the fast lane. 'Shift, you bastard, before I get Traffic out to you,' he snarled.

'I try,' Tony said. 'That's how I do the job. Gradually, the evidence makes me eliminate some of my initial thoughts. Eventually, some sort of pattern begins to form.' He fell silent, already fantasizing about what he would find at the scene of the crime. His stomach felt hollow, muscles fluttering like a musician before a concert. Normally, all he ever got to see were the second-hand, sanitized versions of crime scenes. No matter how good the photographer and the other forensic officers, it was always someone else's vision he had to translate. This time, he was going to be as close to a killer as he'd ever been. For a man who lived his life behind the shield of learned behaviours, penetrating a killer's façade was the only game in town.

Carol said, 'No comment,' for the eleventh time. Penny Burgess's mouth tightened and her eyes flicked round the scene, desperate for someone who would be less of a stone wall than Carol. Popeye Cross might be a male chauvinist pig, but in between the patronizing comments he always salted a few memorable quotes. Drawing a blank, she focused on Carol again.

'What happened to sisterhood, Carol?' she complained. 'Come on, give us a break. Surely there must be something you can tell me apart from "No comment".'

'I'm sorry, Ms Burgess. The last thing your readers need to hear is ill-informed off-the-cuff speculation.

As soon as I've got anything concrete to say, I promise you'll be the first to know.' Carol softened her words with a smile.

She turned to walk away, but Penny grabbed the sleeve of her mac. 'Off the record?' she pleaded. 'Just for my guidance? So I don't end up writing something that makes me look a pillock? Carol, I don't have to tell you what it's like. I work in an office full of guys that are running a book on when I'll make my next cock-up.'

Carol sighed. It was hard to resist. Only the thought of what Tom Cross would make of it in the squad room kept her mouth closed. 'I can't,' she said. 'Anyway, as far as I'm concerned, you've been doing just fine so far.' As she spoke, a familiar Range Rover turned the corner. 'Oh shit,' she muttered, pulling her arm away from the reporter. All she needed was John Brandon deciding she was the police source behind the *Sentinel Times*'s serial-killer hysteria. Briskly, Carol walked towards Brandon's car as it jerked to a halt, waiting for someone to shift the tapes keeping the crowd at bay. She stopped and waited while the constables rushed to impress the ACC with their efficiency. The Range Rover nosed forward, giving Carol the opportunity to spot the stranger in Brandon's passenger seat. As the two men climbed down, she scanned Tony, committing the details to the memory bank she'd trained herself to develop. You never knew when you'd need to come up with a photofit. Around five-eight, slim, good shoulders, narrow hips, legs and trunk in proportion, short dark hair, side parting, dark eyes, probably blue, shadows under the eyes, fair skin, average nose, wide mouth, lower lip fuller than upper. Shame about the dress sense, though. The suit was even more out of fashion than Brandon's. It didn't look worn, however. Deduction: this was a man who didn't spend his working life in a suit. Equally, he didn't like throwing money away, so the suit was going to be worn till it fell to bits. Second deduction: he probably wasn't married or in a permanent relationship. Any woman whose partner needed a suit occasionally would have pitched him into buying a timelessly classic style that wouldn't look so absurd five years after its purchase.

By the time she'd reached this conclusion, Brandon was by her side, gesturing to his companion to join them. 'Carol,' he said.

'Mr Brandon,' she acknowledged.

'Tony, I'd like you to meet Detective Inspector Carol Jordan. Carol, this is Dr Tony Hill from the Home Office.'

Tony smiled and held out his hand. Attractive smile, Carol added to her list of particulars as she shook the hand. Good handshake, too. Dry, firm without the macho need to crush the bones that so many senior officers exhibited. 'Pleased to meet you,' he said.

A surprisingly deep voice, faintly northern. Carol kept her own smile tight. You never knew with the Home Office. 'Likewise,' she said.

'Carol's heading up one of the murder teams we've got on these killings. Number two, is it, Carol?' Brandon asked, already knowing the answer.

'That's right, sir. Paul Gibbs.'

'Tony's in charge of the Home Office National Crime Profiling Task Force feasibility study. I've asked him to take a look at these murders, to see if his experience can give us any pointers.' Brandon's eyes bored into

Carol's, making sure she realized there were lines to be read between.

'I'd appreciate any help Dr Hill can give us, sir. From the brief look I've had at the scene of the crime, I don't think we've got any more to go on than in the previous similar cases.' Carol signalled that she understood what Brandon was saying. They were both walking the same tightrope, but from different ends. Brandon could not be seen to undermine Tom Cross's operational authority, and if Carol wanted a tolerable existence in the Bradfield force, she couldn't openly contradict her immediate superior, even if the ACC agreed with her. 'Would Dr Hill like to see the crime scene?'

'We'll all have a look,' Brandon said. 'You can fill me in as we go. What have we got here?'

Carol led the way. 'It's in the back yard of the pub here. The scene of crime is obviously not the scene of death. No blood at all. We have a white male, late twenties, naked. ID unknown. He appears to have been tortured before death. Both shoulders seem to have been dislocated, and possibly his hips and knees. Some tufts of hair are missing from the scalp. He's lying on his front, so we've not had a chance to see the full extent of his injuries. I'd guess the cause of death is a deep wound to the throat. It also looks like the body had been washed before it was dumped.' Carol ended her flat recitation at the yard gate. She glanced back at Tony. The only difference her words had made was a tightening of his lips. 'Ready?' she asked him.

He nodded and took a deep breath. 'As I'll ever be,' he said.

'Stay outside the tapes please, Tony,' Brandon said.

'The SOCOs will still have a lot to do, and they don't need us dumping forensic traces all over their murder scene.'

Carol opened the gate and waved the two of them through. If Tony had thought her words had prepared him for the sight inside, one look told him otherwise. It was grotesque, made all the more so by the unnatural absence of blood. Logic screamed that a body so broken should be an island in a lake of gore, like an ice cube in a Bloody Mary. He had never seen a corpse so clean outside a funeral parlour. But instead of being laid out calm as a marble statue, this body was twisted into a loose-limbed parody of the human frame, a disjointed puppet left lying where it fell when the strings were cut.

When the two men entered the yard, the police photographer stopped snapping and gave John Brandon a nod of recognition. 'All right, Harry,' Brandon said, seemingly undaunted by the sight before him. No one could see the hands clenched into tight fists in the pockets of his waxed jacket.

'I've done all the long- and medium-range stuff, Mr Brandon. I've just got the close-ups to go,' the photographer said. 'There's a lot of wounds and bruising; I want to make sure I've got it all.'

'Good lad,' Brandon said.

From behind them, Carol added, 'Harry, when you've done that, can you snap all the cars parked up in the immediate area?'

The photographer raised his eyebrows. 'The lot?'

'The lot,' Carol confirmed.

'Good thinking, Carol,' Brandon chipped in before the scowling photographer could say anything more.

'There's always the outside chance that me laddo left the scene on foot or in the victim's car. He might have left his here to collect later. And photographs are that much harder for the defence brief to argue with than a bobby's notebook.'

With a sharp snort of breath, the photographer turned back to the corpse. The brief exchange had given Tony time to get a grip on his churning stomach. He took a step closer to the body, trying to glean some primitive understanding of the mind that had reduced a man to this. 'What's your game?' he said inside his head. 'What does this mean to you? What translations are going on between this broken flesh and your desire? I thought I was the expert in keeping things battened down, but you're something else, aren't you? You are truly special. You're the control freak's control freak. You are going to be one of the ones they write books about. Welcome to the big time.'

Recognizing that he was dangerously close to admiration for a mind so disturbingly complex, Tony forced himself to focus on the realities of what lay before him. The deep slash to the throat had virtually decapitated the man, leaving the head tilted as if hinged at the back of the neck. Tony took a deep breath and said, 'The *Sentinel Times* said they all died from having their throats cut. Is that right?'

'Yes,' Carol said. 'They were all tortured while they were still alive, but it's the throat wounds that have been fatal in each case.'

'And have they all been as deep as this?'

Carol shook her head dubiously. 'I'm only completely familiar with the second case, and that was nowhere near as violent a gash as this. But I have

38

seen the photographs of the other two, and the last one was nearly this bad.'

Thank God for something recognizably textbook, Tony thought. He took a couple of steps back and scanned the area. The body aside, there was nothing to distinguish it from the back yard of any other pub. Crates of empties were stacked against the walls, the lids on the big industrial wheelie bins were firmly closed. Nothing obvious taken away, nothing obvious left behind except for the corpse itself.

Brandon cleared his throat. 'Well, everything seems to be under control here, Carol. I'd better go and have a word with the press. I saw Penny Burgess trying to rip the sleeve out of your coat when I got here. No doubt the rest of the pack are baying at her heels by now. I'll see you back at HQ later. Drop by my office. I want to have a chat with you about Dr Hill's involvement. Tony, I'll leave you in Carol's capable hands. When you're finished here, maybe you can arrange a session with Carol so she can go through the case files.'

Tony nodded. 'Sounds good. Thanks, John.'

'I'll be in touch. And thanks again.' With that, Brandon was gone, closing the gate behind him.

'You do profiling, then,' Carol said.

'I try,' he said cautiously.

'Thank God the powers that be have finally seen sense,' she said drily. 'I was beginning to think they'd never get round to admitting we've got a serial killer on our hands.'

'You and me both,' Tony said. 'I was worried after the first one, but I've been convinced since the second one.'

'And I suppose it's not your place to tell them that,' Carol said wearily. 'Bloody bureaucracy.'

'It's a sensitive point. Even when we have a national task force set up, I suspect we're still going to have to wait for the individual police forces to come to us.'

Carol's reply was cut off by the banging of the yard gate as it was thrown open. They both swung round. Framed in the doorway was one of the biggest men Tony had ever seen. He had the solid brawn of a prop forward run to seed, his beer gut preceding his massive shoulders by a good half-dozen inches. His eyes protruded like boiled gooseberries from a fleshy face, the source of Detective Superintendent Tom Cross's nickname. His mouth, like that of his cartoon namesake, was an incongruously small cupid's bow. Mousey hair fringed a bald spot like a monk's tonsure. 'Sir,' Carol greeted the apparition.

Pale eyebrows furled in a discontented scowl. Judging by the deep lines between his brows, it was a familiar expression. 'Who the bloody hell are you?' he demanded, waving a stubby finger at Tony. Automatically, Tony noted the bitten nail. Before he could respond, Carol spoke smartly. 'Sir, this is Dr Tony Hill from the Home Office. He's responsible for the National Crime Profiling Task Force feasibility study. Dr Hill, this is Detective Superintendent Tom Cross. He's in overall charge of our murder enquiries.'

The second half of Carol's introduction was drowned out by Cross's booming response. 'What the hell are you up to, woman? This is a murder scene. You don't let any old Tom, Dick or Home Office penpusher walk all over it.'

Carol closed her eyes fractionally longer than a

blink. Then she said in a voice whose cheerful tone astonished Tony, 'Sir, Mr Brandon brought Dr Hill with him. The ACC thinks Dr Hill can help us profile our killer.'

'What d'you mean, killer? How many times do I have to tell you? We've not got a serial killer loose in Bradfield. We've just got a nasty bunch of copycat queers. You know what the trouble is with you fast-track graduates?' Cross demanded, aggressively leaning towards Carol.

'I'm sure you'll tell me, sir,' Carol said sweetly.

Cross stopped momentarily, with the slightly baffled air of a dog who can hear the fly but can't see it. Then he said, 'You're all desperate for glory. You want glamour and headlines. You don't want the bother of proper coppering. You can't be arsed grafting on three murder enquiries so you try to knock 'em all into one to minimize the effort and maximize the press coverage. And you,' he added, wheeling round towards Tony. 'You can remove yourself from my crime scene right now. The last thing we need is bleeding-heart liberals telling us we're looking for some poor sod who wasn't allowed to have a teddy bear when he were a lad. It's not mumbo jumbo that catches villains, it's police work.'

Tony smiled. 'I couldn't agree more, Superintendent. But your Assistant Chief Constable seems to think that I can help you target your police work more effectively.'

Cross was too old a hand to fall for civility. 'I run the most effective team in this force,' he retorted. 'And I don't need some bloody doctor telling me how to catch a bunch of homicidal poofters.' He turned back to Carol. 'Escort *Doctor* Hill off the premises, Inspector.' He managed to make her rank sound like an insult. 'And when you've done that, you can come back here and fill me in on what you've managed to find out about our last killer.'

'Very good, sir. Oh, by the way, you might like to join the ACC. He's giving an impromptu press conference round the front.' This time, the sweetness was tinged with acerbity.

Cross gave a perfunctory glance at the body lying exposed in the yard. 'Well, *he*'s not going any place, is he?' he remarked. 'Right, Inspector, I'll expect a report just as soon as I've finished with the ACC and the press.' He turned on his heel and stormed out as noisily as he'd arrived.

Carol put a hand on Tony's elbow and steered him out of the gate. 'This is going to be worth seeing,' she muttered in his ear as she ushered him down the alley in Cross's wake.

Half a dozen reporters had joined Penny Burgess behind the yellow plastic tapes. John Brandon faced them. As they grew closer, they could hear the cacophony of questions the press were hurling at the ACC. Carol and Tony hung back as Cross pushed past a constable standing at Brandon's shoulder and shouted, 'One at a time, ladies and gentlemen. You'll all get heard.'

Brandon half turned towards Cross, his face expressionless. 'Thank you, Superintendent Cross.'

'Have we got a serial killer loose in Bradfield?' Penny Burgess demanded, her voice cutting through the momentary quiet like the cry of some bird of ill omen.

'There's no reason to suppose . . .' Cross started.

Brandon cut across him icily. 'Leave this to me, Tom,' he said. 'As I said a moment ago, this afternoon we have found the body of a white male in his late twenties or early thirties. It's too soon to be one hundred per cent certain, but there are indications that this killing may be connected to three previous homicides that have taken place in Bradfield over the last nine months.'

'Does that mean you're treating these murders as the work of one serial killer?' asked a young man with a tape recorder thrust forward like a cattle prod.

'We are examining the possibility that one perpetrator is responsible for all four crimes, yes.'

Cross looked as if he wanted to hit someone. His hands were bunched into fists at his sides, his brows so low they must have cut his vision to a slit. 'Though it's only a possibility at this stage,' he said mutinously.

Penny chipped in ahead of the opposition again. 'How will this affect your approach to the investigation, Mr Brandon?'

'As of today, we will be amalgamating the three previous murder enquiries with this latest one into a single major incident task force. We will be making full use of the Home Office Large Major Enquiry System computer to analyse the available data, and we are confident that this will enable us to develop new leads,' Brandon said, his lugubrious face belying the optimism in his voice.

'Yo, go for it,' Carol muttered under her breath.

'Haven't you left it a bit late? Hasn't the murderer had a head start because you wouldn't acknowledge he was a serial killer?' a voice from the rear of the pack shouted angrily.

Brandon squared his shoulders and looked stern. 'We're policemen, not clairvoyants. We don't theorize ahead of the evidence. Rest assured, we will be doing everything within our power to bring this killer to justice as swiftly as is humanly possible.'

'Will you be using a psychological profiler?' It was Penny Burgess again. Tom Cross shot Tony a look of pure hatred.

Brandon smiled. 'That's all for now, ladies and gentlemen. There will be a statement later from the force press office. Now, if you'll excuse us, we've got a lot of work to do.' He nodded benevolently towards the press, then he turned away, taking Cross firmly by the elbow. They walked back towards the alley, Cross's back rigid with fury. Carol and Tony followed a few paces behind. As they went, Penny Burgess's voice rang out behind them. 'Inspector Jordan? Who's the new boy?'

'God, that woman doesn't miss a trick,' Carol muttered.

'I'd better keep out of her way, then,' Tony remarked. 'Me ending up front-page news could be a serious health hazard.'

Carol stopped in her tracks. 'You mean the killer could target you?'

Tony grinned. 'No. I mean your Chief Constable would have an apoplexy.'

The irresistible urge to mirror his smile hit Carol. This man was unlike any Home Office Jobsworth she'd ever encountered. Not only did he have a sense of humour, he didn't mind being indiscreet. And close up, he definitely fell into the category her friend Lucy described as 'a bit chewy'. He was showing signs of being the first interesting man she'd met in the Job for a very long time. 'You could be right,' was all she said, managing to sound noncommittal enough for her words not to be held against her.

They reached the corner of the alley in time to see Tom Cross round on Brandon. 'With respect, sir, you just contradicted everything I've been telling them buggers since this sideshow started.'

'It's time for a different approach, Tom,' Brandon said coolly.

'So why not discuss it with me instead of making me look a dickhead in front of that mob? Not to mention my own men.' Cross leaned forward belligerently. His hand strayed upwards, index finger pointed, as if he were going to stab Brandon in the chest with it. But common sense careerism prevailed, and the hand dropped back by his side.

'You think if I'd had you in my office and suggested a different approach I'd have got one?' There was steel beneath the mildness in Brandon's voice, and Cross recognized it.

His lower jaw jutted. 'At the end of the day, operational decisions are down to me,' he said. Beneath the belligerence, Tony pictured a small boy, an aggressive bully resenting the adults who still had the power to sort him out.

'But I'm the ACC Crime and the buck stops with me. I make the policy decisions, and I've just made one that happens to impact on your sphere of operations. From now on, this is one single major incident enquiry. Is that clear, Tom? Or do you want to take it further?' For the first time, Carol saw for herself how John Brandon had climbed so far up the greasy pole. The threat in his voice was no empty posturing. He was clearly prepared to do whatever it took to achieve his ends, and he acted with all the assurance of a man used to winning. There was nowhere left for Tom Cross to go.

Cross rounded on Carol. 'Have you got nothing better to do, Inspector?'

'I'm waiting to make my report, sir,' she said. 'You told me to wait for you after the press conference.'

'Before you get into that . . . Tom, let me introduce you to Dr Tony Hill,' Brandon said, motioning Tony to come forward.

'We've met,' Cross said, sullen as a schoolboy.

'Dr Hill has agreed to work closely with us in this investigation. He's got more experience in profiling serial offenders than just about anybody else in the country. He's also agreed to keep his involvement under wraps.'

Tony gave a self-deprecating, diplomatic smile. 'That's right. The last thing I want is to turn your enquiry into a sideshow. If there's any credit going when we nail this bastard, I want it to go to your team. They'll be the ones doing the work, after all.'

'You're not wrong there,' Cross muttered. 'I don't want you under our feet, getting in the road.'

'None of us want that, Tom,' Brandon said. 'That's why I've asked Carol to act as liaison officer between Tony and us.'

'I can't afford to lose a senior officer at a time like this,' Cross protested.

'You're not losing her,' Brandon said. 'You're gaining an officer with a unique overview of all the cases.

Could prove invaluable, Tom.' He glanced at his watch. 'I better be off. The Chief's going to want a briefing on this one. Keep me posted, Tom.' Brandon sketched a wave and stepped back into the street and out of sight.

Cross pulled a packet of cigarettes out of his pocket and lit up. 'You know your trouble, Inspector?' he said. 'You're not as smart as you like to think you are. One step out of line, lady, and I'll have your guts for a jock strap.' He took a deep drag of his cigarette and leaned forward to blow smoke in Carol's direction. The gesture was ruined by the gust of wind that snatched the smoke away before it reached her. Looking disgusted, Cross turned on his heel and marched back to the scene of the crime.

'You meet a nice class of person in this job,' Carol said.

'At least I know now which way the wind blows,' Tony replied. As he spoke, he felt a drop of rain on his face.

'Oh shit,' Carol said. 'That's all we need. Look, can we meet tomorrow? I can grab the files tonight and skim them beforehand. Then you can get stuck in.'

'Fine. My office, ten o'clock?'

'Perfect. How do I find you?'

Tony gave Carol directions, then watched as she hurried back down the alley. An interesting woman. And attractive too, most men would agree to that. There were times when he almost wished he could find an uncomplicated response in himself. But he'd long since gone beyond the point where he would allow himself to be attracted to a woman like Carol Jordan.

*   *   *

47

It was after seven when Carol finally made it back to headquarters. When she rang John Brandon's extension, she was pleasantly surprised to find him still at his desk. 'Come on up,' he told her.

She was even more surprised when she walked through his secretary's door and found him pouring two steaming mugs from the coffee maker. 'Milk and sugar?' he asked her.

'Neither,' she said. 'This is an unexpected pleasure.'

'I gave up smoking five years ago,' Brandon confided. 'Now it's only the caffeine that holds me together. Come through.'

Carol walked into his office, fired with curiosity. She'd never been across the threshold before. The decor was regulation cream paint, the furniture identical to Cross's office, except that here the wood was gleaming, free from scuffs, scratches, cigarette burns and the telltale rings left by hot cups. Unlike most senior officers, Brandon hadn't decorated his walls with police photographs and his framed commendations. Instead, he'd chosen half a dozen reproductions of turn-of-the-century paintings of Bradfield street scenes. Colourful yet moody, often rain-soaked, they mirrored the spectacular view from the seventh-floor window. The only item in the room that ran true to expectation was the photograph of his wife and children on the desk. Even that was no posed, studio shot, but an enlargement of a holiday snap on board a sailboat. Deduction: in spite of the impression Brandon strove to give as a bluff, straightforward, conventional copper, he was actually far more complex and thoughtful under the surface.

He waved Carol to a pair of chairs in front of his

desk, then sat down in the other one. 'One thing I want to be clear about,' Brandon said without preliminary. 'You report to Superintendent Cross. He's in charge of this operation. However, I want to see copies of your reports and Dr Hill's, and I want to know any theories the pair of you come up with that you're not ready to commit to paper. Think you can handle that balancing act?'

Carol's eyebrows rose. 'There's only one way to find out, sir,' she said.

Brandon's lips twitched in a half smile. He'd always preferred honesty to bullshit. 'OK. I want you to make sure you are given access to everybody's files. Any problems with that, any sense that anyone's trying to stall you and Dr Hill, and I want to know about it, no matter who's responsible. I'll talk to the squad myself in the morning, make sure nobody's in any doubt about what the new rules of the game are. Anything you need from me?'

Another twelve hours in the day would be a start, Carol thought wearily. Loving a challenge was all very well. But this time, it looked like love was going to be an uphill struggle.

Tony closed his front door behind him. He dropped his briefcase where he stood and leaned against the wall. He'd got what he wanted. It was a battle of wits now, his insight against the killer's stockade. Somewhere in the pattern of these crimes there lay a labyrinthine path straight to a murderer's heart. Somehow, Tony had to tread that path, wary of misleading shadows, careful to avoid straying into treacherous undergrowth.

49

He shrugged away from the wall, feeling suddenly exhausted, and headed for the kitchen, pulling off his tie and unbuttoning his shirt on the way. A cold beer, and then he could go through his scanty collection of press clippings on the three previous murders. He had just opened the fridge to grab a can of Boddingtons when the phone rang. He slammed the door shut and snatched up the extension, juggling with the cold can. 'Hello?' he said.

'Anthony,' the voice said.

Tony swallowed hard. 'This isn't a good time,' he said, cutting coldly across the husky contralto coming down the line. He dumped the can on the worktop and popped the ring pull with one hand.

'Playing hard to get? Oh, well, that's part of the fun, isn't it? I thought I'd cured you of trying to avoid me. I thought we'd left all that behind us. Don't say you're going to regress and hang up on me again, that's all I ask.' The voice was teasing, laughter bubbling just beneath the surface.

'I'm not playing hard to get,' he said. 'It really isn't a good time.' He could feel the slow burn of anger rising from the pit of his stomach.

'That's up to you. You're the man. You're the boss. Unless, of course, you want things different for a change. If you catch my drift.' The voice was almost a sigh, teasing him with its elusive quality. 'After all, this is strictly between you and me. Consenting adults, as they say.'

'So don't I have the right to say no, not right now? Or is it only women who have that right?' he said, hearing the tension in his voice as the anger rose like bile in his throat.

'God, Anthony, your voice gets so sexy when you're angry,' the voice purred.

Nonplussed, Tony held the phone away from his ear, staring at it as if it were an artefact from another planet. Sometimes he wondered if what came out of his mouth were the same words that arrived in his listeners' ears. With a clinical detachment he couldn't bring to his caller, he noted that his grip on the phone was so tight his fingers were white. After a moment, he put the receiver back to his ear. 'Just listening to your voice makes me wet, Anthony,' she was saying. 'Don't you want to know what I'm wearing, what I'm doing right now?' The voice was seductive, the breathing more audible than it had been at first.

'Look, I've had a hard day, I've got a load of work to do and much as I enjoy our little games, I'm not in the mood tonight.' Agitated, Tony looked desperately round his kitchen as if searching for the nearest exit.

'You sound so tense, my darling. Let me soothe all that pressure away. Let's play. Think of me as a relaxation technique. You know you'll work better afterwards. You know I give you the best time you've ever had. With a stud like you and a sex queen like me, there's nothing we can't do. And for starters, I'm going to give you the dirtiest, sexiest, horniest phone call we've ever shared.'

Suddenly, his anger found a weakness in the dam and burst free. 'Not tonight!' Tony yelled, slamming the phone down so hard the can of beer jumped. Creamy froth swelled up through the triangular hole in the top. Tony stared at it in disgust. He picked up the can and threw it in the sink. The can clattered against the stainless steel, then rolled from side to side. Beer and foam spurted out in brown and cream gouts as Tony dropped into a crouch, head down, hands over his face. Tonight, faced with staring into the depths of someone else's nightmares, he absolutely did not want the inevitable confrontation with his own deficiencies that the phone calls always brought in their wake. The phone rang again, but he remained motionless, eyes squeezed shut. When the answering machine picked up, the caller disconnected the line. 'Bitch,' he said viciously. 'Bitch.'

When my neighbours go out to work in the morning, they leave their German shepherd loose in the back yard. All day long, he lopes restlessly up and down the yard, quartering the poured concrete with the diligence of a prison officer who really loves the work. He's heavy-set, black and brindle, with a shaggy coat. Whenever anyone enters the yards on either side of his, he barks, a long, deep-throated cacophony that lasts far longer than any intrusion. When the bin men come down the back alley to trundle our wheelie bins to their truck, the dog becomes hysterical, standing on his hind legs, forepaws scrabbling uselessly against the heavy wooden gate. I've watched him from the vantage point of my back-bedroom window. He's nearly as tall as the gate itself. Perfect, really.

Next Monday morning, I bought a couple of pounds of steak and cut it into one-inch cubes, like all the best recipes say. Then I made a small incision in each cube and inserted one of the tranquillizers my doctor insists on prescribing for me. I never wanted them, and certainly never use them, but I'd had the feeling they might come in useful one day.

I came out of my back door and listened cheerfully to the dog's salvo of barks. I could afford to be cheerful; it would be the last time I'd have to endure it. I plunged my hand into the bowl of moist meat, enjoying its cool, slippery feel. Then I tossed it over the wall in handfuls. I returned indoors, washed up and went upstairs to my vantage point by the computer. I chose the atmospheric world of Darkseed, calming my excitement with the gothic and macabre underworld I had come to know so well. In spite of my absorption in the game, though, I couldn't help glancing out of the window every few minutes. After a while, he slumped to the ground, tongue lolling out of his mouth. I exited from my game and picked up my binoculars. He seemed to be breathing, but wasn't moving.

I ran downstairs, picking up the holdall I'd prepared earlier, and got into the jeep. I reversed it down the alley till the tailgate was level with next-door's yard gate. I turned off the engine. Silence. I couldn't resist a certain smug satisfaction as I picked up my crowbar and jumped down. It took moments to force next-door's gate. As it swung open, I could see the dog hadn't stirred. I opened the holdall and crouched down beside him. I shoved his tongue back into his mouth and taped his muzzle shut with a roll of surgical tape. I bound his legs together, front and back, and dragged him to the jeep. He was heavy, but I keep myself in shape, and it wasn't too hard to manhandle him into the back.

His breath was coming in soft snores when we got to the farmhouse, but there was no flicker of consciousness, even when I thumbed back his eyelids. I tipped him into the wheelbarrow I'd left out there, wheeled him through the cottage and emptied him down the flight of steps. I switched on the lights and hauled the dog on to the rack like a sack of potatoes, then turned to study my knives. I'd fitted a

*magnetic strip to the wall, and there they hung suspended,
each sharpened to a professional edge; cleaver, filleting knife,
carving knife, paring knife and craft knife. I chose the craft
knife, cut away the tape from the dog's legs and spread him
out on his stomach. I fastened the strap round his middle to
hold him tightly against the rack. That's when I realized I
had a problem.*

*Sometime in the past few minutes, the dog had stopped
breathing. I thrust my head against the rough hairs of his
chest, searching for a heartbeat, but it was too late. I'd
obviously miscalculated the drug dosage, and given him
too much. I was furious, I have to admit. The dog's death
wouldn't affect the practicalities of scientifically testing my
apparatus, but I had been looking forward to his suffering;
a small revenge for the dozens of times his demented barking
had woken me up, especially when I'd come off a hard night
shift. But he'd died without a moment's suffering. The last
thing he'd known was a couple of pounds of steak. It didn't
please me that he'd died happy.*

*That wasn't all; I soon discovered a second problem. The
straps I'd fitted were fine for human ankles and wrists.
But the dog didn't have hands or feet to stop his limbs
slipping free.*

*I didn't puzzle for long. It was a far from elegant solution,
but it served my purpose. I still had some six-inch nails left
over from the repairs and modifications I'd made to the cellar.
I carefully placed his left front paw so it straddled a gap in
the timbers. I felt for the space between the bones and, with
one blow of my club hammer, I drove the nail through at
right angles to the paw, just above the last joint. I fixed the
strap below the nail, and tugged at it. I reckoned it would
hold for long enough.*

I'd fixed the other legs within five minutes. Once he was

securely strapped down, I was finally able to get started on the business of the day. Even with the bare prospect of a purely scientific experiment, I could feel the excitement rising in me till it was like a hard lump in my throat. Almost, it seemed, without conscious thought, my hand strayed to the handle of the rack. I watched it, detached, as if it were the hand of a stranger. It caressed the cogs, ran lightly over the wheel, and finally came to rest on the handle. The aroma of lubricating oil still hung lightly on the air, melding with the faint smell of paint and the stale, doggy smell of my assistant in the experiment. I took a deep breath, shivered in anticipation, and slowly began to turn the handle.

3

> I do not stick to assert, that any man who deals in
> murder must have very incorrect ways of thinking,
> and truly inaccurate principles.

Don Merrick unzipped his flies. With a sigh of relief, he
relaxed his muscles and let his bursting bladder empty.
Behind him, the cubicle door opened. His pleasure was
abruptly shattered when a heavy hand descended on
his shoulder. 'Sergeant Merrick. Just the man I wanted
to see,' Tom Cross boomed. Inexplicably, Merrick discovered he couldn't finish what he'd started.

''Morning, sir,' he said cautiously, shaking himself
and quickly tucking his manhood out of Cross's
sight.

'Told you about her new assignment, has she, your
guv'nor?' Cross asked, all lads-together bonhomie.

'She mentioned it, yes, sir.' Merrick looked longingly
at the door. But there was no escape. Not with Cross's
hand still clamped on his shoulder.

'I hear you're planning on taking your inspector's
exams,' Cross remarked.

Merrick's stomach clenched. 'That's right, sir.'

'So you'll be needing all the friends in high places you can find, eh, lad?'

Merrick forced his lips apart in what he hoped was a smile to match Cross's. 'If you say so, sir.'

'You've got the makings of a good officer, Merrick. As long as you remember where your loyalties lie. I know Inspector Jordan's going to be a very busy lady over the next few weeks. She might not always have time to keep me fully *abreast* of things.' Cross leered suggestively. 'I'll be relying on you to keep me informed of all developments. You understand, lad?'

Merrick nodded. 'Aye, sir.'

Cross dropped his hand and made for the door. Opening it, he turned back to Merrick and said, 'Especially if she starts shagging our doctor friend.'

The door sighed shut behind Cross. 'Fuck and bollocks,' Merrick said softly to himself as he moved to the washbasin and started scrubbing his hands vigorously under the hot tap.

Tony had been at his desk since eight. So far, all he'd done was make some photocopies of the Crime Analysis Report form he'd devised for the projected task force. Heavily based on the FBI's Violent Criminal Apprehension Program questionnaire, it aimed to produce a standard classification of every aspect of the crime, from the victim through to the forensic evidence. He shuffled the forms absently, then rearranged his newspaper cuttings into a neat pile. He justified his lack of activity by telling himself that until Carol arrived with the police files, there was little he could do. But that was merely an excuse.

The truth was, there was good reason why concentration was eluding him. She was in his head again. The mystery woman. At the start, he'd felt vulnerable, unwilling to take part in her games. Just like his patients, he thought ironically. How many times had he uttered the maxim that everybody was reluctant to cooperate with therapy at some level? He'd lost count of the number of times he'd slammed the phone down in the early days. But she had persisted, patiently continuing to administer her soothing persuasions till he had started to relax, even to join in.

She had completely thrown him off balance. She had seemed from the first to have an instinct for his Achilles heel, yet she never attacked it. She was everything anyone could desire in a fantasy lover, from gentle to raunchy. The key question for Tony was whether he was pathetic because he managed to relate to pornographic phone calls from a stranger, or whether he should congratulate himself on being so well adjusted that he understood what he needed and what worked for him. But he could not escape the fear that, if not yet dependent on the phone calls, he was at risk of succumbing to that danger. Already incapable of sustaining a normal sexual relationship, was he colluding in the worsening of his condition, or was he moving towards recovery? The only way to test which was correct was to attempt the shift from fantasy to reality. But he was still too wary of fresh humiliation for that. For now, it seemed he'd have to settle for the mysterious stranger who managed to make him feel like a man for long enough to drive the demons underground.

Tony sighed and picked up his mug. The coffee was

cold, but he drank it anyway. In spite of himself, he began replaying past conversations in his mind. As if he hadn't run through it enough during the early hours of the morning when sleep had been as elusive as the Bradfield serial killer. The woman's voice buzzed in his ears, inescapable as someone else's Walkman in a train carriage. He tried to close off his emotions and treat the calls with the intellectual objectivity he brought to his work. All he had to do was shut himself off, the way he did when he was examining the perverse fantasies of his patients. He'd certainly had enough experience of refusing to recognize echoes in himself.

Stop the voice. Analyse. Who was she? What drove her? Maybe, like him, she simply enjoyed digging around in messy heads. That at least would explain how she'd wormed her way through his barricades. She was certainly a different animal from the women who worked for the sleazy telephone sex chatlines. Before he'd started this study for the Home Office, he'd been engaged in a piece of research into those chatlines. A significant number of the recently convicted offenders he had dealt with had admitted they were regular callers to the premium-rate phone lines where they could pour their sexual fantasies, however bizarre, obscene or perverse, into the ears of dismally paid women who were encouraged by their bosses to indulge the callers for as long as they were prepared to pay. He'd actually phoned some of the lines himself, just to sample what was on offer, and to discover, using the transcripts of some of his interviews, just how far it was possible to go before disgust overcame the profit motive or the desperate need to earn a living.

Finally, he'd interviewed a selection of the women

who worked the phones. The one thing they all held in common was a sense of being violated and degraded, however some of them dressed it up in the contempt they voiced for their clients. He'd come to several conclusions, but the paper he'd subsequently written hadn't included all of them. Some he'd left out because they were too off the wall, others because he feared they might reveal too much about his own psyche. That included his conviction that the response of a man who had previously called a chatline to a dirty phone call from a member of the opposite sex would be radically different to that of a woman in the same situation. Instead of slamming down the receiver, or reporting it to Telecom, most of these men would be either amused or aroused. Either way, they'd want to hear more.

All he had to work out now was why, unlike the chatline workers, this woman found telephone sex with a stranger so appealing. What he needed was to satisfy the intellectual curiosity that was at least as strong as his urge to explore the sexual playground she had opened up for him. Maybe he should consider suggesting a meeting. Before he could go any further, the phone rang. Tony started, his hand stopping half-way in its automatic journey to the receiver. 'Oh, for God's sake,' he muttered impatiently, shaking his head like a high-diver surfacing. He picked up the phone and said, 'Tony Hill.'

'Dr Hill, it's Carol Jordan here.'

Tony said nothing, relieved that his thoughts had failed to conjure up the mystery woman.

'Inspector Jordan? Bradfield Police?' Carol continued into the silence.

'Hello, yes, sorry, I was just trying to . . . clear a space on my desk,' Tony stumbled, his left leg starting to jitter like a cup of tea on a train.

'I'm really sorry about this, but I'm not going to be able to make it for ten. Mr Brandon's called all the squad together for a briefing, and I don't think it would be politic to miss it.'

'No, I can see that,' Tony said, his free hand picking up a pen and unconsciously doodling a daffodil. 'It's going to be hard enough for you to act as go-between without making it look like you're not part of the team. Don't worry about it.'

'Thanks. Look, I don't think this briefing is going to last that long. I'll be with you as soon as I can. Probably around eleven, if that doesn't interfere with your schedule.'

'That's fine,' he said, relieved he wouldn't have too long to brood before they could get down to work. 'I've no meetings in the diary for today, so take your time. You're not putting me out.'

'OK. See you then.'

Carol replaced the phone. So far, so good. At least Tony Hill didn't seem a prisoner of his professional ego, unlike several of the experts she'd had dealings with. And, unlike most men, he'd perceived her potential difficulty, sympathized without patronizing her, and had happily gone along with a course of action that would minimize her problems. Impatiently, she pushed away the memory of the attraction she'd felt for him. These days, she had neither the time nor the inclination for emotional involvement. Sharing a flat with her brother and finding the time to sustain a few close friendships took as much of her energy as she could spare. Besides, the ending of her last relationship had dealt her self-esteem too serious a blow for her to enter on another one lightly.

The affair with a casualty surgeon in London hadn't survived her move from the Met to Bradfield three years before. As far as Rob was concerned, it was Carol's decision to move to the frozen north. So travelling up and down motorways to spend time together was down to her. He had no intention of wasting any of his valuable off-duty time putting unnecessary mileage on his BMW just to go to a city whose only redeeming feature was Carol. Besides, nurses were a lot less stroppy and critical, and they understood long hours and shift work just as well as a copper, if not better. His brutal self-interest had shaken Carol, who felt cheated of the emotion and energy she'd invested in loving Rob. Tony Hill might be attractive, charming, and, if his reputation was correct, intelligent and intuitive, but Carol wasn't about to risk her heart again. Especially not with a professional colleague. If she was finding it hard to get him out of her mind, it was because she was fascinated by what she could learn from him about the case, not because she fancied him.

Carol ran a hand through her hair and yawned. She'd been home for precisely fifty-seven minutes in the previous twenty-four hours. Twenty of those had been spent in the shower in a futile attempt to inoculate herself against the effects of no sleep. She'd spent a large chunk of the evening out on the knocker with her CID team, pursuing fruitless enquiries among the nervous inhabitants, workers and regular customers of Temple Fields and its gay businesses. The men's reactions had ranged from total noncooperation to abuse. Carol felt no surprise. The area was seething with a mass of contradictory feelings.

On the one hand, the gay businesses didn't want the area swarming with police because it was bad for cash flow. On the other hand, the gay activists were angrily demanding proper protection now the police had belatedly decided that there was a gay serial killer on the loose. One group of customers were horrified to be questioned, since their gay life was a deep secret from wives, friends, colleagues and parents. Another group were happily playing macho men, boasting that they'd never get into a situation where they were slaughtered by some glassy-eyed maniac. Yet another group were eager for details, obscurely and, in Carol's eyes, obscenely excited by what could happen when one man went out of control. And there was a handful of hardline lesbian separatists who made no secret of their glee that this time, men were the targets. 'Maybe now they'll understand why we were so outraged during the Yorkshire Ripper hunt when men suggested single women should have a curfew,' one had sneered at Carol.

Exhausted by the turmoil, Carol had driven back to headquarters to begin her trawl of the files of the existing enquiries. The murder room was strangely quiet, since most of the detectives were out in Temple Fields, pursuing different lines of enquiry or taking advantage of a few hours off to catch up on their drinking, their sex lives or their sleep. She'd already had a quick word with her opposite numbers on the other two murder investigations, and they had reluctantly agreed to give her access to their files provided she had the material back on their desks first thing in the morning. It was exactly the response she'd expected: superficially cooperative, but, in real terms, calculated to cause her even more problems.

When she'd walked through her office door, she'd been appalled by the sheer volume of paper. Stacks of interview statements, forensic and pathology reports, files of photographs virtually buried her office. Why, in God's name, hadn't Tom Cross decided to use the HOLMES computer system for the earlier murders? At least then all the material would be accessible in the computer, indexed and cross-referenced. All she'd have had to do then was to persuade one of the HOLMES indexers to print out the relevant stuff for Tony. With a groan, she closed her door on the mess and walked through the empty corridors to the uniform sergeant's office. The time had come to test the ACC's instruction to all ranks to cooperate with her. Without another pair of hands, she'd never get through the night's work.

Even with the grudgingly granted help of a PC, it had been a struggle to get through the material. Carol had skimmed the investigation reports, extracting everything that seemed to hold the possibility of significance and passing it on to the constable for copying. Even so, there was a daunting pile of material for Tony and her to work through. When her assistant knocked off at six, Carol wearily loaded the photocopies into a couple of cardboard cartons and staggered down to her car with them. She helped herself to full sets of photographs of all the victims and scenes of crime, filling in a form to requisition fresh copies for the investigating teams to replace the ones she'd taken.

Only then had she headed home. Even there, she had no respite. Nelson waited behind the door, miaowing crossly as he wove his sinuous body round her ankles, forcing her to head straight for the kitchen and the tin opener. When she dumped the bowl of food in front of him, he stared suspiciously at it, frowning. Then hunger overcame his desire to punish her and he wolfed down the whole bowl without pause. 'Nice to see you missed me,' Carol said drily as she made for the shower. By the time she emerged, Nelson had clearly decided to forgive her. He followed her around, purring like a dialling tone, sitting down on every garment she selected from the wardrobe and placed on the bed.

'You really are the pits,' Carol grumbled, pulling her black jeans out from under him. Nelson carried on adoring her, his purr not disrupted in the slightest. She pulled on the jeans, admiring the cut in her wardrobe mirror. They were Katharine Hammett, but she'd only paid £20 for them in a seconds shop in Kensington Church Street, where she went on a twice-annual trawl for the designer clothes she loved but couldn't afford, even on an inspector's wages. The cream linen shirt was French Connection, the ribbed grey cardigan from a chain store men's department. Carol picked a few black cat hairs from the cardigan and caught Nelson's reproachful stare. 'You know I love you. I just don't need to wear you,' she said.

'You'd get a shock if he answered you,' a man's voice said from the doorway.

Carol turned to face her brother, who leaned against the doorjamb in his boxer shorts, blond hair tousled, eyes bleary with sleep. His face had a strange congruence with Carol's, as if someone had scanned her photograph into a computer and subtly altered the features away from the feminine and towards the masculine. 'I didn't wake you, did I?' she asked anxiously.

'Nope. I've got to go to London today. The money man cometh.' He yawned.

'The Americans?' Carol asked, crouching down and scratching the cat behind the ears. Nelson promptly rolled over on to his back, displaying his full stomach to be stroked.

'Correct. They want a full demo of what we've done so far. I've been telling Carl that nothing looks very impressive right now, but he says they want some reassurance that they're not just pouring their development money into a black hole.'

'The joys of software development,' Carol said, rumpling Nelson's fur.

'Leading-edge software development, please,' Michael said, self-mockingly. 'How about you? What's happening down the murder factory? I heard on the news last night that you'd copped for another one.'

'Looks like it. At least the powers that be have finally admitted that we've got a serial killer on the loose. And they've brought in a psychological profiler to work with us.'

Michael whistled. 'Fuck me, Bradfield police enter the twentieth century. How's Popeye taking it?'

Carol pulled a face. 'He likes it about as much as a poke in the eye with a sharp stick. He thinks it's a total waste of bloody time,' Carol said, dropping her voice and affecting Tom Cross's Bradfield accent. 'Then when I was appointed liaison officer with the profiler, he perked up.'

Michael nodded, a cynical expression on his face. 'Two birds with one stone.'

Carol grinned. 'Yeah, well, it'll need to be over my dead body.' She stood up. Nelson gave a small miaow of protest. Carol sighed and headed for the door. 'Back to work, Nelson. Thanks for taking my mind off the bodies,' she said.

Michael swung out of the doorway to let her pass and gave her a hug. 'Take no prisoners, sis,' he said.

Carol snorted. 'I don't think you've quite grasped the principle of policing, bro.'

By the time she was behind the wheel, the cat and Michael were forgotten. She was back with the killer.

Now, a couple of hours and a stack of overnight murder team reports later, home seemed a memory as distant as her summer holiday in Ithaca. Carol forced herself out of her chair, picked up the paperwork and walked into the main CID office.

It was standing room only by the time she arrived, detectives normally based in other stations jockeying for position in the crowd. A couple of her detective constables shifted to make room for her, one offering his chair. 'Fucking brown nose,' a voice said audibly from the other side of the room. Carol couldn't see who had spoken, but recognized it wasn't one of her own team. She smiled and shook her head at her junior officer, choosing instead to perch on the edge of his desk beside Don Merrick, who nodded a morose greeting. The clock read nine-twenty-nine. The room smelled of cheap cigars, coffee and damp coats.

One of the other inspectors caught Carol's eye and started to move towards her. But before they could speak, the door opened and Tom Cross barrelled in, followed by John Brandon. The superintendent looked disturbingly benign as he marched in. The troops parted automatically before him, leaving a clear path for him and Brandon to walk to the whiteboard at the far end of the room.

''Morning, lads,' Cross said genially. 'And lasses,' he added as an obvious afterthought. 'There's nobody here that doesn't know we've got four unsolved murders on our hands. We've got IDs for the first three bodies – Adam Scott, Paul Gibbs and Gareth Finnegan. So far, we've not made any progress on the fourth victim. The lads down the path lab are working on him now, trying to come up with a face that won't frighten the horses when we release the picture to the press.'

Cross took a deep breath. If anything, his expression became even more benevolent. 'As you all know, I'm not a man given to theorizing ahead of the evidence. And I've been reluctant officially to connect these killings because of the media hysteria that would bring down about us. Judging by this morning's papers, I was right about that.' He pointed to several of the newspapers the detectives held.

'However, in the light of this latest killing, we're going to have to revise our strategy. As of yesterday afternoon, I have amalgamated the four murder enquiries into one major investigation.'

There was a murmur of support. Don Merrick leaned forward and murmured in Carol's ear, 'Changes his tune more often than a juke box.'

She nodded. 'I wish he changed his socks as often.'

Cross glared in their direction. He couldn't have heard the remarks, but seeing Carol's lips move was enough of an excuse. 'Settle down,' he said sternly.

'I'm not finished yet. Now, it doesn't take much in the way of detective abilities to see that this place is too small for us *and* the normal activities of the station, so as soon as we're finished here this morning, we'll be moving this operation to the former station in Scargill Street, which some of you will remember was mothballed six months ago. Overnight, there's been a team of maintenance workers, computer whizz kids and British Telecom engineers getting it back to temporary operational status.'

A groan went up. No one had shed a tear when the old Victorian building in Scargill Street had been closed down. Draughty, inconvenient, short of parking spaces, ladies' toilets – everything except cells – the building had been earmarked for demolition and redevelopment. Typically, there hadn't been enough money in the budget to push ahead with the project. 'I know, I know,' Cross said, cutting across their complaints. 'But we'll all be under one roof, so I'll be able to keep an eye on you. I will be in overall charge of the enquiry. You'll have two inspectors to report to – Bob Stansfield and Kevin Matthews. They'll be sorting out your assignments in a minute. Inspector Jordan will be otherwise engaged on an initiative of Mr Brandon's.' Cross paused. 'Which I'm sure you'll all want to cooperate with.'

Carol kept her head high and looked around. The faces she could see mostly showed open cynicism. Several heads turned towards her. There was no warmth in their stares. Even those who might support the profiling initiative were brassed off that the prime job had gone to a woman rather than one of the lads.

'So Bob will take over Inspector Jordan's operational

responsibilities for Paul Gibbs and Adam Scott, and Kevin will handle yesterday's body as well as Gareth Finnegan. The HOLMES team have been called in, and they'll be starting to input their data just as soon as the boffins have got the wires in place. Inspector Dave Woolcott, who some of you will remember from when he was a sergeant here, will be the enquiry manager in charge of the HOLMES team. Over to you, Mr Brandon.' Cross stepped back and waved the ACC forward. His gesture was only just on the right side of the border between insolence and politeness.

Brandon took a moment to look around the room. He'd never had to make a more important pitch. Most of the detectives in the room were jaded and frustrated. Many of them had been working on one of the previous murders for months now, with precious little to show for it. Tom Cross's powers of motivation were legendary, but even he was facing an uphill struggle, not least because of his pig-headed refusal to admit before now that the crimes were connected. It was time to beat Tom Cross at his own game. Bluntness had never been Brandon's strong suit, but he'd been practising all morning. In the shower, in front of the shaving mirror, in his head while he ate his egg on toast, in the car on the way to the station. Brandon thrust one hand in his trouser pocket and crossed his fingers.

'This is probably the toughest task of any of our careers. As far as we're aware, this guy is only operating in Bradfield. In a way, I'm glad about that, because I've never seen a better bunch of detectives than we've got here. If anyone can nail this bastard, it's you lot. You've got a hundred and ten per cent support from your senior officers, and all the resources you need are going to be made available, whether the politicians like it or not.' Brandon's note of belligerence won a murmur of agreement from the room.

'We're going to be blazing a trail here in more ways than one. You all know about the Home Office plans for a national task force for profiling repeat offenders. Well, we're going to be the guinea pigs. Dr Tony Hill, the man who's going to be telling the Home Office what to think, has agreed to work with us. Now, I know there are some amongst you who think that profiling is a load of crap. But like it or not, it's part of our future. If we cooperate and work with this guy, we're a lot more likely to see this task force end up something like we want it to be. If we piss him off, we're liable to be lumbered with a bloody great millstone round our neck. Is that clear to everyone here?'

Brandon looked sternly round the room, not missing out Tom Cross. The nods varied from enthusiastic to barely perceptible. 'I'm glad we all understand one another. Dr Hill's job is to assess the evidence we provide him with and to come up with a profile of the killer to help us focus our enquiries. I've appointed Inspector Carol Jordan as the liaison officer between the murder squad and Dr Hill. Inspector Jordan, can you just stand up a minute?'

Startled, Carol scrambled to her feet, dropping her files on the way. Don Merrick immediately got down on his knees and grabbed the spilling papers. 'For those of you from other divisions who don't know Inspector Jordan, there she is.' Nice one, Brandon, thought Carol. As if there were squads of female detectives to choose from.

'Inspector Jordan is to have access to each and every piece of paper on this enquiry. I want her kept fully informed of any developments. Anyone who is pursuing a promising lead should discuss it with her as well as with their own inspector, or Superintendent Cross. And any requests from Inspector Jordan must be treated as urgent enquiries. If I hear that anybody's being a smartarse, trying to freeze Inspector Jordan or Dr Hill out of the investigation, I won't be taking prisoners. The same goes for anybody who leaks anything about this aspect of the investigation to the media. So think on. Unless you've got a burning ambition to climb back into uniform and walk the streets of Bradfield in the rain for the rest of your career, you'll do everything in your power to help her. This isn't a competition. We're all on the same side. Dr Hill isn't here to catch the killer. That's your –'

Brandon stopped in mid-sentence. No one had noticed the door opening, but the words of the communications room sergeant captured everyone's attention faster than a gunshot. 'Sorry to interrupt, sir,' he said, his voice tight with suppressed emotion. 'We've got an ID on yesterday's victim. Sir, he's one of ours.'

It was an American journalist who said, 'I have seen the future and it works.' I know just what he meant. After the dog, I knew Adam wouldn't be any problem.

I spent the rest of the week in a state of nervous tension. I was even tempted to try one of the tranquillizers myself, but I resisted. This wasn't the time to give in to weakness. Besides, I couldn't afford to be anything less than completely in control of myself. My years of self-discipline paid off; I doubt if any of my colleagues noticed anything unusual in my behaviour at work, except that I couldn't bring myself to do the weekend overtime I usually volunteer for.

By Monday morning, I was at a peak of readiness. I was primed and polished, the perfect killer-in-waiting. Even the weather was on my side. It was a crisp, clear autumnal morning, the kind of day that brings a smile even to the lips of commuters. Just before eight, I drove past Adam's home, a new terraced three-storey town house with integral garage on the ground floor. His bedroom curtains were closed, the milk bottle still sitting on his doorstep, half a Daily Mail protruding from his letter box. I parked a couple of streets away outside a row of shops and retraced my journey. I

74

walked down his street, satisfied that so far I was right on time. His bedroom curtains were drawn back, the milk and newspaper gone. At the end of the street, I crossed to the little park opposite and sat on a bench.

I opened my own Daily Mail and imagined Adam reading the same stories that I was staring at unseeingly. I shifted my position so I could see his front door without craning round the paper, and put my peripheral vision on alert. Right on schedule, the door opened at eight-twenty, and Adam appeared. Casually, I folded up my paper, dumped it in the litter bin by the bench and strolled off down the street in his wake.

The tram station was less than ten minutes' walk away, and I was right behind him as he strode on to the crowded platform. The tram glided into the station moments later and he moved forward with the flow of passengers. I hung back slightly and let a couple of people come between us; I was taking no chances.

He was craning his head as he entered the carriage. I knew exactly why. When their eyes met, Adam waved and squirmed through the crowd so they could chatter mindlessly all the way into town. I watched him as he leaned forward. I knew every expression on his face, every angle and gesture of his lean, muscular body. His hair; the little curls in the nape of his neck still damp, his skin pink and glowing from his shave, the scent of his Aramis cologne. He laughed aloud at something in their conversation, and I felt the sour taste of bile rise in my mouth. The taste of betrayal. How could he? It should have been me talking to him, making his face light up, bringing that beautiful smile to his warm lips. If my fixity of purpose had ever wavered, the sight of the pair of them enjoying their Monday-morning encounter would have turned my resolve to granite.

As usual, he left the tram in Woolmarket Square. I was less than a dozen yards behind him. He turned back to wave to his soon-to-be bereaved lover. I swiftly turned away, pretending to read the tram timetable. The last thing I wanted right then was for him to notice me, to realize I was dogging his steps. I gave it a few seconds, then took up the pursuit. Left into Bellwether Street. I could see his dark hair bobbing among the shop and office workers crowding the pavements. Adam cut down an alley to his right, and I emerged in Crown Plaza just in time to see him enter the Inland Revenue building where he worked. Satisfied that this was just another Monday, I carried on through the plaza, past the squat glass and metal office block, and into the newly restored Victorian shopping arcades.

I had time to kill. The thought brought a smile to my lips.

I went off to do some studying in the Central Library. They had nothing new in, so I settled for an old favourite, Killing for Company. *Dennis Nilsen's case never ceases both to fascinate and repel me. He murdered fifteen young men without anyone even missing them. No one had the faintest idea that there was a gay serial killer stalking the homeless and rootless. He befriended them, took them home, gave them drink, but he could only cope with them once they had been perfected in death. Then, and only then, could he hold them, have sex with them, cherish them. Now that is sick. They'd done nothing to deserve their fate; they had committed no betrayal, no act of treachery.*

The only mistake Nilsen made was in the disposal of the bodies. It's almost as if subconsciously he wanted to be caught. Chopping them up and cooking them was fine, but flushing them down the toilet? It must have been obvious to a man as intelligent as he was that the drains wouldn't be able to handle that volume of solids. I've never understood why he didn't just feed the meat to his dog.

However, it's never too late to learn from the mistakes of others. The blunders of killers never cease to amaze me. It doesn't take much intelligence to understand how the police and forensic scientists operate and to take appropriate precautions, especially since the men who earn their living trying to catch the killers have obligingly written detailed textbooks about the precise nature of their work. On the other hand, we only ever hear about the failures. I knew I was never going to appear in those catalogues of incompetence. I had planned too well, every risk minimized and balanced against the benefits it would bring. The only account of my work will be this journal, which will not see printer's ink until my last breath is a distant memory. My only regret is that I won't be around to read the reviews.

I was back at my post by four, even though I'd never known Adam leave work before a quarter to five. I sat in the window of Burger King on Woolmarket Square, perfectly placed to watch the mouth of the alley leading to his office. Right on cue, he emerged at 4.47 and headed for the tram stop. I joined the knot of people waiting on the raised platform, smiling quietly to myself as I heard the tram hoot in the distance. Enjoy your tram ride, Adam. It's going to be your last.

4

> The fact was, I 'fancied' him, and resolved to com-
> mence business upon his throat.

When Damien Connolly failed to turn up at the start
of his shift as local information officer in F Division's
station on the south side of the city, the duty sergeant
hadn't been unduly worried. Although PC Connolly
was one of the best collators in the force, and a trained
HOLMES officer, he was a notoriously bad timekeeper.
At least twice a week, he came hurtling through the
doors of the station a good ten minutes after his shift
was due to start. But when he still hadn't shown up
half an hour after he was due on duty, Sergeant Claire
Bonner felt a twinge of irritation. Even Connolly had
enough sense to realize that if he was going to be more
than fifteen minutes late, he had to phone in. Today of
all days as well, when headquarters were demanding
a full turnout of HOLMES officers on the serial-killer
investigation.

Sighing, Sgt Bonner checked Connolly's home number
in her files and dialled it. The phone rang and rang,
till finally it was automatically disconnected. She felt

a prickle of concern. Connolly was something of a loner outside the job. He was quieter and maybe more thoughtful than most of the officers on Sgt Bonner's relief, always keeping his distance when he joined in the social life of the station. As far as she was aware, there was no girlfriend in whose bed Connolly might have overslept. His family were all up in Glasgow, so there were no relatives to try locally. Sgt Bonner cast her mind back. Yesterday had been a day off for the relief. When they'd knocked off from the previous night shift, Connolly had come for breakfast with her and half a dozen of the other lads. He'd not said anything about having plans for his time off other than catching up on his kip and working on his car, an elderly Austin Healey roadster.

Sgt Bonner went through to the control room and had a word with her opposite number, asking him to have one of the patrol cars swing round by Connolly's house to check he wasn't ill or injured. 'See if they can check the garage, make sure that bloody car of his hasn't come off the jack with him underneath,' she added as she went back to her desk.

It was after eight when the control room sergeant appeared in her office. 'The lads have checked Connolly's house. No answer to the door. They had a good scout round, and all the curtains were open. Milk on the doorstep. No sign of life as far as they could make out. There was only one thing a bit odd that they could see. His car was parked on the street, which isn't like him. I don't have to tell you, he treats that motor like the crown jewels.'

Sgt Bonner frowned. 'Maybe he's got somebody stopping with him? A relative, or a girlfriend? Maybe he's let them stick their car in the garage?'

The control room sergeant shook his head. 'Nope. The lads had a look in the garage window, and it was empty. And don't forget the milk.'

Sgt Bonner shrugged. 'Not a lot more we can do, then, is there?'

'Well, he's over twenty-one. I'd have thought he'd have more sense than to go on the missing list, but you know what they say about the quiet ones.'

Sgt Bonner sighed. 'I'll have his guts for garters when he shows his face. By the way, I've asked Joey Smith to stand in for him in the collator's office for this shift.'

The control room sergeant cast his eyes upwards. 'You really know how to make a man's day, don't you? Couldn't you have got one of the others? Smith can barely manage the alphabet.'

Before Sgt Bonner could argue the toss, there was a knock at the door. 'Yeah?' she called. 'Come in.'

A PC from the control room entered hesitantly. She looked faintly sick. 'Skip,' she said, the worry in her voice obvious from the single word. 'I think you'd better have a look at this.' She held out a fax, the bottom edge ragged where it had been torn hastily off the roll.

Being nearer, the control room sergeant took the flimsy sheet and glanced at it. He drew in his breath sharply, then closed his eyes for a moment. Wordlessly, he handed the fax to Sgt Bonner.

At first, all she saw was the stark black and white of the photograph. For a moment, her mind automatically protecting her from horror, she wondered why someone had gone over her head and reported

Connolly missing. Then her eyes translated the marks on the paper into words. *'Urgent fax to all stations. This is the unidentified murder victim discovered yesterday afternoon in the back yard of the Queen of Hearts public house, Temple Fields, Bradfield. Photograph to follow later this a.m. Please circulate and display. Any information to DI Kevin Matthews at Scargill Street Incident Room, ext. 2456.'*

Sgt Bonner looked bleakly at the other two officers. 'There isn't any doubt about it, is there?'

The PC looked at the floor, her skin pale and clammy. 'I don't think so, skip,' she said. 'That's Connolly. I mean, it's not what you'd call a good likeness, but it's definitely him.'

The control room sergeant picked up the fax. 'I'll get on to DI Matthews right away,' he said.

Sgt Bonner pushed her chair back and stood up. 'I'd better go round to the morgue. They're going to need a formal identification as soon as possible so they can get weaving.'

'This makes it a whole new ball game,' Tony said, his face sombre.

'It certainly ups the stakes,' Carol said.

'The question I'm asking myself is whether or not Handy Andy knew he was giving us a bobby,' Tony said softly, swinging round in his chair to stare out of the window at the city rooftops.

'Sorry?'

He gave a twisted smile and said, 'No, it's me who should apologize. I always give them a name. It makes it personal.' He swung back to face Carol. 'Does that bother you?'

Carol shook her head. 'It's better than the station nickname.'

'Which is?' Tony asked, eyebrows raised.

'The Queer Killer,' Carol said, her distaste clear.

'That begs a lot of questions,' Tony said noncommittally. 'But if it helps them deal with their fear and anger, it's probably no bad thing.'

'I don't like it. It doesn't feel personal to me, calling him the Queer Killer.'

'What does make it personal to you? The fact that he's taken one of yours now?'

'I felt like that already. As soon as we got the second murder, the one I was handling, I was convinced we were dealing with a serial offender. That was when it got personal for me. I want to nail this bastard. I need to. Professionally, personally, whatever.' The cold vehemence in Carol's voice gave Tony confidence. This was a woman who was going to pull out all the stops to make sure he had what he needed to do his job. Her tone of voice and the words she'd chosen were also a calculated challenge, showing him she didn't give a damn what he made of her desire. She was just what he needed. Professionally, at any rate.

'You and me both,' Tony said. 'And together, we can make it happen. But only together. You know, the first time I got directly involved in profiling, it was a serial arsonist. After half a dozen major fires, I knew how he was doing it, why he was doing it, what was in it for him. I knew exactly the kind of mad bastard he was, yet I couldn't put a name or a face to him. It drove me crazy with frustration for a while. Then I realized it wasn't my job to do that. That's your job. All I can do is to point you in the right direction.'

Carol smiled grimly. 'Just point, and I'll be off like a gun dog,' she said. 'What did you mean when you said you wondered whether he knew Damien Connolly was a bobby?'

Tony ran a hand through his hair, leaving it spiky as a punk's. 'OK. We've got two scenarios here. Handy Andy may not have known Damien Connolly was a bobby. It may be nothing more than a coincidence, a particularly unpleasant coincidence for his colleagues, but a coincidence nevertheless. That's not a scenario I'm happy with, however, because my reading, based on the little I know so far, is that these aren't random victims snatched by chance. I think he chooses his victims with care, and plans thoroughly. Would you agree with that?'

'He doesn't leave things to chance, that's obvious,' Carol said.

'Right. The alternative is that Handy Andy knows full well that his fourth victim is a policeman. That in itself leads to two further possibilities. One: Handy Andy knew he'd killed a copper, but that fact is supremely irrelevant to the meaning of the killing for him. In other words, Damien Connolly fulfilled all the other criteria that Andy needs from his victims, and he would have died at this point whether he was a bobby or a bus driver.

'The other scenario is the one I like best, though. The fact that Damien was a copper is a crucial part of the reason why Handy Andy *chose* him as his fourth victim.'

'You mean he's thumbing his nose at us?' Carol asked.

Thank God she was quick. That was going to make

the job so much simpler. She'd done well to get as far up the ladder as she had, given she had looks as well as brains. Either attribute without the other would have made promotion easier. 'That's certainly a possibility,' Tony acknowledged. 'But I think it's more likely to be about vanity. I think he'd started to get pissed off with Detective Superintendent Cross's refusal to acknowledge his existence. In his own eyes, he's very successful at what he does. He's the best. And he deserves recognition. And that desire for recognition has been thwarted by the police's refusal to admit there's only one offender behind these killings. OK, so the *Sentinel Times* has been speculating about a serial killer since the second victim, but that's not the same as being given the official accolade by the police themselves. And I may have unwittingly added fuel to the fire after the third killing.'

'You mean, the interview you did with the *Sentinel Times*?'

'Yeah. My suggestion that it was possible there were two killers at work will have made him angry that he wasn't being acknowledged as the master of his craft.'

'Dear God,' Carol said, torn between revulsion and fascination. 'So he went out and stalked a police officer so we'd take him seriously?'

'It's a possibility. Of course, it can't have been just any police officer. Even though making his point to the powers that be is important to Handy Andy, the prime directive is still to go for victims who fulfil his very personal criteria.'

Carol frowned. 'So what you're saying is that there's something about Connolly that makes him different from most other coppers?'

'Looks like it.'

'Maybe it's the sexuality thing,' Carol mused. 'I mean, there aren't many gays in the force. And those that there are tend to be so deep in the closet you could mistake them for a clothes hanger.'

'Whoa,' Tony laughed, holding up his hands as if to fend her off. 'No theorizing without data. We don't know yet whether Damien was gay. What might be useful, though, is to find out what shifts Damien worked recently. Say, the last two months. That'll give us some idea of the times he was at home, which might help the officers who'll be questioning his neighbours. Also, we should be asking around the other officers on his relief, to check out whether he always left alone, or if he ever gave anyone a lift home. We need to find out everything there is to know about Damien Connolly both as a man and as a bobby.'

Carol pulled out her notebook and scribbled a reminder to herself. 'Shifts,' she muttered.

'There's something else this tells us about Handy Andy,' Tony said slowly, reaching for the idea that had just swum into his consciousness.

Carol looked up, her eyes alert. 'Go on,' she said.

'He's very, very good at what he does,' Tony said flatly. 'Think about it. A police officer is a trained observer. Even the thickest plod is a lot more alert to what's going on around them than the average member of the public. Now, from what you've told me, Damien Connolly was a bright lad. He was a collator, which means he was even more on the ball than most officers. As I understand it, a collator's job is to act like the station's walking encyclopaedia. It's all very well having all the local information about known villains and MOs on file cards, but if the collator isn't sharp, then the system's worthless, am I right?'

'Spot on. A good collator is worth half a dozen bodies on the ground,' Carol said. 'And by all accounts, Connolly was one of the best.'

Tony leaned back in his chair. 'So if Handy Andy stalked Damien without setting any alarm bells ringing, he must be bloody good. Face it, Carol, if somebody was tailing you on a regular basis, you'd pick them up, wouldn't you?'

'I bloody hope so,' Carol said drily. 'But I'm a woman. Maybe we're just a bit more on our guard than the blokes.'

Tony shook his head. 'I think a copper as smart as Damien would have noticed anything other than a very professional tail.'

'You mean we might be looking for someone who's in the Job?' Carol demanded, her voice rising as she spoke the unthinkable.

'It's a possibility. I can't pitch it more strongly than that till I've seen all the evidence. Is that it?' Tony asked, nodding towards the cardboard box Carol had deposited by the door of his office.

'That's some of it. There's another box and some folders of photographs still in the car. And that's after some serious editing.'

Tony pulled a face. 'Rather you than me. Shall we go and fetch it, then?'

Carol stood up. 'Why don't you get started while I go and get the rest?'

'It's the photographs I want to look at first, so I might as well come and help,' he said.

'Thanks,' Carol said.

In the lift, they stood on opposite sides, both conscious of the other's physical presence. 'That's not a Bradfield accent,' Tony remarked as the doors slid shut. If he was going to work successfully with Carol Jordan, he needed to know what made her tick, personally as well as professionally. The more he could find out about her, the better.

'I thought you said you left the detective work to us?'

'We're good at stating the obvious, us psychologists. Isn't that what our critics on the force say?'

'Touché. I'm from Warwick, originally. Then university at Manchester and into the Met on the fast track. And you? I'm not great on accents, but I can spot you're a Northerner, though you don't sound like Bradfield either,' Carol replied.

'Born and bred in Halifax. London University, followed by a DPhil at Oxford. Eight years in special hospitals. Eighteen months ago, the Home Office head-hunted me to run this feasibility study.' Give a little to get a lot, Tony thought wryly. Who exactly was probing whom?

'So we're both outsiders,' Carol said.

'Maybe that's why John Brandon chose you to liaise with me.'

The lift doors slid open and they walked through the underground car park to the visitors' parking area where Carol had left her car. Tony hefted the cardboard box out of the boot. 'You must be stronger than you look,' he gasped.

Carol picked up the folders of photographs and grinned. 'And I'm a black belt in Cluedo,' she said.

'Listen, Tony, if this maniac is in the Job, what sort of stuff would you expect to find?'

'I shouldn't have said that. I was theorizing ahead of data, and I don't want you to place any weight on it, OK? Strike it from the record,' Tony panted.

'OK, but what would the signs be?' she persisted.

They were back in the lift before Tony answered her. 'Behaviour that exhibits a familiarity with police and forensic procedure,' he said. 'But in itself, that proves nothing. There are so many true-crime books and TV detectives around these days that anyone could know that sort of stuff. Look, Carol, please put it out of your head. We need to keep an open mind. Otherwise the work we do is valueless.'

Carol stifled a sigh. 'OK. But will you tell me if you still think that way after you've seen the evidence? Because if it's more than a slim possibility, we might need to rethink the way we're dealing with the enquiry.'

'I promise,' he said. The lift doors slid open, as if placing their own full stop on the conversation.

Back in the office, Tony slid the first set of photographs out of their folders. 'Before you start, could you fill me in on how you want to pursue this?' Carol asked, notebook at the ready.

'I'll go through all the pictures first, then I'll ask you to take me through the investigation so far. When we've done that, I'll work through the paperwork myself. After that, what I usually do is draw up a profile of each of the victims. Then we have another session with these,' he said, brandishing his forms. 'And then I walk out on the high wire and do a profile of the offender. Does that sound reasonable to you?'

'Sounds fine. How long is all that likely to take?'

Tony frowned. 'It's hard to say. A few days, certainly. However, Handy Andy seems to work on an eight-week cycle, and there's no sign that he's accelerating. That's unusual in itself, by the way. Once I've studied the material I'll have a better idea of how in control he is, but I think we've probably got a bit of time to spare before he kills again. Having said that, he may well have already selected his next victim, so we've got to make sure that we keep any progress we make well away from the press. The last thing we want is to be the catalyst for him speeding up the process.'

Carol groaned. 'Are you always this optimistic?'

'It goes with the territory. Oh, and one more thing? If you develop any suspects, I'd prefer not to know anything about them at this stage – there's a danger that my subconscious will alter the profile accordingly.'

Carol snorted. 'We should be so lucky.'

'That bad, is it?'

'Oh, we've pulled in anybody who's got form for indecent assault or violent offences against gay men, but none of them looks even a remote possibility.'

Tony pulled a sympathetic face then picked up the photographs of Adam Scott's corpse and slowly started going through them. He picked up a pen and moved his A4 pad nearer to him. He glanced up at Carol. 'Coffee?' he asked. 'I meant to ask earlier, but I was too interested in what we were talking about.'

Carol felt like a co-conspirator. She had been enjoying their conversation too, in spite of a twinge of guilt that multiple murders shouldn't be a source of pleasure. Talking with Tony was like talking to an equal who had no axe to grind, whose primary concern was finding a path to the truth rather than a way to boost the ego. It was something she'd missed on this case so far. 'Me too,' she admitted. 'I'm probably approaching the point where coffee is a necessity. Do you want me to go and fetch some?'

'Good God, no!' Tony laughed. 'That's not what you're here for. Wait there, I'll be right back. How do you take yours?'

'Black, no sugar. In an intravenous drip, preferably.'

Tony took a large Thermos jug out of his filing cabinet and disappeared. He was back inside five minutes with two steaming mugs and the jug. He handed Carol a mug and gestured towards the Thermos. 'I filled it up. I figured we might be some time. Help yourself as and when.'

Carol took a grateful sip. 'Will you marry me?' she asked, mock romantic.

Tony laughed again, to cover the lurch of apprehension that shifted his stomach, a familiar response to even the most idle of flirtations. 'You won't be saying that in a few days' time,' he said evasively, turning his attention back to the photographs.

'Victim number one. Adam Scott,' he said softly, making a note on his pad. He went through the photographs one by one, then went back to the beginning. The first picture showed a city square, tall Georgian houses on one side, a modern office block on a second and a row of shops, bars and restaurants on the third. In the centre of the square was a public garden, crossed by two diagonal paths. In the middle was an ornate Victorian drinking fountain. The park was surrounded by a three feet high brick wall. Along two sides of the garden was deep shrubbery. The ambience was slightly seedy, the stucco of the houses peeling in places. He imagined himself standing on the corner, taking in the view, smelling the fumid city air mixed with the stink of stale alcohol and fast food, hearing the night sounds. The rev of engines, the sound of high heels on pavements, occasional laughs and cries borne on the wind, the twitter of starlings, conned out of sleep by the sodium light of streetlamps. Where did you stand, Andy? Where did you watch your ground from? What did you see? What did you hear? What did you *feel*? Why here?

The second photograph showed a section of the wall and the shrubbery from the street side. The photograph was clear enough for Tony to make out the little iron squares on the top of the wall, which were all that remained of railings that had presumably been removed during the war to make guns and shells. A section of the bushes showed broken branches and crumpled leaves. The third shot showed the body of a man, face down on the earth, his limbs splayed at strange angles. Tony let himself be drawn into the picture, trying to put himself in Handy Andy's shoes. How did it feel, Andy? Were you proud? Were you scared? Were you exultant? Did you feel a spasm of regret at abandoning the object of your desire? How long did you allow yourself to drink in this sight, this strange tableau that you created? Did the sound of footsteps move you on? Or did you not care?

Tony looked up. Carol was watching him. To his surprise, for once he didn't feel uncomfortable to have a woman's eyes on him. Perhaps because their relationship had so firm a professional base, but without direct competition. The tension in him relaxed a notch. 'The place where the body was found. Tell me about it.'

'Crompton Gardens. It's at the heart of Temple Fields, where the gay village and the red-light district overlap. It's poorly lit at night, mostly because the streetlights are always being vandalized by the sex vendors who want a bit of darkness to cover their activities. There's a lot of sex goes on in Crompton Gardens, in the bushes and on the park benches under the trees, in the office doorways, in the basement areas of the houses. Rent, prostitution and casual pick-ups. There are people around throughout the night, but they're not the sort who are going to come forward about anything unusual they might have seen, even if they noticed it,' Carol explained while Tony took notes.

'The weather?' he asked.

'Dry night, though the ground was pretty damp.'

Tony returned to the photographs. The body was shot from various angles. Then, following the removal of the body, the dumping ground was pictured in close-up sections. There were no visible footprints, but some scraps of black plastic were lying under the body. He pointed at them with the tip of his pen. 'Do we know what these are?'

'Bradfield Metropolitan Council bin bags. Standard issue to businesses, blocks of flats . . . anywhere wheelie bins are inappropriate. That grade of bag has been in use now for the last two years. There's apparently nothing to indicate whether they were already there or if they were dumped at the same time as the body,' Carol said.

Tony raised his eyebrows. 'You seem to have assimilated a helluva lot of detail since yesterday afternoon.'

Carol grinned. 'It's tempting to pretend I'm Super-woman, but I have to confess that I'd already made a point of finding out what I could about the other two enquiries. I was convinced they were linked, even if my boss wasn't. And in fairness to my colleagues, the inspectors leading the other two enquiries had an open mind. They didn't object to me making the occasional trawl through their stuff. Ploughing through it all overnight just refreshed my memory, that's all.'

'You've been up all night?'

'Like you said, it goes with the territory. I'll be fine till about four this afternoon. Then it'll hit me like a sledgehammer,' Carol admitted.

'Message received and understood,' Tony replied, turning back to the photographs. He moved on to the series of shots from the postmortem. The body lay on its back on the white slab, the hideous wounds visible for the first time. Tony went slowly through the whole sequence of pictures, sometimes flicking back to previous shots. When he closed his eyes, he could picture Adam Scott's intact body, slowly breaking out in wounds and bruises like alien blooms. He could almost conjure up the slo-mo vision of the hands that brought flesh to such a pass. After a few moments, he opened his eyes and spoke again. 'These bruises on the neck and chest – what did the pathologist say?'

'Suck marks. Like love bites.'

A head descending, predatory, a bizarre parody of love. 'And these sections of the neck and chest. Three places where the flesh has been cut away?' Tony asked distantly.

'They were removed postmortem. Maybe he likes to eat them?'

'Maybe,' Tony said doubtfully. 'Was there any trace of bruising in the remaining tissues, can you remember?'

'I think there was.' Carol's surprise showed in her voice.

Tony nodded. 'I'll check the pathologist's report. He's a clever lad, our Handy Andy. My first reaction is that these aren't souvenirs, or indications of cannibalism. I think they might have been bite marks. But Handy Andy knows enough about forensic dentistry to realize that identifiable bite marks would be enough to put him away. So once the frenzy's spent, he's cooled down and removed the evidence. These cuts to the genitals – pre or postmortem?'

'Post. The pathologist remarked that they seemed quite tentative.'

Tony gave a small smile of satisfaction. 'Did the pathologist say what has caused the trauma to the limbs? The shots at the site look like a rag doll.'

Carol sighed. 'He didn't want to be pushed to an official conclusion. All four limbs were dislocated, and some of his vertebrae were out of alignment. He said . . .' She paused and imitated the pathologist's portentous delivery, '"Don't quote me, but I'd expect to see injuries like this after the Spanish Inquisition had put someone on the rack."'

'The rack? Shit, we're really dealing with a messy mind here. OK. Next set. Paul Gibbs. This one's yours, I think?' Tony asked as he replaced Adam Scott's photographs and took out the contents of the second folder. He repeated the process he'd gone through before. 'So where is this scene in relation to the first one?' Tony asked.

'Hang on a minute. I'll show you.' Carol opened one of the boxes and picked out the large-scale map she'd thought to bring with her. She unfolded it and spread it out on the floor. Tony got up from his desk and crouched down beside her. She was instantly aware of the smell of him, a mixture of shampoo and his own faint, animal scent. No macho aftershave, no cologne. She watched his pale, square hands on the map, the short, almost stubby fingers, with their neatly trimmed nails and a sparse scattering of fine black hairs on the bottom section of each finger. Appalled, she felt a stirring of desire. You're pathetic as an adolescent, she savagely chided herself. Like a teenager who fancies the first teacher who says anything nice about your work. Grow up, Jordan!

Under the guise of pointing out the sites on the map, Carol inched away. 'Crompton Gardens is here,' she said. 'Canal Street is about half a mile away, over here. And the Queen of Hearts pub is just along here, about midway between the two.'

'Is it safe to assume he knows the area well?' Tony asked, making his own mental map of the murder sites.

'I think so. Crompton Gardens is a pretty obvious dumping ground, but the other two imply quite a high degree of familiarity with Temple Fields.' Carol sat back on her haunches, trying to work out if the pattern of sites implied an approach from one specific direction.

'I need to take a look at the scenes. Preferably around the time the bodies were dumped. Do we know when that was?' Tony said.

'We don't know about Adam. Estimated time of death is an hour either side of midnight, so not before

95

then. With Paul, we know the doorway was clear just after three a.m. Gareth's time of death is estimated at between seven and ten p.m. the evening before his body was found. And with Damien, the yard was clear at half past eleven,' Carol recited, closing her eyes to recall the information.

Tony found himself staring at her face, glad of the freedom her shuttered eyelids gave him. Even without the animation of her blue eyes, he could see that she'd be classified beautiful. Oval face, broad forehead, clear pale skin, and that thick blonde hair, cut slightly shaggy. A strong, determined mouth. A furrow that appeared between her brows when she concentrated. And his appreciation was as clinical as if she were a photograph in a casebook. Why was it that, faced with a woman any normal man would regard as attractive, something in him closed down? Was it because he refused to allow himself to feel the first stirrings that might lead him to a place where he was no longer in control, where humiliation lurked? Carol's eyes opened, registering surprise when she saw him watching her.

He felt his ears tingle with a blush and turned back to the map. 'So he's a night owl,' he said abruptly. 'I'd like to take a look at the area tonight, if I can. Maybe you can get someone else to show me round so you can catch up on your sleep.'

Carol shook her head. 'No. If we can get through here by five, I'll go home and grab a few hours' shut-eye. I'll pick you up around midnight and we can go then. Is that OK?' she asked, belatedly.

'Perfect,' Tony said, getting to his feet and retreating behind his desk. 'As long as you don't mind.' He picked up the photographs and forced himself back behind Handy Andy's eyes. 'He's made a real mess of this one, hasn't he?'

'Paul's the only one who's been beaten up like this. Gareth has cuts to his face, but nothing as extreme. Paul's face has been smashed to a pulp – broken nose, broken teeth, broken cheekbone, dislocated jaw. The anal injuries are horrendous as well; he's been partially disembowelled. The degree of violence is one of the reasons why the Super felt we were looking at a different perpetrator. Also, none of his limbs are dislocated, unlike the other three.'

'This is the one the papers said was covered up with bin bags?'

Carol nodded. 'Same variety as the scraps found under Adam's body.'

They moved on to Gareth Finnegan. 'I'm going to have to give some serious thought to this one,' he said. 'He's changed his pattern in at least two significant ways. First, the dumping ground moves from Temple Fields to Carlton Park. It's still a gay cruising area, but it's an aberration.' He stopped himself short and gave a hollow laugh. 'Listen to me. As if his whole behaviour isn't wildly aberrant. The second thing is his letter and video to the *Sentinel Times*. Why did he decide to announce this body and none of the others?'

'I've been thinking about that,' Carol said. 'And I wondered if it had something to do with the fact that it could have lain there for days, even weeks, otherwise.'

Tony made a note on his pad and gave her the thumbs-up sign with the other hand. 'These wounds to the hands and feet. I know it sounds off the wall, but it almost looks like he was crucified.'

'The pathologist wasn't crazy about going on the record with that one either. But the hand wounds, coupled with the dislocation of both shoulders, makes crucifixion a conclusion that's hard to resist, especially when you remember this probably happened on Christmas Day.' Carol got to her feet, rubbing the sleep out of her eyes. She couldn't manage to stifle a jaw-cracking yawn. She paced round the small office, shrugging her shoulders to loosen the taut muscles. 'Sick bastard,' she muttered.

'The genital mutilations are getting more severe,' Tony observed. 'He's virtually castrated this one. And the fatal wounds, the cutting of the throat. That's getting deeper too.'

'Does that tell us anything?' Carol asked, almost unintelligible through another yawn.

'Like your pathologist, I'm reluctant to speculate just yet,' Tony said. He moved on to the final set of pictures. For the first time, Carol saw his professional mask slip. Horror swept across Tony's face, widening his eyes, drawing his lips back in a hissed intake of breath. She wasn't surprised. When they'd turned Damien Connolly over, a six-foot rugby-playing detective had keeled over in a dead faint. Even the experienced police pathologist had turned away momentarily, visibly struggling not to be sick.

Rigor mortis had frozen Damien Connolly's limbs in a parody of human gesture. The dislocated joints stuck out at crazy angles. But there was more, and worse. His penis had been severed and thrust into his mouth. His torso was branded from chest to groin in a bizarre, random pattering of starburst burns, none more than half an inch across.

'Dear God,' Tony breathed.

'He's really getting the hang of this, isn't he?' Carol said bitterly. 'Takes a pride in his work, doesn't he?'

Tony said nothing, forcing himself to study the appalling photographs as closely as he'd done with the previous sets. 'Carol,' he eventually said. 'Has anybody come up with any theories as to what he's used to make these burn marks?'

'Not a one,' she said.

'They're odd,' he said. 'The patterns vary. It's not like he's used some random object and kept on using it. There are at least five different shapes. Have you got anybody who can do computer pattern analysis? To see if there's any hidden message here? There must be dozens of these bloody burns!'

Carol rubbed her eyes again. 'I don't know. Me and computers are about as compatible as the Prince and Princess of Wales. I'll ask when I go back to the office. And if we don't have someone, I'll ask my brother.'

'Your brother?'

'Michael's a computer genius. He works in games software development. You want a pattern analysed, manipulated, turned into a shoot-'em-up arcade game, he's your man.'

'And he can keep his mouth shut?'

'If he couldn't, he wouldn't be doing the job he does. Millions of pounds depend on his company getting on the next rung of the ladder before anybody else. Believe me, he knows when to button his lip.'

Tony smiled. 'I didn't mean to sound offensive.'

'You didn't.'

Tony sighed. 'I wish to God I'd been brought in sooner on this. Handy Andy's not going to stop here.

He's too much in love with his work. Look at these pictures. This bastard's going to carry on capturing and torturing and killing until you catch him. Carol, this guy's a career killer.'

I walked boldly up the path and pressed Adam's doorbell. In the seconds before he answered the chime, I composed my face into what I believed was an apologetic smile. I could see the fuzzy outline of his head and shoulders as he walked down the hall. Then the door opened and we were face to face. He half smiled quizzically. As if he'd never noticed me before in his life.

'I'm sorry to bother you,' I said. 'Only my car's broken down, and I don't know where there's a pay phone, so I wondered if I might use your phone to call the AA? I'll pay for the call, of course . . .' I let my voice trail away.

His smile broadened and relaxed, his dark eyes crinkling at the corners. 'No problem. Come in.' He stepped back and I moved inside the door. He gestured down the hall. 'There's a phone in the study. Just on the right there.'

I moved slowly down the hall, ears alert for the sound of the front door closing behind me. As the lock snapped back into place, he added, 'There's nothing worse, is there?'

'I'll just look up the number,' I said, pausing in the doorway to reach in my backpack. Adam kept on walking, so that when I pulled out the Mace spray, he was only a

couple of feet away from me. It couldn't have been more perfect. I let him have it full in the face.

He roared in pain and stumbled back against the wall, hands clawing at his face. I moved in swiftly. One foot between his ankles, hands on his shoulders, a quick twist and down he went, face crushed into the carpet, gasping for breath. I was down on top of him in seconds, gripping one wrist and twisting his arm up his back while I snapped the handcuff over it. He was struggling against me by now, tears streaming down his face, but I managed to grab his other flailing arm and snap the other half of the cuffs on it.

His legs were thrashing under me, but my weight was enough to keep him pinned to the floor while I took a ziplock plastic bag from my backpack. I opened it, extracted a pad soaked in chloroform and clamped it over his nose and mouth. The sickly odour drifted upwards into my nostrils, making me feel slightly light-headed and queasy. I hoped the chloroform hadn't gone off; I'd had the bottle for a couple of years, ever since I'd stolen it from the dispensary on a Soviet ship where I'd spent the night with the first officer.

Adam struggled even harder when he felt the cold compress cut off his access to the air, but within minutes his legs stopped their pointless thrashing. I waited a little longer, just to be on the safe side, then I rolled off and fastened his legs together with surgical tape. I returned the chloroform pad to its secure bag, then I taped Adam's mouth shut.

I stood up and took a deep breath. So far, so good. Next, I pulled on a pair of latex gloves and took stock. I am familiar with the theory of the French forensic scientist Edmond Locard, first demonstrated in a murder trial in 1912, that every contact leaves a trace; a criminal will always take something away from the scene of his crime and leave something behind. With this in mind, I had carefully chosen my wardrobe for today. I was wearing Levi 501s, the same brand I'd seen Adam wear often. I'd topped it with a baggy V-necked cricket sweater, the exact double of one I'd watched him buy in Marks and Spencer a couple of weeks before. Any stray fibres I left behind would inevitably be ascribed to the contents of Adam's own wardrobe.

I took a quick look round the study, pausing by his answering machine. It was one of the old-fashioned ones, with a single cassette tape. I opened the machine and helped myself to the tape. It would be nice to have a memory of his voice sounding normal; I knew that the soundtrack on the video wouldn't have that same relaxed quality.

The door to the garage was locked. I headed off up the stairs, where I found the jacket of his suit tossed over the back of a chair in the kitchen diner. The bunch of keys was in the left-hand pocket. Back downstairs, I opened the garage door and unlocked the hatchback of his two-year-old Ford Escort. Then I went back for Adam. He had, of course, come round. His eyes were filled with panic, muffled grunts came from behind the gag. I smiled down at him as I pressed the chloroform pad over his nose again. This time, of course, he couldn't struggle effectively at all.

I pulled him into a sitting position, then brought a chair through from the study. I managed to get him on to the chair, and from there I was able to sling him over my shoulder and stagger through into the garage. I dumped him in the luggage space, and slammed the tailgate shut. Not a trace of his body was visible.

I checked my watch. Just after six. It would be another hour till it was dark enough to be certain none of the neighbours passing casually would notice a stranger driving out of Adam's garage. I filled the time by browsing through his life. Packets of photographs revealed friends, a family

Christmas dinner. I would have fitted into this life perfectly. We could have had it all, if he hadn't been such a fool.

I was startled out of my reverie by the phone. I let it ring, and went through to the kitchen. I helped myself to a bottle of creme cleanser and a cloth and carefully washed down all the paintwork in the hall. I put the used cloth in my backpack, then fetched the vacuum cleaner. I went over the entire hall slowly and carefully, erasing all traces of the struggle from the hard-wearing Berber carpet. I trailed the vac behind me, right into the garage, where I left it in a corner, looking as if it had always lived there. Satisfied I'd removed all traces of me, I climbed into Adam's car, pressed the remote-control button on his keyring and started the engine as the garage door rose smoothly before me.

I shut the door behind me, and drove off. I could hear muffled noises from the back of the car. I raked around in the glove box till I found a Wet, Wet, Wet cassette. I shoved it into the player and turned the volume up high. I sang along with the music as I drove out of the city and on to the moors.

I'd been worried that Adam's car might not make it all the way up the track, and I'd been right. About half a mile from home, the road became too overgrown and rutted. With a sigh, I got out and walked up to collect the wheelbarrow. When I opened the tailgate to tip him into the barrow, his eyes were wide and staring. His muffled calls were wasted on me, however. I dragged him unceremoniously out of the car and into the barrow. It was a hard half-mile up the track, since his constant struggling made steering more difficult. Luckily, Auntie Doris had had the foresight to buy a proper builder's barrow, one with two wheels in front.

When we reached the farmhouse, I opened the trapdoor. The cellar below looked dark and welcoming. Adam's eyes widened in terror. I stroked his soft hair and said, 'Welcome to the pleasure dome.'

5

As to . . . the mob of newspaper readers, they are
pleased with anything, provided it is bloody enough.
But the mind of sensibility requires something more.

After he'd seen Carol to her car, Tony walked across
the campus to the general stores and bought a copy of
the evening paper. If publicity was what Handy Andy
craved, he'd finally achieved it. Fear and loathing
stalked the pages of the *Bradfield Evening Sentinel Times*.
Five of them, to be precise. Pages 1, 2, 3, 24 and 25, plus
an editorial, were devoted to the Queer Killer. If the
nickname was anything to judge by, the police were
already leaking like a Cabinet committee.

'You're not going to like being called the Queer
Killer, are you, Andy?' Tony said softly to himself as
he walked back to his office. Back behind his desk,
he studied the paper. Penny Burgess had had a field
day. The front page screamed, QUEER KILLER STRIKES
AGAIN! in banner headlines. In smaller headline type,
readers were told, POLICE ADMIT SERIAL KILLER STALKS
CITY. Beneath was a lurid account of the discovery of
Damien Connolly's body, and a photograph of him at

his passing-out parade. The turnover on pages two and three was a sensationalist summary of the three previous cases, complete with sketch map. 'Bricks without straw, right enough,' Tony said to himself as he flicked through to the centre spread. GAYS TERRIFIED BY QUEER KILLER MONSTER left the reader in no doubt who the *Sentinel Times* had decided were at risk. The copy focused on the supposed hysteria gripping Bradfield's gay community, complete with interior shots of cafés, bars and clubs that made the scene look seedy enough to pander to the readers' prejudices.

'Oh boy,' Tony said. 'You're really going to hate this, Andy.' He turned back to the editorial.

'At last,' he read, 'police have admitted what many of us have believed for some time. There is a serial killer on the loose in Bradfield, his target the young, single men who frequent the city's sordid gay bars.

'It's a disgrace that the police have not warned the city's homosexuals to be on their guard before now. In the twilight world of anonymous pick-ups and casual sex, it cannot be difficult for this predatory monster to find willing victims. The police's silence can only have made it easier for the killer.

'Their reluctance to speak out has probably increased the gay community's existing suspicion of the police, making them fear that the authorities value the lives of gay men less than those of other members of the community.

'Just as it took the murders of "innocent" women rather than prostitutes to make the police pay full attention to the Yorkshire Ripper, it is wrong that a police officer has had to be murdered before Bradfield Metropolitan Police takes this Queer Killer seriously.

'In spite of this, we urge the gay community to cooperate fully with the police. And we demand that the police investigate these horrific killings diligently and with compassion for the concerns of Bradfield's homosexuals. The sooner this vicious killer is caught, the safer we all will be.'

'The usual mixture of self-righteousness, indignation and unrealistic demands,' Tony said to the Devil's Ivy on his windowsill. He clipped the articles and spread them across the desk. He switched on his micro-cassette recorder and spoke.

'*Bradfield Evening Sentinel Times*, February 27th. At last, Handy Andy has made the big time. I'm wondering how important that is to him. One of the tenets of profiling serial offenders is that they crave the oxygen of publicity. But this time, I'm not so sure he's too bothered about that. There were no messages after the first two killings, neither of which received that much publicity after the initial discovery of the bodies. And although there was a message directing the police to the third body via a newspaper, that note made no claims about the earlier killings. I had puzzled over that until Inspector Carol Jordan offered an alternative explanation for the note and accompanying video, namely that without direction, the body may have lain undiscovered for some time. So, while Handy Andy may not be obsessive about creating headlines and panic, it's clear he wants the bodies found while they are still recognizably his work.' He switched off the cassette with a sigh. Although he'd turned his back on the academic circus years before, he couldn't escape his training; every stage of the process had to be on record. The prospect of this investigation providing the raw material for articles or even a book was something Tony found hard to resist.

'I'm a cannibal,' he said to the plant. 'Sometimes I disgust myself.' He shovelled the clippings together and tucked them into his press-cuttings folder. He opened the boxes and took out the stacks of document wallets they contained. Carol had labelled them all neatly. Fluent capitals, Tony noted. A woman comfortable with the written word.

Each victim had a pathology report and a preliminary forensic report. The witness statements were divided into three groups: Background (victim), Witness (scene of crime) and Miscellaneous. Selecting the Background (victim) files, he walked his wheeled chair across to the table where his personal computer stood. When he'd arrived at Bradfield, the university had offered him a terminal linked into their network. He'd declined, not wanting to waste time learning a new set of protocols when he was perfectly at home with his own PC. Now, he was glad he didn't have to add data security to the list of worries that kept him awake at nights.

Tony called up the customized software that would allow him to make comparisons between the victims, and started the long slog of inputting the data.

Five minutes in the Scargill Street station was enough to make Carol wish she'd gone straight home. To get to the office she'd been allocated for the duration of the investigation, she had to walk the length of the main squad room. Copies of the evening paper were strewn over half the desks, mocking her with their thick black headlines. Bob Stansfield was standing with a couple of DCs halfway down the room and he called to her as she passed. 'The good doctor knocked off already, has he?'

'From what I've seen of the good doctor, Bob, he could give some of our bosses a few lessons in working overtime,' Carol said, wishing she could think of some sharper putdown. Doubtless it would come to her hours later in the shower. On the other hand, maybe it was as well she hadn't come up with something too devastating. Better not alienate the lads any more than her assignment had already done. She stopped and smiled. 'Anything new?' she asked.

Stansfield detached himself from his juniors, saying, 'Right, lads, get on with it.' He moved over to Carol's side and said, 'Not as such. The HOLMES team are working flat out, smacking all we've got so far into the computer, see what correlations they can come up with. Cross has ordered us to pull in all the nonces again. He's convinced one of them's our best bet.'

Carol shook her head. 'Waste of time.'

'You said it. This bastard's not got form, I'd put money on it. Kevin's got a team going out tonight to try something a bit different, though,' he added, taking out and lighting his last cigarette. He tossed the packet in a nearby bin, an expression of disgust on his face. 'If we don't get a fucking break soon, I'm going to have to put in for a raise to cover my bloody nicotine consumption.'

'Me, I'm drinking so much coffee I've got a permanent case of the jitterbug boogies,' Carol said ruefully. 'So what's this idea of Kevin's?' Gently does it. First the rapport, then the question. Funny how getting information out of colleagues followed the same rules as interrogating suspects.

'He's got an undercover team going out on the gay scene, concentrating on the clubs and pubs with a reputation for S&M.' Stansfield snorted. 'They've all been down Traffic this avvy, scrounging leather trousers off the bike boys.'

'It's worth a try,' Carol said.

'Yeah, well let's hope Kevin's not sending in a bunch of closet pansies like Damien Connolly turned out to be,' Stansfield said. 'Last thing we want is a bunch of CID fairies ending up wearing their own handcuffs.'

Carol refused to dignify the comment with a reply and moved off towards her office. She'd got her hand on the door when Cross's voice boomed down the room. 'Inspector Jordan? Get your body in here.'

Carol closed her eyes and counted to three. 'Coming, sir,' she said cheerfully, turning back and walking the length of the room to Cross's temporary office. He'd only been in there a day, but already he'd marked it like a tomcat spraying his territory. The room reeked of cigarette smoke. Half-drunk polystyrene cups of coffee strategically placed on window ledge and desk top had butts floating in them. There was even a girlie calendar on the wall, proof that sexism was alive and well and working in the advertising industry. Hadn't they realized *yet* that it was the women who stood in the supermarkets deciding which brand of vodka to buy?

Leaving the door open in a bid for air, Carol walked into Cross's office and said, 'Sir?'

'What's Wonder Boy come up with then?'

'It's a bit early for conclusions, sir,' she said brightly. 'He's got to read through all the reports I copied for him.'

Cross grunted. 'Oh aye, I forgot he's a bloody professor.' He spat the word out sarcastically. 'Everything in writing, eh? Kevin's got some more stuff on the Connolly business; you'll have to catch up with him. Was there anything else, Inspector?' he asked belligerently, as if she were the one who had imposed herself on him.

'Dr Hill has a suggestion, sir. About the burn marks on PC Connolly's body. He wondered if there was anyone on the HOLMES team who could do statistical pattern analysis.'

'What the bloody hell is statistical pattern analysis?' Cross said, dumping the end of his cigarette into a coffee cup.

'I think it means –'

'Never mind, never mind,' Cross interrupted. 'Go and see if anybody down there knows what the hell you're on about.'

'Yes, sir. Oh, and sir? If we can't do it here, my brother works in computers. I'm sure he could do it for us.'

Cross stared at her, his expression unreadable for once. When he spoke, he was all affability. 'Fine. Go ahead. Mr Brandon gave you carte blanche, after all.'

So that's what a passing buck sounds like, Carol thought as she headed downstairs to the HOLMES room. A five-minute conversation with a harassed

Inspector Dave Woolcott confirmed what she'd already suspected. The HOLMES team had neither the software nor the expertise to carry out the analysis Tony wanted. As Carol walked down to the canteen in search of Kevin Matthews, she hoped Michael could deliver in complete confidence. Keeping quiet about technological developments was very different from resisting the urge to gossip about a high-profile murder enquiry. If he let her down, she could kiss goodbye to a future outside Personnel.

Kevin was hunched alone over a cup of coffee, a plate with the remains of a fry-up next to him. Carol pulled out the chair opposite him. 'Mind if I join you?'

'Be my guest,' Kevin said. He looked up and gave her the ghost of a grin, pushing his unruly ginger curls back from his forehead. 'How's it going?'

'Probably a lot easier than it is for you and Bob.'

'What's this Home Office boffin like, then?'

Carol considered for a moment. 'He's cautious. He's quick, he's sharp, but he's not a know-all, and he doesn't seem to want to tell us how to do our job. It's really interesting watching him work. He looks at things from a different perspective.'

'How do you mean?' Kevin asked, looking genuinely interested.

'When we look at a crime, we look for physical clues, leads, things that point us to who we might want to talk to or where we might want to look. When *he* looks at a crime, he's not interested in all that stuff. He wants to know why the physical clues happened the way they did so he can work out who did it. It's as if we use information to move us forward

113

and he uses it to move him backwards. Does that make sense?'

Kevin frowned. 'I think so. You think he's got what it takes?'

Carol shrugged. 'It's early days yet. But yeah, on first impressions, I'd say he's got something to offer.'

Kevin grinned. 'Something to offer the investigation or something to offer you?'

'Piss off, Kevin,' Carol said, tired of the innuendo that followed her round the job. 'Unlike some, I never shit on my own doorstep.'

Kevin looked momentarily uneasy. 'Only joking, Carol, honest.'

'Jokes are supposed to be funny.'

'OK, OK, sorry. What's he like to work with, though? Nice bloke, or what?'

Carol spoke slowly, measuring her words. 'Considering he spends his working life getting inside the minds of psychopaths, he seems pretty normal. There's something quite . . . closed off about him. He keeps his distance. Doesn't give much away. But he treats me like an equal, not like some thick plod. He's on our side, Kevin, and that's the main thing. I'd guess he's one of those workaholics who's more interested in getting the job done than anything else. And speaking of getting the job done, Popeye says you've turned something up on PC Connolly?'

Kevin sighed. 'For what it's worth. One of the neighbours came home from work at ten to six. She knows the time because the shipping forecast had just started on the car radio. Connolly was on his drive, closing the bonnet of his car. He had overalls on. The neighbour says he must have been working on the car, he was always at it. By the time the neighbour got out of her car and into the house, Damien was reversing his car into the garage. The same neighbour came out about an hour later on her way to a game of squash, and she noticed Connolly's car parked on the street. She was a bit surprised, because he never left the car sitting out, especially after dark. She also noticed that the light was on in Connolly's garage. And that's about the size of it.'

'Is it an integral garage?' Carol asked.

'No, but it's attached to the house, and there's a door from the garage leads into the kitchen.'

'So it looks like he was snatched from the house?'

Kevin shrugged. 'Who knows? There's no sign of a struggle. I spoke to one of the SOCOs who turned the place over, and he said not to hold our breath.'

'Sounds just like the first two.'

'That's what Bob says.' Kevin pushed his chair back. 'I better get weaving. We're going out on the town tonight.'

'I might bump into you later,' Carol said. 'Dr Hill wants a tour of the crime scenes at the sort of time when the bodies were dumped.'

Kevin got to his feet. 'Just don't let him talk to any strange men.'

Tony took the plastic container of lasagne out of the microwave and sat down at the breakfast bar in his kitchen. He'd input all the data that he could find on the four victims, then he'd transferred the files to a floppy disk so he could work on it at home while he waited for Carol to arrive. As soon as he'd reached the tram stop, he'd realized he was ravenous. Then he remembered he'd eaten nothing since his breakfast cereal. He'd been working with such concentration, he hadn't even noticed. He found the hunger curiously satisfactory. It meant he was too involved in what he was doing to be conscious of himself. He knew from long experience that his best work came when he lost self-consciousness, when he could immerse himself in the patterns of another human being, locked into that other's idiosyncratic logic, in tune with a different set of emotions.

He attacked the food with gusto, shovelling it down as quickly as possible so he could get to his computer and carry on with his victim profiles. There were still a couple of forkfuls left in the dish when the phone rang. With no pause for thought, Tony snatched up the phone. 'Hello?' he said cheerfully.

'Anthony,' the voice said. Tony dropped the fork, tipping the pasta out on the worktop.

'Angelica,' he said. He was back in his own world, anchored within his own head at the sound of her voice.

'Feeling more sociable today?' the sweet huskiness asked.

'I wasn't feeling anti-social yesterday. I just had things to do I couldn't ignore. And you distract me,' Tony said, wondering why he bothered to justify himself to her.

'That's the general plan,' she said. 'But I missed you, Anthony. I was so horny for you, and when you discarded me like an old sock, all my pleasure in the day was over.'

'Why do you do this with me?' he demanded. It was a question he'd asked before, but she had always deflected him.

'Because you deserve me,' the voice said. 'Because I want you more than anyone in the world. And because you don't have anyone else in your life to make you happy.'

It was the same old story. Cut off the question with some flannel. But tonight, Tony wanted answers, not flattery. 'What makes you think that?' he asked.

The voice chuckled softly. 'I know more about you than you can possibly dream. Anthony, you don't have to be alone any more.'

'What if I like being alone? Isn't it fair to assume that I'm alone because I want to be?'

'You don't look like a happy boy to me. Some days, you look like you need a hug more than anything in the world. Some days, you look like you haven't slept for more than a couple of hours. Anthony, I can bring you peace. Women have hurt you before, we both know that. But I won't. I can stop it hurting. I can make you sleep like a baby, you know that. All I want is to make you happy.' The voice was soothing, gentle.

Tony sighed. If only . . . 'I find that hard to believe,' he stalled. Right from the start of these conversations, part of him had wanted to slam the phone down on this exquisite torture. But the scientist in him wanted to hear what she had to say. And the damaged man inside had enough self-awareness to know he needed to be cured, and that this might just be the way. He reminded himself of his earlier resolve not to let her get under his skin, so that when the time came, he could walk away without pain.

'But you let me try.' The voice was so self-assured. She was confident of her power over him.

'I listen, don't I? I join in. I haven't put the phone down yet,' he said, forcing artificial warmth into his voice.

'Why don't you do just that? Why don't you put down this phone and go upstairs to your bedroom and pick up the extension there? So we can be comfortable?'

A cold stab of fear hit Tony in the chest. He struggled to frame the question professionally. Not, 'How do you know that?', but, 'What makes you think I've got a phone in the bedroom?'

There was a pause, so brief that Tony couldn't be certain he wasn't imagining it. 'Just guessing,' she said. 'I've got you sussed. You're the kind of man who has a phone by the bed.'

'Well guessed,' Tony said. 'OK. I'm going to put the phone down and I'll pick up in the bedroom.' He replaced the receiver and hurried through to his study, where he switched the answering machine over to 'record' mode. Then he picked up the phone again. 'Hello? I'm back,' he said.

'Are we sitting comfortably? Then I'll begin.' Again that low, sexy chuckle. 'We are going to have some real fun tonight. Wait till you hear what I've got lined up for you tonight. Oh, Anthony,' she said, her voice dropping almost to a whisper. 'I've been dreaming about you. Imagining your hands on my body, running your fingers over my skin.'

'What are you wearing?' Tony asked. It was, he knew, the standard question.

'What would you like me to be wearing? I have an extensive wardrobe.'

Tony bit back the crazy urge to say, 'Fishermen's

waders, a tutu and a rainmate.' He swallowed hard and said, 'Silk. You know how I like the feel of silk.'

'That's why you love my skin. I take a lot of trouble to keep myself in perfect condition. But just for you, I've covered some of my skin with silk. I'm wearing a pair of black silk French knickers and a sheer black silk camisole. Oh, I love the feeling of silk against my body. Oh, Anthony,' she groaned. 'The silk's rubbing against my nipples, gently, like your fingers would. Oh, my nipples are hard as rocks, sticking up, inflamed with you.'

In spite of himself, Tony began to feel the stirrings of interest. She was good, no two ways about it. Most of the women he'd heard on the chatlines had sounded stale and bored, their responses predictable and stereotypical. Nothing in their conversations had aroused anything other than scientific interest in him. But Angelica was different. For one thing, she sounded like she meant it.

She moaned softly. 'God, I'm wet,' she breathed. 'But you can't touch me yet, you've got to wait. Just lie back, that's a good boy. Oh, I love to undress you. I've got my hands under your shirt, my fingers are running over your chest, stroking you, touching you, feeling your nipples under my fingers. God, you're wonderful,' she sighed.

'That's nice,' Tony said, enjoying the caress of her voice.

'That's just the beginning. Now I'm straddling you, unbuttoning your shirt. I'm leaning over you, my nipples inside the silk brushing against your chest. Oh, Anthony!' her voice exclaimed in pleasure. 'You really are pleased to see me, aren't you? You're hard as a rock underneath me. Oh, I can't wait to get you inside me.'

Her words froze Tony. The erection he'd felt hardening inside his trousers died like a snowflake in a puddle. They were there again. 'I think I'm going to disappoint you,' he said, his voice cracking.

That sexy chuckle again. 'No way. You're already more than I dreamed. Oh, Anthony, touch me. Tell me what you want to do to me.'

Tony could find no words.

'Don't be shy, Anthony. There are no secrets between us, nowhere we can't go. Close your eyes, let the feelings flow. Touch my breasts, go on, suck my nipples, eat me, let me feel your hot wet mouth all over me.'

Tony groaned. This was almost more than he could bear, even in the interests of science.

Angelica's voice was more breathy now, as if her words were arousing her as much as they should have been arousing him. 'That's right, oh God, Anthony, that's wonderful. Oh-oh-oh,' she said in a shuddering moan. 'See, I told you I was wet. That's right, plunge your fingers deep into my cunt. Oh God, you're the best . . . Let me . . . let me, oh God, let me get at you.'

Tony heard the sound of a zipper down the phone line. 'Angelica . . .' he started to say. It was falling apart again, just as it always did, spiralling out of control like a wounded bird.

'Oh, Anthony, you're beautiful. That's the most beautiful cock I've ever seen. Oh, let me taste you . . .' Her voice tailed off with the sound of sucking.

The blood rushed to Tony's face in a sudden wave of shame and anger. He slammed the phone down and immediately took it off the hook again. Jesus, what kind of a man couldn't even get it up over the phone? And what kind of scientist couldn't divorce his own pathetic failings from the exercise of objective data collection?

The worst of it was, he recognized his own behaviour. How many times had he sat across the table from a multiple rapist, arsonist or killer and watched them reach the point in their reliving of events where they could no longer face themselves. Just like him, they closed down. They couldn't disconnect a phone, but they closed down just the same. Eventually, of course, with the right therapy, they breached the walls and managed to confront what had brought them there. That was the first step towards recovery. Part of Tony prayed that Angelica knew enough about the theory and practice of psychology to stick with him till he too could break down the barriers and stare into the face of whatever it was that had bred this sexual and emotional cripple.

But the other part of him hoped she'd never call again. Never mind 'no pain, no gain'. He just wanted no pain.

John Brandon scrupulously wiped his plate with the last piece of nan bread and smiled at his wife. 'That was great, Maggie,' he said.

'Mmm,' his son Andy agreed through a mouthful of lamb and aubergine curry.

Brandon shifted awkwardly in his chair. 'If it's all right with you, I think I'll pop back down to Scargill Street for an hour. Just to see how things are going.'

'I thought ranking officers like you didn't have

to work evenings,' Maggie said good-humouredly. 'I thought you said the troops didn't need you breathing down their necks?'

Brandon looked sheepish. 'I know. But I just want to see how the lads are going on.'

Maggie shook her head, a resigned smile on her face. 'I'd rather you went down and got it out of your system than you sat all night fidgeting in front of the telly.'

Karen perked up. 'Dad, if you're going back into town, can you drop me at Laura's? So we can work on our history project?'

Andy snorted. 'Work on how you're going to get off with Craig McDonald, more like.'

'You know nothing,' Karen huffed. 'Will you, Dad?'

Brandon got up from the table. 'Only if you're ready now. And I'll pick you up on my way back.'

'Oh, Dad,' Karen complained. 'You said you were only going to be gone an hour. That's not nearly long enough for us to do all we want to.'

It was Maggie Brandon's turn to snort with laughter. 'If your father's back before half past nine, I'll make Scotch pancakes for supper.'

Karen looked at each parent in turn, the anguish of choice written on her fourteen-year-old face. 'Dad?' she said. 'Can you pick me up by nine o'clock?'

Brandon grinned. 'Why do I feel like I've been stitched up?'

It was just after half past seven when Brandon arrived in the HOLMES room. Even that late, every terminal was occupied. The sound of fingers hitting keyboards clicked away under the quiet conversations taking place at a few of the desks. Inspector Dave Woolcott sat beside one of the collators, who was pointing out some detail on the screen. No one looked up when Brandon entered.

He walked over behind Woolcott and waited till he had finished talking to the constable on the terminal. Brandon suppressed a sigh. It was definitely time he started thinking about retirement. It wasn't just the bobbies that looked young to him now; even the inspectors didn't look old enough to be out of probationer's cap bands. 'Keep trying for a match, Harry, cross-ref with the CROs,' he heard Woolcott say. The lad on the keyboard nodded and stared into his screen.

''Evening, Dave,' Brandon said.

Woolcott swung round in his chair. Registering who the newcomer was, he got to his feet. ''Evening, sir.'

'I was on my way home, and I thought I'd swing by and see how you were doing,' Brandon lied smoothly.

'Well, sir, it's early days. We'll have teams working round the clock for the next couple of days, feeding in all the statement details from the earlier cases as well as PC Connolly's. I'm also liaising with the team manning the hot-line phones. Most of it's the usual spite, vengeance and paranoia, but Sergeant Lascelles is doing a good job of prioritizing the messages.'

'Anything coming out yet?'

Woolcott rubbed his bald spot in the reflex gesture which his second wife claimed had caused the problem in the first place. 'Bits and pieces. We've got a few names of blokes who were out and about in Temple Fields on at least two of the nights in question, and those are being actioned. We've also been hammering the PNC with car index numbers that have shown up regularly around the times of the killings. Luckily, ever since the second killing, Inspector Jordan's had somebody clocking car numbers round the gay village. It's a long job, sir, but we'll get there.'

If he's in there, Brandon thought. It was he who had been adamant that this was a case for the HOLMES team. But this killer was unlike any he'd seen or read about. This killer was careful.

Brandon didn't know much about computers. But one adage had stuck: garbage in, garbage out. He hoped fervently that he hadn't given his men a job that should have gone to the Cleansing Department.

Carol's eyes snapped open, heart pounding. In her dream, a heavy cell door had slammed shut, leaving her a prisoner of cold, sweating windowless walls. Still groggy from sleep, it took her a moment to realize that the familiar weight of Nelson's body wasn't lying across her feet. She heard footsteps, the rattle of keys being thrown on a table. A narrow sliver of light spilled through the few inches of open door Nelson required for his comings and goings. She rolled over with a groan and grabbed the clock. Ten past ten. Robbed of twenty minutes' precious sleep by Michael's noisy return.

Carol stumbled out of bed and pulled on her heavy towelling bathrobe. She opened her bedroom door and walked into the enormous room that made up most of the third-floor flat she shared with her brother. Half a dozen floor-mounted up-lights of different heights cast a warm and elegant glow on the room. Nelson appeared from the kitchen doorway, bouncing lightly on the stripped-wood flooring. Then he crouched and, in a leap that seemed to defy gravity, bounded into the air, touching briefly on a tall thin speaker before landing delicately on top of a blond wood bookcase. From there, he stared superciliously across the room at Carol, as if to say, 'I bet you can't do that.'

The room was about forty feet by twenty-five. At one end, a group of three two-seater sofas covered with quilted throws surrounded a low coffee table. At the opposite end stood a dining table with six chairs in the style of Rennie Mackintosh. Near the sofas was a TV and video on a black trolley. About half of the back wall was occupied by shelves crammed with books, videos and CDs.

The walls were painted a cool dove-grey, except for the far wall, which was exposed brickwork, with five high arched windows looking out over the city. Carol walked across the room till she could just see the edge of the black ribbon of the Duke of Waterford canal below. The city lights glittered like a cheap jeweller's window. 'Michael?' she called.

Her brother stuck his head out of the narrow galley kitchen, looking surprised. 'I didn't realize you were home,' he said. 'Did I wake you?'

'I was getting up soon anyway. I've got to go back to work. I was just grabbing a few hours,' she said resignedly. 'Is the kettle on?' She walked across to the kitchen and perched on a high stool while Michael made tea and carried on building himself a sandwich with ciabatta, beef tomatoes, black olives, spring onions and tuna.

'Eat?' he asked.

'I could handle one of those,' Carol admitted. 'How was London?'

Michael shrugged. 'You know. They like what we're doing, but could we have it finished yesterday.'

Carol pulled a face. 'Sounds just like the *Sentinel Times*'s editorials about the serial killer. What exactly is it you're doing at the moment anyway? Is it explainable in words of one syllable to a techno-illiterate?'

Michael grinned. 'The next big thing is going to be computer adventure games with the same quality as videos. You film real stuff and digitize it and manipulate it to produce gameplay that's as real as a movie. So we're on to the next, next big thing. Imagine you're playing a computer adventure, but all the characters are people you know. You're the hero, but not just in your imagination.'

'You've lost me now,' Carol said.

'OK. When you install the game on your computer, you'll plug in a scanner and scan photographs of yourself and anybody else you want in your game. The computer reads that information, and translates it into screen images. So instead of Conan the Barbarian leading the quest, it's Carol Jordan. You can import pics of your best friends or your lust objects to be your companions in the game. Anybody you don't like, you turn into the baddies. So, you could have an adventure with Mel Gibson, Dennis Quaid and Martin Amis, and fight enemies like Saddam Hussein, Margaret Thatcher and Popeye,' Michael explained enthusiastically as he stuffed the ingredients into the bread. He dumped the sandwiches on plates and together they walked back into the living room and sat staring out over the canal as they ate.

'Clear?' he asked.

'As it needs to be,' Carol said. 'So once you've got

126

this software up and running, presumably you could use it to put people in compromising positions? Like blue movies?'

Michael frowned. 'Theoretically. Your average computer nerd wouldn't even know where to begin. You'd need to know what you were doing and you'd also need seriously expensive hardware to get decent quality stills or videos off your computer.'

'Thank God for that,' Carol said, with feeling. 'I was beginning to think you were creating a Frankenstein's monster for blackmailers and tabloid journalists.'

'No chance,' he said. 'Anyway, close analysis would show it up. So what about you? How's your quest coming along?'

Carol shrugged. 'I could do with a few superheroes to help out, to be honest.'

'What's this profiler like? He going to shake things up a bit?'

'Tony Hill? He already has. Popeye's going around with a face like a melted wellie. But I'm hopeful we might get something constructive out of him. I've had one session with him already, and he's bursting with ideas. He's a nice guy as well, no hassle to work with.'

Michael grinned. 'That must be a refreshing change.'

'You're not kidding.'

'And is he your type?'

Carol pulled a piece of crust off her bread and threw it at Michael. 'God, you're as bad as the sexist pigs I work with. I haven't got a type, and even if I did and Tony Hill was it, you know I won't mix work with pleasure.'

'Given the fact that you work all hours and spend

all your spare time asleep, I guess you're looking at a lifetime of celibacy,' Michael replied drily. 'So is he gorgeous, or what?'

'I hadn't noticed,' Carol said stiffly. 'And I doubt whether he's even noticed I'm female. The man's a workaholic. In fact, he's the reason I'm working again tonight. He wants to see the scenes of crime at around the time the bodies were dumped so he can get a feel for it.'

'Shame you've got to go out again,' Michael said. 'It's ages since we've had a night in with the telly and a few bottles of wine. We see so little of each other just now, we might as well be married.'

Carol smiled ruefully. 'The price of success, eh, bro?'

'I guess so.' Michael got up. 'Oh well, if you're going to work, I might as well do a couple of hours before I sack out.'

'Before you go . . . I need a favour.'

Michael sat down again. 'As long as it doesn't involve doing your ironing.'

'What do you know about statistical pattern analysis?'

Michael frowned. 'Not a lot. I did a little bit when I was doing part-time jobbing work while I was doing my PhD, but I don't know what's state of the art right now. Why? You want something looking at?'

Carol nodded. 'It's a bit grisly, I'm afraid.' She outlined the sadistic injuries to Damien Connolly. 'Tony Hill has an idea they might yield some kind of a message.'

'Sure, I'll have a look for you. I know a bloke who's almost certainly got the latest software in the field. I'm sure he'd let me have some time on his machine to fiddle about with this,' Michael said.

'Not a word to anybody what it's about,' Carol said.

Michael looked offended. 'Of course not. What do you take me for? Listen, I'd rather get on the wrong side of a serial killer than you. I'll keep my mouth shut. Just get the stuff to me tomorrow, and I'll do my best, OK?'

Carol leaned over and rumpled her brother's blond hair. 'Thank you. I appreciate it.'

Michael grabbed her in a quick hug. 'This is seriously weird territory, little sis. Be careful out there, huh? You know I can't afford the mortgage on this place alone.'

'I'm always careful,' Carol said, ignoring the small voice inside her warning not to tempt fate. 'I'm a survivor.'

'I wanted you the first time I saw you,' I said softly. 'I've wanted you for so long.'

Adam's lolling head straightened slightly. I pressed the remote record button on the tripod-mounted video camera. I didn't want to miss a thing. Adam's eyelids, heavy from all that chloroform, struggled open to a slit, then suddenly snapped wide as memory kicked in. His head thrashed from side to side as he tried to see where he was, how he was restrained. As he took in his nakedness, spotted the details of the soft leather wrist and ankle cuffs, and realized that he was fastened to my rack, a moan of what sounded like panic escaped from behind the tape over his mouth.

I stepped out of the shadows behind him and moved into his line of vision, my body oiled and shining in the bright lights. I had stripped down to my underwear, carefully chosen to show off my superb body to its best advantage. When he saw me, his eyes opened even wider. He attempted to speak, but all that came out was a strained mumble.

'But you decided you couldn't allow yourself to want me, didn't you?' I said, my voice hard and accusing. 'You

130

betrayed my love. You didn't have the courage to choose a love that would have exalted us both. No, you ignored your real self and went for a stupid little bimbo, that trashy tart. Don't you realize? I'm the only one in the world who understands, really understands, what you need. I could have given you ecstasy, but you chose the safe, pathetic option. You didn't have the nerve for a marriage of true minds and bodies, did you?'

Drops of sweat were trickling down his temples, in spite of the coolness of the cellar. I moved forward and stroked his body, running my hand over his pale, muscular chest, fluttering my fingers over his groin. He flinched convulsively, his dark-blue eyes pleading. 'How could you betray what I know is in your heart?' I hissed, digging my nails into the soft flesh above the wiry curls of his dark pubic hair. He tensed against me. I thrilled to the sensation. I took my hand away and admired the scarlet half-moons my nails had left in his skin. 'You know you belong to me. You told me. You wanted me, we both know you did.'

Another groan from behind the gag. Now the sweat had spread to his chest, droplets matting the thick dark hair that tapered down his abdomen into a thin line pointing to his cock lying curled and useless as a slug between his legs. Even though it was obvious that he didn't want me, the very sight of his vulnerable nakedness aroused me. He was beautiful. I could feel the blood flowing faster, feel my flesh expanding, ready to take him, ready to explode. I hated myself for that weakness, and I turned away before he could see the effect he was having.

'All I wanted was to love you,' I said quietly. 'I didn't want it to be like this.' My hand strayed to the handle of the rack and caressed the smooth wood. I turned my head and gazed at Adam's beautiful face. Slowly, infinitely slowly, I started to turn the handle. His body, already taut, tightened against the pull of the straps. His effort was wasted. The gears on the winding mechanism multiplied my small exertion till it equalled the strength of several men. Adam was no match for my machine. I could see the muscles of his arms and legs bulge, his chest heaving as he struggled for breath.

'It's not too late,' I said. 'We could still be lovers. Would you like that?'

Desperately, he moved his head. There was no mistaking it, it was a nod. I smiled. 'That's more like it,' I said. 'Now all you have to do is show me you mean it.'

I ran one hand over his damp chest, then rubbed my face against the fine dark hairs. I could smell his fear, taste it in his sweat. I buried my head in his neck, sucking and biting, nibbling his ears. His body stayed rigid, but I felt no trace of an erection beneath me. Frustrated, I pulled away. I leaned over him and, in one swift agonizing movement, I yanked the tape away from his mouth.

'Aagh!' he yelled as the adhesive ripped his skin, rasping on the faint stubble. He licked dry lips. 'Please, let me go,' he whispered.

I shook my head. 'I can't do that, Adam. Maybe if we were really lovers . . .'

'I won't tell anyone,' he croaked. 'I promise.'

'You betrayed me once,' I said sadly. 'How can I trust you now?'

'I'm sorry,' he said. 'I didn't realize . . . I'm sorry.' But there was no penitence in his eyes, only desperation and fear. I'd played this scene so many times in my head. Part of me exulted that I'd predicted the shape of it so well, that the dialogue was almost identical to the scenario I'd conjured up. Part of me felt an inexpressible sadness that he was exactly as weak and faithless as I'd feared. And yet another part of me was almost uncontrollably excited by what lay ahead, whether love or death, or both.

'It's too late for words,' I said. 'It's time for actions. You said you wanted us to be lovers, but that's not what your body's saying. Maybe you're scared. But there's no need to be. I'm a generous person, a loving person. You could find that out for yourself. I'm going to give you one last chance to atone for your betrayal. I'm going to leave you now for a while. When I come back, I expect you to be able to control your fear and show me how you really feel about me.'

I let him go and walked over to the camcorder. I took out the tape that had been recording our encounter and replaced it with a fresh one. At the top of the stairs, I turned back. 'Otherwise, I'll be forced to administer punishment for your treachery.'

'Wait!' he howled desperately as I disappeared from sight. 'Come back,' I heard as I dropped the trapdoor into place. I expect he carried on yelling. But I couldn't hear him. I went upstairs to Auntie Doris and Uncle Henry's bedroom. I slotted the video into the player I'd set up on the chest at the end of the bed, switched on the TV and climbed between the cold cotton sheets. Even if Adam didn't want me, I couldn't escape my desire for him. I watched him on his rack, my hand stroking me, touching myself with all the skill and ingenuity I wanted from him, imagining his beautiful cock swelling in my mouth. Every time I reached the point of orgasm, I stopped, gripping myself tight, forcing myself not to come, to save myself for what lay ahead. After I'd gone through the video for the fourth time, I decided he'd had long enough.

I slipped out of bed and went back downstairs. I looked at him spread-eagled on the rack. 'Please,' he said. 'Let *me go. I'll do anything you want, but let me go. I'm begging you.'*

I smiled and gently shook my head. 'I will take you back to Bradfield, Adam. But first, it's time to party.'

6

> People begin to see that something more goes to the
> composition of a fine murder than two blockheads to
> kill and be killed – a knife – a purse – and a dark lane.
> Design, gentlemen, grouping, light and shade, poetry,
> sentiment, are now deemed to be indispensable to
> attempts of this nature.

Work might not solve anything, but it was a great diversionary tactic. Tony stared into the screen, scrolling
down through the tabulated information he'd gleaned
from the police reports. Satisfied that he'd incorporated
everything useful, he switched on the printer. While it
chattered and stuttered its way through the print-out,
Tony opened another file and started to sketch out
the conclusions he had drawn from the raw data.
Anything, anything to keep her at bay.

He was so absorbed in his work he barely registered
the doorbell's first peal. When it rang out a second
time, he looked up, startled, at the clock. Five past
eleven. If it was Carol, she was earlier than he'd anticipated. They'd already agreed that there was little point
in beginning their trip before midnight. Tony got to his

feet, uncertain. Since she knew his phone number, it wouldn't be too hard for Angelica to discover his address too. He arrived at the front door just as the bell rang for the third time. Wishing he'd installed a peephole, Tony cautiously inched the door open.

Carol grinned. 'You look like you're expecting Handy Andy,' she said. When Tony said nothing, she added, 'Sorry I'm a bit early. I did try ringing, but you were engaged.'

'Sorry,' Tony mumbled. 'I must have accidentally left it off the hook from earlier. Come on in, it's no problem.' He found a smile from somewhere and led Carol into his study. As he reached his desk, he slid the phone back on the hook.

Carol registered that the phone's engaged signal had been no accident. Deduction: he didn't want to be disturbed, not even by the answering machine. Probably, like her, he couldn't resist a ringing phone. She glanced at the sheets of paper sitting on the printer table. 'You've obviously been busy,' she said. 'And there was me thinking you were taking your time answering the door because you'd gone for a quick zizz.'

'Did you get some sleep?' Tony asked, noting that she looked more clear-eyed than she had done earlier.

'Four hours. Which is about ten too few. I've got a couple of bits of information for you, by the way.' She filled him in succinctly on the results of her visit to Scargill Street, leaving out Cross's hostility.

Tony listened carefully, making a couple of notes on his pad. 'Interesting,' he said. 'I don't think there's a lot of point in pulling in the sex offenders again, though. If

Handy Andy's got form, it's more likely to be juvenile offences, petty burglary, minor violence, that sort of thing. Still, I've been wrong before.'

'Haven't we all? By the way, I checked with the HOLMES room, and there's no one there who knows anything about statistical pattern analysis, so I've asked my brother to see what he can do for us. Should I just give him a set of the photographs, or is there some other way of presenting the raw data?'

'I suppose there's less chance of a mistake if he works directly from the photographs,' Tony said. 'Thanks for sorting that out for me.'

'No sweat,' Carol said. 'Secretly, I think he's quite chuffed to be asked. He thinks I don't take him seriously. You know, he writes games software, I do the real thing.'

'And do you?' Tony asked.

'What? Take him seriously? You bet I do. I respect anybody that understands something as far beyond my grasp as computers. Besides, he earns about twice what I do. That has to be serious.'

'I don't know about that. Andrew Lloyd Webber probably earns more in a day than I do in a month, but I still don't take him seriously.' Toby stood up. 'Carol, do you mind if I abandon you for ten minutes? I need a quick shower to wake me up.'

'Fine, feel free. It's me that's early.'

'Thanks. D'you want a brew while you're waiting?'

Carol shook her head. 'I'll pass, thanks. It's cold out there, and there aren't many places a woman can have a pee in Temple Fields in the early hours.'

Almost shyly, Tony picked up the sheaf of a print-out and proffered it to Carol. 'I've started the work on the victims. Maybe you'd like to take a look while I'm gone?'

Eagerly, Carol took the paper. 'I'd love to. I'm fascinated by this whole process.'

'This is just very preliminary,' Tony stressed, backing towards the door. 'I mean, I've not drawn any conclusions yet. I'm working on that.'

'Relax, Tony, I'm on your side,' Carol said as he left the room. She stared after him momentarily, wondering what it was that had unsettled him. By the time they parted in the afternoon, they had built up an easy camaraderie, she'd thought. But now, he was edgy, abstracted. Was it that he was tired, or was it that he was uncomfortable to have her sitting in his home? 'God, does it matter?' she muttered to herself. 'Concentrate, Jordan. Pick the man's brains.' She focused on the first sheet and studied the data.

	Adam S.	Paul G.	Gareth F.	Damien C.
Victim No.	1	2	3	4
Date of crime	6/7.9.93	1/2.11.93	25/26.12.93	20/21.2.94
Bradfield resident?	Yes	Yes	Yes	Yes
Sex	M	M	M	M
Ethnic origin	Caucasian	Caucasian	Caucasian	Caucasian
Nationality	British	British	British	British
Age	28	31	30	27
Star sign	Gemini	Cancer	Scorpio	Capricorn
Height	5'10"	5'11"	5'11"	6'
Weight	147lb	136lb	151lb	160lb
Build	Medium	Slim	Medium	Medium
Musculature	Good	Average	Average	Excellent
Hair length	Abv collar	Collar	Abv collar	Abv collar
Hair colour	Brown	Dark brown	Brown	Reddish brown
Hair type	Wavy	Straight	Straight	Curly
Tattoos	No	No	No	No
Clothing	None	None	None	None
Occupation	Civil servant	University lecturer	Solicitor	Police officer
Place of work	City centre	South of city centre	City centre	Southern suburbs
Car owned	Ford Escort	Citroën AX	Ford Escort	Classic Austin Healey
Hobbies	Working out, angling	Walking	Working out, theatre, cinema	Car restoration
Residence	Modern terraced town house; integral garage	Edwardian terraced house; no garage	Thirties semi; no garage	Modern detached estate house; attached garage
Relationship status	Divorced Lived alone NCP RP	Single Lived alone NCP NRP	Single Lived alone CP NRP	Single Lived alone NCP NRP
Personal items missing?	Wedding ring, watch	Watch	Signet ring, watch	Watch
Items missing from home?	Answering-machine tape	Answering-machine tape	None known	None known
Known sexual history	Hetero	Hetero	Hetero	Not known

139

	Adam S.	Paul G.	Gareth F.	Damien C.
Victim No.	1	2	3	4
Last seen by previous acquaintance	Tram home from work, 6 p.m. approx.	Leaving work, 5.30 p.m. approx.	Home, 7.15 p.m.	Home, 6 p.m.
Criminal record	None	None	None	None
Connection to scene of crime	None known	None known	None known	None known
Status of body-recovery site	Urban	Urban	Suburban/ Rural	Urban
Site of first contact with killer	Unknown	Unknown	Unknown	Unknown
Site of death	Unknown	Unknown	Unknown	Unknown
Disposition of body	Semi-hidden to cause short delay before discovery	Semi-hidden to cause short delay before discovery	Hidden; note to police via newspaper required	Openly displayed but in area unattended until specific time
Body posed?	No	No	No	No
* Has the body been washed?	Yes	Yes	Yes	Yes
Cause of death	Throat cut	Throat cut	Throat cut	Throat cut
** Ligatures?	Wrists Ankles Adhesive gag	Wrists Ankles Adhesive gag	Wrists Ankles Adhesive gag	Wrists Ankles Adhesive gag
Bite marks	No	No	No	No
Putative bite marks (i.e., flesh removed)	Yes	Yes	Yes	Yes
Location of marks	Neck (2) Chest (1)	Neck (2)	Neck (3) Abdomen (4)	Neck (3) Chest (2) Groin (4)
Signs of torture or unusual assault?	Yes (see A)	Yes (see B)	Yes (see C)	Yes (see D)

* BODY WASHING: No fragranced materials appear to have been used, suggesting that the offender is not using the washing process as a means of denial; rather, in line with the rest of his cautious behaviour, I suggest that this washing is intended to obliterate forensic clues, especially since the killer appears to have taken particular care with the fingernails. Scrapings on all four victims showed nothing except traces of unperfumed soap.

** LIGATURES: None were found on bodies, but postmortems reveal bruising consistent with handcuffs on wrists, slight traces of adhesive, missing hairs and bruising round ankles consonant both with parcel tape and with separate ligatures, and traces of adhesive on face around mouth. No traces of blindfolds.

A: *Adam Scott*. Dislocation of ankles, knees, hips, shoulders, elbows and several vertebrae. Consistent with being stretched on a rack. Tentative postmortem cuts to penis and testicles.

B: *Paul Gibbs*. Severe lacerations to rectum, virtual destruction of anal sphincter and partial disembowelment. Suggestive of spiked object repeatedly inserted via anus. Also some burnt tissue internally, suggesting the possibility of heat or electric shock. Face badly beaten before death; bruising, broken facial bones and teeth. Postmortem cuts to genitals, more pronounced than in A.

C: *Gareth Finnegan*. Irregular pierce wounds to

hands and feet, ½″ diameter approx. Lacerations to left cheek and nose, suggestive of glass or bottle being broken across face by right-handed assailant. Shoulders dislocated. ?Possible crucifixion? Postmortem wounds to genitals, virtually castrated.

D: *Damien Connolly*. Dislocations similar to A, but no major spinal trauma, ruling out the idea of a rack. Large number of small, star-shaped burns to torso. Penis severed postmortem and inserted in victim's mouth.
Query: Were Damien Connolly's handcuffs still in his home or police locker?
Query: Why are the bodies always dumped Monday night/Tuesday morning? What happens on Monday that allows him to be free? Does he work nights and have Monday off? Is he perhaps a married man who has Monday free because his wife does things with friends, e.g., girls' night out? Or is it that Monday isn't a traditional 'going out' night and he can be more sure of finding his victims at home?

Carol was aware that Tony had returned, but she carried on reading, simply raising one hand and waving her fingers to indicate she knew he was there. When she reached the end of the report, she took a deep breath and said, 'Well, Dr Hill, you *have* been busy.'

Tony smiled and shrugged himself away from the door-jamb he'd been leaning against. 'I can't believe there's anything in there that you didn't already have filed neatly away in your head.'

'No, but seeing it laid out like that somehow makes it clearer.'

Tony nodded. 'He has a very specific type.'

'Do you want to talk about it now?'

Tony looked down at the floor. 'I'd rather leave most of it for now. I need to let it sink in, and I need to go through all the rest of the witness statements before I can think about a profile.'

Carol couldn't help feeling disappointed. 'I understand,' was all she said.

Tony smiled. 'Were you expecting more?'

'Not really.'

His smile broadened. 'Not even a smidgen?'

The smile was infectious. Carol grinned back. 'Hoping, maybe. Expecting, no. By the way, there was one thing I didn't understand. NCP? CP? NRP? I mean, we're not talking National Car Parks and the Communist Party here, are we?'

'No current partner. Current partner. No recent partner. Acronymitis. It's the disease that afflicts all of us in the soft sciences like psychology, sociology. We have to mystify the uninitiated. Sorry about that. I try to keep things as jargon-free as possible.'

'So you don't confuse us thick plods, eh?' Carol teased.

'It's more about self-preservation. The last thing I want is to give the sceptics another big stick to hit me with. It's hard enough getting people to accept that my reports are even worth reading without alienating them with all that unnecessary pseudo-scientific mumbo jumbo.'

'I believe you,' Carol said ironically. 'Shall we go?'

'Sure. There is one thing I would like to bounce off

143

you now,' Tony said, suddenly serious again. 'The victims. Everybody's assuming this killer is targeting gay men. Now, there are hundreds, probably thousands of openly gay men in Bradfield. We've got the biggest gay scene in the country outside London. Yet every one of those victims has no known history of homosexuality. What does that say to you?'

'He's in the closet himself and he only goes for men who are closeted too?' Carol hazarded.

'Maybe. But if they're all busily passing as straight, how does he meet them?'

Carol straightened the edges of the papers to give herself a moment. 'Contact magazines? Small ads? Multi-user phone chatlines? The Internet?'

'OK, all possibilities. But there was no evidence of any of those interests, according to the reports of the officers who searched their houses. Not in one single case.'

'So what are you trying to say here?'

'I don't think Handy Andy gets turned on by gay men. I think he likes them straight.'

Sergeant Don Merrick decided he'd never felt more fed up. As if it wasn't bad enough that he had Popeye on his back over the guv'nor's new assignment, he was now a servant of three masters. He was supposed to make sure that Inspector Jordan's orders were carried out when she wasn't around, and he was also supposed to be working for Kevin Matthews on the Damien Connolly case as well as liaising with Bob Stansfield on the work that he and Inspector Jordan had already completed on the Paul Gibbs case. To top it all, he was spending his evening in the Hell Hole.

Never, in his opinion, was a club more aptly named. The Hell Hole advertised itself in the gay press as 'The club that dominates Bradfield. One visit and you'll be enslaved. You're *bound* to have the time of your life in the Hell Hole!' All of which was a coy way of saying that the Hell Hole was the place to go to pick up partners if sadomasochism and bondage was how you got your rocks off.

Merrick felt like Snow White at an orgy. He didn't have a clue how he was supposed to behave. He wasn't even sure if he looked right. He'd opted for an old, ripped pair of Levis that normally only saw the light of day when he was doing odd jobs around the house, a plain white T-shirt and the battered leather jacket he used to wear on his motorbike in the days before the kids came along. In his back pocket were his official handcuffs, there in the hope they'd lend some verisimilitude to his pose. Looking round the dimly lit bar, Merrick spotted so much distressed denim and leather that he expected to see an SOS flare rising above the dance floor. Superficially, at least, he thought he might just look the part. Which was worrying in itself. As his eyes grew accustomed to the low lighting, he caught sight of a few of his colleagues. Mostly, they looked as uncomfortable as he felt.

The club had been virtually empty when he'd first arrived just after nine. Feeling incredibly conspicuous, Merrick had asked for a pass-out and gone back on to the streets. He'd wandered round Temple Fields for the best part of an hour, stopping in a café-bar for a cappuccino. He'd wondered why some of the gay clientele had been giving him strange looks until he realized that he was the only customer wearing leather and denim. Clearly he'd transgressed some unwritten dress code. Uncomfortable, Merrick had swallowed the scalding coffee as quickly as he could and got back out on to the streets.

He felt seriously vulnerable, alone on the pavements and walkways of Temple Fields. The men who passed him, either singly, in couples or in groups, all eyed him up and down speculatively as he passed, most glances pausing at his crotch. He squirmed inside, wishing he'd picked a pair of jeans that didn't hug his body quite so tightly. As a couple of black youths walked past, arms entwined, he heard one say loudly to the other, 'Great ass for a white guy, huh?' Merrick felt the blood rise to his cheeks, unsure whether it was anger or embarrassment. In a moment of dreadful clarity, he realized what women meant when they complained of being treated as objects by men.

He returned to the Hell Hole, relieved that the place had filled up now. Loud disco music throbbed, the beat so strong Merrick seemed to feel it inside his chest. On the dance floor, men in leather adorned with chains, zips and peaked caps moved energetically, showing off their Nautilus-hardened muscles, thrusting their groins into empty air in bizarre parodies of sex. Stifling a sigh, Merrick pushed his way through the crowd to the bar. He ordered a bottle of American beer that tasted unbelievably insipid to a palate trained to expect the nutty sweetness of Newcastle Brown.

Turning round to face the dance floor again, Merrick leaned against the bar and surveyed the room, desperately trying to avoid eye contact with anyone in particular. He'd been standing like that for about ten minutes when he became aware that the man standing next to him wasn't actually trying to be served. Merrick glanced round to discover the man's eyes fixed on him. He was almost as tall as the detective, but with a broader, more muscular build. He wore tight black leather trousers and a white vest. His blond hair was cut short at the sides, longer on top, and his body was as tanned and smooth as a Chippendale. He raised his eyebrows and said, 'Hi. I'm Ian.'

Merrick grinned weakly. 'Don,' he replied, raising his voice to combat the music.

'I've not seen you in here before, Don,' Ian said, moving closer so that his naked arm pressed against the worn leather of Merrick's sleeve.

'It's my first time,' Merrick said.

'You new in town, then? You don't sound local.'

'I'm from the North East,' Merrick said carefully.

'That explains it. A bonny laddie from Geordieland,' Ian said, with a bad imitation of Merrick's accent.

Merrick felt his smile grow sick and die. 'You a regular here, then?' he asked.

'Never miss it. Best bar in town for the kind of guy I like.' Ian winked. 'Can I buy you a drink, Don?'

The sweat trickling down Merrick's back had nothing to do with the warmth of the bar. 'I'll have another one of these,' he said.

Ian nodded and turned round to the bar, using the crowd around him as an excuse to thrust himself against Merrick. Merrick stared across the room, his jaw set. He noticed one of the other murder squad detectives watching him. His colleague gave a grotesque wink and mimed one finger pumping into the closed fist of his other hand. Merrick turned away, coming face to face with Ian, who had been served.

147

'There you go, bonny laddie,' Ian said. 'So, you looking for a bit of fun tonight, Geordie?'

'Just checking out the scene,' Merrick said.

'What's the scene like up in Newcastle, then?' Ian asked. 'Bit lively? Cater for all tastes, does it?'

Merrick shrugged. 'I don't know. I'm not from Newcastle. I come from a little village up on the coast. It's not the kind of place where you can be yourself.'

'I get you,' Ian said, laying a hand on Merrick's arm. 'Well, Don, if you want to be yourself, you've come to the right place. And you've found the right guy.'

Merrick prayed he didn't look as terrified as he felt. 'It's certainly busy enough,' he tried.

'We could go somewhere quieter, if you like. There's another room through the back there, where the music isn't so loud.'

'No, I'm fine here,' Merrick said quickly. 'I like the music, if I'm honest.'

Ian moved forward so his torso leaned against Merrick's. 'What is it you're into, Don? Top or bottom?'

Merrick choked on his beer. 'I'm sorry?' he gasped.

Ian laughed and rumpled Merrick's hair. His light-blue eyes glinted wickedly, holding Merrick's stare. 'You really are an innocent abroad, aren't you? What I'm saying is, what do you like best? Handing it out or taking it?' His hand strayed down to Merrick's trousers. Just when the detective thought he was going to be groped in a way that no one apart from his wife had ever done, Ian's hand slid to one side and moved round to stroke Merrick's buttock.

'That depends,' Merrick croaked.

'On what?' Ian asked suggestively, moving so close

that Merrick could feel the other man's erection against his leg.

'On how much I trust the person I'm with,' Merrick replied, trying not to let his revulsion show in voice or expression.

'Oh, I'm very trustworthy, me. And you look like the reliable kind too.'

'Are yez not a bit worried, like, about strangers? With this serial killer doing the rounds?' Merrick asked, using the opportunity of putting his empty bottle back on the bar to move away slightly from Ian's insistent body.

Ian's smile was cocky. 'Why should I be? These guys that are getting topped don't hang out in places like this. Stands to reason that this isn't where this mad bastard's picking them up.'

'How do you know that?'

'I've seen the pictures in the papers, and I've never spotted a single one of them out on the scene. And believe me, I know the scene. That's how I knew you were the new kid in town.' Ian moved closer again and thrust a hand in Merrick's back pocket. He ran his fingers over the hard outline of the handcuffs. 'Hey, that feels interesting. I'm starting to get a picture of what you and me could be like.'

Merrick forced a laugh. 'For all you know, I could be the killer.'

'So what if you are?' Ian said, all self-assurance. 'I'm not the type this fucking nutter goes for. He likes closet queens, not macho men. If he picked me up, he'd want to fuck, not commit murder. Besides, a good-looking guy like you doesn't need to kill somebody to get a fuck.'

'Yeah, well, maybe so, but how do I know you're not the killer?'

'Tell you what, just to prove I'm not, I'll let you top tonight. You'll be in charge. I'll be the one with handcuffs on.'

Carry on like this and you won't be wrong, Merrick thought to himself. He reached down and gripped Ian's wrist hard, removing his hand from the pocket. 'I don't think so,' he said. 'Not tonight. Like you said, I'm the new kid in town. I'm not going home with anybody till I know a bit about them.' He released Ian's wrist and stepped back. 'Nice talking to you, Ian. Thanks for the drink.'

Ian's face altered in an instant. His eyes narrowed and the smile changed to a snarl. 'Wait a minute, Geordie. I don't know what sort of poxy Watch With Mother clubs you're used to, but in this city, you don't get into a clinch with somebody and take drinks off him if you're not prepared to come across.'

Merrick tried to get away, but the press of bodies round the bar made any movement difficult. 'I'm sorry if there's been a misunderstanding,' he said.

Ian's arm shot out and gripped Merrick firmly just below his bicep. The pain was excruciating. Merrick found a moment to wonder what sort of person actively sought out pain like this as part of their sexual pleasure. Ian thrust his face so close that Merrick could smell the bad breath he'd learned to associate with amphetamine abuse. 'It's not a misunderstanding,' Ian said. 'You came here tonight for sex. There's no other reason to be here. So sex is what we're going to do.'

Merrick swivelled on the balls of his feet and jabbed his elbow sharply underneath Ian's ribcage. His breath burst out of him in a sudden 'whoosh', and he doubled over, letting go of Merrick's arm in the reflex of clutching at his solar plexus. 'No, we're not,' Merrick said mildly, moving away through the space that had cleared around him as if by magic.

On his way across the room, one of the other undercover officers fell into step beside him. 'Nice one, Sarge,' he said out of the corner of his mouth. 'You did what we've all been wanting to do ever since we got in here.'

Merrick stopped and smiled at the constable. 'You're supposed to be doing an undercover. Either fucking dance with me or fuck off and let one of these poofters chat you up.'

Leaving the constable open mouthed, Merrick walked over to the far side of the dance floor and leaned against the wall. The commotion he'd left at the bar had died down. Ian pushed his way through the crowd, still holding his stomach, and left the club, shooting venomous glares at Merrick.

Before long, Merrick had company again. This time, he recognized his companion as a detective constable from one of the other divisions who had only joined the murder squad that day. He was sweating under the weight of heavy leather jacket and trousers that looked suspiciously like standard police motorcycle issue. He leaned close to Merrick, so he wouldn't be overheard in the crowd round the dance floor and said urgently, 'Skip, there's a guy I think we should take a look at.'

'Why?'

'I overheard him mouthing off to a couple of blokes that he knew the dead guys. He was boasting about it. Reckoned there weren't many that could say that. And

I heard him say that the killer must be a body-builder like him, on account of lugging bodies around. He was saying he bet there were people here tonight who didn't know they knew a murderer. Boasting, like, all the way.'

'Why don't you bring him in yourself?' Merrick asked, his interest quickened by what he'd heard, but reluctant to deprive the constable of the credit of pulling in a suspect.

'I tried to strike up conversation with him, but he gave me the brush-off.' The constable gave a wry smile. 'Maybe I'm not his type, skip.'

'And what makes you think I am?' Merrick demanded, not sure whether he was being subtly insulted here.

'He's wearing the same kind of gear as you.'

Merrick sighed. 'You better point him out to me.'

'Don't look now, sir, but he's standing over by the disco speakers. IC1 male, five foot six, short dark hair, blue eyes, clean shaven, heavy Scottish accent. Dressed like you. Drinking a pint of lager.'

Merrick leaned back against the wall and slowly scanned the room. He got the suspect on the first pass. 'Got him, I think,' he said. 'OK, son, thanks. Look fucked off when I go.'

He shrugged away from the wall and left the constable practising his depressed look. Slowly, Merrick moved round the room until he found himself next to the man who'd been pointed out to him. He had the bulky build of a weightlifter and the face of a boxer. His outfit was almost identical to Merrick's, save that his jacket had more buckles and zips. 'Busy in here tonight,' Merrick said.

'Aye. Lots of new faces. Half of them probably polis,'

the man said. 'See that jerk you were just talking to? He might as well have come in his Panda car. Did you ever see a more obvious busy in all your born days?'

'That's why I fucked him off sharpish,' Merrick replied.

'I'm Stevie, by the way,' the man said. 'Busy night you're having with the unwanted solicitations. I saw you sort that toerag out earlier. Nicely done, pal.'

'Thanks. I'm Don.'

'Nice to meet you, Don. You new about here, then? Accent like that, you're obviously not a local.'

'Does everybody know everybody else here?' Merrick asked with a wry smile.

'Pretty much. It's a real village, Temple Fields. 'Specially the S&M scene. Let's face it, if you're gonnae let somebody tie you up, you want to know what you're getting into.'

'You're not wrong, Stevie,' Merrick said with feeling. 'Even more so when there's a killer on the loose.'

'My point exactly. I mean, I don't suppose these guys that got themselves killed thought they were up for anything more than a bit of rough. I knew them, you know. Adam Scott, Paul Gibbs, Gareth Finnegan and Damien Connolly. Every last one of them, and let me tell you, I wouldn't have had them pegged for that sort of scene. Just shows you, doesn't it? You can never tell what goes on in people's heads.'

'How come you knew them, then? I thought the paper said they weren't known on the scene,' Merrick said.

'I run a gym,' Stevie said proudly. 'Adam and Gareth, they were members. We used to go out for a drink now and again. That Paul Gibbs, I knew him through a mate of mine, used to have a pint with him and all. And that copper, Connolly, he came round the gym after we had a burglary.'

'I bet there's not many around here that can say they knew all the poor sods,' Merrick said.

'You're right there, pal. Mind you, I don't suppose the killer had anything more in mind than a wee bit of fun.'

Merrick's eyebrows rose. 'You think it's fun to murder folk?'

Stevie shook his head. 'Naw, you're no' following me. See, I don't think he sets out to kill these guys. Naw, it's kind of an accident, if you get my meaning. They're playing their games, and your man just gets carried away, and it all gets out of hand. He's obviously strong, he carts these bodies about and dumps them in the middle of the city, for God's sake. He's not going to be a seven-stone weakling, now is he? If he's a real body-builder like me, he maybe doesn't know his own strength. Could happen to anybody,' he added after a moment's pause.

'Four times?' Merrick demanded incredulously.

Stevie shrugged. 'Maybe they asked for it. Know what I mean? Prick teases and that? Promising what they didnae want to deliver when push came to shove? I've been there, Don, and let me tell you, there've been times when I've wanted to strangle the wee bastards.'

The detective in Merrick was straining at the leash. Carol Jordan wasn't the only Bradfield copper who'd been reading up on the psychology of the serial killer. Merrick had read cases where killers got off on this kind of justification, swaggering in front of a third party. The Yorkshire Ripper, he knew, had boasted to his male cronies about 'doing' prostitutes. He wanted Stevie in an interview room. The only problem was how to get him there.

Merrick cleared his throat. 'I suppose the only way to avoid that is to get to know the people you go to bed with before you get there.'

'My point exactly. You fancy getting out of here? Maybe going for a cup of coffee down the diner? Getting to know each other a wee bit better?'

Merrick nodded. 'Sure,' he said, dumping the remains of his beer on a nearby table. 'Let's go.' Soon as they got outside, he could switch his radio to 'transmit only' and one of the back-up teams would pick them up. Then they could test Stevie's bravado in Scargill Street.

Although it was after midnight, the street outside the Hell Hole was far from deserted. 'This way,' Stevie said, pointing to his left. Merrick slid his hand into his jacket and adjusted the radio switch.

'Where is it we're going?' he asked.

'There's an all-night diner in Crompton Gardens.'

'Great. I could murder a bacon butty,' Merrick said.

'Very bad for your health, all that grease,' Stevie said seriously.

As they rounded the corner into the alley leading into the square, Merrick sensed someone stepping out of a darkened doorway behind him. He started to turn towards the sound of footsteps.

Just like Bonfire Night, was his last conscious thought as a starburst of light erupted behind his eyes.

It didn't last as long as I'd expected. Surprisingly, Adam proved more fragile than the German shepherd. Once he'd lapsed into unconsciousness following the dislocation of his limbs, he proved impossible to rouse. I waited for hours, but nothing seemed to bring him round; not pain, not cold water, not warmth. I was disappointed, I admit it. His pain had been a mere shadow of mine, his punishment not enough for the betrayal that occasioned it.

I finished what I had to do, neatly and swiftly, just after midnight. Then I took him off the rack and folded him into a heavy-duty garden rubbish sack. I put that inside a black Bradfield Metropolitan Council bin bag. It was a struggle to get the dead weight back up the cellar steps and into the wheelbarrow, but my hours pumping iron paid off.

I couldn't wait to get home to my computer, to transform the evening into something transcendent. But I still had work to do before I could relax and indulge myself. I drove into the city centre just above the legal speed limit – not so fast I'd get pulled for speeding, and not so slow that I'd be stopped on suspicion of being a careful drunk driver. I made for the gay cruising area behind the university. Temple

Fields used to be a student area, filled with small cafés, restaurants, shops and bars with low prices and standards. Then, about ten years ago, a couple of the bars became gay. Our left-wing city council responded to pressure and funded a gay and lesbian centre, which moved into the basement of an Indian restaurant. That seemed to trigger a domino effect, and within a year or two, Temple Fields had become Cruising City and the straight students had moved over to Greenholm on the far side of campus. Now, Temple Fields was home to gay bars, clubs, chichi bistros, shops selling leather and bondage gear, and a nightly rent rack right along the canal.

By half past one on a Tuesday morning, there were still quite a few men out on the streets. I drove around a couple of times, concentrating on the area round Crompton Gardens. The square was dark; most of the streetlights had been vandalized for reasons of sexual privacy, and the council was too strapped for cash to repair them. Besides, none of the local businesses was complaining; the darker the square, the more desirable the area, the bigger their profits.

I looked around cautiously. Nothing stirred. I wrestled the bag to the lip of the boot, then half rolled, half carried it on to the low wall. I tipped it over the edge with a rustling thud and closed the tailgate as quietly as I could. I took a penknife out of my pocket, leaned over the wall and slit the bags open. I pulled them free of the body and crumpled them into a ball.

Just after two, I parked Adam's car a couple of streets away from his house then walked back to my jeep, stuffing the bags in a litter bin on the way. I was in bed by three. In spite of my burning desire to carry on with my work, I was overwhelmed with exhaustion. Not surprising, considering the effort I'd expended. I was asleep as soon as I switched off the light.

When I woke, I rolled over and looked at the clock. Then I checked with my watch. I had to accept its corroboration. I'd been asleep for thirteen and a half hours. I don't think I've ever slept for that length of time, not even after general anaesthetic. I was furious with myself. I'd been looking forward to sitting down at my computer to relive and rebuild my encounter with Adam till it more closely resembled my deepest fantasies. But now I barely had enough time to shower and eat.

On my way into work, I picked up a late city final edition of the Bradfield Evening Sentinel Times. I'd made page two of the paper:

NAKED BODY FOUND

The mutilated body of a naked man was found in Bradfield's gay village early this morning.

Council worker Robbie Greaves made the grisly discovery as he made a routine rubbish collection in the Crompton Gardens area of Temple Fields.

Now the city's gay community fears this may be the first act of a gay serial killer like the man who recently terrorized London's homosexuals.

The body was found among shrubs behind a wall in the park, a notorious night-time meeting place for gay men looking for casual sex.

The man, said to be in his late twenties, has not yet been identified. Police describe him as white, 5ft 10ins, muscular build, with short dark wavy hair and blue eyes. He has no distinguishing marks or tattoos.

A police spokesman said, 'The man's throat had been cut and his body mutilated. Whoever committed this callous crime is a violent and dangerous man. The *nature of the victim's injuries mean the killer must have been covered in blood.*

'We believe the man was killed elsewhere and the body dumped in the park sometime during the night.

'We would urge anyone who was in the Crompton Gardens area of Temple Fields last night to come forward for the purposes of elimination. All information will be treated in the strictest confidence.'

Robbie Greaves, 28, the council worker who discovered the body, said, 'I'd only just started work. It was just after half past eight. I was using my grab to pick up litter. When it touched the body, I thought at first it was a dead cat or dog. Then I lifted up the bushes and saw the body.

'It was horrible. I threw up, then I ran to the nearest phone box. I've never seen anything like it in my life and I hope I never do again.'

Well, at least they'd got one thing correct. The body was killed somewhere else and dumped in Crompton Gardens. As for the rest of it . . . If this was any indication of the police's skills, I didn't think I'd have too much to worry about. That was fine by me. The last thing I wanted was to be arrested, since I'd already chosen Adam's successor. Paul, I knew, was going to be different. This time, it wouldn't have to end in death.

7

All his acquaintances afterwards described his dissimulation as so ready and so perfect, that if, in making his way through the streets . . . he had accidentally jostled any person, he would . . . have stopped to offer the most gentlemanly apologies: with his devilish heart brooding over the most hellish of purposes, he would yet have paused to express a benign hope that the huge mallet, buttoned up under his elegant surtout, with a view to the little business that awaited him about ninety minutes further on, had not inflicted any pain on the stranger with whom he had come into collision.

Carol turned off the main drag and cut through the back doubles to emerge in Crompton Gardens. 'Adam Scott was found just there,' she said, pointing to a spot halfway down one side of the shrubbery.

Tony nodded. 'Can you drive slowly round the square, then park up against the wall where the body was found, please?'

Carol did as he asked. As they cruised round the square, Tony gazed out intently, swinging round in his seat a couple of times to snatch a second look. When the car stopped, he got out. Without waiting for Carol, he crossed to the pavement and prowled round the edge of the square. Carol got out of the car and followed in his wake, trying to see what Tony saw.

Neither the murders nor the freezing weather had changed the habits of those who frequented Temple Fields. Doorways and basement areas still held grunting couples, heterosexual and homosexual alike. A few froze momentarily at the sound of Carol's heels on the pavement, but most ignored it. A great place to hang out if you were into voyeurism, Carol thought cynically.

Tony reached the end of the houses and crossed the street to the shop and bar fronts. Here, there were no copulating couples. The city's crime rate dictated heavy shutters and grilles for windows and doors. Ignoring them, Tony looked over towards the gardens in the centre of the square, matching what he'd seen on the photographs with the reality. There were no bushes on this side, only the low wall. He barely noticed two men walking past, wrapped round each other like competitors in a three-legged race. He wasn't interested in anyone else but Handy Andy.

'You've been here,' he said to himself. 'This isn't a place you just happened on, is it? You've walked this pavement, watched these parodies of love and affection that people pay for. But that's not what you were after, was it? You wanted something different, something a lot more intimate, something you didn't have to pay for.' How had they felt, those voyeuristic adventures of Handy Andy? Tony concentrated.

'You've never had a normal relationship with another

person,' he thought. 'The prostitutes don't bother you, though. Or the rent boys. You're not killing them. You're not interested in what you can do with them. It's the couples that get to you, isn't it? I know, you see, I know that for myself. Am I projecting? I don't think so. I think you're looking for coupledom, the perfect relationship, the one where you can be yourself, the one that will value you as highly as you think you should be valued. And then it will be all right. The past won't matter. But it does matter, Andy. The past is what matters most of all.'

He was suddenly aware of Carol standing by his side, looking at him curiously. Probably his lips were moving. He'd better be careful, or she'd be consigning him to the bin marked 'nutter' too. He couldn't afford that, not if he was to keep her on his side long enough to achieve the result he needed.

The last building on that side was an all-night diner, its windows opaque with condensation. In the bright light inside, shapes moved like creatures of the deep. Tony moved forward and pushed open the door. A handful of customers glanced up at him before returning to their fry-ups and chat-ups. Tony stepped back on to the street and let the door sigh shut behind him. 'I don't think you go in there,' he decided. 'I don't think you want to be seen to be alone in a place that's meant for companionship.'

The third side of the square consisted of a couple of modern office blocks. In the doorways, a clutch of homeless teenagers slept, bundled in clothes, newspapers and cardboard boxes. By now, Carol had caught up with him. 'Have they been interviewed?' Tony asked.

Carol pulled a face. 'We tried. My dad used to do a bit of folk singing. When I was a kid, he used to sing me a song with the chorus, "Oh, but I may as well try and catch the wind." Now I know what it means.'

'That good, eh?'

They crossed to the houses on the fourth side of the square, passing a pair of hookers on the corner. 'Hey, gorgeous!' one of them shouted. 'I could give you a better time than that tight-arsed bitch.'

Carol snorted with laughter. 'Now there's a triumph of hope over experience,' she said wryly.

Tony said nothing. The words had barely penetrated his reverie. He continued slowly down the pavement, pausing every few steps to drink in the atmosphere. Conflicting music filtered out faintly into the night from the flats and bedsits. The smell of curry wafted on the breeze that rustled the litter and sent polystyrene fast-food trays tumbling along the gutters. The square was never entirely empty, he noted. 'You despise their messy lives, don't you?' he said to himself. 'You like things clean and neat and orderly. That's partly why you wash the bodies. That's at least as important to you as erasing the forensic traces.' He turned the final corner and walked across to the rear of Carol's car, feeling the first stirrings of confidence that he was capable of mapping this complex and fatally skewed mind.

'He probably had to sit here for a few minutes to make sure he wasn't being watched,' Tony said. 'Depending on what kind of vehicle he's using, it could have taken as little as a minute to get the body out and over the wall. But he'd want to be sure no one was watching.'

'We did a full door-to-door across the street, but

nobody admitted to seeing anything out of the ordinary,' Carol replied.

'Let's face it, Carol, when you look at what's ordinary round here, it leaves plenty of scope for a serial killer. OK, I've seen enough. Shall we go?'

Cross bounded into the squad room, surprisingly light on his feet as fat people often are, as if somehow moving lightly negates the bulk of their body. 'All right, then, where is the scumbag?' he bellowed. Then he caught sight of the thin figure leaning against the wall, his conversation with Kevin Matthews interrupted by Cross's entrance.

'Sir?' Cross said, stopping in his tracks. 'I wasn't expecting you in.' He threw a look of pure venom at Kevin Matthews.

Brandon straightened up. 'No, Superintendent, I don't suppose you were.' He took a couple of steps towards Cross. 'I left instructions with the control room that if any arrests were made in connection with the serial killings I was to be informed at once. This is going to be a high-profile case when it comes to court, Tom. I want us to be seen to be squeaky clean.'

'Yes, sir,' Cross said mutinously. However Brandon dressed it up, what he was saying was that he didn't believe Cross was the man to make sure that over-zealous detectives didn't go too far. With Brandon pacing the corridors, no serial-killer suspects were going to have unfortunate accidents in custody. Cross turned to Kevin Matthews. 'What exactly happened?'

Kevin, so pale with tiredness and stress that his freckles stood out on milk-white skin like some vicious pox, said, 'As far as we can make out, Don Merrick came out of the Hell Hole with some bloke. One of the back-up teams saw them. Don switched his radio on to transmit, so we're assuming he wanted this bloke picked up for questioning. They were heading for the all-night diner in Crompton Gardens, according to the back-up boys. There's an alley that's a short cut through to the gardens, and they went down there. Next thing the back-up hear is a scuffle going on. They leg it round there and find Don on the floor and two blokes slugging it out. They arrested the pair of them and they're kicking their heels in the cells.'

'What about Merrick?' Cross demanded. For all his faults, Cross was a copper's copper. His men were almost as important to him as his own career.

'He's down Casualty getting stitches in a sore head. He came round in the ambulance. I've got one of my lads down there with him taking a statement.' Kevin glanced at his watch. 'He should be back any time now.'

'So what are we looking at here?' Cross demanded. 'Have we got a suspect, or what?'

Brandon cleared his throat. 'I think we can assume that Merrick thought the man he was with was worth a chat. As for the man who attacked them, I suspect we'll need to wait for Merrick's statement. I suggest Inspector Matthews and one of his team talk to the attacker while you and I have a preliminary chat with Merrick's target. That OK with you, Tom?'

Cross nodded, disgruntled. 'Yes, sir. And as soon as your lad gets back from Casualty, Kevin, I want to see him.' He moved towards the door, looking over his shoulder expectantly at Brandon.

Brandon said, 'Before we go, Tom, I think we need Inspector Jordan and Dr Hill in here.'

'With respect, sir, it's the middle of the night. Do we really need to bugger up the man's sleep?'

'I don't want to get into questioning anyone about the murders until I've had the chance to take Dr Hill's advice about how the interview should proceed. Besides, the two of them are probably still out working. DI Jordan was planning to show Dr Hill the crime scenes tonight. Can you fix that, Inspector?'

Kevin glanced at Cross, who nodded slightly. 'No problem, sir. I'll page Inspector Jordan right away. I'm sure she'll be delighted to lend a hand.'

Brandon smiled and walked past Cross into the corridor. 'Just shows what happens to your bottle when you get behind a desk,' Cross muttered, shaking his head in mock-sorrow. 'You get so's you need a bloody psychologist to tell you how to interview some scumbag off the streets.'

Canal Street was still busy. People came in and out of clubs, taxis dropped off and picked up, couples shared their kebabs and chips on street corners, rent boys and hookers watched the slow-moving traffic, pouncing on the least opportunity. 'Interesting, isn't it, how areas become defined?' Tony said to Carol as they walked briskly along the street.

'You mean this is the zone for public encounters, while Crompton Gardens is for the dark side?'

'And ne'er the twain shall cross over,' Tony said. 'It's really quite lively for the time of night, isn't it? Are Monday nights quieter?'

'A bit,' Carol said. 'A couple of the clubs shut on

Mondays. And one of the others has a women-only night.'

'So there's probably not as much street traffic,' Tony mused. As they'd driven round the streets, speculating on Handy Andy's approach route, Tony had been struck by how very public an area he'd chosen for his first two victims. Almost as if he were setting himself challenges. Now, at the corner of the alley leading to the side door of Shadowlands, he looked along the street and mused. 'He's desperate to be the best,' he said softly.

'Sorry?'

'Handy Andy. He just doesn't go for the easy options. His victims are all in the high-risk category. His dumping grounds aren't obscure, deserted hiding places. The bodies are cleaned of forensic clues. He's smarter than us, he thinks, and he has to keep proving it to himself. I'd hazard a guess that the next body's going to be dumped somewhere very, very public.'

Carol felt a shiver run through her that was nothing to do with the cold. 'Don't talk about the next body as if we're not going to find him before then,' she pleaded. 'It's just too depressing to think about.'

Carol led the way into the short dark cul-de-sac. 'Now, the second body, Paul Gibbs, was found just down here. All there is down here is the fire exit for the Shadowlands club.'

'It's dark enough,' Tony complained, stumbling over the edge of a disintegrating cardboard carton.

'We did suggest to the manager that a security light would be a good idea, if only to prevent him being mugged when he's locking up at night, but you can see how seriously he's taken the idea,' Carol replied, raking through her handbag to find her mini-torch. She snapped it on and the narrow beam revealed Tony silhouetted against a hooker in a red rubber dress giving a blow-job to a bleary-eyed businessman in the fire-exit doorway.

'Hoy!' the outraged man shouted. 'Bugger off, Peeping Tom!'

Carol sighed. 'Police. Zip your dick or you're nicked.' Before she'd even finished the sentence, the hooker was on her feet and heading for the mouth of the alley as fast as her stilettoes would let her. Realizing it wasn't worth arguing now the whore had gone, the man quickly fastened his trousers and pushed past Tony. As he turned the corner, he shouted, 'Frigid cunt!' back at her.

'You all right?' Tony asked, his genuine concern obvious.

Carol shrugged. 'When I started in the job, it really shook me when punters abused me like that. Then I realized it was them that had the problem, not me.'

'The theory's sound. How does it work in practice?'

Carol pulled a face. 'Some nights I go home and stand in the shower for twenty minutes and I still don't feel clean.'

'I know exactly what you mean. Some of the messy heads I have to poke about inside leave me feeling like I'll never have a normal relationship with another human being again.' Tony turned away, not wanting his face to betray him. 'So this is where you found Paul?'

Carol moved forward to stand beside him. She shone

her torch into the doorway. 'He was lying there, with a couple of bin bags tucked around him so he wasn't immediately obvious. Judging by the condoms lying around, the working girls had been screwing the night away smack bang next to a corpse.'

'I take it you've talked to the girls?'

'Yes, we've had them all in. The one that scuttled out of here like a cockroach when the light goes on uses this spot most nights. She says she had a punter some time around four in the morning. She knows it was then because this bloke is a regular who comes off his shift at the newspaper-printing plant about then. Anyway, she was going to bring him down here, but there was a car in the way.' Carol sighed. 'We thought we'd cracked it, because she could remember the make, model and the numbers on the licence plate, because it was the same as the number of her house. Two-four-nine.'

'Don't tell me. Let me guess. It was Paul Gibbs's car.'

'Got it in one.'

The insistent bleep of Carol's pager cut into the conversation, demanding as a baby's cry. 'I have to find a phone,' Carol said.

'What is it?'

'One thing you can always say for sure,' Carol said, hurrying back out of the alley. 'It's never good news.'

'Look, I've told youse all I know. I'd just met this guy Don in the Hole, we was going for a cup of tea and suddenly there's footsteps and Don hits the ground like Vinny Jones just tackled him and I turn round and there's this bampot with a brick. So I give him the citizen's arrest with the left hook, and that's when your boys turn up mob-handed, and here I am.' Stevie McConnell spread his hands out in front of him. 'Youse should be giving me a commendation, no' the third degree.'

'And you expect us to believe this . . .' Cross consulted his notes. 'This Ian attacked this Don just because he'd turned him down earlier in the evening?'

'That's about the size of it. Look, this Ian, he's known about the town. He's a heidbanger. He gets out of his brain on speed and thinks he's God Almighty. This Don gave him a right showing up, you know, made him look like a big jessie instead of macho man, so your man was for getting his own back. Look, you gonnae let me go, or what?'

Cross was spared from replying by a knock on the door. Brandon shrugged away from the wall he'd been leaning against and opened the door. He exchanged a few murmured words with the constable outside then came back in. 'Interview suspended at 1.47 a.m.,' he said, leaning past Cross to turn off the tape recorder. 'We'll be back shortly, Mr McConnell,' Brandon promised.

Outside the interview room, Brandon said, 'Inspector Jordan and Dr Hill are upstairs. And DS Merrick has come back from Casualty. Apparently, he says he's well enough to run through the evening's events himself.'

'Right. Well, we'd better hear what he's got to say, and then we can have a proper go at Jock.' Cross marched upstairs to the squad room, where a concerned Carol was hovering over Merrick. Tony sat a few feet away, feet propped up on the rim of a wastepaper bin.

'Bloody hell, Merrick!' Cross roared, seeing the dramatic bandage that turbanned his head. 'You've not turned into one of them bloody Sikhs, have you? Christ, I knew it was a risk sending a team into poofterville undercover, but I wasn't expecting religious mania.'

Merrick smiled weakly. 'I figured that way you couldn't send me back into uniform for cocking up, sir.'

Cross gave a grudging smile in return. 'Let's be hearing it, then. Why have I got a bolshie little sporran-sucker in my nick?'

Brandon, standing a couple of feet behind Cross, interrupted. 'Before DS Merrick runs through the evening's events for us, I just want to explain to Dr Hill why we've dragged him in here at this time of night.' Tony straightened up in his chair and pulled a sheet of paper towards him. 'When you were giving your lecture the other day,' Brandon continued, moving past Cross and sitting on the edge of a desk, 'you mentioned that psychologists can often give pointers to detectives about interview approaches. I wondered if you could apply that to this situation.'

'I'll do my best,' Tony said, uncapping his pen.

'How do you mean, interview approaches?' Cross said suspiciously.

Tony smiled. 'A recent example from my own experience. A force I'd been advising had arrested a suspect in two rape cases. He was the macho type, all bluster and muscle. I suggested that they send in a woman CID officer to interview him, preferably a small, very feminine woman. That made him angry right from the start, because he held women in contempt and thought he wasn't being treated with the appropriate respect. I'd briefed her in advance to suggest in her line of questioning that he couldn't possibly be the rapist since, frankly, she didn't think he had it in him. The result was, he blew his stack and coughed to the two rapes they had him in the frame for, as well as three other offences they didn't even know about.'

Cross said nothing. 'DS Merrick?' Brandon asked.

Merrick took them through his experiences in the bar with frequent pauses for thought. At the end of his recital, Brandon and Carol looked expectantly towards Tony. 'What do you think, Tony? Are either of them a possible?' Brandon asked.

'I don't think Ian Thomson is a starter. This killer is far too careful to get involved in something as ridiculously high profile as a street brawl. Even if Don hadn't been a police officer, the chances are that Thomson would have ended up in trouble for going after someone with a half-brick. Even in a city where attacks on gays are not noted for their high priority in policing terms,' he added drily.

Cross scowled. 'Gays get treated same as everybody else by the lads,' he blustered.

Tony wished he'd kept his mouth shut. The last thing he wanted was to get into a head-to-head with Tom Cross on Bradfield police's 'gays and blacks don't count' policy. He decided to ignore the comment and forged on. 'Also, there's nothing in what we know about the killer's behaviour to suggest that he's an upfront S&M gay man. It's clearly not from the gay scene that he's selecting victims. However, McConnell sounds more interesting from your point of view. Do we know what he does for a living?'

'He's the manager of a gym in the city centre. The same gym that Gareth Finnegan used,' Cross said.

'Hasn't he been questioned before?' Brandon asked. Cross shrugged.

'One of Inspector Matthews's team has spoken to him,' Carol butted in. 'I noticed the report when I was preparing the material for Dr Hill,' she added hastily, when she saw the beginnings of a scowl on Cross's face. God forbid he should think she was trying to undermine him. 'My dustbin memory,' she continued, trying to make a joke of it. 'As far as I can remember, it was simply a routine enquiry, checking up on whether Gareth had had any particular buddies or contacts at the gym.'

'Do we know McConnell's domestic arrangements?' Tony asked.

'He shares a house with another couple of shirt-lifters,' Cross said. 'He says they're both in the body-building game too. So, is he in the frame or not?'

Tony doodled in the margin of his notes. 'It's possible,' he said. 'What are the chances of getting a search warrant?'

'On what we've got at the moment? Not good. And we've no grounds for a search without one. Not even in our wildest dreams can we claim that a street assault gives us grounds to search McConnell's house for evidence relating to serial killings,' Brandon said. 'What would we be looking for in particular?'

'A camcorder. Any indication that he has access to

somewhere isolated and deserted like an old ware-house, factory, derelict house, lock-up garage.' Tony ran a hand through his hair. 'Polaroid photographs. Sado-masochistic pornography. Souvenirs of his victims. The jewellery missing from the bodies.' He looked up and met Tom Cross's sneer. 'And you should check the deep freeze just on the off chance that he's kept the pieces of flesh he removed from the bodies.' He felt a moment's gratification when Cross's expression changed to disgust.

'Charming. But first we have to get something more to go on. Any suggestions?' Brandon asked.

'Send DS Merrick and Inspector Jordan in to interview him. The realization that the man he tried to pick up is a police officer will unsettle him, make him feel that his instincts can't be trusted. There's a chance too that he has problems with women –'

'Of course he's got problems with women,' Cross interjected. 'He's a bloody arse bandit.'

'Not all gay men dislike women,' Tony said mildly. 'But a lot do, and McConnell may be one of them. At the very least, Carol will make him feel threatened. All-male situations offer him the opportunity for cama-raderie, so we take that off him.'

'Let's try it, then,' Brandon said. 'If DS Merrick is up to it.'

'I'm game, sir,' Merrick said.

Cross looked as if he couldn't decide whether to hit Brandon or Tony. 'I might as well bugger off home, then,' he blustered.

'Good idea, Tom. You've had more than your fair share of all-nighters lately. I'll hang on here, see what comes out of McConnell's interview.'

Cross stomped out of the squad room, passing Kevin Matthews on the way. The atmosphere visibly lightened in Cross's absence. 'Sir?' Kevin said. 'Ian Thomson – it looks like he's out of the frame on the murders.'

Brandon frowned. 'I thought I told you not to bring the murders up? At this stage, all we want to front Thomson with is the assault.'

'I didn't bring up the murders, sir,' Kevin said defensively. 'But it emerged during the interview that Thomson works three nights a week as a DJ in Hot Rocks. That's a gay club in Liverpool. He does Monday, Tuesday and Thursday. It should be easy enough to check whether he was working on the nights of the murders.'

'OK, get someone on it,' Brandon said.

'Which leaves McConnell,' Carol said thoughtfully.

'Let's do it,' Brandon said.

'Any tips?' Carol asked Tony.

'Don't be afraid to patronize him. Stay sweetness and light, but make it clear that you're the ranking officer. And DS Merrick – you can afford to play the gratitude card a bit.'

'Thanks,' Carol said. 'OK, Don?'

They left Brandon and Tony together. 'How is it going?' Brandon asked, getting up and stretching.

Tony shrugged. 'I'm starting to get a feel for his victims. There's a definite pattern there. He's a stalker, I'm sure of it. I should have a rough profile in a day or two. It's just bad timing that you've pulled in a suspect now.'

'How do you mean, bad timing?'

'I understand why you wanted my input. But I

175

don't like knowing about suspects before I draw up my profile. The danger is that I skew the profile subconsciously so that it's a better fit for the suspect.'

Brandon sighed. He'd always found it hard to be optimistic in the small hours. 'We'll cross that bridge when we come to it. By this time tomorrow, our suspect might just be a distant memory.'

Getting to know Paul was somehow more exciting than Adam had been. Partly, I suppose, because I knew now I could handle it if things didn't work out the way I wanted. Even if Paul didn't have the insight to see that I could give him more than anyone else, even if he rejected my love, even if he went as far as Adam and actually betrayed the inevitability of our partnership with someone else, I knew that there was an alternative scenario that could give me almost as much satisfaction as the achievement of what I deserved.

But this time, I felt sure that I would get what I wanted. Adam, I now saw, had been immature and weak. Paul was neither of those, I could tell at once. For a start, he hadn't chosen to live in the yuppie part of town like Adam. Paul lived on the south side of the city in Aston Hey, a leafy suburb beloved of university lecturers and alternative therapists. Paul's house was in one of the more inexpensive streets. Like mine, it was terraced, though his two-up and two-down rooms were obviously far bigger. Unlike mine, he had a small garden at the front, and his back yard was twice the size, scattered with terracotta planters and tubs filled with flowers and dwarf shrubs. The perfect place to sit together for a preprandial drink after work on summer evenings.

Now with Paul, I'd have the chance to live in Aston Hey, to enjoy those quiet streets, to walk in the park together, to be just like other couples. He had an interesting job, too – lecturer at Bradfield Institute of Science and Technology, specializing in CAD programs. We already had so much in common. It was a shame I'd never be able to show him what I'd achieved with Adam.

One of the major advantages of having no mortgage is that I have virtually all of my salary to play with. It's a substantial disposable income for someone of my age and with my lack of dependants. That means I can afford a state-of-the-art computer system, with regular upgrades to keep me out there at the leading edge. Given that one software program alone cost me nearly three thousand pounds, it's just as well I don't have anyone leeching off me. With my new CD-ROM system, video digitizer and special-effects software, it took me less than a day to import the videos into my computer. Once they were digitized and installed there, I could manipulate and morph the images to tell any story I wanted to see. Thanks to other video erotica I'd already installed on my system, I was even able to give Adam the erection he'd failed to achieve in life. Finally, I could fuck him, suck him, fist him, and watch him do the same to me. But the knowledge that I would be able to do that still hadn't been enough to save him. Not even my computer and my imagination could give me the joy and satisfaction he could have done if he'd only been honest with himself about his desire for me. And so, every day he had to die all over again. The ultimate fantasy, constantly changing, shaped to fit my every mood and whim. At last, Adam was performing everything he could ever have fantasized about. It was a shame he couldn't share in my pleasure.

It wasn't perfect, but at least I was having more fun than the police. From what I read, it was clear they were getting nowhere. Adam's death barely merited a mention in the national media, and even the Bradfield Evening Sentinel Times *gave up after five days. Adam's body was identified after four days, when anxious colleagues reported him missing after failing to get any reply from his phone or his doorbell. I was interested in their tributes (popular, hard-working, well liked, etc.) and I felt a moment's regret that his stupidity had deprived me of their friendship. The* Sentinel Times's *crime reporter had even managed to track down Adam's ex-wife, a mistake he'd made at twenty-one which he'd extricated himself from by his twenty-fifth birthday. Her comments made me laugh out loud.*

Adam Scott's ex-wife Lisa Arnold, 27, fought back the tears as she said, 'I can't believe this could have happened to Adam.

'He was a friendly man, really sociable. But he wasn't a big drinker. I can't imagine how this weirdo managed to get hold of him.'

Lisa, a primary-school teacher who has since remarried, went on, 'I've no idea what he was doing in Crompton Gardens. He never showed any gay tendencies when we were married. Our sex life was quite normal. If anything, it was a bit boring.

'We married too young. Adam's mother had brought him up to expect a wife who waited on him hand and foot, and that just wasn't me.

'Then I met someone else and I told Adam I wanted a divorce. He was really upset, but I think it was more that his pride was hurt.

'I haven't seen him since the divorce, but I heard he

was living on his own. I know he's had a few affairs over the last three years, but nothing serious as far as I know.

'I just can't get used to the idea that he's dead. I know we hurt each other, but I'm still devastated that he's been murdered like this.'

I didn't rate the chances of Lisa's second marriage lasting the course if she still had as little insight into the workings of the male mind. Boring? Lisa was the only reason sex with Adam could be boring.

And as for calling me a weirdo! She was the one who had turned her back on a charming, handsome man who loved her so much that he was still talking about her to complete strangers three years after she'd rejected him. I knew all about it; I'd listened to him. If anyone was a weirdo, it was Lisa.

8

No unpractised artist could have conceived so bold an idea as that of a noon-day murder in the heart of a great city. It was no obscure baker, gentlemen, or anonymous chimney-sweeper, be assured, that executed this work. I know who it was.

Stevie McConnell ran both hands through his hair in a gesture of desperation. 'Look, how many times do I have to tell you? I was telling porkies. I was trying to make myself sound the big man. I wanted to cop off, I was trying to make myself interesting. I never knew Paul Gibbs or Damien Connolly. I never saw either of them in my life.'

'We can prove you knew Gareth Finnegan,' Carol said coldly.

'OK, I admit I knew Gareth. He was a member down the gym, I can't pretend I'd never met him before. But Christ, woman, the man was a lawyer. He must have known thousands of people in the city,' McConnell said, thumping the table with a solid fist.

Carol didn't even flinch. 'And Adam Scott,' she went on relentlessly.

'Yeah, yeah,' he said wearily. 'Adam Scott had a trial one-month membership down the gym about two years ago. He never joined up. I bumped into him a couple of times in my local pub, we had a jar together, that's all there was to it. I have a drink with a lot of people, you know. I'm not a bloody hermit. Christ, if I killed everybody I've ever stood at a bar with, youse bastards would be busy from now till the next century.'

'We will prove you knew Paul Gibbs and Damien Connolly. You know that, don't you?' Merrick chimed in.

McConnell sighed. His hands clenched, forcing the muscles in his powerful forearms into sharp relief. 'If you do, you'll have to make it up, because you can't prove what isn't true. You're not going to do a Birmingham Six on me, you know. Look, if I was really this mad bastard, do you think I'd have hung around to help you? First sign of trouble, I'd have legged it. Stands to reason.'

Sounding bored, Carol said, 'But you didn't know then that Sergeant Merrick was a police officer, did you? So give us your alibi for Monday night.'

McConnell leaned back in the chair and stared at the ceiling. 'Mondays is my day off,' he recited. 'Like I said, the guys that share my house are on their holidays, so I was on my tod. I got up late, went down the supermarket for my messages, then I went for a swim. About six o'clock, I drove out to the multi-screen off the motorway, and I went to see the new Clint Eastwood film.'

Abruptly, he lurched forward in the chair. 'They'll be able to confirm it. I paid by credit card, and their system's all computerized. They can prove I was at the pictures,' he said triumphantly.

'They can prove you bought a ticket,' Carol said laconically. From the cinema to Damien Connolly's house would take no more than half an hour round the motorway, even allowing for rush-hour traffic.

'I can tell you the whole plot, for fuck's sake,' McConnell said angrily.

'You could have seen it any time, Stevie,' Merrick said gently. 'What did you do after the pictures?'

'I went home. Cooked myself a steak and some vegetables.' McConnell paused and stared at the table. 'Then I went into town for the last hour. Just for a quick drink with a few mates.'

Carol leaned forward, sensing McConnell's reluctance. 'Where in town?' she demanded.

McConnell said nothing.

Carol leaned further forward, the tip of her nose an inch from his. Her voice was quiet but icy cold. 'If I have to stick your face on the front page of the *Sentinel Times* and send a team into every pub in the city, I'll do it, Mr McConnell. Where in town?'

McConnell breathed in heavily through his nose. 'The Queen of Hearts,' he spat.

Carol leaned back, satisfied. She stood up. 'Interview terminated at 3.17 a.m.,' she said, leaning over to switch off the tape recorder. She looked down at McConnell. 'We'll be back, Mr McConnell.'

'Wait a minute,' he protested as Merrick got up and the two of them made for the door. 'When am I going to get out of here? You've got no right to keep me!'

Carol turned back in the doorway, smiled sweetly and said, 'Oh, I have every right, Mr McConnell.

You've been arrested for assault, let's not forget. I have twenty-four hours to make your life a misery before I even have to think about charging you.'

Merrick gave an apologetic smile as he backed out of the room in Carol's wake. 'Sorry, Stevie,' he said. 'The lady's not wrong.'

He caught up with Carol as she was asking the custody sergeant to return McConnell to the cells. 'What do you think, ma'am?' Merrick asked as they walked off together.

Carol stopped and eyed Merrick critically. His skin was pale and clammy, his eyes feverishly bright. 'I think you need to go home and get some sleep, Don. You look like shit on a stick.'

'Never mind me. What about McConnell, ma'am?'

'We'll see what Mr Brandon has to say.' Carol set off for the stairs, Merrick trailing behind her.

'But what do *you* think, ma'am?'

'On the face of it, he could be our man. He's got nothing approaching an alibi for Monday night, he runs the gym where Gareth Finnegan worked out, he knew Adam Scott and by his own admission he was in the Queen of Hearts on Monday night for the last hour. He's certainly strong enough to have carted the bodies in and out of a car. He's got form, even if it is only a couple of breaches of the peace and a Section 18 wounding. And he's into S&M. But that's all circumstantial. And I still don't think we've got grounds for a search warrant,' Carol rattled off. 'What about you, Don? Got a feeling in your water about this one?'

They turned down the corridor towards the murder squad room. 'I kind of like him,' Merrick said grudgingly. 'I can't imagine that I'd take a liking to the bastard that's been doing these murders. But then, I suppose that's a pretty daft reaction. I mean, he's not the two-headed man, is he? He's got to have something about him that lets him get close enough to his victims to do the business. So maybe it *is* Stevie McConnell.'

Carol opened the door to the squad room, expecting to find Brandon and Tony still sitting there, fuelled by coffee and canteen sandwiches. The room was empty. 'Where's the ACC got to now?' Carol said, tiredness lending her voice a note of exasperation.

'Maybe he's left a message at the front desk,' Merrick suggested.

'And maybe he's done the sensible thing and buggered off home to bed. Well, that's us for tonight, Don. McConnell can stew for a bit. See what the bosses have to say in the morning. Maybe we can try for a search warrant now we know McConnell was in the Queen of Hearts. Now, get out of my sight and go home to bed before your Jean accuses me of leading you off the straight and narrow. Get some sleep. I don't want to see you before noon, and if your head's hurting, stay in bed. That's an order, Detective Sergeant.'

Merrick grinned. 'Yes, ma'am. See you.'

Carol watched Merrick walk back down the corridor, worried at the slow deliberation of his movements. 'Don?' she called. Merrick turned enquiringly back to her. 'Get a taxi. My authorization. I don't want you wrapped round a lamppost on my conscience. And that's an order, too.' Merrick grinned, nodded and disappeared down the stairs.

With a sigh, Carol walked down the squad room to her temporary office. There was no message on her desk. Bloody Brandon, she thought. And bloody Tony

Hill. Brandon at least should have waited till she'd finished her interrogation of McConnell. And Tony might have left some indication of when he expected them to meet to discuss his profile. Muttering under her breath, Carol followed Merrick out of the building. As she reached the foyer, the officer minding the front desk called, 'Inspector Jordan?'

Carol turned back. 'I'm what's left of her.'

'The ACC left a message for you, ma'am.'

Carol approached the desk and took the envelope the constable handed her. She ripped it open and pulled out a single sheet of paper. 'Carol,' she read. 'I have taken Tony off on a little mission. I'll drop him at home afterwards. Please be in my office for ten this morning. Thanks for your hard work. John Brandon.'

'Great,' Carol said bitterly. She gave the constable a tired smile. 'I don't suppose you know where Mr Brandon and Dr Hill were headed?'

He shook his head. 'Sorry, ma'am. They didn't say.'

'Wonderful,' she muttered sarcastically. Turn your back for a minute and they were off playing their boys' games. Little mission, indeed. Bollocks to that, Carol thought as she marched back to her car. 'Three can play at that game,' she said as she turned the ignition key.

Tony flicked through the last of the magazines and returned it to the box file in the bedside storage cube. 'S&M always leaves me feeling faintly queasy,' he remarked. 'And this lot's particularly nasty.'

Brandon agreed. McConnell's collection of hard-core pornography consisted mostly of magazines crammed with glossy colour pictures of well-muscled young men torturing each other and masturbating. A few

186

were even more disturbing, with their graphic shots of male couples indulging in full sex with an array of sado-masochistic trappings. Brandon couldn't remember seeing nastier examples, even when he'd done a six-month attachment with Vice.

They were sitting on the bed in Stevie McConnell's room. As soon as Carol and Merrick had left for their interrogation, Brandon had said, 'Would it be helpful to you to see where McConnell lives?'

Tony picked up his pen again and started to doodle on the sheet of paper. 'It might give me some insight into the man. And if he is the killer, there could be evidence that ties him into the crimes. I don't mean murder weapons, or anything like that. I'm thinking more of the souvenirs. Photographs, newspaper clippings, as well as the stuff I was talking about before. But it's academic, isn't it? You said there was no chance of getting a search warrant.'

Brandon's melancholy face lit up in a strange smile, almost a leer. 'When you've got a suspect in custody, there are things you can do to circumvent the rules. You game?'

Tony grinned. 'I'm fascinated.' He followed Brandon downstairs to the cells. The custody sergeant hastily dropped the Stephen King novel he'd been reading and jumped to his feet.

'It's all right, Sergeant,' Brandon said. 'If I only had a couple of prisoners to think about, I'd be enjoying a good read, too. I'd like to have a look at McConnell's property.'

The sergeant unlocked the property cupboard and handed the transparent plastic bag to Brandon. There was a wallet, a handkerchief and a bunch of keys inside. Brandon opened it and removed the keys. 'You haven't seen me, have you, Sergeant? And you won't see me when I come back in a couple of hours, will you?'

The sergeant grinned. 'You couldn't possibly have been here, sir. I'd have been bound to notice.'

Twenty minutes later, Brandon was parking the Range Rover outside McConnell's terraced house. 'Lucky for us McConnell happened to mention that the two blokes he shares the house with are away on holiday.' He took a cardboard box out of the glove compartment and gave Tony a pair of latex gloves. 'You'll need these,' he said, slipping a pair over his own hands. 'If we do get a search warrant, it would be a bit embarrassing when the fingerprint team turn up you and me as prime suspects.'

'There's one thing I'm curious about,' Tony said as Brandon inserted the key in the mortice lock.

'What's that?'

'This is an illegal search, right?'

'Right,' Brandon said, opening the door and stepping into the hall. He groped for the light switch, but didn't turn it on when he found it.

Tony followed him, closing the door behind him. Only then did Brandon snap the light on, revealing a carpeted hall and stairs. There were a couple of framed posters of body-builders on the walls. 'So if we find any evidence, presumably it's inadmissible?'

'Also right,' said Brandon. 'But there are ways round that. For example, if we find a bloodstained cut-throat razor under McConnell's bed, it will mysteriously find its way on to the kitchen table. Then we go to the magistrate, explain that we went to McConnell's house to check he was telling the truth when he said his house-mates were on holiday, and we happened to look through the windows and we spotted what we have reason to believe is the weapon used to kill Adam Scott, Paul Gibbs, Gareth Finnegan and Damien Connolly.'

Tony shook his head in amusement. 'Bent? Us? Never, your honour!'

'There's bent and there's bent,' Brandon said grimly. 'Sometimes you need to give things a shove in the right direction.'

Tony and Brandon moved through the house, room by room. Brandon was intrigued by Tony's method. He would walk into a room, stand in the middle of the floor and slowly scan the walls, the furniture, the floor coverings, the shelves. He almost sniffed the air. Then, meticulously, he opened cupboards and drawers, lifted cushions, examined magazines, checked titles of books, CDs, cassettes and videos, handling everything he touched with the care and precision of an archaeologist. Within seconds, his mind was busy, analysing everything he saw and touched, slowly building a picture in his mind of the men who lived here, constantly matching it against the embryonic picture of Handy Andy that was developing in his mind like a photographic print in developer fluid.

'Have you been here, Andy?' he asked himself. 'Does this feel like you, smell like you? Would you watch these videos? Are these your CDs? Judy Garland and Liza Minnelli? The Pet Shop Boys? I don't think so. You're not camp, I know that much about you. And there's nothing camp or chichi about the house. This place is so aggressively masculine. A living room furnished in eighties chrome and black. But it's not a straight man's house, is it? No girlie magazines, not even car magazines. Just body-building periodicals stacked under the coffee table. Look at the walls. Men's bodies, oiled and shining, muscles like carved wood. The men who live here know who they are, they know what they like. I don't think this is you, Andy. You're controlled, Andy, but not this controlled. It's one thing to keep yourself buttoned up, it's another thing altogether to be strong enough to project so coherent an image. I should know, I'm the expert. If you were as firmly rooted in your identity as the guys who live here, you wouldn't have to do what you do, would you?

'Look at the books. Stephen King, Dean R. Koontz, Stephen Gallagher, Iain Banks. Arnold Schwarzenegger's biography. A couple of paperbacks about the Mafia. Nothing soft, nothing gentle, but nothing off the wall either. Would you read these books? Maybe. I think you'd like to read about serial killers, though, and there's none of that here.'

Tony turned slowly towards the door. It was a small shock to see Brandon standing there. He'd become so absorbed in his scrutiny that he'd lost all sense of being in company. Watch yourself, Tony, he warned himself. Stay inside your head.

In silence, they trooped through to the kitchen. It was spartan, but well equipped. In the sink there was a dirty soup bowl and a mug half full of cold tea. A small shelf of cookery books testified to the occupants' obsession with healthy eating. 'Fart city,' Tony observed wryly, opening a cupboard filled with jars of pulses. He opened the drawers, noting the kitchen knives. There was a small vegetable knife with a blade worn thin from sharpening, a bread knife whose blade was pitted with age, and a cheap carving knife, the handle bleached from the dishwasher. 'These are not your tools, Andy,' Tony said to himself. 'You like knives that do their work properly.'

Without consulting Brandon, he walked out of the kitchen and up the stairs. Brandon watched him stick his head round the first bedroom door and reject it. As he passed, he saw that it was obviously the couple's room. He followed Tony through the door across the landing. In McConnell's bedroom, Tony seemed to drift away altogether into a world of his own. The room was simply furnished with modern pine bed, chest of drawers and wardrobe. An array of weightlifting trophies sat on the deep windowsill. A tall bookcase was crammed with pulp science fiction and a handful of gay novels. On a small table, there was a games computer and a television monitor. On a shelf above was a collection of games. Tony browsed through Mortal Kombat, Streetfighter II, Terminator 2, Doom and a dozen other games whose keynote was violent action.

'This is more like it,' he murmured. He stood by the chest of drawers, hand poised to open one. 'Maybe it's you after all,' he thought. 'Maybe you leave the living room to the other two. What if this is your only domain? What would I expect to find here? I'd want your souvenirs, Andy. You need to keep something by you, otherwise the memory disintegrates too fast. We all need something tangible. The discarded perfume spray that holds her fragrance and summons her before my eyes like a hologram; the theatre programme from the night we first made love and it was all right. Keep the good memories, throw away the bad. What have you got for me?'

The first three drawers were disappointingly innocuous: underwear, T-shirts, socks, jogging suits and shorts. When Tony opened the bottom drawer, he sighed in satisfaction. The drawer contained McConnell's S&M gear – handcuffs, leather restraint straps, cock rings, whips, and a clutch of items that looked to Brandon as if they ought to be in some kind of laboratory or mental institution. As Tony calmly took them out and examined them, Brandon shuddered.

Tony sat down on the bed and looked around. Slowly, cautiously, he tried to construct a picture of the man who lived in this room. 'You like to exercise power through violence,' he thought. 'You enjoy the flow of pain in your sexual experience. But there's no subtlety here. No sign that you're a man who plans things with care and detail. You worship your body. It's a temple to you. You've achieved things, and you're proud of that. You're not socially inadequate. You manage to share a house with two other men, and you're not obsessive about your privacy, since there's no lock on the door. You don't have a problem with your sexuality, and you're comfortable with the idea of picking up a man in a club, provided you have the chance to get to know him a bit first.'

His picture-building was interrupted by Brandon. 'Look at this, Tony!' he said excitedly. The ACC had been painstakingly going through a shoebox full of papers, mostly receipts, electrical guarantees, bank and credit-card statements. The box was almost empty, but now, he held out a flimsy slip of paper.

Tony took it. It was some kind of official police form. He frowned. 'What's this?'

'It's the form you get when an officer stops you in a car and you haven't got your documents with you. You have to take them to a police station within a fixed period, so they can check everything's in order. Look at the name of the officer,' Brandon urged.

Tony looked again. The name that had at first seemed a scrawled jumble suddenly resolved itself into 'Connolly'.

'I recognized his number,' Brandon said. 'You can hardly make out the name.'

'Shit,' Tony breathed.

'Damien Connolly must have stopped him for some minor traffic offence, or just on a spot check, and asked him to produce his documents,' Brandon said.

Tony frowned. 'I thought Connolly was a local information officer? What was he doing dishing out a traffic ticket?'

Brandon looked over Tony's shoulder at the slip of paper. 'It was nearly two years ago. Connolly obviously wasn't a collator then. Either he was doing a stint with Traffic or he was on duty in the area car when he saw McConnell doing something he shouldn't have been.'

'Can you check that out discreetly?'

'No problem,' Brandon said.

'You've cracked it, then, haven't you?'

Brandon looked astonished. 'You mean . . . you think that clinches it? McConnell's the man?'

'No, no,' Tony said hastily. 'Not at all. All I meant was that if you can track that back from the other end, you should be able to get a magistrate to grant you an official search warrant on the basis that McConnell knew three of the four victims, which goes beyond mere coincidence.'

'Right,' Brandon said, sighing. 'So you're still not convinced McConnell's the killer?'

Tony stood up and paced to and fro across the carpet, its jagged geometric pattern of grey, red, black and white reminding him of the one and only migraine he'd ever had. 'Before you found this, I'd come to the conclusion you'd got the wrong man,' he said after a few moments. 'I know I've not had time to sit down and write out a full profile yet, but I felt like I was beginning to get a sense of what this killer's like. And there are too many things here that don't fit that picture. But this is a hell of a coincidence. This is a big city. We've established that Stevie McConnell knew or at least had met three out of the four victims. How many people are going to be in that position?'

'Not many,' Brandon said grimly.

'I still don't like McConnell for the killer, but it's possible that the killer is someone he knows, someone who's met Adam Scott and Gareth Finnegan through him,' Tony said. 'Maybe even somebody who was with him when he got that traffic ticket, or someone that he pointed Damien out to. You know the kind of thing: "That's the bastard who nicked me for speeding."'

'You really don't think it's him, do you?' Brandon said flatly, disappointment in his voice. 'I suppose it's thin. After all, there's no evidence as such to connect the house to the killings,' he said cautiously. 'But you said yourself, he's more likely to be doing his killing somewhere else. That might be where he keeps his souvenirs.'

'It's not just the absence of souvenirs,' Tony said.

'Putting it crudely, John, serial murderers kill to turn their fantasies into reality. Typically, they have fantasies developed to the point where they are more real to them than the world around them. There's nothing here to suggest McConnell is that type of personality. Sure, he's got a stack of porn mags. But so have most single men of his age, regardless of sexual orientation. He's got violent computer games, but so have thousands of teenagers and grown men too. What there is is plenty of evidence to suggest that Stevie McConnell isn't a sociopath. Look around you, John. This whole house reeks of normality. The kitchen calendar has dates for people coming round for dinner. Look at that pile of Christmas cards on his bookshelf. There must be fifty there. Look at his holiday snaps. He was obviously with the same partner for four or five years, judging by the locations and hairstyle changes. Stevie McConnell doesn't seem to have problems forming relationships with people. OK, so there doesn't seem to be anything relating to his family, but a lot of gay people get cut off by their families when they come out. It doesn't mean that his family were dysfunctional in the ways that typically lead to the development of a serial killer. I'm sorry, John. I wasn't sure at first, but the more I've seen, the more this guy just doesn't smell right to me.'

Brandon got to his feet and carefully replaced the slip of paper exactly where he'd found it. 'It grieves me to say so, but I think you're right. When I interviewed him earlier, I thought he was way too calm to be our man.'

Tony shook his head. 'Don't let that mislead you. Chances are when you do pull the right guy, he'll be calm too. Don't forget, this is something he's planned carefully. Although he thinks he's the best, he'll still have made contingency plans. He'll expect to be brought in for questioning sooner or later. He'll be ready for you. He'll be reasonable, pleasant. He won't look like a con. He'll be bland, helpful, and he won't ring alarm bells with your detectives. His alibi will be no alibi. He'll probably say he's been with a tart, or been to an away football match on his own. He'll end up being eliminated from your enquiries because other suspects will be superficially far more appealing.'

Brandon managed to look even more depressed than normal. 'Thanks, Tony. You've really cheered me up now. So what do you suggest?'

Tony shrugged. 'Like I said, it's a possibility that he knows the killer. He may even have his own suspicions. I'd hang on to him for a bit longer, sweat him for what and who he does know. But I wouldn't call off the team. Get a warrant. Do a proper search, under the floorboards, in the loft. You never know what you might turn up. Don't forget, I could be completely wrong.'

Brandon glanced at his watch. 'Right. I'd better get these keys back before the end of the custody sergeant's shift. I'll drop you off on the way.'

With a last look to check they'd left nothing out of place, Brandon and Tony left McConnell's house. As they approached the Range Rover, a voice from the shadows said, 'Good morning, gentlemen. You're nicked.' Carol stepped forward into the light of the streetlamp. 'Dr Anthony Hill, and Assistant Chief Constable John Brandon, I am arresting you on suspicion

196

of breaking and entering. You do not have to say anything . . .' At that point, the giggles took over.

Brandon's heart had thudded into his throat at her first words. 'Hellfire, Carol,' he protested. 'I'm too old for tricks like that.'

'But not for ones like this, I see,' Carol said drily, gesturing with her thumb towards McConnell's house. 'Unauthorized search, and with a civilian? Just as well for you I'm off duty, sir.'

Brandon gave a weary smile. 'So why are you loitering with intent around the suspect's house?'

'I'm a detective, sir. I thought I might find you and Dr Hill here. Any joy?'

'Dr Hill thinks not. What about your interview?' Brandon asked.

'Your suggestions worked really well, Tony. McConnell's got no alibi to speak of for Damien Connolly's murder, apart from one hour late on in the evening, by which time Damien could have been dead already. The significant thing is where he was for that hour. Sir, he was drinking in the pub where the body was dumped.'

Tony's eyebrows climbed and he sucked his breath in sharply. Brandon turned to him. 'Well?'

'It's exactly the cheeky sort of thing Handy Andy could pull. You might want to get someone to check if he's a regular in there. If he isn't, it makes it significant,' Tony said slowly. Before he could say more, he was overwhelmed by a huge yawn. 'Sorry,' he yawned. 'I'm not a night bird.'

'I'll drive you home,' Carol said. 'I think the ACC has something to drop off at the station.'

Brandon looked at his watch. 'Fine. Make it eleven, not ten, Carol.'

'Thank you, sir,' Carol said with feeling as she unlocked her car for Tony. He slumped into the passenger seat, unable to stop the wave of yawns that had engulfed him.

'I'm really sorry,' she made out through a jaw-cracker. 'I can't stop yawning.'

'Did you find anything to make it worthwhile?' Carol said, her tone more sympathetic than her words.

'Damien Connolly nicked him a couple of years ago for a traffic offence,' Tony said heavily.

Carol whistled. 'Gotcha! We've caught him in a double lie, Tony! McConnell originally told Don Merrick he'd met Connolly after a burglary at the gym. Then in the interview he denied ever having seen him. He said he'd been lying to make himself seem interesting. But now it turns out he really had met him! What a break!'

'Only if you believe he's the killer,' he said. 'I'm sorry to disappoint you, Carol, but I don't think he's the one. I'm too tired to go through it all now, but once I've drawn up my profile and we go through it, you'll see why I can't get excited about Stevie McConnell.' He yawned again and leaned his head on his hand.

'When can we do that?' Carol asked, fighting the urge to shake his thoughts out of him.

'Listen, give me the rest of today to myself, and by tomorrow morning I'll have a draft profile for you. How's that?'

'Fine. Anything else you need in the meantime?'

Tony said nothing. Carol gave him a quick sidelong glance and realized he had dozed off. All right for some, she thought. Forcing herself to concentrate, she drove across town to Tony's house, a turn-of-the-century brick-built semi in a quiet street a couple of tram stops away from the university. Carol pulled up outside. The car's slow glide to immobility did nothing to disturb Tony, whose breathing had become audible.

Carol undid her seat belt and leaned over to shake him gently. Tony's head came up in a startled gesture, his eyes wide and frantic. He stared uncomprehendingly at Carol. 'It's all right,' she said. 'You're home. You fell asleep.'

Tony rubbed his eyes with his fists, muttering something unintelligible. He looked blearily at Carol and gave a sleepy, lopsided smile. 'Thanks for bringing me home.'

'No problem,' Carol said, still twisted round in her seat, fiercely aware of his closeness. 'I'll give you a ring this afternoon, we can fix up a time to meet tomorrow.'

Tony, awake now, felt claustrophobic. 'Thanks again,' he said, retreating hastily, opening the car door and almost tumbling on to the pavement, thanks to the combination of haste and sleepiness.

'I can't believe I wanted him to kiss me,' Carol said to herself as she watched Tony open his gate and walk up the short path. 'Dear God, what is happening to me? First I treat Don like a mother hen, then I start fancying the expert witnesses.' She saw the front door open, stuffed a cassette in the stereo and drove off. 'What I need,' she told Elvis Costello, 'is a holiday.'

'You tease, and you flirt, and you shine all the buttons on your green shirt,' he sang back.

'Last night, we were practically sticking the champagne on ice. Now you're telling me you want to let McConnell go?' Cross shook his head in a gesture of exasperation so ancient it probably appeared on a Greek vase. 'What's happened to change everything? Come up with a cast-iron alibi, has he? Out on the razz with Prince Edward and his bodyguards, was he?'

'I'm not saying let him go this minute. We need to question him closely about his associates, check if he introduced anyone to both Gareth Finnegan and Adam Scott. And after that, we have to let him walk. There's no real evidence, Tom,' Brandon said wearily. Lack of sleep had transformed his face into a grey mask that wouldn't have looked out of place in a Hammer Horror film. Cross, on the other hand, looked and sounded as fresh as a toddler who's just had a nap.

'He was in the Queen of Hearts that night. For all we know, he had Damien Connolly's body in the boot of his car, just waiting for closing time. It's got to be grounds for searching his gaff.'

'As soon as we've got enough evidence to get a search warrant, we'll do it,' Brandon said, reluctant to admit that he'd already taken that unorthodox step. Earlier, he'd asked Sergeant Claire Bonner to check all Damien Connolly's arrests and traffic tickets, supposedly on the off chance of a connection to McConnell, but so far, she hadn't unearthed the crucial information that he knew was lurking there.

'I suppose this is all down to Boy Wonder,' Cross said bitterly. 'I suppose the shrink says McConnell's childhood wasn't unhappy enough.'

Carol bit her tongue. It was bad enough being the fly on the wall in this clash of the titans without reminding either of her bosses she was witnessing their conflict.

Brandon frowned. 'I have consulted with Dr Hill, and yes, he does feel that on the basis of what we've got so far, McConnell probably isn't our man. But that's not the main reason why I think we should let him loose. The lack of evidence is a hell of a lot more important to me.'

'And to me. That's why we need time to collect some more. We need to interview these poofters he was drinking with on Monday night, to see what kind of state he was in. And we need to take a look at what McConnell's got under his mattress,' Cross said forcefully. 'We've had him in custody for less than twelve hours, sir. We're entitled to keep him till gone midnight. Then we can charge him with the assault for now, and ask the magistrates for a lie-down in police custody, which gives us another three days. That's all I'm asking for. I'll have nailed him by then. You can't say no to that, sir. You'll have the lads up in arms.'

Wrong, Carol thought. You were doing fine up till then, but the emotional blackmail just scuppered you.

Brandon's ears flushed scarlet. 'I hope no one thinks that because we are questioning someone the work stops,' he said, a dangerous edge in his voice.

'They're dedicated, sir, but they've been working on this a long time without a break in the case.'

Brandon turned away, staring out of the window at the city below. His instincts said to let McConnell go after they'd had one last attempt at digging his contacts out of him, but he had known without Cross's clumsy comments that having a suspect had given the murder squad a new lease of energy. Before he could make a decision, there was a knock at the door. 'Come in,' Brandon called, swinging round and dropping heavily into his chair.

Kevin Matthews's carrot curls appeared round the door. He looked like a kid who's been promised a trip to Disneyland. 'Sir,' he said. 'Sorry to interrupt, sir, but we've just had a report from Forensic on the Damien Connolly killing.'

'Come in and tell us, then,' Cross invited genially.

Kevin gave an apologetic smile and slid his slim frame round the door. 'One of the SOCOs found a scrap of torn leather caught on a nail on the gate,' he said. 'It's a secure area, the public can't just walk in, so we thought it might be significant. Obviously, we had to eliminate the people who work at the pub, and the draymen who deliver there. Anyway, it turns out that the yard was whitewashed and the gates were painted only a month ago, so we didn't have to chase too many bodies. Bottom line is, no one admitted owning anything made from leather like this, so we sent it off to Forensic and asked them to look at it double urgent. The report's just come back.' He proffered the report to Brandon, eager as a Boy Scout.

The relevant passage had been highlighted in yellow. It leapt off the page at Brandon. 'The fragment of dark-brown leather is extremely unusual. For a start, it appears to be deerskin of some sort. More significantly, analysis indicates that it has been cured in sea water rather than a specialist chemical-curing medium. I know of only one source of such leather: the former Soviet Union. Because regular supplies of the correct chemicals are difficult to come by, many tanners there still use the old method of curing with sea water. I would guess that the fragment has come from a leather jacket that originated in Russia. Leather like this is not available commercially elsewhere, since it does not meet the quality levels required by Western retail outlets.' Brandon read it, then tossed it across the desk towards Cross.

'Bloody hell!' Cross said. 'You mean we're looking for an Ivan?'

I read somewhere that murder enquiries cost a million pounds a month. When Paul demonstrated he was every bit as stupid and treacherous as Adam, I began to realize the actions I'd been forced to take might start to have a significant impact on local taxes. Not that I minded a few extra pence a year on my council-tax bills; it was a small price to pay for the satisfaction I gained from dealing with their perfidy.

I was devastated by Paul's defection. Just as I'd set the scene for the triumphant celebration of our love, he turned his back on me and chose another. The night he made his first approach, I don't know how I got home. I can't remember a single detail of the journey. I sat in my jeep outside the farm, raging against his shallowness, his failure to recognize that I was the one he truly loved. My anger was so strong I'd lost all physical coordination. I virtually fell out of the driver's seat and staggered like a drunk towards the haven of my dungeon.

I climbed on to the stone bench and hugged my knees to my chest while the unfamiliar tears rolled down my cheeks and splashed on the raw stone, staining it dark as Adam's blood. What was wrong with them? Why couldn't they let themselves have what I knew they wanted?

I wiped my eyes. I owed it to both of us to make the experience as rich and as perfect as possible. It was time for new toys. Adam had been the dress rehearsal. Paul was going to be the first night.

The ploy of the car that wouldn't start had served me well with Adam, so I used it on Paul. It worked like a dream. Before I was three steps down the hall, he'd even invited me to have a drink while I was waiting for the AA man. But I didn't fall for his blandishments; he'd had his chance, and it was too late now for me to abort my plans for our union on my terms.

When he came round, he was strapped into a Judas chair. It had taken me a few days to construct it, since I'd had to start from scratch. The Judas chair was one of my San Gimignano discoveries. I'd only ever seen a couple of references to it in my books, none of which made it at all clear how exactly it was constructed. But there in the museum, they had their very own working model. I had taken a couple of photographs to augment the one in the museum catalogue, and equipped with those, I had worked out a practicable design on my computer.

It's not a machine that inquisitors have used much, though I can't quite see why. The San Gimignano museum puts forward a theory which frankly seems absurd to me. Coupled with some of the other descriptions on the cards, this daft theory convinces me that the cards have been written by some blinkered, obsessive feminist. The theory goes thus: it was OK to use implements of torture on women such as vaginal pears that shredded the cervix and vagina, so-called 'Chastity' belts which ripped their labia to a bloody pulp, implements that chopped nipples as efficiently as a cigar cutter, because women were a separate species from the inquisitors, and indeed were often creatures of the devil. On the other hand, so this demented theory goes, torture instruments used on men tend not to be directed against their sexual organs, in spite of the tenderness of those areas, because – wait for it – the torturers felt subconsciously connected to their victims and therefore any mutilation inflicted on their cocks and balls was unthinkable. Clearly, the caption writer in San Gimignano is far from au fait with the refinements of the Third Reich.

My Judas chair, even if I say so myself, is a masterpiece of the type. It consists of a square frame with a leg at each corner, with arm supports for the forearms and a thick plank up the back. Much like a primitive carving chair, except that there is no seat. Instead, below the gap where the seat should be, there is a sharply barbed conical spike, attached to the chair legs at its base by a cross-brace of strong wooden struts. For the spike, I'd used one of the large cones that cotton yarn used to be wound round on industrial looms. You can pick them up in the souvenir shop of any outpost of the heritage industry. I'd covered it with a thin, flexible sheet of copper, and fastened thin strands of razor wire in a spiral round the outside. I'd added my own refinement to the example in the torture museum: my spike was wired up to the electrical supply via a rheostat, allowing me to apply electric shocks of varying intensity. The whole thing is bolted to the floor to prevent accidents.

While he'd still been unconscious, Paul had been held above the spike by a strong leather strap under his armpits, binding him to the back of the chair. I'd also strapped each ankle to one of the front legs of the chair. As soon as I *unfastened the strap, he'd be thrown on his own resources, relying on the muscles in his calves and his shoulders to keep him from the savage spike, carefully sited immediately below his anus. Since the chair was so high that only his toes could reach the floor, I didn't expect him to hold out too long.*

His eyes registered the same panic I'd already seen in Adam. But his situation was entirely of his own making. I told him so before I ripped the tape away from his mouth.

'I had no idea, no idea,' he gabbled. 'I'm sorry, I'm so sorry. You've got to let me make it up to you. Just let me out of this thing, and I promise we can make a fresh start.'

I shook my head. 'Robert Maxwell got one thing right. He said trust is like virginity; you can only lose it once. You have a treacherous soul, Paul. How can I believe in you?'

His teeth began chattering, though not, I suspect, from cold. 'I made a mistake,' he forced out. 'I know that. Everybody makes mistakes. Please, all I ask is the chance to make it right. I can make it right, I promise.'

'Show me, then,' I said. 'Show me you mean it. Show me you want me.' I stared at his shrivelled cock, dangling with his balls in the space where the seat should have been. I had looked forward to beauty, but he had failed me there, too.

'N-not here, not like this. I can't!' His voice rose in a pathetic wail.

'It's this or nothing. Here or nowhere,' I told him. 'By the way, in case you're wondering, you're strapped into a Judas chair.' Carefully, I explained how the chair worked. I wanted him to make an informed choice. As I talked, his skin turned grey and clammy with fear. When I explained about the electricity, he lost it completely. Piss dribbled from his cock, splashing on the floor beneath him. The stink of warm urine rose and choked me.

I slapped him so hard his head cracked against the back

board of the Judas chair. He cried out, and tears sprang into his eyes. 'You dirty, filthy baby,' I shouted at him. 'You don't deserve my love. Look at you, pissing and crying like some little girl. You're not a man.'

Hearing my mother's words coming from my mouth shattered my self-control as nothing else could have done. I kept hitting him, revelling in the crunch of cartilage as his nose collapsed under my fist. I was beside myself with anger. He'd fooled me into thinking he was something he wasn't. I'd thought Paul was strong and brave, intelligent and sensitive. But he was just a stupid, cowardly, lecherous pig, a pathetic excuse for a man. How had I ever let myself imagine he could be a worthy partner? He wasn't even resisting, just sitting there mewing like a kitten, letting me hit him.

Panting with exertion and anger, I finally stopped. I stepped back and stared contemptuously at him, watching his tears wash lines through the blood on his face. 'You brought this on yourself,' I hissed. All my careful plans had gone up in smoke.

But now, I didn't want to give him the second chance I'd given Adam. I didn't want Paul's love, not under any circumstances. He didn't deserve me. I stepped round to the back of the chair and grasped the tongue of the strap. 'No,' he whimpered. 'Please, no.'

'You had your chance,' I said angrily. 'You had your chance and you blew it. You've no one to blame but yourself, coming here and pissing on the floor like a baby who can't control itself.' I pulled the strap, tightening it enough to let me slip it free of the buckle. Then I let it slide free.

Paul's muscles instantly clenched, holding him rigidly in place, a scant half-inch above the spike. I moved round into his line of vision and slowly stripped off, caressing my body, imagining what his hands would have felt like. His eyes bulged with effort as he tried to keep himself in place. I sat down and slowly, deliciously began to rub myself, irresistibly turned on by his fight to stay away from the agonizing spike.

'You could have been doing this,' I sneered, aroused still further by the quivering of his thighs and calves. 'You could have been making love instead of fighting to keep your arse in working order.'

If he'd worked out like Adam had, the pleasure would have lasted longer. As it was, his screams of agony mingled with my groans of pleasure. I came like a Guy Fawkes rocket, fire flashing through me and erupting in an orgasm that had me buckling at the knees.

He tried to pull free, but the barbs just cut deeper into his tender flesh. I lay back in the chair, savouring the waves of pleasure that flowed through me after my orgasm, Paul's moans and screams an extravagant counterpoint to my sexual satisfaction.

As time passed, he sank lower on the spike, and his screams moderated to whimpering groans. To my surprise, I felt sexual desire rise in me again. After the exquisite pleasure of my first orgasm, I wanted my excitement matched again. I reached for the control box for the electrical current to the spike, and pressed the button that completed the circuit. Even with a relatively low current, Paul's body convulsed in an arc that wrenched him almost clear of the spike, a fine spray of blood spattering the floor for a couple of feet around.

I matched the rhythms of our two bodies, the speed and intensity of our mutual excitement keeping perfect pace. I felt my muscles quiver like his as I thrust against my hand. As I came, my body arched in sync with his, my gasps echoed by his last agonized cries before unconsciousness came.

I have to confess I was surprised by how much I enjoyed

Paul's punishment. Perhaps because he had deserved so much more than Adam, perhaps because I had had higher expectations of him in the first place, or perhaps simply because I was getting better at what I had to do. Whatever the reason, my second excursion into murder left me feeling as if I'd found my true vocation at last.

9

> We dry up our tears, and . . . discover that a trans-
> action which, morally considered, was shocking, and
> without a leg to stand upon, when tried by prin-
> ciples of Taste, turns out to be a very meritorious
> performance.

'OK, Andy, it's showtime,' Tony said to the blank
screen of his computer. After Carol had dropped him
off, he'd stumbled upstairs, kicking off his shoes and
letting his quilted baseball jacket lie where it fell on
the landing. Pausing only to empty his bladder, he'd
burrowed under the duvet and fallen into the deepest
sleep he'd known for months. When he'd woken, it
had been after noon. But for once, he felt no guilt about
the work he should have been doing. He felt refreshed,
excited, elated even. Searching Stevie McConnell's
house had given him a new certainty that he really
did understand what he was doing. He had known,
with absolute clarity, that Handy Andy did not live like
that. And although it wasn't something he could admit
to anyone outside the tight circle of fellow profilers,
there was a real rush in realizing that he could probably

find his way into Handy Andy's head and map a path through the tortured labyrinth of his unique logic. All he had to do now was find the key to the door.

In the office, Tony powered his way through the remaining piles of documents, making notes as he went along. Then he closed the blinds and told his secretary to hold all his calls. He moved his own chair round the desk so that it faced the visitor's chair. On the desk to one side, he placed his tape recorder, still switched off. He walked over to the door and stood with his back to it, contemplating the room. Some poem he'd once read echoed in his mind. Something about a road that divided in a wood, and the importance of choosing the branch less travelled by. For as long as he could recall, his fascinations had led him down the road less travelled by. It was the road that his patients walked, the dark path that led into the undergrowth, away from the dappled sunshine of the broad path. 'I need to understand why you chose that road, Andy,' Tony murmured. 'This is what I do best, Andy. You see, I know what draws me to that road. But I'm not like you. I can go back when I want to. I can choose the sunny path. I don't have to be here. All I'm doing is studying your footsteps. Or at least, that's what I tell the world.

'But we know the truth, don't we? You can't hide from me, Andy,' he said softly. 'I'm just like you, you see. I'm your mirror image. I'm the poacher turned gamekeeper. It's only hunting you that keeps me from being you. I'm here, waiting for you. Journey's end.' He stood for a moment longer, savouring the admission he'd made to himself.

Finally, he sat down in his chair and leaned forward,

elbows on knees, hands loosely linked. 'OK, Andy,' he said. 'It's just you and me. We're going to skip the preliminaries; all that stuff where we do the verbal arm wrestling and you eventually decide to talk to me. We're going straight for it. First off, I want to say how impressed I am. I've never seen a cleaner job. I don't just mean the bodies, I mean the whole thing. Sweet as a nut, you did it. Never a witness. Let me rephrase that. Never anybody seeing any significance in what they saw or heard, because there must have been people who saw or heard something, but they didn't make the connection. How did you manage to be so invisible?' He pressed 'record' on the cassette recorder, then stood up and stepped across to the other chair.

Tony took a deep breath and deliberately relaxed his body. He used breathing techniques to put himself into a light state of trance. He instructed his conscious mind to let go, to allow his higher self to access directly all he knew about Handy Andy and to answer for him. When he spoke, even his voice was different. The timbre was rougher, the tones deeper. 'I blended in. I took care. I watched and I learned.'

Tony swapped chairs again. 'You obviously did a good job of it,' he said. 'How did you choose them?'

Back into Andy's chair. 'I liked them. I knew it would be special with them. I wanted to be like them. They all had good jobs, a nice life. I'm good at learning things, I could have learned to be like them. I could have fitted into their lives.'

'So why kill them?'

'People are stupid. They don't understand me. I was the one they always laughed at, then they learned to be afraid of me. I don't like being laughed at, and I'm tired of people being wary of me, like I'm some animal that's going to go for them. I gave them a chance, but they didn't give me any choice. I had to kill them.'

Tony sank back in his own chair. 'And after you'd done it once, you realized that was the best thing in the world.'

'I felt good. I felt in control. I knew what was going to happen. I'd planned it all out, and it worked!' Tony surprised himself by the degree of enthusiasm that came out. He waited, but nothing more seemed to emerge.

He returned to his own chair. 'Didn't last for long, did it? The pleasure? The sense of power?'

In Andy's chair, he felt at a loss for the first time. Usually, he found role play loosened up his ideas, let his thoughts flow free. But something was clogging this up. That something was clearly at the heart of the issue. Tony moved back to his own seat and thought about it. 'Serial killers act out their fantasies in their crimes. The crime itself never lives up to the fantasy, so it has limited power. Its details are incorporated into the fantasies, which are then realized in a second, often more ritualistic killing. And so on. But as time goes by, the fantasies have less and less staying power. The killings have to get closer and closer together to keep the fantasies fuelled. But your killings don't get closer together, Andy. Why is that?'

He moved across, not hopeful. He allowed his mind to blank, letting his consciousness drift off, hoping it would come up with an answer that might satisfy his idea of Andy. After a few moments, Tony felt himself slipping away from consciousness. All at once, from what felt like a long way away, a deep chuckle rumbled through him. 'That's for me to know and you to find out,' his own voice mocked him.

Tony shook his head like a diver coming to the surface. Dazed, he got to his feet and snapped the blinds open. So much for alternative techniques. What was interesting, however, was the point at which his brain had snagged. This was one of the factors about Handy Andy that was unique. The gaps stayed constant. Even allowing for his use of a camcorder, it was still remarkable.

The line of thought restored Tony's earlier vigour and he decided to take a side trip to the university library's media-studies section where he went through the back numbers of the *Bradfield Evening Sentinel Times* for the appropriate dates. A careful scrutiny of the entertainments pages revealed little in common between the four evenings in question, unless he was prepared to consider that the local art cinema always showed classic British black-and-white comedies on Mondays. Somehow, he couldn't imagine *Passport to Pimlico* fuelling homicidal sexual fantasies. Finally, just after seven, he was ready to start on the profile.

He started with the usual caveat.

The following offender profile is for guidance only and shouldn't be regarded as an identikit portrait. The offender is unlikely to match the profile in every detail, though I would expect there to be a high degree of congruence between the characteristics outlined below and the reality. All of the statements in the profile express probabilities and possibilities, not hard facts.

A serial killer produces signals and indicators in

215

the commission of his crimes. Everything he does is intended, consciously or not, as part of a pattern. Uncovering the underlying pattern reveals the killer's logic. It may not appear logical to us, but to him it is crucial. Because his logic is so idiosyncratic, straightforward traps will not capture him. As he is unique, so must be the means of catching him, interviewing him and reconstructing his acts.

Tony continued the profile with a detailed account of the four victims. He included everything he'd gleaned from the police reports about their domestic circumstances, employment history, reputation among friends and colleagues, habits, physical condition, personality, family relationships, hobbies and social behaviour. Next, he wrote a short résumé of the pathologist's report on each man, the nature of their injuries and a description of the crime scenes. Then he began the crucial process of organizing and arranging his information into meaningful patterns so he could start to draw his conclusions.

None of the four victims had any history of homosexual relationships, as far as can be ascertained. (We cannot exclude a secret homosexual/bisexual orientation, but there is no evidence in any of the four cases to suggest this.) Yet each body was dumped in an area known primarily for its use by the gay community. In particular, the bodies were dumped in spots which are notorious for the consummation of casual sexual encounters. What does this say about the killer?
  1. He is a man who is not comfortable with his

own sexuality. He deliberately chooses men who are not openly gay-identified. It may well be that he has made a sexual approach to his victims in the past and has been rebuffed. The killer is almost certainly not an out gay; he probably represses his own sexuality at some personal cost. He probably grew up in an environment where masculinity was highly prized and praised and homosexuality condemned, possibly on religious grounds. If he is in a sexual/domestic relationship, it will be with a woman. And he will almost certainly have sexual problems within that relationship, probably ones of potency.

Tony stared bleakly at the screen. Sometimes he hated the way his job constantly forced him to confront his own problems. Did his own sexual failings mean he was really stuck on the road less travelled by? Was there going to be a night when some woman went too far, when her determination to translate his problem into a comment on her womanhood tipped him over the edge? For Tony, it was a scenario that was all too vivid. That's why Angelica was safe. When she drove him to distraction, he could slam the phone down, rather than slap her face. Or worse. Best stay out of risk, he thought. Don't even think about thinking about Carol Jordan. You've seen it in her eyes, she's interested in more than your mind. Don't even think about it, fuck-up. Get back to work.

2. He despises those who express their homo-sexuality openly. At least part of his motivation in using these dumping grounds is to show his

contempt for them, as well as to frighten them. He's also demonstrating his superiority; 'Look at me, I can come and go among you and none of you know me. I can desecrate your places, and you can't stop me.'

3. He is nevertheless familiar with areas where gay men go to socialize and to pick up sexual partners. It may be that his job takes him into the Temple Fields area from time to time, perhaps to make deliveries or to provide some service to businesses. He is fascinated with the gay culture, to the extent that he has scouted out the specific area in Carlton Park where gay cruising goes on.

4. He has a high degree of self-control. He is driving into a populous area and dumping bodies without behaving in a way that draws attention to himself.

'Tell me about it,' Tony said bitterly. He got up and stalked a path from the window to the door. 'I could have written the manual.' Ever since the bullies had started to pick on him, the smallest boy in the street and in his class, he'd learned the harsh lessons of self-control. 'Never show you're hurt, it only encourages them. Never show they've hit the mark, it only reveals your weak points. Learn to be one of the lads. Learn the vocabulary, learn the body language, acquire the attitude. Mix it all together and what do you get? You get a man who hasn't got the remotest idea of who he is. You have a consummate actor, a human impostor who can take on local colour like a chameleon.' The miracle was that it fooled so many people. Brandon clearly thought he was a good bloke. Carol Jordan obviously fancied him. Claire, his secretary, thought he was the best boss she'd ever had. He was passing for human, all right. The only one he couldn't fool was his mother, who still treated him with the thinly disguised contempt which was all he'd ever known from her. His fault his father had left them, and no wonder, according to her. She'd have dumped him in some children's home if it hadn't been for her need to keep in with her parents, the ones who held the purse strings. As it was, she'd dived head first into a career as soon as she'd been able to persuade her mother to mind little Tony. He'd done his best to be good, as Granny had instructed him, but it wasn't always easy. She wasn't a bad woman, just constrained by her own upbringing into the belief that children should be seen and not heard. His grandfather's response to domestic tyranny was to escape to the betting shop, the bowling green and the Legion. Tony had swiftly learned self-control the hard way. Was that what had happened to Andy, too? Rubbing his hand across eyes surprisingly damp, Tony threw himself back into his chair and started typing frantically.

5. His domestic and work situation allows him to be free on Monday evenings, and he does not expect to be spotted in Temple Fields by anyone who knows him. This throws up several possibilities: he may have chosen Monday nights specifically because it's his night off work or because his wife/girlfriend is away from home on Monday nights; he may have decided to kill on Mondays because the first time was a Monday and it worked out for him and now has superstitious power; or he

may have decided to keep on killing on Mondays in the hope that it will skew the investigation. He is obviously intelligent, and such careful planning should not be presumed to be beyond him.

Tony paused for thought, flicking through the pages of notes he'd made. He wasn't thinking like Handy Andy yet, but the elusive mind was getting closer and closer. He wondered again if his involvement in the twisted logic of killers was a surrogacy, the only thing that prevented him from joining their number. God knows, there were times when the inevitable drive that surged through their heads seemed attractive. And there were times enough when he'd felt murderous rage, though it was usually turned against himself rather than the person he was in bed with. 'Enough, already,' Tony said aloud, and returned to the glowing screen.

The offender is an organized serial killer, who is managing to maintain a constant eight-week gap between killings. This consistency is unusual in itself, since the normal pattern is that the space between murders decreases as they lose their power to satisfy the killer's fantasies. One reason for the maintenance of this gap may be that he spends so long stalking his victim before the kill. Thus the delights of anticipation, coupled with the savour of his previous kills, acts as a brake. I also believe that the killer is using his camcorder to record his activities and that this is also fuelling his fantasies between kills.

Tony stopped to consider what he had written. The

stumbling block. His analysis probably looked good enough to convince the lay person, but he was far from satisfied with it. But no amount of dredging of his mind or his data could come up with a better explanation. With a sigh, he continued.

What is the primary intent of his killings? We can rule out killing in the course of criminal activity, such as armed robbery or burglary. We can also rule out emotional, selfish or cause-specific killings, such as self-defence, compassion, assassination or domestic disputes. This places the killings in the category of sexual homicides.

The chosen victims all fall into the low-risk category. In other words, they all had occupations and lifestyles that didn't make them vulnerable targets. The flip side of this is that the killer has to take high-level risks to capture and kill them. What does this tell us about the killer?

1. He is operating under extremely high stress levels.

2. He plans his kills very carefully. He cannot afford to make mistakes, because if he does, his victims will escape and put him at risk, both physically and legally. He is almost certainly a stalker. He chooses his victims carefully, and studies their lives in detail. Interestingly, so far he has not been thwarted in his choice of evening. Is this a result of careful planning, prearrangement or just luck? We know that the third victim, Gareth Finnegan, told his girlfriend he was going on a lads' night out, but none of his male friends or colleagues seemed to know anything about it, and it is not

clear whether he was abducted from his home or if the contact took place at a prearranged point. It may be that the killer has had prior arrangements to meet each of his victims, either at their homes or elsewhere. He may even be posing as an insurance salesman or something similar, though I feel it's unlikely that he would have the people skills to do such a job successfully for a living.

3. He likes the extra excitement that walking out on the high wire gives him. He needs that buzz.

4. He must have some areas of emotional maturity in his make-up that allow him to hold himself under control in these highly stressful situations. This may also allow him to buck the poor work-history pattern so common among serial offenders. (See below.)

Most serial offences demonstrate a degree of escalation, indicating the killer's need for more thrills, better execution of his fantasies. Like a roller coaster, each high needs to be bigger to compensate for the inevitable low that has preceded . . .

Tony looked up, startled. What was that noise? It had sounded like the door to the open-plan outer office, but at this time of night, there shouldn't be anyone on this floor. Nervously, he pushed himself away from the computer desk, steering his chair across the carpet on silent castors till he was behind his desk and out of the pool of light shed by the lamp beside the computer. He held his breath and listened. Silence. The tension gradually began to ooze away. Then, abruptly, a line of light appeared under his office door.

The metallic taste of fear gripped Tony. The nearest thing to an offensive weapon on his desk was a chunk of agate he used as a paperweight. He snatched it up and moved stealthily out of his chair.

When Carol opened the door, she was taken aback to find Tony halfway across the room, hefting a rock in his hand. 'It's me,' she yelped.

Tony's arms dropped to his side. 'Oh shit,' he said.

Carol grinned. 'Who were you expecting? Burglars? Journalists? The bogeyman?'

Tony relaxed. 'I'm sorry,' he said. 'You spend all day trying to get inside some nutter's head and you end up as paranoid as he is.'

'Nutter,' Carol mused. 'Now would that be some technical term you psychologists use?'

'Only inside these four walls,' Tony said, walking back to his desk and putting the agate back where it belonged. 'To what do I owe the pleasure?'

'Since British Telecom don't seem to be able to connect us, I thought I'd better come round personally,' Carol replied, pulling up a chair. 'I left a message on your machine at home this morning. I assumed you'd already left for work, but you weren't here either. I tried again around four, but there was no reply from your extension. At least, I assume that's why the switchboard operator said, "I'm putting you through now," and I ended up in a black hole. And, of course, now the switchboard have all gone home and I never thought to ask for your direct line.'

'And you a detective,' Tony teased.

'That's my excuse, anyway. Actually, I couldn't face another minute in Scargill Street.'

'Want to talk about it?'

'Only if I can talk with my mouth full,' Carol said. 'I'm starving. Could you go a quick curry?'

Tony glanced at his computer screen, then back at Carol's drawn face and tired eyes. He liked her, even though he didn't want to get close, and he needed her on his side. 'Just let me save this file, and I'm out of here. I can come back later and finish this.'

Twenty minutes later they were attacking onion bhajis and chicken pakora in an Asian café in Greenholm. The other customers were students and those of the terminally right-on tendency who hadn't quite adjusted to the fact they were no longer studying anything except political correctness. 'It's not exactly Good Food Guide, but it's cheap and cheerful, and the service is quick,' Tony apologized.

'Fine by me. I'm more egg on toast than Egon Ronay. My brother got the gourmet genes in our family,' Carol said. She glanced quickly around her. Their table for two was less than a foot away from the next. 'Did you bring me here deliberately so we couldn't talk about work? Some psychologist's ploy to refresh my mind?'

Tony's eyes widened. 'I didn't even think of that. You're right, of course, we can't talk about it in here.'

Carol's smile lit up her eyes. 'You can have no idea how much pleasure that gives me.'

They ate in silence for a few minutes. Tony broke the silence. That way, he stayed in control of the subject. 'What made you decide to be a copper?'

Carol raised her eyebrows. 'Because I like oppressing the underprivileged and hassling racial minorities?' she tried.

Tony smiled. 'I don't think so.'

She pushed her plate to one side and sighed. 'Youthful idealism,' she said. 'I had this crazy idea that the police should be there to serve and protect society from lawlessness and anarchy.'

'It's not such a crazy idea. Believe me, if you dealt with the people I used to handle, you'd feel relieved that they weren't on the streets.'

'Oh, the theory's fine. It's just the practice that's such a bummer. It all started when I read sociology at Manchester. I specialized in the sociology of organizations, and all my contemporaries despised the police force as a corrupt, racist, sexist organization whose sole role was to preserve the illusory comfort of the middle classes. To some extent, I agreed with them. The difference was that they wanted to attack institutions from the outside, whereas I've always believed that if you want fundamental change, it has to come from inside.'

Tony grinned. 'You little subversive, you!'

'Yeah, well, I guess I didn't realize what I was getting into. David knocking out Goliath was a piece of piss compared with trying to change things in the police.'

'Tell me about it,' Tony said with feeling. 'This national task force could revolutionize the clear-up rate on serious crimes, but the way some senior officers carry on, you'd think I was setting up a scheme to allow paedophiles to retrain as child minders.'

Carol giggled. 'You mean, you'd rather be back in the locked ward with your nutters?'

'Carol, sometimes I feel like I've never left. You've no idea what a refreshing change it is to work with people like you and John Brandon.'

Before Carol could reply, the waiter arrived with their main courses. As she spooned out lamb and spinach, chicken karahi and pilau rice, Carol said, 'Does your job create the same problems with having a private life as the police service does?'

Instantly defensive, Tony answered with a question. 'How do you mean?'

'Like you said earlier, you get obsessed with the job. You spend your time dealing with shitheads and animals –'

'And that's just your colleagues,' Tony butted in.

'Yeah, right. And you come home at night after dealing with broken bodies and fractured lives and you're expected to sit down and watch the soaps and act like normal people do.'

'And you can't because your head's still plugged into the horrors of the day,' Tony finished. 'And with *your* job, you have the added complication of shift work.'

'Exactly. So, do you get the same problems?'

Was she asking out of idle curiosity or was this an oblique way of finding out about his private life? Sometimes Tony wished he could just switch off the part of his head that had to analyse every statement, every gesture, every intricate piece of body language and just revel in the pleasure of eating dinner with someone who seemed to enjoy his company. Suddenly aware that he had left too long a pause between the question and the answer, Tony said, 'I'm probably even worse at switching off than you. Men generally seem to get much more obsessive than women. I mean, how many female train spotters, stamp collectors or football fanatics do you know?'

226

'And that interferes in your personal relationships?' Carol persisted.

'Well, none of them have ever gone the distance,' Tony said, struggling to keep his voice light. 'I don't know if that's down to the job, or to me. Mostly, the last thing they've screamed at me as they walked out the door hasn't been, "you and your bloody nutters", so I guess it must be me. How about you? How do you handle the problems of the job?'

Carol's fork continued its journey to her mouth and she chewed and swallowed her mouthful of curry before she answered. 'I've found that men aren't very sympathetic towards shifts unless they do them too. You know, you're never there with the tea on the table when they've got to rush out to that vital squash match. Add to that the difficulty of getting them to understand why the job drives you inside your head and what are you left with? Junior doctors, other coppers, fire fighters, ambulance drivers. And in my experience, there aren't many of them who want a relationship with an equal. I guess the job takes too much out of us for us to have much left over. The last guy I was involved with was a doctor, and all he wanted to do when he wasn't working was sleep, fuck and party.'

'And you wanted more?'

'I wanted the occasional conversation, maybe even a movie or a night out at the theatre. But I put up with it because I loved him.'

'So what made you end it?'

Carol stared down at her plate. 'Thanks for the compliment, but I didn't. When I moved up here, he decided that driving up and down the motorway was a waste of good shagging time, so he dumped me for a nurse. Now it's just me and the cat. He doesn't seem to mind the irregular hours.'

'Ah,' Tony said. He had heard the real pain under the surface, but for once, all his professional skills didn't seem adequate to the response.

'How about you? You involved with anyone?' Carol asked.

Tony shook his head and carried on eating.

'Nice bloke like you, I'd have thought you'd have been snapped up ages ago,' Carol said, the tease in her tone covering something Tony wished he was imagining.

'Ah, but you've only seen the charming side. When the moon's full, I sprout hair on the palms of my hands and bay at the moon.' Tony leered melodramatically at Carol. 'I am not what I appear to be, young woman,' he growled.

'Oh, Grandmamma, what big teeth you've got!' Carol said in falsetto.

'All the better to eat my curry with,' Tony laughed. He knew this was the point where he could have moved the relationship forward, but he had spent too long constructing his defences against precisely these moments of weakness to let them down that easily. Besides, he told himself, he had no need of a relationship with her. He had Angelica and bitter experience had taught him that was all he could handle and still function.

'So how did you get into this soul-destroying line of work?' Carol asked.

'I discovered while I was working on my DPhil that I hated getting up on my hind legs and talking to an audience, which kind of ruled out academic work. So I went into clinical practice,' Tony said, slipping easily into a flow of anecdotes about his work. He felt himself relax, like a man walking on a frozen lake who realizes he's back on dry land.

They spent the rest of the meal on the safer ground of their careers, and Carol asked the waiter for the bill when he came to clear off the table. 'I'm picking up the tab, OK? Nothing to do with feminism; you're a legitimate business expense,' Carol said.

As they walked back to Tony's office, he said, 'So, back to work. Tell me about your day.'

The swift switch away from the personal back to the case confirmed to Carol the need to play it cool with Tony. She'd never seen anyone back off so fast at gentle flirtation. It was puzzling, all the more since she sensed he liked her. And she had no doubts about her capacity to attract men. At least tracking Handy Andy with him gave her space and time to build a bridge between them. 'We got a break this morning. At least, that's what we're all hoping.'

Tony stopped abruptly and turned to face Carol. 'What kind of a break?' he demanded.

'Don't worry, you're not being ignored,' Carol said. 'It's something that would be a minor detail in most investigations, but because we've got so little to go on here, it's got everybody excited. There was a torn fragment of leather on a nail by the gate in the Queen of Hearts's yard. Forensic did a rush job on it, and it turns out that it's very unusual. It's deerskin, and it comes from Russia.'

'Oh, my good God,' Tony said softly. He turned away and took a couple of steps. 'Don't tell me, let me guess.

You can't get it in this country, and you'd probably need to send someone to Russia to source it, it's so obscure. Am I right?'

'How the hell did you know that?' Carol asked, catching him up and grabbing his sleeve.

'I've been expecting something like this,' he said simply.

'Like what?'

'An outrageous red herring that'll have the entire police force running around like headless chickens.'

'You think this is a red herring?' Carol almost shouted. 'Why?'

Tony rubbed his hands over his face and ran them through his hair. 'Carol, this guy has been so careful. He's been almost clinical in his obsession with leaving no clues. Serial killers have typically got high IQs, and Handy Andy is certainly one of the cleverest I've ever come across, either personally or in the whole literature. Yet suddenly, out of nowhere we get not just any old clue, but a clue so obscure that it could only possibly be left by a tiny segment of the population. And you're standing here telling me you think this is for real? That's exactly what he's trying to achieve. I bet the lot of you have been running around like blue-tailed flies all day trying to suss out where this obscure piece of Russian leather came from, haven't you? Oh, and don't tell me, let me guess. I bet there's now a whole squad tracking back through Stevie McConnell's life trying to establish where the hell he got it from.'

Carol stared at him. It seemed so blindingly obvious when he explained it like that. Yet not one of them had questioned the validity of the leather scrap.

'Am I right?' Tony asked, more gently this time.

Carol pulled a face. 'Not a whole squad. Just me and Don Merrick and a couple of DCs. I've spent most of the day on the phone talking to governing bodies in weightlifting and body-building, trying to establish if McConnell's ever been on a national or regional team that either competed in Russia or competed against Russians. And Don and the lads have been grilling travel agencies trying to check if he's ever been on holiday there.'

'Oh, Christ,' Tony groaned. 'And?'

'Five years ago, he was one of a team of weightlifters from the North West who competed in an event in what was then Leningrad.'

Tony took a deep breath. 'The poor unlucky bastard,' he said. 'I don't expect the idea that this was deliberately planted to have occurred to any of you,' he added. 'I don't mean that patronizingly. I realize how much closer you are to all of this and how desperately you want to catch this bastard. I just wish someone had told me earlier, before it assumed this major significance for everyone.'

'I did *try* to phone you this morning,' Carol said. 'You still haven't said where you were.'

Tony held his hands up. 'I'm sorry. I'm overreacting. I was in bed, asleep, with the phones turned off. I was exhausted after last night, and I knew I couldn't concentrate on writing the profile unless I had some sleep. I should have checked my answering machine when I got up. Sorry, I shouldn't have had a go.'

Carol grinned. 'I'll let you off this time. Just save the fearsome bit for when we catch Handy Andy, huh?'

Tony pulled a face. 'Shouldn't that be "if"?'

He looked so vulnerable and fallible, his shoulders slumped, his head down, that Carol's impulses overrode the decision she'd taken only minutes before to play it cool. She stepped forward and pulled Tony into a tight hug. 'If anyone can do it, you can,' she whispered, rubbing the side of her head against his chin like a cat marking its territory.

Brandon stared at Tom Cross, his face a mask of horror. 'You did *what*?' he demanded.

'I searched McConnell's house,' Cross said belligerently.

'I thought I said categorically that we had no right to do that? No judge in the land is going to accept that arrest for common assault in the street gives sufficient grounds for suspicion of murder.'

Cross smiled. It was a rictus that would have raised a Rottweiler's hackles. 'With respect, sir, that was then. Once Inspector Jordan had established that McConnell had been to Russia, the picture changed. Not a lot of people have had access to obscure Russian leather jackets, after all. It puts him in the frame. And there's more than one JP around that owes me one.'

'You should have cleared it with me,' Brandon said. 'The last order I gave on the subject was no search.'

'I tried, sir, but you were in a meeting with the Chief,' Cross said sweetly. 'I thought I'd better strike while the iron was hot, being as how we don't have him banged up indefinitely.'

'So you wasted more time searching McConnell's house,' Brandon said bitterly. 'Don't you think you and your men could have been better employed?'

'I haven't told you yet what we found,' Cross said.

Brandon felt his chest constrict. He wasn't a man

232

given to premonitions, but the sinking foreboding that gripped him now was as palpable as any solid fact he'd ever examined. 'Think very carefully about what you say next, Superintendent,' he said cautiously.

A momentary frown of puzzlement flashed over Cross's features, but he was too full of the message he bore to worry about the ACC's words. 'We've got him, sir,' he said. 'Bang to rights. We found one of Gareth Finnegan's firm's Christmas cards in McConnell's bedroom, and a sweater that's a dead ringer for the one Adam Scott's bird says was missing from his house. Plus a traffic ticket with Damien Connolly's badge number on it. Add that to the Russian connection, and I think it's time to charge the little arse bandit.'

Of course, the discovery that one has a natural bent for something does not necessarily mean one should pursue it blindly. While I was disposing of Paul's body, this time in a dark doorway in an alley in Temple Fields, I had already decided who my next target would be. But even after so magnificent an experience as the one I'd just shared with Paul, I had no intention of repeating it with Gareth.

It was going to be third time lucky. Gareth, I already knew, was a man of rich and fertile sexual imagination. Even as I was digitizing Paul's pathetic performance into the computer, I was mourning the fact that, thanks to Gareth, I would never have the opportunity to perfect the extraordinary talent I had discovered in myself. With the resources at my command, I've been making movies like I've never seen. The ultimate snuff stuff. If I could have marketed them, I would have made a fortune. I know there's a market out there. Plenty of people would pay a lot of money to watch Paul fuck me in his death spasms on the Judas chair. And as for what I've done with Adam . . . Let's just say that no one's ever seen sixty-nine like it.

As a treat, I went to the cemetery where Adam had been

buried a few weeks before. The funeral had featured on the local television news, which I'd video-taped and studied so I could be fairly sure where the grave was. After dark, I made my way through the graves, and found Adam's within twenty minutes. I opened the can of red spray paint I'd brought with me and sprayed 'WANKER' on one side of the grey granite, and 'POOFTER' on the other side. That should give the police something to occupy their minds.

The following evening, while I was waiting for Gareth to emerge from the firm of solicitors where he was a salaried partner, I whiled away the time with the hyperbole of the Bradfield Evening Sentinel Times. This time, I'd made the front page.

GAY KILLER STRIKES AGAIN?

The mutilated body of a naked man was found this morning in Bradfield's gay village.

The murder victim had been dumped in the fire-exit doorway of the gay club Shadowlands in an alley off Canal Street in the notorious Temple Fields district.

This is the second time in two months that the body of a naked man has been discovered in the gay cruising area.

Now locals fear a perverted serial killer is stalking the city's large homosexual community.

Today's gruesome discovery was made by nightclub owner Danny Surtees, 37, as he arrived for a meeting with his accountant.

He said, 'I always go into the club through the fire door at the side. I park my car in the alley. This morning, the door was blocked by something covered by a couple of black bin bags.

'When I grabbed hold of the bags to try and pull them away from the door, they just came away in my hands and I saw there was a body under them.

'He was horribly injured. There was no way he was still alive. I'm going to have nightmares about this for the rest of my life.'

Mr Surtees said the doorway had been clear when he locked up his club just after three this morning.

The victim, said to be in his early thirties, has not yet been identified. Police describe him as white, 5ft 11ins, slightly built, with dark-brown collar-length hair and hazel eyes. He has an old scar from an appendicectomy.

A police spokesman said, 'We believe the man was killed elsewhere and the body dumped in the alley between three and eight a.m.

'We would urge anyone who was in the Temple Fields area last night to come forward for the purpose of elimination. All information will be treated in the strictest confidence.

'At this stage of our enquiry, there is no evidence to connect this killing with the murder two months ago of Adam Scott.'

Carl Fellowes, the full-time worker at the Bradfield Gay and Lesbian Centre, said today, 'The police say that they don't think there's a connection between these two murders.

'I don't know what makes me more worried on behalf of the city's gay community – the thought that there's one nutter out there killing gay men, or the thought that there are two of them.'

I didn't know whether to laugh or cry. One thing was clear, though. PC Plod was a long way from covering himself *in glory over this case. I'd obviously done a good job covering my tracks.*

I folded up my newspaper, finished my cappuccino and signalled for my bill. Any minute now, Gareth would emerge from his office and walk through the rush-hour streets to the tram. I wanted to be ready for him. I had something really special planned for him tonight, and I wanted to make sure he was home alone to enjoy it.

10

> The world in general, gentlemen, are very bloody-minded; and all they want in a murder is a copious effusion of blood; gaudy display in this point is enough for them. But the enlightened connoisseur is more refined in his taste.

Penny Burgess topped up her glass of Californian Chardonnay from the bottle in the fridge and walked back through to her living room in time to hear the headlines on the BBC local news. Nothing fresh to worry about, she thought with relief. An armed robbery she could catch up with first thing in the morning. The police were still questioning a man in connection with the gay serial killings, but no charges had been laid yet. Penny sipped her wine and lit a cigarette.

They were going to have to move soon, she thought. By morning, they'd either have had to charge him with something or let him go. So far, no one had got a sniff of the suspect's identity, which was pretty remarkable. The whole pack had been leaning heavily on their personal police contacts, but for once, the reservoir of information had resolutely refused to leak. Penny decided she'd better take a look at the magistrates' court lists in the morning. There was an outside chance that the cops had something fairly innocuous to charge their suspect with so they could hang on to him while they dug around for the evidence they needed to make the serial killing charges stick.

As the news cut away to the weather forecast, the phone rang. Penny reached over to the occasional table by the sofa and grabbed the receiver. 'Hello?' she said.

'Penny? It's Kevin.'

Hallelujah, Penny thought, sitting up and grinding out her cigarette. All she said, however, was, 'Kevin, my man. How's it hanging?' She raked in her handbag for a pencil and her notebook.

'Something's come up you might be interested in,' the police inspector said cautiously.

'It wouldn't be the first time,' Penny said suggestively. Her occasional sexual encounters with the very married Kevin Matthews had provided her with more than an inside track on Bradfield Metropolitan Police. He'd turned out to be one of the best lovers she'd ever had. She just wished he could overcome his Catholic guilt more often.

'This is serious,' Kevin protested.

'So was I, superstud.'

'Listen, do you want this info or not?'

'Definitely. Especially if it's the name of the guy you've got in custody for the Queer Killings.'

She heard the sharp intake of breath. 'You know I can't tell you that. There are limits.'

Penny sighed. It was the story of their relationship. 'OK, so what can you tell me?'

'Popeye's been suspended.'

'He's off the case?' Penny asked, her mind racing. Tom Cross? Suspended?

'He's off the *job*, Pen. He's been sent home pending disciplinary action.'

'Who by?' Jesus, this was a story and a half. Just what had Popeye Cross been up to this time? She felt a momentary panic. What if he'd been caught out giving the suspect's name to one of her rivals? She almost missed Kevin's reply.

'John Brandon.'

'What the hell for?'

'Nobody's saying,' Kevin said. 'But the last thing he did before he saw Brandon was to carry out a search of our suspect's house.'

'A legal search?' Penny probed.

'Far as I know he had grounds under PACE,' Kevin said cautiously.

'So what's going on, Kevin? Has Popeye been planting evidence, or what?'

'I don't know, Pen,' Kevin said plaintively. 'Look, I've got to go. If I hear anything else, I'll call you, OK?'

'OK. Thanks, Kev. You're a star, you know.'

'Yeah, well. I'll speak to you soon.'

The line went dead. Penny dumped the phone back on the base unit and jumped to her feet. She hurried through to her bedroom, pulling off her dressing gown on the way. Five minutes later, she was running down the two flights of stairs from her flat to the underground garage. In the car, she checked the address in her A–Z, then set off, mentally rehearsing what she was going to say on the doorstep.

*   *   *

It was Tony who had pulled away from the clinch first. His body withdrew from hers in a gesture that rendered four inches forty.

Trying to keep it light, to cover the awkwardness that had sprung up between them, Carol said, 'Sorry, you just looked like you needed a hug.'

'Nothing wrong with that,' Tony said stiffly. 'We use it all the time in group therapy.'

They stood for a moment, eyes not quite meeting. Then Carol moved to Tony's side, slipped a hand through his unyielding arm and steered him forwards across the university courtyard. 'So when do I get to look at this profile?'

The conversation was on safe ground again, but Carol was still too close for comfort. Tony could feel the tension inside him, like a cold hand squeezing his chest. He forced himself to speak in a calm, normal voice. 'I want to do another couple of hours' work now, and I'll get stuck into it again first thing in the morning. I should have a draft ready for you by early afternoon. How does three o'clock sound to you?'

'Fine. Look, do you mind if I stick around now while you're working? I could do with rereading some of those statements, and I'll get no peace if I go back to Scargill Street.'

Tony looked doubtful. 'I suppose.'

'I promise not to molest you, Dr Hill,' Carol teased.

'Damn,' Tony said, snapping his fingers in mock-disappointment. Look at you, he thought cynically. Passing for human, sure of all the moves. 'Actually, it's not that. I'm only hesitating because I'm not used to working with someone else in the room.'

'You won't know I'm there.'

241

'I doubt that very much,' Tony said. She might read that as a compliment, but he knew the truth.

Penny pressed the doorbell of the mock-Tudor detached house in one of south Bradfield's more select streets. Even on a superintendent's salary, it should have been beyond Tom Cross's reach. But Popeye's reputation for being lucky had been enhanced a few years back when he'd won a high five-figure sum on the pools. The subsequent party had passed into police mythology. Now, it looked like he'd dropped his lucky pixie somewhere along the road.

A light snapped on in the hallway and someone lumbered towards the door, turned into an amorphous lump by the stained glass. *'Friday the Thirteenth* meets *Hallowe'en,'* Penny muttered under her breath as she heard the lock turn. The door cracked open a suspicious few inches. Penny angled her head round to smile at the shape behind the door.

'Superintendent Cross,' she said, the white cloud of her breath meeting the swirl of smoke issuing from the door. 'Penny Burgess, *Sentinel Times.*'

'I know who you are,' Cross snarled, the slur of drink evident in those few words. 'What the hell do you want, coming round here this time of night?'

'I hear you've had a bit of a problem at work,' Penny tried.

'You hear wrong then, madam. Now, bugger off.'

'Look, it'll be all over the media tomorrow. You're going to be under siege. The *Sentinel Times* has always supported you, Mr Cross. We've been on your side all through this investigation. I'm not some visiting fireman from London, up here to put the boot in. If you've been sidelined, our readers have got a right to hear your side of the story.' The door was still open. If she'd managed to say that much without him slamming it shut in her face, the chances were that she was going to get something usable out of him.

'What makes you think I'm off the case?' Cross asked defiantly.

'I heard you've been suspended. I don't know why, and that's the reason I wanted to hear your side of it, before we get fed the official line.'

Cross scowled, his gooseberry eyes seeming to pop even further out. 'I've got nothing to say,' he told her, grudging every syllable.

'Not even off the record? You're willing to stand by and let them trash your reputation after all you've done for the force?'

Cross opened the door wider and looked down his drive towards the street. 'You on your own?' he asked.

'Not even my newsdesk know I'm here. I only just heard.'

'You'd better come in a minute.'

Penny stepped across the threshold into a hall that looked like a Laura Ashley sample book. At the far end of the hall, a door was half open, the television voices distinct even at that distance. Cross steered her in the opposite direction, into a long sitting room. When he switched the lights on, Penny's eyes were assaulted by more patterns than a knitting shop. The only thing the curtains, carpets, rugs, wallpaper, frieze and scatter cushions had in common was that they were all shades of green and cream. 'What a lovely room,' she stammered.

243

'You think so? I reckon it's bloody hideous. The wife says it's the best money can buy, which is the only argument I've heard for staying potless,' Cross grumbled, heading for a cocktail cabinet. He poured himself a stiff drink from a decanter, then, as an afterthought, said, 'You'll not be wanting one, with you having the car.'

'That's right,' Penny said, forcing the warmth into her voice. 'Can't take chances with your lads out on the roads.'

'You want to know why them gutless bastards have suspended me?' he demanded belligerently, thrusting his head forward like a hungry tortoise.

Penny nodded, not daring to take out her note-book.

'Because they'd rather listen to some poncey bloody doctor than a proper copper, that's why.'

If Penny had been a dog, her ears would have been standing to attention. As it was, she settled for a polite raise of the eyebrows. 'A doctor?' she said.

'They've brought this wanker of a shrink in to do our job. And he says the arse bandit we've got banged up is innocent, so it's bollocks to the evidence. Now, I've been a copper for twenty-odd years, and I trust my instincts. We've got the bastard, I can feel it in my water. All I did was try to make sure he stayed behind bars till we nail down all the bloody loose ends.' Cross downed his drink and banged his empty tumbler on the cabinet. 'And they've got the fucking nerve to suspend *me*!'

Manufacturing evidence, then. Although she was desperate to know more about the mysterious doctor, Penny sensed that she'd better let Cross air his grievances first. 'What did they say you'd done?' she asked.

'I've done nothing wrong,' he said, pouring another massive slug from the decanter. 'Trouble with bloody Brandon is he's been flying a desk for so long, he's forgotten what the job's about. Instinct, that's what it's about. Instinct and hard bloody work. Not some fucking trick cyclist with a head full of daft bloody notions like a fucking social worker.'

'Who is this guy, then?' Penny asked.

'Dr Tony bloody Hill. From the fucking Home Office. Sits in his ivory tower and tells us how to catch villains. He's got no more idea of coppering than I have of nuclear bloody physics. But the good doctor says, let the poofter go, so Brandon says yes, sir, no, sir, three bags full, sir. And just because I don't agree, I'm out on my arse.' Cross swallowed more whisky, his face flushed with anger and drink. 'Anybody'd think we were dealing with bloody Mastermind here, not some fucking dumbshit arse bandit who's had a bit of luck so far. You don't need smartarses with bloody "doctor" in front of their name to catch scum like this. All you do is give the homicidal little fairy ideas above his station.'

'It's fair to say, then, that you don't agree with the line the investigation's taking?' Penny asked.

Cross snorted. 'That's one way of putting it. You mark my words, if they let this little fucker back on the streets, we'll be looking at another body.'

To Tony's surprise, Carol proved to be true to her word. She sat at his desk, working her way through the pile of statements while he carried on working at his computer. Far from distracting him, he found her presence curiously soothing. He had no trouble picking up the profile where he'd left off earlier.

Like a roller coaster, each high needs to be bigger to compensate for the inevitable low that has preceded it. In this instance, there are three principal signs of escalation. The wounds to the throat have become increasingly deep and assured. The sexual mutilation has developed from a few tentative cuts in the genital region to full-scale amputation. And the bites he inflicts then cuts away have increased in number and in depth. Yet he has managed to stay sufficiently in control to cover his tracks.

It is difficult to assess whether or not the level of torture he is administering is escalating, since he seems to be using different torture methods in each case. The fact that he needs the stimulus of these different methods is, however, in itself a form of escalation.

Judging by the pathologist's report, the sequence of events would seem to be:

1. Capture, using handcuffs and ligatures round the ankles.

2. Torture, including sexually motivated acts such as biting and sucking.

3. The fatal blow to the throat.

4. Postmortem genital mutilation.

What does this tell us about the killer?

1. He has sophisticated and highly developed fantasies, which he is exploring through his torture methods.

2. He has a killing place. The amounts of blood and other bodily fluids generated by his activities

could not be readily cleaned away from a normal domestic environment; it would be taking far more of a chance than his other cautious behaviour indicates. It will almost certainly have facilities for him to clean himself up after his killings, and power so he can run lights and a camcorder. We should be looking for something like a lock-up garage, a building that is secure but probably has running water and electricity. It may also be in an isolated location, thus avoiding the possibility of his victims' screams being overheard. (He will almost certainly remove any gags while he is torturing them; he will want to hear them scream and plead for mercy.)

3. He is obsessed with torture, and obviously has enough manual skills to construct his own engines of torture. He does not appear to have either medical or butchery skills, judging by the clumsy and tentative nature of the early throat-cutting and genital mutilation.

Tony turned away from the screen and glanced across at Carol. She was totally absorbed in her reading, the familiar frown line between her eyes. Was he being crazy to back off from what she appeared to be offering? More than anyone he'd ever been involved with she would understand the pressures of his job, the highs and lows that accompanied getting inside the head of a sociopath. She was intelligent and sensitive, and if she committed herself as thoroughly to a relationship as she did to her career, she might just be strong enough to work through his problems with him rather than use them as a stick to beat him with.

Suddenly aware of his eyes on her, Carol looked

up and flashed him a tired smile. In that instant, Tony made his mind up. No way. He had enough problems dealing with the crap in his head without allowing anyone else to make it a hostage to fortune. Carol was just too sharp to let her any nearer. 'Going OK?' she asked.

'I'm starting to get a feel for him,' Tony admitted.

'That can't be a very pleasant place to be,' Carol said.

'No, but it's what I'm paid for.'

Carol nodded. 'And I guess it's satisfying. And exciting?'

Tony smiled wryly. 'You could say that. I sometimes wonder if that makes me as twisted as them.'

Carol laughed. 'You and me both. They say the best thief-takers are the ones who get inside the heads of the villains. So if I'm going to be the best at what I do, I have to think like a villain. That doesn't mean I want to do what they do, though.'

Strangely comforted by her words, Tony turned back to his screen.

The time the killer spends with his victims can also provide pointers. In three of the four cases, the killer appears to have made contact in the early evening and to have dumped the bodies in the early hours of the following morning. Interestingly, in the third case, he spent far longer with his victim, apparently keeping him alive for the greater part of two days. This was the killing that took place over Christmas.

It may be that he is normally unable to spend long with his victims because of the other demands of his life, demands which altered over the Christmas period. These are more likely to be work-related demands than domestic ones, though it is possible that he is in a relationship with someone who returned alone to their family at Christmas, thus giving him time to spend with his victim. Another possibility is that the extended time he spent with Gareth Finnegan was a bizarre Christmas present to himself, a reward for the good performance of his previous 'work'.

The short space of time that elapses between the killings and the dumping of the bodies suggests that he does not use drink or drugs to any significant degree during the torture and murders. He would not risk being stopped by the police for erratic driving while he has a body in the boot, whether alive or dead. Also, although he appears to have used his victims' cars on occasion, it is clear that he also has a vehicle of his own. The chances are that this is a reasonably new vehicle in good condition, since he can't afford to take the chance of being stopped in a routine police check.

Tony hit 'save' on his computer and sat back with a satisfied smile. This was as good a place to stop as any. Tomorrow morning, he'd complete the detailed checklist of characteristics he'd expect to find in Handy Andy, and outline proposals for potential courses of action by the police officers on the case.

'You done?' Carol asked.

He turned to see her leaning back in the chair, her pile of folders closed. 'I didn't realize you'd finished,' he said.

'Ten minutes ago. I didn't want to disturb the flying fingers.'

Tony hated others studying him the way he studied them. The idea of being a patient on the receiving end of his own probing was one of those nightmares that he woke from in a sweat. 'I've had it for tonight,' he said, making a copy of his file on a floppy disk which he then pocketed.

'I'll give you a lift home,' Carol said.

'Thanks,' Tony said, getting to his feet. 'I can never be bothered bringing the car into town. To tell you the truth, I don't much like driving.'

'Can't say I blame you. The city traffic's hell on wheels.'

When Carol pulled up outside Tony's house, she said, 'Any chance of a cup of tea? Not to mention a pee?'

While Tony put the kettle on, Carol slipped upstairs to the bathroom. She came downstairs to the sound of her own voice issuing from his answering machine. She paused at the foot of the stairs, spying on him as he leaned against his desk, pen and paper in hand, listening to his messages. She enjoyed her growing sense of familiarity with his face and the lines of his body. Her voice ended and the machine beeped. 'Hi Tony, it's Pete,' the next voice announced. 'I've got to be in Bradfield next Thursday. Any chance of a bed and a beer Wednesday night? Congratulations on getting on board the Queer Killer investigation, by the way. Hope you catch the bastard.' Beep. 'Anthony, my darling. Wherever can you be? I'm lying here, longing for you. We've got some unfinished business, lover boy.'

At the sound of the voice, Tony straightened up and he turned to stare at the machine. The voice was husky, sexy, intimate. 'Don't think you can –' Tony's hand shot out and cut the voice off abruptly.

So much for not being involved with anyone, Carol thought bitterly. She stepped forward through the doorway. 'Let's just forget the tea. I'll see you tomorrow,' she said, her voice cold and brittle as ice on a winter puddle.

Tony whirled round, panic in his eyes. 'It's not what it seems,' he blurted out without thought. 'I've never even met the woman!'

Carol turned out of the doorway and walked down the hall. As she fumbled with the lock, Tony spoke coldly. 'I'm telling you the truth, Carol. Even though it's actually none of your business.'

She half turned, found a smile from somewhere and said, 'You're quite right. It *is* none of my business. Till tomorrow, Tony.'

The closing of the door reverberated through Tony's head like a jackhammer. 'Thank God you're a psychologist,' he said bitterly as he slumped against the wall. 'A layman might have really buggered that one up. You really believe in making the job a piece of piss, don't you, Hill?'

When Gareth half smiled at me on the tram, I was convinced that my dreams were on the point of fulfilment. Because of an unexpected crisis at work, and all the extra overtime that entailed, I hadn't been able to follow him for more than a week.

His image had lulled me to sleep when I came home at all hours from work, and his voice throbbed hungrily in my ears, but I needed to see him in the flesh. I'd set my alarm clock to give me plenty of time to be outside his house before he left for work, but I was so exhausted I slept right through it. When I started into wakefulness, I realized my only chance was to catch up with his tram a couple of stops further down the line.

The tram was pulling in as I ran on to the platform. I eagerly scanned the first section, but couldn't see him. Anxiety rose in my throat like bile. Then I saw his gleaming head, sitting right by the door of the second carriage. I pushed through the crowd and managed to stand right next to him, my knees brushing his. At the physical contact, he looked up. His grey eyes crinkled at the corners and a smile flickered on his mouth. I smiled back and said, 'Sorry.'

'No problem,' he said. 'This tram gets busier by the day.'

I wanted to continue the conversation, but for once I could think of nothing to say. He returned to the Guardian *and I had to settle for watching him out of the corner of my peripheral vision while I pretended to stare out at the passing cityscape. It wasn't much, I know, but it was a start. He had acknowledged me; he knew I existed. Now, it could be only a matter of time.*

Shakespeare got it right when he said, 'The first thing we do, let's kill all the lawyers.' That way at least there would be fewer liars at large. Even the words sound the same; lawyer, liar. I should have expected nothing else from a man who speaks one day for the plaintiff, the next for the defendant.

I'd parked just round the corner from Gareth's house, where I could watch him come home without being seen, thanks to the tinted windows of my jeep. His house had no hedge, so I could see right into his living room from my vantage point.

I knew his habits by now. He arrived home just after six, went through to the kitchen for a can of Grolsch, and returned to the living room where he drank his beer and watched TV. After about twenty minutes, he'd fetch some food from the kitchen – pizza, TV dinner, baked potato. Cooking clearly wasn't his forte. When we were together, I'd have to take over responsibility for that side of our life.

After the news, he'd leave the room, presumably to do some work in another room of the house. I imagined law books arrayed on pine shelves. Then, he'd either return to the TV later in the evening, or walk down to the pub on the corner for a couple of lagers.

Gareth needed someone to share his life, I thought as I

waited for him to come home. I was just the person to do that. Gareth was going to be my Christmas present to me.

At a quarter past five, a white Volkswagen Golf slipped into a parking place just beyond Gareth's house and a woman got out. She leaned back into the car and picked up a briefcase bulging with files and a shoulder bag. I thought she looked vaguely familiar as she walked down the pavement. Petite, light-brown hair pulled back in a heavy plait, big tortoiseshell glasses, black suit, white blouse with a froth of lace at the throat.

When she turned in at Gareth's gate, I couldn't quite believe it. For the few seconds it took her to get to the door, I told myself she was his estate agent, his insurance agent, a colleague dropping off some papers. Anything. Anything.

Then she opened the flap of her bag and took out a key. My mind screamed 'No!' as she inserted the key into the lock and let herself in. The living-room door opened and she dumped her briefcase by the settee. Then she was gone again. Ten minutes later, she was back, wrapped in Gareth's big white towelling dressing gown.

Frankly, I was with Shakespeare all the way.

'Twas the season to be jolly, so I forced myself not to let my disappointment colour my mood. Instead, I concentrated on researching my next project. I wanted something appropriate to the season, some good old barbaric Christian symbolism. There's not really a lot you can do with a manger and swaddling clothes, so I allowed myself some artistic licence and went for the other end of the life.

Crucifixion as a form of punishment was probably borrowed by the Romans from the Carthaginians. (Interesting, isn't it, how the Romans referred to everyone else as the barbarians . . .) The Romans adopted it round about the time of the Punic Wars, and initially, it was a punishment reserved for slaves only. Which seems appropriate enough, since that was the only role I expected Gareth to be fit for now. Later in the days of empire, it became a more general punishment, meted out to any locals who had the temerity to misbehave after the Romans had kindly come along and conquered – sorry, civilized – them.

Traditionally, the felon was flagellated, then forced to carry the crossbeam through the streets to the place where a tall stake had been driven into the ground. Then he was nailed to the crossbeam and hauled up by a system of pulleys. His feet were sometimes nailed, sometimes tied to the stake. On occasion, death by exhaustion was given a helping hand by the soldiers, who broke the legs of the victim, which must have allowed him a merciful lapse into unconsciousness. For my purposes, however, I decided to opt for the more decorative St Andrew's Cross. For one thing, it would place more interesting stresses on Gareth's muscles. For another, should he rise to the occasion, it would make access a lot easier.

Interestingly, crucifixion was never used as a punishment for soldiers except for the crime of desertion. Maybe the Romans had the right idea after all.

11

But who meantime was the victim, to whose abode he was hurrying? For surely he could never be so indiscreet as to be sailing about on a roving cruise in search of some chance person to murder? Oh, no: he had suited himself with a victim some time before, viz., an old and very intimate friend.

Brandon stared bleakly at the sheet of paper in the typewriter. Tom Cross might have been a long way from the ACC's idea of the perfect copper, but he'd always appeared to be a good thief-taker. Antics like tonight's served only to raise a question mark over his whole career. Just how many other people had Cross fitted up over the years without anyone being any the wiser? If Brandon hadn't himself bent the rules and taken Tony on their illicit search, no one would have doubted the 'evidence' Tom Cross had turned up. No one except Stevie McConnell would have known that two of Cross's three 'finds' had arrived with him. The mere thought of the consequences of that was enough to send a prickle of cold sweat down Brandon's back.

Cross had left Brandon with no option but to suspend him. The disciplinary hearing that would inevitably follow would be painful for all concerned, but that was the least of Brandon's worries. He was far more troubled about the effect on the murder squad's morale. The only way to combat it was to take direct responsibility for the enquiry himself. Now, all he had to do was convince the Chief that he was right. With a sigh, Brandon pulled the last sheet of paper out of the machine and inserted another page.

His memo to the Chief Constable was brief and to the point. That only left one task before he could crawl home to bed. Sighing, Brandon glanced at the clock. Thirty minutes to midnight. He pushed the typewriter away from him and started writing on a sheet of his personal memo paper. 'To Detective Inspector Kevin Matthews. From John Brandon, ACC (Crime). Re: Steven McConnell. Following the suspension of Superintendent Cross, I will assume direct command of the murder squad. There are no grounds for charging McConnell with anything other than assault. McConnell should be released on bail pending a court date for the assault charge, and on separate bail to return to Scargill Street in a week so that we can question him further if more evidence arises. In view of his refusal to give us any information about his contacts, or any names of people he might have introduced to Gareth Finnegan and Adam Scott, we should pursue any contacts he does make. A warrant for a tap on his phone should also be obtained, on the basis of his connection to Scott and Finnegan, and the contact we now know he had with Damien Connolly in a professional capacity. Our enquiries into the four related murders should continue on a broad front, though I suggest that, following his release on bail, we maintain close surveillance of McConnell. There will be a case conference of senior officers tomorrow at noon.' He signed the memo and sealed it in an envelope. How to make friends and influence people, he thought as he walked downstairs to the desk sergeant. Brandon prayed that Tony Hill was right about Stevie McConnell. If Tom Cross had been right to follow his instinct, it would be more than the morale of the CID that would be at risk.

Carol slumped over the dining table, chin resting on her folded forearms, one hand tickling Nelson's belly. 'What do you think, boy? Is he just another lying bastard, or what?'

'Prrrt,' the cat said on a rising intonation, his eyes closed to slits.

'I thought you'd say that. I agree, I know how to pick them,' Carol sighed. 'You're right, I should have kept my distance. That's what happens when you make the running. You get the knockbacks. They don't usually come from that far out of left field, though. At least now I know why he kept backing off. Better off without him, cat. Life's tough enough without playing second fiddle.'

'Mrrr,' Nelson agreed.

'He must think I'm brain dead, expecting me to believe that a total stranger leaves messages like that on his answering machine.'

'Rowrr,' Nelson complained, rolling over on to his back, batting her fingers with his paws.

'All right, so you think it's ridiculous too. But the

man's a psychologist. If he was going to make something up to explain the fact that he'd lied to me, he'd make it a damn sight more plausible than funny phone calls. All he had to say was that it was somebody he'd finished with who wouldn't take the message.' Carol rubbed the sleep out of her eyes, yawned and stood up in one languid movement.

The door to the boxroom Michael used as a study opened and he stood framed in the doorway. 'I thought I heard voices. You could talk to me, you know. At least I answer you.'

Carol gave a tired smile. 'So does Nelson. It's not his fault we don't speak cat. I didn't want to disturb you; I could see you were working.'

Michael walked over to the drinks cabinet and poured himself a small Scotch. 'I was only play-testing, trying to spot the glitches in what we've done so far. No big deal. How's your day been?'

'Don't ask. They've moved us over to Scargill Street. It's a hellhole. Imagine going back to doing your calculations on an abacus, and you get the picture of my current working environment. The atmosphere's shit, and Tony Hill's spoken for. Apart from that, everything's magic.' Carol followed Michael's example and poured herself a drink.

'Want to talk about it?' he asked, perching on the arm of one of the sofas.

'Thanks, but no thanks.' Carol swallowed her drink in one, shuddered at the kick of the spirit and said, 'I've brought you a set of pictures, by the way. How soon can you take a look at them?'

'I've scrounged some computer time with the software tomorrow evening. That do you?'

Carol put her arms round Michael and gave him a hug. 'Thank you, bro,' she said.

'My pleasure,' he said, returning the embrace. 'You know how I love a challenge.'

'I'm going to bed,' she said. 'It's been a long one.'

No sooner had Carol turned out the light than she felt the familiar thud of Nelson landing on the foot of the bed. It was reassuring to feel his warmth against her legs, though it was no substitute for the body she'd hoped for earlier in the evening. Of course, as soon as her head hit the pillow, her sleepiness vanished. The exhaustion was still there, but her mind was racing. Please God, by tomorrow afternoon, the awkwardness between her and Tony would have evaporated. The sting of humiliation would still be there for her, but she was a grown-up and a professional. Now she knew he was off limits, she wouldn't place him in a difficult position again, and now he knew she knew, maybe he'd be able to relax. Either way, the profile should provide more than enough neutral ground between them. She could hardly wait to see what he'd come up with.

On the other side of the sleeping city, Tony too lay in bed, staring at the ceiling, tracing imaginary road maps in the cracks round the plaster rose. He knew there was no point in switching out his bedside lamp. Sleep would elude him, and in the darkness, he'd start to feel the slow choke of claustrophobia closing in on him. Counting sheep had never appealed; the slow watches of the night were when Tony Hill became his own therapist. 'Why did you have to ring tonight?' he murmured. 'I *like* Carol Jordan. I know I don't want her in my life, but I didn't want to hurt her either. Hearing your blandishments on the answering machine must have felt like a smack in the face, after me saying there wasn't anybody in my life.

'An outsider would say we hardly know each other, everything that happened tonight was an overreaction. But outsiders don't understand the bonding, the intimacy that springs out of nowhere when you're working closely together on a manhunt, when the clock's ticking the next victim's life away.'

He sighed. At least he hadn't blurted out the one thing that might have convinced Carol he wasn't lying, the truth he'd so carefully kept locked inside himself. What was it he told his patients? 'Let it out. It doesn't matter what it is, speaking it is the first step in taking away the pain.'

'What a load of crap that is,' he said bitterly. 'It's just another one of the tricks in my magic bag, designed to legitimize my prurient curiosity, tailored to unleash the twisted minds of the fuck-ups who are driven to act out their fantasies in a way society can't accommodate. If I'd told Carol the truth, said the i-word, it wouldn't have taken my pain away. It would only have made me feel even more of a worthless piece of shit. It's all very well for old men to be impotent. Men my age who can't get it up are a joke.'

The phone rang, startling him. He rolled over, scrambling for the receiver. 'Hello?' he said, his voice tentative.

'Anthony, at last. Oh, how I've missed you!'

His surge of anger at the languid, husky voice died as soon as it flared. What was the point in raging at her? She wasn't the problem. He was. 'I got your message,' he said, resigning himself. She hadn't caused the awkwardness with Carol; there would have been no grounds for awkwardness at all if he hadn't been such a pathetic excuse for a man. No point in even thinking about relationships with nice, normal women. He would have blown it with Carol, just as he'd always blown it with women as soon as they got close. The best he could hope for was telephone sex. At least it generated a kind of equality; it allowed men to fake not just orgasm but erection too.

Angelica chuckled. 'I thought I'd leave you something nice to come home to. I hope you're not too tired for some recreation.'

'I'm never too tired for your kind of recreation,' Tony said, swallowing the self-disgust that threatened to overwhelm him. Think of it as therapy, he told himself. Tony lay back and let the voice flow over him, his hand straying down his chest towards his groin.

The cleaners were gossiping by the lift as Penny Burgess emerged on the third floor of the *Bradfield Evening Sentinel Times* office. She walked down the newsroom, snapping on lights as she passed, humming tunelessly under her breath. She tossed her bag on the desk by her computer terminal and logged on. She executed the commands that took her into the library database, and pressed the key for 'search'. Five options were offered: 1. Subject; 2. Name; 3. By-line; 4. Date; and 5. Pictures. Penny hit 2. At the 'surname' prompt, she typed 'Hill'. At the 'forename' prompt, she keyed in 'Tony', and at the 'title' prompt, she entered, 'Dr'. Then she sat back and waited while the computer sorted through the gigabytes of information stored in its huge memory. Penny flipped open her cigarette packet and pulled out her first cigarette of the day. She was only a couple of drags into it when the screen flashed 'Found (6)'.

Penny retrieved the six items and called them up on her screen. They appeared in reverse order of date. The first was a two-month-old cutting from the *Sentinel Times*. It had been written by one of the news reporters. Although she'd read it at the time, she'd completely forgotten about it. As she read it, Penny whistled softly.

INSIDE THE MIND OF A KILLER

The man the Home Office have chosen to spear-head the hunt for serial killers spoke today about the latest slaying that has terrified the city's gay community.

Forensic psychologist Tony Hill is one year into a major study funded by the government which will lead to the setting up of a criminal profiling task force similar to the FBI unit featured in *The Silence of the Lambs*.

Dr Hill, 34, was formerly the chief clinical psychologist at Blamires Hospital, the maximum-security mental unit which houses Britain's most dangerous criminally insane offenders, including mass murderer David Harney and serial killer Keith Pond, the Motorway Madman.

Giving his verdict, Dr Hill said, 'I have not been called in by the police to consult on any of these cases, so I know no more than your readers do about them.'

Either Dr Hill had been lying to her colleague, or his formal involvement with the case came after the interview. If that was the case, Penny could see how to exploit it in a way that would appeal to her editor. She could picture the headline now. 'POLICE FOLLOW BEST'S LEAD IN MURDER HUNT.' She quickly flicked through the rest of the piece. It didn't tell her anything she didn't already know, although she was interested that Dr Hill had speculated that the discrepancies in the third killing might mean there were two killers out on the streets. That was an idea that seemed to have sunk without trace. It was something to ask Kevin about next time she managed to get him on the end of a phone.

The next cutting was from the *Guardian*, and announced the setting up of the Home Office programme for developing a national task force to deal with serial offenders. The project was to be based at Bradfield University. The article gave her more background on Dr Hill, and she jotted down his career details in her notebook. No dummy, this guy. She'd have to handle him carefully. She tapped her teeth with her pen and wondered why the *Sentinel Times* hadn't run a feature on the study, with a profile of Dr Hill. Maybe they tried and had been knocked back. She'd have to check with her colleagues on Features.

The next two cuttings were from a national tabloid, a two-part series on serial killers that had been timed to coincide with the general release of *The Silence of the Lambs*. Dr Hill was quoted in both articles, talking in general terms about the work of psychological profilers.

The last two cuttings dealt with one of his most prominent patients, Keith Pond, the so-called Motorway Madman. Pond had abducted five women from motorway service areas, then savagely raped and murdered them. At the time of his trial, only two of the bodies had been found. But after extensive therapy with Dr Hill, Pond had revealed the whereabouts of the other three bodies. Dr Hill had been hailed as a worker of miracles by the bereaved family of one of the victims. One of the two pieces had attempted a profile of Dr Hill, but they had scant information to go on. As usual, the journalist hadn't let that stand in the way of a good story.

Tony Hill, who has never married, is devoted to his work. A former colleague said, 'Tony's a workaholic. He's married to the job.

'He's totally driven by the desire to understand what makes his patients tick. There's probably not another psychologist in the country who has his knack of getting inside their twisted minds and working out what makes them do what they do.

'I sometimes thought he related better to mass murderers than he did to normal punters.'

The reclusive Dr Hill lives alone and is notorious for not mixing socially with colleagues. Apart from studying the minds of serial killers, the only hobby he apparently indulges in is hill-walking. On weekends off, he regularly drives to the Lakes or the Yorkshire Dales and tramps the fells.

'Sounds like a real barrel of laughs,' Penny said aloud, scribbling more notes on her pad. She returned to the main menu, where she selected the fifth option. Again, she entered Tony's name for a picture search. The data banks revealed there was one stock picture on file. Penny called it up and stared at the face that appeared on her screen. 'Gotcha!' she exclaimed. She had only seen him once before, but now she knew who Carol Jordan's new sidekick was.

Penny leaned back in her seat, savouring her third cigarette, and registered that the newsroom was starting to fill up. One quick phone call, then she could afford the time to treat herself to a fry-up in the canteen. Reaching for the phone, she dialled Kevin Matthews's home number. He picked up on the second ring. 'DI Matthews,' came the sleepy mumble.

'Hi, Kev, it's Penny,' she said, savouring the stunned silence that greeted her announcement. 'Sorry to bother you at home, but I thought you'd rather answer my questions there than in the office.'

'Wh-what?' he stuttered. Then, muffled, 'Yeah, it's work. Go back to sleep, love.'

'How long has Dr Tony Hill been on the team?'

'How did you hear about that? Shit, that's supposed to be top secret!' he exploded, his nervousness transforming itself into anger.

'Tut, tut. Kev, she'll never get back to sleep if you yell like that. Never mind how I know, just be grateful you can put your hand on your heart and deny it came from you. How long, Kev?'

He cleared his throat. 'Just a couple of days.'

'Was it Brandon's idea?'

'That's right. Look, I really can't talk about this. It's supposed to be kept under wraps.'

'He's doing a profile, right?'

'What do *you* think?'

'Working with Carol Jordan? Brandon's blue-eyed girl on this one, is she?'

'She's the liaison officer. Look, I've got to go. I'll talk to you about this later on, OK?' Kevin tried to sound menacing, but failed.

Penny smiled and slowly exhaled a mouthful of smoke. 'Thanks, Kev. I owe you a very special one.' She replaced the handset, cleared her screen and opened a story file.

'Exclusive. By Penny Jordan,' she typed. Never mind breakfast. She had far more interesting stuff to do.

Tony was back in front of his screen by half past eight. Instead of the guilt he'd expected to feel about his erotic encounter, he felt refreshed. Giving himself permission to indulge himself with Angelica had somehow released and relaxed him. Surprising though he found it under the circumstances, he'd actually become aroused as she'd talked him through an outrageous, imaginative sexual encounter. He hadn't actually managed to sustain his erection as far as orgasm, but because there was no one there to share his failure, it hadn't seemed to matter. Maybe a few more calls from Angelica would be all he needed to contemplate the reality with something less than abject panic.

But not at work. What he needed now was complete peace. He'd already instructed his secretary to hold all his calls, and he turned off the ringer on his direct line. Nothing and nobody was going to interrupt the flow of his thoughts. His feeling of satisfaction continued as he read through the work he'd done the day before. He was ready now to put himself on the line and commit his conclusions about Handy Andy to paper. Tony poured himself a cup of coffee from his Thermos and took a deep breath.

We are dealing with a serial killer who will certainly kill again unless he is caught. The next killing will take place on the eighth Monday following the death of Damien Connolly unless some trigger accelerates this. What might push him over the edge into extreme escalation could be some catastrophic event that causes him to lose whatever it is he is using to keep the fantasy alive. Since, for example, he is using videos, loss of or damage to his tapes could lead to loss of control. Another possible scenario is that an innocent person is charged with the killings. That would be such an affront to his sense of himself that he might commit his next murder ahead of schedule.

I believe it is likely that he has already selected his next victim and is familiarizing himself with that victim's movements and lifestyle. The chances are that the chosen victim is a man not known to the gay community. He will be, to all intents and purposes, a straight man living a heterosexual lifestyle.

The fact that his last victim was a police officer is disturbing. It is highly probable that this was choice, not accident or coincidence. The killer is sending a message to the investigation. He is demanding that we take notice of him, that we take him seriously. He is also telling us that he is the best; he can catch us but we can't catch him. There is a theory that such behaviour is a way of inviting capture, but I do not believe that is what is going on in this case.

It is possible that his next target may also be a police officer, perhaps even one who is working on the investigation. This alone will not be sufficient motive for the killer to choose them; they must also fit the victim criteria that he has drawn up in his own mind in order for the killing to assume its full meaning for him. I would strongly recommend that any officers who fit the victim profile employ extra vigilance at all times, noting any suspicious vehicles parked near their homes, and checking to see whether they are being followed to and from work and social events.

The stalking and preparation serves two main purposes for the killer: it cuts down on the potential surprise elements when he comes to carry out the killing, and it also fuels the fantasy that is the all-important area of the killer's life.

Our killer is probably a white male, aged between 25 and 35. He is likely to be at least 5ft 10ins tall, well muscled, with considerable upper-body strength. In spite of this, he probably has a poor body image. He may work out in a gym, but if he can afford it, he would prefer to use his own equipment in the privacy of his home. He is right-handed.

He won't look like a con. He'll look deeply, deeply average. He will have a demeanour that doesn't provoke suspicion. He's the sort of bloke you wouldn't look at twice, and certainly wouldn't suspect of being a multiple murderer. He may have tattoos and/or self-inflicted scars, but these are likely to be fairly discreet.

He is familiar with Bradfield, and his knowledge of Temple Fields is clearly current. This implies someone who lives and probably works in the city. I don't think he's a casual visitor, nor a former resident who simply comes back here to kill. There is no obvious geographical pattern to the homes or workplaces of his victims, except that they all lived in reasonably close proximity to a tram line. The first victim's home is most likely to be geographically closest to where the killer lives or works. Looking at the general background and style of the victims, and working on the principle that he's sticking to the kind of environment he knows and understands, I would suspect that the killer lives in privately owned property rather than rented, a house rather than a flat, in a suburban area of similar properties to those of the victims. The victims' houses are probably worth more than the killer's; these are men that in some way he aspires towards.

He is probably of above average intelligence, though I would not expect him to have a university degree. His school record is probably quite patchy, with poor attendance and highly variable marks. He will never have lived up to his potential or to other people's expectations of him. Most serial killers have a bad employment record, flitting from job to job, being sacked more often than resigning. But this man exhibits an extraordinary level of control in the commission of his murders, so I would expect him to be capable of holding down a steady job, possibly even one with some degree of responsibility and forward planning. However, I don't think his job will involve much contact with his fellow human beings, since his relationships with others will be characterized by their dysfunctional nature. His victims are all white-collar workers, with the marginal exception of Damien Connolly, which indicates to me that he probably operates in a similar working environment. I wouldn't be surprised to find him working in a technology-related area, possibly computers. This is an employment area where people can hold down good jobs without having significant people skills. People who don't fit in are accepted and acceptable in the weird world of software engineers; indeed, they are often highly prized since they are hard to replace. I doubt if our killer is a leading-edge creative person in the software world, but I wouldn't be surprised to find him as a systems manager or a program tester. He probably doesn't get on well with his bosses, being inclined to be insubordinate and argumentative.

He will be middle class in terms of his job, his aspirations, his clothes and his home, although he may be working class in background. He is good with his hands, but I am inclined to think he is not in a manual occupation, if only because of the high degree of planning involved in these murders.

Socially, he feels isolated. He may not necessarily be a loner, but he does not connect with people. He feels like an outsider. He probably has developed superficial social skills, but somehow his behaviour always strikes the wrong note. He's the one who laughs too loudly, the one who thinks he's making jokes when he's actually being deeply offensive, the one who sometimes seems to have drifted off in a daydream all of his own. He's the one who doesn't really have any friends, who will join in with the group but never pair off with one buddy in particular. He has little insight into his social failings. He prefers to be alone with his fantasies,

271

because when others are involved socially, he can't fully control what's happening around him.

It's entirely possible that he does not live alone. If he lives with someone, it will be a woman rather than a man. Because he is sexually attracted to men and cannot accept that, he will not under any circumstances be living with a man, not even in a platonic relationship. His relationships with women may well be sexual, but he will not be an enthusiastic or successful lover. His performance will be barely adequate, and he may regularly experience problems in achieving and/or sustaining an erection. However, he will not be impotent during the commission of his crime, and will almost certainly be able to complete a full sexual act of some sort with his victims.

Tony paused and stared out of the window. Sometimes it felt like the chicken and the egg. Did he empathize with his patients because he too knew the frustrations and anger of impotence, or had his sexual problems increased precisely so that he could do his job better? 'Does it matter?' he said impatiently. He ran a hand through his hair and concentrated once again on the screen.

If he is living with someone, she will almost certainly have no suspicion whatsoever that her partner is the killer. It's therefore quite likely that her first instinct will be to alibi him, since in her heart, she knows it couldn't possibly be him. Any suspects solely alibied by girlfriends or wives should therefore not be eliminated on those grounds alone.

He is mobile, with his own car, which is in good condition (see above). And on Monday nights, he's free to roam without hindrance or obligation to be somewhere.

He is a highly structured personality, a control freak. The sort who has a tantrum because his girlfriend has forgotten to buy his favourite cereal. He believes he's absolutely justified; he thinks that in his crimes, all he is doing is actually committing the actions that everybody else wants to but lacks the bottle for. He has a big chip on his shoulder and feels that the world has conspired against him; how come, since he's so bright and talented, he's not running the company instead of doing this poxy job? How come, since he's so charming, he's not going out with some supermodel? The answer is, the world is out to do him down. He has the egocentric world view of the spoiled child, and has no insight into the impact of his behaviour on others. All he sees is the way events affect him.

He is a persistent fantasist and daydreamer. His fantasies are elaborately constructed and seem more significant to him than reality. His fantasy world is where he retreats both from choice and also whenever he faces any kind of setback or obstacle in his day-to-day life. The fantasies are likely to involve violence as well as sex and may also be fetishistic. These fantasies don't remain static; they lose their power and have to be developed further.

He is certain that he can act out his violent fantasies without anyone being able to stop him. He has supreme confidence that he is smarter than the police. He is not planning for the day he will be caught. He thinks he's too clever for that. He has been very careful to erase forensic traces, which is why, as I have already outlined to Inspector Jordan, I am convinced that the fragment of Russian deerskin left at the scene of the fourth killing is a red herring of the grossest kind. He is almost certainly keeping a close eye on the investigation, and will doubtless be laughing his socks off as we run round trying to source the leather. Even if the police do trace it, I suspect that when we find the killer there will be nothing among his possessions that will remotely connect to it.

If he has any criminal record at all, it is likely to be a juvenile one. Possible offences include: vandalism, minor arson, stealing, cruelty to younger children or animals, assault on teachers. However, somewhere along the line, our killer has learned enormous self-control, and he's unlikely to have an adult record.

He will keep abreast of the investigation as much as possible, and will thrive on publicity as long as it appears to accord him the glamour and respect he craves. It is interesting that Adam Scott's grave was desecrated shortly after the second murder. This may have been an attempt to raise the profile of his crimes. He is possibly someone who has contacts with police officers, and if he does, he will endeavour to use this to gain information about the progress of the investigation. Any officer who feels they are being pumped in this way should be encouraged to report it to senior officers in the murder squad.

Tony saved his file and read the whole thing through

again. Some of the psychologists he'd worked with incorporated great slabs of background about the likely childhood background of the killer, as well as a check-list of behaviours that the killer would possibly have exhibited when he was growing up. Not Tony. There was time enough for that sort of information once there was a suspect ripe for interrogation. Tony never forgot that he was dealing with coppers who were out there at the sharp end. Men like Tom Cross, who didn't give a toss what kind of hideous childhood their suspect had endured.

Thinking of Tom Cross sharpened Tony's critical eye. Convincing him of the value of the profile was going to be a nightmare.

The first edition of the *Bradfield Evening Sentinel Times* hit the street just before noon. The eager searchers after flats, jobs and bargains snatched the first copies from the street vendors without even looking at the front page. They turned straight to the section of small ads that they hoped would meet their needs, holding the front and back pages up to the advantage of passers-by. Anyone curious enough to glance at the banner headlines on the front page would have discovered 'MURDER HUNT BOSS DUMPED. Exclusive, by our Crime Correspondent, Penny Burgess.' Further down the page, the bottom right-hand quarter was taken up with a photograph of Tony, saying, 'MURDER COPS FOLLOW *BEST* LEAD. Exclusive by Penny Burgess.' If they'd been intrigued enough to buy their own copy, they could have read a sub-headline saying, 'Top shrink we chose joins Queer Killer hunt, see story p. 3.'

In an office high above the bustling streets of Bradfield, a murderer stared at the paper, excitement churning inside. Things were working out beautifully. It was as if the police were acting out the killer's own fantasies, proving that wishes do come true.

The world was out in the city streets, buying Christmas presents they'd still be paying for at Easter, the fools. I was in my dungeon, making sure I would have a Christmas I'd never forget. Even though it was to be Gareth's last on this earth, I was sure every detail of it would be as clearly etched on his memory as it was going to be on my video tape.

I'd arranged our meeting with all the care and precision I could. The advent of the bitch meant I couldn't take the chance of capturing him at home as I'd done with Adam and Paul. I'd had to make alternative plans.

I sent him an invitation. I reasoned that Christmas Eve would be spoken for, either by family or by the bitch, so I chose December 23rd. I couched it in terms I knew he wouldn't be able to resist and that he'd never dare show the bitch. The final sentence read, 'Admission by invitation only.' A clever touch, that. It meant he'd have to bring with him the only evidence of contact between us.

The directions on the back led, if he cared to check it out in advance, to an isolated holiday cottage high up on the moors between Bradfield and the Yorkshire Dales; the opposite side of the city to Start Hill Farm and my dungeon. I anticipated that the cottage would be let over Christmas. But I had no intention of allowing Gareth to get that far.

It was a Christmas-cliché sort of night; bone-white crescent moon, stars twinkling like diamond chips on a cocktail watch, grass and hedgerows heavy with rime. I pulled over on to the verge of the single-track moorland road that led up to the holiday cottage and a couple of farms. In the distance, I could see the dual carriageway leading into Bradfield like a ribbon of fairy lights strung across the Pennines.

I turned on my hazard lights, got out of the jeep and opened the bonnet. I placed what I needed near at hand, then I leaned against the front wing and waited. It was freezing, but I didn't care. I'd calculated well. I'd only been waiting for about five minutes when I heard the sound of an engine straining up the steep incline. The lights swung round the bend below me and I stepped out, waving furiously, looking frozen and worried.

Gareth's elderly Escort stopped abruptly in front of the jeep. I took a couple of hesitant steps towards him as he opened the door and got out. 'Some kind of a problem?' he asked. 'I'm afraid I know next to nothing about cars, but if I can maybe give you a lift . . . ?'

I smiled. 'Thanks for stopping,' I said. There was no flicker of recognition in his face as he drew nearer. I hated him for that.

I stepped back towards the jeep, gesturing under the bonnet. 'It's not a big problem,' I said. 'Only, I need three hands. If you can just hold this part in place so I can get a spanner on this nut . . .' I pointed into the engine. Gareth leaned over the bonnet. I picked up the spanner and let him have it.

Within five minutes, he was trussed tighter than a turkey

in the boot of his own car. I had his car keys, his wallet and the invitation I'd sent him. I drove back down through the city to the farm, where I dumped the unconscious body unceremoniously down the cellar steps. I didn't have time to do any more then, not if I was going to get back to the jeep.

I drove Gareth's car into the centre of Bradfield, leaving it in Temple Fields in a back alley off Crompton Gardens. Nobody noticed me; they were all too busy partying. It was a mere ten minutes' walk across town to the railway station.

A twenty-minute train ride and a brisk fifteen-minute walk brought me back to the jeep. Cautiously, I approached. There was no sign of life, no suggestion that anyone had been poking around. I drove back to Start Hill Farm whistling 'Hark The Herald Angels Sing'.

When I switched the cellar light on, Gareth's dark-grey eyes flashed angry fire at me. I liked that. After the pathetic terror of Adam and Paul, it was refreshing to see a man who had some guts. The muffled sound that came from behind the tape on his mouth was more like an angry grunt than a plea.

I stooped over him and stroked his hair back from his forehead. At first, he jerked away from me, then he became calm and still, calculation in his eyes. 'That's more like it,' I said. 'No need to fight, no need to resist.'

He nodded, then grunted, signalling down towards his gag with his eyes. I knelt beside him and picked at one corner of the surgical tape. Once I had a good grip, I ripped it free in one swift movement. It's kinder than doing it gradually.

Gareth worked his jaw, licking his dry lips. He glared at me. 'Some fucking party,' he snarled, his voice a little shaky.

'It's exactly what you deserve,' I said.

'How the fuck do you work that out?' he demanded.

'You were meant for me. But you took up with that slag. And you tried to keep it a secret.'

Light dawned in his eyes. 'You're . . .' he started.

'That's right,' I interrupted. 'So now you know why you're here.' My voice was as cold as the stone floor. I stood up abruptly and walked over to the bench where I'd laid out my equipment.

Gareth was talking again, but I shut out the sound of his voice. I know how persuasive lawyers can be, and I wasn't about to be deflected from my course by any amount of sweet talking. I opened the ziplock bag and took out the chloroform pad. I turned back to Gareth and kneeled beside him. With one hand, I gripped his hair and with the other I applied the pad to his mouth and nose. He struggled so convulsively that I ended up with a clump of hair in my hand before he subsided into unconsciousness. Just as well I was wearing my latex gloves, otherwise his hair would have cut me. The last thing I needed was my blood mingling with his.

When he was out cold, I cut his clothes off. I took the strap from the Judas chair and fastened it round his chest, under the armpits. I'd fixed a rudimentary pulley and hoist to one of the ceiling beams, and I attached the hook to the strap. I raised Gareth's body with the hoist till he swung like mistletoe in a draught. Once he was up in the air, it was the work of moments to undo the handcuffs and fasten him to my Christmas tree.

I'd bolted two planks to the wall in the shape of a St Andrew's Cross, and covered them thickly with prickly boughs of blue Norwegian spruce. To each arm of the cross, I'd attached leather straps, which I fastened around his wrists and ankles. I opened up Gareth's curled fists and taped his hands open to the cross. Finally, I removed the hook and let the wrist straps take the strain. His body slumped alarmingly, and for a moment I was concerned that I hadn't fitted strong enough straps. There was a brief creaking of leather on wood, then silence. He hung like a martyred apostle on the dungeon wall.

I laid out my club hammer and the sharpened cold chisels I'd chosen for the job. We'd be together now till Christmas night. I intended to savour every minute of our forty-eight hours.

12

> Very few men commit murder upon philanthropic or
> patriotic principles . . . As to the majority of murderers,
> they are very incorrect characters.

The four detective inspectors sat stony-faced in what
had been Tom Cross's office as John Brandon gave
them the official version of the superintendent's suspension. Sometimes, Brandon wished he was one of
the lads again, able to explain his reasons without
appearing to undermine his own position by doing so.
'What we've got to do is put this behind us and move
this enquiry forward,' he said briskly. 'Now, what's the
score with McConnell?'

Kevin leaned forward in his seat. 'I did as you
instructed, sir. He left our custody just before midnight,
and I've had a team on him ever since. He hasn't put so
much as a toe out of line so far. He went straight home,
seemed to go to bed, judging by the lights. He was up
at eight this morning, and he's gone off to work. I've
got one lad in the gym, posing as a new member, and
another one out on the street.'

'Stick with it, Kevin. Anything else? Dave, anything

interesting coming out of the computer yet?'

'We're following up a lot of car numbers and blokes with previous for any gay-related offences, both on the gay-bashing and the gross indecency side. We're also about to cross-check those lists with the ones Don Merrick's been getting from travel agents of people who have booked holidays in Russia. Once we get the profile, we might be able to develop some suspects, but it's uphill at the moment, sir.'

Carol chipped in. 'Some of the weightlifting associ-ations said they'd supply us with lists of their mem-bers who'd either been to Russia or competed against Russian teams.'

Dave pulled a face. 'Oh goody, more bloody lists,' he said.

'I've got a contact in the leather business,' Stansfield said. 'Biggest importer in the UK. I asked him about the leather scrap and he said that with it being deerskin, it's probably not your common-or-garden labourer's jacket. He said it was likely to be someone with a bit of clout but not real power. You know. Somebody like a DI,' he grinned. 'Or a town-hall official halfway up the greasy pole. A deputy stationmaster. The second mate on a ship. That sort of thing.'

Dave grinned. 'I'll tell HOLMES to keep an eye out for ex-KGB men.'

Brandon started to say something, but he was cut off by the peal of the telephone. He grabbed it and said, 'Brandon here . . .' His face lost all expression, turning as wooden as the coffins he looked as if he should be carrying. 'Yes, sir. I'll be there right away.' He put the phone down gently and stood up. 'The Chief Constable is interested in hearing how this evening's paper came to look the way it does.' He crossed the room and paused by the door, one hand on the handle. 'I'm sure the person who washed our dirty linen in Ms Burgess's sink will be hoping I can persuade him not to make an example of him.' He gave Carol a frosty smile. 'Or her, come to that.'

Tony locked his office door behind him and gave the project secretary a happy wave and smile. 'I'm going out for a bite of lunch, Claire. I'll probably go to Café Genet in Temple Fields. Inspector Jordan's due at three, but I'll be back by then. OK?'

'You're sure you don't want to return one of these calls from the journalists?' Claire called after him.

Tony swung round, continuing to walk backwards across the office. 'What journalists?' he asked.

'First off, that Penny Burgess from the *Sentinel Times*. She's been trying every half-hour since I came in. Then, in the last hour, they've been on from all the national newspapers, and Radio Bradfield.'

Tony frowned, baffled. 'Why?' he asked. 'Did they say what they wanted?'

Claire held up the copy of the *Sentinel Times* she'd nipped out to buy from the campus newsagent. 'I'm no psychologist, Tony, but I think it might have something to do with this.'

Tony stopped in his tracks. Even across the office he could read the headlines and make out his own photograph splashed across the front page of the paper. Like an iron filing pulled by a magnet, Tony moved closer to the paper till he could read Penny Burgess's name on both stories. 'May I?' he said hoarsely, reaching out for the paper.

Claire relinquished it and watched his reaction. She liked her boss, but she was human enough to relish his discomfort at being exposed in the evening paper. Tony hastily flicked the front page over, hunting for the full story about himself. With a mounting sense of horror, he read:

Dr Hill is well equipped to enter the twisted mind of the Queer Killer. As well as his two university degrees and a wealth of experience in dealing directly with the criminal perverts who have terrorized society, he has a reputation for dogged determination.

A colleague said, 'He's married to the job. It's all he lives for. If anyone can catch the Queer Killer, it's Tony Hill.

'It's only a matter of time now, I'm convinced. Tony is relentless. He won't give up till this bastard is nailed down tight.

'Let's face it, Tony's got a top-class brain. These serial killers might have high IQs, but they're never very smart when it comes to staying out of custody.'

'Dear Christ,' Tony groaned. Apart from the fact that no self-respecting colleague would ever have given quotes like that, the article was tantamount to throwing down the gauntlet to Handy Andy. It read like a challenge. He felt sure Handy Andy would find a way to respond to that. Tony threw the paper down on the desk and scowled at it.

'It is a bit over the top,' his secretary said sympathetically.

'It's bloody irresponsible, never mind over the top,' Tony raged. 'Oh, bollocks to it. I'm going for lunch.

If the Chief Constable rings, tell him I've left for the day.' He walked off again towards the door.

'What about Inspector Jordan? What if she rings?'

'You can tell her I've left the country.' With the door open, he paused. 'No, only joking. Tell her I'll be here for our meeting.'

As he stood waiting for the lift, Tony realized nothing in his experience had prepared him for a direct confrontational challenge with a killer. This was one he'd have to fly by the seat of his pants.

Kevin Matthews drained his pint glass and waved it at the barmaid. 'Even if it is a red herring, he's still got to have had access to this bloody obscure bit of leather in the first place, hasn't he?' he demanded stubbornly of Carol and Merrick. 'Same again?'

Merrick nodded. 'I'll have a coffee this time, Kevin,' Carol said. 'And chuck us a menu, would you? I've got a feeling I'm in for a long session with the doc, and he's got a nasty habit of forgetting about food.'

Kevin ordered the drinks then turned back to Carol. With the persistence that had won him promotion, he said, 'I'm right though, aren't I? To plant the leather like that, not only has he had access to it, he also knows how unusual it is.'

'Agreed,' Carol said.

'So it's not a waste of time trying to source it, is it?'

'I never said it was,' Carol said patiently. 'Now, are you going to fill me in on what happened with Tom Cross, or do I have to copy our murderer and bring out the torture gear?'

While Kevin explained what had happened, Merrick's attention drifted. He'd already heard the tale more times than enough. He leaned against the bar and surveyed the clientele. The Sackville Arms wasn't the nearest pub to the Scargill Street station, but it sold draught Tetleys from Yorkshire and Boddingtons from Manchester, which inevitably made it the police local. The pub was on the outer fringes of Temple Fields, which had given it an added attraction for the local officers when Scargill Street had still been open. The location had meant that hookers or petty villains who wanted to drop a word in the ear of their personal contact on the force could manage it unobtrusively. However, in the few months that Scargill Street had been mothballed, the pub had subtly changed. The regulars had got used to having the place to themselves, and there was a clearly discernible distance between the coppers and the rest of the customers. The officers who'd been using the pub in an attempt to recruit new sources from the community's underbelly had met with a chilly reception. Even with a serial killer on the loose, no one wanted to get back into the habit of informing now they'd kicked it.

With his policeman's eyes, Merrick slowly scanned the room, classifying the drinkers. Hooker, dealer, rent boy, pimp, rich man, poor man, beggar man, wimp. He was jolted out of his scrutiny by Carol's voice. 'What do you think, Don?' he caught.

'Sorry, ma'am, miles away. What do I think about what?'

'That it's about time we developed some of our own snouts among the toms, instead of having to rely on the Vice Squad's girls. They've been round the houses so many times, I'd go outside to check if they told me it was raining.'

287

'Never mind the hookers,' Merrick said. 'We need to know a damn sight more about how the gay community works. I don't mean the lads that are out of the closet and down the Hell Hole. I mean the secretive ones. The ones that don't flaunt it. They're the ones who might have come across this guy before. I mean, from all I've ever read about serial killers, sometimes they don't actually kill the first time, they just have a go. Like the Yorkshire Ripper did. So maybe there's some frightened little guy in the closet who's been on the receiving end of a bit of violence that got out of hand. That might be the road to a break.'

'And God knows we need a break,' Kevin said. 'But if we don't know how the connections are made, how do we connect?'

Carol said thoughtfully, 'When in doubt, ask a policeman.'

'Do what?' Kevin asked.

'There are gay officers in the Job. More than most, they must know about keeping a low profile. They'd be able to tell us.'

'That doesn't answer the question,' Kevin protested doggedly. 'If they're so busy keeping it quiet, how do we know who they are?'

'The Met has an association of gay and lesbian police officers. Why don't we get in touch with them, in confidence, and ask for their help? Somebody must have some contacts in Bradfield.'

Merrick stared at Carol with admiration, Kevin with frustration, both wondering silently how it was that Inspector Jordan always had an answer.

Tom Cross glanced down at the front page of the *Sentinel*

Times, a smirk of satisfaction twitching his cigarette up and down. Ms Burgess might have thought she was in control of their little encounter the night before, but Tom Cross knew different. He'd played the spider to her fly, and she'd done exactly what he expected of her. No, credit where it's due. She'd done better than he'd expected. That line about the police staggering lamely in the wake of the *Sentinel Times* when it came to seeking out Dr bloody Hill was a corker.

There were going to be a lot of angry men in Bradfield police today. That was the revenge element of Tom Cross's game with Penny Burgess. But someone else was going to be angry too. When he read tonight's paper, the killer was going to be more than a little put out.

Tom Cross stubbed out his cigarette and slurped from his mug of tea. He folded his paper and placed it on the table in front of him and stared out of the café window. He lit another cigarette. He'd set out to provoke the Queer Killer. Provoked, he'd start to get careless, to make mistakes. And when Stevie McConnell did that, Tom Cross would be ready and waiting. He'd show those sorry bastards in command how to catch a killer.

Tony was back in the office by ten to three. Even so, he wasn't early enough to beat Carol. 'Inspector Jordan's here,' Claire said as soon as he opened the outer office door. She gestured with her head towards his office. 'She's in there waiting. I told her you'd be back.'

Tony's responding smile was strained. As he gripped the door handle, he clenched his eyes tightly and took a deep breath. Nailing what he hoped was a welcoming smile on his face, Tony opened the door and stepped into his office. At the sound of the door, Carol turned away from the window she'd been staring out of and gave him a cool, appraising look. Tony closed the door behind him and leaned against it.

'You look like a man who's just stepped in a puddle that's deeper than his shoe,' Carol remarked.

'That's an improvement, then,' Tony said with more than a trace of irony. 'Usually I feel like I've stepped in a puddle that's deeper than my head.'

Carol took a step towards him. She'd rehearsed what she was going to say. 'There's no need to feel like that with me. Last night . . . well, you were less than candid and I misread the signals. So can we please forget the whole thing and concentrate on what's important between us?'

'Which is?' Tony sounded impersonal as a therapist, his question conversational rather than challenging.

'Working together to nail this killer.'

Tony pushed himself away from the door and made for the safety of his seat, careful to keep the desk between them at all times. 'That's fine by me.' He gave a crooked smile. 'Believe me, I'm far better at professional relationships than the other kind. Think of it as a lucky escape.'

Carol walked round to the opposite side of the desk and pulled up a chair. She crossed her trouser-clad legs and folded her hands in her lap. 'So let's have a look at this profile.'

'We don't have to behave as if we're strangers,' Tony said quietly. 'I respect you, and I admire the way you're so open to learning new aspects of the job. Look, before . . . before what happened last night, we seemed to be moving towards a friendship that went beyond work. Was that such a bad thing? Couldn't we settle for that?'

Carol shrugged. 'It's not easy making friends after you've exposed your weaknesses.'

'I don't think showing someone you're attracted to them is necessarily a weakness.'

'I feel foolish,' Carol said, not quite sure why she was opening up like this. 'I had no right to expect anything from you. Now, I'm angry with myself.'

'And with me too, I expect,' Tony said. This was proving less traumatic than he had imagined. His counselling techniques hadn't rusted over from lack of use, he thought with relief.

'Mostly with myself,' Carol said. 'But I can deal with that. The important thing for me is that we get the job done.'

'Me too. It's pretty rare for me to find a police officer who seems to have a grasp of what I'm trying to do.' He picked up the papers on his desk. 'Carol . . . This isn't about you, you know. It's about me. I have problems of my own that I need to deal with.'

Carol stared at him long and hard. He felt a quick twitch of panic as he realized he could not read her eyes. He had no idea what she was feeling. 'I hear what you're saying,' she replied, her voice cold. 'Speaking of problems,' she added, 'haven't we got some work to do?'

Carol sat alone in Tony's office with his profile of the serial killer. He had left her to read it while he worked next door with his secretary, catching up on the correspondence that had piled up since Brandon had hijacked him only a handful of days before. She couldn't remember ever having been so fascinated by a report in her entire career. If this was the future of policing, she desperately wanted to be part of it. At last, she came to the end of the main body of text and turned to a separate sheet.

Points to pursue:

1. Had any of the victims ever mentioned to a friend/ relative that they had been the subject of an unwanted homosexual approach? If so, when, where and from whom?

2. The killer is a stalker. His first encounter with his victims probably takes place quite a long time before he kills – weeks rather than days. Where is he encountering them? It may be something as banal as where they take their dry-cleaning, where they have their shoes heeled, where they buy sandwiches, where they have tyres or exhausts put on their cars. Given that they all lived close to the tram network, I think we should check whether the victims regularly used the trams to go to and from work, or to go out in the evenings. I suggest that in-depth background checks are done, going through bank accounts, credit-card statements and anecdotal evidence from colleagues, girlfriends and family members. This may help develop suspects.

3. Is there any indication that the victims were keeping the night in question free for any particular purpose? Gareth Finnegan lied to his girlfriend about it – did any of the others?

4. Where is he doing his killing? It's unlikely to be in his home, since he will have calculated the

possibility of being arrested, and will have taken pains to avoid leaving forensic traces there. It's also got to be big enough for him to build and use the torture engines we are assuming in these cases. It may be an isolated lock-up garage, or a unit on an industrial estate which is deserted at night. Bearing in mind that he almost certainly lives in Bradfield, it's possible that there exists an isolated rural property that he has undisturbed access to.

5. He must have found out about instruments of torture somewhere so that he could construct his own. It might be worth checking with bookshops and libraries to see if any of their customers has enquired about or ordered books on torture.

Carol flicked back a few pages, rereading a couple of paragraphs which had particularly struck her first time through. She found it hard to credit how quickly Tony had assimilated the stacks of files she'd delivered. Not only that, but he'd drawn out of them the key points that created for the first time in Carol's mind a picture, albeit shadowy, of the man she was hunting.

But the profile raised questions in her mind. At least one of those questions didn't seem to have occurred to Tony. She wondered if it wasn't referred to because he had dismissed it out of hand. Either way, she had to know. And she had to find a way of asking that didn't sound like an attack.

I hated to keep Gareth hanging on, but I had to leave him for one little errand. In his car, I'd found a few of the Christmas cards his company sent out to favoured clients, already signed by all the partners. Inside one, with a fountain pen, a stencil set and Gareth's blood, I'd written in block capitals, 'A MERRY CHRISTMAS TO ALL YOUR READERS; YOUR EXCLU-SIVE CHRISTMAS GIFT IS WAITING IN THE SHRUBBERY OF CARLTON PARK BEHIND THE BANDSTAND. COMPLIMENTS OF THE SEASON FROM SANTA CLAWS.' It wasn't easy to write with the blood; it kept congealing on the nib, which I had to clean every few letters. Luckily, there was no shortage of ink.

I addressed a Jiffy bag to the editor of the Bradfield Evening Sentinel Times *and put the card in it, along with a video I'd made a couple of weeks before, when I'd started to plan what to do with Gareth. I'd already decided to change my modus operandi slightly. Temple Fields was bound to be risky now; even if the queens were too drunk or stoned to be vigilant, the police would be keeping an eye open for more than the occasional cottaging poof. But the nature trail through the shrubbery of Carlton Park is almost as notorious a pick-up area.*

294

Early on a rainy Sunday morning, when there was nobody about, I'd driven out to Carlton Park with my camcorder. I started off by the wrought-iron bandstand. I walked around it, filming it from every angle. It wouldn't take long before somebody in the BEST office recognized the landmark. After all, Carlton Park is the biggest park within the city boundaries, and there's a brass-band concert there every Sunday from April to September. I deliberately kept the camcorder at chest level rather than on my shoulder; I've read of instances where correct estimates of height have been made simply from the angle photographs have been taken from. If some forensic scientist was going to draw any conclusions from this video, I wanted to be sure they would be the wrong ones.

Leaving the bandstand behind, I walked down the nature trail towards the shrubbery. I panned across the general area where I thought I'd dump the body, then stopped filming. I passed nobody on my way back to the jeep. That was probably just as well, since I was grinning from ear to ear at the thought of the news editor puzzling over my Christmas message.

The message would also serve two other functions. It would minimize the time it took to identify Gareth's body, which meant the publicity machine would have plenty of fodder to keep it going through what was always a slack news period. Secondly, it would send the police on a wild goose chase, working out who could have had access to the Christmas cards.

The police might even decide that someone connected with Gareth through work had decided to bump him off and make it look like a copycat killing by dumping the body in a gay cruising area. Just the sort of thing a deranged and disillusioned client would do. If I got really lucky, they might even give the bitch a hard time, too.

I drove into the city centre to post the packet at the main post office. There were enough last-minute panicking gift-givers for me to be unremarkable. I stopped at an off licence on the way back to buy a bottle of champagne. I don't normally drink when I'm working, but this was a special occasion.

When I got back, Gareth was semi-conscious, mumbling incomprehensibly. 'Santa's here,' I said cheerfully as I came down the stairs. I popped the cork on the champagne and poured two glasses. I took one over to Gareth and, standing on tiptoe, I gently lifted his lolling head. I held the glass to his lips and tilted it. 'You'll enjoy this,' I said. 'It's vintage Dom Perignon.'

His eyes snapped wide open. For a moment, he looked bewildered, then he remembered and he fixed me with a look of pure hatred. But he was parched, and couldn't resist the champagne. He swallowed it greedily, not savouring it at all. Then he belched in my face, a look of strange satisfaction in his eyes.

'Wasted on you,' I said angrily. 'Like all the fine things in life.' I stepped back and slashed the glass across his face. It shattered against his nose, cutting his cheek to ribbons. I was glad Auntie Doris wouldn't be coming back. She'd had that set of six fragile crystal glasses as a silver-wedding present, and she'd never used them, terrified that someone would break one. She'd been right to be concerned.

Gareth shook his head. 'You're evil,' he slurred. 'Pure evil.'

'No, I'm not,' I said softly. 'I'm justice. Remember justice? It's what you're supposed to stand for.'

'Twisted, evil bastard,' he replied.

I couldn't believe he still had the stamina for bravado. It was time to show him who was boss. I'd already pinned his hands to the cross with a couple of cold chisels. The blood had congealed around them, black and hard. Now it was the turn of his feet.

When he saw me pick up my tools from the workbench, he finally cracked. 'There's no need for this,' he said desperately. 'Please. You could still let me go. They'd never find you. I've no idea where we are. I don't know who you are, where you live, what you do for a living. You could move away from Bradfield and they'd never find you.'

I took a step closer. Tears welled up in his eyes and spilled over, trickling through the blood on his cheek. They must have stung, but he never flinched. 'Please,' he whispered. 'It's not too late. Even if you killed those other men. Was it you who killed them?'

He was smart, I had to give him that. Too smart for his own good. He'd just earned himself some more suffering. I turned away and dropped the chisel and club hammer on the workbench. Let him think I was having second thoughts. Let him spend the night convinced I was going to have mercy. That would make Christmas Day all the sweeter.

I shut the cellar door behind me and went upstairs to bed, armed with my videos and the best part of a bottle of vintage champagne. I was having the best Christmas I'd ever had. I remembered all those years of desperate hope, praying that this would be the year my mother would buy me presents like other children got. But all she'd ever done was let me down. Now I'd worked out that the only person who could give me what I craved was myself; I knew that for the first time in my life, I could look forward to the kind of Christmas other people have, filled with surprises, satisfaction and sex.

13

Reading his acts by the light of such mute traces as he left behind him, the police became aware that latterly he must have loitered. And the reason which governed him is striking; because at once it records – that murder was not pursued by him simply as a means to an end, but also as an end for itself.

The Wunch of Bankers was one of the few city-centre watering holes where Kevin Matthews felt safe meeting Penny Burgess. A fun pub with blaring rap music and decor modelled on soap operas – the Rover's Return Snug, the Woolpack Eaterie, the Queen Vic Lounge, and the Cheers Beer Bar – was the last place he was likely to see another copper or Penny another journalist.

Kevin made a face as his taste buds clenched on the strong bitter coffee that lurked under a swirl of foam that looked more like industrial effluent than a cappuccino. Where the hell was she? He glanced at his watch for the twentieth time. She'd promised she'd be here by four at the latest, and now it was ten past. He pushed the half-empty cup away from him and grabbed his fashionable raincoat from the banquette beside him. He was about to stand up when the pub's revolving door hissed round and disgorged Penny. She waved and headed straight over to his table.

'You said four o'clock,' Kevin greeted her.

'God, Kevin, you're getting really anal in your old age,' Penny complained, giving him a peck on the cheek as she subsided on to the seat beside him. 'Get me one of those mineral waters with a hint of fruits of the forest, there's a love,' she said, her voice mocking the pretensions of her chosen drink.

When Kevin returned with a glass already sweating with condensation, Penny immediately put a proprietorial hand on the inside of his thigh. 'Mmm, thanks,' she said, sipping her drink. 'So what's new? Why the urgent meeting?'

'Today's paper,' he said tonelessly. 'The shit's really hit the fan.'

'Oh, good,' Penny said. 'Maybe we'll get some positive action. Like a suspect you've got some evidence against.'

'You're not understanding. They're hunting for the mole. The Chief had Brandon on the carpet this morning, and the upshot is that Internal Affairs have mounted a leak enquiry. Penny, you've got to cover my back,' Kevin said desperately. Penny took her time lighting a cigarette. 'Are you listening to me?' Kevin demanded.

'Of course I am, sweetheart,' Penny soothed automatically, her mind already planning her story for the morrow. 'I just don't understand why you're getting so worked up. You know a good journalist never reveals her sources. What's the problem? You think I'm not a good enough journalist?' With an effort, Penny forced herself to listen to Kevin's reply rather than the voice in her head reeling off headlines.

'It's not that I don't trust you,' Kevin said impatiently. 'It's inside the force I'm worried about. Everybody will be desperate to put themselves in the clear, so anybody that knows about us will be falling over themselves to tell Internal Affairs. And once they know that we're, well, you know? That'll be it. I'll have had it.'

'But nobody knows about us. Or not from me, they don't,' Penny said calmly.

'I thought nobody knew too. Then Carol Jordan said something that made me think she does.'

'And you think Carol's going to shop you to Internal Affairs?' Penny said, failing to hide the incredulity she felt. She hadn't had many dealings with the CID's most glamorous officer, but what she knew of the inspector didn't incline her to cast her in the role of grass.

'You don't know her. She's totally bloody ruthless. She wants to go all the way, that one, and she'd drop me in it soon as look at me if she thought it would take her a rung up the ladder.'

Penny shook her head in exasperation. 'You're overreacting. Even if Carol Jordan has mysteriously discovered that we're seeing each other, I'm sure she's too busy covering herself with glory from her liaison with Dr Hill to be bothered with shopping you. Besides, if you think about it rationally, she's got nothing to gain from getting herself a reputation with the lads as a grass.'

Kevin shook his head dubiously. 'I don't know. Penny, you've no idea what it's like on this job. We're all working eighteen-hour days, and we're getting nowhere.'

Penny stroked the inside of his thigh. 'Sweetheart, you're under a lot of pressure. Look, tell you what. If it all comes on top and somebody fingers you, Internal Affairs are bound to come to us and front us up. They'll be looking for corroboration. If that happens, I'll make it look like Carol Jordan's my source, OK? That should muddy the waters.'

Kevin's smile was worth the flannel, she decided. That, and one or two other things about him. Reassured, he bounced to his feet. 'Thanks, Pen. Listen, I've got to be a place. I'll call you soon so we can get together, OK?' He leaned over and kissed her deep and hard.

'Keep me posted, lover boy,' Penny said softly to his retreating back. Before he even reached the doors, her intro was taking shape. Oh yes, she could see it now.

Bradfield police are devoting new resources to the hunt for the serial killer who has claimed four victims and placed men in jeopardy as never before.

But the extra officers will not be joining the search for the monstrous Queer Killer. Their job will be to police the police themselves.

Top brass in the force are so alarmed by the accuracy of the *Sentinel Times*'s stories on the killings that they have set up a full-scale mole hunt to uncover the source of our stories. Instead of catching the killer, the mole-catchers will be tracking down fellow officers who subscribe to the view that the terrified public have a right to know what's going on.

Carol opened the door to the outer office and said, 'I'm all done. Can we talk?'

Tony looked up from the computer screen absently, held up one finger and said, 'Yeah, sure, give me a minute,' and finished what he was doing.

Carol retreated and took a deep breath. No matter how professional she tried to be, she couldn't help the surge of attraction she felt for this man. Ignoring it was easier said than done. Moments later, Tony joined her. He perched on the edge of his desk, his hair standing on end like Dennis the Menace from thrusting his fingers through it while he concentrated. 'So,' he said. 'What's the verdict?'

'I'm impressed,' she said. 'It really pulls everything together. There were a couple of things, though.'

'Only a couple?' Tony asked, his voice close to a chuckle.

'You talk a lot about how he must be strong, to over-power his victims and move them around. Also, you speculate about how he gets them into a vulnerable position in the first place. I was wondering if maybe there were two of them.'

'Go on,' Tony said, no hint of frost in his voice.

'I don't mean two men. I mean a man and someone else who appears vulnerable. Maybe an adolescent boy or, more likely, a woman. I don't know, maybe even a person in a wheelchair. A partner in crime. Like Ian Brady and Myra Hindley.' Carol shuffled the papers, putting them back in order. Still Tony said nothing. After a few moments watching his expressionless face, she added, 'I know you've probably thought about it already, I just wondered if it was a possibility we should still bear in mind.'

'Sorry, I didn't mean to look like I was ignoring you,' Tony said hurriedly. 'I was reviewing the thought, weighing it against what we know and against the profile. One of the first things I considered was whether or not it was a solo. On the balance of overwhelming probability, I decided it was. Cases like the Moors Murders where you have two people acting in tandem to carry out atrocities are incredibly rare, for a kick off. Also, I'd expect to find more variation in the methodology and the pathology if there were two people involved; it's hard to believe their fantasies would coincide so exactly. But it's interesting that you've come up with it. You're right in one respect. If he's working with a woman it does explain how he gets close to his victims without them putting up a fight.' Tony sat staring straight ahead, brows lowered in thought.

Carol stayed motionless in her seat. Eventually, Tony turned to face her and said, 'I'm going to stick with my soloist. Yours is an interesting idea, but I can't see evidence that convinces me I should shift from the most highly probable scenario.'

'OK, point taken,' Carol said calmly. 'Moving on from that, have you considered the possibility of a transvestite? Like you just said, a woman could get close without them putting up a fight. What about if the woman was a man in drag? Wouldn't that have the same effect?'

Tony looked startled for a moment. 'Maybe you should think about applying to join the national task force when it's set up,' he stalled.

Carol grinned. 'Flattery will get you nowhere.'

'I mean it. I think you've got what it takes to do this

kind of work. You see, I'm not infallible. I hadn't actually considered a transvestite. Now, why did I ignore that possibility?' he mused, thinking aloud. 'There must be some subconscious reason why I rejected it before it even got to the front of my mind ...' Carol opened her mouth to speak, but he said, 'No, wait a minute, please, let me work this out.' His hands ran through his hair again, rearranging the dark spikes.

She subsided, telling herself he was just as arrogant as all the rest, unable to accept he might just have missed something. Stop kidding yourself he's different, she told herself sternly.

'Right,' Tony said, his voice rich with satisfaction. 'We're dealing with a sexual sadist, agreed?'

'Agreed.'

'Sado-masochism is the power trip of sexual fetishes. But transvestism is the diametric opposite of that. TVs want to assume the supposedly weaker role that women have in society. What underpins transvestism is the belief that women have a subtle power, the power of their gender. It couldn't be further removed from the brute transaction of pain and power that sado-masochists crave. That's not part of a TV's fantasy at all. To convince the victims that they're dealing with a woman and not a man in drag, the killer would have to be an accomplished cross-dresser. But, uniquely in my experience of clinical psychology, he'd also have to be a sexual sadist. The two just don't go together,' Tony explained with an air of finality. 'The same goes for a transsexual. Probably more so, in fact, because of the counselling they have to go through before they're accepted for treatment.'

'So you're ruling it out, then,' Carol said, feeling unreasonably crushed.

'I never rule anything out. That's asking to make a fool of yourself in this game. What I think is that it's so unlikely that I would be loath to include it in a profile because its very inclusion might push people in the wrong direction. But by all means keep it in mind. You're thinking along the right lines.' He smiled, unexpectedly, taking the sting of patronage out of his words. 'Like I said at the start, Carol, together we can crack it.'

'And you're absolutely convinced that it isn't a woman?' she asked.

'The psychology's all wrong. Taking the most obvious point, this killer's an obsessive, and that tends to be a male trait. How many women do you know who hang about station platforms in the rain in anoraks writing down train numbers?'

'But what about that syndrome, what's it called, where people get obsessed with someone else to the point where they make their lives a misery? I thought it was mainly women who suffer from that?'

'De Clerambault's Syndrome,' Tony said. 'And yes, it is principally women who suffer from it. But they only focus on one person, and the only person who's likely to get dead as a result is the sufferer, who sometimes commits suicide. The thing is that women's obsessions and compulsions are different from men's. Men's obsessions are about control; they collect stamps and catalogue them, they collect a pair of knickers from every woman they've slept with. They need trophies. Women's obsessions are about submission; in eating disorders, it's the obsession that takes them over and controls them rather than the other way about. A sufferer from de Clerambault's Syndrome who married the object of her desire would probably be the chauvinist's ideal of the perfect wife. That pattern doesn't fit our killer.'

'I see what you mean,' Carol said, loath to give up the one fresh idea she felt she'd contributed to the profiling process.

'Add to that the sheer physical strength involved here,' Tony continued, seeing her reluctance. 'You're fit. You're probably quite strong for your height. I'm only a couple of inches taller than you. But how far do you think you could carry me? How long would it take you to pick my body up from the boot of a car and dump it over a wall? Could you throw me over your shoulder and carry me through Carlton Park to the shrubbery? Now bear in mind that all the victims have been taller and heavier than me.'

Carol gave a rueful smile. 'OK, you win. I'm convinced. There was one other thing that occurred to me.'

'Let's hear it.'

'Reading your profile, it seems to me that the reason you advance for the maintenance of the gaps between the killings just isn't strong enough,' she started tentatively.

'You noticed that too,' he said wryly. 'It didn't convince me either. But I couldn't think of anything else to explain it. I've never encountered anything quite like it, either face to face or in the literature. All the serial offenders I know about go through escalation.'

'I've got a theory that might cover the problem,' Carol said.

Tony leaned forward, his expression absorbed. 'Speak to me, Carol,' he said.

Feeling like a goldfish in a bowl, Carol took a deep breath. She'd wanted his attention, but she wasn't quite sure if she liked it now she had it. 'I remember what you said to me a couple of days ago about the intervals.' She closed her eyes and recited, '"With most serial killers, the gap between the killings tends to decrease quite dramatically. It's their fantasies that trigger off the killings in the first place, and the reality never quite matches up to the fantasy, no matter how much they refine their killing procedures. But the more extreme they get, the more blunted their sensibilities become and the more stimulus they need to get the sexual buzz that killing provides. So the kills have to become more frequent. Shakespeare said it. 'As if increase of appetite had grown by what it fed on.'" Am I right?'

'Remarkable,' Tony breathed. 'Can you do that with visuals as well, or is it only auditory?'

Exasperated, Carol cast her eyes upwards. 'Auditory only, I'm afraid. Anyway, when I read the bit in the profile where you suggest he might work with computers, something clicked. The question you didn't actually put but is obviously bothering you is, why isn't he getting desensitized to the videos faster as time goes by?'

Tony nodded. The point she'd raised was powerful, and it was precisely what was troubling him. He searched to find an answer that would satisfy them both. Groping for the solution as he went along, he said, 'Suppose, for the sake of argument, that the first video had the potential to keep him stable for

307

twelve weeks. But he'd already set in train the process of capturing his second victim, and the opportune moment came along before he was actually compelled to kill again. He just couldn't resist the chance when it presented itself so perfectly. Afterwards, he realizes he's left eight weeks between the killings and he decides that eight weeks is going to be his pattern. So far, the videos have allowed him to maintain that. Maybe that is going to change now.'

Carol shook her head. 'It's plausible, but I'm not convinced.'

Tony grinned. 'Thank God for that. Neither am I. There's got to be a better explanation, but I don't know what it is.'

'How much do you know about computers?' she asked.

'I know where the on/off switch is and I know how to use the software I need to work with. Other than that, I'm a moron.'

'Well, that makes two of us. My brother, however, is a computer whizz kid. He's a partner in a games software house. The stuff he works on is leading-edge technology. Right now, he and his partner are developing a low-cost system that will allow games players to put images of themselves in the games that they're playing. In other words, instead of it being Arnie kicking the shit out of the bad guys on the screen in *Terminator* 2, it would be Tony Hill. Or Carol Jordan. The point is that there's already the hardware and software around that allows you to scan video tape and import the images into a computer. I think they call it digitized images. Anyway, once you've got that into the computer, you can manipulate it exactly how you want to. You can incorporate still photographs, or bits from other videos. You can superimpose things. When they first got the original hardware about six months ago, Michael showed me this sequence he'd made up himself. He'd taped some of the Tory Party conference and he'd also imported a video sex guide. He'd selected all these government ministers' faces while they were giving their speeches and superimposed them on the sex video.' Carol snorted with laughter at the memory. 'It was a bit choppy, but believe me, you've never seen John Major and Margaret Thatcher getting on so well! It gave a whole new meaning to the word "gobbledegook"!'

Tony stared at Carol in stunned silence. 'You're kidding me,' he said.

'It's the perfect explanation of why the videos manage to keep him under control.'

'Wouldn't that mean he'd have to be a real boffin, like your brother?'

'I don't think so,' Carol said. 'From what I gathered, the actual techniques involved are fairly simple. But the software and the peripherals that you need to do it are incredibly expensive. You could be talking two or three grand just for one piece of software. So he's either working for a company where he has that sort of equipment on tap and the privacy to work on his own stuff, or else he's a computer hobbyist with a lot of disposable income.'

'Or a thief,' Tony added, only half joking.

'Or a thief,' Carol agreed.

'I don't know,' Tony said dubiously. 'It does answer the problem, but it's totally off the wall.'

'And Handy Andy isn't?' Carol said belligerently.

309

'Oh, he's off the wall, all right, but I'm not sure he's that together.'

'He builds torture machines. That would be a lot easier with a computer design program. Tony, something's keeping him stable on his eight-week cycle. Why not this?'

'It's a *possibility*, Carol, no more than that at this stage. Look, why don't you make some preliminary enquiries, see how feasible what you're suggesting would be in practice?'

'You don't want to include it in the profile?' Carol asked, bitterly disappointed.

'I don't want to undermine the things I feel are strongly probable by including something that's really only a bit of kite-flying at this stage. You said yourself, it was triggered off by one of the few bits in the profile that is little more than speculation. Don't get me wrong, I'm not knocking the idea. I think it's brilliant. But we're going to have to work bloody hard as it is to overcome the resistance in some quarters to the profile as a whole. Even people who are broadly in support of the idea aren't necessarily going to agree with some parts of it. So let's not give them any easy targets. Let's bottom it, present it to them gift-wrapped so the snipers can't just knock it straight off the perch. OK?'

'Fine,' she said, knowing in her heart he was right. She picked up a sheet of paper and a pen. 'Check out software manufacturers and consultancies in Bradfield area,' she muttered to herself as she wrote. 'Check with Michael about manufacturers of necessary hardware/software then check sales records. Check recent thefts.'

'Computer clubs,' Tony added.

'Thanks, yes,' Carol said, adding that to her list. 'And bulletin boards. Oh boy, I'm going to be really popular with the HOLMES team.' She got to her feet. 'It's going to be a long job. I'd better get cracking. I'll take this down to Scargill Street now and give it to Mr Brandon. We'll need you to come in and go through it.'

'No problem,' Tony said.

'I'm glad something isn't.'

Tony stared out of the window of the tram, watching the city lights pass in a blur of rain. There was something cocoon-like about the gleaming white interior of the tram. Graffiti-free, warm, clean; it felt like a safe place to be. As the driver approached traffic lights, he gave a blast on the breathy horn. It sounded like a noise from childhood, the sort of hooting that a cartoon train would produce, he decided.

He turned away from the window and covertly studied the half-dozen other passengers on the tram. Anything to take his mind off the curious emptiness he felt now he had delivered his profile. It wasn't as if this would be the end of his involvement with the case. Brandon had told Carol that she was to have a daily briefing with him.

He wished he could have been more encouraging about her computer theory, but years of training and practice had rendered the habit of caution ingrained. The idea itself was brilliant. Once she had done some research into the practicability of what she was suggesting, he'd be only too happy to endorse it with her fellow officers. But for the sake of his profile's credibility, he had to keep his distance from ideas that the average copper would dismiss as science fiction.

He wondered how the police were faring that evening. Carol had called him to say that teams were going out in Temple Fields, trawling the area's regulars, trying to see if the profile suggestions produced any recognition. With luck, they might get some names that would cross-reference to data already in HOLMES, either from previous criminal records or from the car index numbers whose registered keepers had been fed into the system.

'The next stop will be Bank Vale station. Bank Vale station next stop,' the electronic voice from the speakers announced. With a start, Tony realized they had left the city centre far behind and were emerging on the far side of Carlton Park, less than a mile from his home. Bank Vale came and went, and Tony swung round in his seat, ready to make for the exit doors when the next stop was announced.

He walked briskly through the neat suburban streets, past the school playing fields, skirting the small copse that was all that remained of the plantation that had given the Woodside area its name. Tony glanced at the trees as he hurried past, thinking wryly that the path cutting diagonally through the wood would almost certainly be completely deserted. First it was the women walking home alone who had abandoned it. Then it was the children, kept away by anxious parents. Now, in Bradfield, it was the men who were learning the bitter lessons of life in jeopardy.

Tony turned into his street, relishing the quiet of the cul-de-sac. He'd get through the evening somehow.

Maybe drive down to the supermarket and buy the ingredients for a chicken biryani. Pick up a video. Catch up on his reading.

As he turned the key in the lock, the phone started ringing. Dropping his briefcase, Tony ran for the phone, kicking the door to behind him. He picked up the phone, but before he could say anything, her voice trickled into his ear like warm olive oil soothing an earache. 'Anthony, darling, you sound like you're panting for me.'

He'd managed to avoid thinking about it all the way home, but he knew this was what he'd been hoping for.

Brandon had turned out the bedside light less than a minute before the phone rang. 'You should have known better,' Maggie murmured as he dragged himself away from her complaisant warmth and reached for the receiver.

'Brandon,' he growled.

'Sir, it's Inspector Matthews,' the tired voice said. 'We've just picked up Stevie McConnell. The lads have just lifted him at the ferry port in Seaford. He was about to get on a ship for Rotterdam.'

Brandon sat up in a tangle of duvet, ignoring Maggie's protests. 'What have they done?'

'Well, sir, they didn't think there was a lot they could do, being as how he's on police bail and there's no conditions for him to breach.'

'Are they holding him?' Brandon was out of bed and reaching for his underwear drawer.

'Yes, sir. They've got him in the Customs lads' office.'

'What on?'

'Assaulting a police officer.' Kevin's voice somehow summoned up the image of a smirk as disembodied as the Cheshire Cat's smile. 'They rang me to ask what they should do next, and since you've taken such a personal interest in the case, I thought I should ask you first.'

Don't push it, Brandon thought savagely. All he said, however, was, 'I'd have thought it was pretty obvious. Arrest him for attempting to pervert the course of justice and bring him back to Bradfield.' He wrestled into a pair of boxer shorts and leaned over to pick up his trousers from the back of a chair.

'I take it we show him to the magistrates this time and ask that they refuse bail?' Kevin's voice was so sweet it was on the border of costing him his teeth, and not from decay.

'That's what we normally do when we have grounds, Inspector. Thanks for keeping me informed.'

'One other thing, sir,' Kevin said unctuously.

'What?' Brandon growled.

'The lads have also had to make another arrest.'

'*Another* arrest? Who the hell else have they had to arrest?'

'Superintendent Cross, sir. Apparently, he was trying rather forcibly to prevent McConnell from boarding the ferry.'

Brandon closed his eyes and counted to ten. 'Is McConnell hurt?'

'Apparently not, sir, just a bit shaken up. The super has a black eye, though.'

'Fine. Tell them to let Cross go home. And tell them to ask him to call me tomorrow, OK, Inspector?' Brandon replaced the phone and leaned over to kiss his wife, who had reclaimed the duvet and was rolled up tight as a hibernating dormouse.

'Mmm,' Maggie murmured. 'Are you sure you have to go in?'

'It's not my idea of a good time, believe me, but I want to be there when they bring this prisoner in. He's just the sort of bloke who might fall downstairs.'

'A problem with his balance?'

Brandon shook his head grimly. 'Not *his* balance. Other people sometimes get a bit unbalanced, love. We've already had one maverick on the prowl tonight. I'm not taking any more chances. I'll see you when I see you.'

Fifteen minutes later, Brandon walked into the murder squad room. Kevin Matthews was slumped over a desk at the far end of the room, his head cradled in his arms. As Brandon approached, he heard the soft snore of Kevin's breathing. He wondered when any of the squad had last had a straight night's sleep. It was when officers got tired and edgy at the lack of results that the serious mistakes happened. Brandon desperately wanted to avoid his name in lights ten years down the road as the man who masterminded a sensational miscarriage of justice, and he'd go to any lengths to avoid it. There was only one problem with that, he wryly acknowledged to himself as he sat down opposite Kevin. In order to keep his finger on the pulse of the investigation, he had to work the same kind of ridiculous hours that led to the very misjudgements he wanted to avoid. *Catch* 22. He'd read that, a few years back now, when Maggie had decided to go to evening classes and take the A Levels she'd never got round to at school. She'd said it was a wonderful book, funny, savage, sharply satirical. He'd found it almost too painful. It reminded him too strongly of the Job. Especially on nights like tonight when previously sane men turned desperado.

The phone rang. Kevin stirred, but didn't wake. Pulling a sympathetic face, Brandon reached over and lifted it. 'CID. Brandon speaking.'

There was a momentary, confused silence. Then a strained voice said, 'Sir? Sergeant Merrick here. Sir, we've copped for another body.'

Getting Gareth to Carlton Park was less easy than I'd anticipated. I'd done my reconnaissance carefully, I thought, and I'd counted on being able to drive down the access road used by the gardeners. What I hadn't taken into account was the long Christmas break. The road was blocked off by two metal posts slotted into the asphalt and locked in place with heavy padlocks. I could probably have squeezed through on the verge, since the jeep would have had no problem flattening the small shrubs that lined the road. But I would inevitably have left tyre tracks and probably tiny traces of paint. I had no intention of allowing Gareth to deprive me of my liberty, so that option was closed to me.

I parked the jeep round the back of the storage shed where the park staff kept their equipment. At least there I was out of sight both from the road and the park. There weren't many people around at two o'clock on Boxing Day morning, but success is all about taking pains.

I got out of the jeep and scouted around. The shed was out; it had a burglar alarm. But the gods were smiling on me now. Around the side of the shed, there was a low wooden trolley, the kind that porters used to wheel along station platforms in the days when there were railway porters who didn't think shifting luggage was beneath them. The gardeners probably used it to transport plants round the park. I pushed it back to the jeep and tipped Gareth's naked body on to it. I tucked a couple of black plastic bin liners round the body and sprayed the axles with a quick blast of lubricating oil to cure a nasty squeak, then stealthily I set off towards the shrubbery.

Again, I was lucky. I saw no one. I steered the trolley round to the rear of the bandstand towards the shrubs that covered the steep slope behind. At the edge of the path, I pushed the trolley on to the grass verge and into the edge of the shrubs. Then, wary of leaving footprints on the soft ground, I clambered on to the trolley and rolled Gareth's body off the end and into the bushes. I stepped back and jumped down, pulling the trolley after me. The bushes looked a little battered, but there was no sign of Gareth. With luck, he'd remain undiscovered until the postman delivered my Christmas message to the BEST.

Ten minutes later, the trolley was back in place and I was nosing out of the park's rear entrance on to a quiet lane opposite the churchyard. Even though the chances of being spotted were slim, I waited until the main road was in sight before I turned my lights on. Unlike Temple Fields, this was exactly the sort of area where some nosy insomniac would notice a strange vehicle in the early hours.

I drove home and slept for twelve hours, waking up in time for an interesting couple of hours on my computer before I went in to work. Luckily, it was a busy night, so I had plenty of complex problems to take my mind off the anticipation of the following day's Sentinel Times.

They'd done me proud, in spite of the short time they'd had to deal with my message. They'd obviously got on to the plod right away, and managed to persuade them to take it seriously. They'd given me the front page, complete with a photograph of my message, though without anything that would identify who the card had come from.

KILLER ALERTS BEST!

The naked and mutilated victim of a twisted killer has been discovered in a city park following a bizarre message sent to the Sentinel Times.

The killer, who signed himself 'Santa Claws', revealed in a grisly Christmas message that he had dumped the body in Carlton Park.

The sick communiqué appeared to be written in blood. It was scrawled on the company Christmas card of one of the city's leading firms of solicitors.

It was accompanied by a home video of the body's location, which BEST staff immediately recognized from the distinctive bandstand on Park Hill.

Alerted by BEST reporters, police dispatched a squad of uniformed and plain-clothes officers to the area of the park mentioned in the Christmas card.

After a short search among bushes off the nature trail near the bandstand, as indicated in the video, a uniformed constable discovered the body of a man.

According to police sources, the body was naked. The man's throat had been cut and his body mutilated.

It is believed that he may have been tortured before his death.

Although this area of Carlton Park is known as a pick-up area for predatory homosexuals, police are not presently connecting this killing with the murders earlier this year of two young men whose bodies were dumped in the Temple Fields 'gay village' area of the city.

319

The body has not yet been identified, and police have not released a description of the victim, who is believed to be in his late twenties or early thirties.

The package, which had been posted on Christmas Eve in Bradfield, arrived at the offices of the Sentinel Times *in this morning's post, addressed to the news editor, Matt Smethwick.*

Mr Smethwick said, 'My first thought was that someone was playing a sick joke, especially since I know one of the solicitors in the firm concerned.

'Then I realized my friend was out of the country on a skiing holiday, so it couldn't have been him who posted the package.

'I rang the police right away, and luckily they took it seriously.'

I should think they did. I'd never been more serious in my life. In spite of what the police were saying, the thought that Gareth was the third in a series must have made the short journey across their minds. It had certainly not escaped the attention of the journalists, who used the latest discovery as an excuse to rehash the killings of Adam and Paul. By the time the City Final edition hit the streets, they'd even found a rent-a-quote academic to spout forth.

INSIDE THE MIND OF A KILLER

The man the Home Office have chosen to spearhead the hunt for serial killers spoke today about the latest slaying that has terrified the city's gay community.

Forensic psychologist Tony Hill is one year into a major study funded by the government which will lead to the setting up of a criminal profiling task force similar to the FBI unit featured in The Silence of the Lambs.

Dr Hill, 34, was formerly the chief clinical psychologist at Blamires Hospital, the maximum-security mental unit which houses Britain's most dangerous criminally insane offenders, including mass murderer David Harney and serial killer Keith Pond, the Motorway Madman.

Giving his verdict, Dr Hill said, 'I have not been called in by the police to consult on any of these cases, so I know no more than your readers do about them.

'I'm reluctant to make a snap judgement, but if pushed, I'd say it was certainly possible, and possibly likely that the murders of Adam Scott and Paul Gibbs were committed by the same person.

'On the surface, this latest killing looks similar, but there are certain crucial differences. For a start, the body has turned up in a very different sort of location. Even though Carlton Park is also known as a gay cruising area, it's got a very different ambience from the urbanized Temple Fields.

'Also, the sending of the message to the Sentinel Times is a significant variation. Nothing similar happened in the earlier cases, and the killer makes no reference to previous killings.

'That inclines me to think we may be dealing with at least two separate individuals here.'

And so on and so forth, all of it in much the same vein. All of it saying in neon lights, 'We haven't got the faintest idea where to start looking.' I didn't think that worrying about Dr Tony Hill was going to keep me awake at nights. I decided it was time to teach the powers that be a couple of lessons they wouldn't forget in a hurry.

14

> A man is not bound to put his eyes, his ears, and
> understanding into his breeches pocket when he meets
> with a murder. If he is not in a downright comatose
> state, I suppose he must see that one murder is better
> or worse than another, in point of good taste. Murders
> have their little differences and shades of merit, as
> well as statues, pictures, oratorios, cameos, intaglios
> or what not.

Tony lay sprawled in his bath, a snifter of brandy
close at hand. Languid, relaxed, spent, he couldn't
remember the last time he'd felt this comfortable,
this optimistic. His experiences on the phone with
Angelica, coupled with his conviction that he'd done
a good job on the profile, had given him fresh hope.
Maybe he didn't have to be dysfunctional. Maybe
he could join the rest of the world, the ones who
handled things, who assimilated the past and shaped
their world according to what they wanted to see. 'I
can change my life,' he announced.

The cordless phone rang. In a slow, flowing movement, Tony reached for it. It held no terrors for him

now. Strange how he had grown to welcome rather than fear Angelica's calls. 'Hello,' he said cheerfully.

'Tony, it's John Brandon. I'm sending a car round for you. We've got another one.'

Tony sat up, the water swilling up and down like an experiment in a marine laboratory. 'You're sure?'

'Carol Jordan and Don Merrick were at the scene within five minutes of the shout.'

Tony squeezed his eyes shut. 'Oh God,' he groaned. 'Where is it?'

'The public toilets in Clifton Street. Temple Fields.'

Tony stood up and stepped out of the bath. 'I'll see you there,' he said heavily.

'OK, Tony. The car should be with you in five minutes or thereabouts.'

'I'll be ready.' Tony cut off the connection and walked out of the bathroom, towelling himself dry as he went. His mind racing, he pulled on jeans, T-shirt, shirt, sweater and leather jacket, adding an extra pair of socks as he remembered how bitter the night had been earlier. The doorbell rang just as he was tying the laces of his boots.

In the squad car, the atmosphere of tension wrecked any possibility of constructive thought as they sped through the night streets, blue light strobing against the unearthly orange of the streetlights. His escort, a pair of macho traffic cops, maintained a taciturn pose of absolute control that didn't lend itself to conversation. Tyres squealing, they swept into Clifton Street, the driver slamming on the antilock brakes at the sight of the police tapes that cut off access to the central section of the street.

The tape was lifted for Tony, who headed for the

middle of the street where a cluster of police vehicles and an ambulance were parked at seemingly random angles. As he drew closer, he could see the sign for the public toilets, lit up against the looming dark of the building. By the ambulance, he spotted the conspicuous figure of Don Merrick, unmistakable with his bandaged head. Ignored by the milling officers, Tony pushed his way through to Merrick, who was deep in conversation on a mobile phone. He gave Tony a quick wave to signal he'd spotted him, and wound up his phone conversation with, 'All right, thanks, sorry to have bothered you.'

'Sergeant,' Tony said. 'I'm looking for Mr Brandon. Or Inspector Jordan.'

Merrick nodded. 'They're both inside. You'll be wanting a look too, I suppose.'

'Who found the body?'

'One of the street girls. She claims all the ladies loos were full, and that's why she went into the disabled cubicle. Me, I'd lay money she was with a client. He'll have legged it at the first sight of trouble.'

Out of the corner of his eye, Tony saw Carol emerge from the toilets. She made straight for the pair of them. 'Thanks for turning out,' she said as Merrick moved away and continued making his phone calls.

'If I said I wouldn't have missed it for the world, someone would almost certainly take it the wrong way,' Tony replied wryly. 'What makes you think it's Handy Andy?'

'The victim's naked, and his throat's been cut. He'd obviously been brought there in a wheelchair, but he'd been tipped out on to the floor. And lying on top of him, there was a copy of last night's *Sentinel Times* front page,' Carol replied, her voice strained, her eyes haggard. 'We provoked him, didn't we?'

'We didn't. The newspaper might have, but we didn't,' Tony said bleakly. 'I didn't expect him to react this fast, though.'

Merrick approached again and said cheerfully, 'Looks like I've tracked down the wheelchair. One went walkabout from the maternity hospital reception earlier on tonight. With a bit of luck, somebody might have seen it.'

'Good work, Don,' Carol said. 'Shall we take a look, then?' she asked Tony. He nodded and followed her as she shouldered her way through the milling officers towards the toilet entrance. Tony slowly walked into the lavatories, making a mental inventory as he looked around him, conscious of the black rubber tiled floor with its raised circles, the apparently random pattern of the grey and black tiles on the wall, the defiant graffiti, the raw dank air, the smell of disinfectant barely masking the piss. Inside the entrance, the toilets split in two, men to the left, women to the right. The disabled toilet was to the right, just by the entrance to the women's toilets. Brandon and Kevin Matthews stood by the door, looking in through the wide doorway. Tony walked up and joined their glum and silent communion. A photographer was standing just inside the door, off to one side, recording a scene that would shake some jury to the core, provided Brandon's men could deliver Handy Andy to them. Every few seconds, the stark white light of the flash etched the scene on the retinas of the watching men.

Tony stared intently at the body lying sprawled on the floor. It was, as Carol had said, naked, but it was not clean. There were smears of some sort of dark, oily substance on knees, elbows and one ankle. And there were bloodstains on the body too. The cut to the throat was wide, but not, Tony suspected, deep enough to have caused death. As far as he could see, the sexual organs themselves were undamaged, but the man's rectum and anus and the soft flesh around there had been savagely removed with deep cuts from a sharp blade. A warm surge of relief flowed through him, forcing him to recognize what he'd been refusing to think about. Like Carol, he too had been afraid that somehow his activities had provoked Handy Andy to break his cycle and to strike again. Ever since Brandon's phone call, that horror had been sitting on his shoulder like a malevolent bird of prey.

Tony turned to Brandon and said bluntly, 'It's not him. You've got a copycat.'

From the shadows at the far end of Clifton Street, coat collar turned up, Tom Cross joined the ghouls who seemed to spring from under the pavement itself and watched the familiar ritual dance of a murder-scene investigation. His lips pursed in a tight smile and he moved further back into the shadows. He took his diary out of his inside pocket and ripped out a page for notes. In the dim light from a streetlamp, he wrote, 'Dear Kevin; I bet you a bob to a gold clock that the Queer Killer didn't do this one. All the best, Tom.'

Seaford had been embarrassing as well as painful, but Tom Cross was not a man who allowed humiliation to stand in the way of his purpose. He folded the note in four and wrote, 'Detective Inspector Kevin Matthews. Personal', on it. He pushed his way through the crowd till he caught the eye of one of the constables behind the tape. 'You know who I am, don't you, lad?' Cross demanded.

The constable nodded hesitantly, casting a quick glance to either side, to see who was watching his encounter with the force's current leper.

Cross proffered the note. 'See that Inspector Matthews gets this, there's a good lad.'

'Yes, sir,' the constable said smartly, enclosing the note in his gloved fist, finding a moment to wonder who'd had the bottle to give Popeye Cross a shiner like that.

'I'll remember you when I'm back in harness,' Cross said over his shoulder as he pushed back through the spectators.

Cross cut back through an alley to the Volvo, parked in front of a nightclub's fire exit. The day had been far from satisfactory, and the morning held no promises of improvement. But the conviction that his message to Kevin Matthews was the truth made Tom Cross feel there had been some point to his activities.

'The postmortem will back me up,' Tony said stubbornly. 'Whoever killed this guy, it wasn't our serial killer.'

Bob Stansfield scowled. 'I don't see how you can be so sure, just because of a few oil stains.'

'It's not just that the body wasn't clean.' Tony ticked the points off on his fingers. 'He's the wrong age group. He's barely twenty, if that. Far from being in the closet, he was well known on the gay scene. You'd identified him by three this morning.'

Kevin Matthews nodded. 'Well known to Vice. Chaz

327

Collins. An ex-rent boy who worked in a bar and liked rough sex.'

'Exactly,' Tony said. 'Also, there's not a mark on his penis or his testicles, whereas our killer has been progressively violent with those organs. All the press have been told so far is that the victims have been sexually mutilated. We haven't indicated how or where. This killer has interpreted that as a justification for getting rid of the whole anal area. I suspect he's done that because he buggered the victim before he killed him and he wanted to make sure Forensic didn't pick up any semen.' Tony paused to collect his thoughts, and to pour another cup of coffee from the pot that the canteen had sent up with the breakfast trolley John Brandon had ordered for their morning conference.

'The wheelchair,' Carol said. 'He took a big risk stealing that from the maternity hospital. I don't think that fits with the cautious behaviour the serial killer has always displayed so far.'

'And he's not been tortured,' Kevin added, through a mouthful of sausage-and-egg roll. 'Or not obviously, anyway.' He had a note in his pocket that would determine his view as much as anything that was said inside this room. Popeye might be off the job, but Kevin would back his instinct against anyone's.

But Bob Stansfield wasn't giving up. 'OK, what if he's doing it differently to make us think it's a copycat? What if he's deliberately trying to confuse us? After all, you can't ignore the newspaper lying there. And Dr Hill's profile warned us that the stress of inaccurate newspaper coverage might throw his pattern out.'

Tony carried on meticulously building a bacon-and-egg roll. He squirted an aureole of brown sauce round the yolk, closed the lid, squashed it so the yolk broke, then said, 'There's nothing wrong with that as a theory. It's perfectly feasible that he might kill just to flaunt his skills. It wouldn't be planned so far ahead as the others, so his choice of victim might well be very different. But the underlying pattern would be the same.'

'But it is,' Stansfield insisted. 'This kid had his throat cut, same as the other ones. And this bastard had made a right mess of him. How can you say he wasn't tortured when you look at the state of his arse?'

'If I was a betting man, I'd lay you a hundred to one that Chaz Collins didn't die from having his throat cut. I'd bet he was manually strangled and his throat cut afterwards to make it look like he's one of the serial-killer victims. I think what happened here is that some rough sex got a bit out of hand. Chaz was struggling while he was being sodomized, and his sex partner grabs him round the throat to get him to calm down. In the frenzy of orgasm, he squeezes too tight and he has a corpse on his hands. He figures his only chance of getting away with it is making it look like the serial killer's handiwork, and just in case we don't get the message, he dumps last night's paper on the body.'

'It's certainly plausible,' Brandon said, fastidiously wiping his greasy fingers on a paper tissue from a pack in his pocket.

'I think Tony's right,' Carol said decisively. 'My first reaction was that this was the fifth victim, but the more I think about it, the more I think I was wrong. You know what really clinches it for me?' Four pairs of eyes looked quizzically at her. She felt under as much pressure as she ever had in the witness box. 'Last night wasn't Monday.'

Tony grinned. Stansfield cast his eyes upwards. Kevin nodded reluctantly, and Brandon said, 'You think the night of the week's that important to him?'

Carol nodded. 'There's obviously some very strong reason why he goes for Monday, whether it's practical or superstitious. And whatever it is, it means a lot to him. I don't think he'd break it just to stick two fingers up to us.'

'I agree with Carol,' Kevin chipped in. 'Not just because of the night of the week. The other stuff, too.'

Stansfield looked surprised. 'Well, I'm obviously outvoted here,' he said good-naturedly. 'Separate job it is. Who's going to handle it, then?'

Brandon sighed. 'I'll have a word with Chief Superintendent Sharples at Central, pass the buck on to him. If it's not one of ours, it'll be down to their chief inspector.'

'He's off sick,' Kevin reminded him absently.

'So he is. Well, it'll be passed on to whichever inspector drops unlucky this morning. Now, I know the events of last night deprived us of the chance to give Dr Hill's profile the attention it demands, but I think we should –' Brandon was cut short by a knock at the door. 'Come in,' he said, trying to keep the irritation out of his voice.

The uniformed desk sergeant came in with a couple of envelopes. 'These have just come in, sir. One from Forensic, one from the path lab,' he said, laying them on the desk in front of Brandon. He was gone by the time Brandon had taken a sheaf of papers from each.

The others hid their impatience as Brandon skimmed through the pathologist's preliminary findings. ' "Dear John",' he read out, ' "I know you'll be screaming for something on this one, since on the face of it, it looks like your serial killer has finally left some forensic traces. The bad news is, I don't think this is your man's handiwork. The victim was already dead from asphyxiation before his throat was cut. He was probably strangled manually. Also, I don't think he was cut with the same blade as your four earlier victims. From the look of it, this was a longer and thicker blade, more like a chef's vegetable chopping knife. Whereas, as you know, I reckon the earlier ones were done with something more like a filleting knife. Time of death I'd put between eight and ten p.m. last night. I'll let you have a full report as soon as . . ." blah, blah, blah. Well, looks like you were right, Tony.'

'Just as well I'd agreed to go along with you in time, otherwise I'd have looked a right prat,' Bob Stansfield said, extending a hand to Tony. 'Nice one, Doc.' Carol smiled secretly. Thank God the rest of the team were finally starting to accept Tony had something worth saying. It was amazing how different the atmosphere was now that Cross had gone.

Kevin shifted uncomfortably in his chair and said, 'What have Forensic got to say? Anything about our cases, or is it all preliminary stuff on Chaz Collins?'

Brandon flicked through the other papers. 'Prelims . . . prelims . . . prelims . . .' He drew his breath in sharply. 'Jesus Christ,' he said, baffled disgust in his voice.

'What is it, sir?' Carol asked.

Brandon rubbed a hand over his long face and stared at the paper again, as if checking that he hadn't misread it. 'They've been looking at the burns on Damien Connolly's body. Trying to work out what caused them.'

Tony stopped moving, the last bite of his sandwich halfway to his mouth. 'So what's the verdict?' Bob Stansfield demanded bluntly.

'This is totally bloody mental,' Brandon said. 'The only thing the lads in Forensic can come up with is the attachments for a cake-icing kit.'

'Of course,' Tony breathed dreamily, a distant smile lighting up his eyes. 'All the different star shapes. It's obvious, once it's pointed out.' He was suddenly aware that the other four were staring at him. Carol alone looked concerned. On the other faces, he saw expressions he'd seen before. Wariness, repugnance, disgust, incomprehension.

'Twenty-four-carat head banger,' Stansfield said bitterly. No one was quite certain whether he meant the killer or Tony.

The day Penny Burgess took over the *Bradfield Evening Sentinel Times*'s crime beat, she resolved that she was going to have better contacts than any of her male predecessors had managed. She realized that the male rituals of the masonic lodge and the smoker were going to remain closed worlds to her, but she determined that nothing was going to happen of any significance even there without her knowledge.

It wasn't surprising, then, that her home phone had rung twice between six and seven that morning. Both calls were from police officers, telling her that the man who'd been questioned earlier in connection with the Queer Killings had been arrested trying to skip the country. No names, no pack drill, but the anonymous suspect would be up before the magistrates that morning to be remanded in custody on a charge of attempting to pervert the course of justice. Following on from the discovery of a fifth body that had kept Penny out of her bed till gone two that morning, the connection was obvious.

Penny smiled dreamily to herself over her second cup of strong Earl Grey. It would be another front page for her tonight. Provided the editor and the lawyer didn't lose their bottle. She dumped her cup and cereal bowl in the sink and picked up her coat. Either way, it was going to be an interesting day.

Carol had drawn the short straw when it came to going to court to make sure everything went according to plan before the magistrates. Stansfield and Kevin had a backlog of routine enquiries to pursue, and Tony had gone to Leeds to keep a long-standing appointment with a Canadian academic psychologist who was attending a conference in the city. They needed, said Tony, to discuss some esoteric aspect of his task-force study. 'Conceptual mapping,' he'd told her as they'd snatched a few moments together after the group briefing.

He might as well have said 'quantum mechanics,' she thought ironically as she ran up the steps of the court building, her collar turned up against an east wind that promised sleet before dinner. She was going to have to learn a lot if she was going to get anyone to consider her seriously for this task force, that much was clear.

Any thoughts of the task force vanished as soon as she cleared the security check and turned into the long corridor that housed half of the dozen magistrates' courts. Instead of the usual disgruntled and defiant knots of low-level law breakers and their depressed families, she came face to face with a milling mob of journalists. She'd never seen that kind of media turnout at a Saturday-morning court, normally the quietest of the week. At the heart of the crowd, she could see Don Merrick, his back to the courtroom door, looked harassed.

Carol immediately wheeled round on her heel. But she was too late. She'd not only been spotted but also recognized by one of the handful of journalists who weren't visiting firefighters sent up by the national media networks at the sniff of a good tale. As she rounded the corner, they shot after her. All except Penny Burgess, who leaned against the wall and gave Don Merrick a tired smile.

'You weren't the only one that got the early-morning phone call, then,' he said cynically.

'Unfortunately not, Sergeant. At least the lads seem more interested in your guv'nor than they do in you.'

'She's better looking,' Merrick said.

'Oh, I wouldn't say that.'

'So I've heard,' Merrick said drily.

Penny's eyebrows climbed. 'You must let me buy you a drink sometime, Don. Then you can find out for yourself if the gossip's true.'

Merrick shook his head. 'I don't think so, pet. The wife wouldn't like it.'

Penny grinned. 'Not to mention the guv'nor. Well, Don, now the pack's gone off in full cry after Inspector Jordan, are you going to let me exercise my democratic right to report the proceedings of the magistrates?'

Don Merrick stood clear of the door and waved her in. 'Be my guest,' he said. 'Just remember, Ms Burgess, the facts, and nothing but the facts. We don't want innocent people put at risk, do we?'

'You mean, like the Queer Killer's been doing?' Penny asked sweetly as she slipped past him and into the court.

Brandon stared in disbelief at Tom Cross. His face was knitted in an expression of deep complacency, his multicoloured eye socket the only disruption to a picture of smug self-satisfaction. 'Just between ourselves, John,' he was saying, 'you have to admit I was bang on the button about McConnell. That stiff last night – it wasn't down to the Queer Killer at all, was it? Well, it couldn't have been, could it, on account of you had me laddo banged up downstairs.' Ignoring the absence of ashtrays in the ACC's office, Cross lit a cigarette and puffed a happy cloud of smoke into the air.

Brandon struggled, but he couldn't find the words. For once, he was speechless.

Cross looked around vaguely for somewhere to flick his ash, and settled for the floor, rubbing it into the carpet with the toe of his shoe. 'So when do you want me to start back on the job?' he asked.

Brandon leaned back in his chair and stared at the ceiling. 'If it was up to me, you'd never work in this town again,' he said pleasantly.

Cross choked on a mouthful of smoke. Brandon looked back down and savoured the moment. 'By heck, you like your joke, John,' Cross spluttered.

'I've never been more serious in my life,' Brandon said coldly. 'I called you here this morning to warn you off. What you did to Steven McConnell yesterday afternoon was assault. The file stays open, Superintendent. If you come anywhere near this investigation again, I'll have no hesitation in charging you. In fact, I'll enjoy it. I will not have this force brought into disrepute by any officer, serving or under suspension.' As Brandon's words sank in, Cross paled, then turned puce with anger and humiliation. Brandon stood up. 'Now get out of my office and my station.'

Cross got to his feet like a man concussed. 'You'll regret this, Brandon,' he stuttered furiously.

'Don't make me, Tom. For your own sake, don't make me.'

Thinking on her feet, Carol led the journalists round to the small lounge outside the lawyers' cafeteria. 'OK, OK,' she said, trying to damp down their baying with exaggerated hand movements. 'Look, if you'll just give me two minutes, I'll come right back and answer your questions, OK?'

They looked uncertain, one or two at the back showing a tendency to drift back towards the courts. 'Look, people,' she said, gently massaging her jaw, 'I'm in agony. I've got raging toothache, and if I don't ring my dentist before ten, I've got no chance of him fitting me in today. Please? Give me a break? Then I'm all yours, promise!' Carol forced a pained smile and slipped through to the cafeteria. There was a phone on the far wall, which she picked up. She made great play of taking out her diary and looking up a page, while dialling the familiar number of the court. 'Court one, please.' She waited for the connection, then said to the clerk, 'This is Inspector Jordan here. Can I speak to the CPS solicitor?'

Moments later, she was talking to the Crown Prosecution Service lawyer. 'Eddie? Carol Jordan. I've got about thirty hacks here waiting for Steven McConnell to come up. They're dying to jump to all the wrong conclusions, and I think you might prefer to get him on now while I've got them tied up at an impromptu press conference. Can you swing it with the clerk?' She waited while the solicitor muttered with the court clerk.

'Can do, Carol,' he said. 'Thanks.'

Keeping up the pretence, Carol put the phone down and scribbled something in her diary. Then she took a deep breath and headed back towards the pack.

Damien Connolly, the ultimate PC Plod. I couldn't have found a better person to teach the police a lesson if I'd searched for a year. But he was already there, on my list, one of my own personal Top Ten. He was harder to stalk than the others, because his shift pattern was often in conflict with the hours I work. But, as my grandmother always used to say, nothing worth having comes easy.

I trapped him in the usual way. 'I'm sorry to trouble you, but my car's broken down and I don't know where the nearest call box is. Can I use your phone to ring the AA?' It's almost laughably easy to get across the threshold of their homes. Three men dead, and still they fail to take the most elementary precautions. I almost felt sorry for Damien, since of all of them, he is the only one who had not betrayed me. But I needed to make an example of him, to show the police how pathetically useless they are. It was galling to find myself in agreement with the so-called 'gay community', but they were one hundred per cent correct when they said that while supposedly gay men were being killed, the police would do nothing. Killing one of their own would be the one thing that would make them sit up and notice. At last, they'd be forced to give me the recognition and respect I deserve.

To mark this, I had devised something a bit special for Damien. An unusual method of punishment, used occasion-ally to act as a terrible example pour discourager les autres. *It seems to have been most commonly used in cases of high treason, where men had plotted to kill the king. Appropriate, I thought. For what was Damien if not an integral part of the group that would bring me down if only they could?*

The earliest record of this treatment in England was in 1238, when some minor nobleman broke into the royal lodge at Woodstock intent on killing Henry III, there on a hunting trip. To demonstrate to any other potential traitors that the king was serious about attempts on his life, the man was sentenced to be torn limb from limb by horses then beheaded.

Another would-be royal assassin met the same fate in the mid eighteenth century. The aspiring assassin's name just had to be an omen. François Damiens stabbed King Louis XV at Versailles. His sentence read that 'his chest, arms, thighs and calves be burned with pincers; his right hand, holding the knife with which he committed the said attack, burned in sulphur; that boiling oil, melted lead, and rosin and wax mixed with sulphur be poured into his wounds; and after that his body be pulled and dismembered by four horses.'

According to reports of the execution, Damiens's dark-brown hair turned white during the torture. Casanova, that other great lover, reported in his memoirs, 'I watched the dreadful scene for four hours, but was several times obliged to turn my face away and to close my ears as I heard his piercing shrieks, half the body having been torn away from him.'

Obviously, I couldn't get a team of horses down into the cellar, so I'd had to come up with my own arrangement. I'd built a system of ropes and pulleys, attached to floor and ceiling and linked with one of those powered winches that are used on yachts. Each rope ended in a steel shackle that would fasten round wrist or ankle. By adjusting the lengths and tensions on the ropes, I had suspended Damien in midair, his limbs spread in a massive, human X, his pathetic genitals dangling in the middle like something in a butcher's shop.

The chloroform had a worse effect on him than it did on any of the others. As soon as he came round, he vomited violently, not an easy thing to achieve when you're hanging upright four feet above the floor. It was just as well I'd removed his gag, or he'd have choked on his own vomit, which would have cheated me out of my satisfaction in his punishment.

He was completely bewildered. He had no idea why he was there. 'Because I chose you,' I told him. 'You were just unlucky enough to choose the wrong job. Now I'm going to question you the way you question your suspects.'

While I'd been poking around in Auntie Doris's kitchen, vaguely looking to see if she had anything I might find useful, I'd come across her icing set. I remembered that icing set. Every year, her Christmas cakes were a miracle of artistry that any of Bradfield's bakers would have been hard pressed to equal. Once, she'd been called away by Uncle Henry while she was doing the big cake, and I'd picked up the icing bag, determined to help. I can't have been more than six.

When she came back from whatever disgusting farmyard task she'd been helping with and saw my efforts, she went berserk. She grabbed the weighted leather strop that Uncle Henry used to keep his cut-throat razors sharp and beat me so hard she tore my shirt. Then she locked me in my room without any supper, leaving me there for the best part of twenty-four hours with nothing but a bucket to piss in. I knew I had to find an appropriate use for her treasured icing set.

There was a blowlamp in the cellar which I used to heat up the icing attachments so I could leave my mark on Damien, just as the executioner had on his namesake Damiens two hundred and forty years before. There was something quite beautiful about the way his skin blossomed into scarlet starbursts as the red-hot piping rosettes came into contact with his pale flesh. It was also astonishingly effective. He told me everything I wanted to know and lots of rubbish I didn't give a damn about. I was just sorry he wasn't directly involved in the investigation into my previous work. I could have confirmed at first hand how hopelessly at sea the police are.

I decided to deposit the remains in Temple Fields again. I'd used the time since Gareth to find additional safe sites for the disposition of my handiwork. The back yard of the Queen of Hearts was perfect for my purpose; secluded and isolated at night. But it would come alive the next day, ensuring Damien wouldn't be left out in the cold for too long.

The time was ripe for a new game. In preparation for this, shortly after Adam, I went up into the loft and opened the trunk that contains those parts of my past I have retained. One of the things I'd kept as a souvenir was a leather jacket that was given to me by the engineer on a Soviet factory ship, in lieu of payment for a night he won't forget in a hurry. It looks and feels different from anything I've ever seen in this country. I ripped strips of leather from the sleeve until I was satisfied that I'd got something that could have been snagged on a nail or the sharp corner of a lock. I tucked the scrap in

341

a drawer, then I chopped the rest of the jacket into shreds, stuck it in a plastic bag with eggshells and vegetable peelings, and drove into town until I found a skip to dump it in. By the time I needed to use the red herring, the remains of the jacket would be long buried in some anonymous landfill.

I couldn't help feeling a thrill at the thought of how many man-hours the police would waste trying to track down where this strange little piece of leather had come from, but they'd never tie it in to me. Apart from anything else, no one in Bradfield has ever seen me wear it.

This time, the publicity outshone everything I'd achieved so far. At last, the police admitted that one mind was behind all four killings. Finally, they had realized it was time to take me seriously.

With Damien off the planet and in my computer, I still had one more person to deal with before I could return to my original project. I couldn't settle to the task of finding a man worthy of me, a man to share my life as an equal and respectful partner, not until I had punished the man who had publicly treated me with such contempt.

Dr Tony Hill, the fool who hadn't even realized that Gareth Finnegan was one of my bodies, was the target. He had insulted me. He had poured scorn on me, refusing to acknowledge the extent of my achievements. He had no idea of the calibre of the mind he was up against. He was going to have to pay for his arrogance.

I couldn't help but see his disposal as a challenge. Wouldn't anyone?

15

Can they not keep to the old honest way of cutting throats, without introducing such abominable innovations . . . ?

The sound of a roaring crowd greeted Carol as she closed the door of the flat behind her. Michael, sprawled on one of the sofas, didn't even take his eyes off the rugby match on the television. 'Hi, sis,' he said. 'Needle match. Ten minutes, and I'm all yours.'

Carol glanced at the screen where muddy giants in England and Scotland's colours were sprawled across the turf in a collapsed scrum. 'Very hi-tech,' she muttered. 'I need a shower.'

Fifteen minutes later, brother and sister were sharing a celebratory bottle of cava. 'I have some print-out for you,' Michael said.

Carol perked up. 'Anything significant?'

Michael shrugged. 'I don't know what's significant to you. Your killer used five different-shaped objects to make the marks. I separated them out into five separate patterns. You've got what looks like a heart and some rudimentary letters. A, D, G and P. Mean anything to you?'

Carol shivered involuntarily. 'Oh, yes. Plenty. You got the print-out here?'

Michael nodded. 'It's in my briefcase.'

'I'll look at it in a bit. Meanwhile, can I pick your brains again?'

Michael drained his glass and refilled it. 'I don't know. Can you afford me?'

'Dinner, bed and breakfast at the country-house hotel of your choice, first weekend I have off,' Carol offered.

Michael pulled a face. 'At this rate, I could be collecting my pension before I collect on that one. How about you do my ironing for a month?'

'A fortnight.'

'Three weeks.'

'Consider it a done deal.' She offered her hand and Michael shook it.

'So, what do you want to know, sis?'

Carol outlined her theory about the computer manipulation of the killer's videos. 'What do you think?' she asked anxiously.

'It's a can-do,' he said. 'No question about that. The technology's available, and it's not difficult software to use. I could do it standing on my head. But you're talking serious money. Say three hundred for a video capture card, four hundred for a ReelMagic card, another three to five for a decent video digitizer, plus at least a grand for a state-of-the-art scanner. The real killer is the software, though. There's only one package that will do what you're talking about to any real quality. Vicom 3D Commander. We've got it, and it set us back nearly four grand, and that was six months ago. The last upgrade cost us another eight hundred. Manual thick as a house brick.'

'So it's not a piece of software that many people would have?'

Michael snorted. 'Damn right it isn't. It's a serious bit of kit, that. Professionals like us, video production studios and very serious hobbyists only.'

'How readily available is it? Could you buy it over the counter?' Carol asked.

'Not really. We dealt directly with Vicom, because we wanted them to run us a full demo before we committed ourselves to laying out that much dosh. Obviously, some specialist business suppliers sell it, but they wouldn't be shifting it in bulk. That would be mail order, anyway. Most computer stuff is.'

'The other stuff you mentioned – are they things that lots of people would have?' Carol asked.

'They're not uncommon. Off the top of my head, say two or three per cent market penetration on the video stuff, maybe fifteen per cent on the scanner. But if you're thinking of tracking down your man, I'd start with the Vicom end,' Michael advised.

'How do you think they'd be about letting us look at their sales records?'

Michael pulled a face. 'Your guess is as good as mine. You're not a competitor, and this is a murder investigation. You never know, they might be happy to cooperate. After all, if this guy is using their stuff, it'd be bad PR if they didn't. I can dig out the name of the guy we dealt with. He was their sales director. Scottish bloke. One of those names you can't tell which is the Christian name. You know, Grant Cameron, Campbell Elliott . . . It'll come to me . . .'

While Michael searched through his contacts book,

Carol refilled her glass and savoured the prickle of bubbles against her palate. Lately, pleasure seemed to have been in short supply. But if she could come up with some leads on her theory, all of that might change.

'Got it!' Michael exclaimed. 'Fraser Duncan. Give him a ring Monday morning and mention my name. Time you got a break, sis.'

'You're not wrong,' Carol said with feeling. 'Believe me, I deserve it.'

Kevin Matthews lay sprawled across the rumpled kingsized bed, smiling up at the woman straddling him. 'Mmm,' he murmured. 'That was a bit nice.'

'Better than home cooking,' Penny Burgess said, running her fingers through the dark auburn hair that curled across Kevin's chest.

Kevin chuckled. 'Just a bit.' He reached for the remains of the hefty vodka and coke Penny had poured for him earlier.

'I'm surprised you could get away tonight,' Penny said, moving forward languidly so her nipples brushed his.

'We've had so much overtime lately she's given up expecting me home for anything except for a bit of kip.'

Penny let her upper body fall heavily on Kevin, thrusting the breath out of his body. 'I didn't mean Lynn,' she said, 'I meant work.'

Kevin grabbed her wrists and wrestled her off him. When they subsided, lying side by side, giggling breathlessly, he finally said, 'There wasn't much to do, tell you the truth.'

Penny snorted incredulously. 'Oh yeah? Last night Carol Jordan finds body number five, the suspect is arrested trying to leave the country and you tell me there's nothing much doing? Come on, Kevin, this is me you're talking to.'

'You've got it all wrong, darling,' Kevin said magnanimously. 'You and all the rest of your media cronies.' It wasn't often he got the chance to put Penny right and he intended to make the most of it.

'What do you mean?' Penny propped herself up on one elbow, unconsciously covering her body with the duvet. This wasn't a bit of fun any more; this was work.

'Number one. The body Carol found last night wasn't one of the serial killer's victims. It was a copycat job. The postmortem proved that beyond reasonable doubt. It was just another seedy little sex murder. Central should clear it up in a few days with a bit of help from Vice,' Kevin said, the self-satisfaction obvious in his voice.

Penny bit on the bullet and said sweetly through clenched teeth, 'And?'

'And what, darling?'

'If that was number one, there must be a number two.'

Kevin smiled, so smug that Penny made the instant decision that he was on the out just as soon as she had an acceptable alternative lined up. 'Oh yes, number two. Stevie McConnell isn't the killer.'

For once, Penny ran out of words. The information was shocking in itself. But more shocking was the fact that, knowing this, Kevin had said nothing. He had remained silent and let her paper run a story that was eventually going to make her look an ill-informed pillock. 'Really?' she said, in the superior accent she hadn't used since the day she'd gratefully quit boarding school and made the decision to go vocally downmarket.

'That's right. We knew that before he legged it.' Kevin lay back on the pillows, blissfully unaware of the look of distilled hatred that Penny was beaming in his direction.

'So what exactly was that pantomime at court this morning in aid of?' she demanded in tones her elocution mistress would have been proud of.

Kevin smirked. 'Well, most of us had already decided that McConnell wasn't our man. But Brandon had put a tail on him, so when he tried to skip the country, we were more or less obliged to pull him in. By that time, it was starting to look definite that McConnell isn't the Queer Killer. Plus, he doesn't fit the profile that Tony Hill came up with.'

'I don't believe I'm hearing this,' Penny said sharply.

Kevin finally registered that all was not well. 'What? You got a problem, darling?'

'Just a fucking bit,' said Penny, enunciating each syllable crisply. 'You mean to tell me you've not only put an innocent man on remand, you've also let the world's press broadcast the assumption that this man is quite probably the Queer Killer?'

Kevin propped himself up and took another swig of his drink, reaching out to rumple Penny's hair with his other hand. She pulled away with a jerk. 'It's no big deal,' he said patronizingly. 'Nobody can get a lynch mob together and go round his house while he's inside. And we reckon that telling the world between the lines that we've got the killer banged up might just provoke the real killer into getting in touch with us to make sure we know he's still out there.'

'You mean you want to drive him to kill again?' Penny demanded, her voice rising.

'Of course not,' Kevin said indignantly. 'I mean, to get in touch. Like he did after he'd killed Gareth Finnegan.'

'My God,' Penny said wonderingly. 'Kevin, how can you sit there and tell me that nothing bad can happen to Stevie McConnell while he's locked up in prison?'

While Penny Burgess and Kevin Matthews were arguing the morality of Stevie McConnell's remand, in C Wing of Her Majesty's Prison Barleigh, three men were taking turns to show Stevie McConnell what happens to sex cases in prison. At the end of the landing, a warden stood impassively, appearing as oblivious to McConnell's screams and entreaties as a deaf man with his hearing aid switched off. And on the moors above Bradfield, a ruthless killer put the finishing touches to the torture instrument that would help show the world that the man in prison was not the person responsible for four perfectly executed serial punishments.

The HOLMES room was a quiet hum of activity, operators staring into screens and tapping keys. Carol found Dave Woolcott sitting in his office picking listlessly at fish and chips. He looked up when she entered and managed a wan smile. 'Thought you were having a night off,' he said.

'I'm still hoping to. My brother promised to buy me

a bucket of popcorn all to myself if I make it to the multiscreen before the film begins. I just wanted to swing by and run something past you.' She dumped two plastic bags on Dave's desk. Glossy computer magazines spilled out.

'I've got this theory,' she said. 'Well, more of a hunch.' For the third time, Carol outlined her idea about the killer importing videos and transforming them into supports for his fantasies.

Dave listened carefully, nodding as Carol's ideas sank in. 'I like it,' he said simply. 'I've read that profile a couple of times now, and I really can't accept what Dr Hill says about keeping stable just by using videos of the killings. It doesn't make sense. Your idea does. So what do you want from me?'

'Michael reckons that tracing the buyers of Vicom 3D Commander might lead us to him if we're right. I'm not so sure. It's possible that the company the killer works for has the software, and he does the manipulation work there. To be on the safe side, though, he'd need to do all the scanning and digitizing at home. So I thought it would also be worthwhile doing a trawl of the suppliers of video digitizers and video capture cards. We can find suppliers via the ads in these magazines, since virtually all computer stuff comes mail order. We should also contact local computer clubs too. If you've got any bodies to spare, that is.'

Dave sighed. 'Dream on, Carol.' He picked up a magazine and flicked through the pages. 'I suppose I could draw up a list tonight and tomorrow, and first thing Monday morning we could get a couple of DCs to do a ring-round. When my operators will have time

350

to input the data, I don't know, but I will see that it gets done. OK?'

Carol grinned. 'You're a star, Dave.'

'I'm a bloody martyr, Carol. My youngest's cut two teeth that I haven't even seen yet.'

'I could stay and help you go through the magazines,' Carol said reluctantly.

'Oh, bugger off. Go and enjoy yourself. It's about time one of us did. What are you going to see?'

Carol pulled a face. 'It's a Saturday Special double bill – *Manhunter* and *The Silence of the Lambs*.'

Dave's laughter echoed in her ears all the way to the car.

The long howl seemed to come from the pit of his stomach. As his orgasm shuddered through him like a runaway train, Tony felt a glorious sense of release. 'Oh, God,' he groaned.

'Oh, yeah, yeah,' Angelica gasped. 'I'm coming again, again, oh, Tony, Tony . . .' Her voice faded in a gulping sob.

Tony lay back on his bed, chest heaving, the smell of sweat and sex heavy around him. He felt as if he'd been suddenly detached from a burden he had been carrying for so long he had ceased to notice its weight. Was this what being cured felt like, this sense of light and colour, this sensation of having dumped the past like sacks of coal in a bunker? Was this how his patients felt when they'd unloaded their mess on him?

In his ear, he could hear the ragged sound of her breathing. After a few moments, she said, 'Wow. Just wow. That was the best ever. I just love the way you love me.'

'It was good for me, too,' Tony said, meaning it for once. For the first time since they had started this strange combination of therapy and sexual game-playing, he'd had no trouble with his erection. Right from the start, he'd been hard as a rock. No fading, no wilting, no shame. Just the first problem-free sex he'd had for years. OK, so Angelica wasn't actually in the room with him, but it was a giant step in the right direction.

'We make the sweetest music,' Angelica said. 'Nobody's ever turned me on like you do.'

'Do you do this often?' Tony asked languidly.

Angelica chuckled, a husky, sexy gurgle of laughter. 'You're not the first.'

'I could tell that. You're far too much of an expert,' Tony flattered, not entirely insincerely. She'd been the perfect therapist for him, that much was certainly true.

'I'm very choosy about the men I allow to share with me,' Angelica said. 'It's not everyone who appreciates what I have to offer,' she added.

'They'd have to be very strange not to enjoy it. I know I do.'

'I'm glad, Anthony. You'll never know how glad. I have to go now,' she said, her tone changing abruptly to the businesslike one Tony had come to associate with the end of their calls. 'Tonight has been really special. We'll talk soon.'

The line went dead. Tony switched off the phone and stretched out. Tonight, with Angelica, for the first time in his life, Tony had felt a protective care that succoured without smothering. His grandmother, he knew intellectually, had loved him and cared for him, but theirs had never been a demonstrative family, and her love had been brusque and practical, meeting her needs rather than his. The women he'd been involved with in the past had, he now realized, been her emotional doppelgangers. Thanks to Angelica, he dared hope the pattern had been broken. It had caused him enough pain over the years.

His sexual life had started later than most of his contemporaries, in part because his body had been reluctant to mature. Until his seventeenth year, he'd been by far the smallest boy in his class, condemned to dating the thirteen-and fourteen-year-olds who were even more scared of sex than he was. Then, suddenly, he'd shot up five inches in as many months. By the time he'd gone to university, he'd lost his virginity in a clumsy fumble on a single bed, the candlewick bedspread leaving him with uncomfortable friction burns for days afterwards. His girlfriend, relieved to be rid at last of the encumbrance of her virginity, had dumped him days later.

At university, he'd been too shy and hard-working to improve his experience by much. Then, when he'd started work on his doctorate, he'd fallen head over heels with a young philosophy tutor in his college. Because he was bright and interesting, he captured her interest. Patricia made no secret of the fact that she was a woman of the world, just as she made no secret of the fact that she had ended their relationship because of his lacklustre performance between the sheets. 'Face it, sweetheart,' she'd told him, 'your brain might be DPhil material, but your fucking wouldn't earn you an O level.'

It had been downhill from then. The last couple of

women Tony had been involved with had thought he was a perfect gentleman, never pressurizing them into bed. Until they got him there and discovered how seldom he could actually deliver. He had long ago discovered how hard it was to convince a woman that the fact that he couldn't get it up had nothing whatsoever to do with her. 'They just got fed up with having their egos bashed,' he said aloud.

Maybe now he had finally found a way to confront the past and move forward. A few more nights like tonight with Angelica and maybe, just maybe, he'd be ready to try the real thing. He wondered if her services extended to that. Perhaps he should start thinking about dropping a few hints.

Brandon read the sheet of paper on his desk and rubbed the grit of sleep from his eyes. He and Dave Woolcott had spent the evening going through the dozens of reports that had flowed in from the actions Dave had ordered in response to the correlations thrown out by the HOLMES computer. In spite of their determined efforts to find some slender thread of evidence to unravel back to the killer, there was nothing that either of them could identify as a lead.

'Maybe this idea of Carol's will do the business for us,' Dave yawned.

'We've tried everything else,' Brandon said, his voice as depressed as his face. 'It can't hurt to run with it.'

'She's a smart operator, that one,' Dave remarked. 'She'll be running the shop one of these days.' There was no bitterness in his tone, only a tired admiration. Another yawn split his face.

'Go home, Dave. When was the last time you saw Marion awake?'

Dave groaned. 'Don't you start, sir. I was going to knock off anyway, there's not a lot doing. I'll be in tomorrow, finish off listing these computer suppliers.'

'OK, but not too early, you hear? Give your family a treat. Eat breakfast with them.' Before he took his own advice, Brandon wanted to go through the witness statements and officers' impressions once more, unable to believe that there wasn't something lurking in there that would give them their first serious break. By the time he was halfway through he was finding it almost impossible to motivate himself to get through the rest of the pile. The prospect of tucking himself round Maggie's warm body was overwhelmingly appealing.

Brandon sighed and focused on the next sheet of paper. His scrutiny was interrupted by the insistent trill of his telephone. 'Brandon,' he sighed.

'Sergeant Murray here, front desk. Sorry to interrupt you, sir, but none of the inspectors are in the station at the moment. Thing is, there's a gentleman down here I think you'll want to talk to. He's a neighbour of Damien Connolly's, sir.'

Brandon was already out of his chair. 'I'm on my way,' he said.

The man at the front desk was sitting on the wooden bench that ran along the wall, head down, the rough blur of stubble dark along his jaw. As Brandon came round from behind the counter, he looked up. Late twenties, Brandon estimated. Sun-bed tan, bruised circles under his eyes. Some sort of businessman, judging by the expensive but sombre suit and the silk tie hanging askew under the open top button of the shirt. He had the rumpled, red-eyed look of someone who's been travelling so long they've forgotten which day or which city it is. Seeing someone more tired than himself seemed to inject Brandon with fresh energy. 'Mr Harding?' he said cheerfully. 'I'm John Brandon, the Assistant Chief Constable in charge of the investigation into Damien Connolly's death.'

The man nodded. 'Terry Harding. I live a couple of doors down from Damien.'

'My sergeant tells me you might have some information for us.'

'That's right,' Terry Harding said, his voice thick with exhaustion. 'I saw a stranger driving out of Damien's garage the night he was killed.'

I had already started work on Dr Tony Hill even before I had dispatched Damien Connolly. It seemed poetic justice to me that, like Damien, his name was already on my list as a potential partner. If I had needed any kind of reinforcement that I was doing the right thing by punishing him, that was it.

So, I already knew where he lived, where he worked and what he looked like. I knew what time he left the house in the morning, what tram he caught to work, and how long he stayed in his little office in the university.

I only realized how smoothly everything had gone up till now when things started to move in directions I hadn't predicted and didn't like. I suppose I'd made the mistake of underestimating the stupidity of the forces opposed to me. I'd never thought there was much brain power shared out among the officers of Bradfield police, but the latest developments shook even me. They arrested the wrong man!

Their incredible lack of intelligence and perception was matched only by the media, following uncritically like sheep. I couldn't believe it when I picked up the Sentinel Times *to read that a man was in custody helping police enquiries into* my *killings*. The arrest came after a street assault involving a police officer. How on earth could they imagine that someone who had taken as much care as I had would end up in some street brawl in Temple Fields? It was an insult to my intelligence. Did they really think I was some out-of-control street yob?

I read and reread the article, unable to credit the depths of their foolishness. Anger burned inside me. I could feel it in my guts like indigestion and wind cramps rolled into a spiky ball. I wanted to do something vicious and dramatic, something that would prove to them how wrong they were.

I worked out with my weights till my muscles were trembling from effort and my kit was saturated with sweat, but still the anger refused to abate. I stormed upstairs to my computer and worked on the videos of Damien that I'd imported into my system. By the time I'd finished, we'd performed sexual gymnastics that the Russian national team would have been proud of. But nothing satisfied me. Nothing took the anger away.

Luckily, unlike them I'm not stupid. I know how dangerous uncontrolled anger could be for me. I needed to harness my anger, to be creative with it and make it work for me. I forced myself to channel my rage into constructive pathways. I planned in meticulous detail how I would capture Dr Tony Hill, and what I would do with him when I got him. I'd be keeping him in suspense – literally.

Squassation and strappado. The Spanish Inquisition knew exactly how to make the most of what was available. They simply harnessed the most powerful force on the planet, the force of gravity. All you need is a winch, a pulley, a few ropes and a lump of stone. You fasten the victim's hands behind his back and run a rope from them through the pulley. Then you tie the stone to his feet.

In his book The Horrid Cruelties of the Inquisition, *published in 1770, John Marchant described this efficient torture most eloquently:*

He is then drawn up on high, till his head reaches the pulley. He is kept hanging in this manner for some time, that by the greatness of the weight hanging at his feet, all his joints and limbs may be dreadfully stretched, and on a sudden he is let down with a jerk, by the slacking of the rope, but is kept from coming quite to the ground, by which terrible shake, his arms and legs are disjointed, whereby he is put to the most exquisite pain; the shock which he receives by the sudden stop of his fall, and the weight at his feet stretching his whole body more intensely and cruelly.

The Germans added a refinement that attracted me. Behind the victim, they placed a spiked roller, so that as he descended, the rollers cut into and excoriated his back, leaving his body a bloody, dislocated mass. I considered reproducing this effect, but even after a lot of juggling with the layout, I couldn't come up with a design on the computer that I was satisfied would work smoothly, unless I cuffed his hands in front of him, which makes the squassation and strappado far less effective. Keep it simple, that's my motto.

While I was planning and constructing, I took steps to draw my web even tighter around Dr Hill. He might think he could climb inside my head, but he'd got things the wrong way round.

I couldn't wait to get started. I was counting the hours.

16

'Now, Miss R., supposing that I should appear at about midnight at your bedside, armed with a carving knife, what would you say?' To which the confiding girl had replied, 'Oh, Mr Williams, if it was anybody else, I should be frightened. But as soon as I heard your voice, I should be tranquil.' Poor girl; had this outline sketch of Mr Williams been filled in and realized, she would have seen something in the corpse-like face, and heard something in the sinister voice, that would have unsettled her tranquillity forever.

When the phone rang, Carol's first reaction was outrage. Ten past eight on a Sunday morning could only mean work. She stirred, a long, low growl of discontent making Nelson's ears prick. Carol's arm appeared from under the covers, groping around on the bedside table. She connected with the phone and grunted, 'Jordan,' into it.

'This is your early-morning alarm call.' The voice was far too cheerful, Carol decided, before the identity of her caller registered.

'Kevin,' she said. 'This better be good.'

'It's better than good. What would you say to a witness who saw the killer drive away from Damien Connolly's house?'

'Say again?' she mumbled. Kevin repeated his announcement. The second time round, his voice catapulted Carol into a sitting position, on the edge of the bed. 'When?' she demanded.

'The guy walked in late last night. He's been out of the country on business. Brandon interviewed him. He's called a meeting for nine,' Kevin said, excited as a Christmas child.

'Kevin, you bastard, you might have called me before now . . .'

He chuckled. 'I thought you needed your beauty sleep.'

'Bollocks to beauty sleep . . .'

'No, I've only been in five minutes myself. Can you bring the doc in with you? I just tried calling him, but there was no reply.'

'OK, I'll swing round by his place and see if I can raise him. He seems to have a habit of switching the phones off. Fancy thinking he could get away with a decent night's sleep. You can tell he's not a copper,' she added. Carol replaced the phone abruptly and headed for the shower. The thought that Tony might have switched off his phone because he was with the woman on the answering machine crossed her mind. The idea made her stomach hurt. 'Silly bitch,' she muttered to herself as the water cascaded over her.

By twenty to nine, she was leaning on Tony's doorbell. After a couple of minutes, the door opened. Bleary eyed, struggling with the belt of his dressing gown, Tony peered out at her. 'Carol?'

'Sorry to wake you,' she said formally. 'You weren't answering your phone. Mr Brandon asked me to pick you up. There's a meeting at nine. We've got a witness.'

Tony rubbed his eyes, looking bemused. 'You better come in.' He walked down the hall, leaving Carol to close the door behind her. 'Sorry about the phones. I was late getting to sleep, so I switched them off.' He shook his head. 'Can you hang on while I have a shower and a shave? Otherwise, I'll make my own way in. I don't want you to be late on my account.'

'I'll wait,' Carol said. She picked the paper off the mat and flicked through it, leaning against the wall, alert for the telltale signs of a third person's presence. She felt unreasonably pleased when she heard none. Even though she knew her reaction was childish, it didn't mean these responses were going to stop overnight. She was just going to have to learn to disguise them until they died away, as she felt sure they would eventually, starved out of existence by Tony's lack of interest.

Ten minutes later, Tony reappeared in jeans and rugby shirt, hair damp and neatly brushed. 'Sorry about that,' he said. 'My brain doesn't work until I've had a shower. Now, what's all this about a witness?'

Carol told him the little she knew on the way to the car.

'That's great news,' Tony enthused. 'First big breakthrough, isn't it?'

Carol shrugged. 'It depends how much he can tell us. If the guy was driving a red Ford Escort, it doesn't take us a lot further forward. We'd need something solid to cross-match. Maybe something like the computer angle.'

'Oh yes, the computer theory. How goes that?'

'I discussed it with my brother. He reckons it's perfectly feasible,' Carol said coldly, feeling patronized.

'Great!' Tony enthused. 'I really hope that works out. I wasn't trying to pour cold water on it, you know. I have to work with the balance of probabilities, and your idea's way beyond my parameters. But it's the kind of investigative brainwave that we're going to need on the national task force. I really think you should seriously consider signing up when we get the show on the road.'

'I didn't think you'd be comfortable with the idea of working with me after this,' Carol said, eyes firmly fixed on the road.

Tony took a deep breath. 'I've never met a police officer I'd rather work with.'

'Even if I do trespass on your personal space?' she asked bitterly, hating herself for picking at the hurt like an old scab.

Tony sighed. 'I thought we'd agreed we could be friends? I know I . . .'

'Fine,' she interrupted, wishing she'd never opened up the conversation. 'I can do friends. What do you think of Bradfield Victoria's chances in the Cup?'

Startled, Tony twisted in his seat and stared at Carol. He saw a smile twitching at the corner of her mouth. Suddenly, they were both laughing.

The latest government threats to the prison service meant the officers at HM Prison Barleigh had started to work to rule. That in turn meant that prisoners were banged up for twenty-three hours in every twenty-four. Stevie McConnell lay on his side on his bunk bed in the cell he had to himself. Following the attack that had left him with two black eyes, a couple of cracked ribs, more bruises than he could count, and the kind of sexual damage that made sitting down an option too painful to contemplate readily, he had asked for and been granted solitary confinement.

It didn't matter how much he protested that he wasn't the Queer Killer. Nobody cared, neither cons nor screws. He'd realized that the warders held him in as much contempt as his fellow prisoners when he'd heard the sounds of slopping-out all along the wing. But no officer had unlocked his cell door to allow him to empty the stinking bucket of his sewage that sat in the corner, its smell insistent and somehow more disgusting than any of the dozens of public toilets where Stevie had picked up strangers for sex.

As far as he could see, his prospects were bleak. The very fact that he was behind bars was enough to condemn him in most people's eyes. Probably the whole world was convinced that the Queer Killer had taken his last victim now that Stevie McConnell was in jail. After he'd been released following his first stretch of questioning, he'd been painfully aware that everyone at work, staff and clients, were giving him a wide berth, refusing to meet his eyes. One drink in a Temple Fields bar where he'd been a regular for years had been enough to show him that gay solidarity had mysteriously deserted him too. The police and the press clearly thought he was their psychopath. And until they caught the Queer Killer, Bradfield wasn't going to be a welcoming place for Stevie McConnell. The decision to move out to Amsterdam where an ex-lover ran a gym had seemed to make sense at the time. It hadn't occurred to him that they'd be tailing him.

The irony that this had all happened to him because he'd rushed to the defence of a police officer in the first place was not lost on Stevie. He gave a bitter bark of laughter. That big Geordie sergeant was probably counting his blessings that he'd been smacked with a half-brick, figuring that that was the only thing that had saved him from being the Queer Killer's next victim. The reality was that Stevie McConnell was the only victim around that night. And it wasn't going to get any better. Even his shocked family didn't want to know, according to his solicitor.

Lying there, examining his future dispassionately, he came to a decision. Grimacing with pain, Stevie rolled off the bunk and took off his shirt, wincing at the stab of pain from his ribs. With his teeth and nails, painstakingly he unpicked the seams that held the denim together. On the sharp end of a bed spring, he ripped the edges of the material so he could tear it into thin strips, which he plaited together for extra strength. He tied one end of the makeshift ligature round his neck in a tight noose, then climbed on to the top bunk. He fastened the other end of his short rope to the bottom rail of the upper berth.

Then, at seventeen minutes past nine on a sunny Sunday morning, he threw himself head first over the edge.

Like an ailing company which has won a life-saving tender against all odds, Scargill Street was buzzing with excited activity. At the heart of it all was the HOLMES

365

room, where officers stared into screens, manipulating the new information, evaluating the new correspondences the system was throwing out.

In his office, Brandon held a council of war with his four inspectors and Tony, all of them clutching a photocopy of Brandon's notes on his interview with Terry Harding. The ACC had only had five hours' sleep, but the prospect of movement on the enquiry had given him a new energy, betrayed only by the heavy shadows around his deep-set eyes. 'To recap, then,' Brandon said. 'At about quarter past seven the night Damien Connolly was killed, a man drove out of his garage in some kind of big four-wheel drive jeep, dark in colour. He got out of the jeep to close the garage door, and that's when our witness got his best look at him. The description we've got is white, five ten to six feet, aged between twenty and forty-five, possibly with his hair tied back in a ponytail. Wearing white trainers, jeans and a long waxed coat. Overnight, the HOLMES team have been going through the vehicles clocked in Temple Fields that fit the description. Most of these drivers have already been interviewed, but they're all going to be followed up and questioned more thoroughly now we've got Terry Harding's evidence. Bob, I want you to take charge of that, and I want alibis checking too.'

'Right, boss,' Stansfield said, flicking the ash off his cigarette with a determined motion.

'Oh, and Bob? Can you get someone to check that Harding really has been in Japan all week on a business trip? I want to make sure we cover all the bases on this one.' Stansfield nodded.

'I'm sending a car round for Harding at eleven

o'clock,' Brandon went on, checking the list he'd made in the kitchen at seven. 'Carol, I want you to do the interview. Check what taxi firm Harding used to take him to the airport; let's see if we can get that time narrowed down a bit more. Tony, I'd like you to sit in on it. Maybe you can help us with strategies to improve his recollection, see if we can get any firm description of what this character looks like.'

'I'll do my best,' he said. 'At least I can probably distinguish between what he really remembers and what he thinks he remembers.'

Brandon gave him an odd look, but carried on regardless. 'Kevin, I want you to organize a team to hit the car showrooms, get as many brochures and posters as you can of four-wheel drive jeeps, so we can show them to Mr Harding and see if he can give us a positive ID.'

'Will do, sir. Do you want us to go back to the neighbours in the earlier cases, see if anyone noticed the same vehicle there?' Kevin asked eagerly.

Brandon considered for a moment. 'Let's see how we go on today,' he said after a few moments. 'It'll take a lot of bodies and time to go over the old ground again, and we might not need it. It's probably worth having a word with the rest of the neighbours in Connolly's street, though. Now we've got something positive to hit them with. Good idea, Kevin. Now, Dave. What can you do for us?'

Woolcott outlined the actions the HOLMES team were already carrying out. 'With it being Sunday, I'm holding back on contacting Swansea until we've tried to get the vehicle narrowed down. The more information we can give them, the fewer possibilities we'll have to deal with. If this Harding bloke can give us make, model and year, or at least eliminate some models, we can ask DVLC to let us have a list of all the matches throughout the UK. Then we can start interviewing registered keepers, starting with Bradfield and moving out from there. It's a helluva big job, but we should get there in the end.'

Brandon nodded his acknowledgement. 'Anybody got anything else?'

Tony lifted a hand. 'If you're questioning neighbours anyway, it might be worth extending the enquiries slightly.' All eyes were on him, but he was only aware of Carol's. What had happened between them had sharpened his desire to be instrumental in capturing Handy Andy. 'This guy is a stalker, I don't think anyone would dispute that now. I think he'd been watching Damien Connolly for a while. Given that we're in the middle of winter and it's not the ideal weather for standing around in the open, chances are he did the bulk of his spying from his car. He probably didn't park up in the close itself, since he'd be too noticeable in such a short street. I'd guess he parked on the street that runs along the bottom, somewhere that he had the house in his line of sight. Maybe someone there noticed an unfamiliar vehicle parked outside for long stretches.'

'Good thinking,' Brandon said. 'Kevin, can you cover that?'

'Will do, sir. I'll get the lads on to it.'

'And the lasses,' Carol said sweetly. 'And maybe we should ask them not to concentrate on the four-wheel drive motor. If this guy's as careful as we think he is, he might only use the jeep for the actual snatches and go for something different when he's doing the stalking, just in case a nosy neighbour has clocked him.'

'What do you think, Tony?' Brandon asked.

'It wouldn't surprise me,' he said. 'It's important we don't forget how competent this killer is. He might even be using hired cars.'

Dave Woolcott groaned. 'Oh God, don't do this to me.'

Bob Stansfield looked up from the pad where he'd been scribbling the names of his team. 'I take it that the other lines of enquiry that Dr Hill suggested are on the back burner for now?'

Brandon pursed his lips grimly. The euphoria had died somewhere during the briefing. The weight of the work ahead seemed unbearable, the idea of finding the killer almost as distant as it had before Terry Harding walked into the station. 'That's right. No disrespect, Tony, but your suggestions are hypotheses, and what we've got now is our first solid set of facts.'

'No problem,' Tony said. 'Hard evidence always comes first.'

'And Carol's idea about the computer stuff? Should we still pursue that?' Dave asked.

'Same thing applies,' Brandon said. 'It's a hunch, not a fact, so yes, it goes on the back burner.'

'With respect, sir,' Carol chipped in, determined not to be sidelined. 'Even if Terry Harding gives us a positive ID on the make and model of the vehicle, we might be no further forward. We need other elimination factors before we can narrow things down. If I'm right about the computer, we'd be looking at such a small segment of the population that it would be significant if we did get a cross-match.'

Brandon considered for a moment. Then he said, 'Point taken, Carol. OK, we can pursue it, Dave, but not as a priority. Only as and when we have bodies freed up from the main enquiry. Right, are we all clear what we've got to do?' He looked around expectantly, registering the series of nods. 'OK, team,' Brandon said, his voice stern. 'Let's go for it.'

'And may the force be with you,' Kevin said under his breath to Carol as they emerged from the office.

'I'd rather have the force than the gutter press,' she said drily, turning her back on him. 'Tony, can we find a quiet corner and plan our strategy for this interview?'

'The only way you're going to get more out of him is by hypnosis,' Tony told Carol as they talked in the corridor after an hour with Terry Harding.

'Can you do that?' Carol asked.

'I've got the basic technique. Judging by his eye movements and body language, he was telling the truth about what he saw, not making anything up or exaggerating, so he might come across with more detail under hypnosis, particularly if we have pictures to show him.'

Ten minutes later, Carol was back with a sheaf of car brochures that Kevin's team had scavenged from city dealerships. 'This what we need?'

Tony nodded. 'Perfect. You sure you want me to give this a go?'

'It's got to be worth a try,' Carol said.

They walked back into the interview room, where Terry Harding was finishing a mug of coffee. 'Can I go now?' he said plaintively. 'Only I'm due to fly out to Brussels tomorrow and I haven't even unpacked my bag.'

'Not much longer, sir,' Carol said, sitting down to one side of the table. 'Dr Hill would like to try something with you.'

Tony smiled reassuringly. 'We've got some pictures of the kind of jeep you saw leaving Damien's garage. What I'd like to do, if you're agreeable, is to put you in a light hypnotic trance and ask you to look at them.'

Harding frowned. 'Why can't I just look at them as I am?'

'The chances are better that you'd recognize the particular model,' Tony explained soothingly. 'Thing is, Mr Harding, you're obviously a very busy man. Since you saw the incident, you've travelled to the other side of the world, you've had a series of important business meetings, and you've probably not had enough sleep. All of that means your conscious mind has probably filed away the details of what you saw last Sunday. Using hypnosis, I can help you retrieve that information.'

Harding looked dubious. 'I don't know. Always supposing you could get me to go under, you could make me say anything.'

'Unfortunately, that's not the case. If it was, hypnotists would all be millionaires,' Tony joked. 'Like I said, all it does is free up the stuff you've buried because it's not important.'

'What do I have to do?' Harding said suspiciously.

'Just listen to my voice and follow what I tell you,' Tony said. 'You'll feel a little strange, a little spaced out, but you'll be in control at all times. I use a technique called neuro-linguistic programming. It's very relaxing, I promise you.'

'Do I have to lie down, or what?'

'Nothing like that. And I'm not going to wave a watch in front of you. Are you prepared to give it a try?'

Carol held her breath, watching Harding as an assortment of expressions chased each other across his face. Finally, he nodded. 'I doubt you'll be able to get me under,' he said. 'I'm a man who knows his own mind. But I'm willing to try.'

'OK,' said Tony. 'I want you to relax. Close your eyes if it feels more comfortable. Now, I want you to go deep down inside yourself . . .'

Elated with their success, Tony and Carol bounced into the murder squad room. Bob Stansfield was standing by the window, staring out at the rain-drenched street below, his shoulders slumped, a cigarette burning unheeded in his hand. He glanced round and Carol called, 'Cheer up, it might never happen.'

Stansfield swung round and said bitterly, 'You obviously haven't heard the news.'

'What news?' Carol asked, walking over to him.

'Stevie McConnell topped himself.'

Carol rocked on her heels and stumbled against a desk. Her ears were ringing and she thought she was going to faint. Instinctively, Tony moved forward and steered her into a chair. 'Deep breaths, Carol. Deep and slow,' he said softly, leaning over her, staring intently at her white face.

She closed her eyes, dug her nails into her palms

and obeyed. 'Sorry,' Stansfield said. 'It knocked me for six too.'

Carol looked up and pushed her hair away from a forehead suddenly clammy. 'What happened?'

'Apparently he took a beating yesterday. A sex-case special, by all accounts. So, this morning he tore up his shirt and hung himself. The fucking warders never noticed, on account of they're playing at work to rule,' he added savagely.

'The poor bastard,' Carol said.

'There's going to be hell to pay,' Stansfield predicted. 'I'm glad it was fuck all to do with me. At least it won't be my arse in the fire. I mean, Brandon's bombproof, so it's going to be some poor fucker of an inspector who's going to carry the can.'

Carol looked at him as if she'd like to hit him. 'Sometimes, Bob, you really fuck me off,' she said coldly. 'Where's Brandon?'

'Down in the HOLMES room. Probably hiding from the Chief.'

They found Brandon and Dave Woolcott closeted in the inspector's cubby hole off the main room. 'We've got a positive make, sir,' Carol said, her initial exuberance flattened by Stansfield's news. 'We know what car he was driving.'

Penny Burgess turned off the main road on to the Forestry Commission track that led deep into the heart of the woodland. She was aiming for a car park and picnic area in the middle of the woods. It was one of her favourite spots from which to strike off through the trees and up on to the bare gritstone edges where the wind could blow away all the accumulated dross of the week. She certainly needed it after the last few days of hard graft, big stories and not enough sleep.

The record on the radio finished and the announcer said, 'And now, over to the newsroom for the headlines on the hour.' The news ident followed, then a woman said in a voice altogether too bright for her subject matter, 'Northern Sound news on the hour. A man who was questioned by Bradfield police in connection with the serial killings that have terrorized the city was found dead this morning in his cell at Barleigh jail.'

In her shock, Penny took her foot off the accelerator and pitched forward as the car stalled. 'Shit!' she exclaimed, her hand shooting out to twist the volume higher.

'Steven McConnell is thought to have committed suicide by hanging himself with a noose made from his own clothes. McConnell, the manager of a body-building gym in the city, was arrested last week after a street brawl involving an undercover police officer in the city's gay village,' the newsreader continued, sounding for all the world as if she were announcing the results of the Eurovision Song Contest. 'He was released on bail, but rearrested after attempting to flee the country. A Home Office spokesman said there would be a full enquiry into the circumstances of his death.

'The economy has never been in a better position,' the Prime Minister said today . . .' Penny turned the key in the ignition and did a perilous five-point turn in the narrow lane before stamping on the gas and shooting back towards the road. It was just as well, she thought, that she'd already decided to dump Kevin.

After the story she was about to write, she couldn't imagine him ever wanting to see her again anyway.

Tony drummed his fingers on the back of the cab's seat, a curious restlessness possessing him. Leaving Scargill Street hadn't been easy, but he knew he had no role while the police worked on their one piece of solid evidence. The last thing they needed in that maelstrom of reproach and driven activity was for him to sit around reminding them of all the reasons why he'd never been convinced that Stevie McConnell was their man.

His consolation was that he felt certain that Angelica would phone tonight. As the taxi hissed through the wet and empty streets, Tony rehearsed the conversation. He felt a new confidence, a certainty that tonight he would have no problems, that he had finally wrestled his demon into submission thanks to her strange erotic therapy. He would tell her she had no idea how much her phone calls had meant to him. That she had helped him more than she could know. Satisfied that he had things under control, Tony sighed comfortably and cleared his mind of Handy Andy.

Penny Burgess popped the top on a can of Guinness, lit a cigarette and switched on her computer. After making a handful of phone calls to firm up the version of events she'd heard on the radio, she was fired with the self-righteous enthusiasm that only politicians, journalists and fundamentalist preachers seem capable of harnessing for professional advancement.

She inhaled a long stream of smoke, thought for a moment, then started to hammer the keys.

Bradfield's serial killer claimed his fifth victim yesterday (Sunday) when gay body-builder Stevie McConnell killed himself in a prison cell.

Police had implied that McConnell was himself the Queer Killer in a cynical bid to force the real killer's hand.

But their twisted exercise ended in tragedy when McConnell, 32, hung himself with a makeshift rope woven from his own torn shirt. He tied it to the top bunk in his solitary-confinement cell at Barleigh prison and threw himself off, strangling himself.

And last night, a police officer involved in the Queer Killer investigation admitted, 'We've known for several days that Stevie McConnell wasn't the killer.'

McConnell had pleaded with prison staff to put him in solitary after a barbaric attack by fellow inmates the previous day.

A source inside Barleigh prison said, 'He took a real beating. The word on the grapevine when he arrived was that he was the Queer Killer, only the police didn't have enough evidence to charge him yet.

'Prisoners don't like sex killers, and they tend to make their feelings known. McConnell got a brutal hammering. He was badly beaten up, and sexually assaulted too.'

Warders are said to have turned a blind eye to McConnell's savage battering. Then yesterday (Sunday) because of a prison officers' work to rule, he was left unattended in his cell for long enough to end his life. A Home Office spokesman said there would be a full enquiry into the incident.

McConnell managed Bodies gym in the city centre, where the killer's third victim, solicitor Gareth Finnegan, was a member.

McConnell faced a minor assault charge after coming to the rescue of an undercover police sergeant who was attacked by a third man in the Temple Fields gay village.

He then tried to flee the country while he was out on bail. Police rearrested him as he was about to board a ferry for Holland, and persuaded magistrates to remand him in custody.

A police source revealed, 'What we did made people think that McConnell was the killer, and that's what we wanted.

'Serial killers are very vain, and we thought that the killer would be so outraged that we had pointed the finger at the wrong person that he would break cover and make contact.

'It's all gone horribly wrong.'

A friend of McConnell's said last night, 'Bradfield police are murderers. As far as I'm concerned, they killed Stevie.

'The police really grilled him about the serial killings. They put him under all kinds of pressure.

'Even though they let him go afterwards, mud like that sticks. He got the cold shoulder at work, and out in the gay bars.

'That's why he decided to leg it. It's a tragedy. Worse than that, it's a pointless tragedy.

'This hasn't taken the police an inch closer to finding the killer.'

Penny lit another cigarette and read through her

copy. 'Pick the bones out of that, Kevin,' she said softly, hitting the keys that would save the file and transmit it via her modem to the office computer. Then, as an afterthought, she typed:

Memo to newsdesk.
From Penny Burgess, Crime Desk.
I am taking tomorrow (Monday) as time off in lieu of working extra hours last week and today. Hope this doesn't pose too many problems!

'A Land Rover Discovery, metallic grey or dark blue?' Dave Woolcott confirmed, making a note on a pad.

'That's what the man said,' Carol agreed.

'Right. With it being Sunday, I can't get a full run-down from Swansea on every vehicle like that on our patch,' Dave said.

'What we could do, though, is get a team going round the main dealerships and the quality second-hand dealers asking for their records of anyone who's bought one,' Kevin suggested. Like all of them, he was fired with an excitement only slightly tempered by the tragic news from Barleigh.

'No,' Brandon said. 'That's a waste of time and personnel. There's no guarantee that the killer bought his vehicle locally. We wait until tomorrow morning. Then we go flat out.'

Everyone looked disappointed, even though they recognized the force of Brandon's argument. 'In that case, sir,' Carol said, 'I'd like to work with Dave compiling lists of computer hardware and software suppliers so we're ready to roll with that as soon as there are some spare bodies to hit the phones.'

Brandon nodded. 'Good thinking, Carol. Now, why don't the rest of us go home and rediscover what our houses look like?'

Tony was stretched out on the sofa, trying to persuade himself he was enjoying the luxury of watching TV when the doorbell rang. The hope of company come to rescue him from his restless boredom catapulted him to his feet and down the hall. He opened the door, a smile already spreading across his face.

The smile died halfway as he registered that he was out of luck. There was a woman on the doorstep, but she wasn't one of his friends or colleagues. She was tall, bigboned, with heavy, blunt features and a strong, square jaw. She pushed her long dark hair away from her face and said, 'I'm really sorry to trouble you, only my car's broken down and I don't know where there's a pay phone. I wondered if I might use your phone to call the AA? I'll pay for the call, of course . . .' Her voice trailed off and she smiled apologetically.

When I clocked Sergeant Merrick in the Sackville Arms, I thought I was going to pass out. I'd only gone there because I knew the detectives from Scargill Street use it. I wanted to hear what the gossip was among the murder squad. I wanted to hear them talk about me and my accomplishments. The last thing I expected was to see so familiar a face staring out at me.

I was sitting unobtrusively in the corner when I saw Merrick come in. I debated whether to leave, but I decided that might make me noticeable. The last thing I wanted was for him to recognize me and follow me for whatever reasons of his own. Besides, why should I let a policeman drive me away from my lunch break?

But I couldn't stop the churning in my stomach in case he caught sight of me and moved across to speak to me. I wasn't afraid of him, but I just didn't want to draw attention to myself. Luckily, he was with two of his colleagues, and they were too busy discussing something – me, probably, had they but known it – to pay much attention to anybody else. I recognized the woman from the papers. Inspector Carol Jordan. She looks better in the flesh than in print, probably because her hair's a lovely shade of blonde. The other man I hadn't seen before, but I filed his face away for future reference. Carroty-red hair, pale skin, freckles, boyish features. And of course, Merrick, head and shoulders above the others, some kind of dressing on his head. I wondered how he'd come by that.

I'd never hated Merrick the way I hated some of the others, even though he'd taken me into custody a couple of times. He'd never treated me with the contempt they had. He'd never sneered at me when he arrested me. But I could see he still saw me as an object, someone not worthy of respect. He never understood that when I sold my body to sailors it was for a purpose. But whatever I did then is irrelevant now. I am different now, I am a changed person. What happened back in Seaford feels as irrelevant and remote as something I'd seen at the cinema.

In a strange way, being in the presence of the very officers who are trying to track me down was quite exciting. I got a real buzz out of being only feet away from my hunters, who didn't sense their prey. They didn't even have enough sixth sense to realize there was something extraordinary happening, not even Carol Jordan. So much for women's intuition. I see it as a sort of test, a measure of my ability to delude my pursuers. The notion that they can catch me is so absurd, it's unthinkable.

I felt so strong after that encounter that the next day's paper hit me like a blow with a sandbag. I was walking through the main computer room when I saw an early edition of the Sentinel Times lying on some junior engineer's desk. FIFTH BODY IN QUEER KILLER'S RAMPAGE screamed out at me.

I wanted to rage and shout, to throw things through windows. How dare they? My handiwork is so individual, *how could they mistake some blundering copycat's body for one of mine?*

I was trembling with suppressed fury when I made it back to my own office. I'd wanted to ask the engineer if I could have a look at his paper, but I didn't trust myself to speak. I wanted to rush out of the office to the nearest newsagent's and snatch a copy off the counter. But that would have been unforgivable weakness. The secret of success, I told myself, was to behave normally. To do nothing that would make my colleagues think there was something peculiar going on in my life.

'Patience,' I told myself, 'is the cardinal virtue.' So I sat at my desk, fiddling with the intricacies of a piece of software that needed rewriting. But my heart wasn't in it, and I know I wasn't justifying my salary that afternoon. By four o'clock, I could stand it no longer. I grabbed my phone and dialled the special number that broadcasts Bradfield Sound to callers.

The story was the lead item on the news bulletin, as it ought to have been. 'The body of a man found in the Temple Fields area in the early hours of the morning is not the fifth victim of the serial killer who has brought terror to Bradfield's gay community, police revealed this afternoon.' As the newsreader's words sank in, I felt my anger depart, the hollowness inside me whole once more.

Without waiting for more, I slammed the phone down. They'd got something right at last. But I'd gone through four hours of hell because of their mistake. Every hour I'd suffered would be an hour added on to the agonies of Dr Tony Hill, I vowed.

Because the Bradfield police have now committed the ultimate absurdity. Dr Tony Hill, the stupid man who hadn't

even recognized that all my crimes belonged to me, has been
appointed the official police consultant to the serial-killer
enquiry. The poor, deluded fools. If that's their best hope,
then they clearly have no hope.

17

> In a murder of pure voluptuousness, entirely disinter-
> ested, where no hostile witness was to be removed, no
> extra booty to be gained and no revenge to be gratified,
> it is clear that to hurry would be altogether to ruin.

The agony was so extreme Tony wanted to believe he
was in a nightmare. He had never understood before
how many different kinds of pain there were. The dull
throb in his head; the harsh rasp in his throat; the
screaming, wrenching rip in his shoulders; and the
knives of cramps in his thighs and calves. At first,
the pain blocked all his other senses. His eyes screwed
up tight, all he knew was suffering so stark it made the
sweat pop out on his forehead.

Gradually, he learned to bear the extremes of his
pain, realizing that if he took his weight on his feet,
the cramps would slowly subside and the excruciating
tearing in his shoulders grow less. As the torment
became more tolerable, he grew aware that he felt
nauseous, a deep queasiness that sat in his stomach
and threatened to spill over at any moment. God alone
knew how long he'd been hanging here.

Slowly, fearfully, he opened his eyes and raised his head, a movement which sent a spasm of agony through his neck and shoulders. Tony looked around. Instantly, he wished he hadn't. He knew immediately where he was. The room was brightly lit, spotlights mounted on the ceiling and walls revealing a white-washed room, its rough stone floor marked with dark stains that he knew without examination were the visible remains of the blood that had pooled and splashed there. Facing him was the blind eye of a camcorder on a tripod, a red light on the side indicating that his scrutiny was not going unrecorded. Fixed to the far wall was a magnetic strip with a selection of knives hanging neatly on it. In one corner of the room, he saw the unmistakable implements of torture. A rack; a strange contraption like a chair which he recognized but could not name at first. Something religious? Something vaguely Christian? Something treacherous, not what it seemed? A Judas chair, that was it. And on the wall, a huge wooden saltire, like some hideously perverted holy relic. A soft moan escaped from his dry lips.

Now he knew the worst, he took stock of his own position. He was naked, his skin gooseflesh in the chill of the cellar. His hands were fastened behind his back; judging by the hard edges cutting into his wrists, by handcuffs, held taut in their turn by a rope or chain or something that was obviously fastened to the ceiling. This hawser was tight enough to force his upper body forward, leaving him doubled over at the waist. Tony managed to push himself on to the tips of his toes and twist his body sideways. Out of the corner of his eyes, he could see a strong nylon rope leading from behind him, through a pulley, along the ceiling, through another pulley on to a winch.

'Jesus Christ,' he croaked. He was afraid to look at his feet, lest his worst fears should be confirmed, but he forced his eyes downwards nevertheless. As he had feared, each ankle was encased in a leather strap. The straps in their turn were attached to a rope cradle that held a heavy stone flag. An involuntary shudder of fear rippled through him, stressing his tortured muscles even further. He knew about torture; to treat his patients he'd had to study the history of sadism. Not even in his worst moments had he imagined he would face so inhuman a fate.

His mind was already racing ahead. He would be winched up till he reached the ceiling. His muscles would wrench and tear, his joints strain to their utmost limit. Then the winch would be released, letting him drop a few feet before the brake was applied. The weight of the stone flag, still hurtling downwards accelerating at thirty-two feet per second, would finish the job, ripping his joints apart, leaving him dangling in a jumble of dislocated limbs. If he was lucky, the shock and pain would thrust him into unconsciousness. Strappado, brought to a fine art by the Spanish Inquisition. No need for high tech in torture.

In a bid to escape the blind panic his knowledge had brought him to, he forced himself to cast his mind back to what had happened. The woman at the door, that was where it had started. As he had let her into the house, Tony had felt a niggle of familiarity. He felt sure he'd seen her somewhere, but he couldn't imagine having seen someone so distinctively ugly and not remembering. He'd walked ahead of her down the hall and into his study. Then, the faintest whiff of a strangely medicinal, chemical smell, before a hand had sneaked round his neck and clamped a cold, disgusting pad on his face. A kick behind his knee to buckle his legs and bring him down. He'd struggled, but with her weight on top of him, it had only lasted for moment before he had lost consciousness.

Then he had drifted in and out of a half-world of light and dark, aware only of the pad that seemed constantly to send him out as soon as he struggled into consciousness. Until, finally, he had come round. In Handy Andy's torture chamber. Out of nowhere, a quotation sprang into his mind. 'Depend upon it, sir, when a man knows he is to be hanged in a fortnight, it concentrates his mind wonderfully.' Somewhere, he knew there was a clue in what had happened that might just allow him to escape what seemed inevitable. All he had to do was to find it.

Had he been completely wrong in his profile? Was the woman who had kidnapped him Handy Andy? Was she the one? Or was she just the decoy, the willing accomplice who got off on her master's vice? Again, he replayed what his memory would allow him to snatch back. He summoned up the woman's image again. Clothes first. Beige mac, cut continental style, just like Carol's, swinging open to reveal a white shirt, enough buttons undone to reveal the swell of full breasts and a deep cleavage. Jeans, trainers. Trainers. They were the same make and model as his own. But none of this was significant, Tony told himself. They were only outward symbols of the care Handy Andy took not to be caught. The woman's garb had been chosen so that if she did leave any stray fibres, they wouldn't show up as having any significance, being identifiable as having come from either Carol's clothes or his. And Carol had been in his house often enough now for her to have left stray fibres.

The woman's face didn't really ring any bells either. She was tall for a woman, at least five feet ten, with chunky bone structure to match. Not even her mother could have called her attractive, with her heavy jaw, slightly bulbous nose, wide mouth and eyes set curiously far apart. Even though she was skilfully, if heavily, made up, there wasn't a lot she could do with the basic building materials. He was sure they'd never been in a room together, though he couldn't rule out having passed her in the street, at the tram station or on campus.

The trainers. For some reason he kept coming back to the trainers. If only the pain would stop long enough for him to focus properly. Tony locked his legs straight, trying to relieve the agonizing strain on his shoulders. The fraction of an inch he gained wasn't nearly enough. Again, visceral fear gripped him and he blinked away a tear.

What was it about the trainers? Tony summoned every ounce of concentration he could master, and called up the image of the woman again. With a slow gasp of understanding, he realized what it was. The feet were too big. Even for a woman of that height, the feet were too big. As soon as he grasped that, he remembered the hands too. First, black leather, later thin latex gloves covering big hands, fingers thick and strong. The person who had brought him here had not always been a woman.

*   *   *

388

Carol pressed the doorbell again. Where the hell was he? The lights were on, the curtains drawn. Maybe he'd nipped out to pick up a pizza, post a letter, buy a bottle of wine, rent a video? With a frustrated sigh, she turned away and walked down to the end of the street, turning into the ginnel that ran between Tony's street and the houses behind. She walked down to his back yard, where a previous owner had demolished the wall and concreted half the area to provide the hard standing where Tony had told her he always kept his car.

The car was in place, exactly where it should have been. 'Oh, bloody hell,' Carol complained. Edging past the car, she walked up to the house and peered through the kitchen window. The light from the open door into the hall cast a pale glow over the room. No sign of life. No dirty dishes, no empty bottles.

On the off chance, Carol tried the back door. No joy. 'Bloody men,' she grumbled as she strode back to her car. 'Five minutes, pal, then I'm off,' she said, throwing herself into the driver's seat. Ten minutes crawled by, but no one appeared.

Carol started the engine and drove off. At the end of the street, she glanced across at the pub on the other side of the main road. It was worth a try, she supposed. It took less than three minutes to check the smoky, crowded rooms and discover that wherever Tony Hill was, it wasn't in the Farewell to Arms.

Where else could he be within walking distance at nine o'clock on a Sunday night? 'Anywhere,' she told herself. 'You can't be his only friend in the world. He wasn't expecting you; you only called round to arrange a meeting for tomorrow.'

Giving up, Carol drove home. The flat was empty. Michael, she remembered, was out to dinner with some woman he'd met at a trade fair. She decided to give up on the world and go to bed. But first, she'd better leave a message on Tony's machine. If she turned up two mornings running without warning, he might start to get twitchy. The answering machine checked in after a couple of rings, but there was no outgoing message, just a series of clicks followed by the tone. 'Hi, Tony,' she said. 'I don't know if your machine's working properly, so I don't know if you'll get this message. It's twenty past nine, and I'm about to have an early night. I'll be in the office first thing, working on the computer supplies stuff. Mr Brandon's called a case conference for tomorrow at three. If you want to get together before then, give me a call. I'll be in the HOLMES room if I'm not in the squad room.'

Sitting down with Nelson on her lap and a stiff drink by her side, Carol thought about the job that lay ahead. The list of computer supplies companies who sold the peripherals and hardware Handy Andy would need to construct his own images was depressingly long. She had told Dave not to start work on it until she'd had a chance to check out the software company. Their list of customers would be shorter, and they would have the Discovery to cross-reference that list with. Only if that came up blank would she set Dave's team loose on the dozens of numbers she'd painstakingly compiled that evening. 'We'll get there, Nelson,' she told the cat. 'It just better be worth the trip.'

The clatter of high heels on stone cut through the delirium of pain like a wire through cheese. So everyday a sound, translated by its location into a threat. He had no idea whether it was day or night, or how long had passed since he had been snatched from his life. Tony forced himself into alertness as the sound approached him from behind. She was coming downstairs. At the foot of the stairs, the clicking ended. He heard a low chuckle. Slowly, one step at a time, the footsteps crossed behind him. He could sense the scrutiny he was under.

She took her time, skirting round his trussed body until she moved into his line of vision. Tony was momentarily taken aback by the magnificence of her body. From the neck down, she could have been a model for a soft-porn magazine. She stood with legs apart, arms akimbo. She wore a loose red silk kimono, which fell open to reveal an extraordinary red leather basque with peephole nipples and a split crotch. Black stockings sheathed shapely, muscular legs which ended in black stilettoes. Even under the kimono, he could see the clear outline of strong, well-muscled arms and shoulders. From where he was hanging, she was as erotic as a kaolin poultice.

'Worked it out yet, *Anthony*?' she drawled, the warmth of suppressed laughter evident in her voice.

The stressing of his full name was the last turn in the Rubik's cube of his memory. His mind racing, Tony said, 'I suppose a couple of paracetamol would be out of the question, Angelica?'

The low chuckle again. 'Glad to see you haven't lost your sense of humour.'

'No, only my dignity. I wasn't expecting this, Angelica. Nothing in our phone conversations led me to imagine this is what you had in mind for me.'

'You had no idea who I was, did you?' Angelica said, pride unmistakable in her tones.

'Yes and no. I didn't know you were the person who killed those men. But I did know you were the woman for me.'

Angelica frowned, as if uncertain how to respond. She turned away and checked the camcorder. 'You took long enough to get that far. Do you have any idea how many times you slammed the phone down on me?' Her voice was angry, not hurt.

Tony sensed the danger and tried to find emollient words. 'That was because I had a problem, not because of you.'

'You had a problem with me,' she said, moving over to the stone benches that ran along one wall. She picked up another cassette and walked back to the camera.

Tony tried again. 'Quite the opposite,' he said. 'I've always had trouble with relationships with women. That's why I didn't know how to treat you in the beginning. But it got so much better. You know it did. You know we were wonderful together. Thanks to you, I feel like all my problems are behind me.' He hoped she wasn't alive to the unintentional irony in his words.

But Angelica was no fool. 'I think you can safely say that, Anthony,' she said with a wry smile.

'You outsmarted me, you know. I was convinced the killer was a man. I should have known better.'

With her back to him, Angelica swapped the cassettes in the camcorder. Then she wheeled round and said, 'You'd never have caught me. And with you out of the way, no one else will either.'

Ignoring the threat, Tony continued to chat, straining to keep his voice warm and even. 'I should have realized you were a woman. The subtlety, the attention to detail, the care you took to clear up after yourself. It was stupid of me not to grasp that those were the hallmarks of a woman's mind, not a man's.'

Angelica smirked. 'You're all the same, you psychologists.' She spat the word out as though it were an obscenity. 'You've got no imagination.'

'But I'm not like them, Angelica. OK, I made that one crucial mistake, but I bet I know more about you than any of them ever did. Because you've shown me the inside of your mind. And not just through the killings. You've shown me the real woman, the woman who comprehends love. But I guess they didn't understand you, did they? They didn't believe you when you told them you had a woman's spirit trapped in a man's body. Oh, I expect they pretended to, I expect they patronized you and talked down to you. But deep down, they wrote you off as a freak, didn't they? Believe me, I've never done that.' Tony's voice cracked as he reached the end of his speech, his mouth dry with a mixture of fear and chloroform. At least the adrenaline coursing through his veins seemed to be acting as an analgesic.

'What do you know about me?' she said roughly, the pain on her face a strange contrast with the coquettish pose she had adopted.

'I need a drink if we're going to talk,' Tony said, gambling that her narcissism would demand that she share her exploits, that she needed to hear his version of herself. If he was to have any chance of escaping with his life, he needed to build up a relationship with her. A drink would be the first brick in the wall. The more he could get her to see him as an individual, not as a cipher, the higher his chances rose.

Angelica scowled suspiciously. Then, with a toss of her head that sent her long hair swirling, she turned away and walked to a slop sink set against the wall. She turned on the tap and looked around vaguely for a drinking vessel of some kind. 'I'll get a glass,' she muttered, passing him and clattering up the steps again.

Tony felt a surge of relief at his small victory. Angelica was gone for less than thirty seconds, returning with a thick white mug. Kitchen above, Tony deduced as she walked back to the sink. She moved well in the heels, her stride measured and feminine. It was interesting, since she had obviously reverted to more masculine movements under the stress of kidnapping and killing. That was the only way to account for Terry Harding's conviction that he'd seen a man driving off from Damien Connolly's.

Angelica filled the mug and approached Tony cautiously. She gripped his hair, pulled his head back agonizingly and tipped freezing water into his mouth. As much went down his chin as his throat, but the relief was palpable. 'Thanks,' he gasped as she withdrew.

'One should always be hospitable to one's guests,' she said sardonically.

'I hope to remain one for some time,' Tony replied. 'You know, I admire you. You've got style.'

She frowned again. 'Don't bullshit me, Anthony. You won't get round me with stupid flattery.'

'It's not bullshit,' he protested. 'I've spent days and

nights poring over the details of what you've achieved. I'm so deep inside your head, how could I not admire you? How could I not be impressed? The other ones you brought here, they didn't have a clue about who you are, what you can do.'

'That's true, I'll grant you that. They were like babies, frightened, stupid babies,' Angelica said contemptuously. 'They didn't appreciate what a woman like me could do for them. They were treacherous, lecherous fools.'

'That's because they didn't know you like I know you.'

'You keep saying that. Prove it. Prove you know anything about me.'

The gauntlet was well and truly down now, Tony thought. Never mind singing for your supper, talk for your life. This was the proving ground, the place where he would discover if his psychology was indeed a science or just bullshit.

'Fraser Duncan? Hello, this is Detective Inspector Carol Jordan of Bradfield police,' she said. Carol had never grown used to referring to herself by her full title. She felt as if, any moment, someone was going to jump out and shout, 'Oh no, you're not! We found you out at last.' Luckily, that didn't seem to be happening today.

'Yes?' The voice was cautious, the single syllable drawn out in a question.

'Actually, it was my brother, Michael Jordan, who suggested you might be able to help me with an enquiry we're pursuing.'

'Oh, yes?' The climate was getting warmer. 'How is Michael? Is he enjoying the software?'

'I think it's absolutely his favourite toy,' Carol replied.

Fraser Duncan laughed. 'An expensive toy, Inspector. Now, what can I do for you?'

'It's the Vicom 3D Commander I wanted to talk to you about. In strictest confidence, you understand. We're pursuing a major murder investigation, and one of the theories I'm looking at is that our killer might be using your software to edit his own videos, maybe even to import other material into them. That would be possible, wouldn't it?'

'More than possible. It would be perfectly straightforward.'

'So, do you keep records of all your customers?' Carol asked.

'We do. We don't sell all the packages direct, obviously, but anyone who buys the Commander should register their purchase with us since that gives them access to a free customer helpline and also means they get priority mailings when we develop upgrades.' Duncan was positively expansive now. 'Do I detect a request for access to our customer database, Inspector?'

'You do indeed, sir. This is a murder enquiry and the information could be crucial to us. Can I stress too that it would be completely confidential? I would personally undertake to ensure that your data is removed from our system as soon as we have finished with it,' Carol said, trying not to sound as if she was begging.

'I don't know,' Duncan said hesitantly. 'I'm not sure I like the idea of you and your colleagues hammering on the doors of my customers.'

'It wouldn't be like that, Mr Duncan. No way. What

we would do is input the list into our Home Office Major Large Enquiry System and cross-match it against existing data. We would only act on any correlations that came up with people who are already in there.'

'Is this the serial killer you're after?' Duncan asked abruptly.

What did he want to hear, Carol wondered momentarily. 'Yes,' she said, taking a gamble.

'Let me call you back, Inspector. Just to make sure you are who you say you are.'

'No problem.' She gave him the main police switchboard number. 'Ask them to put you through to me in the HOLMES room at Scargill Street.'

The next five minutes passed in a fever of impatience. The phone barely chirruped before Carol had it to her ear. 'Inspector Jordan?'

'You owe me, sis.'

'Michael!'

'I've just been telling Fraser Duncan what an honourable little person you are and despite what he's heard about the police, he can trust you.'

'I love you, bro. Now get off the phone and let the man talk to me!'

Within the hour, Vicom's data was inside the HOLMES computer network, thanks to Dave Woolcott and the miracles of modern technology. Carol had passed Fraser Duncan on to him after they had agreed the ground rules for the data use, and Carol had listened uncomprehendingly to Dave's end of a conversation which consisted of alien expressions like 'baud rate' and 'ASCII files'.

Carol sat by Dave's side as he worked on one of the terminals. 'OK,' he said. 'We've got the list from

Swansea of everyone within a twenty-mile radius of Bradfield who has one of these Discoveries. We've also got the list of names from Vicom of people who have bought their software. I hit this key, and go down this menu to this option, wild-card match, and now we sit back and let the machine talk to itself.'

For an agonizing minute, nothing happened. Then the screen cleared and a message flashed up. '[2] matches found. List matches?' Dave hit the 'y' key and two names and addresses appeared on the screen.

1: *Philip Crozier, 23 Broughton Crag, Sheffield Road, Bradfield BX4 6JB*
2: *Christopher Thorpe [sort criterion 1]/Angelica Thorpe [sort criterion 2], 14 Gregory Street, Moorside, Bradfield BX6 4LR*

'What does that mean?' Carol asked, pointing to the second option.

'The Discovery is registered to Christopher Thorpe and the software was bought by Angelica,' Dave explained. 'Using the wild-card option means that the machine sorted by address as well as by name. Well, Carol, you've got something. Whether it means anything or not, we'll have to see.'

Penny Burgess strode over the rough, fissured limestone of Malham Pavement. The sky was the bright blue of early spring, the rough moorland grasses starting to look more green than brown. From time to time, larks shot out into the air and poured their songs into her ears. There were two occasions when Penny really came alive. One was on the trail of a hot story. The other was up on the high moorlands of the Yorkshire Dales and the Derbyshire Peak District. Out in the open air, she felt free as the skylarks, all pressure gone. No newsdesk demanding copy by an hour ago, no contacts to be appeased, no looking over her shoulder to be sure of staying ahead of her rivals. Just the sky, the moors, the extraordinary limestone landscape, and her.

For no reason, Stevie McConnell burst into her thoughts. He'd never see the sky again, never walk a moor and watch the turning of the seasons. Thank God she had the power to make sure that someone would pay for that inhuman deprivation.

Philip Crozier's house was a narrow, terraced three-storey modern town house, the ground floor consisting mainly of an integral garage. Carol sat in the car, eyeing it up and down. 'We going in, ma'am?' the young detective constable in the driving seat asked.

Carol thought for a moment. Ideally, she'd wanted Tony to be with her when she interviewed the people whose names the computer had spat out. She'd tried ringing him at home. No reply. Claire said he hadn't come into the office yet, which surprised her since he'd had a nine-thirty appointment. Carol had swung round by the house, but it looked exactly the same as it had the night before. Off having fun with his lady friend, she'd decided. Serves him right if he misses out on the showdown with Handy Andy, she thought maliciously, then immediately regretted her childishness. Failing Tony, she'd have liked to have had Don Merrick with her. But he was out pursuing other lines of enquiry that had flowed from the identification of the Discovery. The only person she could find who wasn't urgently involved with something else was DC Morris, on the third month of his secondment to CID.

'We might as well see if he's in,' Carol said. 'Though he's probably at work.'

They walked up the path, Carol taking in the details of the neatly trimmed lawn and the smart paintwork. The house didn't really fit Tony's profile. It was more like the victims' houses in terms of value and status, rather than the home of someone who aspired to their lifestyles. Carol pressed the bell and stepped back. They were about to give up and return to the car when Carol heard feet pounding downstairs. The door swung open to reveal a stocky black man dressed in grey sweat pants and a scarlet T-shirt, his feet bare. He couldn't have looked more different from Terry Harding's description. Carol's heart sank momentarily, then she reminded herself that Crozier might not be the only person with access to his software and his Discovery. He was still worth interviewing. 'Yeah?' he said.

'Mr Crozier?'

''S right. Who wants to know?' His voice was relaxed, the Bradfield accent strong.

Carol produced her warrant card and introduced herself. 'I wonder if we could come in and have a word, sir?'

'What about?'

'Your name has cropped up in some routine enquiries and I'd like to ask you some questions for the purposes of elimination.'

Crozier's brows furrowed. 'What sort of enquiries?'

'If we could just come in, sir?'

'No, hang on, what's all this about? I'm trying to get some work done here.'

Morris stepped to Carol's side. 'There's no need to be difficult, sir, it's just routine.'

'Mr Crozier isn't being difficult, Constable,' Carol said coolly. 'I'd feel just the same in your shoes, sir. A car answering the description of yours has been involved in an incident, and we need to eliminate you from our investigation. We're speaking to several other people in connection with this enquiry, sir. It won't take long.'

'All right then,' Crozier sighed. 'You'd better come in.'

They followed him up stairs carpeted in functional cord carpet into an open-plan living-room-cum-kitchen. It was furnished in expensive but minimalist style. He waved them to two leather and wood armchairs and dropped into a leather bean bag on the polished wood floor. Morris pulled out his notebook and ostentatiously opened it to a fresh page.

'You work from home, then?' Carol asked.

''S right. I'm a freelance animator.'

'Cartoons?' Carol said.

'I do mostly science animations. You want something for your Open University course that shows how atoms collide, I'm your man. So what's all this about?'

'You drive a Land Rover Discovery?'

''S right. It's in the garage.'

'Can you tell me if you were driving it last Monday night?' Carol asked. God, was it only a week ago?

'I can. I wasn't. I was in Boston, Massachusetts.'

She went through the routine questions that established precisely what Crozier had been doing, and who she could check the information with. Then she stood up. Time for the key question, but it was important to keep it looking casual. 'Thanks for your help, Mr Crozier. One more thing – is there anyone else who has access to your house while you're away? Someone who could have borrowed your car?'

Crozier shook his head. 'I live on my own. I don't even have a cat or plants, so nobody has to come in when I'm away. I'm the only one with keys.'

'You're sure of that? No cleaning lady, no colleague who drops in to use your system?'

'Sure, I'm sure. I do my own cleaning, I work alone. I split up with my girlfriend a couple of months back and I changed the locks, OK? Nobody's got keys except me.' Crozier was starting to sound tetchy.

Carol persisted. 'And no one could have borrowed your keys without your knowledge and had them copied?'

'I don't see how. I'm not in the habit of leaving them lying around. And the car's only insured for me, so nobody else has ever driven it,' Crozier said, his irritation clearly mounting. 'Look, if somebody did anything criminal in a car with my number on, they were using faked-up plates, OK?'

'I accept what you're saying, Mr Crozier. I can assure you that if the information you've given me checks out, you won't be hearing from us again. Thanks very much for your time.'

Back at the car, Carol said, 'Find me a phone. I want to try Dr Hill again. I can't believe he's gone AWOL the one time we really need him.'

It's laughable. They pick a man who can't even tell whether I've carried out a particular punishment or not and they employ him to help them catch me. They could at least have shown me the respect of employing someone who has some reputation, an opponent worthy of my skills, not some idiot who has never encountered someone of my calibre.

Instead, they insult me. Dr Tony Hill is supposed to be producing a profile of me, based on his analysis of my killings. When this account is published, years hence, after my death in my bed from natural causes, historians will be able to compare his profile with the reality and laugh at the gross inaccuracies of his pseudo-science.

He will never come close to the truth. For the record, I set down that truth.

I was born in the Yorkshire port of Seaford, one of the busiest fishing and commercial docks in the country. My father was a merchant seaman, the first officer on oil tankers. He went all over the world, then he would come home to us. But my mother was as bad a wife as she was a mother. I can see now that the house was always in chaos, the meals irregular and unappetizing. The only thing she was good at, the only thing they could share, was the drinking. If there was an Olympic pairs event for pissheads, they'd have walked off with the gold.

When I was seven, my father stopped coming home. Of course, my mother blamed me for not being a good enough son. She said I'd driven him away. She told me I was the man of the house now. But I could never live up to her expectations. She always wanted more from me than I was capable of, and ruled me by blame rather than praise. I spent more time locked in the cupboard than most people's coats do.

Without my father's pay cheque, she was thrown on the resources of the welfare system, which was barely enough to live on, never mind get drunk on. When the building society repossessed the house, we went to live with relatives in Bradfield for a while, but she couldn't handle their disapproval, so we moved back to Seaford, when she turned to the town's other boom industry, prostitution. I grew accustomed to the procession of disgusting, drunken sailors traipsing through the succession of grubby flats and bedsits where we lived. We were always behind with the rent, usually doing a moonlight flit just before the bailiffs got really heavy.

I grew to hate the ugly, grunting copulation that I was a constant witness to, and stayed out of the house as much as I possibly could, often sleeping rough down by the docks. I used to pick on kids that were younger than me to get their money off them so I could afford to eat. I moved schools almost as often as we moved house, so I never did too well there, in spite of the fact that I knew I could run rings round most of the other kids, who were just stupid.

As soon as I was 16, I left Seaford. It wasn't a wrench; it wasn't as if I'd ever managed to make many friends, what with moving all the time. I'd seen enough of men to know that I didn't want to grow up like them, and I felt different inside. I thought if I moved back to a big city like Bradfield I'd find it easier to work out what I wanted. One of my mother's cousins got me a job at the electronics firm where he worked.

About that time, I discovered that dressing in women's clothes made me feel good about myself. I got my own bedsit so I could do it whenever I wanted to, and that calmed me down a lot. I started studying computer science at evening classes, and eventually got some proper qualifications. About that time, my mother got left a house in Seaford in her brother's will.

I got the chance of a job back in Seaford, working in computer systems for the local private phone company. I didn't really want to go back there, but the job was too good to turn down. I never went near my mother. I don't think she even knew I was there.

One of the few good things about Seaford is that it's handy for the ferry to Holland. I used to go there every other weekend, because in Amsterdam I could go out dressed as a woman and nobody batted an eyelid. Over there, I met a lot of transsexuals as well as transvestites, and the more I talked to them, the more I realized that I was just like them. I was a woman trapped in a man's body. That explained why I'd never had much sexual interest in girls. And although I found men attractive, I knew I wasn't a poof. They disgust me, with their pretence at normal relationships when everybody knows that it's only men and women that can fit together properly.

I went to see the doctors at Jimmy's in Leeds, where they do all the sex-change operations in the north, and they turned me down. Their psychologists were as stupid and blinkered as all the rest of their brotherhood. But I managed to find a private doctor in London who prescribed the hormone treatment I needed. Of course, I couldn't go on working while this was going on, but I spoke to the boss and he said he'd give me a good reference for another job when I'd had the operation and I was a woman.

I had to go abroad for the operation, and it was all much more expensive than I expected. I went to my mother and asked her if she'd mortgage the house to lend me the money and she just laughed at me.

So I did what I'd learned from her. I sold myself on the docks. It's amazing how much money sailors will pay for a travesti. They get out of their heads with excitement at the thought of someone who has breasts and a cock. I wasn't like the other hookers either; I didn't blow it all on drink or drugs or a pimp. I stashed it all away till I could afford the operation.

When I came to Seaford, not even my own mother recognized me at first. I'd only been back a few days when she took that tragic accidental overdose of drink and pills. Nobody was surprised. Yes, Doctor, you can add her to the list.

With my qualifications, experience and reference, I had no trouble getting a job as a senior systems analyst with the phone company in Bradfield. The money I made from the sale of the house in Seaford bought me my home in Bradfield, and I started the task of finding a worthy man to share my life.

And Dr Tony Hill presumes to understand me, without knowing any of this? Well, in a very short time, I'll share it all with him. Such a shame he won't have the chance to write it down for himself.

18

> The truth is, I am a very particular man in every-
> thing relating to murder; and perhaps I carry my
> delicacy too far.

Don Merrick walked into the HOLMES room munching
a two-inch-thick double cheese and Bar-B-Q bacon
burger. 'How do you do it?' Dave Woolcott asked.
'How do you get those slack Alices down the canteen
to cook you edible food? They could burn a cup of tea,
that lot, but you always manage to twist them round
your little finger.'

Merrick winked. 'It's my natural Geordie charm,'
he said. 'I just pick on the ugliest one and tell her
she reminds me of my mother when she was in her
prime.' He sat down and stretched his long legs. 'I've
checked out the half-dozen Discoveries your sergeant
gave me. They're all in the clear. Two of them are
women, two of them have got rock-solid alibis for at
least two of the nights in question, one's got multiple
sclerosis, so he couldn't have done the jobs, and the
sixth sold his to a dealership in the Midlands three
weeks ago.'

'Great,' Dave said heavily. 'Give the list to one of the operators so we can update the file.'

'Where's the guv?'

'Carol or Kevin?'

Merrick shrugged. 'I still think of Inspector Jordan as my guv'nor.'

'She's off chasing wild geese,' Dave said.

'She got a result, then?' Merrick asked.

'Two cross-matches.'

'Let's have a look,' Merrick said.

Dave rummaged among his papers and found three sheets of paper stapled together. The first listed the two correlations. Merrick frowned and flicked over a page. The second was a print-out of the result of a criminal records search on Philip Crozier. Nothing known. Hurriedly, he turned to the third page, which listed two Christopher Thorpes. One had a last-known address in Devon and several convictions for burglary. The second had a last-known address in Seaford. There were a string of juvenile convictions; assaulting a football referee, breaking windows at a school, shoplifting. There were half a dozen adult convictions, all for soliciting prostitution. Merrick sucked in his breath sharply and turned back to the front page. 'Fuck,' he said.

'What is it?' Dave asked, suddenly alert.

'This here. Christopher Thorpe, the Seaford one?'

'Yeah? Carol reckoned it wasn't the same one as ours. I mean, he's got convictions for being a male prostitute, but this one in Bradfield looks to be married, because the woman at the same address has his surname. And let's face it, you don't get dockland rent boys driving around in serious motors like the Discovery.'

Merrick shook his head. 'No, you've got it all wrong. I know this Christopher Thorpe from Seaford. I worked on Vice in Seaford before I came here, remember? I was the arresting officer on two of these charges in soliciting. Christopher Thorpe was halfway to a sex change at the time. He had the tits and everything, he was trying to earn enough money to get the operation. Guess what his working name was? Dave, Christopher Thorpe isn't *married* to Angelica Thorpe, he *is* Angelica Thorpe.'

'Fuck,' Dave echoed.

'Dave, where the hell is Carol?'

Angelica stood in front of him, hands on hips, chewing one corner of her mouth. 'You can't, can you? You can't prove it because you know nothing about my life.'

'In one sense you're absolutely right, Angelica. I don't know the facts of your life,' Tony said carefully, 'but I think I know a bit about the shape of it. Your mother didn't do a very good job of loving you. Maybe she had a problem with drink or with drugs, or maybe she just didn't understand what a little kid needed. Either way, she didn't make you feel loved when you were little. Am I right?'

Angelica scowled. 'Go on. Dig yourself a hole.'

Tony felt a prickle of fear tingle at the base of his skull. What if he'd got it wrong? What if this woman was the exception to every statistical near certainty Tony had held at the front of his mind during the whole enquiry? What if she was the one serial killer who had come from a happy, loving family? Dismissing his doubts as a luxury he couldn't afford right now,

Tony ploughed on. 'Your father wasn't around much when you were growing up, and he never showed you he was proud of his son, even though you did everything you knew how to make him feel that pride. Your mother expected too much of you, kept telling you you were the man of the house, and giving you a bad time when you behaved like the child you were instead of the man she wanted to pretend you were.' Angelica's face twitched in a spasm of recognition. Tony paused.

'Go on,' she grated between clenched teeth.

'It's not easy for me to talk, doubled over like this. Can't you slacken the rope a bit, let me stand upright?'

She shook her head, her mouth sulky as a child's.

'I can't look at you properly like this,' Tony tried. 'You've got a fabulous body, you must know that. If it's going to be the last thing I see, at least let me appreciate it.'

She cocked her head to one side, as if replaying his words to check them for truth or trickery. 'All right,' she conceded. 'It doesn't mean anything's changed, though,' she added as she moved to the winch and released it. She let out about a foot of slack.

Tony couldn't bite back the scream of pain that shot through his shoulders as the muscles were released from the strain that had stretched them to their limit. 'It'll wear off,' Angelica said roughly as she returned to her station by the camcorder. 'Keep talking,' she instructed him. 'I've always enjoyed fantasy fiction.'

He eased himself upright, struggling against the pain. 'You were a bright kid,' he gasped. 'Brighter than the rest of them. It's never easy making friends when you're so much smarter than the other kids. And maybe you moved around a bit. Different neighbours, maybe even different schools.'

Angelica was back in control of herself, her face impassive as he continued. 'It wasn't easy to make friends. You knew you were different from everybody else, special, but you couldn't work out why at first. Then as you grew up, you realized what it was. You weren't the same as the other boys because you weren't a boy at all. You had no interest in girls sexually, but it wasn't because you were gay. No way. It was because you were really a girl yourself. What you discovered was that dressing up in women's clothes made you feel like you'd come home, like this was how you were meant to be.' He paused and gave her a crooked smile. 'How am I doing so far?'

'Very impressive, Doctor,' she said coldly. 'I'm fascinated. Carry on.'

Tony flexed his shoulder muscles, relieved to discover that the damage so far seemed to be only temporary. The pins and needles that raged across his back seemed no more than a minor irritation after what he'd been through. He took a deep breath and carried on. 'You decided to become the person you were inside, the woman you knew you really were. God, Angelica, I've got so much respect for you, putting yourself through that. I know how hard it is to get the medical profession to take the idea seriously. All the hormone therapy, the electrolysis, living as a half-man, half-woman while you waited for the operations, and then all the pain of the surgery.' He shook his head, wonderingly. 'I know I wouldn't have the courage to put myself through all that.'

'It wasn't easy.' The words escaped from Angelica's lips, almost against her will.

'I believe you,' Tony said sympathetically. 'And after all that, to find yourself wondering if it had been worth it after all, when you realized that the stupidity, the insensitivity, the lack of insight you'd identified in men didn't just disappear because you were a woman. They were still the same old bunch of bastards, incapable of recognizing an exceptional woman when they were offered her love and affection on a plate.' He paused, studying her face, deciding if the time was right for the big gamble. The coldness had left her eyes, replaced by a look almost of misery. He softened his voice and lowered the volume. Please God, let his training pay off.

'They rejected you, didn't they? Adam Scott, Paul Gibbs, Gareth Finnegan, Damien Connolly. They turned you down.'

Angelica shook her head violently, as if by activity she could deny the past. 'They *let* me down. They *let* me down, they didn't turn me down. They betrayed me.'

'Tell me about it,' Tony said softly, praying that his hard-earned techniques weren't going to fail him now. 'Tell me about it.'

'Why should I?' she shouted, stepping forward and slapping him so hard he tasted blood as his cheek impacted against his teeth. 'You're no better than them. What about that slag? That blonde bitch, that fucking plonk you've been giving one to?'

Tony swallowed the warm salty blood that filled his mouth. 'You mean Carol Jordan?' he said, playing for time. How should he play this? Should he lie or tell the truth?

'You know full well who I mean. I know you've been with her, don't fucking try lying to me,' she hissed, raising her hand again. 'You treacherous, faithless bastard.' Her hand cracked him across the face again, so hard he heard his neck crick under the force of it.

Tears sprang to his eyes involuntarily. The truth wasn't going to work. It would only earn him more punishment. Praying he could lie with conviction, Tony pleaded, 'Angelica, she was just a fuck, just someone to scratch the itch. You'd got me so horny with your phone calls. I didn't know when you were going to call again, or even if you were.' He allowed anger to creep into his voice. 'I wanted you and you didn't tell me how I could get hold of you. Angelica, it's like you with the other ones. I was filling in time, waiting for my equal. You can't believe that a mere cop would answer my fantasies, do you? You should know, you've had one too.'

Angelica stepped back, shock on her face. Sensing he had made some kind of a breakthrough, Tony pursued her with his words. 'We were different, you and me. They weren't worthy of you. But we were special. You must know that, from our phone calls. Didn't you sense that we had something extraordinary? That this time it would be different? Isn't that what you really want? You don't want the killing. Not really. The killing only happened because they weren't worthy, because they let you down. What you really want is a worthy partner. What you want is love. Angelica, what you want is me.'

For a long moment she stared at him, eyes wide, mouth open. Then confusion took over, as obvious to Tony as a hooker's come-on. 'Don't use that word to me, you worthless scumbag,' she stuttered. 'Don't fucking say it!' Her voice was a low, throaty scream. Suddenly, she turned on her heel and ran from the room, her heels clattering up the stairs.

'I love you, Angelica,' Tony shouted desperately after her retreating footsteps. 'I love you.'

Carol and DC Morris stood on the doorstep of the small terraced house in Gregory Street. She didn't need to be a psychologist to read his body language. Morris was fed up at trailing round pursuing Carol's daft hunch. 'They must be out at work,' he remarked after their fourth assault on the doorbell.

'Looks that way,' Carol agreed.

'Shall we come back later?'

'Let's go on the knocker,' Carol suggested. 'See if any of the neighbours are around. Maybe they can tell us when the Thorpes get back from work.'

Morris looked as if he'd rather be on crowd control at a student demo. 'Yes, ma'am,' he said in a bored voice.

'You take across the street, I'll go for this side.' Carol watched him trudge across the street as wearily as a miner at the end of his shift, shook her head with a sigh and turned her attention to number twelve. This was much more the kind of territory Tony had suggested for their killer. Thinking of Tony just made Carol cross again. Where the hell was he? She really needed his input today, not to mention a bit of support for an idea that everybody else seemed to think was a complete waste of time. He couldn't have picked a worse moment to go on the missing list. It was unforgivable. At least he could have phoned his secretary and not left her having to field his calls and make excuses for him.

There was no bell on the door of number twelve, so Carol bruised her knuckles on the solid wood. The woman who opened it looked like a caricature from a soap opera. In her forties, her make-up would have been over the top for dinner in LA, never mind mid-afternoon in a Bradfield back street. Her dyed platinum blonde hair was piled high in a lopsided beehive. She wore a tight black sweater with a scoop neck revealing a cleavage the texture of crumpled tissue, shiny blue skin-tight leggings, white stilettoes and a thin gold ankle chain. A cigarette dangled from a corner of her mouth. 'What is it, love?' she said nasally.

'Sorry to trouble you,' Carol said, flashing her warrant card. 'Detective Inspector Carol Jordan, Bradfield police. I'm trying to get in touch with your next-door neighbours at number fourteen, the Thorpes, but there doesn't seem to be anybody home. I wonder if you happen to know what time they get in from work.'

The woman shrugged. 'Search me, love. That cow comes and goes at all hours.'

'What about Mr Thorpe?' Carol asked.

'What Mr Thorpe? There's no Mr Thorpe next door, love.' She gave a croak of laughter. 'It's easy seen you've never clapped eyes on her. Any man that married that ugly cow would have to be blind and bloody hard up. So what've you got her for?'

'It's just routine enquiries,' Carol said.

The woman snorted. 'Don't give me that fanny,' she said. 'I've watched enough episodes of *The Bill* to know they don't send inspectors out on routine enquiries. It's

415

about time you put that cow behind bars, if you want my opinion.'

'Why is that, Mrs . . . ?'

'Goodison, Bette Goodison. As in Bette Davis. Because she's an ugly, anti-social cow, that's why.'

Carol smiled. 'I'm afraid that's not a crime, Mrs Goodison.'

'No, but murder is, isn't it?' Bette Goodison crowed triumphantly.

Carol swallowed, hoping the effect of the word wasn't as visible as it was palpable. 'That's a very serious accusation.'

Bette Goodison took a final drag of her cigarette and expertly flipped the dog end across the narrow pavement and into the gutter. 'I'm glad you think so. It's more than your mates at Moorside nick did.'

'I'm sorry you feel you've not been well served by my colleagues,' Carol said in a concerned tone. 'Perhaps you could tell me what you're talking about?' Please God, let this not be a rerun of the Yorkshire Ripper case, where the killer's best friend told the police they suspected he was the Ripper and the police paid no attention.

'Prince, that's who we're talking about.'

For one wild moment, Carol had a vision of the diminutive American rock star buried in the back yard of a Bradfield terrace. Pulling herself together, she said, 'Prince?'

'Our German shepherd. Always complaining about him, that Angelica Thorpe was. And she had no grounds. That dog was doing her a service. Anybody so much as walked down our ginnel and that dog let you know about it. She'd have paid a fortune for a

416

burglar alarm as efficient as that dog. Any road up, a few months back . . . August, it were, weekend before Bank Holiday, we come home from work, Col and me, and Prince is gone. Now, there's no way he could have got out of that yard, and he'd have gone for anybody that came in. There's only one way he could have disappeared, and that's if he was murdered,' Mrs Goodison said, stabbing Carol in the chest with her finger for emphasis. 'She poisoned him and then she got rid of the body so there would be no proof. She's a murderer!'

Normally, Carol would have walked a mile barefoot to avoid this conversation, but she was in pursuit of Handy Andy, and any oddity was something to be grasped eagerly. 'How can you be so sure it was Mrs Thorpe?' she asked.

'Stands to reason. She were the only one that ever complained about him. And the day he went missing, me and Col were out at work, but she were home all day. I know that for a fact, because she were on nights that week. And when we knocked on her door to ask did she know anything about him going missing, she just smiled all over that ugly gob of hers. I could have put her face in for her,' Mrs Goodison said emphatically. 'So what are you going to do about it?'

'I'm afraid that without evidence, there's not much we can do,' Carol said sympathetically. 'You're sure, are you, that Mrs Thorpe lives alone?'

'Nobody'd want to live with an ugly cow like that. She never even has visitors. Not surprising, mind, she looks like a brick shithouse in drag.'

'Do you happen to know what kind of car she drives?' Carol asked.

'One of them bloody yuppie jeep things. I ask you, who needs a bloody great jeep in the middle of Bradfield? It's not like we live up some farm track, is it?'

'And do you know where she works?'

'I don't know and I don't care.' She glanced at her watch. 'Now, if you don't mind, my serial's starting.'

Carol watched the door close behind Bette Goodison, an unpleasant suspicion starting to form in her mind. Before she could try number ten, her pager bleeped insistently. 'Phone Don at Scargill Street. Double urgent,' she read.

'Morris!' Carol shouted. 'Get me to a phone. Pronto monto.' Whatever was going on in Gregory Street could wait. Don clearly couldn't.

Exhausted, Tony had slipped into some nightmare delirium doze. A gout of freezing water thrown in his face smacked him straight to agonized attention, his head snapping back painfully. 'Augh,' he groaned.

'Wakey, wakey,' Angelica said roughly.

'I was right, wasn't I?' Tony said through swollen lips. 'You've had time to think about it, and you know I'm right. You want the killing to stop. They had to die, they deserved to die. They let you down, they betrayed you, they didn't deserve you. But all that can change now. It can be different with me, because I love you.'

The rigid mask of her face crumpled before his eyes, becoming softer, more tender. She smiled at him. 'It's never been about sex, you know. I could always have sex. Men paid me for sex. They paid me a lot of money for sex. That's how I paid for the surgery, you know. They always wanted me.' Her voice was filled with a strange mixture of pride and anger.

'I can see why,' Tony lied, arranging his face in what he hoped was an expression of hunger and admiration. 'But what you really wanted was love, wasn't it? You wanted more than loveless sex on the streets or faceless sex down the phone. You deserve that. God, you deserve it. That's what I can give you, Angelica. Love isn't just physical attraction, though God knows you're attractive. But love's about respect, admiration, fascination, and I feel all of that for you. Angelica, you can have what you want. You can have it with me.'

Her warring emotions were written plainly on her face. He could see that part of her desperately wanted to believe him, wanted to escape into the normal world of relationships. But that part had to contend with a level of self-esteem that was so low she couldn't imagine anyone worth loving wanting to love her. And, underlying it all, suspicion that he was trying to entrap her. 'How can we?' she demanded harshly. 'You've been trying to hunt me down. You're with the police. You're on their side.'

Tony shook his head. 'That was before I realized you were the same woman I'd fallen in love with on the phone. Angelica, love is the one emotion that overrides duty. Yeah, I've worked with the police, but I'm not one of them.'

'You lie down with dogs, you get up with fleas,' she sneered. 'You've been trying to put me away, Anthony. You expect me to believe you? You must think I'm really stupid.'

'Quite the opposite. If you want to talk about stupid, talk about the police. Mostly, they're one-dimensional, boring bigots who couldn't keep a psychologist interested for more than five minutes. I don't have anything in common with them,' he argued desperately.

She shook her head, more in sorrow than in anger. 'You work for the Home Office. Your whole career, you've spent catching serial offenders and treating them. And you expect me to believe you'd suddenly change sides and stay loyal to me? Come on, Anthony, I'm not going to fall for crap like that.'

Tony felt his powers flagging. His brain just wasn't fast enough any longer to keep her at bay. Wretchedly, he said, 'I've not made a career of catching people, only treating them. I had to do that, don't you understand? Inside the places where I've worked is the only place where I can find minds that are complex enough to be interesting. It's like going to see animals at the zoo. You want to watch them in their natural habitat, but if the only way you are ever going to see them is at the zoo, you go. I've always had to wait till they were in captivity before I could study them. But you, you're still in the wild, still the way you want to be, perfected in your craft. And compared to them, you're the cream of the crop. You're exceptional. I want to spend the rest of my life being excited by your mind. I can't imagine ever finding you boring.' Terrifying, maybe, but never boring.

Her lower lip thrust out, bringing an expression of calculating petulance to her face. She nodded in the direction of his groin, where his penis hung limp. 'So if you find me that attractive, how come it doesn't show?'

It was the one question to which Tony had no answer at all.

'What have we actually got, Carol?' Brandon challenged.

Carol paced the floor of Brandon's office, ticking off her points on her fingers. 'We've got a transsexual. Not a transsexual who went through the controlled, counselled National Health Service process, but one who, according to Don, was turned down for a sex change here and had to finance an operation abroad by selling sex. So right from the start, we know we've got someone who has been examined by psychiatrists and found to be unstable. We've got this transsexual driving a vehicle identical to the one driven by a suspect in Damien Connolly's murder. We've got a neighbour who's convinced that Angelica Thorpe offed her dog. The dog was killed a fortnight before the first murder. Angelica Thorpe bought software that would allow her to manipulate videos in her computer system, which fits a theory of the killer's behaviour developed by me and endorsed by our psychological profiler. She even lives in the kind of house Tony said she would,' Carol argued vehemently.

'When she was Christopher, she was definitely a few butties short of a picnic,' Don chipped in.

'I wish we could ask Tony about this,' Brandon said, stalling.

'So do I,' Carol said through her teeth. 'But he's obviously found something more important to do today.' A sudden thought hit Carol like a sandbag to the neck. Her knees started to buckle and she collapsed into the nearest chair. 'Oh, my God,' she gasped.

'What is it?' Brandon asked, concerned.

'Tony. He hasn't been in touch with anybody since he left here yesterday. He had two task-force meetings arranged for today, according to his secretary, but he hasn't shown up at work, and he hasn't phoned in. He wasn't home last night, and he's not there now.' Carol's words hung in the air like a cloud of poisonous smoke. A wave of nausea lurched up from her stomach, almost choking her. Somehow, she maintained her composure under Brandon's concentrated stare.

With fingers that trembled, Carol picked up Brandon's copy of the profile from his desk. Urgently, she flicked through the pages till she found what she was looking for. '"It is possible that his next target may also be a police officer, perhaps even one who is working on the investigation. This alone will not be sufficient motive for the killer to choose them; they must also fit the victim criteria that he has drawn up in his own mind in order for the killing to assume its full meaning for him. I would strongly recommend that any officers who fit the victim profile employ extra vigilance at all times, noting any suspicious vehicles parked near their homes, and checking to see whether they are being followed to and from work and social events." Think about it, sir. Think about the victim profile. Sir, Tony fits it perfectly.'

Not wanting to believe what Carol was suggesting, Brandon said, 'But it's not eight weeks. It's not time!'

'But it *is* a Monday. Don't forget, Tony also pointed out that his timetable could be accelerated if something happened to traumatize him. Stevie McConnell, sir.

422

Think of all the publicity. Someone else was getting the credit for his crimes. Look, it's in here, sir: "Another possible scenario is that an innocent person is charged with the killings. That would be such an affront to his sense of himself that he might commit his next murder ahead of schedule." Sir, we've got to move on this now!'

Brandon's hand was on the phone before she'd even started her last sentence.

The front door opened directly into the house. Downstairs couldn't have looked more normal. The small living room was furnished inexpensively but comfortably with a two-seater sofa and matching chair upholstered in moss-green Dralon. There was a TV, video, mid-priced stereo system and a coffee table complete with a copy of *Elle*. A pair of framed posters of whales in the ocean hung on the walls. The single bookshelf contained a selection of science-fiction classics, a couple of Stephen King novels and a trio of Jackie Collins bonkbusters. Carol, Merrick and Brandon moved cautiously through the room, past the stairs and into the kitchen diner. It was surgically neat as a showroom, work surfaces clean and uncluttered. On the drainer, one mug, one plate, one fork, one knife.

With Brandon leading the way, they climbed the narrow stairs built between the two downstairs rooms. The front bedroom was pink and frothy as a strawberry milkshake. Even the kidney-shaped dressing table, with its skirt of lace, was pink. 'Barbara Cartland, eat your heart out,' Merrick muttered. Brandon opened the wardrobe and flicked through the array of women's clothes. Carol headed for the drawers in a pink tallboy and worked her way down. They contained nothing more disturbing than a selection of tacky underwear, much of it in red satin.

It was Merrick who first broached the back bedroom. As soon as he opened the door, he knew no one was going to be screaming to the papers about magistrates granting warrants on non-existent evidence. 'Sir?' he shouted. 'I think we've cracked it.'

The room was arranged as an office. A large desk held a computer and assorted peripherals that none of them could identify. To one side was a telephone linked to a sophisticated tape recorder. A small video-editing desk was in one corner, next to a filing cabinet. A wheeled trolley carried a television and video, both state of the art and top of the range. Shelves lined two walls, filled with computer games, videos, cassettes and computer disks, each box labelled neatly in firm capitals. The only alien object in the room was a leather recliner, the material slung hammock-like on a steel frame.

'Bingo,' Brandon breathed. 'Well done, Carol.'

'Where the fuck do we start?' Merrick said.

'Do either of you know how to work the computer?' Brandon asked.

'I think we should leave that to the experts,' Carol said. 'It might be programmed to crash the data if someone else tries to log on.'

'OK. Don, you take the filing cabinet, I'll take the videos, and Carol, you take the cassettes.'

Carol moved across to the shelves of cassettes. The first couple of dozen seemed to be music tapes, ranging from Liza Minnelli to U2. Next were a dozen marked 'AS' and numbered from one to twelve. Fourteen marked 'PG' followed, then fifteen with 'GF', eight with 'DC' and six with 'AH'. The concatenation of initials was far beyond the boundaries of coincidence. Carol picked the first 'AH' tape and, heart heavy with misgivings, slotted it into the cassette player. She picked up the headphones plugged into the machine and gingerly pushed them into her ears. She heard the sound of a telephone ringing, then a voice so familiar she could have wept. 'Hello?' Tony said, his voice reduced by the telephone line.

'Hello, Anthony,' a voice not entirely strange to her said.

'Who is this?' Tony asked.

A chuckle, low and sexy. 'You'll never guess. Not in a million years.' Got it, thought Carol, grim foreboding gripping her. The voice on the answering machine.

'OK, so tell me,' Tony said, his voice curious, friendly, joining in the game.

'Who would you like me to be? If I could be anyone in the world?'

'Is this some kind of wind-up?' Tony demanded.

'I've never been more serious in my life. I'm here to make your dreams come true. I'm the woman of your fantasies, Anthony. I am your telephone lover.'

There was a moment's silence, then the phone slammed down at Tony's end. Over the dialling tone, Carol heard the strange woman say, '*Hasta la vista*, Anthony.'

She stabbed the stop button and violently pulled out the headphones. She turned round to see Brandon transfixed by the image of Adam Scott stretched out on a rack, naked and apparently unconscious. Part of her mind could not comprehend what she was seeing. Evil, she thought, should be drenched in blood, not prosaically displayed on a suburban television screen.

'Sir,' she forced out. 'The tapes. She's been stalking Tony.'

Tony tried a laugh. It came out more like a sob, but he carried on regardless. 'You expect me to get an erection? Trussed up like this? Angelica, you chloroformed me, kidnapped me and left me to come round alone in a torture chamber. I'm sorry to disappoint you, but I've got no experience of bondage. I'm too bloody scared to get a hard-on.'

'I'm not letting you go, you know. Not to run straight back to them.'

'I'm not asking you to let me go. Believe me, I'm happy to be your prisoner if that's the only way I can spend time with you. I want to get to know you, Angelica. I want to prove my feelings to you, I want to show you what love feels like. I want to show you whose side I'm really on here.' Tony tried to turn on the kind of smile he'd learned that women responded to.

'So show me,' Angelica challenged, letting one hand run caressingly down her body, lingering over her nipples and edging towards her crotch.

'I'm going to need your help. Just like I needed you on the phone. You made me feel so good, like a real man. Please, help me now,' Tony pleaded.

She took a step towards him, moving sinuously as a stripper. 'You want me to turn you on?' she drawled in a ghastly parody of seduction.

'I don't think I can do it like this,' Tony said. 'Not with my arms pinned behind me like this.'

Angelica stopped dead and scowled. 'I said, I'm not letting you go.'

'And I said I'm not asking you to. All I'm asking is that you cuff my hands in front of me. So I can touch you.' Again, he forced the gentle smile.

She looked at him consideringly. 'How do I know I can trust you? I'd have to set your hands free so I could cuff them in front of you. Maybe you're trying to double-cross me.'

'I won't. I give you my word. If it makes you feel safer, chloroform me again. Do it while I'm uncon- scious,' Tony said, gambling again. Her reaction would tell him all he needed to know about his chances.

Angelica moved behind him. An exultant voice in his head screamed 'Yes!' He felt the warmth of her hand between his as she gripped the cuffs and painfully jerked them up. 'Shit!' Tony yelled as new arrows of pain shot up his arms and through his shoulders. He heard a click of metal as the shackle connecting the rope to the handcuffs snapped free. Angelica released the handcuffs and Tony collapsed to his knees, his legs buckling under him. 'Jesus Christ!' he swore as he crashed forwards on to his face, feeling the rough stone graze his cheek.

Moving swiftly, Angelica unlocked one side of the handcuffs, seized the back of his hair and pulled him upwards. Still holding the arm with the handcuffs attached, she stepped in front of him and roughly gripped his other arm just below the bicep, drag- ging it across his body. Seconds later, his hands were cuffed again, this time in front of him. He knelt like a supplicant, his discomfort doubled by the tight leather straps round his ankles. 'You see?' he gasped. 'I told you I wouldn't try anything.'

Panting slightly, Angelica stood in front of him, legs apart. 'So show me,' she demanded.

'You'll have to help me up. I can't do it by myself,' he protested weakly.

She bent down and grabbed his hair again, hauling him up on to legs whose muscles trembled with the effort of staying upright. They stood, inches apart, the silk of her kimono brushing his hands. He could feel the warmth of her breath on the raw flesh of his grazed cheek. 'Kiss me,' he said softly. Whores never get to kiss, he told himself. This'll make it different.

Something flickered in Angelica's eyes, but she leaned over him, releasing his hair and pulling his face to hers. It took every ounce of his willpower not to flinch as her lips met his, her tongue invading his mouth, exploring his teeth and tongue. Your life depends on it, he told himself. You've got a plan. Tony forced himself to kiss her back, thrusting his tongue into her mouth, telling himself there were worse things in the world, and this woman had made her previous victims endure some of them.

After what felt like the longest kiss of his life, Angelica pulled away, looking critically down to his groin. 'I'm going to need some help here,' Tony said. 'It's not been an easy day.'

'What kind of help?' Angelica asked, panting slightly through parted lips. It was clear that she was having no difficulty with the sexual arousal that was beyond him.

'Give me head. That's the one thing that always

works when I'm having trouble. I've felt your mouth now; I just know you'll be terrific. Please, I really want to make love to you.'

Almost before he'd finished speaking, she was on her knees, hands flickering over his balls. Tenderly, she lifted his flaccid penis and slipped it into her mouth, not taking her eyes from his face. Tony reached out and began to stroke her hair. Then, with what felt like infinite slowness, he pulled her head forward on to him, forcing her head down, her eyes away from him.

Then, summoning up what remained of his strength, Tony raised his hands and brought the handcuffs crashing down on the back of Angelica's head.

The blow caught her completely off guard and she went crashing forward between his legs, her teeth snagging agonizingly on him. Tony let himself fall backwards, feeling a tearing in his ankles as they protested against a movement they were never designed to make. As he hit the ground, he doubled forwards and grabbed Angelica's head, banging it hard on the stone floor till her body stopped thrashing.

He dragged himself over her prone figure till his numb fingers could reach the ankle straps. With maddening clumsiness, he struggled to unfasten the sets of buckles that fixed him to the stone slab. After what felt like hours, he was finally free. As he tried to stand, his ankles refused the challenge, turning over and catapulting him to the floor again, sending excruciating daggers of pain up his legs. Moaning, he dragged himself across the floor towards the steps. He had barely travelled a couple of yards when the body on the floor groaned. Angelica lifted her head, blood and mucus turning her face into a grisly Hallowe'en mask. When she saw him, she roared like a wounded animal and started scrambling to her feet.

The search for a clue to Angelica's killing ground was growing more desperate as their fear and concern for Tony grew. They had emptied out the contents of the filing cabinet on to the floor. Every scrap of paper was scrutinized for any hint of the location of the cellar revealed in the video. Invoices, guarantees, bills and receipts all got the treatment. Carol was wading through a file of official correspondence, hoping to come across some lease or mortgage details, anything that related to another property. Merrick was ploughing through the files relating to Thorpe's sex change. Brandon had already had one false alarm, coming across a stack of solicitor's letters relating to a property in Seaford. It soon became clear, however, that they concerned the sale of Thorpe's late mother's home in the town.

It was Merrick who found the key. He'd finished with the sex-change files and started on a bundle of assorted letters, filed under 'Tax'. When he came across the letter, he had to read it twice to make sure wishful thinking wasn't making him imagine things.

'Sir,' he said cautiously. 'I think this might be what we're looking for.'

He handed the letter to Brandon, who read the letterhead of Pennant, Taylor, Bailey and Co., Solicitors. 'Dear Christopher Thorpe,' it said. 'We have received a letter from your aunt, Mrs Doris Makins, in New Zealand, authorizing us to pass on to you the keys for Start Hill Farm, Upper Tontine Moor, by Bradfield, W. Yorkshire. As her agents, we are empowered to allow you access to said property for the purposes of maintenance and security. Please make arrangements with this office to collect the keys at your convenience . . .'

'Access to an isolated rural property,' Carol said, looking over Brandon's shoulder. 'Tony said that's what the killer might have. And now she's got him there.' A wave of anger poured through her, displacing the slow burn of fear that had been eating through her from the moment they'd unlocked the macabre secrets of that superficially normal office.

Brandon closed his eyes momentarily then said tightly, 'We don't know that, Carol.'

'And even if she has got him, he's a clever bloke. If anyone can keep himself out of trouble with his gob, it's Tony Hill,' Don chipped in.

'Never mind whistling in the bloody dark,' Carol said sharply. 'Where the hell is Start Hill Farm? And how soon can we get there?'

Tony looked around in desperation. The rack of knives was over to his left, impossibly high up. As Angelica got to her knees, he clawed at the stone bench and hauled himself upright. His hand closed on the haft of the knife as she staggered to her feet and threw herself at him, still bellowing like a cow bereft of its calf.

Her weight and the momentum of her charge bent Tony backwards over the bench. Her hands scrabbled for his throat, gripping his windpipe so tightly that white lights started to dance in front of his eyes. Just when he thought he could hold on no longer, he felt the warm, sticky gush of blood against his stomach and Angelica's grasp became flabby as a wet newspaper.

Before he could take it all in, he heard footsteps crashing down the stone steps. Like a mad vision of paradise, Don Merrick crashed downstairs, rapidly followed by John Brandon, his jaw dropping at the tableau in front of him.

'Fucking hell,' Brandon breathed.

Carol pushed past the two men and stared uncomprehendingly at the carnage before her.

'You lot took your time,' Tony gasped. As he passed out, the last thing he heard was his own hysterical laughter.

Epilogue

Carol pushed open the door of the side ward. Tony was propped up on a pile of pillows, the left side of his face swollen and bruised.

'Hi,' Tony said, a wan half-smile the best he could manage without too much pain. 'Come on in.'

Carol closed the door behind her and sat down on a chair by the bed. 'I brought you some bits and pieces,' she said, dumping a plastic bag and a padded envelope on the coverlet.

Tony reached out for the bag. Carol winced inside as she saw the bracelet of bruises round his inflamed wrists. He took out a copy of *Esquire*, a can of Aqua Libra, a tin of pistachio nuts and a Dashiel Hammett omnibus. 'Thanks,' he said, surprised by how her choice touched him.

'I wasn't sure what you liked,' she said defensively.

'Then you're obviously a good guesser. The perfect taskforce officer.'

'If a little slow on the uptake,' Carol said bitterly.

Tony shook his head. 'John Brandon was here earlier. He told me how you worked it all out. I don't see how you could have got there any quicker.'

'I should have realized sooner that you wouldn't have done a disappearing act at such a crucial time. Come to that, I should have realized as soon as I saw that profile that you could be a target and taken steps to protect you.'

'Bollocks, Carol. If anyone should have realized that, it was me. You did a bloody good job.'

'No. If I'd been on the ball, we'd have got there in time to save you having to . . . to do what you did.'

Tony sighed. 'You mean, you'd have saved Angelica's life? For what? Years in a secure mental hospital? Look on the bright side, Carol. You've saved the state a fortune. No expensive trial, no years of incarceration and treatment to pay for. Shit, they'll probably give you a medal.'

'That's not what I meant, Tony,' Carol said. 'I meant you wouldn't have to live with the knowledge that you've killed someone.'

'Yes, well, I can't pretend it was the perfect outcome, but I'll learn to live with it.' He forced a smile. 'Don't take this the wrong way, but the first thing I'm going to do when I can walk again is go out and buy you a new mac,' he said. 'Every time I look at that coat of yours, I get the urge to scream.'

'Why?' Carol frowned in puzzlement.

'Didn't you know? She was wearing the identical mac when she turned up on the doorstep. That way, if she left any fibres at the scene, Forensic would assume they'd come from you.'

'Terrific,' Carol said ironically. 'How are the ankles, by the way?'

Tony pulled a face. 'I don't think I'll ever play the violin again. I managed to make it to the loo on

434

crutches, but I had to sit on the edge of the bath to pee. They're saying there probably won't be any permanent damage, but it'll take a while for the torn ligaments to heal. How was your day?'

Carol pulled a face. 'Grisly. I suspect you'd have been in your element. You were right about keeping the fantasy alive. She, he, it, had tapes of all the telephone-sex conversations she'd had with her victims, and she'd stolen the outgoing message tapes from the men who had answering machines.

'It took the boffins a little while to crack the computer stuff. We didn't have anybody who really knew what they were doing, but my brother Michael came in and sorted it out for us.'

Tony gave a twisted smile. 'I didn't want to say anything at the time, but for a wild moment, I actually wondered about your brother.'

'Michael? You're kidding!'

Embarrassed, Tony nodded. 'It was when you posited the idea of the computer manipulation of the videos. Michael had the expertise to do that, no question. He's in the right age group, he lives with a woman but not in a sexual relationship, he's got access to all the information the killer needed about the way the police and forensic scientists work, his job is in the general area where I'd expect the killer to work, and he was in a position to know exactly what the police were up to and be involved in the investigation. If we hadn't caught Angelica when we did, I'd have been scrounging an invitation to dinner to check him out.'

Carol shook her head. 'See what I mean about being slow on the uptake? I had access to all the same information as you, and Michael never even crossed my mind as a possibility.'

'Not so surprising. You know him well enough to know he's not a psychopath.'

Carol shrugged. 'Do I, though? It wouldn't be the first time a close family member, a wife even, has made the same mistake.'

'Usually, they're either deluding themselves or they're emotionally unstable and dependent on the killer in some way. Neither of which would have applied in this case.' He gave a tired smile. 'Anyway, tell me about what your Michael uncovered.'

'The computer was a total goldmine. She'd kept her own diary of the stalking and the murders. It even says that she wanted it published after her death. Can you beat that?'

'Easily,' Tony said. 'Remind me to show you some of the academic papers I've got on the subject of serial killers.'

Carol shivered. 'Thanks, but no thanks. I got a print-out of the diary for you. I figured you'd be interested.' She gestured to the envelope. 'It's in there. Also, as you'd surmised, she had video-taped the killings, and as I suggested, she'd imported them into her computer and manipulated the images to keep the fantasy alive. It was absolutely gruesome, Tony. It went way beyond nightmare.'

Tony nodded. 'I won't say you get used to it, because you never do if you're going to be any use at this job. But you do get to the stage where you can lock it away, so it doesn't jump out and wreck your head unawares.'

'Oh, yeah?'

'That's the theory. Ask me again in a few weeks,' he said grimly. 'Was there anything in there about how she chose her victims?'

'Just a fucking bit,' Carol said bitterly. 'She'd been at this for months before she even picked out the first victim. She worked for the phone company, a computer systems manager. Apparently, she used to work for a small private phone company back in Seaford, which gave her the experience to get the job in Bradfield. She was what they call a super-user of the computer system, so she had access to every piece of data in there. She used the phone company's computer to extract all the residential numbers who had made regular calls to sex chatlines in the past year.' Carol paused, letting the obvious question hang in the air.

'It was research,' Tony said wearily. 'I published a paper on the role of chatlines in the development of fantasies among serial offenders. Someone should have told Angelica not to jump to conclusions.'

Reading his remark as a veiled reproach, Carol moved on. 'She cross-referenced that against the electoral roll and came up with men who lived alone. Then she just checked them out by watching their houses. She had a clear picture of the physical type she wanted, and she wanted one with his own house, a decent income and good career prospects. Can you believe it?'

'Only too well,' Tony said grimly. 'Her rationale was that she never wanted to kill them, she only wanted to love them. But they made her murder because they betrayed her. She kept telling herself that what she really wanted was a man who would love her and live with her.'

Don't we all, Carol thought but didn't say. 'Anyway, once she'd decided on the likely candidate, she paved the way with the dirty phone calls. She got them on the hook that way, on account of all you sleazy men can't resist anonymous sex.'

'Ouch,' Tony said, wincing. 'In my defence, I'd have to say that a large part of my interest was purely academic. I was interested in the psychology of a woman who would do what she did on the phone.'

Carol smiled tightly. 'At least I know now that you were telling the truth when you said you didn't know the woman who was leaving the sexy messages on your answering machine.'

Tony looked away. 'And the discovery that a man you were attracted to was getting his rocks off in kinky telephone sex with a stranger must have been delightful for you.'

Carol was silent, unsure what to say. 'I've heard the tapes now,' she admitted. 'Yours are very different from the others. You were clearly uncomfortable a lot of the time. Not that it's any of my business.'

Still unable to meet her eyes, Tony spoke, his voice clipped and clinical. 'I have a problem with sex. To be precise, I have problems with achieving and maintaining an erection. The honest truth is that only part of me was treating the calls with professional interest. The other part of me was trying to use them as a kind of therapy. I know that makes me sound like a pervert, but part of the trouble with doing the job I do is that it's virtually impossible to find a therapist I can respect and trust who isn't connected in some way to the world I work in. And however much they verbally espouse the principle of client

438

confidentiality, I've always been reluctant to expose myself to the risk.'

Realizing the difficulty Tony had had in making his confession, Carol reached out for his hand and covered it lightly with hers. 'Thank you for telling me that. It won't go any further. And if it makes you feel any better, the only people who have heard the tapes in full are me and John Brandon. You don't have to worry about what people are saying about you behind your back within the force.'

'That's something, I suppose. So, go on. Tell me about Angelica's phone calls to the other victims.'

'It was obvious that the men thought this was sex without any commitment or comeback. Angelica's analysis was completely different. She'd convinced herself that their responses meant they were falling in love with her. Unfortunately for the guys, they decided otherwise. As soon as they showed any interest in another woman, they signed their death warrants. Apart from Damien, that is. She killed him to teach us a lesson. You were going to be the other lesson.'

Tony shuddered. 'No wonder she had to go abroad for the sex-change operation. The NHS psychologists she saw must have had a field day with her attitudes and aspirations.'

'Apparently, they decided she was not an appropriate candidate for a sex change because of her lack of insight into her sexuality. They concluded that she was a gay man who couldn't cope with his sexuality because of cultural and family conditioning. They recommended counselling with a sex therapist rather than a sex change. There was an ugly scene at the time. He threw one of the psychologists through a glass door,' Carol revealed.

'Pity they didn't press charges,' Tony said.

'Yes. And you'll be pleased to hear they're definitely not going to charge you.'

'I should think not! Like I said, think of the tax-payers' money I've saved. Maybe we should have dinner to celebrate when I get out of here?' he asked tentatively.

'I'd like that. There is one other good thing that came out of all of this,' Carol said.

'What's that?'

'Penny Burgess took the day off yesterday to go walking in the dales. Apparently, her car broke down and she got stranded in the middle of a forest all night. She missed the whole shooting match. There's a dozen by-lines in the *Sentinel Times* tonight, and not a single one of them is hers!'

Tony lay back and stared at the ceiling. Papering over the cracks, that's what they were doing. He suspected Carol knew that as well as he did, and he wasn't sorry for the effort she was making. But he'd had enough for now. He closed his eyes and sighed.

'Oh God, I'm sorry,' Carol said, getting to her feet. 'I wasn't thinking. You must still be exhausted. Look, I'm out of here. I'll leave you this stuff to read when you feel up to it. I could drop in tomorrow if you like . . .'

'I think I'd like that,' Tony said wearily. 'It just comes over me in waves sometimes.'

He heard her feet cross the floor and the click of the door opening. 'Take care,' Carol said.

The door closed behind her and Tony pushed himself

back up till he was leaning against the pillows. He reached for the padded envelope. While he couldn't cope with conversation, his curiosity wouldn't let him ignore Angelica's diary. He pulled out a thick wedge of A4 paper. 'Let's see what you were really made of,' he said softly. 'What's the story? How did you justify, what did you hide behind?' Hungrily, he began to read.

Wading through the outpourings of the psychologically damaged was normally a routine exploratory experience for Tony. But this was different, he realized after only a few paragraphs. At first, he couldn't pin down what it was. The writing was more literate, more controlled and more immediate than most of their ramblings, but that didn't explain why his response was so different. He moved on a few pages, fascinated and repelled equally. It was no more or less self-obsessed than other things he'd read, but there was a chilling relish here that was unusual. Most killers whose writings he'd read had gloried far more in their own bloody role, reflecting less on what they'd done to their victims and its effect on them, but here was someone who identified herself as much in terms of them. But even that couldn't entirely explain why he felt so unsettled by what he was reading. Whatever it was, it was making him more reluctant to continue the more he read, the opposite to his normal response. He'd been so obsessively keen to get inside the head of the killer he'd dubbed Handy Andy, but now it was laid out before him, it was as if he didn't want to know.

As he forced himself to read on, mentally chalking up the correct assumptions he'd made in his profile, it eventually dawned on him that what he was feeling was personal. These words were touching him in ways he'd never experienced before because the life outlined in these pages had touched him with a directness he'd never known before. These were the footsteps of his own personal nemesis that he was tracing, and it was an uncomfortable journey.

He tossed the papers to one side, unable to keep going, seeing his own fate mirrored in the broken bodies Angelica had meticulously described. The trouble with being a psychologist was that he knew exactly what was happening to him. He knew he was still in shock, still deep in denial. Although he couldn't get the events in the cellar out of his mind, there was still a distance between him and the memory, as if he were watching them from a long way off. One day the horror of the previous night was going to come roaring back in stereo, splashed across his inner eye in Cinemascope. Knowing that, this numbness was a blessing. Already, he knew, his answering machine would be crammed with lucrative offers for the story of how the hunter turned killer. One day, he was going to have to tell that story. He hoped he'd have the strength to save it for a psychiatrist.

It was no comfort to rationalize that having been the target of one serial killer, he was statistically unlikely ever to find himself in that position again. All he could think of was the hours in the cellar, dredging his experience and knowledge for the magic words that would give him a few minutes longer to try for the key to his freedom.

Then that kiss. The whore's kiss, the killer's kiss, the lover's kiss, the saviour's kiss, all rolled into one. A kiss from the mouth that had been seducing him for weeks, the mouth whose words had given him hope for his future, only to leave him finally stranded in this place. He had spent his working life worming his way into the heads of those who kill, only to end up one of them, thanks to a Judas kiss.

'You've won, haven't you, Angelica?' he said softly. 'You wanted me, and now you've got me.'